TOGETHER AGAIN

IRENE HANNON

CHERYL WOLVERTON

DEB KASTNER

Love Inspired

Published by Steeple Hill Books™

STEEPLE HILL BOOKS

Steeple
Hill®

ISBN 0-373-78525-9

TOGETHER AGAIN

Copyright © 2003 by Steeple Hill Books, Fribourg, Switzerland

The publisher acknowledges the copyright holders
of the individual works as follows:

IT HAD TO BE YOU
Copyright © 1999 by Irene Hannon

A FATHER'S LOVE
Copyright © 1998 by Cheryl Wolverton

DADDY'S HOME
Copyright © 1999 by Debra Kastner

This edition published by arrangement with Steeple Hill Books.

® and TM are trademarks of Steeple Hill Books, used under license. Trademarks indicated with ® are registered in the United States Patent and Trademark Office, the Canadian Trade Marks Office and in other countries.

Visit us at www.steeplehill.com

Printed in U.S.A.

CONTENTS

Books by Irene Hannon

Love Inspired

*Home for the Holidays #6
*A Groom of Her Own #16
*A Family To Call Her Own #25
It Had to Be You #58
One Special Christmas #77
The Way Home #112
Never Say Goodbye #175
Crossroads #224

*Vows

IRENE HANNON

has been a writer for as long as she can remember. This prolific author of romance novels for both the inspirational and traditional markets began her career at age ten, when she won a story contest conducted by a national children's magazine. Today, in addition to penning her heartwarming stories of love and faith, Irene keeps quite busy with her "day job" in corporate communications. In her "spare" time she enjoys performing in community musical theater productions.

Irene and her husband, Tom—whom she describes as "my own romantic hero"—make their home in St. Louis, Missouri.

IT HAD TO BE YOU
Irene Hannon

With deepest gratitude to the
One who makes all things possible.

Prologue

"I'm sorry, Maggie, but...I just can't go through with it."

Maggie Fitzgerald stared in shock at the man standing across from her, his words echoing hollowly in her ears. He looked like Jake West, the man she'd loved since she was sixteen years old. But he didn't sound like that Jake. Not even close.

Maggie felt a cold chill crawl up her spine despite the Midwest heat and humidity, and she wrapped her arms around her body for warmth. He was only an arm's length away, close enough to touch, and yet she suddenly felt more alone than ever before in her life. Because always, through all the losses in her life—her mother, her father, and just three weeks before, the tragic deaths of her sister and brother-in-law in a small-plane crash—she'd still had Jake. He'd been her friend for as long as she could remember, and though their relationship had transitioned—quite unexpectedly—to romance, their friendship remained strong and sure.

But now he was leaving—less than five weeks before she was scheduled to walk down the aisle as his bride. It was inconceivable. Incomprehensible. But true. The stoic expression on his face told her so more eloquently than his words.

The knot in Maggie's stomach tightened as she sank down onto the couch, her legs suddenly too shaky to support her willowy five-foot-six, hundred-and-ten-pound frame. Nothing in her twenty-four years had prepared her for this...this *betrayal*. Maybe that was a harsh term. But what else could you call it when the man you loved bailed out just because things got a little rough?

Even in her dazed state, however, Maggie had to admit that "a little rough" wasn't exactly an accurate description of the situation. The sudden responsibility of raising six-year-old twins—one of whom needed ongoing medical care—wasn't a minor complication. Not when they'd planned to spend the first ten years of their marriage child-free, exploring some exotic new corner of the world each year on vacation, living the adventures they'd always dreamed of. It was a situation that demanded huge compromises, and Maggie knew it marked the death of a dream for both of them. But she had wanted to believe that Jake would realize there simply was no other option. As their only living relative, Maggie *had* to take her sister's girls. But clearly Jake hadn't been able to accept it. And where did that leave her?

Apparently alone.

As Jake sat beside her and reached for her hand, she glanced at him with dazed eyes, blind to the anguish in his. The strongly molded planes of his dear, familiar face were only a misty blur. When he spoke, the appealing, husky cadence of his voice—edged with that smoky quality that was distinctly his—sounded suddenly foreign to her ears, and his words seemed to come from a great distance.

"Maggie, I'm sorry," he whispered, knowing the words were inadequate, his gut twisting painfully at the wretched, abandoned look in her eyes.

So was she. Ever since her sixteenth birthday, when their relationship changed forever—from childhood friends to sweethearts—she'd never even looked at another man. She'd built her whole future around Jake. A future that was now crumbling around her.

"This…situation…doesn't change how I feel about you," he continued when she didn't respond. "But…well, I guess I never expected a ready-made family. It would be bad—" He cut himself off and deliberately changed the term. "Hard…enough if they were normal kids. But they've just lost both parents, and Abby has years of medical treatment ahead of her. And what about our plans for seeing the world? For not being tied down by responsibilities, at least in the beginning? And I'm not ready to take on the responsibilities of parenthood. I just feel so...trapped,'' he finished helplessly. With a sigh, he reached for her cold hands, his gaze locked on hers. "Do you understand at all?"

Slowly Maggie shook her head, trying desperately to restrain her tears. "No," she replied brokenly. "No, Jake, I don't. I thought...well, I know we haven't actually said the vows yet, but I thought, in our hearts, we'd already made a commitment. For life. For better or for worse. What if this had happened six weeks *after* the wedding instead of six weeks before? Would you have walked out then, too?"

Jake cringed, and he felt his neck grow hot. He deserved that. It was more or less the same question his father had coldly asked. Though his mother had been less vocal in her disapproval, he had seen the look of disappointment in her eyes, as well. But if the vows had actually been spoken, he would have stuck it out.

"You know better, Maggie."

She looked at him, suddenly skeptical. "Do I? I'm not so sure anymore, Jake." She shook her head and gave a short, mirthless laugh. "But I guess it was a lucky thing for you it happened now. You won't be put to that test. You're free to walk away."

God forgive him, but he'd thought that very thing. That he *was* lucky this had happened *before* the wedding. He felt like a heel for even thinking it, but he couldn't deny that he'd been relieved.

Maggie watched his face, realized that though her words had been spoken harshly, they did, in fact, mirror his thoughts. Her stomach clenched even tighter. Until this very minute she'd half expected him to rethink his decision and do what she considered the honorable thing. But as her gaze searched his eyes, she knew he wasn't going to bend, and a powerful wave of fear suddenly crashed over her.

When she spoke again, her voice was tinged with desperation. "Jake, I—I don't want to lose you. I don't know why the Lord gave us this burden, why He's testing our commitment like this. I wish I did. I wish there was an easy answer to this problem. But I can't see any other option. Can you?''

He stared at her helplessly. There was only one other option as far as he could see: put the two bereft six-year-olds into the hands of a foster family. But leaving them in the care of strangers would be wrong, and he knew it. That was why he hadn't asked her to choose between that or him. After much soul-searching he had decided that the best solution was for him to break the engagement. He didn't feel particularly noble about it, and his father's few choice words about duty and honor were still ringing in his ears, but in the end he had to make his own decision. And as much as he loved Maggie, he feared that if he went into this marriage feeling trapped, it would lead to resentment and, ultimately, heartbreak.

But now, sitting here with her ice-cold hands in his, her vulnerable eyes pleading with him to reconsider, he wondered if this was any better.

"Maggie, are you sure Charles didn't have any relatives who might take the girls?'' he asked, already knowing the answer. They'd been over this before.

She shook her head. "He was an only child, born late in life. His parents died years ago. There isn't anyone else, Jake.''

With a sigh of frustration, Jake rose and strode restlessly across the room, stopping at the window to stare unseeingly into the night.

Maggie watched him, frantically searching for words that might change his mind. She couldn't lose Jake! Since her sixteenth birthday, all she'd wanted out of life was to be Mrs. Jake West. Maybe modern women were supposed to want a career and independence. But those things paled in comparison to being Jake's wife. What better ''career'' could she find than spending her life loving Jake, first traveling with him all over the world and then creating a home for him and their children? Her throat tightened painfully, and she choked back a sob.

"Jake...maybe we should just postpone things. Maybe if we give it a little time..."

Her voice trailed off as he turned to face her. There was a tightness to his jaw, a sudden resolve in his face, that made her realize there was something he hadn't told her yet, something that she knew intuitively was going to seal their fates.

"That's not really an option, Maggie. I..." He paused, and she could see the struggle on his face as he searched for the words to tell her the thing that was going to make her world fall completely apart.

"Jake." The panic in her voice was obvious, even to her own ears. She didn't want to hear what he was going to say. "Please, can't we think about this a little more?"

She heard him sigh, saw the sudden sag in his shoulders, watched with trepidation as he walked slowly back to the couch and sat beside her again. More than anything in the world she wanted him to pull her into his arms and tell her that everything was going to be all right, as he had on so many other occasions through the years. But she could see that wasn't his intent. He kept himself purposely at a distance and made no attempt to touch her.

Jake lifted a hand and wearily rubbed his forehead, then drew in a deep, unsteady breath. When he spoke, his voice was gentle but firm. "Maggie, I joined the navy. I leave in five days."

Maggie stared at him blankly, her eyes suddenly confused. "Leave?" she parroted. "You're leaving? You joined the navy?"

"Yes. I signed all the papers this morning. I've known for a week I was going to do it, but I just couldn't seem to find the words to tell you."

"But...but why?"

"It's my chance to see the world, Maggie. It won't be the same as if we were going together, I know, but with my advanced degree I should get plum assignments. That's what they told me at the recruiting office, anyway. I go directly to officer training school. It's a great opportunity."

"But...but you have a job already."

"I know. But it's just a job, Maggie. In two years the most exciting thing I've done with my engineering skills is design hydraulic systems for elevators. I don't want to do that the rest of my life."

"But...but why the navy?" she asked, still trying to make sense of this unexpected twist.

Because I knew if I didn't do something irrevocable like that, I wouldn't be able to go through with the breakup, not when you look at me like this, he thought in silent anguish. But he couldn't say that.

He studied her now, this woman he loved, as he debated how to answer. From the first time he kissed her, Maggie had been the only woman he ever wanted. They'd played together as toddlers, hung around as teenagers and fallen in love that one magical day on Maggie's sixteenth birthday when he'd suddenly begun to realize that she was growing up. For the first time, he had really looked at her—the way a man looks at a woman who attracts him. Maggie wasn't exactly a great beauty, with her wavy, flyaway red hair and turned up nose. But those attributes were more than offset by her gorgeous, deep green eyes and porcelain complexion. Suddenly she wasn't just a "pal" anymore, but a woman who brought out unexpected feelings and responses in him.

And as time went by, he'd begun to notice other things, too. Like how close to the surface her feelings lay, how transparent they were, clearly reflected in her expressive eyes. And he'd noticed something else in her eyes, too—a maturing passion, flashes of desire, that set his blood racing. But she had a discipline he could only admire. For, in an era of questionable morals, she made no apology for her traditional Christian values, believing that the ultimate intimacy should be reserved for marriage, expressed only in the context of a lifetime commitment. He'd always respected her for that.

Yet despite Maggie's strong faith, she had a certain air of fragility, an aura of helplessness, that always brought out his protective instinct. And it was this latter quality that he knew would do him in tonight unless he had an airtight out, an ironclad escape—like joining the navy.

And *escape* was an accurate word, he admitted. He was running away because he was running scared. It was as simple as that. But he couldn't very well tell her all that.

"The navy seemed to offer some great career and travel opportunities," he replied, the reason sounding lame—and incomplete—even to his own ears.

Maggie stared at him, wide-eyed and silent. She'd hoped he'd at least help her get settled with the twins. She'd even begun to think that maybe he would change his mind if he saw that caring for them wasn't so bad after all. But he wasn't going to give himself that chance. He was bailing out.

An aching sadness overwhelmed her as she recalled all the tender words they'd said to one another, all the plans they'd made with such eager anticipation. She thought of the hours they'd spent poring over maps, dreaming of places that would take them far from their Midwest roots, planning their future travels around the world—beginning with their honeymoon in Paris. A honeymoon now destined never to take place, she realized. Cold fingers clutched at her heart and tightened mercilessly, squeezing out the last breath of hope. He'd made his decision. It was done. There was nothing more to say.

She gazed at Jake, and suddenly she felt as if she was looking at a stranger, as if the man she'd fallen in love with had somehow ceased to exist. That man had been caring and kind, someone who could be relied upon to stand beside her, no matter the circumstances. The stranger sitting beside her seemed to possess none of those qualities. He'd said he loved her. And maybe he thought he did. But his actions didn't even come close to fitting her definition of love.

Maggie took a deep breath, struggling to make sense of everything that was happening. Her life had changed so dramatically in the last three weeks that there was an air of unreality about it. She'd lost her only sister. She'd been given responsibility for two young, newly orphaned children, one of whom needed ongoing medical care. And now the final blow. She was losing the man she loved. Only her faith kept total despair at bay. But even *with* her faith, she was finding it hard not to give in to self-pity. Why was the Lord testing her this way? she cried silently. She just couldn't see any purpose to it.

Unless…unless it was the Lord's way of letting Jake show his true character now, before they formalized their commitment, she thought, searching desperately for an explanation that made *some* sense. She supposed it was better to find out now how he reacted in adversity. But frankly, at this moment, it didn't give her much consolation.

"Maggie?"

Jake's concerned voice drew her back to the present. The familiar warmth and tenderness were back in his eyes, and for just a moment she was tempted to tell him she'd do whatever he wanted, just so long as they could be together.

But with sudden resolve, she straightened her shoulders and lifted her chin. She'd already practically begged him to rethink his decision, and he'd rejected her plea. Well, she had *some* pride. If Jake didn't love her enough to stick by her through this, then she didn't want him, either. She could survive on her own. Okay, so maybe she'd relied too much on Jake to take care of things, make all the decisions. That didn't mean she couldn't learn to do those things herself. Especially since it was clear she *had* to. She needed to take her life in her own hands. Beginning right now.

Abruptly Maggie rose, and Jake stared up at her, startled by her sudden movement.

She took a deep breath, willing herself to get through the next few minutes without breaking down. Her heart might be tattered, but there would be time for tears later, when she was alone. Plenty of time, in fact. Like the rest of her life.

"Jake, I don't see any reason to prolong this, do you? You've said what you came to say. It's obvious you've set a new course for your life. I have to accept that. And I wish you well."

Jake rose more slowly, his face troubled. There was a quality in Maggie's voice he'd never heard before—a quiet dignity, tinged with resignation. This wasn't at all the reaction he'd anticipated. He'd expected tears and pleading right up to the final goodbye.

"Look, Maggie, I don't want to just walk out and leave you to totally fend for yourself. I'd like to at least help you out financially, make sure you're settled."

As far as Maggie was concerned, offering money was the worst thing Jake could have done. Maybe it would appease his conscience, but she wanted nothing from this man who, until half an hour ago, had been the center of her world, whose love she had mistakenly believed to be unshakable and true.

"I don't want your money, Jake. I have a job. A good job. Graphic design is a growing field. I might even branch out into illustration. And Becky and Charles had insurance, so the girls will be well provided for. We'll be fine."

Jake looked at Maggie, noting the uncharacteristic tilt of her chin. She'd always been so compliant, so accepting of his help, that he was a bit taken aback by her refusal. And he was even more surprised when she removed her engagement ring and held it out to him.

"I think this is yours."

"Keep the ring, Maggie," he protested, surprised at the unevenness of his own voice.

"Why? It's a symbol of something that no longer exists. I'd rather you take it back." She reached over and dropped it into his hand. Then she walked to the door, opened it and turned to face him. "I don't think we have anything else to say to each other, do we?"

Jake looked at Maggie. Her beautiful eyes were steady, and for once he couldn't read her feelings in their depths. But he knew she was hurting. Knew that she must feel exactly as he felt—devastated and bereft. But she was hiding it well. Slowly he followed her to the door.

"I'll take care of canceling all the…arrangements." He could at least spare her that.

"Thank you," she said stiffly.

"I'm sorry, Maggie." He knew words were inadequate. But they were all he could offer.

"So am I." Her voice caught on the last word, and for a moment he thought she was going to lose it. He almost wished she would. He didn't know how to deal with this aloof, controlled Maggie. He wanted to take her in his arms one last time, wanted to cry with her at the unfairness of life, wanted to mourn the passing of their relationship. It was clear, however, that she had a different sort of parting in mind.

"Well...I guess there's nothing left to say."

"No."

"Maggie, I hope..." His voice trailed off. What did he hope? That someday she would find it in her heart to forgive him? Unlikely. That she would eventually be able to remember with pleasure their good times? Again, unlikely. That a man worthy of her love would one day claim her heart?

That thought jolted him. No, that wasn't at all what he wanted. His Maggie in the arms of another man? The idea repelled him. And yet, how could he wish her less? She deserved to find happiness with a man who would love her enough to stand by her through the tough times as well as the happy ones. Someone who would do a much better job at that than he had.

"What do you hope?" she asked curiously, a wistful note creeping into her voice.

He considered his answer, and settled for one that didn't even come close to expressing the myriad of conflicting emotions in his heart. "I wish you happiness, Maggie."

The smile she gave him was touched with bitterness, telling him more eloquently than words that she considered that a vain hope. "Thanks, Jake. Goodbye."

And then she very gently, very deliberately, shut the door behind him.

Maggie walked numbly back to the couch and sat down. She felt chilled to the bone and suddenly she began to tremble. For the first time in her life she was truly alone. She'd told Jake that she would be all right. But those words had been spoken with more bravado and pride than confidence. She didn't have a clue how she was going to cope. Not without Jake.

Jake, with his gentle touch and laughing eyes, his confidence and optimism, his sense of adventure. He had filled her world with joy and brightness. The events that had transpired in this room during the last hour couldn't erase the memory of all they'd shared, of the love she had felt for him. Without Jake, the future stretched ahead like a dark, aching void, filled with overwhelming responsibilities, yet empty of the warmth and companionship and love that made all trials bearable. How could she go on alone?

And then she thought of the twins. They needed her. Desperately. They, too, had been deprived of the people they loved most. She had to be strong for them, if not for herself. Together they would move forward. For the three of them, love had died—for the twins, physically; for her, emotionally. But the death was equally final in both cases.

Which meant that, for the first time her life, her future lay solely in her own hands. She had no one to consult, no one to make decisions for her, no one to reassure her that she could handle the task before her. It was up to her alone.

Well, maybe not quite alone, she reminded herself suddenly. There *was* Someone she could rely on, Someone who would stand by her through whatever lay ahead. And so she took a moment, before the demands of her new life came crashing down on her, to close her eyes and ask for His guidance.

Please, Lord, show me what to do. Help me be strong. Help me to know that I'm never truly alone. That You're always with me. And help me to accept, even without understanding, the hardships You've given me, and to believe in my heart that You would never give me a cross too heavy to bear.

The short prayer brought Maggie a momentary sense of peace and renewed confidence. She could almost feel the Lord's loving presence beside her. And for that she was immensely grateful. For she knew, beyond the shadow of a doubt, that she would need Him desperately in the months and years to come.

Chapter One

Twelve Years Later

Give it up.

The word's echoed in Jake's mind as the swirling Maine mist wrapped itself around his small rental car, effectively obscuring everything beyond a thirty-foot radius. He frowned and eased his foot off the accelerator. Should he continue the short distance to Castine or play it safe and pull in somewhere for the night?

A sign appeared to his right, and he squinted, trying to make out the words. Blue Hill. He glanced at the map on the seat beside him. Castine was less than twenty miles away, he calculated. But he suspected that these narrow, winding—and unfamiliar—roads weren't too forgiving, and dusk was descending rapidly. Not a good combination, he decided. Besides, he was tired. He'd driven up from Boston, then spent what remained of the day exploring the back roads and small towns of the Blue Hill peninsula. If he wanted to feel rested and fresh for his interview at the Maine Maritime Academy tomorrow, it was time to call it a day.

As if to validate his decision, a sign bearing the words Whispering Sails B&B providentially loomed out of the mist. Talk about perfect timing! he mused. He pulled into the gravel driveway and carefully followed the gradual incline until he reached a tiny parking area, where one empty space remained. Hopefully, the space was a good sign.

Jake eased his six-foot frame out of the compact car and reached into the back seat for his suit bag, slinging it effortlessly over his shoulder. As he made his way up the stone path, he peered at the house, barely discernible through the heavy mist. The large Queen Anne-style structure of weathered gray clapboard was somewhat intimidating in size, its dull color offset by the welcome, golden light spilling from the windows and the overflowing flower boxes hugging the porch rail. Definitely a haven for a weary traveler, he decided.

Jake climbed the porch steps, read the welcome sign on the door and entered, as it instructed. A bell jangled somewhere in the back of the house, and he paused in the foyer, glancing around as he waited for someone to appear. The house was tastefully decorated, he noted appreciatively, with none of the "fussiness" often associated with this style of architecture. In fact, the clean, contemporary lines of the furnishings set off the ornate woodwork beautifully, and he found the subtle blending of old and new eminently pleasing. A soft, warm color palette gave the house a homey feel—no small accomplishment for high-ceilinged rooms of such grand proportion. Clearly the house had been decorated by someone with an eye for design and color.

His gaze lingered on the ample fireplace topped by a marble mantle, which took up much of one wall, and he was sorry the month was July instead of January. He wouldn't mind settling into the large overstuffed chair beside it with a good book on a cold night. There was something...restful...about the room that strongly appealed to him.

As Jake completed his survey, a door swung open at the back of the foyer and a young woman who looked to be about twenty hurried through.

"I thought I heard the bell," she greeted him breathlessly, her smile apologetic. "I was on the back porch changing a light bulb. Sorry to keep you waiting."

He returned the smile. "Not at all. I was hoping you might

have a room for the night. I was trying to make it to Castine, but the weather isn't cooperating.''

She made a wry face and nodded. "Not exactly Maine at its best," she concurred sympathetically as she slipped behind a wooden counter that was half-hidden by the curving stairway. "You're in luck for a room, though. We're always booked solid in the summer, but we just received a cancellation." The young woman smiled and handed him a pen. "If you'll just fill out this card, I'll help you with your bags."

"No need. I just have a suit bag. But thanks."

He provided the requested information quickly, then waited while the young woman selected a key and joined him on the other side of the desk.

"I'll show you to your room. It has a private bath and a great view of the bay—well, it's a great view on a clear day," she amended with a rueful grin over her shoulder as she led the way up the steps. "Maybe by tomorrow morning it will be clear," she added hopefully. "Anyway, breakfast is between eight and nine in the dining room, which is next to the drawing room. Checkout is eleven. My name's Allison, and I'll be on duty till ten if you need anything. Just ring the bell on the desk." She paused before a second-floor door at the front of the house and inserted the key, then pushed the door open and stepped aside to let him enter.

Jake strolled past her and gave the room a quick but thorough scrutiny. It seemed that the hand of a skilled decorator had been at work here, as well. The room was done in restful shades of blue. A large bay window at the front of the house would afford a panoramic view of the sea in clear weather, he suspected, and a cushioned window seat beckoned invitingly. A four-poster bed, antique writing desk, intricately carved wardrobe and comfortable-looking easy chair with ottoman completed the furnishing. His gaze paused on the fireplace, noting the candle sconces on the mantle, and again he wished it was cool enough for a fire.

"I hope this is all right," Allison said anxiously.

He turned to her with a smile. "Perfect. The room is very inviting."

Allison grinned. "My aunt has a way with color and such. Everybody says so. And she makes all the guests feel real welcome. That's why we have so many regulars. You know, you're really lucky to get this room. It's the most requested one. Especially with honeymooners."

Jake grinned. "I can see why. It's quite...romantic."

Allison blushed and fumbled with the doorknob. "Well, if you need anything, just let me know. Have a pleasant evening, Mr. West."

As the door clicked shut, Jake drew a deep breath and stretched tiredly, flexing the tight muscles in his neck. He'd been on the road since early morning, but the time had been well spent. Before he decided to make this area his permanent home, he intended to check it out thoroughly.

He strolled over to the window and stared out thoughtfully into the gray mist. Home, he repeated silently. Surprisingly enough, the word had a nice sound. After twelve years of roaming the globe, his worldly possessions following him around in a few small boxes, the thought of having a home, a place to call his own, had a sudden, unexpected appeal. But he shouldn't be too surprised, he supposed. For the last couple of years he'd been plagued with a vague feeling of restlessness, of emptiness, a sense of "Is this all there is?" Even before his brother's phone call, the notion of "settling down" had crept into his thoughts, though he'd pushed it firmly aside. It wasn't something he'd seriously considered—or even *wanted* to consider—for a very long time. In fact, not since he was engaged to Maggie.

Jake frowned. Funny. He hadn't really thought much about Maggie these last few years. Purposely. During the early years after their breakup, she'd haunted his thoughts day and night, the guilt growing inside him with each passing month. It was only in the last three or four years that he had met with some success in his attempts to keep thoughts of her at bay. So why was he thinking of her now? he wondered, his frown deepening.

His gaze strayed to the chocolate-chip cookies, wrapped in clear paper and tied with a ribbon, resting between the pillows on the bed. He'd noticed them earlier, had been impressed by the thoughtful touch. Maybe they had triggered thoughts of the woman he'd once loved, he reflected. She used to bake him chocolate-chip cookies—his favorite—he recalled with a bittersweet smile.

But Maggie was only a memory now, he reminded himself with a sigh. He had no idea what had become of her. She'd moved less than a year after their parting, breaking all ties with the town which held such unhappy memories for her. Even his parents, to whom she had always been close, had no idea where she went. It was better that way, she'd told them. They understood. And he did, too. But though he'd initiated the breakup, he had nevertheless been filled with an odd sense of desolation to realize he no longer knew Maggie's whereabouts. He didn't understand why he felt that way. Didn't even try to. What good would it do? All he could do was hope she was happy.

Jake walked over to the bed and picked up the cookies, weighing them absently in his hand. Here he was, in the honeymoon suite, with only memories of a woman he'd once loved to warm his heart. For a moment, self-pity hovered threateningly. Which was ridiculous, he rebuked himself impatiently. His solitary state was purely his own doing. He'd known his share of women through the years, even met a few who made him fleetingly entertain the idea of marriage. But that's as far as it ever went. Because, bottom line, he'd never met anyone who touched his heart the way Maggie had.

He sat down in the chair and wearily let his head fall against the cushioned back. He'd never really admitted that before. But it was true. Maybe that was the legacy of a first love, he mused, that no one else ever measured up. Most people got over that, of course, moved on to meet someone new and fall in love again. He hadn't. As a result, he'd never regretted his decision to remain unmarried. Until now. Suddenly, as he contemplated a future that consisted of a more "normal" land-bound existence instead of the nomadic life he'd been living, the thought of a wife and family was appealing. For the first time in years, he felt ready to seriously consider marriage—and fatherhood.

Of course, there was one little problem, he thought with a humorless smile. He hadn't met the right woman.

Then again, maybe he had, he acknowledged with a sudden, bittersweet pang of regret, his smile fading. But it was too late for regrets. To be specific, twelve years too late.

"I mean, this guy is gorgeous!"

Abby looked at her sister and grinned as she scrambled some eggs. "Are you sure you're not exaggerating?" she asked skeptically.

"Absolutely not." Allison peeked into the oven to check the blueberry muffins, then turned back to her twin. "Tall, handsome, dark hair, deep brown eyes. And you know what? I think he's single."

"Yeah?" Abby paused, her tone interested. "How old is he?"

Allison shrugged. "Old. Thirty-something, probably. But for an older guy, he's awesome."

"Let me serve him, okay?" Abby cajoled.

"Hey, I saw him first!" Allison protested.

"Yes, but you had your chance to talk to him last night. It's my turn. That's only fair, isn't it, Aunt Maggie?"

Maggie smiled and shook her head. "You two are getting awfully worked up about someone who will be checking out in an hour or two."

Allison sighed dramatically. "True. But we can dream, can't we? Maybe he's a rich tycoon. Or maybe he's lost his beloved wife and is retracing the route they traveled on their honeymoon. Or maybe he's a Hollywood producer scouting the area for a new movie. Or…"

"Or maybe you better watch those muffins before they get too brown," Maggie reminded her with a nod toward the oven.

Allison sighed. "Oh, Aunt Maggie, you have no imagination when it comes to men."

"I have plenty of imagination. Fortunately, I also have a good dose of common sense."

"But common sense is so...so boring," Allison complained.

"He just came in," Abby reported breathlessly, peering through a crack in the kitchen door. She grabbed the pot of coffee before Allison could get to it, and with a triumphant "My turn," sailed through the door.

Maggie smiled and shook her head. One thing for sure. There was never a dull moment with the twins. At eighteen, the world for them was just one big adventure waiting to happen. And she encouraged their "seize the moment" philosophy—within reason, of course. Because she knew that life would impose its own limitations soon enough.

When Abby reentered the kitchen a few minutes later, she shut the door and leaned against it, her face flushed.

"Well?" Allison prompted.

"Wow!"

"See? Didn't I tell you? What's he wearing?" Allison asked eagerly.

"A dark gray suit with a white shirt and a maroon paisley tie."

"A suit? Nobody ever wears a suit here. He must be a business tycoon or something."

"Sorry to interrupt with such a mundane question, but what does he want for breakfast?" Maggie inquired wryly.

"Scrambled eggs, wheat toast and orange juice," Abby recited dreamily.

Maggie was beginning to regret that she'd missed this mysterious stranger's arrival. But the church council meeting had run late, and their unexpected guest had apparently retired for the night by the time she arrived home. It *was* unusual for a younger, apparently single, man to stay with them. Most of their guests were couples. Maybe she ought to check this guy out herself, she thought, as she placed two of the freshly baked blueberry muffins in a basket. Just for grins, of course. It would be interesting to see how she rated this "older guy" the twins were raving about.

Maggie picked up the basket of muffins and a glass of orange juice and headed for the door. "Okay, you two, now the mature woman of the world will give you her expert opinion."

The twins giggled.

"Oh, Aunt Maggie. You've never been anywhere but Missouri, Boston and Maine," Abby reminded her.

Maggie felt a sudden, unexpected pang, but she kept her smile firmly in place. "True. But that doesn't mean I haven't had my romantic adventures."

"When?" Allison demanded pertly.

When, indeed? There'd only been one romantic adventure in her life. And that had ended badly. But she'd never told the girls much about it. Only when they reached the age when boys suddenly became fascinating and they'd begun plying her with questions about her own romantic past had she even mentioned it. And then only in the vaguest terms. Yes, it had been serious, she'd told them. In fact, they'd been engaged. But it just hadn't worked out. And that was all they ever got out of her, despite their persistent questions. She never wanted them to know that it was because of their arrival in her life that her one romance had failed. They'd had a hard enough time adjusting to the loss of their parents; she never wanted to lay the guilt of her shattered romance on them, as well. And she wasn't about to start now. "I think I'll remain a woman of mystery," she declared over her shoulder as she pushed through the door to the sound of their giggles.

Maggie paused on the other side, taking a moment to compose herself. For some reason their innocent teasing had touched a nerve. She'd always claimed she had no time for romance, that she was perfectly happy living her life solo. She'd pretty much convinced them of her sincerity through the years. She'd almost convinced herself, as well. In many ways, her life *was* easier this way. Only occasionally did she yearn for the life that might have been. But she'd learned not to waste time on impractical "what-iffing." Her life was the way it was, and for the most part she was happy and content and fulfilled. The Lord had blessed her in many ways, and she was grateful for those blessings. In fact, she had more in the "blessings" department than most people.

Her spirits renewed, she glanced around the small dining room. All the tables were filled, but it was easy to spot their "mystery" guest. He sat alone, angled away from her, his face almost completely obscured by the daily paper he was reading. Yet she could tell that for once her assessment matched that of the girls'. They'd been right on target in their description of his physical attributes. He was impeccably dressed, his dark hair neatly trimmed above the collar of his crisp white shirt. His long legs stretched out beneath the table, and his hands seemed strong and capable.

As Maggie started across the room, the man lowered the paper and reached for his coffee, giving her a good view of his strong, distinguished—and very familiar—profile.

It was *Jake!*

Even as her mind struggled to reconcile his presence with the astronomical odds of him appearing in her dining room, her heart accepted it. She knew that profile—the firm chin, the classic nose, the well-shaped lips. It was him.

Maggie felt suddenly as if someone had delivered a well-placed blow to her chest, knocking every bit of wind out of her lungs. Her step faltered and the color drained from her face. She had to escape, had to get back to the kitchen and regain some control, before he spotted her.

But it was too late. As he lifted the coffee cup to his lips he glanced toward her, and their gazes connected—Maggie's wide with shock, Jake's changing in rapid succession from mild interest to curious to stunned.

Jake stared at the red-haired woman standing less than ten feet away from him and his hand froze, the coffee cup halfway to his lips. His heart stopped, then raced on. *Maggie!*

Maggie didn't even realize her hands were shaking until the basket of muffins suddenly slipped out of her grasp. She tore her gaze from his and bent down, just as he rose to join her. Some of the juice sloshed out of the glass, leaving a sticky residue on her fingers as it formed a puddle on the floor. She looked at it helplessly, but a moment later Jake was beside her, wiping it up even as he retrieved a wayward muffin. Then he reached over and took her hand.

Her startled gaze collided with his, their eyes only inches apart.

"Let me," he said softly, the husky cadence in his voice exactly the same as she remembered it. With difficulty she swallowed past the sudden lump in her throat as he carefully wiped the sticky juice off her fingers with the clean side of the napkin. She stared down numbly, watching his strong, bronzed hand gently hold hers. She used to love the way he touched her, she recalled, her breath lodging in her throat. His hands—possessive, sure, tender—could work magic. A sudden, unexpected spark shot through her, and in confusion she jerked free of his grasp and rose unsteadily to her feet.

He stood up, as well, and then gazed down at her, his eyes warm, a shadow of incredulity lingering in their depths.

"Maggie." The way he said her name, gently and with wonder, made her heart lurch into triple time. "It's been a long time."

"Yes. It has." A tremor ran through her voice, but she didn't care. She was just grateful she could speak at all.

"Is this your place?"

"Yes. Listen, I'm sorry about the muffins and juice. I'll go get you some more. Excuse me." And then she turned and fled.

Jake watched her go, aware for the first time that the two of them were drawing curious looks from the other guests. With one last glance toward the kitchen, he slowly turned and walked back to his table. His first inclination had been to follow Maggie, but he understood that she needed some time to adjust to this strange turn of events. He knew he did.

Jake reached for his coffee, noting that his hand was trembling. He wasn't surprised. A bizarre coincidence like this was more than a little unsettling. Only yesterday he'd been thinking of Maggie, and his dreams last night had been filled with her. Then he'd awakened to a reality that didn't include her, reminding himself that she was part of his past. Until now.

For twelve years, Jake had felt as if the two of them had

unfinished business. Now, after all these years, it seemed he was being given a second chance to make amends. And he intended to take it. He didn't expect her to welcome him back with open arms. But he hoped they could at least find some sense of resolution and inner peace.

Peace wasn't exactly the word Maggie was thinking as she burst through the kitchen door, breathless and pale. Her emotions were anything *but* peaceful. Her heart was banging against the wall of her chest as furiously as if she'd just finished a hundred-yard dash. She felt strangely light-headed. And more than a little annoyed. What was wrong with her? Why should a man whom she hadn't seen in twelve years, who had walked out when she'd needed him most, still have such a powerful effect on her? It didn't make any sense. And Maggie didn't like things that didn't make sense.

"Aunt Maggie?" Allison's concerned voice penetrated her thoughts, and she glanced up.

"What's wrong?" Abby asked, her face alarmed at her aunt's pallor.

Maggie forced herself to take a deep breath. "I'm fine. I just…well…that man you two have been talking about, I—I used to know him."

"You *know* him?" Allison repeated incredulously. "How? When?"

"A long time ago. I haven't seen him in years. It was just a…shock, that's all. I'll be okay in a minute."

Abby sent Allison a worried frown. Maggie never got rattled. "So who is he?" Abby persisted.

Maggie walked over to the center island and put two new muffins in the basket, then filled a glass with orange juice, aware that her hand was shaking. She knew the twins would notice. She also knew they weren't going to let her get away without explaining this uncharacteristic behavior. With a sigh, she turned to find them staring at her, their expressions intent—and concerned.

"He's a man I used to date…a long time ago."

Suddenly the light dawned on Allison's face. Though Maggie teased them about her past beaux, as far as they knew she'd only been really serious about one man in her entire life. Certainly none since they could remember. And it would take someone who had once been important to her to make their aunt…well, come unglued.

"Aunt Maggie, this is *him,* isn't it?" Allison's voice was slightly awed.

"Him who?" Abby demanded.

Allison turned to her twin, suddenly excited. "*Him.* You know, the guy Aunt Maggie was engaged to once."

Now it was Abby's turn to look incredulous. "Aunt Maggie, is that true?"

Maggie had always been glad that the twins had grown into insightful, perceptive young women. Until now. She might as well admit the truth, she thought with a sigh. They'd get it out of her sooner or later.

"Yes, it is."

"Wow!" Allison breathed.

"Yeah, wow!" Abby echoed. "It's so romantic!"

Maggie could think of other words to describe it. *Disruptive,* for one. *Upsetting,* for another. *Scary,* for a third, although why that word popped into her mind she had no idea. She turned to the twins and gave them a stern look.

"Now look, you two, the man is leaving shortly. It's just sheer coincidence that he turned up on our doorstep last night. I'll admit I was surprised. Shocked, even. But don't make a big deal out of this."

"But Aunt Maggie, don't you think it's…well, like a movie or something, that he appeared out of the mist at your B&B after all these years? You know, where long-lost lovers are reunited and rekindle an old romance?" Abby asked dreamily.

"First of all, we are *not* long-lost lovers. We didn't get lost. We broke up. On purpose. And second, neither one of us has any interest in rekindling an old romance. I'm perfectly content with my life just as it is. And even though he's not wearing a ring, Jake could very well have a wife and five kids somewhere."

"I'll bet he doesn't," Allison predicted smugly.

"Now why on earth would you say that?" Maggie demanded impatiently, turning to find the other twin peeking through the crack in the door.

"Because he keeps looking this way, like he's waiting for you."

"He probably just wants his orange juice," Maggie pointed out, trying desperately to keep her voice from reflecting the turbulence of her emotions.

As she picked up the glass and added it to the tray with the basket of muffins she could feel the twins' gazes on her back, knew they were silently communicating with each other about this exciting development in their aunt's lackluster love life. But in truth, she didn't want to go back out there. Talking to Jake would only stir up old, painful memories best left at rest. Yet, refusing to see him would be childish. Their relationship was history, after all. Whatever they once felt for each other had long since evaporated. They would simply carry on a calm, mature conversation, and then she'd bid him farewell. She could handle that, she thought as she lifted the tray and walked toward the door.

Couldn't she?

Chapter Two

Jake was on his feet the moment Maggie stepped through the door, but when she was detained by guests at another table, he slowly sat back down. In a way he was grateful for their intervention, because as they engaged her with questions about local sights, he had a chance to look at her unobserved.

She's changed, he reflected, as his discerning gaze swept over her. She was still slender, her trim figure shown to good advantage in a pair of well-fitting khaki slacks and a green, long-sleeved cotton blouse that was neatly tucked in and secured with a hemp belt. But the girlish figure he remembered had changed subtly—and attractively—as she'd matured.

His appreciative eyes moved to her hair. The vibrant red color had mellowed slightly, but was no less striking, he noted with pleasure. He'd always been partial to red hair, and Maggie's was especially beautiful, shot through with gold highlights. Apparently she'd never quite tamed its waves. Despite her efforts to pull it sedately back, loose tendrils had escaped around her face, giving the no-nonsense style a winsome, feminine appeal. She still had her freckles, too, he observed with a smile, but they appeared to have faded slightly. He assumed she was grateful for *that* change, recalling how she'd always complained about them.

But there was something else…different…about her, he realized. The Maggie he remembered had been dependent, always waiting for him to take the initiative. The woman he now observed seemed anything *but* dependent. She was gracious, poised and self-confident. A woman who not only took charge of *things* but was quite capable of taking care of *herself*. It was a surprising—but intriguing—transformation.

There was one thing, though, that hadn't changed at all, he discovered a moment later when their gazes connected and his pulse flew into overdrive. He found her every bit as attractive as he had twelve years before. His spirits took a swift and surprisingly strong upswing—only to nose-dive a moment later. Just because *he* felt the old chemistry didn't mean *she* did. And even *if* she did, he doubted that she'd want to renew their friendship, let alone anything more. Why should she, after what he'd done to her twelve years ago? Yet, he couldn't quite stifle the hope that suddenly surged through him.

Maggie moved toward him then, and he stood as she joined him, noting the slight flush on her cheeks. One more thing that hadn't changed, he tallied with pleasure. She still blushed. It was a quality he'd always found endearing.

"I wasn't sure you'd come back out," he confessed quietly.

She served the juice and muffins, avoiding his gaze. "Why wouldn't I?"

There was a moment of silence before he responded. "I wouldn't have blamed you if you hadn't," he told her, instead of replying to the question.

She risked a glance at him then, praying that her fragile composure would hold. "That was a long time ago, Jake." Much to her surprise—and relief—her voice was steady, and she congratulated herself for sounding so calm and controlled when her insides were churning.

Jake eyed her speculatively, debating whether to pursue the subject. "Maybe so," he responded carefully. "But some things are hard to forget."

A shadow crossed her eyes, come and gone so quickly he almost missed it. Anyone else would have. But once he had been keenly attuned to the nuances of her emotions. Apparently he still was. No matter what she said next, he knew that the hurt was still there, possibly buried so deeply in her heart even *she* didn't realize it still existed. But it clearly did, and his gut twisted painfully as he came face-to-face with the lingering effects of his actions twelve years before.

Instead of responding directly to his comment, she shrugged, and when she spoke, her tone was straightforward. "Life goes on, though. We all learn to cope."

He wanted to ask if life had been good to her, if she'd found the happiness she deserved, if she'd had much trouble raising the twins…if her heart belonged to another man. She wore no ring. He'd noticed that right away. But you didn't ask someone personal questions after twelve years. Not when you'd long ago forfeited the right. He had to settle for a less probing query. "So you've managed all right, then, Maggie?"

Maggie looked into his eyes—warm and compelling and intense—and remembered with a bittersweet pang how easily she used to get lost in his dark gaze. How, with a simple look, he could make her heart soar. His eyes were still expressive, still powerful, she realized. But she wasn't susceptible to their magnetism anymore, she told herself resolutely. A lot of things had changed. She'd changed. And this man, once the center of her world, was really nothing more than a stranger to her now.

She tucked the tray under her arm and forced herself to smile. "Well, as you can see, I have a business. The girls are well. We've done fine. I hope your career has been as satisfying as mine."

"The navy has given me a good life," he acknowledged. "I have no regrets about that choice, anyway."

But he had regrets about other choices? Better not to ask, though, she decided quickly.

"Well, I have things to attend to, Jake," she said brightly. "I hope your stay with us has been pleasant—"

The words died in her throat as he reached out and touched her arm.

"I know this situation is somewhat…awkward…but I can't help thinking our paths crossed again for some reason." He paused, searching for a convincing way to phrase his request. Finally he drew a deep breath, his eyes reflecting the intensity of his feelings. "I don't want to walk away without at least talking to you," he told her honestly, his gaze steady and direct. "Will you give me half an hour or so? For old times' sake, if nothing else?"

Maggie tried to ignore the entreaty in his eyes as she considered his request. But it was hard to think rationally when the warmth of his hand was seeping through the sleeve of her blouse. She really didn't want to talk to him. What good would it possibly accomplish after all these years? It seemed far...safer...to leave the past where it belonged—in the past.

But she had to admit that, like him, she was thrown by the odd coincidence that had brought them together. A coincidence so odd that it seemed somehow more than coincidence. She recalled how she'd prayed for just such a "coincidence" more often than she cared to admit in the early years, when she was struggling to earn a living and cope with the challenges of single parenthood. There were so many times when a simple touch, a warm, caring hand holding hers, would have lightened her burden immeasurably. But the Lord hadn't answered those prayers. Not in the way she'd hoped for, at least. Instead, He had helped her find hidden reserves of strength, spirit and determination that had seen her through the rough times. In the end, she'd made it on her own, and in so doing, discovered that she was a capable and competent woman who didn't need to rely on a man to survive. The experience had bolstered her self-esteem, and she had learned to make choices and plans decisively and with confidence.

So why had the Lord sent Jake now, long after she'd stopped asking? Why disrupt her world now, when she had not only resigned herself to a solitary life, but made her peace with it? Maggie didn't have a clue. But there must be a reason for this unexpected meeting, and maybe she should at least try to find out what it was.

"Please, Maggie," Jake persisted. "It would mean a lot to me."

She drew a deep breath and nodded. "All right, Jake. The girls can finish up the breakfast."

His answering smile was warm and grateful—and relieved.

"Thank you." He glanced at his watch. "I need to make a quick call. Then we can talk."

"There's a phone in the drawing room. Next to the fireplace."

He nodded. "I'll be right back."

Maggie watched him leave, then sank down into the closest chair. Her seat afforded her a discreet view of the drawing room. He was turned slightly away from her as he used the phone, and she took advantage of the opportunity to observe him.

He's changed, she noted thoughtfully. He'd filled out, the lanky frame she remembered maturing into a trim, well-toned body. The style of his dark brown hair was familiar, though shorter than it used to be. And a faint brush of silver at both temples gave him a distinguished air. The few lines on his face, which hadn't been there when they parted, spoke more of character than of age. Maggie had to admit that he was even more handsome now than he had been twelve years before.

But there was something else different about him, something beyond the physical that she couldn't quite put her finger on, she realized with a frown. He radiated a quiet confidence, a decisiveness, a sense of determination and purpose. It was reflected in his body language, in the very way he moved, she thought, as he hung up the phone and made a few quick notes on the pad beside it. The Jake she had known was eager, restless and searching. This Jake was polished, self-assured and at peace with his place in the world.

And yet...there was a certain indefinable sadness in his eyes, a world-weariness, that tugged at her heart. It was almost as if he'd searched the world for something but had come up empty, and ultimately had resigned himself to that fact.

Maggie had no idea where that insight came from, or even if it was accurate. Nor did she have a clue what it meant. Still, she knew instinctively there was a void of some sort in Jake's life that troubled his soul.

But the state of Jake's soul was *not* her concern, she reminded herself sternly as he walked toward her. Her energies would be better focused on conducting a civil, rational conversation.

Jake smiled as he sat down across from her. "Well, that buys me an hour."

"You have an appointment?"

"Mmm-hmm. But I wish I didn't."

His comment, as well as the familiar tone in his voice, startled Maggie. She didn't know how to respond, so she remained silent, uncomfortably aware that he was studying her.

"The years have been good to you, Maggie," he said finally. "You look great."

This wasn't at all the polite, impersonal conversation she'd expected, and the warm, husky note in his voice rattled her. "Th-thanks. So do you," she replied, berating herself for letting him fluster her.

"So tell me about this place." He made an all-encompassing gesture. "Have you been doing this long?"

That was more like it, she thought with relief. Questions like that she could handle. "Eight years. I moved to Boston about a year after..." She started to say, "after you left," but changed her mind. The less she talked about *them,* the better. "...after I got the twins," she continued. "I worked in a graphic design firm there for three years. By then Abby was finished with all her operations and therapy, so there was less need to stay in a big city. And I thought it would be better for the girls to grow up in a small town. We'd visited Maine on vacation once and loved it, so we came up and looked around one summer. This place happened to be on the market at a good price. It had been vacant for a while, and even though it was structurally sound, it needed lots of cosmetic help and some updating. Before I knew it, I was the proud owner of a B&B. I did freelance design work for a while to tide us over until we established a clientele, and I still sell some of my watercolors to a greeting card company."

She paused and took a deep breath. "The early years here were a little rough, and it took a lot more hard work than I expected to get established, but I've never regretted the move," she finished.

Jake eyed her speculatively, making no attempt to conceal his admiration. "I'm impressed, Maggie. It took a lot of courage to make such a radical life-style change. Not many people would have risked it."

She shrugged dismissively, but was oddly pleased by the compliment. "I did a lot of research before I made the move. This is a popular area, and the B&Bs do well. I drew up a pretty solid business plan, so it wasn't too difficult to get a loan for the necessary improvements. And I found ways to keep the capital expenditures reasonably low."

Jake stared at the woman across from him, struggling to reconcile the Maggie he knew with this savvy business-woman. His Maggie would not have had a clue about business plans or capital expenditures. Apparently she'd changed even more than he suspected. But it wasn't an unpleasant change, he realized, a faint smile touching his lips.

Maggie noted the smile and eyed him cautiously. "What's wrong?"

"Nothing. It's just that the Maggie I remember had very little interest in business. I'm surprised, that's all."

"The Maggie you knew didn't *need* to be interested in business, Jake. This one does."

There was no hint of recrimination in her matter-of-fact tone, but the old, familiar guilt tugged at Jake's conscience. If he'd honored his commitment to her, Maggie wouldn't have had to struggle alone to build a life for herself and the twins. It couldn't have been easy, though she'd downplayed the difficulty. Which only made him admire her more.

"You seem to have done a good job," he said quietly. "This place is obviously a success. And the twins seem like fine young women. Abby looks as if she's recovered fully from the accident."

Maggie nodded. "She has. She needed two more operations after...after I took them in, and therapy after that for three years. But she's fine now." She glanced toward the kitchen, her eyes softening. "They've been a tremendous help to me through the years. I couldn't have made this place a success without them. And they've brought a great deal of joy to my life.''

Now was the perfect opening to ask the question that was most on his mind. He reached for his coffee and took a sip, trying to phrase it the right way. "Has it just been the three of you all these years, then?"

Maggie turned and looked at him directly. "If you're asking me whether I'm married, or have ever been married, the answer is no."

"Why not?" The indiscreet question came out before he could stop it, and he felt hot color steal up the back of his neck. He shook his head and held up his hands. "Listen, forget I asked that, okay? It was way out of line."

She toyed with the edge of a napkin, then gave a little shrug. "It's all right. The simple fact is, you weren't the only one who didn't want to take on a ready-made family, Jake. Especially one with medical problems."

He flinched. She'd scored a direct hit with that comment, whether she intended to or not. "I guess I deserved that," he admitted.

She frowned. "I didn't mean it that way. It's just that I eventually realized my situation was an awful lot for anyone to take on, especially in the early years. And as time went by, I simply lost interest in romance. I have a nice life. Why should I change it? But tell me about you," she urged, adroitly shifting the focus before he could pursue the subject. "What are you doing here?"

He took her lead readily, grateful she hadn't taken offense at his rash question. "Actually, I'm interviewing this afternoon at the Maine Maritime Academy."

Her eyes widened in surprise. "For a job?"

"Yes. To make a long story short, I'm leaving the navy and Dad is coming to live with me."

"What about your mom?"

"She died five years ago, Maggie."

"Oh." Her face looked suddenly stricken, and he reached across and laid his hand over hers. Maggie had always gotten along famously with his parents. They'd held a special place in her heart, especially after her own parents died.

"It was a shock to all of us," Jake continued gently. "She had a stroke about five years ago. She lived for about six months after that, and Dad took care of her at home. That's where she wanted to be. Mom was a great believer in families taking care of their own. In fact, before she died, she made Rob and me promise that if Dad ever got to the point where he couldn't live alone, one of us would take him in rather than relegate him to a retirement or nursing home."

"And he isn't able to live alone now?"

Jake shook his head regretfully. "No. He had a heart attack about eight months ago and went down to stay with Rob and his family in Atlanta while he recovered. Except that he never did recover very well. He's gotten pretty frail and a little forgetful, and Rob and I finally realized that he couldn't ever go home. Rob was perfectly happy to have Dad live with them—the kids love having their grandpa around—but three weeks ago he lost his job in a corporate downsizing, and Jenny—Rob's wife—had to go back to work. What with three kids and lots of uncertainties, life has been pretty stressful for them. And they really can't give Dad the attention he needs. So the younger son—namely me—was called in to pinch-hit. That's why I'm here."

"You mean you're giving up your navy career to take care of your dad?"

Jake dismissed the implied sacrifice with a shrug. "I never intended to spend my life in the service. And even though it was a good life in many ways, I have to admit that I'm getting a little tired of being a nomad. The idea of settling down in one place is beginning to appeal to me. Rob may be having some career problems at the moment, but I'm starting to envy his life—the wife, the kids, the picket fence."

"So you've been…alone all these years?" she said tentatively.

"I never married, either, Maggie," he told her quietly.

A strange feeling of lightness swept over her, but she ignored it and focused on a less volatile topic. "So how does your dad feel about this move?"

Jake's face grew troubled. "Not happy, I'm afraid. You know how independent Dad always was. He hasn't taken kindly to having to rely on his kids to take care of him. Rob says it wasn't too bad at first, when Dad thought he'd eventually be able to go home. But since we decided that's not an option, he's been pretty despondent. He knows we're right, but that hasn't made it any easier for him to accept. And it's even worse now that he realizes he'll be stuck with me instead of Rob, at least for a while."

Maggie eyed Jake assessingly. His last comment had been made lightly, but she suspected his tone masked deeper feelings. She knew his parents hadn't been happy when he'd walked out on her. They'd apologized on his behalf more times than she could count. But surely, after all these years, his father didn't still hold a grudge against his son on her behalf. There had to be more to their troubled relationship than that.

"I take it you and your dad don't get along that well," she probed carefully.

Jake gave a short, mirthless laugh. "You might say that. As I'm sure you know, Dad was very disappointed in me after I...after we broke up. And he didn't hold back his feelings on the subject, either. So I made fewer trips home, which only seemed to fuel the fire. I did go home more often after Mom's stroke, but not enough to suit Dad. He figured I'd abandoned them, too, I guess."

Maggie looked at him in surprise. Abandoned them, too? That was an incriminating word choice. Did it mean that he regretted his decision twelve years ago to break up with her? Had guilt followed him all these years as he roamed around the world? She'd never really considered that. She figured once he'd made his decision he's simply gone on with his life, that eventually memories of her and their time together had faded. But his words implied otherwise.

"Anyway, like it or not, we're stuck with each other," Jake continued. "And I'm determined to make the best of it. In fact, to be perfectly honest, I hope we can mend the rift between us. Dad and I used to be close, and…well, I've missed that all these years."

Once again, Maggie was taken aback by Jake's admission. He'd never been the kind of man who talked much about feelings. Maybe the willingness to do so had come with maturity, she speculated. Once you felt comfortable with your life and had proven your abilities, it was easier to admit other limitations without feeling threatened. Jake struck her as being a very secure man in most aspects of his life. Confident and in control. Yet he'd been unable to reestablish a good relationship with his father. And he wasn't too proud to admit it.

"Well, the opportunity will certainly be there now," Maggie pointed out encouragingly. "I'm sure your dad will come around."

Jake shook his head skeptically. "I'm not so sure. But I have to try at least. Rob has his hands full, and we can't go back on our promise to Mom. Besides, Rob's done more than his share with Dad since Mom died. It's only right I take my turn."

Maggie stared at Jake. The man was full of surprises. Through the years she'd gradually convinced herself that he was a self-centered, spoiled, irresponsible man who had probably grown even more so with age. But the decisions he'd made regarding his father, his acceptance of his duty, his willingness to honor the promise to his mother at the expense of his career, weren't the actions of a selfish man. They spoke of integrity and principal and dependability. Maggie had to admit that his behavior was admirable. But it was a grudging admission, and certainly not one she cared to verbalize.

"Excuse me, but there's a call for you, Mr. West," Abby interrupted, pausing beside the table, her gaze blatantly curious as it moved from Jake to Maggie. "A man named Dennis Richards."

Jake frowned. "He must not have been able to switch the time for the first interview after all. Will you wait, Maggie? I'll be right back."

"Yes."

"You can take the call on the phone in the foyer, at the desk," Abby told him.

She watched Jake leave, then turned to Maggie, her eyes shining. "Were you really engaged to him once?" she asked incredulously.

Maggie briefly glanced in the direction Jake had disappeared and nodded. "It's a long story, honey. And it happened a long time ago."

"But he's back now," Abby pointed out eagerly. "Who knows? Maybe—"

"Maybe we should try not to let our imaginations run away with us," Maggie advised, cutting off her niece's fanciful speculations.

"But what's he doing here?" Abby persisted.

"He's on his way to Castine. He's considering a job at the Maritime Academy."

"You mean he might be living less than twenty miles away?" Abby was clearly elated.

"Maybe," Maggie admitted reluctantly.

"Wow!" Abby repeated. "Wait till I tell Allison!"

Before Maggie could respond, Abby turned on her heel and disappeared into the kitchen. Maggie shook her head helplessly, then propped her chin on her hand, a pensive frown on her face as she considered the situation.

Jake had reappeared in her life after twelve years. "Shock" was hardly adequate to describe her reaction. But somehow she'd made it through the last half hour or so. Perhaps the Lord had taken pity on her and sent an extra dose of courage her way. Still, it had taken every ounce of her willpower and fortitude to act as if Jake's presence hadn't been a jolting experience that left her reeling emotionally.

She had succeeded, though, and congratulated herself for that. But a thirty-minute encounter was one thing. How on earth would she cope if the man lived just down the road? If she knew every time she went out that she might run into him—at the grocery store, on the street, in the park? The thought unnerved her completely.

What unnerved her even more was the realization that the

man still had the *power* to unnerve her. She resented that. After all, he was nothing to her anymore. Her life was full and rich as it was. She had two loving "daughters," an artistic talent that gave her great joy, a satisfying career and a solid faith that continued to sustain her. What more could she ask for?

But Maggie knew the answer to that question, she admitted with a sigh. Though she'd long ago reconciled herself to the fact that the single life seemed to be God's plan for her, deep in her heart she still yearned for someone to share it with. Having once loved deeply, she knew what joy love could bring. She didn't think about it often, though. Idle wishing was fruitless. But seeing Jake again had reawakened those yearnings, made her recall the heady feeling of being in love.

Her lips curved up into a wistful smile as she thought back. It had been a wonderful time, those days of awakening emotions and eager plans for a future together, when the world stretched before them, infinite in its possibilities. How differently her life would have turned out if those plans had come to fruition. But the Lord had had a different future in store for her. And she shouldn't complain. Her life had been blessed in many ways.

"It looks like I'll have to leave sooner than I wanted to." Jake's regretful voice interrupted her reverie.

"I understand."

"Listen, Maggie, I'd like to continue our conversation. We barely got started. Can I call you tomorrow?"

She frowned and slowly shook her head. "I'm not sure that's a good idea."

"I guess you've been kinder to me already than I have any right to expect," he acknowledged soberly. "You probably still hate me, and I can't say I blame you."

"I never hated you, Jake. I was just...hurt. But I got over that a long time ago."

He looked at her, wanting to believe that was true, but finding it difficult to accept. In her place, he doubted he'd be that forgiving. "Really?"

She nodded. "Really."

"Then why won't you talk to me?"

Because I'm scared, she cried silently. *I feel like a tightrope walker who's about to lose her balance. And I don't want to fall, Jake. Not again. Not ever again.*

But of course she couldn't say that. "It's awfully busy this time of year. I just don't have the time to socialize."

"How about a phone call, then? Surely you can spare a few minutes for that."

They both knew she could. And Maggie didn't want to give Jake the impression that she still held a grudge. That would make her seem small and unforgiving. Not to mention un-Christian. With a sigh, she capitulated.

"All right, Jake. Give me a call when you have a few minutes."

She was rewarded with a smile so warm it seemed like sunshine on a lazy summer day. "Thank you, Maggie. I appreciate it. I've already taken care of my bill and loaded my car, so I'll say goodbye for now." He stood up and held out his hand. She had no choice but to take it, trying to still the rapid beating of her heart as her fingers were engulfed in his firm, warm grip.

"I know this encounter has upset you, Maggie," he murmured, the familiar husky timbre of his voice playing havoc with her metabolism as his discerning gaze locked on hers. "And I'm sorry for that. I never want to upset you again. But I'm not sorry our paths crossed. I think it happened for a reason."

Maggie didn't respond. She couldn't.

Jake held her gaze a moment longer, then released it—as well as her hand. "I'll call you soon," he promised. With that he turned and strode away.

Maggie sank back into her chair, his words echoing in her mind. He'd said he thought their paths had crossed for a reason. She couldn't dispute that. It was too odd a coincidence to accept at face value. He'd also said he was glad it had happened. On that point she disagreed. Maggie wasn't glad at all. Because now that Jake had walked back into her life, she somehow knew it would never be the same again.

Chapter Three

"Earth to Maggie, earth to Maggie. Are you with me over there?"

Maggie abruptly returned to reality, blushing as she sent Philip, her lunch partner, an apologetic look. "Sorry about that," she said sheepishly.

"No problem. So what if you don't find my company fascinating? Why should I be insulted?"

Maggie grinned at his good-natured teasing. "You're a good sport, you know that?"

"So I've been told. So what gives?"

She shifted uncomfortably. "What do you mean?"

"Maggie, I've known you for what...seven, eight years? In all that time I've never once seen you distracted. So I figure something's happened—something pretty dramatic. Therefore, I repeat...what gives?"

Maggie looked down and played with her fork. She should have known she couldn't hide her inner turmoil from Philip. He was way too perceptive. And maybe it wasn't such a bad idea to tell him about Jake. Philip had been a trusted friend and firm supporter for years. Without his encouragement, she might never have taken up serious painting again. Even now he had several of her pieces displayed in his gallery. He'd been a good sounding board through the years, too. A widower with two grown daughters, he'd offered her valuable advice about the girls on numerous occasions. Maybe it wouldn't hurt to run this situation by him, get his take on it.

"Okay, you win," she capitulated. "Something pretty… dramatic…did happen today."

He tilted his head and eyed her quizzically. "Well, I can't say you look unhappy exactly. It must not be anything too terrible."

"I'm not so sure about that," she murmured, shaking her head. She stirred her ice tea and took a deep breath. "You remember I mentioned once that years ago I was engaged?"

"Mmm-hmm."

"Well…Jake—that was his name—he…he stayed at the inn last night."

Philip frowned. "You mean he came to see you?"

"No, nothing like that," she said quickly. "He got caught in the fog and just happened to stop at our place. Allison checked him in. I didn't even know he was there until this morning at breakfast, when the girls kept talking about this…this nice-looking man who'd checked in. It turned out to be Jake."

Philip stared at her. "That must have been a terrible shock."

Maggie gave a short, mirthless laugh. "That's putting it mildly. I've been off balance ever since it happened. Which is odd, since my relationship with him was over long ago. I can't figure out why his reappearance has disturbed me so much."

Philip studied her for a moment. "It does seem strange," he concurred. "After all, whatever you two shared is obviously history."

"Right."

"And it isn't as if he even means anything to you anymore."

"Right." This time there was a hint of uncertainty in her voice.

"What was he doing here, anyway?"

"He's interviewing for a job at the Maritime Academy."

"You mean he might actually move up here?"

"Yes. And that makes me even more nervous. Which is

ridiculous, because we're really no more than strangers to each other now."

"It's probably just the shock of seeing him," Philip reassured her. "Where has he lived all these years?"

"All over, I guess. He's been in the navy. I think he still would be if it wasn't for his father." Maggie briefly explained the situation to Philip.

"Hmm" was his only cryptic comment when she finished.

Maggie tilted her head and looked at him quizzically. "What's that supposed to mean?"

He shrugged. "I guess I'm a little surprised. And impressed. Not many people would give up their career, start over, change their whole life to keep a promise basically made under duress. He sounds like a very honorable man."

Maggie frowned. "Yes, he does," she admitted. "And it's so at odds with the image I've had of him all these years."

"Well, people do change."

"I suppose so," she admitted reluctantly. "I just wish I didn't feel so off balance."

"Things will work out, Maggie," he told her encouragingly. "They always do. You've successfully weathered a lot of storms though the years, and you'll ride this one out, too. I know. And I'm always here if you need a sympathetic ear. Don't forget that." He touched her hand lightly and smiled, then switched gears. "In the meantime...when do I get a preview of the new painting?"

"Will next week be okay?"

"Perfect. I'll reserve a spot right near the front for it. You know, you have a large enough body of work now to consider your own show."

Maggie grimaced. "I just don't feel...well...good enough...to have an official show."

"Why don't you let me be the judge of that? Besides, you'll never know till you try. It's not like you to back off from a challenge."

"I know. But my painting is so...personal. If I got bad reviews it would be devastating. I'm not sure I'm ready to face that."

"First of all, they wouldn't be bad. And second of all, you can face anything, Maggie Fitzgerald. Because you are one of the strongest women I know."

Maggie wanted to believe him. As recently as yesterday she might have. But a lot had happened since then. And at this particular moment, she didn't feel very strong at all—thanks to one very unforgettable man named Jake West.

"Jake called twice. Will call again tomorrow."

Maggie's heart leapt to her throat as she read the note on the kitchen counter. She should have figured he'd call while she was out. She hoped the girls had explained where she was. She didn't want him to think she was trying to avoid him. It was just that she led a very busy life. Her days—and evenings—were filled. Like tonight. The zoning board meeting had run far later then she expected, because of some heated discussion. And she still had a few breakfast preparations to make, even if it was—she glanced at her watch and groaned—ten-thirty. There always seemed to be too much to do and not enough time.

As Maggie methodically set about assembling the egg and cheese casseroles that were tomorrow's breakfast entrée, she reflected on the hectic pace of her life. For most people, simply running an inn and raising twins would be a full-time job. But she had made other commitments, as well. Like serving on the church council. And on the zoning board. Not to mention the watercolors she did for the greeting card company and, in recent years, pursuit of more serious art in her limited "spare" time. Why did she take so much on? she wondered with a frown. Could it be that she wanted to keep herself so busy that she had little time to dwell on the one thing that was lacking in her life?

With an impatient shake of her head, Maggie beat the eggs even harder. She didn't usually waste time trying to analyze her life choices. If some of them were coping mechanisms, so be it. They worked, and that was all that mattered. Or they'd worked up until today, she amended. Jake's reappearance had changed everything and, much to her surprise, rattled her badly.

But what surprised her even more was the fact that when she looked at him, it wasn't the hurt she remembered, but the intense, heady joy of being in love. In some ways, it would almost be easier to remember the pain. Because that had no appeal. But love—that was a different story. That had a whole lot of appeal. It was just that the opportunity had never come along again. And it wasn't here *now,* she reminded herself brusquely as she slid the casseroles into the refrigerator. Jake had had his chance. She wasn't about to give him another.

Abby looked up from her seat in a wicker chair on the porch and grinned as she saw Jake stride up the path.

"Did you come to see Aunt Maggie?" she asked eagerly, laying her book aside.

"Please don't tell me I missed her again?" He'd been trying unsuccessfully for the past two days to reach her, and the frustration was evident in his voice. If every minute of his stay in Castine hadn't been packed, he would have simply driven over and planted himself in her drawing room until she had time to talk to him. But he knew one thing for sure. He wasn't leaving Blue Hill until he saw her again, even if that meant tracking her down wherever she might be now.

"Don't worry, you didn't. She's in the studio, Mr. West."

He felt the tension in his shoulders ease, and he smiled. "Call me Jake. And where's the studio?"

"It's the little room off the kitchen."

"Would it be all right if I go back?"

"Sure. Aunt Maggie won't mind," Abby said breezily, ignoring the worried look that Allison sent her way as she stepped outside. "It's just down the hall and through the door at the end."

"Thanks." Jake turned to find Allison in the doorway.

"Hello, Mr. West," Allison greeted him.

Jake grinned at her. "No one's called me 'Mr.' in years. Just Lieutenant. And both of those sound too formal now. So how about we just make it Jake?"

Allison smiled. "Okay."

"Good. I'll see you ladies later."

Allison watched him disappear, then turned to her sister with a worried frown. "Why did you send him back there?" she demanded urgently. "You know Aunt Maggie said never interrupt her when she's painting, unless it's an emergency."

Abby gave her sister a condescending look. "Allison, Aunt Maggie's love life *is* an emergency."

Allison clamped her lips shut. How could she argue with Abby—especially when her sister was right?

Maggie tilted her head and frowned. She wanted the seascape to convey restlessness, inner turbulence, the sense of impending fury. But she wasn't quite there yet. Considering her firsthand knowledge of the ocean, and given that her own emotional state paralleled the scene she was trying to paint today, it ought to be easy to transfer those feelings to canvas. But the mood was eluding her, and that was frustrating.

A firm tap sounded on the door, and Maggie glanced toward it in annoyance. Why were the twins bothering her? They were old enough now to handle most of the so-called crises that occurred at the inn. But maybe there truly was an emergency of some kind, she thought. In sudden alarm she reached for a rag to wipe her brush, psyching herself up to deal with whatever crisis awaited her. "Come in."

The "crisis" that appeared when the door swung open was *not* one she was prepared for, however. What on earth was Jake doing here, in her private retreat? She stared at him in surprise as her heart kicked into double time. Try as she might, she couldn't control the faint flush that crept onto her cheeks, or stop the sudden tremble that rippled over her hands.

Jake smiled engagingly. "Abby said I could come back. I hope you don't mind. But I'm on my way back to Boston, and this was my last chance to see you before I left. We didn't seem to have much success connecting by phone."

"Y-yes, I know." Why did her voice sound so shaky? "Sorry about that. I was at a zoning board meeting the first night you called, and running errands the other times.'' That was better. Steadier and more in control.

''So the girls told me.'' He propped one shoulder against the door frame and folded his arms across his chest. ''You continue to amaze me, Maggie. I don't remember that you ever had any interest in politics or government, local or otherwise, and now you're on the zoning board?''

She carefully set the brush down and reached for a different rag to wipe her hands on, using that as an excuse to escape his warm, disquieting gaze. ''Well, I'm part of the business community of this town. It's my home. I feel a certain sense of responsibility to do my part to make sure Blue Hill retains the qualities that attracted me in the first place.''

''Once again, I'm impressed.''

''Don't be. A lot of people do a whole lot more than me.''

He didn't agree, but rather than debate the point, he strolled into the studio, his gaze assessing. It was a small room, illuminated by the light from a large picture window on one side. Unlike his image of the stereotypical messy artist's studio, however, this one was neat and orderly. A couple of canvases in various stages of completion stood on easels, and several other finished works were stacked against one wall.

But what captured his attention most were the posters. Vienna. Florence. Rome. Paris. London. Athens. As his gaze moved from one to another, he realized that these were the places he and Maggie had planned to visit together. And he realized something else, as well. He'd seen most of them, while Maggie had been confined to rural Maine, coping with responsibilities that even now her slender shoulders seemed too fragile to bear. His dream of travel had become reality; hers had remained a dream.

He looked down at her slim form silhouetted against the window, the sun forming a halo around her hair, and his throat tightened. He wished with all his heart that he could take her to all the exotic places pictured on her walls. She would love them, he knew, would be as awed as he had been on his first visit. But maybe…maybe she'd managed to see one or two, he thought hopefully.

He nodded toward the walls. "Nice posters," he remarked casually. "Are any of them souvenirs?"

She gave him a wry smile and shook her head, dashing his hopes. "Hardly. B&B owners may cater to travelers, but they do very little traveling themselves. Especially with two girls to raise. I've stayed pretty close to home all these years. I expect you've made it to some, or all, of these spots, though."

He nodded, trying to stem the surge of guilt that swept over him. "Yes."

"Are they as wonderful as we...as people say?" she asked, the slightly wistful note in her voice producing an almost physical ache in his heart.

"Mmm-hmm." He cleared his throat, but still the huskiness in his voice remained. "I'm sorry you never got to see them, Maggie."

"Oh, but I will," she said brightly, suddenly aware that he felt sorry for her. She didn't want his sympathy. "I'm going to Europe right after Christmas. Actually, the trip's been in the works for years. I decided what with the twins going away to college this fall, it was time I started a new phase of my life, as well. I'm going to close the B&B for four months and visit all the museums and take some art classes and just soak up the ambiance. It should be wonderful!"

The sudden spark of enthusiasm in her eyes lit up her face, giving it a glow that warmed his heart. "That sounds great. I know you'll enjoy it, especially with your art background." He nodded toward the canvases stacked around the room. "I guess I never realized just how talented you are. I remember you sketching and doing some watercolors, but not painting. I don't know that much about art, but these look very impressive to me."

Despite herself, Maggie was pleased by his compliment. "Thanks. I'm not that good, though. I really don't have any formal training. But Philip—he owns a local gallery—has encouraged me. He even displays some of my work. And he's been trying for the last year to convince me to have a show at a gallery in Bangor that's owned by a friend of his. But I'm just not sure I'm ready for that."

"You look ready to me," Jake told her sincerely. There was a quality to her work, an emotion, a power, that radiated compellingly from the canvases. Even with his untrained eye he could sense it.

"Philip says so, too. But I haven't committed to it yet."

"Is this Philip someone whose judgment you trust?"

She nodded confidently. "Absolutely. About everything except my painting, that is. We've been friends for a long time, and I'm afraid he may not be completely impartial."

An alarm bell rang in Jake's mind. Maggie had used the term *friend,* but when she spoke of this Philip, the warmth and familiarity in her voice implied something more. And that possibility disturbed him. Which was wrong. He certainly had no claim on her heart. He should be glad that she'd found a male companion. Considering all the love she had to offer, Maggie wasn't the kind of woman who should spend her life alone. But even as he acknowledged that his reaction was selfish and wrong, he couldn't change the way he felt. The thought of Maggie in love with another man bothered him. It always had.

"Well, I think he's right," Jake said, biting back the question that he longed to ask her about Philip.

"We'll see," Maggie replied noncommittally. "So... you're heading back to Boston. How did the interview go?"

"I'll tell you all about it in exchange for a cup of coffee," he bartered with a smile.

"Oh! Sure. I thought maybe you only had a few minutes."

"I've got an early flight out of Boston tomorrow morning, so I'd like to get back at a reasonable hour. But I can stay for a little while," he told her as he followed her into the large, airy kitchen.

"Flight?" she asked over her shoulder as she filled two cups.

"Rob and I are meeting at the old house. Before we put it on the market we have to sort through everything and decide what we want to keep. The rest will be sold at an estate sale."

Maggie turned to him with a troubled frown. "This must be awfully hard on your dad."

"I'm sure it is," he agreed with a frown. "He's accepted the necessity of it, though, and other than a few specific items he's asked us to save, he's pretty much left the disposition of everything in Rob's and my hands."

"That won't be an easy job, Jake," Maggie empathized.

Jake hadn't really thought that far ahead. But he'd been gone from his childhood home for a long time. The emotional ties had loosened long ago. He expected he'd cope just fine. He couldn't very well say that, though. It would sound too coldhearted somehow.

"Well, Rob and I will be doing it together. That should help," he replied.

She placed his coffee on the table and sat down, motioning for him to join her. "So how did the interview go?"

"I guess it went well. They offered me the job."

Her breath caught in her throat as her heart stopped, then lurched on. "So you'll be moving to Castine?" she said carefully.

He nodded. "In about three weeks."

Three weeks! That hardly even gave her time to adjust to the idea! "That fast?"

"Well, Rob's in a bind. The sooner I take Dad off his hands, the better. And I think I'll like the job a lot. I've been an instructor for a few classes in the navy, and I enjoy teaching. And this job will let me stay close to the sea, which is a real plus."

His voice had grown thoughtful, and Maggie looked at him curiously while he took a sip of coffee, again struck by the sense of maturity and quiet confidence that he radiated. The high energy she remembered—exhilarating but sometimes undirected—seemed to have been tamed and channeled toward specific goals.

"So, since I had a lot of leave accumulated, I'm taking a month off while they process my discharge—to get things squared away for my new life. I found a nice two-bedroom cottage that's available right now and signed the papers yesterday,'' he finished.

"It seems like you have everything pretty much under control.''

"Logistically, yes. Dealing with my father…that's another story.''

"Well, he's had an awful lot to adjust to, Jake. Maybe he just needs some time.''

"Time I can give him. I'm just not sure that's all it will take.'' He glanced at his watch regretfully and drained his cup. "I've got to go. It's a long drive back to Boston. But I'll be back, Maggie. And I was hoping…well, I thought maybe we could have dinner then to finish catching up and celebrate my new job.''

She looked into warm brown eyes that, with a single glance, had once been able to fill her heart with light and hope and promise. But that was then. This was now. And she wasn't the starry-eyed bride-to-be that she'd been twelve years ago.

And yet…sitting here with him now, she felt an awfully lot like the young girl she used to be. Which was not a good sign at all. Her best plan would be to avoid him until she straightened out the emotional tangle she'd felt ever since his reappearance.

"So what about it, Maggie? How does a dinner celebration sound?''

She looked down and ran a finger carefully around the rim of her cup. "I'm not sure that's a good idea, Jake.''

He didn't respond immediately, and she refused to meet his gaze, afraid that if she did, her resolve would waver. Finally she heard him sigh, and only when he made a move to stand up did she look at him.

"Would you think about it at least?'' he asked quietly. "Don't give me an answer now. I'll call you when I get back. And I'm sorry about interrupting your work. I'll let myself out.''

Maggie didn't protest. And as she watched him disappear through the door, she took a sip of her cold coffee. She had no intention of changing her mind. For one very simple reason. She wasn't at all sure there was anything to celebrate.

Chapter Four

With a weary sigh, Jake flexed the muscles in his shoulders, then reached for yet another dusty box. Thank heavens Rob hadn't been called back to Atlanta for that job interview until all of the big items at the house had been dealt with. Only a couple of closets remained for Jake to clean out alone. But it was slower—and more difficult—going than he'd expected.

It seemed that Maggie had been right. Even though he'd cut most of his ties with this small house and the town where he grew up, for some reason he found it surprisingly difficult to be in his childhood home for the last time. He'd come to realize that though his ties to this place were few, they were stronger than he'd suspected. The process of cutting his roots with such finality was unexpectedly unsettling.

As he and Rob pored over the old scrapbooks, sometimes laughing, sometimes lapsing into quiet, melancholy remembrance, the good days came back to Jake with an intensity that startled him. The days when they'd all lived here together under this roof, happy and content. The days when he and his dad were not only father and son, but friends.

He'd lingered longest over the faded photos. The photos of himself, flanked by his parents at high school graduation, their eyes shining with pride. Photos older still, of his dad teaching him to ride a bike and to pitch a baseball. For years, Jake hadn't allowed himself to remember those happier times. The memories only made him sad. Though he'd denied it to himself for more than a decade, the truth was he'd always cared what his father thought about him. But he'd failed him twelve years ago, and many times since in the intervening years.

Jake sighed. He almost wished he didn't care. It would make things easier. But he did. He still loved his father, despite the older man's opinionated views and stubborn disposition. Not that he'd done much to demonstrate that in the last decade, he admitted. After his father's sound rejection of his initial overtures, he hadn't wasted time or energy on further attempts.

His mother was a different story. She had been disappointed in his choices, as well, but she'd never let that interfere with her love for him. The rift between her youngest son and husband had always caused her distress, and in her quiet way she'd tried—unsuccessfully—to bring them together on several occasions. One of her greatest disappointments was that she hadn't lived to see a reconciliation.

Maybe his father would have softened over time if Jake had admitted he'd made a mistake. And maybe Jake would have admitted his mistake if his father's attitude had softened a little. But instead it became a standoff. It was a shame, really, Jake thought with a pang of regret. Because as he'd grown older he'd come to realize the enormity of his betrayal in walking out on the woman he had professed to love.

Jake had considered admitting that to his father a few times through the years, but the older man had never offered him an opening. And Jake didn't want it thrown back in his face.

Sometimes he wondered if his father harbored regrets, too. If he did, he'd never let on. Jake suspected that pride was at the root of their problem. But knowing the source didn't necessarily suggest a solution. And dwelling on the past wasn't helping him finish today's job, he reminded himself.

Jake glanced at the box he had just withdrawn from the closet and was surprised to find his name written on it in his mother's neat, careful hand. As he sifted through the contents, he realized that she had saved every letter he'd written, as well as every clipping he'd sent. He blinked rapidly to clear the sudden film of moisture from his eyes. His mother's death had been hard on him. He missed her deeply, as well as the direct link she had provided to home. Although he'd continued to write, his father never responded. It was only through Rob that Jake kept tabs on him. He wasn't sure if his father even opened his letters.

Suddenly Jake's gaze fell on the clipping announcing his promotion to lieutenant two years before. His mother couldn't have put that in the box. Nor the article about the special commendation he'd received last year, he realized, shuffling through the papers. Which only left one possibility. His father had not only *opened* his letters, but *saved* them. Which must mean he still cared.

With a suddenly lighter heart, Jake worked his way steadily through the remaining boxes, eating a hastily assembled sandwich as he made one more circuit of the house to ensure that none of the furnishings had gone untagged. Most items were to be sold. A few were to be shipped to his cottage in Maine. Everything seemed to be in order, he thought with satisfaction, as he stepped into the garage and glanced around. There really wasn't much of value out here, certainly nothing he planned to take to Maine. Unless...

His gaze lingered on the boxes containing his father's woodworking tools. He knew from Rob that they had lain unused since his mother's death. But why not hang on to them, just in case? Without stopping to reconsider, Jake quickly changed the instructions on the boxes, then headed back inside.

By the end of the emotionally draining day, Jake had reached the last "box"—a small fireproof safe stored in the far corner of the closet in his parents' bedroom, under the eaves. He read the label, written in his mother's hand, with a puzzled frown. "Important Documents." As far as he knew, he and Rob had already located and dealt with all the "important documents."

But the mystery was cleared up a moment later when he opened the lid. He should have guessed the kinds of things this box would contain, knowing his mother's definition of "important," he thought with a tender smile. Carefully, one at time, he withdrew the items. Her own mother's handwritten recipe for apple pie. A poem she'd clipped from the newspaper about taking time to enjoy a quiet summer night. Jake's kindergarten "diploma." An embossed copy of the Twenty-third psalm, given to her on her wedding day by her father. These sentimental items were his mother's real treasures, Jake knew. These "important documents"—not expensive rings or necklaces—had been her jewels.

Every item touched his heart—but none more so than the last one. As he withdrew the single sheet of slightly yellowed paper, memories came flooding back of a hot summer day more than a quarter of a century before. The document contained few words, but as his eyes scanned the sheet he remembered with bittersweet intensity the strong emotions and deep sincerity that had produced them.

It had been a long time since that document had seen the light of day. But as he carefully replaced the paper and gently closed the lid, he hoped that its time would come again soon.

"Is Maggie here?"

The unfamiliar woman behind the desk at Whispering Sails shook her head. "No, I'm sorry. Is there something I can help you with?"

Jake sighed wearily. It had been a hectic and emotionally taxing three weeks since he'd left Maine, and he'd had a very long drive up from Boston. He should have just gone directly to his cottage in Castine and contacted Maggie tomorrow. This was obviously a wasted detour.

"No. I was just hoping to see her for a minute. I should have called first."

The woman looked at him uncertainly. "Are you a friend of hers?"

"Yes." Jake wasn't sure Maggie would agree, but from his perspective the statement was true.

"Well…then I guess it's okay to tell you what happened. Allison was in a car accident, and Maggie's at the hospital."

Jake's face blanched. "How badly is she hurt?"

"I don't know. Maggie got the call about two hours ago, and I haven't heard from her yet."

"Where's the hospital?"

The woman gave him directions, and with a clipped "Thank you," he strode out the door and to his car. Less than a minute later he pulled out of the driveway in a spray of gravel, his foot heavy on the gas pedal, oblivious to the speed signs posted along the route.

By the time he reached the hospital, his body was rigid with tension. He scanned the emergency room quickly, but there was no sign of Maggie.

"Sir...may I help you?"

He glanced at the woman behind the desk. "I'm looking for Maggie Fitzgerald. Her niece, Allison Foster, was brought in some time ago. A car accident."

"Oh, yes. Ms. Fitzgerald is just around the corner." She inclined her head to the right.

"How is Allison?"

"The doctor is still with her, sir. We'll let you know as soon as we have any word."

He acknowledged her reply with a curt nod, then covered the length of the hall in several long strides, pausing when he reached the door to the cold, sterile waiting room. It was empty except for the lone figure huddled in one corner.

Jake's gut clenched as he looked at Maggie's slim form, every muscle in her body tense, her face devoid of color. He tried to swallow, but it was difficult to get past the sudden lump in his throat. How many of these kinds of crises had she endured alone, without even the reassuring clasp of a warm hand for comfort?

Jake had never thought of Maggie as a particularly strong woman. But his assessment of her had changed radically in the last few weeks. She was clearly capable of handling emergencies alone. If she wasn't, she couldn't have survived the last twelve years. But that didn't mean she had to, not anymore. Not if he had anything to say about it, he decided, jamming his hands into his pockets, fists clenched, as a fierce surge of protectiveness swept over him.

The sudden movement caught Maggie's eye and she jerked convulsively, half rising to her feet as she turned to him. The frantic look in her eyes changed to confusion as his identity registered. Was that Jake? she asked herself uncomprehendingly. And if so, why was he here? She hadn't prayed for him to miraculously appear to comfort her, to hold her, to help her survive, as she had so many times in the past during times of trauma. And yet...here he was. Or was it just a dream? she wondered, closing her eyes as she wearily sank back into her chair and reached up to rub her forehead.

The warm hand that clasped her icy one a moment later wasn't a dream, though, and her eyelids flew open.

"Jake?" Her voice was uncertain, questioning, as if she couldn't believe he was really there.

"Yeah, it's me," he confirmed softly as he reached over and pried a paper cup of cold coffee out of her other hand, then took that hand in his warming clasp, as well.

"But...what are you doing here?"

"I stopped by Whispering Sails, and the woman on duty told me you were here. What happened, Maggie?"

She drew a deep, shuddering breath and spoke in short, choppy sentences. "Some guy ran a stop sign. Rammed Allison's car on the passenger side. He walked away. But her...her head hit the window. It knocked her out. She was still unconscious when they brought her in. They haven't told me anything yet. But I'm afraid.... She's so young, and... Oh, Jake!" A sob rose in her throat and she bowed her head as a wave of nausea swept over her. *Dear God, please let Allison be all right,* she prayed fiercely. *Please! She has her whole life still to live!*

Jake watched helplessly as Maggie's slender shoulders bowed under the burden of desperate worry. Without even considering what her reaction might be, he put his arm around her and pulled her close.

For a moment, Maggie was sorely tempted to accept the comfort of his arms. A part of her longed to simply let go, to burrow into the haven he offered, to let his solid strength add stability to a world that at the moment seemed terribly shaky. Part of her wanted that badly.

But another part sounded a warning. *Don't get used to this,*

Maggie. Don't even think about leaning on this man. You did that once, remember, and where did it leave you? Alone, to pick up the pieces. You've handled crises before. You don't need him to make it any easier. Because even if he helps you through this one, he won't be there the next time. And it will be that much harder to face if you accept his support even one time.

Jake felt her go absolutely still, and he waited, holding his breath. He hoped she would simply let him hold her, that she would accept his actions at face value—as the compassion of a friend. But when her body grew rigid and she pulled away, he knew he'd lost this round. Reluctantly he let her go.

"Ms. Fitzgerald?"

Maggie's head shot up and she was on her feet instantly. "Yes."

The white-coated figure walked into the room and held out his hand. "I'm Dr. Jackson." He turned to Jake quizzically as he took Maggie's hand.

"Th-this is Jake West," Maggie told him. "He's a...a friend of the family."

The two men shook hands, and then the doctor turned his attention back to Maggie. "Let's sit down for a minute, okay?"

Jake watched her carefully. He could tell from the rapid rise and fall of her chest that she was scared to death, and despite her rejection moments before, he decided to risk taking her hand. Maybe she'd allow that minimal intimacy. He wanted—needed—her to feel a connection between them, a tactile reassurance that she was not alone. And this time she didn't protest his touch, he noted with relief. In fact, she almost seemed unaware of it, though she gripped his hand fiercely.

"Your niece has a slight concussion, Ms. Fitzgerald, and a bruised shoulder. Nothing more, it appears. She was very lucky that the other driver hit the passenger side of the car. We'd like to keep her overnight for observation, but she should be fine."

Jake could sense Maggie's relief as her body went limp. "Thank God," she whispered fervently.

"You can see her now if you'd like."

"Yes." She nodded and rose quickly. "If you'll just show me the way, Doctor..."

"Of course."

"I'll wait here for you," Jake told her.

She stopped and turned back to him with a frown. "You don't have to."

"I want to."

Maggie was too exhausted to argue. Besides, she had a strong suspicion it wouldn't do any good anyway. "I'm not sure how long I'll be."

"I'm in no hurry." Before she could argue further, Jake settled into one of the chairs and picked up a magazine.

Short of telling him to get lost, Maggie was left with no choice but to follow the doctor.

She reappeared in thirty minutes, and Jake looked at her in surprise, rising quickly when she entered. "Is everything all right?" he asked.

"Yes. Allison's all settled now. She wanted me to go home and get some rest." She didn't tell him that when Allison found out Jake was there, she'd just about pushed her aunt out the door.

"I think she's right. You look done in, Maggie."

"Yeah, well, it's been a long day." She brushed a hand wearily across her eyes, and Jake noted that her fingers were still trembling. She was clearly in no condition to drive, he realized.

"Listen, Maggie, why don't you let me take you home?"

Her startled gaze flew to his. "But...my car is here."

"Do you need it for anything else today?"

"No."

"Then leave it here. I'll bring you back tomorrow to pick up Allison."

"That's too much trouble, Jake. I couldn't let you do that."

Couldn't or wouldn't? he wondered, deciding to try a different tact. "Come on, Maggie," he cajoled. "I know you're a strong woman and very capable of running your own life, but it's okay sometimes to let other people help. Besides, my mother always taught me to do at least one good deed a day. If you cooperate, I can count this for today."

, Maggie was torn. In all honesty, she felt too shaky to drive. And she *was* exhausted. But she definitely did *not* want to feel indebted to Jake, didn't want to owe him *anything*.

"Look, Maggie, this is an offer with no strings, okay?" he assured her, as if reading her mind. He'd been pretty good at that once, she recalled. It was rather disconcerting to think he still was. "And if you feel that you have to do something to repay me, here's a suggestion. You can go with me to pick up Dad at the airport next week. A familiar face might help smooth over what's sure to be a rocky beginning."

Maggie considered his request. It seemed like a reasonable trade.

"Okay," she agreed. "That seems fair."

A relieved smile chased the tension from his face. "Great. Let's head home."

When he took her arm and guided her toward the door, she didn't pull away as she had earlier. His protective touch felt comforting. Not that she'd let it happen again, of course. Tomorrow, after a good night's sleep, she'd feel stronger. And then she'd keep her distance.

"Well, this is it."

Maggie turned to look up at Jake as they waited near the exit ramp of the plane, noting his tense expression. She wanted to reassure him that everything would be all right, but she wasn't sure that was true. From what Jake had told her, he and his father wouldn't have an easy time of it. Still, she wished there was some way to ease his mind, offer him some hope. With sudden inspiration she reached up and touched his arm.

"Jake, do you remember the verse from Proverbs? 'Entrust your works to the Lord, and your plans will succeed.' It's been a great comfort to me through the years. I know you face an uphill battle with your dad, and I'm not sure anyone can make it any easier for you. But there is a greater power you can turn to, you know. Prayer might help.''

Jake glanced down at her with a wry smile and covered her hand with his. "Well, it sure couldn't hurt.''

Just then the passengers began to emerge, and Maggie felt Jake stiffen, almost as if he was bracing for a blow.

A few moments later Howard West appeared. At least she thought it was Jake's father. But the frail figure trudging wearily toward the waiting area bore little resemblance to the robust man Maggie remembered. There was nothing in his dejected posture or delicate appearance to suggest the man she had once known. Maggie's grip on Jake's arm tightened, and she felt a lump rise to her throat.

Jake looked down at her. He should have prepared Maggie for his father's deteriorated appearance, he realized.

"He's changed a lot since Mom died," Jake murmured gently. "And even more since the heart attack.''

She nodded silently and he saw the glint of unshed tears in her eyes. "I guess I should have expected something like this," she admitted, a catch in her voice. "But somehow I never thought that…well, I don't know, he just seems so…so lost…"

Jake glanced back toward his father and nodded. When he spoke, his own voice was slightly uneven. "I know. He should have made a better recovery. But after Mom died, he lost interest in a lot of things, and once he had the heart attack he just sort of gave up on life. He keeps getting more frail. It's hard to accept sometimes. He was always so strong.''

Howard looked up then. His gaze fell first on Jake, and his eyes were so cool, Maggie could almost feel the chill. His mouth tightened into a stubborn line and he lifted his chin slightly, defiantly as the two men looked at each other across a distance that was more than physical. They remained like that for several seconds, until finally, sensing a need to break the tension, Maggie took a step forward and smiled.

Howard transferred his gaze to her, and the transformation in his face was astonishing. The glacial stare melted and the line of his lips softened as a genuine smile of pleasure brightened his face.

"Hi, Pop," she greeted him, using her pet term of endearment for him.

"Maggie." He held out his arms. "Nobody's called me that in years. Aren't you going to give this old man a hug?"

She stepped into his embrace, and his thin, bony arms closed around her. There was almost nothing to him, she realized in alarm as she affectionately returned the hug. When they finally drew apart there was a telltale sheen to his eyes.

"Maggie girl," he repeated, still holding her hands. "You look wonderful. A sight for sore eyes, I can tell you. I heard you were here, but I didn't expect you to come and meet me. I'm glad you did, though. It does a body good to see such a friendly face in a strange place."

Maggie knew Jake was right behind her, knew he'd heard his father's comment. She was sure it had cut deeply. And she was equally sure that was Howard's intent. Clearly the gulf between the two of them had widened dramatically through the years, she thought in dismay.

"Hello, Dad."

Howard reluctantly transferred his gaze from Maggie to Jake. "Hello," he said flatly.

"Did you have a good trip?"

"It was bumpy. And long."

"Then let's get your luggage and head home so you can rest."

"I don't need to rest."

Before Jake could respond, Maggie tucked her arm in Howard's and began walking toward the luggage carousels. "You're a better traveler than me, then," she declared with a smile. "I'm always tired after a long plane trip. And Atlanta to Maine certainly qualifies."

"Well, I might be a little tired," he admitted.

"Maybe a short nap would be nice when you get home."

"Maybe it would."

Although Howard conversed readily enough with Maggie, and his eyes even took on their old sparkle a couple of times, she quickly became aware that he was doing his best to ignore his son. Several times she tried to draw Jake into the conversation, but Howard would have none of it. Finally she gave up.

When Jake pulled into the parking lot of Whispering Sails, Howard leaned forward interestedly. "Is this your place, Maggie?"

"Yes. And the bank's," she teased.

"Well, it's mighty pretty. And a nice view, too."

"Thanks, Pop. It's been our home for a long time now. We love it here."

"I can see why. What's that over there?" He pointed to a small structure of weathered clapboard about a hundred yards from the house.

"That's our cottage. It's a little roomier and more private than the house. Some of our guests come back and stay there every year. I'll give you a tour soon, if you'd like."

He nodded eagerly. "That would be great."

She reached back then, and clasped his hand warmly. "You take care now, okay, Pop?"

He held on to her hand as if it was a lifeline, the strength of his grip surprising her. "Is that tour a promise, Maggie?"

The plea in his eyes made her throat tighten, and her heart was filled with compassion and affection for this man she'd once loved like a father. Cutting her ties with Jake's parents had been very painful, but at the time it had seemed the best way to preserve her sanity and start a new life. She'd never stopped missing them, though. And she was more than willing to do what she could to ease the difficult transition for this man who had lost not only his wife, but his health, his home and now his independence.

"Of course. Give me a call once you're settled and we'll have lunch."

"I'd like that." When he at last reluctantly released her hand, she reached for the door handle.

"I'll walk Maggie to the door, Dad."

"That's not necessary, Jake," she said quickly.

"I insist."

"At least some of your good manners stuck with you," Howard muttered.

A muscle in Jake's jaw clenched, but he didn't respond. Maggie quickly stepped out of the car and met him at the path to the house, deciding not to protest when he took her arm. She wasn't going to give him the cold shoulder, too.

"It's pretty bad, isn't it?" she conceded quietly.

"And not apt to get much better any time soon, I'm afraid."

He paused when they reached the porch and raked his fingers wearily through his hair. "Thanks for going today, Maggie. I think it was good for Dad to see a friendly face, as he so bluntly put it."

There was a touch of bitterness—and despair—in Jake's voice, and though Maggie had her own unresolved issues with this man, she couldn't help but feel compassion for his plight. Impulsively she reached over and laid a hand on his arm. "I'll keep you both in my prayers, Jake," she promised with quiet sincerity.

"Thanks. We could use them. Goodbye, Maggie."

As he walked back to rejoin his father, Jake thought about Maggie's last comment. He wasn't much of a praying man, not anymore. In fact, it had been so long since he'd talked to the Lord that he doubted if his voice would even be recognized. But maybe the Lord would listen to Maggie.

Jake hoped so. On his own, he wasn't sure he could ever make peace with the stony-faced man waiting in his car. It would take the intervention of a greater power to bring about such a reconciliation. In fact, it would take a miracle. And unfortunately, Jake thought with a sigh, he hadn't witnessed many of those.

Chapter Five

Jake slowly opened his eyes, glanced at the bedside clock with a groan, then pulled the sheet back over his shoulder and turned on his side. Even after all his years in the navy, living by rigid timetables that often included unmercifully early reveille, he'd never adjusted to getting up at the crack of dawn. Okay, so maybe eight o'clock didn't exactly qualify as the crack of dawn. But it was still too early to get up on a Sunday morning.

He had just drifted back to sleep when an ominous clatter in the kitchen rudely awakened him. Obviously his father was up, he thought wryly. As he'd discovered in the last couple of days, Howard was an early riser. But he usually tried to go about his business quietly until Jake appeared. Clearly, however, his father was in no mood to humor him this morning.

With a resigned sigh Jake swung his feet to the floor. He supposed he should look on the bright side. At least they hadn't come to blows yet. On the other hand they'd barely spoken since Howard's arrival. Jake had tried to engage his father in conversation, but the older man's responses were typically monosyllables or grunts.

Jake frowned as Howard noisily dropped something onto the counter. For whatever reason, his father appeared to be in a worse mood than usual today.

Jake pulled on his jeans and combed his fingers through his hair. Might as well find out what was in the old man's craw.

Whatever it was, Jake had a sinking feeling that it had something to do with him.

He padded barefoot toward the kitchen, pausing on the
threshold to survey the scene. Howard had apparently already
eaten breakfast, judging by the toast crumbs on the table and
the almost-empty cup on the counter. A crusty oatmeal pot
added to the unappetizing mess. Jake jammed his hands into
his pockets and took a deep breath.

"I would have made breakfast for you, Dad."

"I might starve waiting for you to get up," the older man
replied brusquely.

Jake felt a muscle tighten in his jaw, but he tried to maintain
a pleasant, civil tone. "I spent a lot of years in the navy
getting up early, Dad. I like to sleep in when I can. I'll be on
my new job in less than a month, back to a regular schedule.
I'm enjoying this while I can."

"At the expense of God, I see."

Jake frowned. "What's that supposed to mean?"

Howard spared him a disparaging glance, disapproval evident in his eyes. "It doesn't look to me like you plan on going
to church today. I guess you've turned your back on God,
too."

So that explained why his father was wearing a tie, Jake
thought distractedly as he considered Howard's caustic remark. The fact was, the older man was right—and Jake felt
guilty about it. Since he'd left home, he'd slowly drifted away
from his faith. Oh, he still believed all the basics. He just
hadn't seen much reason to demonstrate those beliefs by going to church. And gradually, as time went by, his faith had
become less and less a part of his life. But clearly it was still
very much a part of his father's.

"Give me a few minutes to get dressed," he said shortly,
turning on his heel and retreating to his bedroom.

"What time are the services?" his father called.

Jake ignored the question—because he didn't have a clue.
But Maggie would. He knew beyond the shadow of a doubt
that her faith still played a pivotal role in her life. There was
probably a church somewhere near Castine, but if he had to

go, he figured he might as well use it as an excuse to see her. He reached for the phone, praying she hadn't left yet.

By the time Jake reappeared in the kitchen fifteen minutes later, in a navy blue blazer and striped tie over khaki slacks, his father had cleaned up the kitchen and was sitting at the table reading the paper. He looked up and adjusted his glasses when Jake stepped into the room, and for the briefest second Jake could have sworn he saw a flash of approval. But it was gone so fast, he couldn't be sure.

"So what time are services?"

"Ten o'clock."

"When do you want to leave?"

"Nine-thirty should be fine. I'm going to grab some breakfast first."

His father silently perused the paper as Jake toasted a bagel and poured some coffee. Except for the rustle of paper as he turned the pages, the house was quiet. Jake didn't even try to converse with him this morning. The last few days had been draining, and he was tired. The tension in the air between them was so thick, he could cut it with the proverbial knife. Jake found himself on edge all the time, constantly bracing for his father's next dig.

The drive to the church also passed in strained silence. But the sight of Maggie waiting outside for them, just as she'd promised, brought a wave of relief. Funny. As far as he was concerned, Maggie had more reason than his father did to treat him badly. Yet despite her wariness and her obvious attempts to keep him at arm's length emotionally, she was at least civil. That was more than he could say for his father.

"Hello, Pop. Hi, Jake."

Jake smiled at Maggie as they approached. She looked especially lovely today, in a teal green silk dress that clung to her lithe curves, her hair sending out sparks in the sun when she moved. In the soft morning light, she hardly looked older than she had twelve years before.

"Hi." He smiled at her, and their gazes connected for a brief, electric moment before hers skittered away.

"Maggie, you're a sight for sore eyes." Howard's tone was

warm, and for the first time since the day they'd picked him up at the airport, the older man smiled. It was amazing how that simple expression transformed his face, Jake reflected. Gone was the cold, prickly, judgmental man who shared his house. In his place was a congenial stranger, easygoing and good-natured. He seemed like the kind of person who could get along with anybody. Anybody but his youngest son, that is, Jake thought grimly.

"How have you been, Pop?"

He shrugged. "Kind of hard to adjust to a new place. I'm looking forward to that lunch and tour you promised me, though."

"How about tomorrow?"

"That would be great!" His eyes were actually shining and eager, Jake noted.

"Jake, would you like to come, too?" Maggie asked politely, turning to him.

The idea of spending time with Maggie under any circumstances was appealing to Jake. But he knew his presence would ruin the treat for the older man. Slowly he shook his head. "I'm afraid I can't. I need to go over to school and get some things squared away." Without even looking, he could sense his father's relief.

"Another time, then," Maggie replied.

Did she mean it? he wondered. She'd done little to encourage his attention since that first morning at the B&B when he'd reappeared in her life. She was polite, pleasant, completely civil. But he sensed very clearly that she'd also posted a No Trespassing sign on her heart. She would be nice to him because she was a lady and because she'd been brought up in a faith that taught forgiveness. But he suspected that she had set clear limits on their relationship.

Maggie took Howard's arm and led him into the church, leaving Jake to follow in their wake. In Maggie's presence Howard stood up straighter, walked more purposefully, Jake realized. It was obvious that Maggie was good for his father. And maybe...maybe that was why their paths had crossed, he speculated. Not because the two of them were destined to renew a failed romance, but because Maggie would be able to help Howard.

It was a sobering thought, and not one Jake especially liked. It wasn't that he begrudged his father the joy Maggie seemed to give him. But somehow he'd hoped that…well, he didn't know exactly what he'd hoped would come out of their chance meeting. He only knew it had something to do with him and Maggie—*not* Maggie and Howard.

As Jake took a seat beside Maggie, he tried to recall the last time he'd been to a Sunday service. Eight or ten years ago, maybe? Probably during one of his few visits home on leave. It felt strange to be back. Strange, and yet… He couldn't quite put his finger on it. It was just that here, in this peaceful place, with the familiar words of Scripture ringing in his ears and Maggie and his father beside him, he felt oddly as if he'd come home. Which made no sense, given that his father hated him, Maggie—though polite—was distant, and he hadn't darkened a church door in years. The Lord probably didn't even recognize him. Nevertheless, he couldn't shake the sense of homecoming. For whatever reason, being in this place with these people felt good. And right.

When the service ended, Maggie accompanied them outside, then turned to say goodbye. But Jake didn't want her to leave, not yet. She was the only bright spot in his day, and he was in no hurry to return to the silent, tension-filled house with his father.

"Where are the girls today?" he asked, trying to buy himself a few more minutes in her presence.

"Minding the store. We take turns going to services on Sunday. What time would you like me to pick you up tomorrow, Pop? We don't take guests on Sunday night, so my Monday mornings are free."

"I'll drop Dad off, Maggie. It will save you a trip," Jake said.

She considered his offer for a moment, then gave a shrug of concession. "All right. How about ten o'clock, Pop?"

"The sooner the better as far as I'm concerned."

"I'll see you tomorrow, then." She reached over impulsively and gave Howard a hug, and for a moment Jake actually envied the older man. Though she was only a whisper away from him, she was as distant as some exotic locale where he'd been stationed. The breeze sent a whiff of her perfume his way, and he inhaled the subtle, floral scent. Nothing dramatic or sophisticated, just refreshing and filled with the promise of spring. It seemed somehow to capture her essence.

"Goodbye, Jake," she said pleasantly as she stepped out of his father's embrace. The sizzling connection was there again as their gazes met, sending a surge of electricity up his spine. His eyes darkened, and her own dilated ever so slightly under the intensity of his gaze, her lips parting almost imperceptibly. How was it possible that she could move him so after all these years with no more than a look?

"See you tomorrow, Maggie," Howard said brightly.

With a nod, she turned and walked rapidly away. Too rapidly, Jake thought. It was as if she was running away from him. He knew she didn't want to feel anything for him. He understood that. He also understood that she had no choice. *They* had no choice. The emotional ties that had once bound them might be tattered. But the chemistry was most definitely still there.

"She always was a real special girl," Howard declared warmly as he watched her disappear around the corner. "It sure is nice to see that some things never change."

Jake glanced at his father, prepared to take offense. But for once the older man's potentially barbed remark didn't seem to be directed at Jake. His eyes were thoughtful, sad even, as he stared after Maggie. Maybe his father was thinking of all the things that had changed in his life these last few years, Jake mused. Death, illness, loss of independence—they'd all taken their toll.

Both his father and Maggie had clearly changed through the years. And so had he. For the better, he thought. The challenge was to convince these two very special people of that.

* * *

"This sure is a wonderful place, Maggie," Howard complimented her as they finished their tour of Whispering Sails. "And you did all this yourself?"

"All the decorating. And a lot of the minor renovations. It's amazing what you can learn from a library book. Plumbing, wallpapering, electrical repairs, carpentry—it's all there."

Howard shook his head. "I would never have believed it. I don't recall you ever showing an interest in that kind of thing in the old days."

"Well, what's that old saying—'Necessity is the mother of invention'? You can learn an awful lot when you have to. And it's a whole lot more economical than paying someone to do it. So how about a quick look around town before we have lunch?"

By the time Maggie pulled up in front of Jake's cottage to drop Howard off, it was nearly three o'clock. She could tell that the lonely older man was reluctant to see their outing come to an end, and her throat tightened in empathy. If only he and Jake could reach some understanding. This rift had to be hard on both of them.

"Maggie, would you come in and have a cup of coffee?" Howard asked, the plea in his eyes tugging at her heart. "Jake's not back yet. His car's still gone."

Maggie hesitated, but only for a moment. As long as she didn't have to worry about running into Jake, she could spare a little more time for Howard. And maybe she could find some words that would help these two strong-willed men breach the gap between them. "All right. For a few minutes," she agreed.

Half an hour later, sitting at the kitchen table with Howard, Maggie carefully broached the subject. "So how have you and Jake been getting along?"

Howard's response was a wry face and a shrug. Which pretty much confirmed her suspicion. She took a sip of her coffee, then wrapped her hands around the mug, choosing her words carefully. "You know, Pop, it would be easier if you and he could find a way to make some sort of peace."

He glanced down at his coffee. "Not likely."

"I feel guilty about the two of you, you know. Like the rift between you is my fault."

"That's not true, Maggie. At least not now. Jake's decision to walk out on you did *start* everything. What kind of man would do a thing like that? I thought I raised him better." He shook his head sadly and sighed. "But things just went downhill from there. I guess I made my feelings pretty clear—I never have been one to mince words—and he just quit coming around. Oh, once in a while on leave he'd show up for a few days. More for his mother than anything else. He did love her, I'll give him that. But he should have come around more often. She was always sad he didn't. It was almost like he cut us off because we reminded him of something he was ashamed of. Even when Clara was sick, we didn't see much of him. Not till the end. Barely made it home before she died, in fact. That wasn't right."

"Where was he at the time, Pop?" Maggie asked gently.

"Japan."

"That's pretty far away," she reflected. "I don't suppose the navy would have looked kindly on too many trips home."

Howard studied her curiously. "Seems strange, you defending him, Maggie. After what he did to you."

She shrugged and took a sip of her coffee. "It was a long time ago, Pop. We were different people then. I was devastated for a long time. But in the end I put it in the hands of the Lord, asked for His help. And eventually I was able to leave the past behind and move on. I won't lie to you, Pop. The scars are still there. It was a very tough road alone. But the girls, and my faith, helped a lot."

"I can see you've made a nice life for yourself, Maggie. But…well, I hope you won't think I'm being too nosy…I just wondered how you feel about living this close to Jake again after all these years."

Maggie took a moment to consider that question as she poured herself another cup of coffee. It was the same question she'd been asking herself for weeks. And it was a question that became even harder to answer after Sunday services, when one sizzling look from Jake had not only sent her blood pressure skyrocketing, but made her feel as shaky as a new-born colt.

So far she hadn't come up with an adequate answer. Her feelings were all jumbled together…shock, anger, trepidation. She was nervous and jumpy and confused. Mostly confused. Because she'd long ago relegated her relationship with Jake to history. She'd even gotten to the point where weeks went by when she didn't think of him. She had finally convinced herself that he no longer meant anything to her. So she had been stunned and unsettled to discover that the powerful attraction between them hadn't died after all. It had simply lain dormant—and undiminished. She felt it spark to life every time he was near her. She sensed that he did, too. And she didn't like it. Not in the least. But she didn't know what to do about it.

Maggie glanced up and realized that Howard was still waiting for an answer. "I really don't know, Pop," she replied honestly as she stood and gathered up their cups. "I'm still trying to sort it out." She deposited the cups in the sink and turned on the faucet. "I suppose I'm still in…" She paused and peered down. "Say, Pop, did you know your sink isn't draining too well?"

He rose and joined her. "Yeah. We called the owner but he hasn't done anything about it yet."

"This could back up anytime. Let me take a quick look in the garage. There might be a few tools."

Howard showed her the way, but after poking around between the boxes Jake had shipped from his father's house, she gave up. "I don't see anything. But I have some in the… Pop, what's this?" she asked curiously, leaning close to examine a label on a box. "Do you still do woodworking?"

Howard peered at the box. "Haven't in years. Not since Clara died. Hmmph. Can't imagine why Jake brought all that stuff. Guess I ought to look around and see what else he dragged up here." He glanced at the small accumulation of boxes, and his shoulders sagged dejectedly. "Not much to show for a lifetime, is it? A couple dozen boxes of junk."

Maggie reached over and gently touched his arm. "Pop,

you know the important things aren't in boxes. They're here.'' She laid her hand on her heart.

He nodded. "You're right about that. But I haven't done too well on that score, either, I guess.''

"It's never too late.''

He considered that in silence for a moment, then turned to her and planted his hands on his hips. "But first things first. What about my clogged-up sink?''

She smiled. "I have some tools in the car. Let me run out and get them.''

A few minutes later Maggie was wedged under the sink, Howard standing over her. "Can you hand me the wrench?'' she asked, her voice muffled.

He rummaged around in her toolbox and passed it to her. "Maggie, are you sure you know how to do this?''

She grinned. "Trust me. Now, do you think you could round up some rags or old towels? There's probably water in here that will run out when I loosen the pipes.''

"I'm pretty sure there are some rags out in the garage. I'll check.''

Maggie shifted into a more comfortable position as she waited. It was too dark under the sink to get a clear view of the pipes. When Howard returned she'd ask him to hold the flashlight while she worked. In the meantime, she might as well see how tight the corroded connections were, she decided, reaching up to clamp the wrench onto the pipe.

When Jake pulled up in front of the cottage, he was pleasantly surprised to discover Maggie's car still parked in front. He had expected her to be long gone by the time he returned. He had no idea how his father had convinced her to come inside, but he owed the older man one for that coup. Just seeing her would brighten up his otherwise mundane day.

Jake strolled into the house, pausing in the living room to listen for voices. But the house was totally silent. Maybe they were sitting out back.

Jake strode quickly through the living room, heading toward the back door. But he came to an abrupt halt when he reached the kitchen doorway and his gaze fell on a pair of long, clearly feminine legs, in nicely fitting tan slacks, extending out from under his sink. Maggie, of course. But what in heaven's name was...

"Pop? Listen, could you hold the flashlight for me? It's pretty dark under here. And hand me the rags. I think the wrench did the trick. It's starting to give."

Silently Jake walked over to the sink, sorted through the items in the unfamiliar toolbox on the floor and withdrew a flashlight. He clicked it on, then squatted beside the prone figure, impressed by her deft handling of the wrench. She was full of surprises, that was for sure. As he recalled, she didn't know pliers from a screwdriver in the old days. With a smile he pointed the light toward the tumbled mass of red hair. "Sorry. I don't have any rags," he said in an amused tone.

Maggie's startled gaze flew to his, and she tried to sit up, whacking her forehead on the pipe in the process. "Ouch!" She clapped her hand to her head and let the wrench drop to the floor.

Jake was instantly contrite. "Maggie, are you all right?" Without waiting for a reply, his hands circled her slender waist and he gently tugged her into the open until she sat on the floor beside him, her head bowed.

"I can't believe I did that," she muttered, rubbing her forehead. "After all the sinks I've been under, to pull a stupid stunt like that..."

"I shouldn't have startled you. Let me check the damage." He pried her hand off her forehead and frowned at the rapidly rising lump. "This needs ice right away." He rose and reached for her hand, drawing her swiftly to her feet in one smooth motion, then guided her to a chair. "Sit tight. What were you doing under there, anyway?" he asked over his shoulder as he headed toward the freezer.

"Pop said it was clogged. I figured I could probably fix it. I was checking it out when you walked in."

"I found some rags, Maggie. They were right where..." Howard stopped abruptly at the garage door. "What happened?" he asked in alarm.

"I hit my head," Maggie explained quickly. "Jake is fixing me an ice pack."

"I knew I shouldn't let you tackle that plumbing. That's not woman's work," Howard fretted.

"Oh, Pop, don't be silly. I do this all the time at home. Women are liberated these days, you know." Jake handed her the homemade ice pack—ice cubes in a plastic bag wrapped in a dish towel—and she clamped it against her head, wincing as the cold made contact with her tender skin. "Thanks. I think."

Howard snorted in disgust. "Liberated! You mean free to do all the dirty work? Doesn't sound very liberating to me."

Maggie chuckled. "I've never heard it put quite that way, but you have a point," she conceded.

"We seem to be in short supply when it comes to tools around here, Maggie, but if you'll let me borrow a couple of these, I'll fix the drain," Jake said.

"Are you sure? I really am pretty good at this. I don't mind finishing up."

"Let Jake do it," Howard told her. "He should have done it in the first place anyway."

Maggie looked at Jake, saw his lips compress into a thin line at the criticism, and decided that this was a good time to make her exit. "Well, in that case, I'll head home. We have a full house tonight, and I need to be on hand to greet the guests."

"I'll bring the tools back in a day or so," Jake promised as he walked her to the door.

"No hurry. Hopefully I won't need them before then anyway." She turned and smiled at Howard, who had followed them. "Goodbye, Howard."

"Goodbye, Maggie. Thank you for the tour. And lunch. It was real nice."

"You're very welcome. I enjoyed it a lot."

Maggie turned to go, only to find Jake's hand at her elbow. She looked up at him questioningly.

"I'll see you to your car."

Maggie shrugged. "Suit yourself."

They walked in silence, and even though Maggie's head was starting to throb, she was acutely conscious of Jake's nearness, of the warmth of his hand on her bare skin and the faint, woodsy scent, uniquely his and achingly familiar. She had all but forgotten that scent. But standing so close to him now, she was reminded with startling intensity of all the times this man had held her in his arms, had caressed her face, had claimed her lips. But how could she still find him attractive after what he'd done to her? She'd been burned once. Shouldn't she be immune to his appeal?

Jake glanced down at Maggie's bowed head as they approached the car. She seemed lost in thought. *Where are you, Maggie?* he asked silently. *Are you remembering, as I am?* Gently, as unobtrusively as possible, he rubbed his thumb over the soft skin on her arm, recalling a time when she'd welcomed his touch. His happiest memories, his times of greatest contentment, were linked with this woman, he realized.

His gaze lingered on her glorious hair, as beautiful as ever. It was the kind of hair a man could get lost in—full and thick and inviting his hands in to play. But those old, sweet days were gone, he reminded himself. And yet…he felt the same as he had twelve years before. The astounding attraction—physical, emotional and intellectual—was still there. Did she feel it as intensely as he did? he wondered. And was it real? Or was it just fed by memories of what had once been, reawakened temporarily by the strange coincidence of their reunion?

"I'll hang on to the ice bag, if that's all right," Maggie interrupted his thoughts when they reached the car, trying with limited success to keep her voice steady.

With an effort he forced his lips up into a grin as he opened her door. "Such as it is. And thanks for taking time for Dad today. I know he appreciated it."

"It was no effort. He's a good man, Jake. He's just dealing with an awful lot right now."

"I know it's tough for him. I wish I could make it easier. But I can't reach him, Maggie. He shuts me out." He sighed and raked the fingers of one hand through his hair as he glanced back toward the cottage. "I had hoped that if we actually lived under the same roof he might come around. But I'm beginning to lose hope."

"Give it some time," she urged, impulsively laying her hand on his arm. "You and he have been apart for so long that you need to get to know each other again before you can feel comfortable together."

Jake smiled gently as he glanced down at her hand resting on his arm, then covered it with his. "You know, when I talk to you, I don't feel quite so hopeless. Why is that, Maggie?"

Her gaze locked with his, and for just a moment, the tender look in his eyes, the warmth of his voice, made her feel sixteen again. Made her want to *be* sixteen again. Which was bad. What was past could never return. She needed to remember that. She was not going to get caught up in the romantic fantasies that Abby and Allison were weaving. They were eighteen. She was almost thirty-seven—far to old to believe in fairy tales and happy endings.

With an abruptness that momentarily startled Jake, Maggie removed her hand and stepped away.

"I don't know. But maybe I should bottle it," she said with forced brightness as she slid into the car. "Call it Dr. Maggie's elixir. See you later, Jake." She started the engine, put the car in gear and drove away without a backward look.

Jake watched her go, a troubled look on his face, then slowly walked back to the house. His father met him at the door.

"She going to be all right? That was a nasty bump."

"She'll be fine, Dad." Physically, at least. Emotionally, he wasn't so sure. About either of them.

Chapter Six

Great. Just great.

Maggie stared down in disgust at the decidedly flat tire. Naturally this couldn't have happened in town. That would be too easy. It had to happen in the middle of nowhere— namely, an isolated spot on the remote Cape Rosier loop.

A drop of water splashed onto her cheek, and she closed her eyes with a sigh of resignation. Now it was raining. That figured. And it only made sense that the air would take a turn toward the chilly side. Where was the warm sun and lovely light she'd had earlier while she was painting?

Gone, obviously, she thought with a disgusted glance at the rapidly darkening sky. As were her hopes of anyone appearing along this stretch of deserted road, she concluded. Other than walking two or three miles to a house, her only option was to change the tire herself. Suddenly she sneezed, groping in her pocket for a tissue as she sniffled. On top of everything else, she seemed to be coming down with a bug of some kind. So what else could go wrong today? she wondered in dismay.

Maggie climbed back into the car, allowing herself a moment to regroup before tackling the job ahead of her. She put her forearms on the wheel and wearily rested her cheek against them, angling her head away from the bruised spot on her temple that was a souvenir of her plumbing adventure the week before. She hadn't seen Jake since then, although Howard had called once in the middle of the week. He said he was just checking to see how she was, but she suspected that he was simply lonely. It was so sad, the two of them sharing a house yet both so alone. Jake was trying—she knew that. But his attempts at reconciliation were rebuffed at every turn. In a way she felt sorry for him.

It was odd, this feeling of sympathy she had for Jake. And it was certainly a surprising—and ironic—twist, considering their history. But what surprised her even more was the spark between them. How could her response to him suddenly reactivate after lying in disuse for so long? One smoky look from those deep brown eyes was all it had taken to make her feel sixteen again. It has been so long since she'd felt the tremulous, breathless sensation of physical attraction that she'd even forgotten how to handle it. And she didn't want to relearn that lesson. What she *wanted* to do was turn those feelings off. That, however, didn't seem to be an option, she admitted with a sigh. But she *could* choose not to act on them. And she so chose.

For the moment, though, she would do better to focus her attention on a more pressing problem. The flat tire wasn't going to fix itself, after all. So, with a resigned sigh, she got out of the car and opened the trunk.

Maggie eyed the spare tire and jack uncertainly. She'd changed a tire before, of course. Once. A long time ago. In a basic car-maintenance class she'd taken. Under the watchful eye of the instructor. The procedure was a bit hazy after all this time. But it would come back to her, she told herself encouragingly.

Maggie removed the spare tire without too much difficulty, then got down on her hands and knees to look under the car, trying to figure out where to put the jack. She was so intent on her task that she didn't even realize a car had stopped until she heard a door shut. Before she could fully extricate herself from under the car to check out the new arrival, an amused voice spoke beside her.

"How is it that I always seem to find you repairing things?"

Maggie scooted back and turned to stare up at Jake.

"What are you doing here?" she asked in surprise.

"I think the more important question is, what are *you* doing here?"

"At the moment, changing a tire," she replied dryly.

"I can see that. What I meant was, what are you doing on this road? It's pretty isolated."

She shrugged. "I come here to paint. There are some lovely coves out this way." Suddenly she sneezed again, then reached into the pocket of her jeans for another tissue.

Jake frowned. He'd noticed right off that her voice was a bit husky, and a closer look revealed that her eyes were red. "Are you sick, Maggie?"

She wiped her nose and shook her head. "Of course not. I never get sick."

He reached for her hand then, and before she could protest he drew her to her feet and placed a cool palm against her forehead. It was warm—too warm—and his frown deepened.

"You have a temperature."

"No, I don't. I'm fine." She pulled away, disconcerted by his touch. If her face hadn't been flushed before, it was now. She walked around him toward the trunk and started to reach for the jack, but his hand firmly restrained her.

"Yes, you do. And standing out here in the drizzle isn't going to help matters. Go wait in my car while I change your tire."

"You don't have to do that," she protested.

He sighed in frustration. "Maggie, just accept the help, okay? I would have stopped no matter who it was."

In all honesty, she really wasn't feeling that great. In fact, she was fading fast. With a sigh, she capitulated. "All right. Thank you."

Maggie couldn't believe that she actually dozed in Jake's car while he changed her tire, but he had to nudge her shoulder gently to wake her up when he finished. Her eyelids felt extraordinarily heavy as they flickered open.

"All done," he declared as he slid in beside her.

The drizzle had escalated into a steady rain during her brief nap, producing a soft, rhythmic cadence on the roof. Her gaze flickered to Jake's blue shirt, which had darkened in color with moisture and now clung damply to his broad chest, and stuck there as her pulse accelerated.

"How are you feeling?" he asked solicitously.

"Your shirt's wet," she murmured inanely, her gaze still on his chest.

He shrugged her concern aside. "It'll dry. I'm more worried about you. Are you okay to drive?"

With a supreme effort, she transferred her gaze to his face. "Sure. I—I guess I picked up a bug or something. I felt fine this morning. This just came over me in the last hour or two. I'll be okay by tomorrow."

"I don't know," he replied doubtfully. "You look pretty under the weather."

"As opposed to under the sink? Or under the car?" she teased.

That drew a brief smile in response, but then he grew more serious. "You don't have to put on an act in front of me, you know. I can tell you're feeling rotten. You always got a certain look when you were sick. Something in your eyes..." His gaze locked on hers, and for a moment her heart actually stopped beating. Here, in this cocoon of warmth, sheltered from the rain, she felt as if they were alone in the world. He was only a few inches away, close enough to touch, to lean on, to kiss...

Her breath caught in her throat as the impulse to do just that intensified. This was all wrong. She didn't want to feel this way, not about Jake. How could she even consider letting herself get involved with him again? Yes, he seemed different. More responsible, more mature. But it was too soon to know. Far too soon. But even though her mind accepted that logic, her heart stubbornly refused to listen.

Jake watched Maggie's face, his perceptive gaze missing nothing. She had always been easy to read. She wanted him to kiss her just as badly as he *wanted* to kiss her. But it was too soon. One of the things he'd learned in the navy was to control his impulses, think things through. An impulsive move in battle could cost you your life. And an impulsive move right now could cost him Maggie. Intuitively he knew that, and it wasn't a risk he was willing to take.

Reluctantly he released her gaze and turned to look at the road, which was now partially obscured by fog. He took a deep breath, willing his pulse to slow down, struggling to control his erratic respiration. He didn't want to scare Maggie away by revealing the depth of his attraction.

"I think we'd better head back or we might be marooned here," he said conversationally, striving for a light tone. "Not that I'd mind, you understand, but I think you need to change into some dry clothes and get some rest."

Maggie drew a shaky breath and reached for the door handle.

"You're right." She started to push the door open, then turned back to him with a frown. "By the way, you never did tell me how you happened to be out here today. It's not exactly a well-traveled route."

He sighed and wearily shook his head. "Dad and I had an argument. Again. I decided to go for a drive until I cooled down, and this road caught my eye. Lucky for you, I guess."

"I take it things haven't improved much in the last week between you two?"

"I think that would be a fair assumption."

"I'm sorry, Jake. I wish there was something I could do."

He shrugged. "We'll just have to work it out between the two of us. But I appreciate your concern."

"Well, tell Pop I said hi. And...thanks, Jake."

"You're welcome. Now go home and get some rest."

"I'll try, although I do have a business to run, Jake. But Eileen—you met her the night Allison was in the hospital, remember?—she comes by to fill in when we need someone, and she helps with the cleaning every day for a couple of hours. So I don't have to do much when I get home. Since I don't take guests on Sunday night, I'll actually be a lady of leisure until tomorrow afternoon."

"Good. Take advantage of it. The best way to fight a virus is to rest."

"Yes, Doctor," she teased.

"Hey, I learned a lot in the navy. One of my best buddies was a medic." He reached across to push her door open, and as his arm brushed against hers her heart lurched.

"I'll follow you until we get to the main road." Did his voice sound huskier than usual, or was it only her imagination? she wondered. "And Maggie...don't worry about my problems. I'll deal with the situation. I'm sure you have enough problems of your own to handle."

He was right, of course, she thought, as she dashed through the rain to her own car. She did have her own problems. And a glance into the rearview mirror revealed her biggest one.

With a sinking feeling, Maggie played back the answering machine again. As she listened a second time, her spirits nosedived. Eileen had the flu, too, and wasn't going to be able to come over in the morning to help with the cleaning.

Maggie hit the erase button and wearily pushed her hair back from her face. This had most definitely *not* been a good day, she decided. A flat tire, a flu bug and four guest rooms plus the cottage to clean before two o'clock tomorrow. If the twins were here it would be manageable. But they had signed up months ago to volunteer for a week at a camp for disadvantaged children, and they wouldn't be home until tomorrow afternoon. Which meant the housecleaning chores fell squarely on her shoulders.

She trudged into the kitchen to make herself a cup of tea, detouring for two aspirin on the way. She was generally able to overlook minor aches and pains and work right through normal fatigue, but this was different. She honestly felt that if she didn't lay down, she might fall down. Maybe Jake was right. A little rest might help. Perhaps if she gave herself an hour or so she'd feel good enough to tackle a couple of the rooms tonight. Then she could finish up in the morning.

Maggie dragged her protesting body up to the third floor, which had been divided into two dormer bedrooms—one for her, one for the girls. She sank down onto her bed, too tired even to remove her shoes as she stretched out. The twins would give her a hard time about that, she thought with the ghost of a smile as her eyelids drifted closed. She'd always been such a stickler about keeping shoes off beds and furniture. But the thought didn't linger long. In less than fifteen seconds she drifted into oblivion.

* * *

As consciousness slowly returned, Maggie lifted her heavy eyelids and stared at the ceiling feeling disoriented. Then she turned her head to look at the clock on her bedside table. When it finally came into focus, she frowned. Eight o'clock? She'd slept for two hours? But no, the light wasn't right, she thought in confusion, glancing toward the dormer window. It was at the wrong angle.

With a sudden jolt, the truth hit home. It was *morning!* Propelled by panic, she quickly sat up and swung her legs to the floor. The room tilted crazily, and she dropped her head into her hands as she waited for everything to stop spinning.

The sudden ringing of the phone on her nightstand made her jump, and she groped for the receiver with one hand.

"Hel…" Her voice came out in a croak and she tried again. "Hello?"

"Maggie? Is that you?"

"Yes," she replied groggily. "Hi, Jake."

She could hear the frown in his voice. "You sound awful."

"Thanks a lot."

"How are you feeling? Or does your voice tell the story?"

Yes, she thought to herself, it does. The numbing lethargy still had a grip on her body, and her aches hadn't dissipated much, if at all. "I'll live," she assured him, striving for a flippant tone. "It's just a flu bug or something. And in this business there are no sick days. The guests just keep coming." She reached for a tissue and tried to discreetly blow her nose.

Jake realized that he'd never really thought about that. The few times he'd been under the weather in the navy he'd simply gone on sick call. But Maggie didn't have that luxury. In fact, as far as he could see, she didn't have many luxuries, period. And that bothered him. "I guess you're right," he admitted. "But the girls can help, too, can't they?"

There was no way to avoid such a direct question. "They could if they were here. But they've been gone all week and won't be back until late this afternoon. So I'm the official greeter today."

"But your cleaning woman is coming today, isn't she?"

"Monday is one of her regular days to come," Maggie hedged.

"Well, try to take it easy, okay?" he replied.

"I'll try," she said, knowing that she could try all she wanted to—the house still had to be cleaned. It was a daunting task when she was well; "impossible" was a more appropriate descriptor today, considering how she felt. But she'd manage somehow. She always did.

"I'll check back with you later, Maggie."

"Okay. Thanks for calling, Jake."

Slowly she replaced the receiver. Then, summoning all her reserves of energy, she forced herself to stand up. At least she was already dressed, she thought wryly as she made her way unsteadily down the stairs to the utility closet. *You can do it,* she encouraged herself. *The girls will be back to help later today. Just make it through the next few hours, take it one room at a time, and you'll be fine.*

And with that she reached for the mop.

By the time Maggie started on the third room, however, she was on autopilot. She went through the motions mindlessly, every movement more of an effort than the last. In fact, she was so out of it that it took several rings before she realized someone was at her front door. Her gaze flew to the steps in panic. *Please, Lord, not a guest,* she prayed as she made her way stiffly down the stairs. *Not yet. Not this early.*

This time her prayers were answered. When she swung the door open, she found Jake, not a guest.

In one swift, assessing glance he came to the obvious conclusion. She was sick as a dog and, judging by the faint scent of disinfectant cleaner drifting his way and the mop in her hand, she was *not* resting. Without a word he took her arm and ushered her inside, forcing her to sit in the closest chair before he knelt beside her. He put his hand on her forehead, and this time it was not only hot but clammy. A muscle in his jaw clenched and he frowned.

"What are you doing with that mop?" he demanded.

"Cleaning."

"What happened to Eileen?"

"She has the bug, too."

"Why didn't you tell me that earlier?"

"What good would that have done?"

He ignored that comment for the moment. "Have you called the doctor?"

"It's just a bug, Jake. Something's been going around. I was just lucky till now. I guess it was my turn."

He didn't look convinced, but he didn't argue the point. Instead, he stood up and held out his hand. "Come on. You're going back to bed."

She shook her head. "Jake, you don't understand. I have ten guests arriving this afternoon beginning at two o'clock. I've only cleaned two of the four rooms and I still have the cottage to do. I'll barely make it as it is. I can't lay down now."

"Maggie, you're sick. You should never have gotten up today in the first place."

She sighed, blinking away the tears of weariness that sprang to her eyes. "Jake, try to understand. Eileen and the girls are my only backup. There isn't anyone else I can call."

"Yes, there is."

She gave him a puzzled look. "Who?"

"Me. I learned to wield a pretty mean mop in the navy. They don't tolerate slobs, you know," he said, flashing her a brief grin.

She stared at him. Jake West cleaning a house? It was incomprehensible. As she recalled, he had always put house-keeping duties on a par with going to the dentist.

"Don't look so shocked," he admonished her gently, with that disconcerting habit he had of reading her mind. "Times change. People change. You can trust me to do a good job. I promise your guests won't complain."

"It's not that…" She was still having a hard time comprehending his generous offer. And even if he was sincere, it was too much to ask. "Jake, I can't let you do my work. It's not right. And don't give me that good deed business. This goes way above and beyond that."

He crouched down beside her once again, his warm, brown eyes level with hers, and took her cold hand in his. "Maggie, I *want* to do this, okay? You're sick. You'll only get sicker if you push yourself." He paused a moment, then took a deep breath. "Look, I know that you're still trying to grapple with this whole situation between us. To be honest, so am I. But fate, or whatever you care to call it, brought us back together. I don't know why. But at the bare minimum I'd like to be your friend—whatever that takes, and despite the fact that I don't deserve it. And friends take care of each other. Let me take care of you today, Maggie. As a friend."

She listened to Jake's heartfelt speech in silence, unable to doubt the sincerity in his eyes—or ignore the tenderness. He cared for her, that was clear. And, God help her, she was beginning to care for him again. She didn't want to. She told herself it was unwise. That it was risky, that she could get hurt again. But she couldn't help it. Because the Jake that had walked back into her life not only had all the good qualities she remembered, he had become even better. Under other circumstances, he was the kind of man she could easily fall in love with. There was nothing in his present behavior to make her cautious.

It was his past behavior that worried her. His track record wasn't good. And that made her *very* cautious. Her wariness wasn't something that could be overcome in a week, or a month, or maybe even a year. She'd been burned once before by this man and left with scars—plus a very real fear of fire.

Jake scrutinized her face, but for once he couldn't read her thoughts. He didn't want to push himself on her, but he'd already decided he wasn't going to walk away and let her face the housecleaning task alone. If necessary, he would insist—and deal with the consequences later. But he hoped she would just accept her limitations and be sensible.

"Maggie?" he prodded gently, exerting slight pressure on her hand when she didn't respond.

Jake's voice brought her back to the present. She was deeply touched by his offer, whatever his motivation. And like it or not, she needed help today. The Lord had obviously seen that need and provided for it. Maybe the help wasn't in the form she would have chosen, but who was she to question His motives?

"All right, Jake. Thank you. To be honest, I—I'm not sure I could have made it anyway."

Considering how she prided herself on her self-reliance,

Jake knew she must be a whole lot sicker than she was letting on, to admit that she wasn't able to handle the task in front of her. Once more he stood and gently reached for her hands, drawing her to her feet. He put his arm around her shoulders, and as they walked slowly up the stairs she leaned on him heavily—another indication of her weakened physical state. No way would she lean on him—literally or figuratively— unless she was in bad shape.

He paused at the landing, giving her a chance to catch her breath.

''Where's your room?''

She nodded toward the back stairway at the end of the hall. ''Third floor.''

By the time they made it up the much narrower stairway to her bedroom, he could feel her quivering. They passed an open door that revealed a spacious, gaily decorated dormer room with two twin beds. Obviously the twins' domain, he thought with a smile, noting the posters of the girls' latest movie heartthrobs.

Maggie's room was much smaller, squeezed under the eaves near the front of the house. It was very simply furnished and decorated, as if she'd poured all of her attention into the rest of the house and simply not bothered with her own little piece of it. As he gently eased her down onto the narrow twin bed, his throat contracted with tenderness and admiration for this woman who had struggled against all odds to overcome traumas and challenges that would have overwhelmed most people. Jake didn't know where she had found the strength to face each day, especially in those early years. But as he knelt to remove her shoes, his eyes fell on the Bible on her nightstand, and he suspected that was probably its source. She'd always had a strong faith, and it clearly had sustained her spiritually through the difficult years.

But how had she managed emotionally? he wondered. Maggie had so much love to give. Had it all been directed to the girls? He suspected so. As he tucked the covers around her shoulders, he felt that the single bed in the small attic room spoke more eloquently than words of her solitary state. He started to speak, then realized that she had already fallen asleep. Gently he reached down to brush a wisp of hair off her forehead, his fingers dropping to linger on her cheek. As he gazed at her pale face, a fierce surge of protectiveness washed over him.

Ever since their paths had crossed, Jake had felt increasingly drawn to the woman who had once, long ago, claimed his heart. At first he'd looked upon their reunion as a chance to at last find a way to ease the guilt that had plagued him for so long. Only a few minutes ago, he'd told Maggie that he hoped they could be friends. But now, as he stood beside her, he knew that his interest wasn't motivated by guilt, and that his feelings went far beyond friendship.

He loved her. It was as simple—and as complicated—as that.

As he gazed tenderly down at her, he thought of the Maggie he'd once loved. All the essential qualities he'd cherished were still there. But she'd changed, too. And he found that he loved the new Maggie, with her self-reliance and confidence and decisive manner, even more than he had loved the dependent young woman who had once deferred to his every decision. He liked her grit and her spunk and her strength—and her soft heart, which hadn't changed one iota.

Jake walked slowly to the door, pausing at the threshold to glance back once more at Maggie's sleeping form. She was quite a woman, he thought. She deserved to find a man who would love her and stand by her no matter what, who believed in honoring commitments and wasn't afraid of responsibility, who could be counted on to stand with her through good times *and* bad.

Jake had failed her once on that score, but he vowed silently that he never would again. The question was, how could he convince her of that?

Jake didn't have the answer. But he knew one thing with absolute certainty. He would find a way. Because suddenly a future without Maggie was not something he was willing to consider.

Chapter Seven

"See, Allison, I told you it was him!"

Abby's triumphant voice heralded the arrival of the twins at the kitchen door, and Jake glanced up from the pot he was stirring. "Hello, ladies," he greeted them with an engaging grin.

They simultaneously dumped their knapsacks on the floor and joined him.

"What are you doing here?" Abby asked curiously. "And where's Aunt Maggie?"

"She's in bed with the flu. I'm making her some soup."

"You're cooking?" Allison was clearly impressed.

Jake grinned. "I don't think heating up a can of soup exactly qualifies as cooking."

"How sick is she?" Abby asked with a frown of concern.

"Pretty sick."

"Where's Eileen?"

"She's got the same bug."

"But...but what about the cleaning?" Allison asked in alarm. "What will we tell the guests when they arrive?"

"The guests have already arrived and they're all settled in," Jake informed them calmly as he transferred the soup to a bowl and put it on a tray. "Your aunt started the cleaning, and I finished up."

"You mean...you mean *you* helped clean the rooms?" Abby asked incredulously.

Jake gave them a look of mock indignation. "Don't you think I'm capable of wielding a mop and broom?"

"It's not that," Allison said quickly. "It's just that…well, guys don't usually offer to pitch in on stuff like that."

"Well, let me tell you ladies a little secret," Jake said conspiratorially. "Men know how to clean. They just pretend they don't. So keep that in mind whenever you meet Mr. Right."

"I bet you had trouble convincing Aunt Maggie to let you help," Allison speculated.

"A little," he admitted with a grin.

Suddenly Abby frowned. "Gosh, she must be really sick if she gave in and went to bed."

"It's just the flu," Jake assured them as he added a cup of tea and some crackers to the tray. "But she's probably not going to have a whole lot of energy for a few days. Do you think you two can pick up the slack?"

"Sure. No problem. This is our summer job, anyway. We'll just put in a little overtime. Aunt Maggie's done it often enough for us."

They really were good kids, Jake reflected. Maggie had raised them well. "Great. Now, if you two can get the breakfast preparations under way, I'll take this up to your aunt."

The twins watched him disappear through the door, then Allison sank down on a convenient chair and sighed. "Wow! Talk about Sir Galahad!"

Abby joined her on an adjacent chair and propped her chin dreamily in her hand. "Yeah."

There was silence for a moment while they both mulled over this latest turn of events, and then Allison turned to her sister. "Do you think maybe something might come of this after all? I mean, I know Aunt Maggie keeps saying that their relationship is in the past and all that, but how many guys would clean toilets for a woman they don't care about?"

"I think it has very interesting possibilities," Abby replied with a thoughtful nod. "I think Aunt Maggie still cares, too. She just won't admit it—to us or herself. But maybe we can find a way to give her a nudge."

"And how do you propose we do that?"

Abby smiled smugly. "Well, as a matter of fact…I have a plan."

Jake eased Maggie's door open with one shoulder and cast a worried glance toward the bed. He'd checked on her a couple of times during the afternoon, and she'd been sleeping soundly. Now, however, she was sitting up, bent over, struggling to tie her shoes.

He pushed the door all the way open and strode inside. "What are you doing?" he demanded with a frown. He deposited the tray on the dresser and turned to face her, clamping his hands on his hips.

She looked up, startled. "Jake, it's after five! I'm surprised none of the guests have arrived yet," she said, her voice edged with panic.

"They have arrived. All of them."

Her eyes widened in alarm. "Oh, no! What did you tell them?"

"I told them hello. Then I welcomed them to Whispering Sails and asked if I could help with their luggage. I think that's the spiel, isn't it?"

Her frantic hands stilled on the laces and she stared him. "You mean…you checked everyone in?"

"Mmm-hmm. I looked them all up in the guest book on the desk in the foyer. It was a piece of cake." He picked up the tray and came to sit beside her. "Dinner," he explained, placing it on her lap.

She stared down at the soup, then back at him. "Jake, I…" Her voice choked, and she looked down in embarrassment. She was usually able to keep her emotions under control, but she couldn't stop the tears that sprang to her eyes. It had been a long time since anyone had stepped in as he had to ease her burden. The twins were great, of course. And they certainly would have helped if they'd been here. But they were family. Family members did those kinds of things for each other. But Jake wasn't family. He was… Well, she wasn't sure exactly what he was. He said he wanted to be her friend. But a moment later, when he took her chin in gentle fingers and turned her head toward his, the look in his eyes said a whole lot more than friendship.

"Did I pick the wrong kind of soup?" he asked with a tender smile.

She shook her head. "No. Th-this is fine."

"Then, what's wrong?"

She swallowed with difficulty. "It's just that I—I appreciate all you did today, Jake. It was too much to ask."

"You didn't ask."

"No, but...well, I feel like you were sort of forced into this."

"I wasn't forced into anything," he assured her firmly. "I wanted to help."

"I guess I owe you now," she replied with a sigh. "Bigtime."

Jake cupped her flushed face with both hands, and his gaze locked on hers. It was difficult to concentrate on his words when his thumbs began to stroke her cheeks. But she tried.

"Maggie, you don't owe me a thing. If I spent the rest of my life trying to ease your burdens, I could still never make up for what I did to you."

Maggie's spirits took a sudden, unaccountable nosedive. Was that the only motivation for Jake's good deed—to make amends? Was that the reason he'd offered her his friendship?

Jake saw the sudden dark cloud pass over her eyes and frowned. "What's wrong now?"

She shrugged and transferred her gaze to her soup, playing with the spoon. "Nothing. Just tired, I guess."

Jake studied her a moment, then nodded toward the tray. "Well, eat your soup and get back in bed. Everything's under control downstairs. The girls will take care of breakfast."

"I feel better since I slept, Jake. I can—"

"Maggie." He cut her off, his voice gentle but firm. "I want you to promise me you'll take it easy until at least tomorrow afternoon. You need the rest." When she didn't reply, he sighed. "Look, if you won't do it for yourself, do it for me, okay? Otherwise I'll be awake all night worrying about you."

She looked at him curiously, started to ask "Why?" but stopped herself in time. She could deal with those kinds of questions later, when she'd regained her strength. In the meantime, after all he'd done for her today she could at least give him some peace of mind in return.

"All right, Jake," she agreed.

"Good." He glanced at his watch, then grinned ruefully. "Well, I better get home and put together some dinner for Dad and me. Or maybe I can convince him to go out. He hasn't been in the mood yet, but it's worth a try tonight," he mused. "Now eat your soup."

She gave a mock salute. "Aye, aye, sir."

He grinned sheepishly. "Sorry. I got used to giving orders in the navy. It's a hard habit to break. How about, please eat your soup?"

"That's better," she conceded.

He sat there for another moment, his eyes soft on her face, and Maggie felt her breath catch in her throat. She knew that look. It was the look he used to get at his most tender moments, right before he kissed her, and her pulse went into overdrive.

Jake's gaze dropped to her full lips and a surge of longing swept over him. With a supreme effort he forced his gaze back to hers.

His eyes had deepened in color, Maggie noted, and she stared back into their unfathomable depths as he reached over to stroke her cheek with a featherlike touch. A pulse began to beat in the hollow of her throat as he slowly, very slowly, leaned toward her.

Maggie knew she should resist while she still could. But instead of listening to logic, her eyelids fluttered closed and she leaned ever so slightly toward him, inviting his kiss. She felt powerless to stop herself.

And then his lips, warm and tender, gently—and briefly—brushed her forehead. That was it. The kiss was over in an instant, so quickly that Maggie, who had expected so much more, was momentarily left off balance. Her eyelids flew open and she stared at him as he abruptly stood up.

"Good night, Maggie. I'll call you tomorrow."

And then he was gone.

She stared after him, still trying to figure out what had just happened. She thought he was going to kiss her. Really kiss her. And she'd offered no resistance. But instead of the passionate kiss she'd expected, he'd given her a brotherly peck on the forehead.

Why? Was it because he really did care about her only as a friend? Or was he just being noble, refusing to take advantage of her weakened physical condition?

Maggie didn't have a clue. But she knew one thing very clearly. Jake's brotherly kiss on her forehead just hadn't cut it. For better or worse, she wanted more.

Jake pulled up in front of his cottage and turned off the engine. It had taken the entire drive from Maggie's place to his for him to regain some semblance of control over his emotions. And he was still shaken by how close he had come just now to blowing it with her. Thank God he had found the discipline to back off, to stop at that brotherly kiss on the forehead, when what he really wanted to do was claim her tender lips with a kiss that expressed all the passion and love that was in his heart.

As each day passed, he knew with greater certainty that his feelings for this special woman had never died. During all the years of separation they had simply been stored in a quiet corner of his heart, growing in intensity as they waited for the opportunity to be given full expression. Now that the opportunity was at hand, they were clamoring for release.

But he had to be cautious. He felt sure that Maggie wasn't yet ready to accept such an admission on his part, that she was still very confused about her own feelings, grappling with questions and doubts, just as he had been initially. She needed time. He needed patience.

Jake drew a slow, deep breath. Only now was his pulse returning to normal, his respiration slowing. He'd known any number of women through the years who attracted him, but he'd never come this close to losing control. The only woman who had ever been able to do that to him was Maggie, beginning that summer when he was seventeen. She obviously hadn't lost her power over him.

Jake stepped out of the car and walked toward the house, trying to psyche himself up for the long evening ahead with his father. He didn't feel up to that ordeal—or to cooking. Wearily, he pushed the door open, took one step inside, then stopped in surprise. Appetizing aromas were wafting his way, and he frowned in puzzlement. Warily he made his way to the kitchen door, where a quick survey revealed the table neatly set for two and his father at the stove.

"Dad?"

Howard turned in surprise. "Oh. Didn't hear you come in. Dinner will be ready in fifteen minutes. You have time for a shower if you want one."

His father turned back to the stove and Jake stared at him, speechless. "Dad...are you making dinner?"

"Looks that way, doesn't it?" he replied gruffly.

"But...why?"

The older man shrugged. "You worked all day over at Maggie's. That was a nice thing to do, with her sick and all. Figured you'd probably be hungry when you got home. I didn't have anything else to do anyway."

Jake struggled to grasp this unexpected turn of events. His father actually sounded...well, if not friendly, cordial at least.

"Dad...I bought some sparkling cider when you first arrived," he said on impulse. "I thought we could have it with our first dinner here in the cottage. But...well, things didn't quite work out. If you'd like to have it tonight, it's in the cabinet next to the dishwasher."

His father's only response was a grunt, which Jake couldn't interpret. But when he reappeared ten minutes later after a quick shower, dinner was on the table. And so was the cider.

"Maggie, my dear. How are you feeling today?"

Maggie glanced toward the familiar voice of Millicent Trent and smiled at the older woman seated in a wicker settee on the front porch.

"Hello, Millicent! Welcome back to Whispering Sails. I'm much better today, thank you. And I'm sorry I wasn't on hand to greet you when you arrived."

"Don't give it a thought. The young man who showed me to my room last night was very nice. And he seemed quite concerned about you."

Maggie flushed. "It was just a flu bug, I think."

"Well, I must say you still look a bit peaked," Millicent observed, peering over her glasses.

"I'm a little tired, but I feel fine," Maggie assured the older woman. "I'm sure I'll be completely back to normal by tomorrow. The girls won't let me lift a finger today, so I'm getting lots of rest."

"Well, then, can you spare a few minutes to visit with an old lady?"

Maggie smiled. "I don't know about an old lady, but I certainly have time to visit with you."

Millicent chuckled. "You do have a way with words, my dear. Oh, Allison, would you mind bringing your aunt and me some tea?" she called when the younger girl stepped outside.

"Not at all, Ms. Trent. I'll be back in a jiffy."

"Now then, we can have a nice visit. Let's start with that young man. Who is he, my dear? I've never seen him around here before, and you know I've been a regular since the first year you opened."

Maggie took a moment to settle into an adjacent wicker chair, trying to decide how to answer the older woman's question. Millicent had become almost part of the family through the years, her annual two-week visits as predictable as the tides. She'd retired ten years before, apparently from a very prestigious position in publishing, and she had no family to speak of, as far as Maggie knew. But although she and Millicent had shared many a cup of tea and discussed everything from philosophy to the latest books and plays, they never talked about more personal matters. But for some reason, Maggie felt comfortable confiding in her about Jake.

"Jake is...an old friend," Maggie replied carefully. "He's

recently moved to this area, and our paths just happened to cross.''

Millicent eyed her shrewdly. ''A friend, eh? His interest seemed somehow more than friendly to me.''

Maggie blushed. Millicent might be old in body, but her mind was still as sharp and perceptive as someone half her age.

''To be honest, Millicent, I'm not sure what his interest is,'' Maggie admitted. ''The fact is, we were…well, we were engaged once, many years ago.''

''My dear, I had no idea!'' Millicent exclaimed, laying her hand on the younger woman's arm. ''I always suspected there was an unhappy romance in your past, but I never wanted to pry.''

''It wasn't an unhappy romance,'' Maggie corrected her. She leaned back against the cushions and gazed thoughtfully into the distance as Allison deposited their tea, her lips curving into a sweet smile as she retreated to memory, oblivious to the view of the bay spread out before her. ''It was a wonderful romance. Jake was my first love. In fact, he was my only love. But a few weeks before we were to be married, he… Something happened, and we… The wedding was called off. Jake joined the navy and I left the Midwest and moved to Boston, then eventually here. I hadn't seen him in twelve years when he literally appeared out of the fog at the inn a few weeks ago.''

''My!'' Millicent breathed softly, clearly mesmerized by the story. ''What an odd coincidence.''

Maggie nodded. ''I still have a hard time believing it myself.''

''And he lives here now?''

''Yes. In Castine. He'll be teaching at the Maritime Academy in the fall.'' Maggie briefly explained the events that had precipitated his move.

''My!'' Millicent repeated. ''That's quite a story, my dear. I take it your Jake has never married?''

''No.''

"Hmm. And what do you intend to do about the situation?"

"Do?" Maggie repeated with a frown.

"Yes. Do. I would say the man is quite taken with you still, my dear. I can see it in his eyes when he talks about you."

Maggie flushed. "You sound like the twins," she declared.

"Well, the young and the old often have a clearer vision of life than you people caught in the middle," Millicent observed. "But I suppose the most important thing is how you feel about this young man."

Maggie sighed. "I really don't know, Millicent. I loved him once. With all my heart. But...well, I got hurt. He...he wasn't there when I needed him the most. I'm afraid to...well, take that risk again."

Millicent nodded sagely. "I can understand that, my dear. Perhaps the best thing to do is give yourself some time to become acquainted again. People can change, you know. And twenty years from now you don't want to look back with regrets."

Maggie studied her curiously. The bittersweet quality in the older woman's voice tugged at Maggie's heart. "Millicent...I don't want to pry, either, but...well, it sounds like maybe you had a similar experience."

The older woman took a sip of tea and nodded slowly. "Yes, Maggie, I did. Many years ago. Long before you were born, in fact. It's one of the reasons I come back here each year, in fact. You see, this is where I fell in love."

"You lived in this area?"

The older woman smiled. "Actually...I lived in this house."

Maggie stared at her. "Here?" At the woman's nod of confirmation, Maggie frowned. "But...but I researched the history, and I never saw the name Trent."

"That's because I took my mother's name when I moved to New York. I thought it had more of a literary ring to it."

"You mean you actually lived at Whispering Sails?" Maggie repeated incredulously.

"Yes. It wasn't Whispering Sails then, of course. It was just home. My father owned a very successful shipping company, and Robert—that was my beau's name—was a merchant seaman who sometimes worked on my father's ships."

She paused, a smile of sweet remembrance lifted the corners of her mouth.

"We met the summer I was twenty-two. He was a handsome man, with sun-streaked brown hair, tall and strong, with the bluest eyes you could ever imagine. Bluer than the sea on a cloudless day. We fell in love, madly, passionately, with the intensity reserved for the very young. But my father would have none of it. His daughter deserved better than a seaman, he informed me. And what of the career I'd planned? He'd sent me to college, much against his better judgment, and now that I had the degree I'd so desperately wanted, he expected me to do something with it.

"Robert and I had a wonderful summer together, and when it was drawing to a close he asked me to marry him. I thought about it a long time, Maggie. I loved him as I had loved no one before or anyone since. But he was poor, and content with his lot, and I was wealthy and ambitious. I wanted to make something of my life outside of Blue Hill, and I had just been offered a prestigious position with a publishing company in New York. Plus, much as I hate to admit it, my father had finally convinced me that I was too good for a mere seaman. So in the end, I turned him down."

She gazed out over the water, and her voice grew quiet. "I regretted my decision within a year. New York wasn't nearly as glamorous as I'd expected, and living among so many different kinds of people made me realize how arrogant my attitude had been. I wasn't any better than anyone else. Not as good as most, in fact. And I missed Robert desperately. To love with such intensity…what a gift that is. And what a sin to waste it."

Her voice faded, and Maggie leaned toward her. "But why didn't you tell him you'd changed your mind?" she pressed.

Millicent turned to her with a smile of regret. "At first I was too ashamed—and too proud, I suppose—to admit my mistake. But eventually, after two years, I realized what a fool I'd been. And so I wrote to him, and asked him to meet me on his next trip to New York. I didn't tell him why, because I wanted to apologize in person, to beg him to give me one more chance.''

"And did he come?''

She shook her head. "No. You see, by then he was engaged to another woman. He was an honorable man, my Robert, and I knew he wouldn't break his engagement. Nor would I ask him to. So I simply wished him well.''

"And you never saw him again?''

"No,'' she replied sadly. "But we corresponded after that, each Christmas, until he died five years ago.''

"So you...you never married, Millicent?''

She shook her head. "No. Not that I didn't consider it. But no one ever again touched my heart the way Robert did. And I wasn't willing to settle for less.''

Maggie knew exactly what she meant. It was the same legacy Jake had left with her.

"I'm so sorry, Millicent,'' she murmured, deeply touched by the sad story.

The older woman nodded. "So am I. Especially after I received this.'' She withdrew a slender chain from beneath her blouse and fingered two jagged pieces of silver which, when fitted together, formed one heart. "Robert gave me half of this in the middle of our special summer,'' she related softly. "He said that part of his heart now belonged to me and asked me to keep this always, and that he would do the same with his. I've worn my half faithfully, all my life.

She paused and gently fingered the two pieces of silver. "When he died I received a package with the other half from his daughter, along with a letter saying that her father had always carried it in his wallet and had left instructions for it to be sent to me when he died.''

Maggie's eyes filled with tears as Millicent brought her story to a close. Her heart ached for the older woman and the sailor named Robert, whose abiding love had never been fulfilled.

Millicent leaned toward her then, her gaze earnest and intent. "My dear, love is a precious and beautiful gift, but it's easily lost. Pride, ambition, fear—so many things can get in the way. I don't know what made you and Jake break up years ago. I don't know how deeply he hurt you. But a lot can happen in twelve years. People change. Circumstances change. But true love endures. And if that's what you have, don't let it slip away. Because not very many people get a second chance at love."

Chapter Eight

A second chance at love.

Those words had been playing over and over in Maggie's mind ever since Millicent Trent planted the thought. And especially so today. Birthdays always made her wonder what the next twelve months would hold. But even in her wildest imagination she'd never considered on her last birthday that before the next one Jake would be back in her life.

Maggie took a quick glance in the rearview mirror and shook her head. She didn't feel thirty-seven. Not physically, anyway. Emotionally…well, that was a different story. She'd lived through a lot, especially in the last dozen years. But she honestly didn't think she looked her age.

Obviously, though, the twins did, she mused with a rueful smile. Why else would they have given her a day of "rejuvenation" at the new one-day spa that had opened in Bangor? Frankly, she'd been taken aback by the gift—not to mention appalled at the cost. Maggie wasn't accustomed to such self-indulgence, had opened her mouth to point out that the money could have been better spent on more practical items for the upcoming school year. But the girls had been so excited about their gift, had received so much pleasure from the giving, that she couldn't dampen their spirits. So she'd bitten her tongue and accepted it with a smile.

Then they'd topped off the first indulgence with a second— they were going to cook her a special birthday dinner tonight. Since neither of the girls was particularly interested in cooking, the chore usually fell to Maggie. And she was pretty good at it, if she did say so herself. Jake had always liked her cooking, she recalled with a smile.

Jake. He'd been more and more in her thoughts these last few days. Did he remember that today was her birthday? she wondered wistfully. Probably not. In general, men weren't very good about those kinds of things. But he'd changed a lot in the last dozen years. She thought of Millicent's words. Was Maggie being offered a second chance at love? And if so, was it a chance she was willing to take?

She didn't have the answer to those questions. And she didn't even want to think about them for the next few hours. The twins had told her to relax and enjoy the spa experience, and she couldn't very well do that if she thought about Jake. So with a discipline that surprised her, she forced all disruptive thoughts from her mind and focused on the moment. She wanted to get her money's worth—make that the twins' money, she corrected herself—out of this extravagant gift.

And as it turned out, she did. She was coddled and massaged and manicured, then treated to a facial, makeup session and haircut and style. It was pure indulgence, pampering like she had never before experienced, but much to her surprise she enjoyed it. Thoroughly. She emerged feeling invigorated, renewed, pretty and—strangely enough—younger than when she went in. It was wonderful!

By the time she climbed into her car for the drive back to the inn, Maggie was completely relaxed and looking forward to the special dinner the twins were preparing. She loved them dearly for the effort, no matter the result.

They were obviously watching for her, because when she stepped inside they were waiting, their faces shining, eyes expectant.

"Wow!" they breathed in unison, their voices reflecting their awe at the glamorous transformation in their aunt.

Maggie grinned. "Not bad for a thirty-seven-year-old innkeeper, huh?" she teased.

"Aunt Maggie, you look great!" Abby enthused. "That

makeup really brings out your coloring. And I love your hair!''

"Yeah," Alison agreed. "It's a great cut. It looks re-ally...sophisticated."

Maggie smiled. The haircut *was* good, she had to admit as she glanced at her reflection in the oven door. Nothing dramatically different than before, but expertly shaped and tamed to bring out her gentle, natural waves. She rarely left it down around the inn, but now, as it softly brushed her shoulders and flatteringly framed her face, she had to admit that wearing it loose and full made her feel younger. And very chic.

"Thanks. And thank you both for today. I hate to admit this, since it was such a wild extravagance, but I loved every minute of it!''

The girls beamed.

"We hoped you would. Now go up and dress for dinner. We laid out your clothes. And take your time," Abby instructed. "We aren't going to eat for an hour."

"Well, I won't argue," Maggie replied, trying to ignore the chaotic mess. "I may not be going to a ball, but I must admit I feel a little like Cinderella at the moment. So I'll enjoy it while it lasts."

As Maggie closed the kitchen door she heard the girls begin to whisper, and she smiled indulgently. They were terrific young women, she thought, allowing herself a moment of pride. Despite her novice-level child-rearing skills, despite her many mistakes, despite the absence of a father figure in their home, the girls had turned out just fine. It hadn't been easy to raise them alone, she reflected, but she'd done okay.

Then again, she'd never been totally alone, she reminded herself, as she stepped into her room and her gaze fell on the Bible beside her bed. She'd turned to the Lord many times through the years, asking for His guidance and support. And He'd always answered her. Not necessarily in the way she expected, but always with a wisdom that it sometimes took her years to appreciate.

She picked up the volume and opened it to the well-worn pages in Matthew that had given her comfort and calmed her troubled soul on so many occasions. "Ask, and it shall be given you; seek, and you shall find; knock, and it shall be opened to you. For everyone who asks, receives; and he who seeks, finds; and to him who knocks, it shall be opened." She flipped forward a few pages. "Come to me, all you who labor and are burdened, and I will give you rest. Take my yoke upon you, and learn from me, for I am meek and humble of heart, and you will find rest for your souls. For my yoke is easy, and my burden light."

Maggie couldn't remember the number of times through the years when she had read those pages before going to bed, asking the Lord to help her make the right decisions, to ease her burden. And always she had felt His loving presence beside her. She paused now to thank Him in the silence of her heart for His steadfast presence throughout her life, but especially during these last twelve, often tumultuous years.

When Maggie gently closed the book, she felt even more renewed. She replaced it on the nightstand, then turned her attention to the clothes the girls had laid out. Her eyebrows rose in surprise when she realized that they had chosen her fanciest dress—a black chiffon, with rhinestone-studded spaghetti straps and a straight-cut bodice softened with a cowl-like draping of fabric. The full skirt swirled softly beneath a wide belt that was also studded with rhinestones. It was a lovely outfit—but good heavens, what were the girls thinking? she wondered in amusement. This was a cocktail dress, better suited to an elegant black-tie affair than an at-home dinner, no matter how "fancy" they were trying to make it. In fact, she'd only worn the dress once before, to an opening at an art gallery Philip had invited her to a couple of years before. She smiled and shook her head. Obviously the girls were trying to make this as nice an evening as possible. She couldn't find it in her heart to disappoint them.

She reached for the dress, and discovered a small, gift-wrapped package from the girls. It was a bottle of her favorite perfume, one she rarely bought because of the high cost. The twins had really outdone themselves this year, she thought with a soft smile.

When she was dressed, Maggie paused to glance in the mirror behind her door. She felt a little silly, all dressed up and nowhere to go. But she had to admit that her rejuvenating day at the spa, her new makeup and expertly styled hair—along with the dress, which emphasized her trim figure—made her feel terrific.

Suddenly she wondered what Jake would think if he saw her now. Would he be awed by her "glamour"? Would that flame of desire she so clearly remembered from years ago spark to life in his eyes? Would he be tempted to pull her into his arms and kiss her fiercely, with the simmering, barely restrained passion she recalled so well?

Although Maggie impatiently dismissed those questions, the answers were nevertheless waiting for her a few moments later when she walked into the dining room and came face-to-face with the man himself. They were obvious from the look in his eyes—yes, yes and highly likely.

Jake rose slowly from the table set for two in the center of the dining room, his gaze smoldering, hers confused. What on earth…?

A movement to her left caught her eye, and she turned to find the twins watching the proceedings with undisguised glee.

"Surprise!" they chorused.

I'm going to ground them until they're thirty, Maggie thought fiercely, hot color suffusing her face as she realized what they'd done. Now everything made sense. The spa. The clothes. The perfume. The two conspirators had decided to fill their aunt's social vacuum by planning a romantic evening for her—down to the fresh flowers and candles on the table and the bottle of sparkling cider chilling in the silver cooler, she noted with a dismayed glance. What must Jake think? she wondered, her mortified gaze meeting his. But he didn't look upset. Not in the least. In fact, he seemed amused. He was wearing that lopsided smile he used to give her when they were sharing a private joke. Thank goodness he was being a good sport about the whole thing! she thought gratefully. But she was so embarrassed, she wished the floor would just open up and swallow her.

"There's cheese and crackers on the table to start," Abby announced. "Take your time. We'll bring in the salad in a little while."

And then the twins disappeared.

Maggie stared helplessly at the tall, distinguished man in the dark gray suit who stood across from her.

"Jake...I'm so sorry," she choked out apologetically, her blush deepening. "I had no idea.... This isn't at all what..." Her voice trailed off and she shook her head. "Wait till I get my hands on them," she added vehemently.

He chuckled, a deep, pleasing rumble that somehow helped soothe her tattered nerves. "Oh, don't be too hard on them. Their hearts were in the right place."

"Maybe. But I've explained to them over and over that we're...well, that our relationship was in the past...they knew better than to pull a stunt like...I just can't believe they did this," she finished in exasperation, realizing how inarticulate her disjointed jumble of words sounded. But she was so upset, she couldn't think straight, let alone form a coherent sentence.

Jake, on the other hand, seemed the epitome of calm as he strolled toward her. But his casual stance was at odds with the flames flickering around the edges of his eyes, and her breath caught in her throat. "Let's humor them," he said quietly. "They've gone to a lot of trouble, Maggie. And it is your birthday. What will one dinner together hurt?"

Maggie was afraid it might hurt a great deal. But she couldn't very well say that. And Jake was right. The girls meant well, even if their intentions were misguided.

"I suppose you're right," she capitulated with a sigh.

He smiled, then tucked one of her hands through his arm as they strolled back to the table. He pulled out her chair with a flourish and wink before sitting down next to her. The girls had set the two places at right angles instead of across from each other, Maggie noted. Another transparent attempt to make this an intimate dinner.

Jake poured their drinks, then raised his glass in a toast.

"To Maggie—the most beautiful thirty-seven-year-old I've ever known—and the most memorable woman I've ever met," he murmured huskily.

Maggie watched as he took a sip, his gaze never leaving hers, and suddenly she found it difficult to breathe.

"You really are beautiful, you know," he said softly. "Especially tonight. I like your hair down, Maggie. It's too lovely to pull back all the time."

She swallowed with difficulty. "Th-thanks." Despite her best efforts, she couldn't stop her voice from betraying her turbulent emotions. She glanced down and played with the edge of her fork. It had been a long time since anyone had treated her as a desirable woman. It had been an even longer time since she *felt* like one. But with Jake...it was different. He made her feel special...and alluring...and not at all like Maggie the aunt, or Maggie the innkeeper. With him she felt like Maggie the woman.

Suddenly his hand covered hers, stilling her restless fingers. "Maggie?"

She took a deep breath and looked up.

"Do I make you nervous?"

Of course he made her nervous. But she couldn't say that without saying *why,* so she forced herself to smile. "I'm just embarrassed by this whole thing, Jake. It's very...awkward. You must feel very uncomfortable."

"Frankly I don't."

She looked at him in sudden suspicion. "Did you know about this?"

"No. The girls just invited me to a birthday dinner. I had no idea it was only going to be the two of us. But to be honest, I'm not sorry. I've been wanting to..."

Suddenly soft music began to play, and Jake paused as Maggie uttered a soft groan. "Oh, no! Now we have music, too."

He listened for a moment, then another chuckle rumbled out of his chest. "Mmm-hmm. Can you place this singer?"

Maggie focused on the music, and then she, too, had to

smile. The vocalist was one who had been popular in her parents' courting days.

"Just how old do they think we are?" Jake asked in a low tone, his eyes glinting with mirth.

"Ancient," she replied dryly, struggling to contain her own smile.

"Oh, well." He stood up and held out his hand. "I have a feeling the twins conveniently cleared the floor so we could…do the minuet maybe? That's a little beyond my capabilities, but I have mastered a pretty mean fox-trot. So… may I have this dance?"

"Jake, you'll only add fuel to the fire," she admonished him. "The girls' imaginations are active enough without any encouragement."

"Oh, come on, Maggie. One dance. It's a nice song—even if it *is* old."

When he had the beguiling look in his eyes, she found him difficult to refuse. And he *was* being a good sport about the whole thing. After being brought here under false pretenses, he had a right to be angry. Instead, he was playing along, taking the whole thing in stride. In fact, he seemed to be enjoying it. She supposed she might as well try to, as well. It was her birthday, after all. But dancing with Jake, being held in his arms—the mere thought of it made her feel shaky inside.

"One dance, Maggie?"

Face it, Maggie, she told herself as she stared up into his warm, brown eyes. *You want to dance with the man. Don't fight everything so much. Remember Millicent's advice. Give it a chance.*

With a sigh of defeat, she rose silently, and Jake gave her a smile of encouragement as he led her to the center of the floor. Then he took her into his arms, and for just a moment, Maggie thought every bone in her body was going to dissolve simultaneously.

She closed her eyes to better savor the sensations washing over her. His hand was firm but gentle in the small of her back, feeling familiar to her yet new. He entwined the fingers of his other hand with hers and pressed her trembling hand against his solid, muscled chest. The scent of him—masculine, unique, utterly appealing—surrounded her and set a swarm of butterflies loose in her stomach. She could easily stay like this forever, she decided, as a wave of pure contentment washed over her. With a small, almost inaudible sigh, she let her cheek rest against his shoulder and slowly relaxed in his arms, putting aside for just a moment all of the doubts and questions that plagued her about this man. For once, for the space of this brief dance, she would simply enjoy being held in his sure, strong arms.

Jake felt the stiffness in her body ease as she nestled against his shoulder. He dropped his chin and brushed his cheek against her hair, inhaling the subtle, sweet fragrance that clung to it. She felt so good in his arms. She always had. Soft and appealing and somehow fragile, in a way that brought out his protective instinct and made him want to keep her safe and sheltered. In fact, he would like nothing better than to spend the rest of his life doing exactly that.

For the first time all evening, he relaxed, too. Until this very moment he'd been afraid that she would bolt. It was obvious that she was uncomfortable with the contrived situation. And he was sure the twins would hear about it later. But personally, he had no complaints. In fact, he'd been trying for weeks to figure out a way to get Maggie alone so that he could try to begin rebuilding a relationship with her. So far he'd failed miserably.

He couldn't fault her caution. And at least she was pleasant to him, which was more than he would probably be in her place, he admitted. It was a start. But only a start. Before he could hope to make any progress, he had to find a way to break through the barrier she'd erected between them so that he could begin to rebuild her trust level, make her realize that he was a different man than the one who had walked out on her twelve years ago. And tonight was a good time to start, thanks to the twins.

When the music ended they drew apart reluctantly, and Jake smiled tenderly down into her dreamy eyes.

"See? That wasn't so bad, was it?" His tone was teasing, but unmistakably husky.

She shook her head, not trusting her own voice.

The twins appeared with their salads then, and slowly, as they worked their way through the meal that had been prepared with love, if not finesse, Maggie began to truly relax. Jake told her amusing stories about his travels, and she found herself admiring his wit and self-deprecating humor. He also gave her an update on his relationship with his father—still strained, though improving—and the progress he was making on his lesson plans for the coming school year.

But he also drew her out, skillfully and with sincere interest. Maggie didn't know if it was the romantic atmosphere that loosened her tongue, or just Jake's adept probing, but she opened up more than she expected. She even admitted her secret aspiration to give serious art a try, now that the girls were grown and ready to leave for college.

"I think you should, Maggie. I've seen some of your work, and I'm very impressed. I'm no expert, but didn't you say that your friend—the gallery owner—had encouraged you, too?"

She nodded. "But Philip and I...well, we go back a long way. He has a wonderful eye for art, but I'm afraid he may not be that impartial when it comes to my work."

This was the opening Jake had been waiting for ever since the day in her studio when she'd made a similar remark, and he wasn't about to let it pass. Even though he wasn't sure he wanted to hear the answer, he had to know. "You've mentioned him before," he remarked with studied casualness. "I suppose you might have a point about the impartiality issue if you and he are...well, close."

Maggie tipped her head and studied him.

"If you want to know whether Philip and I are romantically involved, why don't you just ask, Jake?" she said bluntly.

He felt his neck grow red. "I guess I didn't want you to think I was prying, and take offense."

She shrugged. "Actually, we explored a romantic relationship once. Shortly after I moved here. But there just wasn't any...*passion* might be the best word, I suppose. Philip's wife died ten years ago, and even though he's lonely, no one ever came along who compared to her, I guess. As for me, well, it was kind of the same story. Plus, I had a ready-made family in tow.'' Before he could ask a follow-up question about her "same story" comment, she quickly asked one of her own. "And what about you, Jake? Why didn't you ever marry?"

He looked at her steadily. "For the same reason you didn't, I suspect."

They gazed at each other for a moment in silence, and then she glanced down, suddenly uncertain. Did he mean what she thought he meant? Had he cared about her all these years, as she had cared about him, held back unconsciously by a love that had never died?

He reached for her hand then, and she was forced to meet his gaze. "However, lately I've been thinking more and more about settling down, getting married, raising a family—the whole nine yards."

His implication was clear. But even clearer was his comment about wanting a family, Maggie thought with a frown, that single reference suddenly casting a pall over her evening. She vaguely recalled that he'd mentioned a family once before, but it hadn't really registered at the time. Now it hit home.

He saw the sudden furrow on her brow, and a mirror image appeared on his own. Had he revealed too much too soon? "Maggie? Is something wrong?"

She forced herself to smile. "No. It's probably a good time for you to...to get married and start a family, if that's what you want. Raising kids is an experience everyone should have."

One time. She hadn't said that, but the implication was clear, Jake realized. She was telling him that she'd done the family scene, that if a family was in his future, it wouldn't be a future that was linked with hers. He could understand how she felt. Raising twins, especially when one had had a medical problem, would have been difficult enough for two people, let alone one. But it was different when the responsibility was shared.

Before he could suggest that, however, the twins appeared at the door carrying a birthday cake topped with glowing candles. As they launched into a spirited rendition of "Happy Birthday," Jake gave her a look that said, "We'll continue this later" before joining in the refrain.

The twins set the cake before Maggie with a triumphant flourish.

"Make a wish, Aunt Maggie," Allison instructed.

"But don't tell," Abby added. "Or it won't come true."

It was the same instruction she'd always given them, and she smiled. Her gaze met Jake's over the golden light of the candles, but she couldn't read the enigmatic expression in his eyes. Was he wondering whether her wish would have anything to do with him? she reflected. But that would remain her secret.

She took a deep breath and blew out the candles on the first try, to the applause of her small audience. Then Jake reached down next to the table and retrieved two small packages, which he held out to her.

"Happy birthday, Maggie."

"Oh, Jake, you didn't have to do this!" she protested.

"Of course I did. What's a birthday party without presents? Actually, the small one is from me and the larger one is from Dad, who sends his best wishes."

Maggie took them as the girls quickly and efficiently cut and served the cake. Then, despite her entreaties to stay and join the celebration, they whisked the cake away and returned to the kitchen to enjoy their dessert, leaving the guest of honor once more alone with her dinner companion. Maggie shook her head resignedly.

"Their single-minded determination is amazing. Especially when I think about all the years I struggled to get them to concentrate on their homework," Maggie noted wryly.

Jake chuckled. "I have to admit, I'm impressed by their thoroughness." He took a sip of coffee and nodded toward the packages on the table. "Aren't you going to open your presents?"

She chose Howard's first, exclaiming over the intricate pair of wooden candlesticks that were nestled in tissue. "Oh, Jake, these are lovely! Did Pop make them? I thought he didn't do woodworking anymore?"

"He doesn't. He's had these for years. He made them right before Mom died."

Maggie's face grew thoughtful. "I saw all his woodworking equipment in the garage the day I tried to fix your plumbing," she reflected. "You know, it would probably be really good for him to get back into this. It's not too taxing physically, and it would give him something productive to do."

"I agree. But he hasn't show any interest in picking it up again."

"There's a fair coming up at church," Maggie mused aloud. "We have it every fall. A lot of area crafters exhibit and sell their work. And the church sponsors a booth where we sell donated items. Maybe Pop would make a few things for us, since it's for charity. It might be a way to get him back into it."

"It's certainly worth a try," Jake concurred. "But I doubt he'll be receptive to the idea if it comes from me."

"Then I'll talk to him tomorrow," Maggie decided, carefully laying aside the candlesticks as she turned her attention to Jake's present. When she tore the wrapping off she was delighted to discover a leather-bound travel diary, with a note scrawled on the first page.

To Maggie,
May all your travels be exciting—and may they all lead you home.
Jake.

She looked over at him, touched by the thoughtful gift—and the thought-provoking inscription. "Thank you, Jake."

"You're welcome. I hope your upcoming trip is the first of many."

They focused on the cake, then, and just as they finished the twins made another appearance.

"Why don't you two go sit on the porch while we clean up," Abby suggested.

Jake grinned. "Sounds good to me." He stood up and reached for Maggie's hand. She glanced over at the twins who were, as she expected, positively beaming. She intended to have a long talk with those young women later, but for the moment she'd let them hold on to their misguided romantic fantasy. So, with a "Why fight it?" look, she placed her hand in Jake's and stood up, strolling with him in silence to the front door.

Once outside, she carefully withdrew her hand from his. The evening was drawing to a close, and though she'd enjoyed spending the time with Jake, she didn't want to get used to it.

"Those two," she declared in exasperation, stepping away from him to stand at the porch railing and look out over the moon-silvered bay. "What would they have done if my birthday hadn't been on a Sunday? Any other day the inn would have been full of guests."

Jake noted the physical separation she'd established. And he knew why. Her defenses had started to crumble just a bit tonight, and she was scared. But he wasn't about to let that wall come back up, not yet, anyway. He moved behind her and brought one hand up to rest lightly on her shoulder.

"Somehow I think they would have found a way."

Maggie heard the amusement in his voice, felt his breath close to her ear. So much for her plan to put some space between them. He was so close that she was afraid he would be able to tell that she was trembling. "You're probably right," she admitted, grateful that at least her voice wasn't shaking.

"Well, shall we sit? Or would you rather walk a little?"

Maggie glanced at the wicker porch swing, a perfect invitation to romance—obviously what the twins had in mind—and quickly made her choice. "Let's walk."

"I think the girls will be disappointed," Jake countered with a grin.

"Too bad. They've had their way all evening."

Maggie moved purposefully toward the porch steps, certain that walking was a far safer alternative than sitting next to Jake on the porch swing. But when he reached for her hand, laced his fingers through hers and led her into the moonlit night, she suddenly wasn't so sure.

Chapter Nine

"Are you chilly?"

Maggie glanced up at Jake. Obviously he'd felt her shiver, but she could hardly tell him it was caused more by the warm, tingly feeling his presence evoked than by the cool night air. She swallowed and shook her head.

"No. I'm fine."

Which wasn't true, either. Not when he was stroking her clasped hand with his thumb and smiling at her with that tender look in his brown eyes.

"Well, you're welcome to my jacket if you need it."

That was the *last* thing she needed at the moment, Maggie decided. Having him place his jacket around her shoulders would not do a thing to calm her rapidly accelerating pulse rate.

"Thanks."

Jake seemed content to stroll in silence after that, and Maggie gladly followed his lead. She didn't trust her voice anyway.

After a few minutes, Jake paused and nodded toward the water. "Looks like a good spot for a view of the bay. Can your shoes handle the path?"

Maggie glanced down at her slender-heeled pumps, then at the gravel path he'd indicated. Her shoes would handle the detour with no problem, she decided. But she wasn't so sure about herself. The path led to a small dock that jutted out into the silver-flecked water—the perfect spot for a romantic tryst.

Is that what Jake had in mind? she wondered nervously. Better to play this safe and take the out he'd offered her, she concluded. But when she opened her mouth to decline, different words emerged instead.

"They should be okay."

He smiled then, a smile so warm and tender, it made her toes tingle and her stomach flutter—and convinced her that she'd just made a big mistake.

But he didn't give her time for second thoughts. He took her arm and silently guided her down the narrow path to the water's edge, then onto the rough wooden planks of the dock. They walked to the railing, and as she gazed over the moonlit sea, she realized that the gentle cadence of the waves lapping against the shore was much steadier than her pulse. That was even *more* true when Jake draped an arm casually around her shoulders, making her heart jump to her throat. What had she gotten herself into? she thought in sudden panic. She was attracted to Jake, yes. But she wasn't ready for this. Not yet. And maybe never. She still had too many tangled issues and emotions to work through.

Jake felt Maggie trembling, knew she was scared, knew she was still grappling with her feelings for him and fighting their mutual attraction every step of the way. He couldn't blame her. She was afraid of being hurt again, afraid to let herself believe that maybe this time things would be different. But they had to get past that eventually if anything was ever to develop between them. Which was exactly what he had in mind.

Once upon a time, he had never even considered a future without Maggie. He felt the same way now. The challenge was to convince her of that.

A drop of water flicked against his cheek, and he glanced up at the sky with a frown, surprised to discover that a dark cloud had crept up behind them. But he wasn't ready to go back to the inn. He nodded toward the small, abandoned shed they'd passed at the end of the dock and took Maggie's arm.

"Come on. I'd hate to see that spectacular dress ruined."

She followed his lead unprotestingly, pausing only when

he stopped to push open the rickety door of the structure. The hinges objected with a loud squeak, but the door reluctantly gave way, and he ushered her inside.

Maggie took a quick inventory of the shed as she stepped over the threshold. When the girls were younger she'd brought them to this dock a few times to fish, not wanting to deprive them of any of the experiences they might have had with a father. She'd peeked into the old fishing shack, but never ventured inside. It looked more dilapidated than ever, she assessed, noting that the spaces between the weathered gray clapboards had widened considerably through the years. The floorboards had long since rotted away, leaving hard-packed dirt and rock in their place. But at least it was relatively even, she thought, as she walked over to a framed opening in the wall that had once been a window. Amazingly enough, the roof still seemed reasonably watertight. It would do as a shelter from the storm, she decided.

But what about the storm inside of her? she wondered, as memories of another rainy day suddenly came flooding back with an intensity that took her breath away. In a shed much like this one, her life had changed forever, she recalled. It was her sixteenth birthday—twenty-one years ago—but right now it seemed like yesterday.

Maggie glanced up at the sky and wrinkled her nose as the first raindrops splattered again the asphalt, leaving dark splotches in their wake.

"Oh, great! Now it's going to rain on my birthday!" she complained as they pedaled side by side down the country lane.

Jake laughed. "Sorry about that, squirt. But I have no control over the weather."

She made a face at him. "Very funny. And will you please stop calling me that?"

He grinned. "Why?"

"Because I'm not. At least, not anymore."

"My, my. Aren't we getting uppity now that we're sixteen," he teased.

Maggie made another face, then pointed to a small, seemingly abandoned shed off to the side of the road. "Let's go in there till the rain stops." Without waiting for him to reply, she rode off the pavement and onto the bumpy ground.

Jake followed her lead, and as they reached the ramshackle structure the rain suddenly turned into a downpour. They dropped their bikes and dashed for cover.

"Wow! Where did *that* come from?" Maggie said breathlessly. When they'd loaded their bikes into the rack on Howard West's car earlier in the day, there hadn't been a cloud in the sky. Nor had there been any when they'd started their ride an hour ago.

"I guess the clouds crept up behind us while we were riding," Jake replied easily. He glanced up at the sky. "I think it will pass quickly. Might as well make ourselves comfortable in the meantime."

Maggie glanced around skeptically. The rain beat a noisy refrain on the rusted tin roof, but at least the floor was dry, she noted, as she started to sit down.

"Watch that mouse!" Jake exclaimed, then laughed when Maggie jumped. "Just kidding."

She glared at him. "Very funny."

He looked around. "Actually, I think we're alone here. But I promise to defend you if any cheese eaters show up." He lowered his tall frame to the floor and leaned back against the wall, drawing his knees up and clasping his hands around his legs.

Maggie looked around doubtfully, then sat down gingerly in the middle of the floor where she could keep a three-hundred-and-sixty-degree lookout for small, unwanted visitors. She dusted her hands on her khaki shorts and crossed her legs, then glanced at Jake. Her eyes widened in alarm and she gasped, pointing behind him.

"Is that a poisonous spider?"

Jake jerked away from the wall and turned to look. Maggie's sudden eruption of giggles told him he'd been had.

"Gotcha!" she declared gleefully.

Jake's eyes narrowed and he gave her a disgruntled look. "How old are you again? Sixteen—or six?"

"You did it to me," she pointed out.

"Once is okay. Getting back isn't," he declared with a tone of superiority.

Maggie gazed at him speculatively. In a way she was glad it had rained, glad they'd found this isolated shelter. Because she had something she wanted to ask him. After all, Jake was more than a year older than she was. He was popular with the girls, dated a lot. In another week he'd be going off to college. Today would be her best chance to pose the question that had been burning in her mind for weeks. But she just wasn't quite sure how to go about it.

"Jake?" Her voice was suddenly tentative, uncertain. "Can I ask you something?"

"Sure." His eyes were closed now, his head dropped back against the rough planks of the wall. He looked very comfortable, and Maggie hated to bother him with this, but he was her only hope.

"Um…well, I've been wondering…I mean, I know this is kind of a weird question, but…well…how do people learn how to kiss?"

That got his attention. His eyelids flew open and he stared at her, startled.

"What?"

Her face grew pink and she dropped her gaze. "I need to find out how people learn to kiss," she repeated, acutely embarrassed.

He grinned. "Ah, the squirt must be growing up."

She blushed furiously and scooted back against the far wall, suddenly wishing some poisonous creature *would* bite her and put her quickly—and mercifully—out of her misery. "Just forget I asked, okay?" she muttered, her shoulders hunched miserably.

Jake looked over at her bowed head, instantly contrite. He and Maggie had been friends since his parents moved onto her block when he was six, and he'd enjoyed their easy give-and-take ever since. She was a good sport and lots of fun to be with. More fun than anyone he'd ever met, in fact. But she was also easily hurt. Obviously she'd had to muster all of her courage to ask him about such a personal subject, and instead of realizing how embarrassed she was, he'd given her a hard time. Jake scooted over and sat in front of her, reaching out to touch her stiff shoulder.

"Maggie, I'm sorry." His voice was gentle, all traces of teasing gone.

She refused to look at him. "It was a dumb question anyway."

Her voice was muffled, and she seemed on the verge of tears. Which only made him feel worse.

"It's not a dumb question."

"Yes, it is."

"No, it's not. And I'm sorry I made a joke of it. I guess I just never thought about you growing up and thinking about those kinds of things."

She sniffed and risked a glance at him, her eyes frustrated. "Well, I am, Jake. And I do. Most of my friends date now. They talk about...stuff...and I feel so ignorant. I don't even know how to kiss, and they...they're way past that stage. I even turned down a date with Joe Carroll last week because I'm afraid he'll think I'm...well, that I don't know what I'm doing. And I don't!" she wailed.

Jake frowned darkly. "Joe Carroll asked you out?"

She nodded. "Why are you so surprised? Don't you think I'm the kind of girl guys would want to ask out?"

Actually, he'd never thought about it one way or the other. But the idea of Maggie going out with Joe Carroll, who acted like he was the next Casanova, made his blood run cold. Maggie was too sweet and innocent to go out with a guy like that.

"I'm not pretty enough. Is that what you think?" Maggie's miserable voice interrupted his thoughts when he didn't respond.

Jake stared at her. He'd never thought about that, either, to be honest. Maggie was...well, Maggie. She was cute. She had pretty hair. He liked her turned-up nose. He'd just never thought about her in those kinds of terms. But clearly she needed some reassurance, and the least he could do was build up her confidence—and give her some warnings.

"Of course you're pretty," he declared gallantly. "Too pretty, maybe. You need to be careful around guys like Joe. He expects a whole lot more out of a date than a kiss, from what I hear."

"Really?" She stared at him wide-eyed.

"Uh-huh."

She sighed. "Oh, well, it doesn't matter anyway. I don't even know how to do *that,* let alone anything else."

"You just need to practice," Jake told her. "That's how I learned."

"Yeah?"

"Mmm-hmm."

"But…who would I practice with?"

He looked at her for a moment as an idea suddenly took shape in his mind. "Well, I suppose you could practice with me," he offered slowly. "*I* could teach you."

She stared at him again. "You?"

"Yeah. What's wrong with me?" he asked, offended.

"Well…I don't know. It just seems kind of…weird, you know? I mean, it's not exactly…romantic…or anything."

"So? That's probably good. This way there's no pressure."

She considered the idea for a moment, her head tipped to one side. "Yeah, you're right," she conceded. In fact, the idea made a lot of sense, the more she thought about it. She scooted closer and looked up at him expectantly. "Okay. What do I do?"

Jake shifted uncomfortably. He was in this too far now to back out, but it *was* weird, as she said. Besides, *she* might think he was an expert at this. But at the moment his limited experience seemed hardly adequate to qualify him as an instructor. However, his seventeen-year-old ego wasn't about to let him admit that. He'd just have to try and pull this off.

"You don't really have to *do* anything. The guy usually takes the lead." Like Joe Carroll, Jake thought grimly. He took more than the lead if he had half a chance, to hear him boast. Maggie needed to be prepared for guys like that, had to learn not to be swept away by their nice words and what, to her, would be sophisticated technique. The more she knew before she got into a situation like that, the better.

"So when he *does* take the lead, is that when the kissing starts?"

"Yeah. Usually."

"Okay." She looked up at him, but when he remained unmoving she frowned. "So...are you going to show me?"

Jake took a deep breath. Maggie now seemed at ease. He was the one who suddenly felt uncomfortable. He *had* made a promise, though. "Yeah, I am." He took a deep breath and leaned forward, and she followed his lead. But instead of their lips connecting, their noses collided. Maggie threw back her head and erupted into a fit of giggles.

"This isn't how it happens in the movies," she declared, her shoulders shaking with laughter.

Jake gave her a stern look. "This isn't going to work if you keep giggling," he admonished her.

Maggie stifled the giggles—with difficulty. "Sorry. Can we try that again?"

This time their lips briefly connected, but when Jake backed off and checked out her reaction, *disappointed* was the only word that came to mind. He frowned at her in irritation.

"Now what's wrong?"

"Is that it?" she asked, crestfallen.

Jake's seventeen-year-old pride took a nosedive. This lesson was getting a lot more complicated than he'd anticipated.

"Maggie, are you really sure you want me to teach you all this?"

Her face fell. "I don't have anyone else to ask, Jake," she replied quietly. Then she dropped her gaze and played with the edge of her shorts. "But if you don't want to, that's okay. I understand."

The plaintive note in her voice tugged at his heart, and he reached down and tilted her chin up with a gentle finger. "I said I'd teach you, and I will," he told her softly. Then, calling on every bit of his limited experience, he set out to do just that.

He reached over and touched her hair, surprised at its softness as it drifted through his fingers. Then he cupped her face with this hands and combed back through her flame-colored tresses, loosening her barrettes in the process until her hair tumbled freely around her shoulders. He stroked her face, the skin soft and silky beneath his fingers. But she was too far away, he decided. He reached down to her waist and pulled her toward him, until her knees touched his as they sat cross-legged facing each other, their faces only inches apart.

At this range, Jake noticed the flecks of gold in her deep green eyes. Funny, he'd never even paid any attention to their color before. But they were beautiful eyes, he realized, expressive and—at the moment—a bit dazed. So maybe his technique wasn't so bad after all, he thought, pleased. His confidence bolstered, he reached over and traced the outline of her lips with his fingertip, a whisper-soft touch that made her gasp. Her lips parted ever so slightly—and oh-so-invitingly. She'd be putty in Joe Carroll's hands, he thought, suddenly glad they'd pursued this today. At least now she'd have some idea what to expect, be a little more prepared if some guy tried to take advantage of her innocence and inexperience.

Jake let his hands drop to her shoulders, then framed her face with his hands, marvelling at the incredible softness of her skin. As she gazed up at him, so trustingly, his heart suddenly did something very strange. It stopped, just for a second, then raced on.

Jake didn't pause to analyze his reaction. Instead, he leaned forward to claim her lips, softly tasting them, before he captured her mouth in a kiss that was perhaps a bit short on technique but very long on passion.

Maggie had no idea what was happening to her. This had all started out so innocently, two old friends out for a bike ride. Her request of Jake had seemed simple enough: Tell me how people learn to kiss. But the results were far from simple. From the moment he'd begun running his fingers through her hair, her heartbeat had gone haywire. Her stomach felt funny, and she couldn't seem to breathe right. And now...now, as his lips possessed hers, she thought she was going to drown in the flood of sensations washing over her.

How could he never have noticed before that she had grown up? Jake wondered in amazement. It was obvious in her delicate curves, in her softness, in the small sounds she made as he continued to kiss her. He'd always thought of Maggie as a kid, a pal, someone to ride bikes and shoot baskets with. But he didn't think of her as a kid right now. The frantic beat of the rain on the tin roof couldn't compete with the beating of their hearts as their embrace escalated.

It was Jake who finally realized that things were moving too fast and he broke away abruptly. Somewhere along the way this "lesson" had gotten out of hand, their roles changing from instructor and student to man and woman. And as Jake gazed down into Maggie's dazed eyes, he realized something else had changed, as well. Namely his life. Somehow he knew it would never be the same again.

Maggie stared up at him, then reached out to wonderingly trace the contours of his face. She heard his sharply indrawn breath, then he captured her hand in his, stilling its sensual movement. She could see the tension in his face, feel the thudding of his heart and realized with awe that she had drawn this passionate response from him. But she felt no less moved. She drew a deep, shaky breath, and when she spoke her voice was unsteady.

"Wow!" she breathed.

He tried to smile but couldn't quite pull it off. "Yeah. Wow!"

"Jake, I…I never expected to feel like…well, anything like this. I feel so…I don't know…fluttery inside. And shaky. And scared. But good, too. All at once. Is it…is it because I've never done this before?"

Slowly he shook his head. "I don't think so, Maggie. I feel the same way, and I've kissed a fair number of girls."

She struggled to sit up, and he saw with a frown that her hands were shaking badly. He should have been gentler, moved more slowly, he chided himself. She'd never even been kissed before. Of course, better him than Joe Carroll, he consoled himself. At least he'd had the decency to back off. He doubted Joe would have been as noble.

Jake put his arm around Maggie and pulled her against him until her head rested on his shoulder, smiling as he rubbed his cheek against her hair.

"You know, I never thought of you—of us—romantically before," she said in a small, uncertain voice.

"Me, neither. But I do now." He stroked her arm. "And you know what? I like it."

"So do I," she replied softly.

"You know something else? I have a feeling this may be the start of something pretty wonderful."

She snuggled closer. "I have the same feeling."

He backed off just far enough to look down into her emerald eyes, and the warmth of his smile filled her with joy. "Happy birthday, Maggie." And then he leaned down and claimed her lips in a tender kiss filled with sweet promise.

Maggie drew a deep, shaky breath as she stared at the silvered bay through the rough opening in the wall. She wrapped her arms around her body, holding the memories close for just a moment longer, memories of the day their friendship had ripened into romance. The images had seemed too vivid, so real—so lovely. She hated to let them go.

Had taking shelter in the old fishing shack prompted similar memories in Jake? she suddenly wondered, turning toward him. He was gazing at her silently.

"Seems like old times, doesn't it, squirt?" he said quietly, and she had her answer.

Maggie swallowed with difficulty, and turned back to the window. "Yes," she whispered.

She felt him move behind her, and her breath caught in her throat as he placed his hands on her shoulders and stroked them lightly.

"It's still there, isn't it, Maggie?" he murmured, his voice rough with emotion.

"What?" she choked out, knowing only too well what he meant.

With firm but gentle hands he turned her to face him so that she had to look directly into his eyes.

"This," he replied, and slowly reached over to trace the soft curve of her mouth with a whisper touch.

She closed her eyes and shuddered, willing herself to walk away, knowing she couldn't.

"Jake, I...things have changed. We're not the same people anymore."

"Not everything has changed."

She swallowed, and a pulse began to beat erratically in the delicate hollow of her throat. His gaze dropped to it for a moment, swept over the expanse of skin that had turned to alabaster in the moonlight, then came back to her eyes.

"We should go back," she suggested, a touch of desperation in her voice.

"I wish we could," he replied, and she knew he wasn't talking about the inn. "But the best we can do is start over. Tonight. Right now."

And then slowly, very slowly, he leaned toward her until his lips, familiar and warm and tender, closed over hers.

With a soft sigh, Maggie gave up the fight and melted into his arms. She'd intuitively known this moment would come since the day she stepped into the dining room seven weeks ago and found him there. It had been a losing struggle from the beginning, she acknowledged. Right or wrong, she wanted this moment in the arms of the man she'd always loved.

She was aware that the muscular contours of his chest were more developed, harder, than she remembered. And his arms were stronger, more sure, than she recalled, holding her with a practiced skill that had been absent twelve years ago. His mouth moved over hers with a new adeptness. The passion, though—that was the same. Just more intense.

Mostly she simply gave herself up to the moment, reveling in the exquisite joy of Jake's embrace. She returned his kiss tentatively at first, but his lips coaxed hers into a fuller response. She sighed softly as he cradled her head in one palm, his fingers tangled in her hair. Jake deepened the kiss, and she could feel the hard, uneven thudding of his heart as he pressed her closer. She offered no resistance. Couldn't have even if she'd wanted to.

Jake wasn't usually a man who lost control. He'd learned a great deal about discipline over the last dozen years, but it was a virtue that deserted him at the moment. Even as he told himself not to push, it was almost as if he was trying to make up for twelve long, parched years in one kiss. He had been so afraid she would reject his overture, that her fear would make her back off. But the fact that she had allowed him to claim her lips gave him hope for the future.

With a shuddering sigh, Jake at last raised his head and pressed hers close against his chest, holding her tightly. He had to stop now, before this got out of hand. He wasn't seventeen anymore, even if he felt like he was.

For several minutes neither spoke. Jake could feel Maggie trembling in his arms, and he didn't feel any too steady himself. Not only had their attraction endured through the years, it had intensified, he realized. The question now was, what were they going to do about it?

When her quivering finally eased, and when he finally felt able to carry on a coherent conversation, he gently pulled away from her, though he kept his arms looped around her waist. Their gazes met—his smoldering, hers dazed. With great effort, Jake summoned up the semblance of a smile.

"Wow."

"I…I think that's my line," she replied in a choked voice.

"I'm stealing it."

"Jake, I—I don't know if this is wise. I don't think I'm ready to…to…"

"Trust me again?" he finished softly, when her voice trailed off.

She stared at him, and warm color suffused her face at his blunt—and accurate—assessment of her feelings.

"It's okay, Maggie," he assured her softly. "I'm not asking you to—not yet, not after all these years. We need to give this some time. But the magic is still there. We both know that. I'd like to see where it leads."

Maggie swallowed. He was being direct about his intentions, and she respected that. She owed him no less. "Jake, I have a good life now. I've been…content. I thought that love had…that it wasn't the Lord's will for me. But I think I could…that we might…" She paused and turned away in frustration, reaching up to swipe at an errant tear. "See what you do to me? I'm a wreck. And it will be worse if I let myself…if I let myself care and then…" She paused, and Jake stepped in to finish the sentence again, much as he hated to.

"And then I disappear."

She turned to look at him and nodded slowly.

"I'm not going to leave again, Maggie," he promised her, his intense gaze locked on hers. "I'm here to stay this time."

She searched his eyes, wanting desperately to believe him. But he'd turned her world upside down once, and she had vowed never to let anyone do that again. How could she be sure this time?

Jake read the uncertainty in her eyes. "Just give me a chance, Maggie. That's all I ask. Spend some time with me. Just the two of us."

Maggie sighed. After tonight, there was no way she could refuse. She might be foolishly walking headfirst into danger, but Millicent Trent was right. Not very many people got a second chance at love. She'd be a fool to let it slip by without even considering it.

"All right, Jake. But right now we really do need to get back. The twins will be wondering what happened to us."

He grinned. "I think their imaginations will fill in the blanks. They're probably celebrating the success of their strategy right now."

Maggie took the hand he extended, and as he laced his fingers with hers, she suspected he was right. She knew that the notion of a rekindled romance between their aunt and Jake made the twins feel hopeful and excited. She ought to chastise them for their unrealistic expectations. But how could she, when her heart suddenly felt the same way?

Chapter Ten

Jake tossed his jacket onto the couch, set his briefcase on the floor and reached up to massage his neck. It had been a day full of meetings as the faculty prepared for the new school year, and he was tired. Classes started in a week and Jake was inundated with lesson plans and paperwork. The latter was no problem, of course. His years in the navy had prepared him for that, he mused, his mouth quirking up into a wry smile.

The lesson plans were another story. Teaching a course here and there during his career in the service was one thing. Planning a full load of classes for an entire semester was another. But not much could dampen his spirits after yesterday's dinner with Maggie. His heart felt lighter than it had in years.

A sudden thud from the direction of the garage drew his attention. What in the world was his father up to? he wondered, heading out to investigate.

When Jake reached the door to the garage, he paused only long enough to note that Howard was struggling to lift one of the boxes containing his woodworking tools. Then he strode rapidly across the floor and reached for it before the older man could protest.

"This is too heavy for you, Dad."

"I could have managed it," Howard declared stubbornly.

Jake didn't argue the point. They both knew he wasn't supposed to do heavy lifting or strenuous work of any kind. Making an issue out of it would only lead to an argument or cause his father to retreat into miffed silence. So instead, Jake nodded toward the once neatly stacked boxes, which were now in disarray. "What are you doing anyway?"

Howard stuck his hands in his pockets. "Maggie called. They need some craft items for a booth at the church fair, and she asked me if I'd make a few things. I couldn't say no, not after she's been so nice and all since I got here. But I need to set up my equipment."

Jake deposited the box on the floor and surveyed the garage. There was a workbench in one corner, and he nodded toward it. "Will that spot work?"

"That'll do. I just need to set up the saw and lathe."

"I'll take care of it for you after dinner."

"I can do it myself."

Jake planted his hands on his hips and turned to face his father. They were going to have to address the issue anyway, it seemed. "Dad, this equipment is too heavy for you to lift," he said evenly. "You know that. Why didn't you just wait until I got home?"

Howard shrugged. "Didn't want to be a bother."

Jake's tone—and stance—softened at the unexpected response, and he reached over and laid a hand on his father's stiff shoulder. "You're not a bother, Dad."

The older man glanced down, his shoulders hunched. "I just feel in the way these days. Maybe I can at least do something productive for the church."

Jake frowned. Did his father really feel that useless? Maggie had intimated as much, but Jake had been so busy getting ready for school—and worrying about his relationship with her—that he hadn't really thought much about how his father was feeling. Maybe he needed to.

"Well, we'll set it up tonight. Tomorrow we can run into Bangor and buy whatever wood and supplies you need. And a couple of space heaters, so you can work out here when the weather gets cooler."

Howard looked at him warily. "I don't want to put you out."

Jake's gaze was steady and direct. "I'm glad to do it, Dad," he said firmly.

As Jake prepared for bed later that night, he thought about his conversation with his father and how they'd worked side by side earlier in the evening to set up the workshop, Jake doing the physical work, Howard providing the direction. It reminded him of younger, happier times with his father. Maybe, just maybe, they were finally taking the first tentative steps toward a true reconciliation, he thought hopefully.

He recalled Maggie's promise to pray for them, and his own conclusion that it would take a miracle to put things right between him and his father. Jake had always been skeptical of miracles. But perhaps he was about to see one come to pass after all.

"Please, Aunt Maggie?"

Maggie stared at the twins. They'd ganged up on her again, and she couldn't seem to come up with a reason to say no. Ever since her birthday the week before, they'd been grinning like the proverbial Cheshire cat, dropping hints about her and Jake, urging her to call him, to accept his invitations for dinner, to sit on the porch with him when he dropped by unexpectedly in the evening. But she needed some space to mentally regroup after their last tumultuous encounter. Those few minutes in the fishing shed had caused her too many sleepless nights.

"Won't you do it for *us,* Aunt Maggie?" Allison cajoled.

Maggie sighed, realizing she'd lost this battle. If the twins wanted her to invite Jake to accompany them to the airport in Bangor when they departed for college in two days, how could she disappoint them?

"All right. You guys win. I'll ask. But remember, he's getting ready for school, too," she warned. "So don't be surprised if he can't make it."

"He'll make it," Abby predicted with a knowing smile.

And she was right. In fact, he not only agreed to go, he offered to drive.

When the big day arrived, Jake showed up right on time,

dressed in a pair of khaki slacks and a cotton fisherman's sweater that emphasized the broadness of his chest and enhanced his rugged good looks. His smile of welcome for her was warm and lingering, and the smoky look in his eyes wasn't missed by the perceptive twins. She saw them exchange a secret smile and shook her head. Hopeless romantics, the two of them.

The twins chattered excitedly all the way to Bangor, plying Jake with questions about his overseas travels, and Maggie was content to just sit back and listen to the lively banter. Between her sleepless nights and the rush to take care of all the last-minute details that going off to college entailed—not to mention running the inn—she was exhausted. Up till now the girls' enthusiasm had been contagious and had kept her adrenaline flowing. It was a happy, exciting time for them—the start of a new life—and she was pleased that their excellent academic performance had earned them both scholarships to the universities of their choice. Those scholarships, combined with their parents' insurance money—most of which had been put into a trust fund—would offer them security for many years to come. Their futures looked bright, and they had much to be happy and thankful for.

But late at night these last couple of weeks, when all the tumult ceased and she lay alone in bed, Maggie was overcome with a vague sense of melancholy. For the twins, college was a beginning. For her, it was an ending. Their departure marked the end of the life she had known for most of her adult years. Their laughter and teasing had filled her days, and the girls had provided her with an outlet for the bountiful love that filled her heart. Now they would build their own lives, apart from her, and eventually, special men would come along to claim their hearts. That was what she hoped for them anyway. She wanted their lives to be full and rich, filled with love and a satisfying career and children. It was just that she would miss them terribly. They had been her purpose, her anchor, and she felt suddenly adrift and strangely empty.

It wasn't until Abby was getting ready to board the plane that the girls themselves got teary-eyed. They'd never been apart for any great length of time, and now they were heading in two different directions, away from each other and the only home they could remember. Abby clung first to Allison, then to Maggie, as Jake stepped discreetly into the background.

"I'll miss you both so much!" she said, her voice suddenly shaky and uncertain.

"Call me every day, okay?" Allison implored.

"I promise."

"Goodbye, Aunt Maggie. And thank you...for everything."

Maggie's own eyes grew misty, but she struggled to maintain her composure as she hugged Abby again. She wanted this to be a happy moment for them, not a sad one. "Believe it or not, I loved every minute of it. Even the old days, when you and Allison used to delight in confusing me about who was who."

"I guess we were pretty bad about that," Abby admitted with a sheepish grin.

"Well, I survived. I even managed to guide two girls through adolescence at once without losing my sanity. Don't I get a medal or something?"

"Would a kiss and a hug do instead?" Abby asked with a laugh.

Maggie smiled. "I think that would be an even better reward."

Abby embraced her, and Maggie blinked back her tears.

"Now get on that plane before it leaves without you. I can't run after the plane like I used to run after the school bus!"

Abby grinned. "Yeah, I remember. Alli, you'll call, right?" Her voice was anxious as she hugged her twin.

"Count on it."

"You too, Aunt Maggie?"

"Absolutely. Now scoot. The bus is leaving," Maggie teased, trying valiantly to keep her smile in place.

"Okay." She hefted her knapsack and headed down the ramp.

Maggie and Allison waved until she was out of sight, and then, half an hour later, it was Allison's turn.

As Jake watched in the background, giving the two a moment alone, he wondered what was going through Maggie's mind. She seemed upbeat, happy. But he'd caught the glimmer of tears in her eyes more than once today. And as Allison disappeared from view, the sudden slump in Maggie's shoulders confirmed his suspicion that saying goodbye to the twins was one of the more difficult moments in her life. She suddenly looked lost—and very alone. He tossed his empty disposable coffee cup into a nearby receptacle and quickly strode toward her.

Maggie felt Jake lace his fingers through hers, and she blinked rapidly before looking up at him, struggling to smile. The understanding look in his eyes made it even more difficult to keep her tears at bay.

"You did a good job with them, you know," he said quietly, brushing his thumb reassuringly over the back of her hand. "They're lovely, intelligent, confident young women with their heads on straight and hearts that reflect an upbringing filled with kindness and love."

How was it that he'd known exactly the right thing to say? she wondered incredulously, trying to swallow past the lump in her throat. In the moments before he'd walked over, she'd been asking herself those very kinds of questions. Had she done everything she could to prepare them for what was ahead? Would the values she'd instilled in them survive their college years? Had their single-parent upbringing provided enough love and support and stability? Had she given them an adequate sense of self-worth, a solid enough grounding in their faith, to sustain them through whatever lay ahead? Jake seemed to think so. She didn't know if he was right. But hearing him say it made her feel better, and for that she was grateful.

"Thank you. I tried my best. I suppose that's all any of us can do. And I hope you're right. I hope it was good enough."

He draped his arm around her shoulders. "I don't think you have to worry about those two, Maggie. You raised them to be survivors. But then, they had a good example to follow."

Suddenly she was immensely grateful that the girls had insisted Jake come along today. His presence somehow helped ease the loneliness of their departure.

"Thank you for coming today, Jake. It was a lot tougher than I expected, saying goodbye. I—I'm going to miss those two! It will be so strange to be alone after all these years."

Jake turned to face her, letting one hand rest lightly at her waist as he tenderly stroked her cheek. "You're not alone, Maggie."

She searched his eyes, discerning nothing but honesty in their depths. His intense gaze seemed to touch her very soul, willing her to believe the sincerity of his words. And she wanted to. Dear Lord, she wanted to, with every fiber of her being! But she had to be cautious. She had to be sure. She still had too many doubts, too many questions. She would move forward, yes. But slowly. Because only time would provide the answers—and the assurance—she needed.

"By the way, the date's set."

"What date?" Maggie asked distractedly as she snagged another forkful of chicken salad. The mid-September weather was absolutely balmy, and when Philip had called and asked her to meet him for lunch at the outdoor café overlooking the bay, she couldn't refuse. Even now, her attention was focused more on enjoying the warmth of the sun seeping into her skin than on their conversation.

"The date for your show."

She stared at him. "What show?"

"The show we've been talking about for a year—remember?"

"You mean the show I never agreed to?"

"That's the one," he verified cheerily, reaching for his iced tea.

Maggie set her fork down with a clatter. "Philip, you didn't! You know I'm not ready!"

"You're ready, Maggie. You have been for a couple of years."

"But...but I never agreed to a show!"

"True. And why is that?"

Maggie bit her lip. "This is too close to my heart, Philip. You know that. I just can't take the chance. What if...what if I fail?"

Philip leaned forward and took her hand. "Maggie, there's no growth without risk. You've lived a very predictable, quiet life here for as long as I've known you. You think things through and try as hard as you can to make everything perfect. And that's worked well for you with the inn. You have a successful business and a comfortable life. But some things can't be worked out on a spreadsheet. Sometimes you have to just trust your heart. I know it's risky. I know how much your art means to you. It comes right from your heart, exposes your soul. That's why it's so good—and also why rejection is so scary. But I'm telling you, as your friend and a professional art dealer, that the risk of a show is minimal. I've shown some of your work to my friend in Bangor, and he agrees with my assessment. It will be a great opportunity for you to launch a more serious career. I'll cancel the show if you really want me to, but I think it would be a big mistake."

She frowned. "When is this show supposed to be?"

"The opening is scheduled for the first Friday in December. It will run for a month."

Maggie took a deep breath. It was a scary commitment, but Philip was right. If she ever wanted to pursue serious art, she had to make her work available for critique and review. She needed to take this opportunity.

"All right, Philip. I'll do it," she told him with sudden decision. "I guess it's time to test the waters, take a chance."

He smiled. "You won't be sorry, you know."

"I hope you're right."

"And what about the other...risky...situation in your life at the moment?" he asked, purposefully keeping his tone casual.

"What situation?"

"Jake."

Maggie glanced down and played with her chicken salad. "I'm not so sure about that one. It's even scarier."

"Well, it would be a shame to walk away from something

good just because you're afraid. And that's true for every-thing—from a show to a relationship. Now, suppose I get off my soapbox and change the subject to something less heavy. Tell me about the girls. How are they adjusting?''

The rest of the lunch passed in companionable conversa-tion. But Philip's words kept replaying in her mind. Was her fear protecting her—or keeping her from something good, as he had suggested? Maggie didn't know. But as she left Philip in front of the restaurant and returned to her car, she turned to the source of guidance she always relied on in times of uncertainty.

Lord, I'm confused, she confessed in the silence of her heart. *I'm starting to fall in love with Jake again, but I don't know if that's wise. He hurt me badly once, and I don't ever want to go through that pain again. But I feel You sent him here for a reason. If it's Your will that I give our love a second chance, please help me to find the courage to trust again. Because otherwise I'm afraid I'll let it slip through my fingers. And I don't want to live the rest of my life with regrets, the way Millicent has. Please—please—show me the way!*

''Pop! Over here!''

Jake turned at the sound of the familiar voice and smiled at Maggie.

''She's over there, Dad.'' He laid one hand on Howard's shoulder and gestured toward the church booth with the other.

''Well, let's go say hello.''

Jake was more than happy to comply. He hadn't seen enough of Maggie these last two weeks, not since the girls left. September was a popular month at the inn, and she was busier than ever, without the girls to help. But no more busy than him. He had been a bit overwhelmed by the workload at school and had been left with virtually no free time. It was not a situation he was pleased about, but until he adjusted to school and her business slowed down for the winter, there didn't seem to be much he could do about it. He had to take whatever limited time he could get with her. And accompa-nying his father to the church fair—especially knowing Maggie was working at the booth—was as good an excuse as any to take a break from correcting papers.

He gave her a lazy smile as they approached. "Hi, Maggie."

The smoky, intimate tone in his voice brought a flush to her cheeks. "Hello, Jake." With an effort she dragged her gaze from his and turned her attention to Howard. "Hi, Pop."

"Hi, Maggie. How's business?"

"That's what I wanted to tell you. All of the things you made sold already!"

"Really?" he asked, clearly pleased.

"Yes. And not only that, Andrew Phillips—he owns the local craft alliance—wants to talk to you. They'd like to take some of your things on consignment, and he was even interested in having you teach a class."

Howard's eyes lit up. "He liked my work that much?"

Maggie nodded emphatically. "Absolutely. He said…wait, there he is over there. Andrew!" She waved at a tall, spare young man with longish hair and gestured for him to join them. He strolled over, and she made the introductions.

"I told Howard you were interested in talking with him," Maggie explained.

"Yes, I am. Could you spare me a few minutes now? Maybe have a cup of coffee or something?"

Howard was actually beaming. "Sure, sure. That is, if my son doesn't mind waiting." He glanced at Jake, suddenly uncertain.

Jake propped his shoulder against the corner of Maggie's booth and folded his arms across his chest. "Not at all. Take your time, Dad."

He watched the two men wander off toward the refreshment area, then turned to Maggie with a smile and shook his head. "Now that, Ms. Fitzgerald, is a miracle. Did you see the way my dad's face lit up?"

She smiled. "Yes. It makes all the difference in the world when a person believes they have something to contribute. Pop just needs to feel like he can still do something worthwhile."

"Thanks to you, he does."

Maggie blushed again and shook her head. "No. You were the one who thought to bring the woodworking tools."

"But you were the one who convinced him to use them."

She shrugged. "Well, it doesn't really make any difference where the credit belongs. The important thing is that Pop seems interested in something again. And he's looking better, too, Jake. Are…are things improving at all between you two?"

"They're better. But even though we're more comfortable with each other, there's still a…a distance, I guess is the best way to describe it. I don't feel like we ever really connect at a deeper level. And frankly, I'm not sure what else I can do. School is pretty demanding right now, and I just don't have the time to focus on Dad the way I'd like to. I'm not used to dealing with boys that age, and it's a real challenge. In fact, to be perfectly honest, I sometimes feel like I'm in over my head."

"Your father raised two boys," Maggie said thoughtfully. "Maybe he could offer you a few tips. Have you talked to him about your job, or any of the kids?"

Jake frowned and shook his head. "I don't think he's interested. He's never asked about my work."

"Maybe he's afraid that you don't want his advice."

Jake considered that. She might have a point. During the last twelve years he hadn't exactly shared a lot of his life with his father. Why should the older man expect him to start now?

"I guess it couldn't hurt to try," Jake conceded.

"Well, most people are flattered when asked for advice. And your father really does have a lot of experience with boys. You might actually…"

"Next Wednesday, then?"

Andrew's voice interrupted their conversation, and they turned as the two men approached.

"Let me check with my son." Howard looked at Jake. "Andrew would like me to come by the shop next Wednesday and look things over, maybe work out a schedule for a class. Would it put you out to run me over after school?"

"I'd be happy to, Dad."

Howard turned back to Andrew and stuck out his hand. "It's nice to meet you, young man."

"My pleasure. I'll see you Wednesday."

"Sounds like things went well," Maggie observed with a smile.

Howard nodded, looking pleased. "Yes, they did. Nice young fellow. He's a potter. It's good to talk to people who appreciate handcrafted work."

"Could be a whole new career for you, Pop," Maggie pointed out.

"Could be, at that." He turned back to Jake. "I appreciate the ride Wednesday," he said stiffly.

"No problem, Dad."

"Well, if I'm going to be making things for the shop, I need to take inventory. You ready to go?"

"Sure." Jake turned to Maggie, the warmth of his smile mirrored in his eyes. "Thanks."

Before she realized his intent, he reached over and touched her cheek, then let his hand travel to her nape. He exerted gentle pressure and drew her close for a tender kiss. When he backed off she was clearly flustered, and Jake wondered if he'd been too impulsive. But it had been three long weeks since her birthday, three weeks with nothing but the memory of their embrace in the fishing shack to sustain him. He needed to reassure himself that she hadn't had second thoughts about pursuing their relationship.

He searched her eyes, and when their gazes locked for a mesmerizing moment, he had all the reassurance he needed. "I'll be by later this week, Maggie," he said in a voice only she could hear. "We need to talk."

She nodded, unwilling to trust her voice.

He smiled, then glanced at his father. "Ready, Dad?"

The older man nodded. "Whenever you are." Howard looked at Maggie quizzically, then turned and walked away.

"I'm surprised she let you do that," he muttered as Jake fell into step beside him.

"I think she's beginning to realize that I've changed, Dad," Jake replied quietly. "At least, I hope she is."

The older man paused and regarded his son silently for a moment. Jake tensed, waiting for a derogatory comment, but instead Howard simply turned and continued toward the car. "Let's go home," he said gruffly, over his shoulder. "I've got some projects to start."

Jake followed, trying to absorb the significance of what had just occurred. Not only had his father refrained from making a disparaging remark, but even more important, he had used the word *home* for the first time. It was a small thing, Jake knew. But it was a start.

Chapter Eleven

Jake dropped his briefcase on the couch and sniffed appreciatively. Since the beginning of the school year, his father had taken over the chore of cooking dinner. The meal was never fancy, given Howard's limited culinary skills, but the gesture was greatly appreciated by Jake. He was usually tired when he got home, and definitely not in the mood to cook. His father's willingness to step in and handle KP was a godsend. Especially tonight.

As Jake strolled toward the kitchen, he mulled over the encounter he'd had with one of the freshmen this afternoon. Actually, *confrontation* might be a better description, he thought grimly. The last thing he needed in this "learning-the-ropes" phase of his new career was a smart-aleck kid mouthing off at him. He supposed he could—and perhaps should—report the insubordination to the dean. But that could be the death knell for a budding maritime career, and he was reluctant to take such a drastic measure so early in the semester. Besides, there was something about the boy that troubled him. A look in his eyes of…bleakness; that was the word that came to mind. And desperation. They were barely discernible under his veneer of insolence, but they were there, Jake was certain. He just didn't know what to do about it.

"Hi, Dad." He paused in the doorway. "What's for dinner?"

His father shrugged. "Just meat loaf. I used to make it for

myself at home sometimes, after your mother died. She made it better than I do, though.''

"Well, it sure smells good.''

Howard turned to set the table, pausing for a moment to study Jake. ''You look tired.''

Jake sighed and reached around to rub the stiff muscles in his neck. ''It was a long day.''

"Well, I imagine teaching is quite a change from the navy. Takes a while to get used to, I expect.'' Howard placed the cutlery beside the plates. ''Go ahead and change if you want. Dinner'll be ready in fifteen minutes.''

When Jake reappeared a few minutes later wearing worn jeans and a sweatshirt, his father nodded to the table. ''Have a seat. It's almost ready.''

"Can I help with anything?''

"Two cooks in the kitchen is one too many. That's what your mother always used to say, and she was right.''

Jake eased his long frame into the chair, watching as Howard bustled about. His father was moving with much more purpose and energy these last few days, he realized. Thanks to Maggie. Getting his father back into woodworking had been a terrific idea, and she had known just how to go about it. Considering the success of that strategy, he decided to talk to his father about school, ask his advice. Maggie had been batting a thousand so far, after all. And he *was* at a loss about how to deal with his problem student. Perhaps his father could offer a few insights. It couldn't hurt to ask anyway.

Halfway through the meal, his father gave him the perfect opening.

"I saw some of the students from the academy walking down the road today. They look like fine young men,'' he observed.

Jake nodded. ''They are. Most of them. But I've got one freshman—I just can't figure out what's going on in his head.''

Howard looked over at Jake quizzically. ''What's his problem?''

Jake sighed. ''I wish I knew. I checked his transcripts, and he's obviously bright. But he's only doing the bare minimum to survive in my class—and apparently in his other classes, as well. He's sullen and withdrawn and just itching for a fight. We had a confrontation after class today, as a matter of fact. I told him I expected more, and essentially he said that as long as he turned in the assignments it wasn't any of my business how well he did. That I should just grade his papers and buzz off."

"Sounds like somebody needs to give that boy a good talking to."

Jake nodded. "You're right. But he doesn't let anybody get close enough. Whenever I see him he's alone."

"Well, I'm not surprised, with that kind of attitude."

"The thing is, Dad, he has a sort of...hopeless...look in his eyes," Jake said pensively, his brow furrowed. "Like he's worried and scared and...I don't know. I just sense there's something wrong. I'd like to reach out to him, try to help, but I don't know how," he admitted with a frustrated sigh.

Howard stopped eating and peered across the table at Jake, obviously surprised by his son's admission. There was a moment of silence, and when he spoke, his voice was cautious.

"Sounds like something's on his mind, all right. Probably could use a sympathetic ear. But you're a stranger, Jake. It's pretty hard to trust a stranger, especially one who's an authority figure."

"Yeah. I suppose so."

"You know, going away to school can be a pretty scary thing. That could be part of it. But it sounds to me like maybe something's going on at home, too. Something that's tearing him up inside. Lots of times people get belligerent when they're faced with a situation that scares them, especially if it's something they can't control."

Jake wondered if his father realized that insight might apply in his own case, but as the older man thoughtfully buttered a piece of bread, his focus was clearly in the past.

"I remember one time when Rob was in sixth grade, the teacher called us up and said he was picking fights," he recalled. "Well, you know that wasn't like Rob at all. So I took him out to the woods the next weekend to help me chop some logs. Just the two of us. Your mother packed a nice lunch, hot chocolate and sandwiches, and while we were eating I started to ask about school, casual-like, and how things were going. Just kind of opened the lines of communication, I think they call it these days. Anyway, 'fore we left, I found out Rob was scared to death your mother was sick. Overheard us talking about the Nelsons, but misunderstood and thought it was your mom who had to have surgery. Amazing how things improved once he got that worry off his mind.''

Jake stared at his father. ''I never knew anything about that.''

Howard shrugged. ''No reason for you to. Anyhow, might not be a bad idea, if you really want to find out what's going on with this boy, to take him out for a cup of coffee or something. Let him know you're willing to listen, away from the classroom. More as a friend than a teacher—you know what I mean? Sounds like he could use a friend.''

Jake looked at his father speculatively. Maggie was right, it seemed. Not only did the older man have some good insights, but he'd been more than willing to share them.

''That sounds like good advice, Dad,'' he said with quiet sincerity. ''Thanks. I'll give it a try.''

The older man gave what appeared to be an indifferent shrug, but Jake knew his father was flattered.

''Might not work. But it couldn't hurt to try,'' Howard replied. Then he rose and began clearing the table. ''How about some apple pie? Can't say I baked it myself, but you'll probably be just as happy I didn't.''

Jake sent his father an astonished look. This was the first time in years he had shown Jake any humor. Could a gesture as simple as a mere request for advice make such a difference? Jake marveled. Apparently it could. Because as Howard deposited the dishes in the sink and prepared to cut the pie, something else astonishing happened. For the first time in years, Jake heard his father whistle.

Maggie glanced at her watch for the tenth time in fewer minutes and told herself to calm down. Just because Jake was coming over was no reason for her nerves to go haywire. Unfortunately, her nerves weren't listening to reason, she thought wryly, as another swarm of butterflies fluttered through her stomach.

She sat down in the porch swing, hoping its gentle, rhythmic motion would calm her jitters. She was certain that Jake wanted to pick up where they'd left off the night of her birthday, and she was afraid. Afraid that by allowing their relationship to progress, she was exposing her heart to danger. But she still cared for him. To deny it was useless. She still found him attractive, still responded to his touch. But more than that, she still felt as she had so many years ago—that God had meant Jake and no one else to be her husband. In fact, she felt it even more strongly now than before. Which seemed odd, after all they'd been through.

The crunch of tires on gravel interrupted her thoughts, and her heartbeat quickened as her gaze flew to the small parking lot. She recognized the small, sensible car Jake had purchased—a far cry from the impractical sporty number he used to crave—and watched as he unfolded his long frame and stood gazing out to sea, his strong profile thrown into sharp relief by the setting sun. He stayed there, motionless, for a long moment, seeming to savor the scene. It was a lovely view, and Maggie herself had often paused to admire it. But it was not something Jake would have appreciated—or even noticed—a dozen years ago, she reflected. It was just one of the many things about him that had changed.

And yet, at least one thing had stayed the same. He was every bit as handsome as he'd always been—tall, confident in bearing, with an easy, heart-melting smile that could still turn her legs to rubber. He was the kind of man who would stand out in any gathering—and who could have had his pick of women through the years.

And yet...he'd never married. Had even implied that she was the reason for his single status. Maggie wanted to believe that was true, wanted to think that the love he'd once felt for her had endured—just as hers had for him.

At the same time, she wasn't a starry-eyed sixteen-year-old anymore. She was an adult who knew better than to let her emotions rule her life. She was determined to approach the situation as logically and as objectively as she could. It was true that everything she'd seen since he'd returned indicated that Jake had matured, that he was now a man who understood the concept of honor and responsibility, who could be counted on in good times *and* bad. And Maggie *wanted* to believe the evidence that was rapidly accumulating in his favor. But only time would tell if the changes were real—and lasting.

He didn't notice her in the shadows, so as he reached to press the bell she spoke softly.

"Hello, Jake."

He turned in surprise, and a slow, lazy smile played across his lips. She looked so good! he thought. Her shapely legs, covered in khaki slacks, were tucked under her, and she'd thrown a green sweater carelessly over her shoulders to ward off the evening chill. In the fading light, her flame-colored hair took on a life of its own. She wore it down tonight, as he preferred, and it softly and flatteringly framed her porcelain complexion. Right now, at this moment, she looked no older than she had that summer twenty-one years before, on the day of their eventful bike ride. And she made him feel exactly as he had on that same memorable, long-ago day—breathless, eager and deeply stirred. But he wasn't a seventeen-year-old bundle of hormones anymore, he reminded himself. Even if he did *feel* like one. *Control* was the operative word here.

"Hi." The deep, husky timbre of his voice was something he *couldn't* control, however. And it wasn't lost on Maggie, he realized, noting the soft blush that crept up her cheeks.

"Would you like some coffee?"

He shook his head. "No, thanks. Why don't we just sit out here for a while?"

"Okay." She lowered her feet to the floor and scooted over to make room for him. The swing creaked in protest as he sat down, and he turned to her with a grin.

"Are you sure this is safe?"

No, she thought in silent panic as he casually draped an

arm across the back of the swing and gently brushed his fingers over her shoulder. *It isn't safe at all. Not for me!*

"Perfectly safe," she replied, struggling to keep her voice even. "We check it every season."

He smiled at her then, that tender smile she knew so well. "I've missed you," he told her softly.

"You just saw me at the fair."

"That was four days ago. And besides, there were too many people around."

The corners of her mouth tipped up. "That didn't stop you from…"

When her blush deepened and her voice trailed off, he grinned. "Kissing you? No, as a matter of fact it didn't. It could easily become a habit," he warned, reaching out to seductively trace the contours of her lips with a gentle finger.

Maggie's breath caught in her throat at the intimate gesture, and her heart began to bang painfully against her rib cage.

"But I have to admit I prefer more privacy. Take this spot, for instance. I think the twins had the right idea on your birthday. It's very romantic here." He cupped her chin in his hand and let his gaze lovingly, lingeringly caress her face. The conflict in her eyes, the war between desire and prudence, was apparent. But equally apparent was the longing in their depths—and the invitation.

Jake tried to resist. Valiantly. He told himself that she wasn't even aware of her silent plea. That he needed to move slowly. That he needed to reach deep into his reserves of discipline and simply back off. But he was only human, after all. And desire suppressed for twelve long years was a difficult thing to control, especially when the object of that desire sat only inches away, looking so appealing and ready to be kissed.

With a sigh of capitulation to forces stronger than he seemed able to resist, Jake gave up the fight and leaned down to tenderly claim the sweet lips of the woman he loved. His intention was to keep the kiss simple and swift. Make it long enough to let her know he cared and had missed her, but short enough not to make her nervous, he cautioned himself. But somehow it didn't turn out that way.

Because from the moment their lips met, Jake was overwhelmed by a sense of urgency that took his breath away. Maggie felt so good in his arms, so right, as if she belonged there always. He framed her delicate face with his strong hands, his lips eager and hungry as he kissed her with an abandon that surprised them both. The initially gentle, tentative touching of lips escalated rapidly to an embrace that spoke eloquently of love and longing, reflecting twelve long years of parched emotions.

What surprised Jake more than his unexpected loss of control was Maggie's acquiescence. He had felt her tense initially, as if taken aback by the intensity of his embrace, but within seconds she was returning his kiss with a passion that equaled his own. Without breaking contact with her lips, he shifted their positions so that she was cradled in his arms. She sighed softly, and he continued to kiss her, with a hunger that only Maggie's sweet lips could satisfy.

Maggie was only vaguely aware of their change in position. All she knew was that she wanted to stay in Jake's embrace forever, feeling cherished and loved and desired. With a sigh, she put her arms around his neck and strained to draw him even closer, letting her fingers explore the soft hair at the base of his neck. Jake reciprocated by combing his fingers through her thick tresses, and she felt her heartbeat quicken at his touch.

Jake was thrown by the feelings of tenderness and desire that nearly overwhelmed him. How had he lived without her sweet love to sustain him all these years? he asked himself wonderingly. Now that he'd found her again, he couldn't imagine a future without her.

When at last Jake reluctantly released her lips, she lay passively in his arms, staring up at him with a slightly dazed expression that he suspected mirrored his own. He hadn't intended their evening to begin this way. But once in her presence, all his good intentions had evaporated, he acknowledged, as he gently brushed a few errant tendrils of hair back from her face. She tentatively reached up, as if to touch his cheek, then dropped her hand.

"Why did you stop?" He took her hand and laced his fingers through hers, then pressed it against his cheek.

She colored and removed her hand from his, then eased herself to the other side of the swing. She wasn't sure what had come over her just now, but if taking things slowly was her plan, this was not exactly the way to start. Distractedly she ran her fingers through the tangled waves of her hair, trying futilely to restore it to order.

"Jake...I think that...well, I think it's obvious that we're still...attracted to each other on the...on the physical level," she stammered. "But there are other levels that are equally important—if not more important. I—I need to focus on those, but I can't even think straight when you...when I'm...when we're close," she said haltingly, obviously flustered. "And there are issues we need to deal with—*I* need to deal with—things I still need to work through. I don't want to lose sight of those."

That wasn't exactly what Jake wanted to hear, but he saw her point. All of the other realities of his life—and their relationship—got pretty fuzzy for him, too, when her soft, pliant body melted against him and her lips were warm and willing beneath his. He drew a deep, slightly unsteady breath.

"So...no more kissing—is that what you're saying?" He tried for a teasing tone but didn't quite pull it off.

"No, of course not. It's just that...well, I think we need to keep it in perspective, that's all."

He wondered if she had any idea just what she was asking. Maintaining his perspective—let alone his equilibrium—around Maggie was almost impossible. But if that's what she wanted, he'd give it his best shot, he resolved. With a crooked grin, he draped his arm casually around her shoulders, though he felt anything but casual. His body was clamoring with unfulfilled needs—which weren't going to be fulfilled anytime soon, it appeared. So he'd better just get used to it.

"How about the old arm around the shoulder? Is that out of bounds, too?"

"No." She snuggled close and pulled her legs up beside her as Jake set the swing gently rocking.

It was sweet agony to have her soft curves cuddled so close, but he'd get through this, he resolved, gritting his teeth. He had to. *Change the subject,* he told himself desperately. *Focus on something else.* He struggled to find a topic, and was immensely grateful when Maggie took the initiative.

"Your dad seemed pleased about the fair Sunday."

"He was. He spent the rest of the afternoon making a list of supplies. I drove him over to Bangor to pick up everything yesterday. He's happy as a clam—or should I say lobster, here in Maine?—now that he's got a project. I have to practically force him to stop every night. You were right about him needing to have something to do that would make him feel worthwhile. And you were right about something else, too."

She turned to look up at him. "What?"

"Your idea to talk to dad about school. I tried it Monday night. I think he was a little shocked, but he did open up. And offered some pretty good advice along the way, I might add. Thanks to him, I think I'm finally starting to connect with one of my problem students."

"Really?" Her eyes were bright, her smile warm and genuine. "I'm so glad, Jake! What did he suggest?" She listened interestedly as he recapped his father's suggestion. "And it's working?"

"So far. I invited Paul—that's the student's name—to meet me in the canteen for coffee yesterday. I wasn't sure he'd come, but he did. He hasn't said much yet, but I picked up enough to suspect that there was a major trauma of some sort in his life shortly before he left for school. Something to do with his parents, I think. I invited him to meet me again tomorrow between classes, and I'm hoping he'll come. I'd like to help him through this, whatever it is, if I can."

"Did you tell your father?"

He chuckled. "You've heard the phrase, 'Pleased as punch'?"

Maggie smiled and settled back against Jake. "That's good. I'm glad you two are getting along better."

"We still have a long way to go, Maggie."

"But at least you're moving in the right direction."

They swung quietly for a few minutes, her head nestled contentedly on his shoulder, the muffled night sounds peaceful and soothing. When Jake finally broke the silence, his husky voice was close to her ear.

"It's good to have you in my arms again, Maggie."

She swallowed past the lump in her throat. "I was just thinking the same thing," she confessed softly.

"I know you need some time. And I'm not trying to rush you. But I think you know where I hope this is heading."

She'd have to be a fool not to. But there was so much still to be dealt with. So much that she wasn't yet *ready* to deal with. And she hadn't expected him to be quite so up-front about his intentions—not yet, anyway. "There are…issues… Jake."

"You mean beyond the obvious?" They both knew he was referring to her struggle to overcome lingering doubts about his reliability and honor.

She nodded. Maggie hadn't really planned to get into a heavy discussion tonight. But there was one issue in particular that had to be discussed sooner or later, and sooner was probably better from a self-preservation standpoint. Jake wasn't going to like what she had to say. In fact, he might dislike it enough to reconsider his feelings. But it would be better to know that now, before she got any more involved, she told herself resolutely as she drew a deep breath.

"You mentioned once that you wanted a family." Her voice was quiet, subdued. "But I've already had a family, Jake. I don't regret a minute of it, but it's a demanding job, and I've spent the last twelve years doing it. So much of my adult life has been spent doing what I *had* to do. Now…now I want to focus on the things I *want* to do for a while. Like go to Europe, pursue my art." She paused and stared down unseeingly, absently running her finger over the crease in her slacks. "I guess that sounds selfish, doesn't it?" she finished in a small voice.

Jake frowned and stroked her arm comfortingly. "No. *Self-ish* is hardly a word I would use to describe you, Maggie."

She leaned away and looked up at him in the dim light, trying to read his eyes. "Do you understand how I feel, Jake?" she asked anxiously.

"Well, it's not exactly what I wanted to hear," he admitted, "but I do understand." He stroked her cheek and gave her a rueful smile that was touched with melancholy. "Our timing always seems to be off, doesn't it? First you were saddled with responsibilities that tied you down. Now you're free, and I'm saddled with responsibilities that tie me down. And as for a family—it would be different this time, you know. Two people sharing the responsibility for one child is a whole lot easier than one person trying to raise two children."

"I accept that in theory, Jake," she conceded. "But life has a way of tearing theories to shreds. And plans can fall apart in the blink of an eye."

He couldn't argue with that. Their own broken engagement was a perfect example of plans gone awry. And his presence here in Maine was another. Three years ago, if someone had told him he'd end up being a land-bound teacher, sharing a cottage with his father in rural Maine, he'd have laughed in their face.

Maggie frowned as the silence between them lengthened. She'd known since the day he talked about a family that her feelings on the subject could be a major hurdle to their relationship, had dreaded having to deal with the issue. They were at two ends of the spectrum. Jake wanted a family. She didn't—at least, not in the near future. And with her biological clock beginning to tick rather loudly, it might come down to the near future—or not at all.

Maggie felt a wave of despair sweep over her. Why did the Lord always make the choices so difficult? she wondered helplessly. Twelve years ago, her choice had been a family or Jake. Now it seemed that it might come down to Jake and a family—or no Jake. That thought chilled her, but she saw no way around it. Not unless she gave up her own dreams.

And she'd done that once. She couldn't do it again—not even for Jake.

"I'm sorry, Jake," she said quietly at last. "I do understand your desire for a family. It's a beautiful thing, raising children, watching them develop and grow and become caring, responsible adults. But I—I can't make any promises. Maybe in a year or two I'll feel differently, but right now I'm just not ready to even consider it."

Jake absently brushed his fingers up and down her arm, his frown deepening. He'd been so caught up in his rediscovery of Maggie that he really hadn't thought much about the family issue, though she had alluded to her feelings on the subject a few weeks before, he admitted. It just hadn't been something he wanted to deal with at that moment. Or at all, if he was honest. There had been enough barriers already between himself and the woman he loved. Why did life often seem to consist entirely of hurdles and detours? he railed silently.

Jake sighed. The evening had taken an unexpectedly heavy turn. He still hoped that when her trust level grew, the notion of a family based on shared responsibilities would become more palatable. In the meantime, she needed the space, the freedom, that the twins' departure had given her. He didn't begrudge her that. She'd earned it. He wanted her to make that trip to Europe, to see all the places she'd always dreamed of. He only wished he could go with her.

"I'm not sure what the answer is, Maggie," he admitted, gently stroking her arm. "But maybe it's one of those things we should just place in the hands of the Lord. I can't help but believe He brought us together for some reason. Maybe, if we give this some time, He'll eventually let us in on His plans and show us the way."

She turned and looked up at him, tipping her head. "That's funny, Jake. I can't ever remember you talking about faith or trust in the Lord before."

He chuckled softly. "Well, Dad's been dragging me to church every Sunday. Some of it must be rubbing off." Then his voice grew more serious. "Besides, the older I get, the more I realize how much help I need finding my way through this maze of a world. Going back to church, thinking about my faith again—well, it's been a great help. It seems to give me more of a sense of direction. I'm beginning to realize what I've been missing all these years by not turning to the Lord when I needed help.''

Yet another new dimension to Jake, Maggie thought wonderingly. And he was right about trusting in the Lord. He would reveal His plan for them in His own time—which, as she'd learned through the years, wasn't always *her* time. She just needed to be patient.

"All right, Jake. Let's just give it some time.''

"How about starting Sunday? We could go hiking over on Isle au Haut. I hear it's spectacular.''

She nodded. ''It is. The twins and I have spent some lovely days over there. It's wild and rugged and isolated—a wonderful spot to get away from it all.''

They swung in silence for a few moments, and when he spoke, his voice was thoughtful. ''Maggie?''

"Mmm-hmm?''

"You know that comment you made earlier? About keeping kissing in perspective?''

"Mmm-hmm.''

"It's not going to be easy, you know. Not when it's the first thing I think of every time I'm near you—and most of the time when I'm not.''

She blushed at his frankness. ''It's—it's a problem for me, too,'' she admitted.

She heard a chuckle rumble deep in his chest and was relieved that at least he seemed to be taking her ground rules in good humor. ''Well, as long as I don't have to suffer alone, maybe it won't be so bad.''

"Besides, I didn't rule out kissing entirely, you know,'' she reminded him. She doubted whether she could even if she wanted to.

"Are good-night kisses acceptable, then?'' he inquired hopefully, a smile tugging at the corners of his mouth.

"Absolutely.''

"Well, in that case…" He glanced at his watch and feigned a yawn. "I think it's time to say good-night. Don't you?"

She chuckled and shook her head. "You're incorrigible, you know."

"Guilty," he admitted promptly. And then his eyes grew serious. "At least when it comes to you." He reached over and drew a finger gently down the line of her cheek. "Good night, Maggie," he murmured softly, and then his lips closed over hers.

This time the kiss was gentle, a thing to be slowly savored as they absorbed each exquisite nuance of sensation. Now that they had agreed to let time be their friend, the earlier urgency of their embrace was replaced by a tender exploration and leisurely rediscovery that spoke of understanding and promise and hope.

Maggie had no idea what the future held for them. But for the first time since Jake had come back into her life, she felt a sense of peace and calm. For now that she had stopped struggling so hard to resolve their issues on her own and had put her trust in the Lord, her soul felt refreshed. She didn't know the destination of their relationship, but her heart felt sure that He would guide them in right paths.

Chapter Twelve

As the blaze of fall colors began to burn brightly on the coastal landscape, so, too, did the blaze of love burn with ever-growing fervor in Maggie's heart. Sundays became "their" day, and after early-morning services together she and Jake explored the back roads and quaint byways of their adopted state. Sometimes Howard went with them, but usually he declined their invitation, insisting that three was a crowd.

And so, from popular Acadia National Park to remote Schoodic Point, their love blossomed once again on the splendor of the Maine coast. The twins regularly demanded progress reports, and though Maggie tried to play it low-key, even *she* could hear the joyful lilt in her voice every time she mentioned Jake. The girls, of course, were delighted—but no less so than Maggie. She'd been so afraid that her fragile bubble of happiness would burst, that one day she'd wake up to find herself once more alone. Yet her fears seemed groundless. Each moment she spent with Jake was more perfect than the last.

In fact, everything seemed almost *too* perfect. And life was far from perfect, as she well knew. Yet her hours with Jake disputed that reality. Each time he protectively enfolded her fingers in his strong, bronzed hand; each time his warm, brown eyes smiled down into hers; each time he held her in his arms and tenderly claimed her lips, Maggie felt a renewal, a rebirth, a reawakening. Joy and hope filled her heart as the love she'd kept locked away for so long gradually began to find release. For Maggie, who had long ago ruthlessly stifled romantic fantasies and the notion of happy endings, it was a dream come true.

That "dream-come-true" quality was brought home to her most clearly on Thanksgiving Day when she glanced around the table, her heart overflowing with love. The twins looked radiant and vivacious, chattering about college life and clearly thriving in the challenging academic environment. Howard had filled out and looked well on the road to recovery. And Jake… Maggie's eyes softened as they met his warm, intimate gaze across the table. Jake made her understand the real meaning of Thanksgiving. Loving him, and being loved in return, filled her with gratitude—and hope. For Maggie sensed they were close to a resolution of their issues.

In fact, she had a feeling this Christmas might bring a very special present her way, one she'd thought never to receive again. She glanced down at her bare left hand as she reached for the basket of rolls. Maybe…maybe in a month it wouldn't look so bare, she thought, as a delicious tingle of excitement and anticipation raced along her spine. And wouldn't the girls love a spring wedding?

Jake turned the corner and drove slowly through the pelting, icy rain, a troubled frown on his face. Though Paul had eventually opened up and taken Jake into his confidence, in the end it hadn't made much difference. He was withdrawing at the end of the semester.

Jake let out a long, frustrated sigh. The boy had been dealing with a lot, no question about it. First, a few weeks before leaving for school, his parents had announced their intention to divorce. That was hard enough to accept. But the reason had made it even worse. His father, whom Paul had always looked up to and admired, had admitted to an affair and made it clear that he wanted to marry the other woman. Paul had not only felt betrayed and abandoned himself, but as the only child he'd been left to comfort his devastated mother. It was a difficult position to be in at any age, but especially for a seventeen-year-old still in the process of growing up himself.

Jake believed that his talks with Paul had helped a great deal, that the sympathetic ear he'd offered had provided a much-needed outlet and sounding board for the angry, hurt young man. Slowly, over the last few weeks, he had begun to calm down, settle in. His work improved and he began to socialize more.

And then he'd been hit with the news that his mother had cancer, so far advanced that there was nothing the doctors could do. She'd been given four to six months, at best. And because she had no one else to love and support her through the ordeal to come, he had decided to go home, to be with her during the difficult days ahead. Jake knew Paul had struggled with the decision, knew he didn't want to withdraw from school. In the end he'd made a courageous choice, and Jake admired him for it. But it was just so unfair, he thought in frustration, his fingers tightening on the wheel as he pulled to a stop in front of the cottage.

Jake forced himself to take a long, steadying breath before he slowly climbed out of the car and turned up his collar against the biting wind and cold rain. He slammed the door and strode up the walk, stopping abruptly when he realized that there was a ladder directly in his path. He frowned and glanced up—to find his father perched precariously on one of the top rungs, at roof level. A sudden gust of the relentless wind slapped a stinging sheet of sleet against his face, and he shivered.

"Dad!" he shouted, trying to be heard above the gale.

His father half turned and peered down at him.

"What are you doing up there?" Jake demanded angrily, his lips taut.

"The gutter's blocked. Had a waterfall right above the front door," the older man called in reply.

It wasn't the first time lately that Jake had found his father engaged in an activity that was far too strenuous for him. Now that the older man was feeling better, he was beginning to act as if he'd never had a heart attack. But today was the worst transgression so far. He shouldn't be on a ladder in *any* weather, let alone what seemed to be the beginning of a south-wester.

"I'll fix it later. Come down here right now!"

Even through the gray curtain of rain and sleet, Jake could see the sudden, defiant lift of the older man's chin. "I was only trying to help. And you're not in the navy anymore, you know. So stop giving orders."

A muscle in Jake's jaw clenched and he took a deep breath, struggling for control. "Will you *please* come down and go inside where it's warm? We're both getting soaked and I, for one, don't intend to get pneumonia."

With that he skirted the ladder and strode into the house, banging the door behind him.

By the time Howard followed a couple of minutes later, Jake had stripped off his wet coat and hung it to drip in the bathroom. His father glared at him as he entered, then stomped into the bathroom and threw his own drenched coat into the tub. When he returned, Jake was waiting for him, his fists planted on his hips, his lips compressed into a thin line.

"Okay, Dad. Let's talk about this. I can't be here to watch you all day. You know what you're supposed to do and what you're not supposed to do. This—" he gestured toward the front door "—is *not* on the list of 'do's,' and you know it."

Howard gave him a resentful glare. "I'm not one of your students, Jake. Or some enlisted man you can order around. I feel fine. I'm tired of being treated like an invalid. I can do what I want. You're not my keeper."

"Yes, I am. I promised Mom years ago—and Rob more recently—that I'd take care of you. And I intend to do just that."

"That's the only reason you let me come up here, isn't it? Because you promised your mother and Rob. Well, I don't need charity. I can do just fine on my own."

"Right," Jake replied sarcastically. "Like that little escapade I just witnessed outside. Suppose you'd fallen? Or put too much strain on your heart? You could be dead right now—or at the very least, in the hospital."

"Maybe I'd be more welcome there."

"That's a fine thing to say."

"Well, it's true. You haven't wanted me around in years," the older man declared bitterly.

"I invited you to live with me, didn't I?"

Howard gave a snort of disgust. "Sure. But only because you promised your mother and Rob. Maybe if you'd bothered to come around once in a while, Clara wouldn't have died— five years ago today, not that you'd remember. You broke her heart, Jake. Just like you broke Maggie's."

Jake drew in a sharp breath. His father's harsh words cut deeply, leaving a gaping wound in his soul. He struck back without even stopping to think, wanting to hurt as badly as he'd just been hurt. "You didn't exactly act like you wanted me around. It wouldn't have killed you to try and understand how I felt. Maybe if you hadn't been so stubborn, we could have worked this out years ago. Maybe it's as much your fault as mine that Mom's gone."

Howard's face went white with shock and anger. He gripped the back of the chair and the look he gave Jake was scathing. Yet there was pain in his eyes as well, raw and unmistakable. "That's a terrible thing to say," he rasped hoarsely.

Yes, it was, Jake admitted, silently cursing his loss of control, shocked at the words he'd just uttered. And more were poised for release, despite his efforts to hold them back. Words that, once spoken, could never be retracted. They'd said too much already, possibly irreparably damaging the fragile relationship they'd built these last few weeks. It was time to stop this tirade, before it got even more emotional and hateful. With one last look at his father, Jake brushed past him and retrieved his damp coat from the bathroom, shrugging into it as he headed toward the front door.

"Where are you going?" Howard demanded, his voice quivering with anger.

"Out. I need to cool down before I say anything else I'll end up regretting."

And then he stepped outside, slamming the door shut behind him.

The sleet continued unabated, but Jake hardly noticed as he drove mindlessly to a nearby spot that overlooked the turbulent, storm-tossed coast. He sat there for a long time as the elements battered his car much as his father's words had battered his soul. So many old hurts had surfaced, so many suppressed emotions had been released. But not in a healthy way. They'd ended up accusing each other of terrible things. All this time, while Jake thought their relationship was stabilizing, his father had been harboring a deep-seated anger against him, borne of blame and resentment. And, in many ways, Jake had felt the same toward the older man, he admitted. No wonder their ''progress'' had been so slow. Now it had not only come to a grinding halt, but regressed dramatically.

Jake sighed and raked his fingers helplessly through his hair as a wave of despair washed over him. His father clearly didn't enjoy living with him. Was only doing so under duress. But he couldn't go back to Rob's—not yet, anyway. Though Rob had finally connected with a firm that seemed interested in hiring him, his life was still in an uproar and there was a strong possibility he and his family would have to move. So what options did that leave for Howard?

Jake didn't have the answer to that question. And he probably wasn't going to come up with one in the next few hours, he thought with a weary, dispirited sigh. He might as well go home, as unappealing as that prospect was.

All in all, he decided, it had been one lousy day.

And it didn't get any better when he stepped inside the door and his glance fell on his father's suitcase. Now what was going on? He closed his eyes and drew in a long breath, then let it out slowly.

He could hear his father rattling pans in the kitchen, and slowly, with reluctance, he made his way in that direction, pausing at the doorway just in time to see his father emptying what appeared to be a pot of beef stew into the garbage disposal. The act seemed somehow symbolic of far more than dinner going down the drain, he thought, his gut twisting painfully.

"What's with the suitcase, Dad?" he asked, striving for an even tone.

"I'm going to visit Rob for a week. I called, and he said it was okay. There's a flight out of Bangor in the morning. I'll take a cab."

Jake sighed. "I'll drive you."

"That's not necessary," the older man replied stiffly.

"I'll drive you, Dad. Let's not argue about that, too."

Howard reacted to that statement with silence. And *silence* was the operative word during the drive to Bangor the next morning. The few comments Jake tried to make were promptly rebuffed, so he finally gave up. Only when Howard was preparing to board the plane did he get more than a grunt for an answer.

"When are you coming back, Dad?"

"I'll take a cab to the house."

"I'll pick you up. Just tell me the day and time. Or I'll call the airline and find out."

Howard gave him a withering look, but provided the information—with obvious reluctance.

"Have a good trip," Jake said.

Howard didn't reply, and as Jake watched him trudge down the ramp to the plane, he jammed his hands into his pockets in frustration. How would the two of them ever work out their differences? Or maybe the real question was whether they even could, he acknowledged with a disheartened sigh. He desperately wanted to make things work between them, but he was beginning to think this was one mission that was destined for failure.

Jake was oblivious to his surroundings as he drove back to Castine, his mind desperately seeking a solution to a situation that appeared to have none. Why the retirement home caught his eye he didn't know, but he eased his foot off the accelerator slightly and looked at it with a frown as he drove past. He'd seen it before, of course, but for the first time he examined it with a critical eye. It seemed to be a nice place. Well kept, with spacious grounds in an attractive setting. Maybe... But even as the thought crossed his mind, Jake pushed it aside. How could he even consider such a possibility when he'd promised his mother that he'd never send Howard to an ''old folks'' home, as she called them?

And yet...he'd also promised to take care of his father. Given the recent turn of events, he was beginning to doubt whether it was possible to keep both promises. His father clearly didn't want to live with him. And Jake couldn't be there all the time to take care of the older man, who was beginning to take chances with his health. Maybe, in the short term, a retirement home was the best solution. His father would have companionship, and better care than Jake could provide. They certainly wouldn't let him climb on ladders, for one thing. And it would only be temporary, until Rob was settled again. His father liked living with Rob. Rob liked having him. Ultimately Jake was sure Howard would move back in with his first-born. Until then, he might be a lot happier—and healthier—away from his younger son.

Yet the thought of packing the older man off turned Jake's stomach. Yes, things were bad between them. But surely there was a way to smooth out their relationship. There had to be. Only, he didn't have a clue what it was, not after last night. And he was reaching the point of desperation. They couldn't live as they had those first few weeks. The tension had been almost unbearable. That in itself was bad for his father's health. The retirement home wasn't a great solution, Jake acknowledged. But maybe his father would welcome the chance to get out from under Jake's roof. At the very least, Jake decided to check the place out. He didn't think it was the answer, but it couldn't hurt to consider all the options.

Maggie's gaze sought and came to rest on Jake's tall, distinguished form across the gallery, and she smiled. He was half turned away from her, engaged in conversation with a patron, looking incredibly handsome in a crisply starched white shirt and dark gray suit that sat well on his broad shoulders. It was the first time all evening that Maggie had been alone, and she savored the respite, heady with elation at the praise her work had received during the opening reception for her show, basking in this moment of glory. And yet...as she lovingly traced the contours of Jake's strong profile, she knew that her happiness tonight was magnified because he was here to share her moment of triumph. His presence made her joy complete.

"And you were worried about having this show."

Maggie turned at Philip's gently chiding voice and smiled. "You were right. I guess I was ready after all."

Philip glanced at Jake, then back at Maggie, and smiled. "For a lot of things, it seems. I take it you two have worked things out?"

She colored faintly and turned to gaze again at Jake, a whisper of a smile softening her lips. "We're getting there. We still have issues, but...I don't know. Somehow I sense we'll work them out."

Philip put his hand on Maggie's shoulder. "I'm happy for you, you know. About this—" he gestured with one hand around the gallery "—and about that." He nodded toward Jake. "You deserve all the happiness life has to offer, Maggie."

"Thank you, Philip," she said softly. "But I'm trying not to rush things. I want to be sensible about this."

Just then Jake turned and glanced around the room, his gaze restless and searching until it came to rest on Maggie. He gave her a slow, lazy smile that warmed her all the way from her toes to her nose, and she heard Philip chuckle.

"Maggie, honey, I know your intentions are good. But trust me. Jake is past the sensible stage. And forgive me for saying it, but so are you. In fact, I'm guessing that wedding bells will be in the air in the not-too-distant future."

Maggie blushed. She didn't even try to deny Philip's words. Because the truth was she felt the same.

Maggie's eyes were glowing as she set the Sunday paper down on the kitchen table. A review of her work—brief, but highly complimentary—had made the Boston paper! A wave of elation washed over her, and she was filled with a deep sense of satisfaction and accomplishment—and a compelling need to share the news with Jake—in person. He would be thrilled, too. She'd see him in church in two hours—but she couldn't wait!

With uncharacteristic impulsiveness, she tucked the paper carefully into a tote bag, added four of the large cinnamon rolls she'd baked last night and headed out the door. Maybe her impromptu visit would cheer Jake up, even without the news she was bearing. He hadn't shared many of the details about the latest falling-out with his father, sparing her the worry during this last week as she fretted about her opening, but she knew it was serious if Howard had actually gone down to Rob's. She hoped Jake would tell her more about it now that the opening had passed.

Maggie grinned at Jake's look of surprise half an hour later when he answered her ring. She'd never shown up uninvited before, and he was clearly taken aback—but just as clearly pleased.

"Maggie!" He drew her inside, pulling her into his arms as he kicked the door shut with his foot and buried his face in her hair. For a long moment he just held her, loving the feel of her soft, slim body wrapped in his arms. Less than five minutes ago he'd been wishing—praying—for just such a visit, and it seemed the Lord had heard his plea. The last week had been hell as he'd wrestled with the problem of what to do about his father, and he was running out of time. Howard was returning late this afternoon, and Jake still hadn't figured out how to deal with the situation. All he knew with absolute certainty was that they couldn't go on as they had before.

But now, with Maggie in his arms, her sweetness enveloping him, he somehow felt better.

Maggie snuggled closer against Jake's broad, solid chest. His embrace today spoke less of passion than of the need for comfort and solace, almost as if he was drawing strength from her mere physical presence. It was a much different sensation than the usual amorous nature of their touches, but oddly enough, Maggie found it as powerfully affecting in a different way. She remained motionless as he held her, his hands stroking the curve of her slender back.

When at last he drew away, he looped his arms loosely around her waist and smiled down at her.

"Hi." His eyes were warm and tender, his voice husky and intimate.

"Hi yourself," she replied softly, playing with a button on his shirt.

"I'm glad you're here."

"I sort of got that impression. Do you want to talk about it?"

"About what?"

"About why you're so glad to see me."

"You mean beyond the obvious reason?"

"Mmm-hmm."

"Actually, I'd rather talk about you. What's the occasion?"

"What do you mean?"

"Well, you've never shown up on my doorstep uninvited before. Not that you need to wait for an invitation, you understand. It's just a first. And I hope not a last."

She smiled and blushed. "I had some good news, and I wanted to share it with you."

"I could use some good news. Let's have it."

She reached into her tote bag and withdrew the Boston paper, already turned back to the right page, and handed it to him, her eyes glowing.

He tilted his head and smiled, loving the way her eyes lit up when she was happy. She was like a warm ray of sun, a balm on his troubled soul. He reached over and gently stroked her face, letting a long, lean finger trace its way from her temple to her chin, following the delicate curve of her jaw. Her eyes ignited at his touch, and he was tempted to take her in his arms again, to taste her sweet lips until all coherent thoughts were driven from his mind and he was lost in the wonder of her love.

But first he needed to focus on the paper, he told himself. If it was important enough to bring her over without an invitation, it deserved his full attention. So, reluctantly he transferred his gaze. As he scanned the complimentary article, his lips curved into a slow smile, and when at last he turned to her, his eyes held a special warmth.

"I would certainly call that an auspicious beginning, Maggie. I'm very proud of you," he said with quiet honesty. "And in case I haven't told you lately, you are one amazing and incredible woman—not to mention talented, intelligent and drop-dead gorgeous."

Maggie flushed with pleasure at his compliments. "That might be overstating it just a bit."

"Nope. I never exaggerate."

She laughed, so filled with joy that it simply came bubbling to the surface. All of the pieces of her life were finally falling into place. She'd raised the girls well and sent them on their way in the world. She'd taken a bold step and successfully launched a serious art career. And the only man who'd ever touched her heart had come back into her life and offered her his love. The long, dry years, often filled with drudgery, seemed suddenly a distant memory. She'd made it through the hard times, and now, at last, it seemed that the Lord was rewarding her for her diligence and hard work. Her heart felt lighter than it had in years, and her face was radiant as she looked up at Jake.

"I think you're pretty special, too, you know. In fact, now that we've formed a mutual admiration society, I would say a celebration is in order." She lifted the bag. "I brought some homemade cinnamon rolls."

"Now that's the best offer I've had all day," Jake declared with a grin. He draped an arm around her shoulders and guided her toward the kitchen. Maggie's enthusiasm and euphoric mood were catching, and he found himself feeling better—and more hopeful—by the minute. "I'll pour the coffee if you want to nuke those for a minute."

"Okay."

Maggie tore the foil off the cinnamon rolls, put three of them on a plate and set the timer on the microwave. "Jake, do you have some plastic wrap? I want to leave one of these for your dad."

"Sure. In the drawer, on the right. Boy, they smell great already!"

Maggie smiled and pulled out the drawer. "They're pretty hard to resist, if I do say so myself. My guests always…"

Maggie's voice faltered and her smile froze as the words *Water's Edge Retirement Community* screamed up at her from a brochure, Jake's name prominent on the mailing label. Her stomach clenched into a cold knot, and she gripped the edge of the counter as the world tilted strangely. All of her dreams, all of her hopes, suddenly seemed to dissolve like an ethereal vapor on a frosty morning.

Maggie wanted to shut the drawer again, pretend she'd never seen that brochure, but she knew she couldn't erase it from her memory so easily. Nor could she deny its implication. The man she loved, the man she had come to believe was honorable and could be counted on to remain steadfast in bad times, was reneging on his promise to his mother. He was throwing in the towel on his relationship with his father because things had gotten rough. Or at the very least *considering* throwing in the towel. And as far as she was concerned, that was bad enough. The future that had moments before looked so full of hope and promise now seemed bleak and empty.

"Your guests always what?" Jake prompted over his shoulder as he poured their coffee. When she didn't respond, he frowned and turned toward her.

Jake knew immediately that something was wrong. Very wrong. Her body was rigid, and she was gripping the edge of the counter so fiercely that her knuckles were white. Her face was mostly turned away from him, but what little he could see was colorless. His gut clenched in sudden alarm, and he moved toward her in three long strides, placing one arm around her shoulders.

"Maggie? What's wrong?" he asked urgently.

She looked up at him, and he was jolted by her eyes, dull and glazed with shock. Panic swept over him and he gripped her shoulders, his gaze locked on hers.

"Maggie, what is it? Tell me. Let me help."

As she stared at him, Jake was able to read beyond the shock in her eyes. There was pain and confusion and disillusionment in their depths as well. His frown deepened as he mechanically reached down to close the drawer that separated them. And that's when he saw the brochure.

With a sickening jolt, he came to the obvious conclusion. Maggie had finally given him her trust, had come to believe that he was man who kept his promises and could be counted on to stand fast no matter what the circumstance, and now she had found stark evidence to the contrary.

Silently Jake cursed his carelessness. He'd meant to put that brochure in his room, had barely looked at it when it arrived, feeling in his heart that it wasn't the answer to his dilemma. But Maggie wasn't going to believe him, not now, not considering the look of betrayal in her eyes. And he couldn't blame her. He'd made a mistake in a moment of weakness, and though he recognized it as such now, he knew that for her, the fact that he'd even *considered* such an option indicated that he held his promise as less than sacred.

She began to tremble, and Jake tried desperately to think of something, anything, to undo the damage. But no words came to mind. Instead he silently guided her to the table and gently forced her to sit down, then pulled up a chair beside her. Jake reached for her hand, and she looked at him dully as he laced his fingers through hers.

"Maggie, will you listen if I try to explain?"

"Is there an explanation?" Her voice was flat and lifeless.

"Yes. Although it's not one you'll want to hear, I suspect. But I'd like to tell you anyway. Will you listen?" he repeated.

When she didn't respond, Jake took a deep breath and spoke anyway. "You know that Dad and I have had a rough time of it from the beginning, Maggie. I've made no secret of that. But I was really starting to think that we'd turned a corner. I won't say things between us were completely comfortable, but we were getting along. Life was pleasant enough.

"Then, last Monday, everything just fell apart. I'd had a bad day at school, and I came home to find Dad up on a ladder in the middle of that sleet storm. I was a little too heavy-handed in my reaction, I guess, and Dad took offense. The next thing I knew we were accusing each other of some pretty terrible things. Including the death of my mother.''

Maggie gasped, and Jake nodded soberly. ''Yeah, it got that bad. On top of everything, it was five years to the day Mom died. Emotions were running pretty high on both sides. Suffice it to say, the situation was pretty tense by the time I walked out to cool off. When I got back, Dad's bags were packed. He left the next morning for Rob's.''

Jake paused and stared down unseeingly at the oak table. ''I don't know what made me request that information on the retirement home, Maggie. Desperation, I guess. I just felt that I couldn't keep my promise to Mom *and* make sure Dad was taken care of. And I think living with me is the last thing in the world he wants. He's unhappy here, and stressed, which isn't good for his health. I just didn't know what to do. I passed that retirement home on the way back from the airport, and figured it couldn't hurt to check it out. The brochure came yesterday. To be honest, it's not something I even want to consider. But I just don't know what's best for Dad anymore. Do you understand at all how I feel?''

Maggie tried. Desperately. But she was too numb to even think. ''At the moment, Jake, not very much is clear to me,'' she said shakily. ''But I know one thing. A promise is a promise. No one ever said life was easy. But we can't just walk away from our commitments. If you give your word, you keep it. Period. It's a matter of honor. And if people don't honor their promises, how can there ever be any trust?''

Jake flinched. Maggie's words had been said without rancor, but they hit home nonetheless. And she was right. He'd made a mistake—and it was apparent that it was going to cost him dearly. Maybe even the woman he loved.

She stood up then, and Jake was instantly on his feet, as well. ''Don't go yet, Maggie. Please.''

''I need to be alone for a while, Jake.''

''Will you call me later?''

There was a pause, and when she looked at him her eyes were guarded and distant. ''I don't know.''

Jake felt like someone had just delivered a well-placed blow to his abdomen. He couldn't let the woman he loved walk out of his life. But he didn't know how to stop her.

She gathered up her purse and bag, and he followed her to the door, futilely searching for something to say that would make her reconsider. When she turned on the threshold and looked at him, her eyes were filled with anguish and brimming with tears. His stomach tightened into a painful knot, and he wanted to reach out to her, gather her in his arms, tell her that he loved her and would never do anything to hurt her. But he doubted whether she would believe him. Why should she? He'd hurt her once before. And now he'd done it again. What was that old saying? Fool Me Once, Shame On You; Fool Me Twice, Shame On Me. And Maggie was no fool. Hurt and betrayed a second time, he was afraid she would simply choose to cut her losses and go on alone. She was strong enough to do it. But he wasn't strong enough to go on without her. He needed her. Desperately. For the rest of his life.

"Goodbye, Jake." Her voice was quiet, and though a tremor ran through it, he heard the finality in the words.

And as he watched helplessly while she turned and walked out into the cold rain, the rest of his life suddenly loomed emptily before him.

Chapter Thirteen

Jake turned into the church parking lot and pulled into a vacant spot by the front door.

"What are we doing here?" Howard demanded, giving his son a suspicious look.

Jake shut off the engine and angled himself toward his father, resting his arm on the back of the seat. Ever since the fiasco with Maggie this morning, he'd been praying for guidance about how to mend the rift with his father. But no one upstairs seemed to be listening. And then suddenly, on the drive to Bangor, a plan had formed in his mind. He wasn't sure it would work. In fact, he figured the odds were fifty-fifty at best. But he knew in his heart that this was the only way he and his father might have a chance at a true reconciliation. And so he had to try. He took a deep, calming breath and gazed steadily at the older man.

"I'd like to talk with you, Dad. On neutral ground. In a place where we can't shout, and where maybe some greater power will guide our conversation. I couldn't think of a better spot than here, in the house of the Lord."

His father's eyes were guarded. "What do you want to talk about?"

"Us."

Howard shifted uncomfortably and turned away, staring straight ahead. "Seems like we've done enough talking already. Maybe too much."

"Too much of the kind you're referring to," Jake agreed.

"I have something different in mind. Will you give me a few minutes?"

While Howard considered the request, Jake waited quietly, his physical stillness giving away none of his inner turmoil. Only when his father grunted his assent did he realize he'd been holding his breath, and he let it out in a long, relieved sigh.

They didn't speak again until they were seated in a back row in the quiet, dim church. It was peaceful there, and conducive to the kind of talk Jake had in mind. He just prayed that his father would be receptive.

Jake hadn't really prepared the speech he was about to give. There hadn't been time. So he silently asked the Lord to help him find the right words to express what was in his heart.

"I guess it's no secret that things have been rough between us for a long time, Dad," he began slowly, a frown creasing his brow. "Twelve years, to be exact. You didn't approve of my decision to leave Maggie and join the navy, and pretty much told me to my face that I was being selfish and irresponsible. I didn't want to hear that then. It hurt too much. The truth often does."

His father turned sharply to look at him, his face registering surprise.

Jake smiled wryly. "I guess you never expected me to admit that you were right, did you? There's stubborn blood in this family, you know. And a lot of pride. Too much, sometimes. I think that's what got us into trouble through the years. I was too stubborn and proud to admit I was wrong, even though in my heart I knew it was true. Then, to make things worse, the man I had always loved and admired, who I never wanted to disappoint, had rejected me. So...I rejected him.

"It wasn't a rational decision, Dad. It was reactive, a way to protect my heart from the pain of knowing that I had disappointed you and hurt Maggie. After that, we just seemed to grow further and further apart. It's not something I ever wanted. The truth is, I missed you all these years. I missed your humor and your kindness and your guidance. And I missed your love."

He reached over and gripped the older man's hand, the hand that more than thirty-five years before had been extended to him in encouragement as he took his first few struggling steps. Jake was breaking new ground today, too, taking new, faltering steps in their relationship, and he was as much afraid of falling now as he probably had been then.

"Dad, I'm sorry for all the pain I've caused you through the years. I'm sorry I wasn't there for Mom—and you—when you needed me most. I want to try and make things right, but I need your help. That's what I'm asking for today. I've been on my own for twelve years now, and one of the things I discovered is that I need you now as much as I ever did. Maybe more. Please give me another chance."

Jake thought he saw the glint of moisture in the older man's eyes before he averted his glance, but he couldn't be sure. *Please, Lord, if ever you listened to a prodigal son, hear my voice today,* he prayed fervently. *I want Dad back in my life— not to make things right with Maggie, but because it's the right thing to do. For Dad and me.*

Several long moments of silence passed, and Jake saw this father's Adam's apple bob. When Howard at last turned back to his son, he seemed less stiff, less aloof than he had at any time since coming to Maine.

"I know your mother would have wanted this, Jake," he said, his voice catching. "It was one of the last things she prayed for before she died. Fact is...I always wanted it, too. But it was like you said, we sort of took our positions and just dug in. Neither of us was willing to budge. Can't say it did either of us any good. And it sure did make your mother sad. She called me a stubborn fool more than once, told me you'd come back in a flash if I gave you half a chance. Guess she was right after all. Clara had a way of knowing about those things. I should have listened to her. But that West pride got in the way, I expect. Couldn't bring myself to admit that maybe I was a little too hard on you. Not that I agreed with what you did. Still don't. But it was a lot to take on at such a young age. Looking back, I can understand how it must

have been pretty overwhelming. I guess Maggie can, too, seeing as how you two are getting along so well these days.''

Jake didn't correct him. The situation with Maggie was too
fresh, too raw, to even discuss. He would find a way to deal
with it later. He had to. His future depended on it. But at the
moment, he had another relationship to mend.

''Does that mean you're willing to make a fresh start?''

Howard nodded slowly, his face thoughtful. ''I expect we'll
still have our differences, though,'' he warned.

Jake smiled wryly. ''I'm sure we will. The key is to agree
up front that we'll work them out instead of building walls.
We just need to keep the lines of communication open, just
like you did with Rob all those years ago.''

Howard smiled, and the bleakness that had earlier been in
his eyes was replaced by a new warmth. ''Even if it takes hot
chocolate and sandwiches in the woods?''

Jake grinned. ''*Especially* if it takes that. Maggie's con-
verted me to hot chocolate. I even prefer it over a gin and
tonic.''

''That girl always was a good influence on you,'' Howard
declared with a smile. ''I'm glad she's back in your life.''

A shadow crossed Jake's eyes, but he kept his smile firmly
in place. ''So am I, Dad. But we have run into a bit of a
roadblock,'' he admitted. He couldn't say much more, not
without revealing *why* they were having a problem, and there
was no need to tell his father about the retirement home. That
idea was already history, had been almost from the moment
he'd sent for the brochure.

''Nothing serious, I hope,'' his father said in concern.

''We'll work it out,'' Jake replied with more confidence
than he felt. But he had to think positively. Because he
couldn't face the alternative. ''Are you ready to go home?''
he inquired, changing the subject before his father probed
more deeply.

Howard nodded. ''I don't want to overstay our welcome
here in the Lord's house. I expect He has more important
problems to deal with than ours.''

"I expect He does," Jake agreed as he stood up. "But I'm grateful He helped us through this one."

Now if only He would do the same for him and Maggie.

Maggie paced back and forth in the living room, agitated and unsettled. This time, when Jake called, he hadn't let her put him off as he had on the numerous other occasions he'd phoned. Tonight he'd simply asked if she would be home and announced he was coming over.

She paused in front of the fireplace and gazed down into the flickering flames, a troubled frown creasing her brow. Since the day she'd walked out of Jake's house almost three weeks ago, her emotions had been on a roller coaster. They'd run the gamut from devastation to bleakness to loneliness to grief to anger. She'd berated herself over and over again for allowing her trust to be betrayed a second time—and by the *same* man! How big of a fool could she be?

She'd asked herself repeatedly if she had overreacted. And always the answer came back the same. No. Jake had made a sacred promise to his mother, literally as she was dying, and until recently he had gone to admirable lengths to keep it. Everything he'd done and said in the months he'd been here had seemed to indicate he was a changed man, a man who understood the meaning of duty and honor and responsibility.

Maggie understood Jake's frustration and sense of helplessness over his relationship with his father. She'd had similar moments during the girls' growing-up years, when they'd clashed and said things they'd later regretted. It happened. But you didn't deal with it by turning your back on the problem, by simply shoving it out of sight. You talked about it. You worked things through. You made amends and went on. You didn't walk out.

Yet that's exactly what Jake had contemplated doing when things got rough. The very fact that he'd even *considered* breaking his promise scared Maggie to death. Because if he'd done that with Howard when things got dicey, how did she know he wouldn't do it with her?

And that was one fear she couldn't handle. Life was filled

with uncertainties. She knew that. But if she ever married, she wanted to do so secure in the knowledge that the sacred vows of "for better, for worse" would be honored by the man to whom she'd given her heart. And she was no longer sure Jake was that man.

The doorbell interrupted her thoughts, and she jerked convulsively, one hand involuntarily going to her throat. She didn't feel ready to face Jake. Then again, she doubted she ever would. So they might as well get this over with, she thought resignedly.

When she reached the front door, she took a slow, deep breath, then pulled it open.

For a long, silent moment, Jake simply looked at her, his breath making frosty clouds in the still, cold air. He was wearing a suede, sheepskin-lined jacket over dark brown corduroy slacks, and his hands were shoved deep into the pockets. The shadowy light on the porch highlighted the haggard planes of his face, and Maggie suspected he'd suffered as many sleepless nights as she had.

"Hello, Maggie."

She moved aside to let him enter. "Hello, Jake."

He stepped in and shrugged out of his jacket, watching as she silently hung it on a hook on the wall. Except for Sunday services, he'd seen nothing of her since the day she walked out of his house. The faint bluish shadows under her eyes, the subtle lines of tension around her mouth, were mute evidence of the strain she'd been under, and his gut clenched painfully. It seemed all he ever brought this woman he loved was pain and uncertainty, when what he really wanted to give her was joy and peace.

Of all the failures in his life, his relationship with Maggie was the one that affected him most deeply. He wanted to take her in his arms right now, to hold her until she knew beyond the shadow of a doubt that he loved her with every fiber of his being. But that was not the way to convince her. He had another plan in mind. Not one he particularly liked, but at least he felt it had a chance to succeed.

She turned back to him then, her eyes guarded and distant. "Let's go into the living room. I have a fire going."

She chose a chair set slightly apart from the others, and Jake sat down on the couch. He leaned forward intensely, his forearms resting on his thighs, his hands clasped.

"Thank you for seeing me, Maggie."

"I suppose we had to talk sooner or later."

"Well, it was tonight or not for several months. Dad and I are going to Rob's tomorrow for Christmas. We won't be back until after you leave for Europe."

That jolted her, and Maggie's eyes widened in surprise. "When did you decide to do that?"

"Last week. Rob invited us, and Dad wanted to go. It will be a good chance for all of us to have some family time together. It's not the way I anticipated spending Christmas, but given the circumstances, I thought it might be for the best."

Maggie's throat constricted, and the ache in her heart intensified as she turned to gaze unseeingly into the fire. She blinked to hold back the tears that suddenly welled in her eyes, berating herself for her lack of control, and took a deep breath before she spoke.

"You're probably right." How she managed such a calm, controlled tone when her insides were in turmoil she never knew.

Jake nodded wearily. "But I couldn't leave with things so unresolved between us." He frowned and raked his fingers through his hair, then restlessly stood and moved beside the fire, gripping the mantle with one hand as he stared down into the flickering flames. When at last he turned to her, his eyes were troubled. "The fact is, Maggie, the whole retirement home idea was a bust, from start to finish. I'm not even sure why I sent for that brochure, except that I was desperate. I wanted to keep my promise to my mother, but I also knew Dad was unhappy, which wasn't good for his health. I was between the proverbial rock and a hard place.

"I guess what it comes down to is this—I'm human. I make mistakes. And that was a big one. But I never pursued it beyond sending for that brochure. Because I realized, even before you walked out, that I had to try harder to make things work with Dad. The two of us had been living under the same roof for months, but we'd never really connected, never really opened up and been honest with each other, never dealt directly with the issues that divided us. And so I decided to tackle them head-on when he got back.''

He paused and dropped down on the ottoman in front of her, his eyes so close that she could see the gold flecks in their depths. As well as the sincerity.

"It worked, Maggie. The last three weeks have been the best we've had in twelve years. We admitted to each other where we'd fallen short and agreed to try our best to make things work. And we are. I know we'll still have some rough times. I think that's the nature of any human relationship. But we'll get through them. Because we both want it to work.''

He reached for her hand then, and Maggie's breath caught in her throat. It took only this simple touch to reawaken all the longing she'd so ruthlessly crushed since she'd walked out of his house.

"The fact is, Maggie, I feel the same about us. I have almost since the day I took shelter here from the mist. I never realized how lonely the last twelve years had been until then. I know you're disappointed and disillusioned right now. I know you think I betrayed your trust. But I do honor my commitments. I'm a different man in a lot of ways than the twenty-five-year-old who walked out on you twelve years ago. What I did then was wrong, and I make no excuses. All I can do is give you my word that it will never happen again. The retirement home fiasco notwithstanding, I've learned a lot about duty and honor and responsibility in these last dozen years. I can't promise that I won't make mistakes. But I can promise you that in the end I'll always do the right thing. Because I love you with all my heart. And I always will.''

The tears in Maggie's eyes were close to spilling over. With every fiber of her being she wanted to believe him. But hurt had made her cautious. And so had the need for self-preservation.

Jake watched the play of emotions across Maggie's face. He saw the yearning and the love in her eyes, but also the uncertainty and fear. It was what he expected. What he had come prepared to address. Slowly he reached into the pocket of his slacks and withdrew a small, square box, then flipped it open to reveal a sparkling solitaire.

Maggie's eyes grew wide as she gazed at the dazzling ring. "Isn't that…that's the ring…" Her voice trailed off.

"It's the same ring, Maggie. I kept it all these years. I never knew why—until I came to Maine and found you again."

Maggie's voice was thick with unshed tears, and a sob caught in her throat when she spoke. "Jake, I…I don't know what to…"

He reached over and placed a gentle fingertip against her lips. "I'm asking you to marry me, Maggie. But I'm not asking you for an answer right now. In fact, I don't want one tonight. Because whatever you decide, I want you to be absolutely sure. No second thoughts, no regrets. All I'm asking is that you take the ring with you to Europe, as a reminder of my love. Think about my proposal. Give yourself time. And then, when you get back, we'll talk about it again."

Maggie's mind was whirling. This was the Christmas present she'd anticipated with such joy at Thanksgiving. Now… now it left her confused and uncertain—yet filled with a sudden, buoyant hope. But there was still a major unresolved issue between them that had nothing to do with their recent falling-out.

"Jake…there's still something we haven't dealt with," she reminded him in a choked voice. "The family issue. I haven't changed my mind on that."

He looked at her steadily. "But I have. I've given it a lot of thought, Maggie. And bottom line, while I'd like to have children, if it comes down to a choice between you and a family, there's no contest. I love you, and that's enough for me. Anything else would be a bonus. Whatever you decide is fine with me."

Maggie felt her throat tighten at the love and tenderness— and absolute certainty—reflected in Jake's eyes.

"You seem awfully sure."

"That's because I am. It's not so hard to make compromises when you love someone as much as I love you. Besides, I don't come without strings, either."

She frowned. "What do you mean?"

"Think about it, Maggie. I'll bring an aging parent to this union. A lot of women wouldn't want to take that on. You faced marriage once before saddled with a pretty overwhelming responsibility. In a way, you will again."

Maggie smiled and shook her head. "Jake, I love Pop. I don't consider him a burden in any way. In fact, before...well, before we had this problem, I was thinking down the road that maybe if things...well...progressed between us, we might want to live here. And we could turn the little guest cottage into a place for your dad. That way he'd be close by, but still have a sense of independence."

Jake's heart overflowed with love for this incredible woman who was so giving, who always thought of others. Dear Lord, how was he going to survive the next three months without her? And he couldn't even bring himself to consider beyond that if, in the end, she rejected his proposal.

"You are one special woman, Maggie Fitzgerald," he declared huskily. He was tempted to demonstrate the depth of his feelings in a nonverbal way, but he restrained himself—with great effort. Calling on every ounce of his willpower, he stood up, then reached down and pulled her to her feet. For a long moment they simply gazed into each other's eyes, both wanting more, both trying desperately to remain in control.

"Will you take the ring, Maggie?" Jake finally asked, his voice rough with emotion. "Not as a commitment—but as a reminder of my love?"

She nodded. "Yes." Her voice was a mere whisper, and she clutched the small velvet box tightly to her breast. "You know, I...I almost wish I wasn't going now," she admitted tremulously.

Jake shook his head firmly. "Don't feel that way. Savor every minute of this experience. You owe that to yourself after all these years. And I'll be here when you get back."

"I'll...I'll miss you, Jake."

He reached for her then, groaning softly as he pulled her fiercely against him and buried his face in her hair. How could he leave without at least one brief kiss to sustain him during the long months to come? That wasn't too much to ask, was it?

He backed up slightly and gazed down into Maggie's eyes. They were filled with yearning, and his own deepened with passion. No, it wasn't too much. They both wanted this. Needed it. Silently he let one hand travel around her neck, beneath her hair, to cup the back of her head. And then he bent down and gently, tenderly claimed her sweet lips.

Maggie responded willingly, knowing that this moment would be a memory to take with her, to hold in her heart, during the long, solitary months ahead. His lips, warm and lingering, moved over hers, seeking, tasting, reigniting the flames of desire that had smoldered in her heart these last few weeks. But all too soon, with evident reluctance, he drew back. The smile he gave her seemed forced, and his voice sounded strained.

"I'd better go."

Several more moments passed before he released her, however, and when he did it was with obvious effort. She followed him to the hall, watched silently as he shrugged into his coat, walked beside him to the door. He turned there, reaching out once more to touch her face, his gaze locked on hers.

"Bon voyage, Maggie. Think of me."

And then he was gone.

Maggie knew that Jake was doing the right thing, the noble thing, giving her time to sort through her feelings and be sure of her decision. But for just a moment, she was tempted to throw caution to the wind, fling open the door and run impulsively into his arms. It was what her heart told her to do. But her heart had led her astray before, she reminded herself. And so, with a decisive click she locked the door and turned back to the living room. She would take the time he'd offered her to think things through. It was the wise thing to do.

But it wouldn't be easy.

Chapter Fourteen

Jake smiled as he read Maggie's account of her adventures at the Trevi Fountain in Rome. He wasn't surprised that several locals had tried to pick her up. She might be nearing forty, but she was still one gorgeous woman.

"Good news from Maggie?" his father inquired, setting a mug in front of Jake. They had gotten into the habit of sharing hot chocolate—and some conversation—each evening before going to bed.

Jake chuckled. "Seems the Italians are a good judge of beauty after all."

Howard raised his eyebrows. "Oh? Are they asking her for dates?"

Jake smiled. He doubted that "dates" were what they were after, but he let it pass. "Mmm-hmm. But she's holding her own. Sounds like she's having a wonderful time. The art classes are going well, and she says she's made some great strides with her painting."

"Glad to hear it. But I'll sure be glad when she comes back. Seems kind of quiet around here without her."

Jake's smile faded. "Yeah."

"You never said much the night you went to say goodbye to her, Jake," Howard said carefully. "I don't want to pry, but...did you two work things out?"

Jake glanced down into his half-empty mug and sighed. "I don't know, Dad. But...well, I guess there's no reason to keep it a secret. I asked her to marry me."

Howard's eyes widened in surprise. "You did? What did she say?"

"I didn't ask for an answer. All I asked her to do was think about it while she was gone, and let me know when she got back."

Howard drained his cup and rose thoughtfully. He paused by Jake's chair and placed a hand on the younger man's shoulders. "Maggie will come around, son. You'll see. You're a good man, and she'll realize that in time."

Jake stared after his father, his throat tightening with emotion. The future of his relationship with Maggie might still be uncertain, but at least he and his father had reconnected. His father had just touched him with affection for the first time in years. And he'd called him "a good man." That small gesture, those few words, meant more to Jake than all of his other accomplishments combined.

Now if only Maggie would come to the same conclusion.

Maggie tipped her face back to the sun and sighed contentedly as Parisian street life bustled around her. Her fabulous European adventure was drawing to a close, but it had been everything she'd hoped. She felt steeped in great art, had soaked it up until her soul was satiated. And she'd learned so much! The classes had been tremendous, and she'd produced some of her best work on this trip, shipping it home to Philip as she completed it. His enthusiastic response had reaffirmed her opinion that she'd made great strides.

With only two weeks left in her sojourn, her thoughts were now beginning to turn to home, and she reached up to finger the ring that hung on a slender gold chain around her neck. Soon she would have to make her decision. Maggie knew, with absolute certainty, that she loved Jake. She also knew, with equal certainty, that she was afraid. So the question came down to this: Was she willing to take the risk that love entailed? To trust her heart completely to this man who had walked out on her once before? A man who she had come to believe was now capable of true commitment—but whose unexpected lapse had shaken her trust?

Maggie knew what the twins thought. They'd summed it up in three pithy words. *Go for it.* Philip had said much the same thing. And Maggie felt in her heart they were right. She knew that nothing good came without risk. Yet she was still afraid. She'd prayed daily for guidance, asked for a sign, for direction, but so far the Lord hadn't responded to her plea.

Maggie sighed and reached for the mail she'd just picked up. There was a letter from Jake, she noted, her lips curving up into a smile. He wrote practically every other day. And one from Pop, she saw with surprise. Those would be letters to savor. So she put them aside and opened the large brown envelope from Philip, who sorted through her mail at home and passed on things that looked important. She peered inside and withdrew a small package with an unfamiliar New York return address. Curiously she tore off the brown wrapping to find a little box cocooned inside a letter. Quickly she scanned the single sheet of paper.

Dear Ms. Fitzgerald,
Millicent Trent gave this to me and asked that I send it to you. I am sorry to inform you that she passed away last week after a brief illness. But she did so at peace with the Lord, and with joy. She said she wanted you to have this because you would understand, and that she hoped your story turns out happier than hers. She also asked me to remind you that very few people get a second chance, and to consider carefully before you let yours slip away. I confess I don't understand the message, but Millicent said you would. May the Lord keep you in His care.

The letter was signed by a Reverend Thomas Wilson.

Maggie's eyes filled with tears as she removed the lid from the small box and gazed down at the two-part heart pendant nestled inside. She was deeply touched by Millicent's gift, for she knew that of all the woman's possessions, this was the one that meant the most to her. Perhaps in death she would at last find the reconciliation that had eluded her in life, Maggie thought wistfully, as she silently asked the Lord to watch over her friend.

Wiping a hand across her eyes, Maggie reached next for Pop's letter. It was brief, and written very much in character.

Hi, Maggie.
I got your address from Jake. I hope you're having fun. We're not. Don't get me wrong. Things are good between Jake and me. Real good. Jake turned out fine after all, and I'm proud to have him for a son. But he's been moping around the house like a lovesick puppy, and it's driving me crazy. So please come home soon and put him out of his misery. He misses you a lot. So do I.

Maggie smiled through her tears. Obviously Pop and Jake were getting along fine. Jake had told her he'd make it work, and he had. There was an undertone of affection in Pop's letter that conveyed even more clearly than the words that the two of them were back on track.

And then she settled back in her chair and opened Jake's letter. His notes were typically chatty and warm as he filled her in on his daily life, making her feel that she was sitting next to him on the couch while he shared his day's adventures. But it was always the opening and closing that she reread several times. He never failed to remind her how much he missed her or that he was counting the days until her return. Though he never pressed for an answer to his proposal, she could sense hope—and anxiety—in every line. The closing of today's letter especially tugged at her heart.

The days are long, Maggie, and without the sound of your voice and your sparkling eyes, they seem empty. The nights are even worse. I find sleep more and more elusive as I anticipate your return. I hope that you're faring better than I am on that score. And then again, maybe I don't. In my heart, I hope you miss me as desperately as I miss you. I don't know what hell holds for those who sin, but I feel that in the agony of uncertainty

I've endured during these last few weeks I have somehow made reparation for at least some of my transgres-
sions. I love you, Maggie. More with each day that
passes. I look forward to the moment I can tell you that
again face-to-face. Until then, know that thoughts of you
fill my days—and nights.

Maggie's eyes grew misty again, and she drew in a long,
unsteady breath. This was the most direct Jake had been about
his feelings. Until now his letters had been mostly light-
hearted, written to make her smile, not cry. But now he was
baring his soul, letting her know just how much her answer
meant to him. It was a courageous thing to do, giving someone
the power to hurt you that way. But it was honest. And from
the heart. And it touched her deeply.

Maggie pressed his letter to her breast as she extracted Millicent's pendant from the tiny box and cradled it in her hand.
She thought about the gift of love Jake was offering her. And
she thought about Millicent's sad story of love thrown away.
She thought also about all that Jake had done in the last few
months to prove his steadfastness and his ability to honor a
promise. How he had diligently cared for his father and pains-
takingly rebuilt that relationship. How he came to her aid
when she was ill. How he stayed by her side at the hospital,
and was there for her to lean on during the twins' emotional
send-off to college. Since coming back into her life, he had
never once failed to be there when she needed him.

And suddenly the image of the painting she was just now
completing came to mind. With a startling flash of insight,
she realized that while she had been asking the Lord for a
sign to help her make her decision, it had literally been in
front of her for weeks. For she now knew that she had made
her decision long ago, in the hills above Florence. She'd just
been too afraid to admit it. But today's letters had brought
everything sharply into focus and banished her fear.

With a sudden, joyful lightening of her heart, Maggie gathered up her letters and headed back to her room.

* * *

Jake shoved his hands into his pockets and drew a long, unsteady breath. It had been three months since he'd said goodbye to Maggie. Three eternal, lonely months. She'd written regularly, but letters didn't ease the ache in his heart, nor did they fill his days with joy and laughter and his nights with tenderness and love.

He sighed and reached up to loosen his tie as he gazed out into the night. Nothing seemed right without Maggie. He needed her. The thought that she might ultimately reject his proposal had plagued him incessantly, etched faint lines of worry at the corners of his eyes. And yet he knew he had done the right thing. He'd given her the time she needed to be sure. Because he didn't want her to commit to him unless she felt the same absolute certainty, trust and deep, abiding love for him that he felt for her.

Jake heard a door open and he turned slowly, his gaze softening into a smile as Maggie entered. She always looked beautiful to him, but never more so than right now, as she walked toward him resplendent in her wedding finery. He held her at arm's length for a moment when she joined him, letting his gaze move over her slowly and lingeringly, memorizing every nuance of her appearance as she stood before him, more dazzling in her radiance than the illuminated Eiffel Tower visible behind her through the French doors on the balcony.

Her hair was drawn back on one side with a cluster of sweetheart roses and baby's breath, a miniature reflection of the bouquet she'd carried as they were married just hours before. Her tea-length white silk gown, subtly patterned to shimmer in the light, was simply but elegantly cut, with slightly puffed sleeves and a sweetheart neckline. Around her neck she wore Millicent's heart pendant, the two halves seamlessly joined by the hands of a master jeweler. Jake would never forget the expression of joy and certainty on her face as they'd exchanged their vows in the tiny chapel she'd reserved. Illuminated only by the mosaic of late-afternoon light as it filtered through the intricate stained-glass windows, with the fragrance of roses sweetly perfuming the air, it had been the perfect, intimate spot for them to exchange the vows that had been so long delayed.

"You look breathtaking," Jake said huskily, the warmth in his eyes making her tremble with joy—and anticipation.

She smiled, and a becoming blush rose in her cheeks. "Actually, I feel pretty breath*less*," she admitted.

He chuckled. "It has been a bit of a whirlwind, hasn't it?" Since her phone call a week ago, life had moved into high gear. Thank heaven her call had coincided with Spring Break! But even if it hadn't, nothing could have kept him from her side.

"Everything happened so fast that I can hardly believe it's real."

"You're not sorry, are you?" he asked worriedly. "Would you rather we had waited, been married at home?"

She smiled and shook her head. "No. We waited long enough. And once I decided, I was determined to have that Paris honeymoon after all."

His eyes deepened with passion, and he reached for her. But when she held back, he looked down at her questioningly.

"Jake, before we...we...well, I have something I'd like to give you first," she stammered.

He smiled indulgently. "Since I've already waited years for this moment, I suppose I can hold out a few more minutes."

"I'll be right back," she promised, extricating herself gently from his arms. She disappeared into the bedroom of their suite, and returned a moment later with a large package wrapped in silver paper. As she held it out to him, she noticed that he'd placed two small packages with white bows on the coffee table.

"Looks like we both had the same idea," he commented with a smile.

"I didn't expect a present, Jake. Not on such short notice," she protested.

"I've had these for a long time, Maggie," he told her quietly. "They were just waiting for this moment."

He sat on the couch and drew Maggie down beside him,

then tore off the shiny paper of his package to reveal an impressionistic painting of a man, woman and small child on a hillside picnic, visible only from the back, surrounded by a golden light. The man and woman were seated, and he had his arm around the child. He was pointing into the distance, and the woman's hand rested on the man's shoulder as she leaned close to him. A feeling of intrinsic love and serenity and unity pervaded the painting, making the viewer yearn to be part of the idyllic family scene.

Jake examined the exquisite painting silently, then drew a deep breath as he turned to his wife and shook his head in awe. "This is wonderful, Maggie!" he said in a hushed voice. "All of your work is excellent, but...well, this stands apart. You always paint from the heart, but this...it captures something, some essence, I've never seen before in your work."

"It comes even more from the heart than you realize, Jake," she told him softly.

He looked at her curiously. "What do you mean?"

"I thought a lot about us while I've been here. I knew from the beginning that I loved you. That was never a question. But I was so afraid of being hurt again. I just couldn't decide what to do. I asked the Lord for guidance, but I never seemed to get an answer.

"And then last week I was sitting at a sidewalk café, and I thought about this painting, which I started in Florence. Suddenly I realized I'd made my decision—about a couple of things—a long time ago."

She drew a deep breath and looked at him, her gaze steady and certain. "That's us, Jake. You and me...and our child. I never even realized it until a few days ago. My heart's known for weeks what I wanted to do. It just took a little longer for the message to reach my mind."

Carefully Jake set the painting down, then he reached for her and pulled her close.

"Oh, Maggie." His voice broke, and he buried his face in her hair, holding her tightly. "Are you sure? You're not doing this just because you know I want it?"

"Partly," she admitted, her voice muffled against his chest.

"But I'm doing it for me, too. I want to raise our child—together—if the Lord chooses to bless us with one. I want part of us, what we have together, to live on. And I want to share our love with a child."

He drew a deep, shuddering breath, and when he pulled back, the tenderness, love and gratitude reflected on his face brought a lump to her throat.

"I love you, Maggie."

"I love you, too. With all my heart." Her own voice broke on the last word, and he reached over to frame her face with this strong hands, his thumbs gentle as they stroked her damp cheeks.

"Now it's your turn." He retrieved the two small packages, handing her the smaller one first.

Maggie tore off the wrapping and lifted the lid of the small box to reveal an antique, gold-filigreed locket. She flipped it open to find two tiny photos—one of she and Jake taken when they were about nine and ten, and one of them taken by the twins on her last birthday. Those two photos seemed to re-affirm what her heart had long known—that their lives had always been destined to join.

"That was Mom's locket," Jake told her. "I found it when I was cleaning out the house for Dad. Her mother gave it to her when she turned twenty, and it was always one of her most treasured possessions. I know she'd want you to have it. And so do I."

"Oh, Jake! It's lovely! Thank you."

He handed her the other package and waited silently as she tore off the wrapping, raised the lid and carefully folded back the tissue paper. With unsteady hands she withdrew a small, framed document, and her breath caught in her throat as she was immediately transported back to another time and place. At the top, in careful lettering, were the words *Official Document.* Below that it read, "I, Jake West, and I, Maggie Fitzgerald, promise to always be friends forever and ever, no matter what happens." It was dated twenty-eight years before, and they'd each signed it in their childish scrawls. Their mothers had signed also, as witnesses.

"I'd forgotten all about this," she whispered.

"I found it in my mother's fireproof 'treasure box' the same day I found the locket," Jake said quietly. "I meant those words then, Maggie. And I mean them now."

Maggie could no longer hold back her tears. They streamed down her cheeks unchecked as she stared down at the yellowed document in her hands. She thought about the gifts they had just exchanged—the locket that had once belonged to Jake's mother, this sentimental document, her painting. None of them had much, if any, monetary value. But they were worth far more than gold to her, for they came from the heart and were born of love. A cherished line from Matthew came suddenly to mind—"For where thy treasure is, there also will thy heart be."

Maggie looked up at Jake, and he reached over to gently brush her tears away.

"No more tears, Maggie. There've been enough of those in this relationship." He reached down and drew her to her feet, guiding her to the French doors that looked out onto the lights of Paris, the illuminated Eiffel Tower rising majestically into the night sky.

"Remember how we used to talk about Paris? How we thought it was so romantic, and how we dreamed of spending our honeymoon here?" he asked softly.

She nodded, a smile of gentle remembrance touching her lips. "Mmm-hmm."

He turned to face her, his hands resting gently at her waist. She looked up at him, and the intensity—and fire—in his eyes made her breathless. "Well, our honeymoon might have been a little delayed. But I promise you this, my love. I'll spend the rest of my life making up for lost time. Starting right now."

Then he took her hand and drew her back inside, closing the door on the lights of Paris before he pulled her into his waiting arms. And as his lips claimed hers, in a kiss filled with promise and passion, Maggie said a silent prayer of thanks. After all these years, she had at last come home to the man she loved. And it was where she belonged. For always.

Epilogue

Two and a half years later

"Allison, will you run down to the cottage and tell Pop dinner's almost ready?"

"Sure." Allison pulled off a piece of the turkey that stood waiting to be carried to the table and popped it into her mouth. "Mmm. Fantastic! Sure beats the food in the dorms," she declared with a grin.

"Well, you'll only have to put up with the food for one more semester," Maggie reminded her with a smile. "I still can't believe you two are graduating in less than six months!"

"We can't, either," Abby chimed in. "Watch out, world, here we come!"

Maggie laughed. "Amen to that!"

Jake ambled into the kitchen, sniffed appreciatively and headed straight for the turkey. "That smells great!" he pronounced.

But just as he reached for a piece, Maggie stepped in his way. "If everyone eats their turkey in the kitchen, I'll end up having mine alone in the dining room," she complained good-naturedly. "And that's no way to spend Thanksgiving."

"Well, I have to nibble on something," Jake declared. Without giving her a chance to elude his grasp, he reached for her and pulled her into a dip. "I guess your ear will have to do."

Abby giggled. "You two act like you're still on your honeymoon."

Jake's eyes, only inches from Maggie's, softened and he smiled tenderly. "That's because we still feel like we are," he replied as he held her close.

Abby sighed dramatically. "That's s-o-o-o romantic. I sure hope I meet somebody like you when I'm ready to get married," she told Jake.

"I hope you do too, honey," Maggie agreed before Jake muffled her lips in a lingering kiss.

"Mmm," he murmured. "I like this idea. Start with dessert."

Maggie laughed softly. "That's all you're going to get if you don't let me up before everything burns."

"That's all I need," he countered, raising one eyebrow wickedly.

She blushed. "Well, I don't think the others would agree to defer dinner until after you have...dessert."

With an exaggerated sigh, he slowly released her. "Oh, all right. I suppose I have to be a good sport about this."

"Pop's on his way," Allison informed them as she breezed back into the kitchen.

"Okay, let's get this show on the road, then. Everybody grab a dish and let's eat!"

It took a few minutes for everyone to settle in, and then they joined hands and bowed their heads as Jake spoke.

"Lord, we thank You today for all the blessings You've given us this past year. For the joy You've sent our way, for good health, for the family ties that bind us to one another with deep, abiding love. Thank You also for watching over us and guiding us through each day, for letting us feel Your loving presence so strongly in our lives. Help us always to be grateful for all that we have, not only today, but every day of the year. Amen."

As Maggie raised her eyes, she was filled with a sense of absolute peace and deep contentment. All of the people she cared about most were with her today, and that alone made her heart overflow with gratitude. Her gaze moved around the table. Pop, who loved living in his own little cottage and now had a thriving woodworking business. Allison and Abby, still incurable romantics, ready to launch their own careers. And Jake. She gazed at him lovingly as he carved the turkey. Every moment with him had been a joy. Each day their relationship grew and deepened and took on new dimensions.

At that moment, one of those dimensions began to loudly demand attention, and Maggie's gaze moved to the high chair next to Jake. Her lips curved up softly and her eyes took on a new tenderness as she gazed at the newest member of their family. For the last nine months, Michael had joyfully disrupted their household, and they'd loved every minute of it. True to his word, Jake had gone out of his way to make sure that this time raising a child was a shared experience. He'd attended every childbirth class, coached her through labor, took most of the night feedings and changed more than his share of diapers. And Maggie loved him more every day.

As Michael demonstrated his hunger in a particularly vocal way, Jake turned to him with a smile. "Hold on there, big fella," he said, reaching over to tenderly ruffle the toddler's auburn locks.

Then he glanced at Maggie, and they smiled across the table at each other. It was a smile filled with tenderness, understanding, joy and love. Especially love. Because both of them realized how very blessed they were to have been given a second chance to find their destiny. And how close they'd come to losing it.

Though no words were spoken, Maggie knew what Jake was thinking. She could read it in his eyes. And it mirrored her thoughts exactly.

It didn't get any better than this.

*   *   *   *   *

Dear Reader,

When my husband and I were married nine years ago, the priest who officiated at the ceremony spoke about the extraordinary gift of ordinary love—how remarkable it was that love could flourish amid the stresses and tribulations of day-to-day life. He went on to point out that it was the everyday kindness and caring gestures—more than the fleeting euphoric moments—that formed the solid foundation of lasting love. And he said that this "ordinary" love was to be celebrated and held up as an example to others.

Although I was too caught up in the "euphoric moment" of the wedding to fully appreciate his message that day, ultimately I recognized its truth—and broadened my definition of "romance." Yes, it's still that enchanted evening when you see a stranger across a crowded room. And it's still that heart-stopping moment when two hearts touch for the first time. But it's so much more! It encompasses all of the levels on which two lives intertwine—intellectual, emotional and spiritual, as well as physical.

I try to capture this multidimensional nature of love in all of my books. But it is perhaps especially present in *It Had to Be You,* which focuses on growth and change in a long-term relationship. I hope you enjoy reading about Jake and Maggie's reawakening love as much as I enjoyed writing about it.

Sincerely,

Irene Hannon

Books by Cheryl Wolverton

Love Inspired

A Matter of Trust #11
A Father's Love #20
This Side of Paradise #38
The Best Christmas Ever #47
A Mother's Love #63
*For Love of Zach #76
*For Love of Hawk #87
*For Love of Mitch #105
*Healing Hearts #118
*A Husband To Hold #136
In Search of a Hero #166
A Wife for Ben #192
Shelter from the Storm #198
Once Upon a Chocolate Kiss #229

*Hill Creek, Texas

CHERYL WOLVERTON

RITA® Award finalist Cheryl Wolverton has well over a dozen books to her name. Her very popular Hill Creek, Texas series has been a finalist in many contests. Having grown up in Oklahoma, lived in Kentucky, Texas and now Louisiana, Cheryl and her husband of twenty years and their two children, Jeremiah and Christina, consider themselves Oklahomans who have been transplanted to grow and flourish in the South. Readers are always welcome to contact her via P.O. Box 207, Slaughter, LA 70777 or e-mail at Cheryl@cherylwolverton.com. You can also visit her Web site at www.cherylwolverton.com.

A FATHER'S LOVE
Cheryl Wolverton

ACKNOWLEDGMENTS

Wow. A second book. And so many people to thank.
My GEnie pals, Kathi Nance, Judy DiCiano,
Shannon Lewis and Nancy aka Igor; and
Yvonne Grapes, my mail critique partner. And
Gayle Anderson, who willingly read over the
manuscript for mistakes. They are wonderful
to bounce ideas off.

And of course, Jean Price, my agent, and Anne,
my editor, who have been unfailingly patient with me
as I learn the process of what goes into publishing
a book. And Anita Slusher and Debbie Weaver.

But most of all, my daughter, Christina,
my son, Jeremiah, and my husband, Steve,
who are so wonderful about eating spaghetti
or leftovers when I'm at the computer.

Chapter One

The shrill cries woke him.

Multimillionaire bachelor Max Stevens rolled over in bed and listened.

It couldn't be the television since his twin brother, Rand, and Rand's new wife, Elizabeth, were on an extended honeymoon. Besides, the sound of the TV wouldn't reach his suite of rooms.

None of the staff at the house he shared with his brother would dare turn on a TV while on duty. And gauging from the sky's pale light it was probably about 6:00 a.m.

Cats, he decided. Despite the gardener's attempts, strays had obviously gotten onto the grounds again and were fighting. Max pushed himself up in bed, the silk sheet sliding down his chest and pooling at his waist. It looked as if he would have to break up the fight himself since he could still hear the noise down on the patio.

Swinging his bare legs over the edge of the bed, his toes sank into the lush tan carpet. He slid his feet into slippers and grabbed his silk robe, shrugging it on over his paisley shorts. He doubted anyone was up yet. However, in a house this size, he could never be certain of not running into the staff. It was safer to stay decently covered.

As he walked to the balcony, he rubbed a weary hand over his face. This was not how he liked to be awakened early in the morning. He had a hard day of work ahead of him. Stevens Inc. was planning two more store openings across the country and with Rand gone, all the extra work fell to Max. Not that he begrudged Rand his vacation for a moment. Rand had been in a tailspin after losing his wife, Carolyn, almost two years ago. Blind and bitter, it had taken his occupational therapist, Elizabeth, who was now Rand's wife, to lead him back to the living. Eventually, Rand's sight improved and he began working at the office. Max had been grateful for Rand's help again. He wholeheartedly approved of his brother's extended honeymoon before coming back to work full-time. Max had held down the fort for over a year, what difference did a few extra months make?

Still, it would've been nice to have been done with his morning devotions and prayer *before* this interruption. His whole day would feel off-kilter now.

Padding down the balcony stairs, Max followed the wrought-iron railing around the curve to the patio below. But when he turned the corner, he stopped and stared in stunned amazement.

"Sarah!" It was his housekeeper's fault. It had to be. "Sarah, where are you!"

He continued to stare, rooted to the spot until he heard hurried footsteps. "Oh, mercy," the housekeeper said.

Her gasp told him he'd been wrong. "Do you have grandkids?"

"Certainly not. You know my husband and I wouldn't keep that a secret." She stood by him and stared too.

"Well, do something," he finally said.

"Like what?" she asked.

"You're a woman. Don't you know what to do about these things?"

"That's a sexist remark, Mr. Stevens."

Realizing she didn't intend to move from her position as an observer, he stepped forward. The sounds stopped. He raised an eyebrow as he peered into the laundry basket that contained the two toddlers.

"Well?" Sarah prodded.

He shot her a look that told her to mind her tongue and

took another step forward. "They're sorta small, aren't they?"

"I guess. But you would know better than me."

He glanced over his shoulder. "And what do you mean by *that?*"

Sarah had been with the household since Max was five so Max's scowl didn't faze her in the least. Plopping her hands on her ample hips, she replied, "What do you think I mean? They look just like…look, there's a note."

Max plucked the piece of paper off the side of the laundry basket and began to read:

Dear Max,
    I had no one else to leave them with. I'm in trouble, and have to leave. I know you'll take care of them and love them for me. Please don't tell anyone the secret. I've always thought they looked like my knight in shining armor. I've never forgotten you. Thank you. You're a kind man.
P.S. Meet Maxwell Robert and Madeline Renée.

Max stared in disbelief at the note until a gurgle from the basket drew his attention.

Maxwell and Madeline?

Two cherubic faces stared back at him. He wasn't sure how old they were but he knew they were too big to be newborns. And the writer of the note was right. They did look like him. They both had dark hair and one had deep brown eyes, hinting at a Cajun lineage.

But his?

Impossible! He knew that for certain. He wasn't promiscuous.

"Well, Mr. Stevens," Sarah said, her voice reeking with disapproval. "Are you just going to leave your kids here on the porch or bring them into the house?" She pivoted and marched away before he could answer.

His kids.

Dear Father, he thought, staring at the two children who

were beginning to squirm against the bonds that held the
backs of their overalls to the handles of the basket. *I know
these aren't my kids. I* know *it. So, would You mind telling
me what I'm getting myself into this time?*

God didn't answer.

Max took that to mean he would find out in time. Inching
forward, not sure if his nearness would set the kids off, he
picked up the two bulky blue-striped bags that sat nearby and
the laundry basket that held the two tiny children.

The one with the brown eyes, he thought it was the girl
since it had a pink ribbon in its hair, gurgled and kicked its
feet.

The other one chewed on its toe and studied Max with a
serious expression.

"Well, uh, kids, I don't quite understand this, but for some
reason your mommy left you with me. She sounded scared in
the note. But don't worry. Hopefully, she'll be back soon
because...to be honest, I don't have the faintest idea what to
do with you. But maybe we can get along fine until...until
we get this all worked out."

The blue-eyed child frowned and released his foot, kicking
Max in the nose.

Max froze, afraid they'd start crying again.

The child wiggled his toes against Max's mouth as if offering him a taste.

Max grimaced and started to move slowly toward the door,
deciding the kids would be better off on the floor inside, instead of trying to jam their feet down his throat.

Madeline laughed, which caused the other child to gurgle,
too.

Relieved that they weren't going to throw a fit at his movements, Max hurried to the door. "I'm just going to take you
inside now, and sit you down. I bet you're hungry. I am."

He paused at the doors leading into the study that overlooked the balcony. Fumbling, he managed to get the door
open and make it inside. "I'm not sure exactly what you eat."

Suddenly, he sniffed, his nose wrinkling as his eyes narrowed suspiciously. "You're still in diapers, aren't you?"

Kicking the door closed, he juggled the basket for a firmer grip.

"We're going to have to do something about that right now," he said, though he wasn't sure what. Smiling in relief at the accomplishment of getting them into the house without another bout of crying, he decided maybe this baby stuff wasn't going to be so bad—except for the odor emanating from one of them.

Setting the basket down by the sofa, he hollered, "Sarah!"

Both children immediately jumped, then burst into tears. The terror any bachelor immediately feels at the sight of such small children had been held at bay—until those shrieks. His eyes widened and he reached out and patted first one, then the other's shoulder. Yes, there was no doubt about it, he was in way over his head. He needed help.

"Sarah! Find me the employment agency's number."

Kaitland Summerville ran a hand wearily through the straight strands of her honey blond hair, pushing it back from her face. The action did no good, the blunt cut allowed it to fall right back against her smarting jaw.

Adjusting the ice pack, she tried to shuffle the paperwork that she was currently working on, but to no avail.

"Why don't you take a break?" her assistant, Shirley, asked, her lips quirking in exasperation. "If I'd just been through what you'd been through, I would. I still can't believe you've been temporarily pulled from working with the kids—"

Kaitland smiled, a weary smile. "I don't blame Jake one bit, Shirley. True, I did nothing to provoke Johnnie's daddy. He was drunk. But he and his wife are separated, and he doesn't have custody. And what happened *was* very traumatic for the kids. It's only natural that I step back until everything is settled. At least for the sake of the other kids and their parents. I wouldn't want to stay and risk any censure falling on the day care or the church."

Kaitland set the ice pack down on the table and pulled out a compact to examine the swelling.

Today had started out a rotten day and had gone downhill from there. First thing this morning, her stepbrother, Robert had called, trying to get her to go to a society function with him. She smiled wryly thinking of their conversation. She rarely went anywhere like that anymore. Still, he knew she did her best to have a forgiving nature and he was always wheedling, trying to get her to do things for him whenever he needed help. Sometimes she thought she'd rather be bitten by a rattler than to again circulate at the society events he frequented. These outings always ended in disaster. It was simply that he wasn't a Christian. They had nothing in common except their parents had married each other when Kaitland was a preteen. When she'd managed to avoid a commitment to attending the function with her stepbrother, she had thought things were looking up.

However, she'd gone out to her car, running late, only to find it wouldn't start. Just her luck. The water pump had been on its last legs for at least six months and she didn't have the money to pay for a new one. True, she was the director of the local day care in the small town of Zachary, Louisiana, but that wasn't always enough to make ends meet.

Disgusted, she'd called a cab, then a mechanic, hoping she could work out some sort of payment plan with him. The mechanic had agreed. But unfortunately for her, George had been driving the cab. George was the slowest driver in the world, she was sure of it. How he'd kept his license she didn't know. The ten-minute trip to work had taken twenty minutes.

Because of that she had been running even later. The chapel service they held for the older kids was therefore late starting, which threw everything else behind. And right into the middle of that had come Johnnie's daddy while she was outside; the daddy that had skipped out of town two months ago and left his wife and child destitute. He wanted his boy, as he'd said. She couldn't allow him to take the child and had sent Shirley to call the police.

That's when she'd been injured. Oh, she didn't think Johnnie's daddy had meant to hurt her. He'd only meant to move her aside so he could get to his boy. As far as she knew,

Johnnie's father had never been of a violent nature. However, he'd pushed her and in the process he had tripped over one of those stupid shrubs that all businesses put out to look nice but only ended up getting in the way.

Trying to stop their fall by counterbalancing, Kaitland had shoved back against him, but the maneuver hadn't worked. She'd ended up with a table on top of her and he'd ended up going through a plate-glass window.

And some of the children had witnessed the scene.

The man was now at the hospital getting stitches—and sobering up—and she was sitting in the office nursing a bruised jaw.

And a temporary removal from the eyes of the parents and kids until her battered face healed. Instead of overseeing the day care for the rest of the week, her pastor, Jake, had suggested she stick with the paperwork until everything blew over. There had already been two calls from concerned parents—boy, did news travel fast in a small town. Since there was a board meeting scheduled in a few weeks, the pastor suggested they discuss the incident then. But he didn't expect any trouble. By then any worries would be gone, Jake had assured her, and she would be able to go back to work with no problems. But she still had to wait that long.

It couldn't get any worse.

Of course, looking at her jaw now, Kaitland saw only a very faint coloring to it. She didn't bruise easily. She knew that from five years ago....

Her eyes still held a slightly dull glaze, no doubt from the pain in her jaw.

"Well, at least you're not losing any pay while you're working in here with me, though you're probably going to be bored to death."

Kaitland smiled at Shirley, knowing she was right. Shirley was short, no more than five foot and had bright red hair and green eyes, fitting her Irish heritage. She also possessed the energy of ten people, one of the reasons Kaitland was so glad to hire her in the first place. Kaitland hated the paperwork and was glad when the day-care center had been able to afford a full-time bookkeeper/secretary, taking the burden off Kaitland's shoulders. Since Kaitland had helped found the day care, she'd done all the extra work. She could honestly say it was nice to be the director. Now she worked overseeing so much of what she hadn't particularly loved to do before. The only thing she really missed was working with the kids on a one-to-one basis.

"You're right," Kaitland told Shirley. "I'll be bored to death. I'd go ahead and take vacation right now, but I don't want Jake to think I'm bailing out on him."

"How about another job then?" a voice said.

Both women gasped. Kaitland's eyes shot to Jake, who'd just entered the room, afraid to believe what she'd just heard. As if realizing his mistake, he said, "I didn't mean that the way it sounded. I had a call from a friend who runs an employment agency. We have a mutual friend in need of a temporary nanny... Why don't you come into my office?"

Temporary nanny? She shot Shirley an odd look and followed the pastor into his office. Once they were seated, he continued, "I didn't mean to blurt that out. Sometimes my humor falls flat."

Jake Mathison was thirty-two, single, but also single-minded in his dedication to his job. He'd been enthusiastic four years ago when Kaitland had approached him about the idea of opening a day-care center in their church. He'd supported her every step of the way. So, Kaitland knew he didn't mean anything by what he'd said, but was curious anyway about what he'd meant. She sat patiently and waited as he rubbed one hand over his face.

"This is confidential." Jake leaned forward in the chair, his gaze meeting hers and showing her the seriousness of his statement. "That's why I brought you in here. This is something I *don't* want overheard by anyone." Placing his hands on the desk, he allowed a small smile to ease Kaitland. "As I said, a friend called the employment agency, needing a nanny. The person requires immediate help at his house. It seems that some kids were abandoned on his doorstep."

Kaitland's mouth dropped open. "Has he called Child Services?"

"No. No, there was a note. Um, well, the note intimated that the kids were his, though he denies it. He wants to find out what's going on before he does anything with the children. And the first thing he needs is a nanny."

"Why me?"

"He didn't ask for you. He just asked the agency for someone who's not gossipy. I've known you for five years now, Kaitland," he said, calling her by the name everyone at church called her by. "I've never heard a word of gossip out of you. I feel I can trust you." He leaned slightly forward again, and with earnest eyes, added, "I also know you can use the extra money. Not only can you take your paid vacation if you want, but you'll be getting a salary, almost double what you're earning now, while you're on the job there."

"Double?" Kaitland gaped. She could sure use the money. Her grandmother's medical bills over the last year and a half, and then her funeral, had put Kaitland in debt. She was barely managing each month, which was ironic, considering her stepbrother was rich. But he'd refused to help their grandmother after she had disowned him. So, it was left to Kaitland to see to her grandmother's bills now that she was gone. And the taxes were past due on the house her grandmother had left her. She hated the thought of losing the place. Yet, now she was being given a possible solution to her dilemma. "Why is he willing to pay so much?" Then another thought crossed her mind. "Just who is he?"

"Discretion is part of his need. And he'd want you to live in. As for who he is..."

Jake leaned back and folded his hands across his flat stomach. Why did that gesture make her feel so uneasy?

"It's been a long five years for you, Kaitland."

Kaitland knew he was talking about the *incident,* as she thought of it.

"I've watched you recover from the circumstances, pull your life back together and conquer almost all of your fears. You're a strong woman, willing to work hard at the work God has called you to. Not only that, but you're devoted in your personal life, too. Sometimes we don't understand the trials we go through, but we have to remember that God lets us go through things to mold us how He wants us, into His image.''

"What are you getting at, Jake?'' Nervously, she gripped her damp palms together in her lap. She didn't like talking about that time. She had overcome most of what had happened.

That was the catch, though.

Most.

She knew there was still some bitterness and hurt there, but was at a loss how to let go of it.

"Getting on with your life, Kaitland,'' the pastor said. "I would never suggest anything that might hurt you. I feel you're ready for this.'' He paused, then, "The man is rich. I know your ex-fiancé was rich, too. I thought this might be the perfect opportunity for you to get out around that social set again and see that not all of them are like your ex-fiancé. Since I know this family and would trust them with my own sister, I feel you'd be safe. What do you say?''

Perspiration broke out on Kaitland's skin. She'd never told her pastor the name of her ex-fiancé as she'd started at this church after that fiasco. But her pastor talked about his friends a lot. It couldn't be…it just couldn't be.

Still, she so desperately needed the money, she knew before she asked the next question that she was going to take the job. "Who is it?''

"You've heard me talk about Rand and Max Stevens?'' he asked easily.

Her stomach sank to her toes even as she said, "I believe I have.''

"Well, it seems there's been some sort of mix-up and Max Stevens needs you out there immediately.''

Kaitland smiled. Max Stevens might need someone immediately, but she doubted he was going to appreciate seeing the woman he had jilted five years ago.

Nope, he wasn't going to want to see Kaitland at all.

But her pastor was right. Though he didn't realize it, he was giving her the perfect opportunity to lay her past to rest. Kaitland took a deep breath. She was going back into the lion's den and would come out unscathed this time.

Chapter Two

"Come here, che'rie. Just give me the baby powder and we'll be okay."

Max Stevens, covered from head to toe in white dust, was down on all fours near the edge of the queen-size bed, holding out his hand coaxingly as he peppered his speech with Cajun words, trying to persuade the diaper clad little girl to hand over the dusting powder.

Kaitland stood at the door and held back her laugh.

"*No!* No! No! No! No!" The toddler accentuated each no with a bounce of her knees and a squeeze of the powder container, which puffed out its fine white sheen all over the forest green carpet.

Max winced, shook his dark glossy hair in exasperation then promptly sneezed when he inhaled the dusty powder that floated in the air. Only a few hours had passed since he'd discovered the children, yet somehow, it felt longer. *Much* longer, Max reflected.

"Come on, che'rie. Just give it to Uncle Max and let me change your diaper."

"No!" the little girl squealed, then threw the container at him and turned, dancing away on her toes toward the bed.

"Thank you," he said with the desperation of one totally besieged, but saw relief in sight when the little girl started to crawl up on the bed. He placed his hand on the mauve and green comforter to push himself up, but the other twin, who had been trying to pull off his shirt, suddenly decided it was playtime.

"Horsey!" the young boy whooped. With a lunge, he shot forward, landing in the middle of Max's back.

"Oooaf!"

Max went down.

Kaitland burst into peels of laughter. "Felled by your own son, Max. I'm surprised. And you, who used to play football."

Max's head jerked around at the familiar voice and his eyes widened incredulously. "Katie?" he gasped.

"That's right, Max. At least you remember my name...or should I say the name *you've* always called me."

She strode into the room, gliding into it as if she had every right to be there. Ignoring him, she crossed to where the little girl was lying on the bed, one toe in her mouth, the other foot waving around as she waited for a diaper. Grabbing a diaper bag, Kaitland pulled out the wipes and then quickly, efficiently cleaned and diapered the child.

Max couldn't get over how good Katie looked as he knelt there in the middle of the powder-caked floor.

It had been five years. She hadn't aged, just gotten more graceful. Her honey blond hair was now straight instead of permed, but it was more beautiful, swaying to and fro with every step she took. She'd filled out a little, was more rounded, softer-looking, not as coltish as he remembered. Long, graceful hands worked quickly and expertly to diaper and dress the girl in a pink romper that was in the bag she'd pulled up onto the bed.

Her high cheekbones were slightly flushed with color and her lips were puckered as she made cooing noises to Maddie. Maddie laughed and kicked both feet in approval to whatever Kaitland had said.

And those eyes.

Her green eyes still sparkled like jewels when she laughed.

Five years and he'd thought never to see her in his house again... His eyes widened. "What are you doing here?" he blurted out, realizing he was seeing her in his house and had no idea why.

Kaitland glanced over her shoulder, a sardonic brow lifted. "I'm changing a diaper, Max. Don't tell me you've never seen a diaper changed."

Chagrined by her answer, Max opened his mouth to tell her he knew exactly what she was doing and that was not what he'd meant, but Kaitland continued, "The girl doesn't look much like you, but now the boy... My, Max, he could be your twin, but you already have one of those, don't you?" Her light tone was in contrast to her sudden intense stare at the child.

"They're not mine."

"Oh, really?" Kaitland asked, lifting Maddie in her arms. "And what is this one's name?" she asked, bouncing the little girl on her hip.

"Madeline Renée."

"And the boy?"

"Maxwell Robert," he replied, suddenly realizing how Kaitland would take the fact that the boy's first name was the same as his own.

"And he's not yours," she said so falsely that Max flushed. She was always able to goad his temper.

"No. *They are not!*" He enunciated each word.

"I see, little Max," she said, winking at the boy.

"I've been calling him Bobby."

"Bobby?" Kaitland asked before giving Maddie a peck and letting her down on the floor.

"Well, it would seem rather odd to call him Max, now, wouldn't it?" Max demanded as she crossed the room.

"I don't know," Kaitland mused aloud, pausing to tap her chin as if in deep thought. Then, for the first time, she pierced him with those deep green eyes. "A lot of people name their firstborn son after themselves."

"He's not my firstborn son!"

"You have another?" she asked, all innocence.

"I don't have any son," he growled, then took a deep breath. "Look. It's hard to explain. I woke up to what I thought was a cat brawl and found these two at the bottom of the balcony steps near the kitchen."

"I see."

"No. You don't see. I have no idea who they belong to. Though it's probably someone who reads those stupid rag magazines and believes I'm out to populate half of Louisiana."

"You sure it's not the other half that believes you're Mr. Perfect?"

He frowned at her words.

"I'm sorry, it was only a guess."

"I don't know," he finally said, brushing off his pants. "It doesn't really matter. All I can figure out is some woman dropped off her kids hoping I'd give them a better life. For all I know, Max and Maddie aren't their real names."

Both children turned at those words. Kaitland laughed. "I'd say that's their correct names, all right. Now, as to their parentage—"

"They're not mine!" he said so forcefully that Kaitland's eyes widened.

"I wasn't going to say that."

"You've already said it twice."

"No. I said the boy looks like you." She smiled. "But if the shoe fits—"

"Things aren't always as they look," he muttered.

Kaitland suddenly lost her smile and even paled slightly. "Don't I know that," she murmured, the air in the room suddenly charged with memories, a time when things hadn't been like what they'd looked.

Max remembered that time with clarity, and remembered the irrefutable proof that he'd produced to show her he knew she had been lying to him. Pain that he thought long dead and buried resurfaced, grabbing his heart and giving it an unexpected squeeze. Longing swept through him. *If it could only have been different. If you hadn't lied to me, had even just trusted me a little.* But that was in the past, the best place for it to remain. These children were the present. *And* Katie's presence in his house.

Kaitland walked over to the door where he only now realized Sarah stood. "Someone needs to sweep up here, Sarah," Kaitland said. "Will you see to it?"

"Of course," his housekeeper replied, and with an infinitesimal nod turned crisply on her heel and strode off down the hall.

"Thank you," Kaitland called out and then returned her attention to the room as she surveyed it through narrowed eyes.

"Wait a minute," Max protested as Kaitland looked around as if the room were a bug under a microscope. "You can't go ordering my servants around."

Max stepped away from the bed, attempting to disengage Bobby from where the child hung on to his pant legs. Looking down, he realized the child had drooled all over his trousers. "Aw, no," he moaned. "These are two-hundred-dollar slacks."

Grimacing, he pulled the child away and then, not knowing what to do, he lifted the boy into his arms.

"Have they had lunch?" Kaitland asked as she went around the room, picking up objects on lower tables and moving them to higher places and rearranging other things.

Max stared in disbelief, unable to figure out just what she thought she was doing. The baby suddenly grabbed Max's paisley tie and jerked. He tried to disengage the choke hold Bobby had on him. Looking distracted, he glanced away from the deceivingly cherubic bundle in his arms. "What?" he asked, already forgetting what Kaitland had said.

"Lunch, Max? Have you fed the children yet?" Kaitland looked downright exasperated with him. "I don't remember you having a memory or hearing problem. Has that changed lately?"

Max growled low in his throat, managed to disengage the child's unnaturally strong grip then snapped rather curtly, "No, Katie. That hasn't changed. I'm a little overwhelmed at the moment. I've never been around kids before, and never two at once... Watch out!"

He went running across the room to where Maddie had just grabbed a tablecloth and pulled. Potpourri spilled everywhere.

"No, no, Maddie, che'rie," he said. "Don't put that in your mouth."

Kaitland strolled over and picked up the cute little girl, easily removing the dried rose petals from the child's mouth. "This room is definitely not meant for children. Where are you keeping them?"

"Um…" He looked around the room, then shrugged sheepishly.

"Oh, Max. They can't stay in here. They need baby beds, and there are no child protectors in the plugs—"

"Child protectors?" He looked thoroughly confused.

"And those lamps won't last an hour. Kids tend to gravitate toward the forbidden. You need to get your staff up here and have them baby-proof this room right now. Get rid of all these tablecloths that hang down and replace them with shorter ones. The kids look to be about fifteen months, is that right?" Kaitland stared at him expectantly.

"I don't know." He felt like a helpless green recruit in an army full of generals—or one general in particular, he thought sourly, eyeing Kaitland with a suddenly wary eye.

She shot him a reproachful look, and he had the vague thought that she was thoroughly enjoying his discomfiture. This was the first time cool, debonair Max had ever been less than the perfect sophisticate in front of her.

"Well, that's about the right age," she continued. "They can walk, but still use things to pull themselves up."

Bobby began to fuss and Max looked panicked.

"Bounce him gently on your hip, like this," Kaitland instructed.

Max watched Katie bounce Maddie, then imitated her.

Bobby immediately threw up. "Ugh!" Max hollered and thrust the child out at arm's length.

"What did you feed them for lunch?" Kaitland demanded, instantly setting down Maddie and gathering Bobby to her.

Max looked at the brown stain with revulsion. "Cookies."

"And?" she asked when he didn't say anything else.

"And milk." What did she want? A whole list down to the bug Maddie had tried to eat from the floor the last time she'd gotten out of the chair that he'd had to sit her in every two minutes.

"That's all?" Kaitland's eyes widened.

"They seemed to like it," he added defensively, realizing belatedly that his mother had never allowed him cookies for any meal when he had been a child...or, come to think of it, as an adult, before she'd died.

"They'll both have tummyaches," she warned.

As if out of sympathy with her brother, Maddie suddenly tossed her own cookies, all over the green carpet. Kaitland gathered her up in her free arm. "There there, little one," she comforted as the baby began to whimper.

"Well, this room is definitely out for a while. Find me a nearly empty room for these two...maybe your library, and bring some blankets. It's nap time. I need to put them down and then we'll talk."

"Talk? About what?"

"Why, their schedule. What else?"

"Their schedule? You make them sound like army recruits."

"You really don't know anything about babies, do you?"

Max ran a weary hand through his hair. "You know I don't. But I've sent for someone from the agency. I was assured they'd have someone out here by this afternoon."

Max's eyes suddenly narrowed. "Which brings me back to the original question I was going to ask you before you sidetracked me. What are you doing here?"

"Surprise," Kaitland said brightly and headed toward the door.

"Surprise? What does that mean?" he asked, grabbing the diaper bags and starting after her.

"It means, Max, that I'm the new nanny."

The thud of the bags hitting the floor could be heard all the way out in the hall.

Chapter Three

"No! No way! You're not staying."

Kaitland winced at Max's adamant tone. However, that didn't stop her from heading down the stairs. She refused to stand there and argue, with two sleepy kids in her arms.

"Katie, are you listening to me? I said no way!"

"I'm not deaf, nor do I even pretend to be," she replied, entering the library. "Oh, my, have you changed this into an office?" Papers covered the tops of two desks and new equipment had been added.

"Rand and I do a lot of day-to-day work here. I tend to go into the office only two or three times a week."

Ignoring him, she went to the plush tan sofa. Setting the children down on their feet, she quickly pulled the throw blanket off the back—this used to be Max's favorite spot to relax when she'd known him, and he always kept a blanket there—and spread it over the leather. Picking the children up, she lay them down one by one and tucked the blanket around them.

"No!" Maddie yelled, then immediately stuffed two fingers in her mouth, closing her eyes.

Bobby whined, then, grabbing the blanket, he curled it against his cheek and with a shuddering sigh was out.

"They were exhausted," Max whispered, stunned, absently handing Kaitland the blanket he'd grabbed on his way out the bedroom door.

"I imagine they've had a full day and night," Kaitland murmured softly, putting the blanket and some throw pillows as padding on the floor next to the sofa in case one of them accidently fell off.

She heard Max inhale and knew he was about to blast her. "Shh," she said, and motioned toward the door.

Max nodded curtly and went into the hall. With the door pulled almost closed, she turned to him. "It's been a long time, Max."

Looking disconcerted, Max stared for a moment then sighed. "Yeah, Katie, it has. Long enough that I had decided I'd never see you again."

He started toward a small sitting room where the family gathered at night to watch TV.

"Surely you knew someday we'd see each other again, Max?"

"I hadn't expected it under these circumstances," he muttered.

Kaitland laughed. "You were expecting these circumstances?"

"Of course not," Max said curtly, then apologized. "I'm sorry for snapping. But you could have given me a warning you were coming."

"What would you have said if I'd called and told you it was me the agency hired?"

He scowled.

"That's what I thought."

"Surely you don't want to work for me, do you?"

Kaitland's smile turned wistful. *I'd like a lot more,* she thought. "What do you think?"

Inside the cozy room he went straight to the phone and dialed the agency.

"Max, wait," she pleaded.

His gaze turned tortured for only an instant before hardening. "Yes, this is Max Stevens," he said to the person on the other end of the phone. "When I called this morning, I asked for an older woman, Christian, fifty or so, the grandmotherly type." He paused. "I see." There was another pause. "There's *no one* else?" Casting a harassed look at Kaitland, he replied, "Thank you."

Kaitland stared at Max, waiting for the ax to fall. When he didn't speak, she took hope and pleaded her case. "It's not going to be that bad, Max. The kids won't be any trouble. And as you've said, you don't know the first thing about them. Besides, I'm an emergency foster parent. I'm used to dealing with kids in stressful situations."

"What happened to your job at the day-care center?"

"You know about that?" She had been his secretary years ago, before the incident, but hadn't realized he knew anything about her life after they'd broken up.

He shrugged. "Jake talks about his church."

"I still work there. I'm on a leave of absence."

"What happened? Why?"

It was her turn to shrug. "I had an accident with a belligerent parent. My pastor thought it best to keep me out of the spotlight. Especially if my cheek bruises."

Max's gaze sharpened and he came forward. "You were hit?" he demanded, taking her face in his hands and tilting it toward the east window.

His hands felt good. His touch awoke old memories in her, memories of when he'd held her tenderly within his embrace and kissed her good-night, leaving her with his own reluctance to part for even so short a time. Longing, deep and painful, filled her chest. His scent was still the same, spicy, musky. *Oh, Father, how can I stand this?* she silently asked.

Max's thumb ran over the slight swelling that her hair almost concealed. His breath fanned her face as his thumb stroked back and forth. Suddenly, realizing what he was doing, he released her and stepped back.

"I wasn't hit," she replied, just a little husky, despite her accelerated heart rate. "A table fell on me when the man and I tripped."

He said nothing for a moment, then, "I don't see how this can work, Katie. There's just too much past between us."

Panicked, she decided to play her trump card. Max was a good man despite his unwillingness to forgive her so many years ago and his determination in suspecting her of lying. She didn't want to tell him this, but seeing him now, she realized there was something still between them, something that had to be settled one way or another. And if he wasn't willing to make the effort, she suddenly was.

"I need the job, Max. If I can't get a new one within the month..." she paused. Should she tell Max she'd lose her house? No, she decided, it seemed too much like begging. She had some pride, after all. "I'll have some serious problems," she concluded.

Max whipped around to stare at her. "But why? Your stepbrother—"

"Refuses to help me," she replied before he could remind her how rich her stepbrother was.

That was a sore point she'd not quite gotten over in reference to her grandmother's health. Her grandmother had disowned Robert just before she fell ill with cancer. Kaitland was never sure why. Her grandmother never told her the cause of it. Somehow her grandmother had her will changed without Kaitland knowing it. When it was read, Kaitland was stunned to find out the house and almost all of the money that was left belonged to her. What little money there was ran out before the hospital bills and funeral were paid for.

"If you need money—" Max said, interrupting her thoughts.

"Don't even say it," Kaitland warned, her eyes narrowing. "After what *has* gone on between us, it would be wrong if you offered me anything."

"But you'll *work* for me."

Kaitland flushed just a little. "Yes."

She knew it didn't make sense to Max. They had almost married, which should have made her more amenable to accepting a loan, but for her it was just the opposite. No, it would be easier to work for him and not feel indebted.

"You aren't making this easy for me, Katie," he finally said, running a weary hand through his hair.

"I hope not," she replied brightly, despite the tension.

He shot her an exasperated look. "Fine. You have the job. But, before you celebrate, I want to lay down some ground rules. The past is the past. We leave it there. This is strictly an employer-employee relationship. Your job is to take care of the children, see they are cared for and want for nothing. You only need to tell me what to get and it'll be done. Is that understood?''

"Yes, Max."

"Well, good."

She hid her smile. Max looked as if he thought he'd lost the battle but couldn't figure out why. She knew why. Just by being in the same house, the past was going to creep up until it was dealt with and taken care of.

"First we'll need cribs for the children. With that they'll need sheets and bumper pads and a couple of light blankets. What about some clothes? Do you want me to run over to the church and check their clothes closet—''

"I can certainly buy anything the children need," Max replied, affronted.

Kaitland paused, then asked the question that had been burning in her since she'd first arrived. She'd known the kids weren't Max's. He lived by the moral code of his faith. She took his word, too, for Max also didn't lie. "Why do you insist on seeing to this problem? You could call Child Services and the children would be taken away and you'd never have to be responsible for them again."

"But I am responsible."

Her eyes widened in shock, thinking she had misjudged him.

"Not that way," he replied, clearly exasperated. He dropped wearily onto the couch. Leaning his head back, he closed his eyes. "Someone left them on my patio with a note addressed to me. I don't know if the person was a crackpot or someone who really thought I could help the children. But whoever it was put their trust and faith in me. I won't palm that off on some overworked agency that would probably separate the children out of necessity."

Kaitland nodded. That would probably happen. Though Child Services didn't like to do that, they had to find somewhere for the children.

"I have plenty of money," he said. "Enough to last two

lifetimes. And this house is big enough to hold forty or fifty people. So there's plenty of room. It won't hurt to keep them here."

She smiled, gently, doing her best to hide the misting of her eyes. "You're a good person, Max Stevens."

"No, just practical," he argued gruffly, refusing praise as he always did. "I'm going to call one of the investigative people we use in our business. I'll put him on the case and see if he can find out what happened to the mother. After all, how hard is it going to be to track down a set of twins that were born about…fifteen months?" At her nod, he continued, "About fifteen months ago."

"I honestly don't know. I imagine easier than tracking down a single child."

"My thoughts exactly. So, I figure within a week, maybe two, we'll have this all cleared up."

She hoped they had more than just that cleared up, but she didn't say so. "Are you going to order the cribs and clothes, or do you want me to go shopping. I should warn you, if I go shopping, the children will be left here with you."

His eyes widened. "I'll call my store immediately. It's nice owning a large chain of retail stores." He suddenly grinned. "I'll have my secretary at the office go downstairs to the store and find someone who knows about babies and send over everything they'll need. *Two* of everything," he amended. "That should work."

Kaitland shook her head in disbelief.

"Now, about my office. When do I get it back?"

Kaitland shrugged. "I imagine when the kids wake up, which could be anywhere from an hour to two hours."

"But I've got a lot of work to do," he began.

"Bring it in here," she replied.

Grumbling, he stood and walked out of the room, listing to her or himself, she wasn't sure, what he needed to accomplish today.

Same old Max, except she didn't remember him taking quite this much interest in the business five years ago.

She headed up the stairs to the room where the children

had been. She found the maid, Lavina, in there finishing cleaning up the mess. "You'll need to get someone up here to take all the knickknacks out of this room, Lavina. They'll also need to remove the bed. Mr. Stevens is turning it into a nursery for the twins."

"I'll get Tim from the stables to help me this afternoon," the maid said.

"You'd better go ahead and do it now," Kaitland told her. "Mr. Stevens is ordering cribs and I imagine they'll be here in an hour or two. Also, do you know which room I'm staying in?"

"Oh, I'm sorry, Miss Summerville. Sarah told me to put your bags in the room across the hall, unless you want the one across from Mr. Stevens?"

She knew Max's room was next door to the babies' room. The one next to her would be across the hall from him and larger than the one she was in. "No. This is fine. I need to be close to the children. As a matter of fact, if you could find a small twin bed I might just sleep in here."

"Oh, no, ma'am. Sarah wouldn't approve of that at all. She was telling me how much she likes you and has missed you around here. She'd be very upset if you weren't completely comfortable while you were here."

Kaitland grinned. That sounded just like Sarah. "Very well. Thank you, Lavina."

"And Darlene is to help you with the babies whenever you need it. Sarah said those two are too much for one person. She said of course Mr. Stevens, being a bachelor, wouldn't know, nor would he remember how much of a handful he and his brother were. She said that he deserved a taste of what he'd put her through growing up. I think she's quite excited about having the little mites in the house."

Kaitland's grin turned into a full-blown smile. "I'm glad. You tell Sarah I'm sure Max is going to get a great big taste of what it's like to have two toddlers underfoot. Now, go on. I need to unpack."

She walked across the hall to her suite. Pushing open the door, she immediately smiled in pleasure. Light mauves and browns decorated the space. There were no balcony doors like the room across the hall, but the shutters on the large window made it possible for her to keep the room as bright as day or dimly lit. A large overstuffed, floral-print couch sat near two armchairs, creating a comfortable sitting area. A polished oak armoire held a TV and VCR, as well as a stereo. A low bookcase held a collection of interesting titles. She knew the door to the right was the bedroom and bathroom.

Crossing the plush carpet, she found out she was right. Max's room was larger. She knew he had a small gym in the second room off the main room, as did Rand. Max had explained the layout of the house once to her.

"Oh, my," she breathed, looking in the room. Yellows and green pastels decorated the bedroom, along with pink and blue pastel watercolors hanging on the walls. She wondered who had decorated this. Certainly not an interior decorator. Her bag was sitting on the bed. She unpacked, putting everything in the cherry-wood armoire as she went. Her last thing to unpack was the first thing she had packed—her Bible.

Taking it out, she sat down on the bed and opened it. She was surprised to find she had opened it to a familiar scripture, *"You will not fear,"* it started, and ended with, *"I will be with him in trouble, I will deliver him and honor him."*

Smoothing her hand over the worn pages, she prayed, "Father, please help me, guide me in what You would have me do. I thought this would be so easy, coming here and facing the past. But, well, I've discovered I still have some kind of feelings for Max. Oh, I'm not sure what they are, but they're there. I don't want to hurt Max again, but I refuse to put myself in the path of hurt, either. Open the doors for healing between us even if that means we solve the problems and never see each other again. All I know is this has to come to a head. Thank You, Father."

She laid her Bible down and stood. Taking her suitcase, she tucked it under the bed and then turned toward the door.

"Round one goes to Daniel," she whispered. She had faced the lion in his den and come out unscathed.

"Now let's see what happens in round two," she murmured.

Chapter Four

"I've got Dugan Lawrence, head of security at our stores, checking into the twins' background," Max said, hanging up the phone and turning to where Kaitland had just entered the den. "And Jennifer is buying the store out, if I know her."

"Jennifer?" Kaitland asked quizzically.

"My secretary. She loves kids and became my secretary when Rand had his accident."

Max watched Kaitland digest that as she seated herself across from him in one of the overstuffed chairs. He couldn't get over how good she looked. His heart beat a staccato as he unobtrusively studied her again. She was like manna for a starved soul. He thought he'd gotten over her, was no longer empty without her, but seeing her now... He forced himself to push those feelings aside and remember how she'd betrayed him. It would not be good to act the fool again. "Do you have any problems with living in? What about your own house or your job?"

"Jake gave me time off. I'm on vacation. I have four weeks built up but hadn't taken any of it until now. As for my house, I imagine if I can run by once or twice a week, it'll be okay. I can call and stop the paper, and my mail all goes to a post-office box anyway." She shrugged daintily. "There's nothing else to worry about."

"What about personal phone calls and such? Do you need to forward your phone?"

"No. The only people who would need to get in touch with

me are at the church. Jake will forward any urgent messages
to me.''

He nodded. ''About publicity. I'd like to keep this situation
quiet. You know how the news media constantly hounds Rand
and me. This would be a field day. Not that I have anything
to hide. But I'd like to have some answers, know who these
kids belong to before this hits the papers.''

''I understand.''

''But?'' he asked, seeing the look on her face.

She hesitated. ''I'd as soon not be in the middle of a media
feeding frenzy, either. If you'll remember, I almost was, five
years ago…''

''I thought we agreed to keep the past in the past?'' Max
asked, his tone harsher than he'd intended.

Kaitland sighed. ''I'm sorry. You asked.''

''Yes, I did. And yeah, I wondered why those pictures
never hit the newsstands.''

''Oh, Max, you had that all figured out. Remember, I was
in on the conspiracy with whoever it was that slipped you the
pictures. They were angry at me and wanted to make sure you
knew I didn't really love you.''

''Katie,'' Max began.

''You brought this up, Max,'' Kaitland said, remembering
those years when she had waited day after day then week after
week until she had figured out that the sick person who had
snapped pictures of her and ruined her soon-to-be marriage
was not planning to release the photos to the media and ruin
the rest of her life, as well.

''I don't want to fight,'' he warned.

''Oh, no, of course not,'' Kaitland said gently, defeat in her
voice. ''It was easier to accept what you saw in those pictures
and find me guilty.''

''You can't deny you were in Senator Richardson's arms
kissing him,'' Max said desperately, the old pain boiling up
anew. ''I saw the pictures. How can you explain it?''

Kaitland smiled, but it wasn't a smile of pleasure. She remembered that night. Going up to her stepbrother's room.
She'd thought, at the time, that the note sent to her had been

from her stepbrother. Who else would call her to his bedroom in the middle of a party? Of course, later she realized that the person had simply gotten their rooms mixed up. Her and her stepbrother had connecting rooms. But at the time, she had simply thought her brother might be ill.

She'd found out differently. Going into the darkened room, looking around, she had been surprised when large muscular hands had closed around her shoulders. Gasping, she had spun around, only to see Senator Richardson, very drunk, standing there smiling at her. She remembered his words about *inviting, her room* and *cook up our own little fun.* Realizing his intentions, she had backed away, but he'd thought it funny, some grand game. It was during that struggle that someone had snapped shots of their intimate embrace.

She almost shuddered, remembering how close she'd come to getting raped. Shame had prodded her not to tell anyone of the fiasco in the bedroom. Since she was spending the night, she had escaped to her room and changed her ruined gown. But she'd not gone back down to the party. She'd hidden in her room, crying over what had almost happened.

And if she'd pulled away from Max's touch for the next few weeks it had only increased her shame, and her inability to explain why she suddenly didn't want to be touched.

She hadn't been able to tell him, certain he would look at her differently. When she'd finally decided to confess, it was too late. That someone else who had evidently witnessed her humiliation and taken pictures had sent them to Max. Yeah, she didn't much like the media, either, for whoever the scum was that had taken the pictures had certainly gotten revenge. She still couldn't understand why one of the magazines hadn't bought them...assuming that is what happened, as she was almost certain it was.

"That's the problem, isn't it?" she said sadly now. "You never once asked me to explain the pictures. You just waited until I showed up for our date that night and then dropped the pictures in my lap and told me they had been delivered to you, anonymously. And since they were pictures of the bash over a month before, the one you didn't go to with me, it was obvious, according to you, that I was not as committed to the relationship as you were.''

"You never even offered an explanation," Max argued.

"You should have trusted me," Kaitland said unhappily.

"But the pictures..." Max raised his hands helplessly, then let them fall back to his sides.

Kaitland saw the hurt and pain that she was sure was mirrored on her own face. She remembered her terror when she'd seen the pictures, the sinking sensation in the pit of her stomach when Max had stared so coldly down at her. She had opened her mouth to explain, but suddenly realized all of her fears were coming true. Max was not going to believe whatever she said. She was doomed to even try. And belatedly, she realized the main reason he wouldn't believe her was because she had not been the one to tell him. Still, the pictures were so incriminating.

"Yet you won't explain?" he said now.

Pride stiffened Kaitland's spine. It would do no good. She knew his mind was set against her. Had those pictures not shown up, they would have worked through the situation, but all Max could see was that she had not come to him until someone else had implicated her so he believed what he saw in the photos. "No," she finally said, thinking it useless to argue further.

He shook his head. "Then it's best we forget it and remember this is only a job between us."

Kaitland's heart breaking, she nodded. "Agreed, again."

"Very well." Max cleared his throat and wiped the emotion from his face. Kaitland could still see what he thought of as her betrayal burning in his eyes. "I told Jennifer to have the furniture delivered by noon today. I'll be calling my lawyers to make sure we're not breaking any laws by keeping the kids here. Would you be willing to act as an emergency foster parent should the need arise?"

Kaitland inclined her head. "Of course. I imagine, though, you won't have any problem housing them here temporarily since the note was left for you."

"How do you know about the note?" he asked, surprised.

"Sarah showed it to me."

Max rolled his eyes. "I should have known."

Kaitland giggled, the tension between them finally easing. "She was ecstatic at the thought that you might be getting served back some of what you put her through when you were a child."

"Hey, it was Rand, not me, that drove the woman to gray prematurely."

"Not according to her," she replied. "You were, after all, the one with all the broken bones each time something went awry."

"But it was Rand who masterminded the situations."

"We only have your word for that," she said, smiling with the good memories they had once shared. "As I remember, Rand has a completely different story."

"Ask Elizabeth. I'm sure Rand has told her the truth."

"I know Elizabeth," Kaitland said. "And I'm sure she wouldn't divulge a secret Rand might share."

Max's smile immediately dimmed. Kaitland realized the issue of trust between Rand and Elizabeth had reminded Max of the betrayed trust he felt Kaitland had dealt him. "If you'll excuse me, Max. I need to get upstairs and make sure everything has been moved," she said abruptly. "I've got Darlene sitting with the little ones right now. She'll be helping me out as I need it. After making sure Sarah has a menu for the children, I'll go relieve Darlene. Bobby and Maddie should be awake by then and I'll take them outside to play until the room is ready. You'll have your office back and can work in peace."

Max nodded. "If they need anything, come tell me."

Kaitland imitated Max's nod, so formal, polite and distant. "I'll do that."

She stood and strode from the room.

Max sighed, his rigid posture deflating the minute Kaitland was out of sight. She'd just had to bring up those pictures. It seemed like only yesterday when a courier had hand-delivered the package to him. Thinking it was something Rand had sent over from the store, Max had strolled into his office/gym in his room upstairs. He was running late. Kaitland was due any minute and he still had his cuff links to apply and his jacket to slip into. He'd bought a special gift, a matching necklace to go with the ring he planned to give her tonight. Oh, they were engaged, but the ring she had worn was his mother's. He'd asked her to wear that until he found the perfect ring for her—which he'd discovered and which had just been delivered that day. A beautiful teardrop emerald surrounded with diamonds. The wedding band was emeralds with clusters of diamonds around them. It was exquisite. And to go with the ring was a matching necklace. He knew the color would bring out the glow of Kaitland's eyes, accentuate the gold highlights in her hair.

He could hardly wait to present it to her over dinner.

Grabbing his letter opener, he'd slit the manila envelope, tipping it so the papers would slide out.

Pictures had slid out instead. Pictures and a note demanding money.

Pictures of Kaitland and Senator Richardson as he kissed her, his arms wrapped around her, holding her tightly to him. A picture of Richardson falling onto the bed with her while her hands tangled in his jacket, her own leg showing up to her thigh. Another of the senator's hand pulling her dress from her shoulder while her head was flung back in abandon.

His face had flushed hot before every bit of blood had drained from it. He'd dropped into a chair, certain he was going to pass out. Then he'd thrown up.

His stomach had twisted with rage. He'd wanted to go out and destroy the senator with his bare hands. And Kaitland. He'd almost cried over the pain of her betrayal. He probably would have, had Sarah not chosen that moment to tell him Kaitland was there.

Instead, holding on to every shred of dignity he could muster, he'd marched downstairs and dropped the pictures in her lap, wanting her to break down and tell him they were a lie. Even though he *knew* they couldn't be, he wanted her to tell him that.

But when she'd paled and looked guiltily up at him, he'd

known the truth. She was seeing the senator. All of her odd skittishness the past month suddenly made sense. And he'd thought it had been because he hadn't given her the official engagement ring yet. The joke had been on him. She hadn't wanted a ring, was probably flinching at the thought of having to wear it when she was interested in someone else.

He'd never felt such pain or betrayal as in that moment, especially when he accused her and she didn't deny it. No, she'd simply stood, with an unfathomable look in her eyes, and turned and walked out the door.

And he hadn't seen her since.

In five long years.

Except in his dreams. Yet those dreams were less and less frequently, and through prayer he had been certain he had put her behind him.

Then she showed up on his doorstep, just when he was finally going forward again with his life. He'd found his niche at work, had plenty to keep him busy, had even been thinking about asking his secretary out, though he wasn't really interested in her romantically.

"Katie." He whispered her name out loud, shuddering at the feelings just saying her name evoked. "And I'm fool enough to keep you on, even when I realized what you're here for."

Well, what had he hoped her to be here for? To start up their relationship again? Preposterous. It was way too late for that. He should have known she was here for the kids, not to see him. But for one tiny moment he had forgotten everything. When she'd first walked through the door, he had remembered the feeling of joy, of contentment, before the ugly memories had rushed in.

"I was a fool," he repeated. "A total fool if I think I'm going to get any work done with you in this house."

Hearing his own weak voice, he vowed not to let Kaitland Summerville interrupt his life in the least. No, he *would* continue to work, *would* ignore her presence, *would* get on with his life as he'd been doing for the past five years. And she wasn't going to stop him.

Standing, he left the library, heading toward his office. She was not going to bother him in the least. Everything was going to proceed according to his neat little schedule, and peace would again reign in his house.

Chapter Five

"Sarah! Katie! Get in here!"

Peace, indeed, he thought sourly. Had it only been a half hour ago he had thought that? "Darlene, grab Maddie. No! Not the fax—"

The crash sounded all the way into the hall.

"I'm so sorry, Mr. Stevens. I thought they were asleep so I just ran to the bathroom..."

Max looked in dismay to the overturned fax machine. The beep of an incoming fax had obviously been the culprit behind the kids' untimely wakening. But the fax wasn't the only casualty. His desktop had been cleared and Bobby sat in the middle of it, eating a pencil.

Maddie was covered with dirt from the plant she had dug up, one of his Easter lilies or prayer plants or something. He wasn't sure of the name of the plant that opened only occasionally. The tan carpet was dotted with little footprints that reminded him of a bear cub. It looked as if one of the children—probably Maddie since he knew her propensity for dancing—had padded in little circles all over the floor.

Running to Bobby, Max immediately removed the pencil from the child's mouth, only to find a rubber band in his mouth, too, and... "Ouch!" He jerked his finger back, looking at the red swollen digit.

Bobby simply grinned toothily at him then spit out what looked like his eraser...or what was left of it. "Open up,"

Max said, wanting to check, but afraid to stick his finger back in there.

"Oh, no, Maddie. No. No!"

Max looked over at Darlene and groaned. The contracts his secretary had sent over were demolished. Even now Darlene was digging pieces of paper out of Maddie's mouth. Those that the little girl hadn't tried to eat were covered with muddy little paw prints.

"What happened?" Kaitland came running into the room, her eyes widening in despair at the signs of chaos. She hesitated, not sure which child to take until Max held Bobby up.

"I'm sorry. I didn't know they were awake. I was in with Sarah—" She stopped midsentence, looking at Max with growing dismay.

Max didn't have to ask why. He felt the warm liquid running down Bobby's leg wetting his tan shirt. "His diaper is leaking," Max said bleakly, thinking that at this rate his dry-cleaning bill was going to bankrupt his company.

"I'm sorry, Max," Kaitland said. "I'll just take him. Darlene, bring Maddie. I'll, uh, come back and clean up..."

"Let Darlene or Sarah see to that."

"Of course, Max."

She turned toward the door, talking to Bobby as she hurried out.

"And Katie?" Max called, picking up the ruined contracts and looking at the chew marks on them.

Kaitland paused, glancing warily back at Max. "Yes?"

"I think Maddie's hungry."

"Yes, Max," she said and scuttled out the door. Then to Sarah, "Could you get the children some carrot sticks. I'm going to take these two out back where they can wear off some of their energy."

Toting one child in each arm, Kaitland went into the library and grabbed the checked quilt then went out back. She avoided the formal gardens—no telling what they'd eat there—and the pool area. Instead, she went farther out toward the outer wall where there was a huge section of green lawn. The children could run there and do little damage.

"Here you go," Sarah called, huffing up behind Kaitland.

"Oh, thank you," Kaitland said, gratefully seeing not only the snacks, but drinks, a washcloth and a diaper bag, too.

She spread the blanket then called both children.

Maddie immediately came over and plopped down on the quilt. "It's going to take a little longer for little Bobby to get used to his nickname," Sarah said, bringing Maxwell Robert over to where Kaitland was. She dropped by her with a groan. "Should have gotten closer to a bench, young lady," Sarah grouched good-naturedly.

"I'm sorry, Sarah," Kaitland responded, even as she wiped up Maddie. She exchanged children with Sarah and went to work on Bobby, including changing the sopping-wet diaper.

She pulled out the snacks and sipper cups from the bag and said a quick prayer with the children. Amazingly, they both settled right down and began munching their snacks. "Good thing they like this. I wasn't sure what to fix them. I guess it's just going to take time for us to figure out what food they like."

"The way those two wolfed down the cookies Max fed them earlier, I doubt you're going to find very little those two don't like to eat."

Kaitland sighed as she watched the two little ones exchange snacks and resume eating. "They're so adorable," she said. "But at the rate everything has gone this morning, I'm afraid Max will let me go before I have a chance to find out their likes and dislikes."

"Oh, pshaw," Sarah said. "I have to disagree with you, Kaitland, dear. I haven't seen Max this animated in years. Not since you left his life."

"Since he dismissed me from it, you mean."

Sarah leaned forward and patted Kaitland's hand. "Don't know why you've waited so long to come back and straighten it out. Should have been taken care of a long time ago, if you ask me. But of course, Max is so closemouthed. It doesn't matter what happened back then. It's obvious Max still cares for you."

Kaitland raised surprised eyebrows. "What in the world

makes you say that? It's obvious every time I'm in the room that Max is in a foul mood and can't wait to get away.''

"Exactly."

Kaitland wrinkled her forehead in confusion. "You're not making sense."

"Of course I am. Ever heard the old saying, where there's a spark, you can get a fire going?"

Kaitland laughed. "Yeah, but don't you know an out-of-control fire can destroy everything around it?"

"Not this, dear. Max is led by God, and so are you. You're both just too stubborn to forgive and forget, though. When Max finally let's go of his hurt, I think you're gonna find that fire back. But with God tempering it, it ain't gonna get too out of control that either one of you gets hurt again, if you both remember to rely on God this time."

Kaitland blinked back sudden tears. *If they relied on God this time.* How true. When they'd had their problems before, instead of turning to God for help, they'd both allowed their wounded pride to stand in the way. That had caused untold problems. However, unlike Sarah, Kaitland didn't believe this was a second chance. She just wanted to make peace so she could get on with her life. She knew Max would never trust her again, not that she couldn't really blame him. Her mistake had cost her someone very dear to her. If she and Max could part as friends, she would take that and be happy. If Max could only forgive and forget. That was the key. And with her in the house, around him every day, that might happen.

"I hope you're right, Sarah. I'd like the pain between us healed."

"Ms. Summerville?"

Kaitland glanced up to where Darlene stood. "I wanted to let you know the furniture has arrived. I've got some people working on arranging the room right now. And there's someone here to see you."

"Me?" The only person Kaitland could think of was Jake. "Could you stay with Bobby and Maddie?" she asked Darlene.

"Sure. I led the person to the gardens. I wasn't sure where to put him…"

"That's fine," Kaitland said, wondering where Timms, the butler, was.

"And I have to get back to cooking," Sarah said. "Don't you let them young 'uns outta your sight, Darlene. You hear me?" Sarah added, heaving her body up off the ground.

"Yes, ma'am," Darlene said, sitting down next to the children. Bobby immediately plopped into her arms. Maddie, obviously feeling left out, pushed her brother then squirmed up next to him on Darlene's lap.

Kaitland laughed and, with a kiss to each one's head, she turned and headed toward the gardens. Who in the world could it be that had come to visit her?

Then she spotted the dark brown head and knew.

Her stepbrother, Robert.

Robert and Max didn't get along. Darlene wouldn't want to leave him where Max might run into him. Kaitland had never understood the hostilities between the two men. She knew Max didn't approve of Robert's lifestyle, but he'd never discussed it with her, just told her to be careful around Robert. What could her stepbrother do to her that Max worried about—or had worried about, she amended.

Except take her to a party where she ended up getting attacked, she told herself. Well, Max had been right and she'd learned her lesson.

"Robert," she said, stopping at the garden gate where Robert stood. "What are you doing here?"

"I couldn't believe it when your pastor told me where to reach you," he said. In many ways, his dark brown eyes and dark complexion reminded her of Max. He, too, had Cajun blood in him from his mother's side of the family. Whereas Kaitland was light and fair, taking after her mother, Robert took after his mother. Her father, who was Irish, left only his green eyes and gold highlights to Kaitland.

Robert, being no blood relation, had no look of the family about him. Of course, her grandmother had raised them most of their life as their parents had died in a tragic car accident not long after they married. With no relatives, Robert had been raised by Kaitland's grandmother, too.

That was part of the ongoing tension between them now. Robert had never thought Kaitland's grandmother cared for him. And Kaitland refused to listen to Robert bad-mouth the woman who had raised them both. That was one reason she was so surprised to see him.

"Max Stevens needed a sitter. I was available."

"Those his kids?" Robert asked, nodding toward where the two little children sat playing with Darlene.

"No, those aren't his kids."

"Then what's he doing with them?"

Kaitland sighed. "Don't ask me to gossip about my boss, Robert. You know I won't do it. Suffice it to say, they aren't his children."

"Your boss, huh?" Robert asked.

"Yes, my boss."

"He was once much more."

"Robert," Kaitland warned. Robert was not a Christian, and scorned anything to do with church. He loved to find anything at all to needle Kaitland with when it came to morals.

"Okay, okay," Robert finally relented. "I don't know how you could work for the man after what he did, but that's up to you. I just wanted to check on you and find out what happened at the day care to send you running off."

"I wasn't running off." Pushing open the gate, she headed down the curving pathway, ignoring the sweet fragrance of roses and azaleas, the climbing honeysuckle bushes, until she arrived at a bench. Seating herself, she motioned to Robert, who had followed her, then told him about the confrontation she'd had with the man at the day care. "Jake felt it was better for the children who witnessed the incident, and their parents, if I took some time off," she finished. "This job was available. So, after reassuring the children that there was no harm done, I came out here for the next few weeks. Besides, Jake has been encouraging me to relax. The pressure of the expansion project we're planning has been exhausting and he thought that coming here and straightening everything out might give me a chance to clear the air of the past. Satisfied?'' Though that wasn't the entire story. Kaitland had wanted to do something new and different. Jake had known that, too.

"Your pastor thinks you need rest?" Robert asked, a conniving look on his face.

Instantly wary, for Robert rarely showed such interest in her, she said, "Yes, why?"

Robert reached out and took her hand. "I have a function to attend next week. You know my girlfriend deserted me a year and a half ago and I haven't found anyone to replace her at these social occasions."

"Is this one of those dinner parties?" she asked suspiciously.

"Please, Kaitland. Senator Bradley will be there. It's very important I talk to him. He's one of the men against the gambling issue and I need a chance to sway his decision."

Of course. She should have guessed that Robert's desperate need of her company had to do with his work as a lobbyist.

Kaitland removed her hand from her brother's grip. "You know I told you after what happened with Senator Richardson that I'd not go to those parties. I hate them."

"That was an accident. Richardson was drunk. Things like that don't normally happen."

"So you say. I don't like the way everyone judges me by what I wear, eyeing me, attaching a price tag to my dress. It's demeaning. Besides, I don't have the money to buy a dress for one of those functions."

"I'll buy you the dress," he said, grabbing her hand again. "And it's only because you don't know anyone that you're uncomfortable. Max Stevens attends those parties sometimes. I bet if he was there you'd attend."

"If I went with Max, then I might," Kaitland agreed. "But I'm not going with Max. I'm his employee. Therefore, the point is moot."

Robert's face turned red. "You'd go with him, yet you won't go with your brother." He shot to his feet, his hands fisted. "Your grandmother brainwashed you against me. It's always been like that, you know. I've always been the outsider.''

Kaitland shot to her feet, too, dismayed at the turn of the conversation, though not surprised. ''That's not true, Robert. You know Mimi loved you just like she did me.''

''No. She loved you, tolerated me. And you're the same way. I come here begging for one small favor and you turn me away like she always did. You'd think you'd care a little more about me than that, you who profess to love thy neighbor. Or is that it? You can love your neighbor—'' he motioned toward the mansion ''—but not your own brother.''

With that, he stormed down the path.

Kaitland collapsed back against the bench. It would do no good to chase Robert right now. He'd only argue more. And she did feel a little guilty about what he'd said. She loved her stepbrother. But her grandmother *had* disinherited Robert, and left everything to Kaitland.

However, she was terrified of those parties. Why couldn't Robert understand the burden she carried inside her after that night? She didn't want any part of what had caused the pain and fear in her life. Not again, not just when Max had come back into her life.

If she went to a party like that now, it would only dredge up more hurt and probably get her fired faster than she could blink.

Wearily, her shoulders drooped. ''Why now, Father? It looks like I might have a chance to clear the air between Max and myself and suddenly all of these old problems are making themselves known again. Why?''

With a sigh, she rose from the bench and went back out the gate and toward where Darlene sat with the children. She wondered how she could have thought it would be so easy coming back here, seeing Max and then going on with her life after this temporary job was over. She was afraid this was just the beginning of more momentous things to come.

Chapter Six

Max was avoiding her and the children.

Kaitland juggled the diaper bag as she arranged Maddie in her arms and urged Bobby onward down the long carpeted hall of the building that housed Stevens Inc.

Oh, it had not been obvious at first as Kaitland had adjusted herself to the children's rigorous schedules. But as Maddie and Bobby had settled into a routine, it had quickly become apparent to Kaitland that Max wasn't just missing supper and spending more time than usual at the office. She had no doubt he was doing his best to detach himself from the situation.

The children didn't notice, as they had not grown used to Max yet. But Kaitland noticed. He'd taken to coming up the balcony stairs to his room in the evenings. And if he did pass through the house when she and the children were still up, and happened to run into them, he made some excuse about being tired, or making it an early night and they'd discuss anything that might need discussing at a more opportune time.

And to think, that first night she'd caught him unawares, she had only planned to ask him if she could take the children to the zoo.

Well, he was done avoiding her. She was about to put an end to that, she thought again determinedly. After all, Max had made the decision to keep the children until their mother, whoever that was, could be located. He should at least spend time with them. The children had no one else. It was up to her to make Max realize that, whether he wanted to or not.

She assured herself that was her only motivation and that she wasn't upset that he'd been treating her as if she had the plague every moment since that first day.

"Door!"

Kaitland, brought abruptly out of her reverie by the lunging child as she pointed at the door, glanced at the squirming Maddie in her arms and noted how intently she examined each door they passed. "Yes, Maddie. Door. No, Bobby," she admonished gently as the toddler on her right reached toward the leg of a very delicate table with a very expensive china vase sitting on top of it. "Come on. Take my hand," she urged him, grabbing hold of his chubby little hand just in time.

She swerved to avoid the cherry-wood table that sat just outside the main doors leading to Max's office.

Taking a deep breath, she nodded to the receptionist who was just coming out of a side room, then barged into the secretary's office before the receptionist could stop her.

A young girl, no more than twenty-three years old, Kaitland guessed, looked up from her computer. "May I help you?" she asked, her glance taking in one child, then the other. Surprised, Kaitland watched the woman smile sweetly at both children with a gaze that was soft and loving. Maddie clapped and squealed.

"Go!" Bobby said, reaching toward the secretary.

The secretary winked before glancing back in query at Kaitland.

"I'm here to see Max...Mr. Stevens." Kaitland suddenly realized she didn't even know if Max was in. In the past, he had rarely done the traveling for the company. He had held simple nine-to-five hours unless problems cropped up. Of course, back then, Rand had been around to take care of most of the problems. Now, Max was doing the bulk of the work. Maybe he wasn't here.

"I'm sorry, Jennifer," the receptionist said, coming into the office almost on Kaitland's heels, but the young blonde interrupted her.

"It's all right, Mary." With a small nod, the younger girl

dismissed the older woman. "You must be Ms. Summerville?" she inquired politely if a little coolly.

The children were both squirming and despite her resolve, Kaitland suddenly felt like squirming, too. She knew how much Max demanded of his secretaries. How could a woman so young be in such a position of responsibility? Long blond hair coiled in a French twist at the back of her head gave the woman an air of sophistication. Remarkable blue eyes regarded her with wisdom beyond her years. Her long slender hands were more suited to modeling than typing, Kaitland thought. She in her plain jeans and short-sleeve sweater, suddenly realized how underdressed she must look compared to the woman's tailored suit and silk blouse. "Yes, I'm Kaitland Summerville. I know Max said he had to work today, but I needed to see him…"

The girl frowned over Kaitland's use of Max's first name, causing Kaitland to wonder if maybe there wasn't more going on between the secretary and Max than she realized. She watched as the woman buzzed the office. "Yes, Jennifer?"

Kaitland watched the way the girl's face softened and grew just the tiniest bit dreamy as she responded to Max's query. "Ms. Summerville is here to see you. Would you like me to schedule an appointment with her? Or maybe have her come back…"

"Katie?" The astonishment was quickly covered. "Go ahead and send her in."

Obviously distressed at the sound of Kaitland's nickname on Max's lips, Jennifer nodded toward the door. Maddie squealed again and clapped her hands. Kaitland immediately released Bobby's hand to steady Maddie.

Faster than any toddler should be able to, Bobby toddled around Jennifer's desk.

Kaitland started to race after Bobby, but watched as Jennifer reached down and lifted the boy into her lap. Any jealousy Kaitland had felt melted away as she watched the genuine warmth spread across Jennifer's face. Maddie immediately wiggled from her grasp and followed her brother.

"You like children?" Kaitland smiled when Jennifer glanced up as if startled to see Kaitland still standing there.

"Yes, I do," Jennifer replied. Staring at Kaitland, sizing her up, clearly deciding if she could trust her or not, she finally confided, "I used to work in a day care, was the administrator until it closed down."

Kaitland's disbelief must have shown because Jennifer smiled. "I'd been working there since I was fifteen. My mother owned it. Unfortunately, when she died two years ago, most of the parents and even the staff thought I was too young to run it. We lost too much business and I had to shut the place down."

"You owned it?" Kaitland was amazed.

She shrugged. "My mother owned it. I practically grew up in it. I only ended up here because a friend of mine knew that Rand Stevens needed a temporary secretary while his own was on maternity leave. He liked how levelheaded I was so much he kept me on."

Kaitland flushed. "I shouldn't have judged you by your age."

"Everyone does, even Max." Jennifer's frown returned. Kaitland suddenly realized the girl, despite how responsible she appeared to be, was still very young otherwise. She evidently had a huge crush on her boss. Kaitland was almost envious of the sweet innocence that glowed briefly in Jennifer's eyes.

"Well," she said, uncomfortable with the knowledge that this young girl liked the same man she herself had almost married. "Come on Maddie, Bobby. Come with me," she coaxed, holding out her hands. She wasn't surprised when the children ignored her.

"Oh, please," the secretary said. "They're no trouble. If you're only going to be a few minutes, you can leave them with me."

Kaitland didn't miss the girl's hopeful expression. So, she felt threatened by Kaitland, did she? She would have liked to reassure her there was no reason to worry. Max didn't trust her anymore. And there was no chance of that happening in the near future, either. Instead, she nodded. "Five minutes at the most. But be careful, they're very active."

Kaitland dropped the diaper bag by the desk and strode in the door. Max was sitting behind his desk, papers spread out everywhere. She was certain they had been placed there in the last few seconds to make him look busy, for she remembered Max *never* let his desk become the least bit unorganized.

The desk was centered in a large, airy room, decorated with green plants everywhere. She'd always liked that about Max's office. Expensive mahogany bookcases lined one wall and on the other end of the office was what he liked to call his negotiating corner. A large fireplace—that was totally electric— was surrounded by soft leather chairs and a tan sofa. It was a place to put someone at ease. Max used to spend a lot of time in that corner when she'd come to visit him. He'd jokingly say they were going to have to find somewhere else to sit and talk, because remembering her sitting there caused no end of distraction when he was trying to make a case for something with one of his business associates.

Reluctantly, she drew her mind away from the fond memories and braced herself for the confrontation ahead. Turning back to Max, she saw he, too, had been staring at the sofa. Did it hold the same memories for him? He focused on her, quickly shuffling his papers to one side of the desk. "What can I do for you, Katie? Is something the matter with the kids? By the way, where are they?"

She smiled. "They're with Jennifer."

"What?" He frowned and stood. "You know I'm trying to keep this quiet. Jennifer won't talk, but running through the offices...and besides, can she even handle those two?"

Kaitland laughed. "She's not a kid," she replied, belying her own thoughts of a minute ago. "Besides, don't you know *anything* about your secretary?"

"What do you mean?" Max had come around the desk and headed toward the door. At her words, he turned back to her.

"She used to own a day care, or at least, her mother did.

She misses it terribly. It was obvious in the way she took to Maddie and Bobby.''

"I didn't know," he murmured, slowly strolling over to his desk. Turning, he leaned against it. "So, what are you doing here?"

"I came to invite you to the zoo."

Handing him a spitting cobra would have surprised him less. His mouth fell open. "You *are* kidding, right?"

Kaitland's smile left. "No, I'm *not* kidding. Max, I don't think you've thought out this idea."

"I certainly have," he said. "Kaitland, I appreciate that you think I need a break, but I'm very behind because of Rand's honeymoon. He'll be back in a couple of days or so and I've got to get all of this work caught up."

She realized the work on his desk must be real. Biting her lip in indecision, she glanced at his desk, but then firmed her resolve. The kids needed him, whether he realized it or not, and she was done with him hiding out. "Your needing a break is not what I'm worried about. Actually, it's the kids."

"Are they sick? What is it? You're not making any sense."

"Max!" His eyes widened at her sharp tone. She sighed. "Let me finish."

He nodded.

"You hired me to take care of the kids. I understand that. I love taking care of Maddie and Bobby. However, there is something I think you've neglected in their care."

He frowned and when she didn't say anything more, he finally asked, "What have I neglected?"

"Your presence."

She had definitely caught him by surprise. The hand that was rubbing his chin paused. He stared at her intently, then said, "That's preposterous. They don't even know me."

"Exactly," Kaitland responded. "I'm a nanny, not their mother."

"We're not going through this again, are we, Katie? I told you, I'm not their father."

"But you're the closest thing to a relative they have right now. Don't you see that?" she pleaded, her hands going out in supplication. "I'm temporary. I'll leave soon. But you'll be left behind. Think how hard that will be on the children. They need to bond with you, have someone to hold on to until their mother can be located. And that someone should be you, not me. You do remember I have a job to go back to in a few weeks, don't you?"

"But what do I know about kids? I'm a bachelor," Max complained helplessly. "That's why I hired you."

"I know that, Max. But what would you have done when we had children?" she asked softly, trying to make a point.

His eyes darkened. "That would've been different. I could have learned day by day."

She smiled. "Tell me why you refused to let them be turned over to Child Services?"

Max pushed away from his desk and paced toward the fireplace. "I didn't want them separated."

"But why?"

Casting her a harassed look, he replied, "They need each other... I don't know. You had to see them that morning when I found them. They are part of each other, depending on each other. I can't explain how it is to be a twin. I just *know* how it is and it would've been cruel to separate them."

"I agree."

"Then why did you ask me?" he replied.

"To remind you it was you who wanted them living at your house, you who went out of your way to make sure you could keep them."

Max sighed, but Kaitland wasn't done. "And to remind you that whether you want to admit it or not, you feel something for them."

"I'm not afraid to admit that," he grumbled.

Kaitland thought that was at the heart of his problem. He didn't want to care. He wanted to hide in his own world where he could be nice, have fun, but have no close attachments.

Why, she'd never understood, but later, after their breakup, she'd wondered if there wasn't more driving Max than just the thought of those pictures. He'd never tried to work it out, never tried to find out why.

She didn't say anything about his reasons for avoiding the children. Instead, she said, "I didn't think you were. But just imagine how much easier it'll be for the children if you're there when I leave. They need someone steady so they won't be hurt."

Walking over to where he was standing, she looked up into his dark brown eyes and said, "I'm not asking much, Max. I know you're a very busy person. But if Rand is going to be gone a couple more days, what will it hurt to play hooky? He won't know. And I doubt he'd care if you did. You've held up the business admirably the past couple of years. You've taken on many responsibilities, just like you have with those kids out in the reception area. What will it hurt to cut loose for a few hours, escort us to the zoo and have some fun?"

She smiled when his lips twitched. That was a sign he was weakening. She knew him too well. "It's not like I'm asking you to adopt them," she drawled. "Just get to know them, spend a couple of hours a day with them."

"If I agree, will it keep you out of the office and away from the possible exposure to the media that's always lurking here?" he asked seriously.

A slow smile spread across her face and Max looked just a little stunned. Had it been that long since he'd seen her smile? she wondered. "I can guarantee it, Maxwell Edward Stevens," she replied. "And you've just given me a weapon. If you start neglecting us, I promise to come down here and bug you until our pictures are plastered in every magazine west of the Mississippi!"

His lips curved into a reluctant smile. "And you would, too, wouldn't you, Kaitland Amanda Summerville."

Grinning sweetly, she didn't answer. He knew she'd never go to the press, with his hating them as much as he did.

"Okay, che'rie, you win, despite your obvious lies. Let me straighten that up—" he motioned toward the desk "—and we'll go. Luckily, today was a light load. No appointments, just paperwork that needed catching up on and I decided to do it here..." He winced as if suddenly realizing what he was revealing.

"To avoid me," she supplied, refusing to let him see how much his reasons for frequenting the office hurt. "But we've put an end to that," she said lightly, letting him read into her words that she thought it was only the kids he was avoiding and not her. "So, I'll expect to see you at home around the children more often."

She turned toward the door. "Well, I'd better go check on the demolition team—"

"Katie." His hand on her arm stopped her. Biting her lip to hold in the hurt, she did her best to put on a smile.

"It's okay, really, Max."

"Look, I'm sorry. I know this is difficult."

Letting go of her arm, he ran a hand wearily through his hair. "This was one reason why I wanted someone else. It would have been easier—"

"Not to see each other again?" she asked, the smile still intact though her face felt as set as concrete.

"Yes. We had broken it off, gotten on with our lives. It would have been a lot easier not to be thrown together again."

"If we really had gotten on with our lives, Max, if we had actually gotten over the past and were living again, would our being together really hurt this much?"

Max opened his mouth to reply but he never got the chance. A loud crash on the other side of the door held his words within.

Both Max and Kaitland stared at each other in shock then in unison groaned.

"The kids!" Max said.

"The kids," Kaitland confirmed.

Chapter Seven

Max jerked open the door to his office. "What's going on out here?" he said, then stopped, his stunned shock turning to dismay.

"Oh dear," Kaitland said, scooting past Max and going toward the children.

Max wasn't surprised at the state of the office. Not really. Hadn't he learned since the children's arrival in his life what to expect?

"I should have warned you, Jennifer, that Maddie likes plants," Kaitland said. "That's not poisonous, is it?"

Maddie, sitting near the far end of the office, was covered in dirt and stuffing a leaf in her mouth as Jennifer tried to clean up the mess.

Seeing Max, Bobby squealed and made a beeline for him. Absently, Max lifted Bobby into his arms. The little boy promptly dropped his head to Max's shoulder.

The feeling Max had been running from all week was immediately present again. These kids had the power no one else had, to slip past his guard and wind their way around his heart.

Something soft and squishy, grainy, touched his chest. "Well, I guess I'll be leaving work now instead of later," Max said resignedly.

"What... Oh, no, Max!" Kaitland sighed.

Max looked down at the handful of dirt Bobby had been

holding in his hand. Half was down the child's trousers, the rest smeared on Max's jacket and shirt.

Cutting his eyes toward the toddler he held, he was met by an impish grin. Then the wetness came. "He's leaking—again."

Kaitland rushed over. "I'm so sorry. I don't know why he keeps leaking out of his diapers every time you hold him..."

"Not to worry," Max said. "I have some casual clothes in the office. I wear them sometimes when I have somewhere to go after work and don't want to run home and change. So, while I clean up, how about cleaning these two up?"

Without waiting for a reply, he went back into his office and headed for the private bathroom. He hoped this was not a sign of what was to come. He'd never met two little kids who could get into more trouble than those two. With a small smile, he remembered some of his and Rand's antics. Well, almost no one, he amended. He and his brother had certainly turned his parents' hair gray.

But these were only babies. And he was beginning to think Bobby had some delicate condition. Every time he picked that child up, Bobby spit up or had an accident on him. Kaitland didn't seem to think there was anything wrong with Bobby. Maybe if Max spent more time around the children, he would find out that Bobby didn't get sick every time he picked up the boy. Maybe it was just coincidence since he'd held him so little.

He pulled his dark slacks and green pullover off the hanger and slipped into them. Then he washed off all traces of dirt and grime. It wasn't often he wore casual clothes anymore. He had started keeping an outfit at work when Kaitland and he had been dating. She would often show up just as he was getting off and suggest some outrageous place to go where a suit would definitely be out of place. After their breakup, he had continued to keep clothes here out of habit.

Kaitland.

Even now his heart ached for her. She was so beautiful, so sweet, so generous. He wanted to take her in his arms and kiss her and tell her the past could be forgotten.

But it couldn't.

Kaitland was right. The past was like some big silent monster than hung between them.

Arranging his suit on a hanger, he gave himself one last check. He reminded himself that no matter what, the past was not going away. There was no way to heal the hurt, was there? Too much pain and damage had passed between them for him to reach out and pull her into his arms and offer comfort. *Father, what am I going to do? Why this temptation now?*

Max didn't wait for an answer. Instead, he took out his soiled suit and laid it over the couch.

He buzzed Phil, his driver, on the phone. "Meet me downstairs in five minutes."

Going out to his secretary's office, he was glad to see both children being held by Jennifer and Kaitland. "Jennifer, have my suit cleaned, please, and have housekeeping come clean up this mess. If anyone has any questions, direct them to my vice president, Hunter. You'll be able to reach me later at home. If it's an emergency, page me." He indicated the small pager on his belt.

Holding out his hands, he watched as Maddie lunged at him, just as he knew she would. Contrary to what Kaitland thought, Max spent a lot of time watching her and the children as they played. He knew Maddie loved to lunge, liked plants and was the leader in mischief. Bobby liked to stick things in his mouth, but was not as likely to dance as Maddie. He loved to be held, whereas Maddie liked to be free and wild. So, he expected the lunge and caught Maddie up in his arms. "Ready to go, Katie?"

She picked up the diaper bag. "Ready."

They left the office and started down the hall. She nodded to three people they passed and was confused by how cautious they were to respond, hurrying off to another office or disappearing behind doors.

It was unusually quiet, only Maddie babbling and Bobby noisily sucking his thumb. "So much for prudence," Max finally murmured dryly.

"I didn't remember you having this large a staff," Kaitland agreed, nodding again to a woman they passed.

"That all of them had so many errands to run at least," Max added as they reached the elevators. "I imagine I'm going to add greatly to the rumor mill."

"They won't take it to the papers, will they?" Kaitland glanced warily around at the secretaries as they went to the copier or peeked out of offices. She could hear the low hum of conversation as a possible explanation came to her. "There weren't this many people around when I came up," she added.

"The people that work on this floor are picked for discretion as well as skills. No, they won't go to the paper," he added darkly. "If they value their jobs."

The private elevator opened. Max stepped back to let Kaitland pass him. He stepped in behind her. "As for the number of people on the floor...I imagine every person on this end of the building was on the phone right after you passed, calling everyone on Rand's end of the building to inform them that an unknown woman—for those who don't remember you—was seen entering my office with twins."

Kaitland blushed when he confirmed her suspicions. "I'm sorry, Max. I guess I forgot how much attention you attract."

Max chuckled and finally met Kaitland's gaze. "Che'rie, it's not me. Anyone that's single who has a beautiful woman show up at his door toting twins who resemble him in coloring would be speculated about. Just relax. It's none of their business. I don't have to explain myself."

Kaitland shook her head.

"What?" Max asked, bouncing Maddie when she squirmed in his arms.

"You. I wish I could be as easygoing about what people thought about me. How do you do it?"

"I've had practice. There's an article at least once a month in the papers about me, wondering about my job, my life, my brother, or my private life. You learn to ignore it."

"It never bothered you?"

Max shrugged, chucking Maddie under the chin when she

hit him on the face and burbled something excitedly. "That's right, che'rie," he murmured, then said to Kaitland. "Occasionally. But not enough that I'm going to make myself sick over it. The only time it really matters is if it hurts my family. And then, I can be very unforgiving if it is done by someone I know."

"I remember Rand telling me once about an old friend selling articles about your childhood…"

"Old friend is right. I let him know how displeased I was. He got angry. It ruined our friendship, even though later I did apologize for my temper. It was still wrong of him, though."

"He shouldn't have betrayed your trust. But you need to forget it, Max. Forgetting is part of forgiving," she murmured.

"Private information that hits the papers is hard to forget." Max was thinking of the last time he'd been ill over any upsetting news. That had been with Kaitland five years ago. Katie's pictures had been the last time he'd been ill over what people thought. And that had been personal, it didn't deal with papers at all, though some photographer had been responsible for destroying his future.

The elevator opened in the private parking lot where the company's executives parked. Max stepped out and started toward his car.

"We need to take my car," Katie said.

Max glanced to his limo, which was just pulling up.

"You don't have car seats," she explained.

"Car seats? I hadn't thought."

"Well, I keep them in my car since I'm the one who usually does any running with the children. I suppose we could put the seats in your car. But let's face it, the press know that car. They don't know mine."

"A good idea," he replied.

Kaitland watched as he walked over to the limo. Relieved, she let out a sigh. Max had been withdrawn even though he'd agreed to go with her to the zoo. She wasn't sure what he was thinking, or what he had wanted to ask, but she did know she was afraid of that faraway look he had in his eyes. It meant he was thinking about things she didn't want to confront right now.

The limo pulled off and Max returned. She gratefully led the way to her car, a white compact. She noticed how old it looked compared to Max's sleek Mercedes that was parked in the garage back at the house. She was a little embarrassed to have him see this vehicle.

"What happened to your other car?" he asked.

"It proved to be too expensive," she replied lightly.

Max looked at her, his eyes narrowing. "Too expensive?"

She shrugged. Taking Bobby, she easily slipped him into his car seat and buckled him in. Max had a more difficult time with Maddie. She was glad it distracted him from her answer, though, or she thought it did, until he closed the door and looked over the hood at her.

"I don't like asking this, Katie, but just how tight did your grandmother's illness leave you?"

Kaitland smiled grimly. "Since you don't like asking it, you'll be relieved to know I have no intention of answering. Shall we go?" She held up the keys, grinning. She knew he didn't like her driving. He'd always complained she went too fast.

He slid into the passenger's seat while she got behind the wheel. "You sure you don't want me to drive?" he asked.

"Absolutely," she replied. "I thought you liked being chauffeured," she added.

"By a chauffeur," he muttered.

Her laughter tinkled out in the small car. Maddie immediately echoed the sound. Bobby just grunted, which caused Max to smile.

"It's not far to the zoo so I don't see why you're worried," Kaitland said.

"I'm not," he said, and she knew he was lying.

"So," Kaitland said once they were on the interstate, "have you heard anything from the private investigator you hired?"

"Nothing good." Max adjusted in his seat, turning a little so he could see her. Kaitland unconsciously tensed. Having

Max so close was not something she'd bargained on when they'd entered the car. She could smell his spicy aftershave, almost feel the breaths he was taking as he faced her. Memories swamped her but she forced them to the recesses of her mind.

"As far as Dugan can tell, there were several births in the area that might just be our person. He's narrowed it down to eighteen—assuming the woman who had the children wasn't married. We're guessing that's the case since she left the kids with me instead of the father. There were thirty-one people he was checking out. We'll have to get lucky soon."

"Why would it take so long?" she questioned, easily flowing in and out of traffic as she traversed the busy road.

"Some had moved from the area, a few were given up for adoption. It's hard to track down that type of information and confirm it by talking with these people. Plus, he had a few favors to call in to get some of this information in the first place."

Kaitland glanced in her rearview mirror at the two children playing contentedly in their seats. "Why would someone run like that, giving up her children?"

Max was quiet a long time. "Maybe she thought they'd have a better life with someone who had money."

"But that's awful," Kaitland replied.

"Not if she believes that person would provide for her children when she couldn't."

Kaitland shook her head. "I can't imagine having to give my children away."

"If the mother was sick, or dying, maybe that was the most generous thing she could have done."

Kaitland sighed. "They miss her, you know."

Max didn't comment. He was looking out the window, gazing off in the distance.

She continued, "Some nights they wake up fussy and just don't want anything to do with me. I notice it more in Bobby. I've found putting the two of them in the same crib helps. They're pretty stable otherwise, but it's those little things. The second day on the job, Maddie just kept crying for her mother, right in the middle of eating a plant or playing patty-cake. She'd sniffle and call out, 'Mama'. It's so sad.''

"We'll find her," Max said in a low tone. "We'll find out why she had to leave, help her if we can. I won't let her desert these children if we can help her."

Kaitland took the exit to Baker, a small suburb between Baton Rouge and Zachary, and in minutes was at the zoo.

"You know, they've been rather good," Max commented as they climbed out of the car.

"Very good," Kaitland agreed.

They carried the children to the gate, where they bought tickets. Inside, Max surprised Kaitland by taking the stroller and strapping Bobby in. When he reached for Maddie, their hands touched. Kaitland couldn't help sucking in a sharp breath. His skin was so warm, his hands so masculine against her own feminine size.

Their eyes met. His eyes warmed until they were suddenly banked by the memories of their past. "Let me just strap this little girl in," Max said.

Kaitland walked on ahead looking at the peacocks. Max was right behind her.

"You know, it's been years since I've been to the zoo."

He paused near the Louisiana State University mascot's cage and allowed the children to look at the tiger. "I'd forgotten they kept Mike the Tiger here," he said.

"If it's been very long since you've been here, you're in for a surprise. They have elephant rides, and a hands-on room. It's really fun. I love to come here myself."

Max sighed. "It's always going to be there, isn't it?"

Kaitland knew he was referring to their past. "I don't want it to be, Max. But I don't know what to do to help you get over your hurt."

"I don't know what to do, either," Max said. "You're a great woman, Kaitland. But what you did…"

She waited to see what he said. It hurt her that he still didn't believe her.

"Why, Katie? Why?" he asked, the words torn from him.

Kaitland ached with remorse. "Would you believe me if I

said it was an accident? I went upstairs looking for my brother and the senator was there.''

"I can maybe believe that, but why did you let him kiss you. I *saw* the pictures. You and he were kissing. He had you on the bed. Katie, I'm not blind.''

"No, you're not, are you?'' she said sadly. It did no good to try to explain. He didn't believe her. And besides, she was ashamed of what had happened and feared the disbelief or coolness that would enter his eyes when she told him everything. Still, in her own hurt, she added, "Maybe you could have trusted me and asked me before dropping the pictures in my lap.''

"And what would you have said? It had been over a month, Katie. Why didn't you come to me immediately? I mean, what was I to think? This happens. A month later I get the pictures and a blackmail note. I confront you and you don't deny the pictures? What was I suppose to believe?'' He paused, then, "You know how often weirdos try to blackmail my family. Remember, this has happened before. That's why I now have Jennifer instead of my last secretary. The woman was saying it was my child she carried and was intending to blackmail me. Of course, we found out who had planned the extortion. But can't you see, Katie, how common this kind of thing is in my life?''

"Is it common for the woman you love to try and blackmail you?''

"I don't know. There was only one woman I'd ever loved.''

Loved. Past tense. Her heart constricted with pain. Kaitland pasted a smile on her face. "Well, that's all in the past. I just want us to be friends. Can't we manage that?''

"I don't know.''

Kaitland glanced at him. "Look. It's obvious you no longer have feelings for me. That's fine. But you were always so much fun to be around. Can't we just enjoy that?''

Finally, Max nodded.

Forcing herself to smile brightly, Kaitland said, "So, how about an elephant ride?'' She would do her best to be the happy, easygoing woman he remembered. Maybe, in time, he would see she wanted nothing to do with him except to bury the past and be friends again while she was working for him.

A slow smile spread across his face. "Just let me run back to the souvenir shop and buy a camera. I think Maddie and Bobby will need a picture of this for later."

She laughed at the boyish look in his eyes. "You just want a camera in case I fall off."

His grin widened, the past temporarily forgotten as both Kaitland and Max focused on the children and making today a memorable one. "That, too. I know how clumsy you can be." He chuckled. "And I'd love to get it on film. Now stay there. If you're good, I'll bring us all back some cotton candy."

"Oh, Max, I don't think that would be a good idea."

Max paused on the sidewalk, stepping out of the way as a group of schoolkids trudged past with their teachers. When they were gone he stepped back over to Kaitland. "Why not? I know you love cotton candy."

Kaitland smiled, the last of the tension finally leaving her. "Of course I love cotton candy. But remember the kids?"

"I'm sure they'll love it," Max reassured.

"I'm sure they will, too. But they'll make a mess."

Max glanced down at the children, then shrugged. "They're calm enough now being pushed around out here in the open. I think we can keep the cotton candy off them."

"It wasn't them I was worrying about."

"Come on, Katie. Where's your sporting adventure? You wanted to go to the zoo. No zoo trip is complete without cotton candy. Are you going to let two little kids intimidate you?"

Famous last words, she thought, and smiled wanly.

Chapter Eight

"What happened to you?"

"Rand! Welcome home." Max stuck out his hand and grasped his brother's hand. Rand, who had been eyeing the children, now looked down at his hand in disgust. Holding his hand up, he studied it as if some foreign creature had attached itself to it. "What is so sticky? And why is your hair sticking up in tufts? And, if I may be so bold, who is the child... Kaitland..."

Rand's voice fell away as Kaitland entered behind Max. Max watched Rand's eyes go to the twins, then back to Kaitland as if speculating, then negating what his mind was conjuring up.

"Hello, Rand," Kaitland said softly, shifting Maddie from one hip to the other. She reached out with her other arm and took the sleeping child from Max. "I'll just go put them down for a nap, Max," she said and turned toward the stairs.

Max didn't like the incredulous look on Rand's face. "Let me explain," he said. "It's a long story."

A curious smile crossed Rand's face. "I'd like to hear you try." Going toward the den, Max studied his brother as they walked.

"You look tanned and fit," he said. Rand did indeed look good again. Beige pants and a green shirt, more casual than what Max was wearing, showed his body had filled out again and his clothes no longer hung on a gaunt frame. They looked more like identical twins once more.

"I had a wonderful time," Rand told him. "But that's not what we're talking about so don't try to change the subject."

Max rolled his eyes. Rand was only minutes older but could really act superior sometimes. "You were wondering about Kaitland," Max said, going into the den.

"Actually, I was wondering about those children *and* Kaitland."

"Like I said, it's a long story." Max seated himself on the leather sofa, stretching out his feet in front of him. He was hot, tired and covered in cotton candy. All he wanted to do was bathe. Kaitland had been right. Only someone eligible for psychiatric care would attempt to feed sticky cotton candy to toddlers.

But instead of a bath, he now had to explain to his brother who had arrived back two days early, not that he'd taken off work, but that he'd taken off work to bond with two kids who weren't even his. This was going to be just great.

"The babies were left on my doorstep, so to speak."

"On the doorstep?" Rand asked, shock evident in his voice.

"Well, actually, they were left at the bottom of the stairs on the patio."

"How did someone get in?"

Max shrugged. "The security was off that night. It was Sarah's night out and she remembers leaving it off."

"Do you have any idea who..."

Again Max shrugged, easily accepting how flabbergasted Rand was at the explanation. "You know I'm not promiscuous. I sent for a nanny, deciding to do nothing drastic until I figured out what was going on."

"There wasn't a note or anything?"

"Oh, yeah, brother," he said, his accent thickening. "There was a note. *Mais oui,*" he said, nodding again for emphasis. "It was an introduction to Madeline Renée and Maxwell Robert."

"One of them is actually named Max?" Rand sounded as if he was strangling on his own voice.

"We call him by his middle name—Bobby."

"There's no chance they can be yours?" Rand asked, though earlier Max was certain Rand had discounted that notion.

"No chance at all."

"And they're not, um..." He looked uncomfortable as his voice trailed off.

Max's face hardened. "They're not Katie's, either."

"I wondered. They do have a look about them that reminds me of the old Katie, that look of mischief she used to wear."

Max stiffened, the old pain rearing its head. "No. They're no relation to either one of us."

"So, why haven't you sent them to a social worker by now if that's the case?" Rand asked when Max added nothing else to their identity.

"I couldn't do that, Rand," Max said. "The mother left them with me for some reason. I have Dugan Lawrence out looking for her. I need to care for them, at least until we have an explanation. Besides, if I sent the children to the state system, chances are they'd be broken up and sent to different foster parents. The kids can't handle that. They shouldn't have to handle that," he amended. "Just think what it was like for us as kids when Mom or Dad put us in separate rooms to punish us. I can't imagine any kids going through that kind of separation right after losing their mom."

"Since when have you become so paternal?" Rand asked wryly.

"I'm not," Max argued. "Just concerned for those kids." Though he did remember how awful it had been that last year his mom and dad had been alive, and how Sarah had done her best to give Max and Rand the stability they had needed. Maybe, Max silently admitted, that was behind some of his reasoning to help these kids. He didn't want them going through the insecurity of being tossed about. True, the children's parents were gone, not going through problems the way his had been.

But still, the memories, the one thing he hadn't shared with Rand, of how frustrated and angry—and scared—he'd felt when his mom had gotten tired of the newspaper articles and decided she needed to get away from everyone—including him and Rand. And his father, worried about failing her, insisting it was all his fault, convincing her to go on one last vacation to try to work it all out. Then their deaths and feeling bereft, alone in the world...

"So, you weren't carrying a little boy in your arms when you walked in."

Max shrugged.

"What's in your hair?" Rand asked.

"Cotton candy."

Rand smiled. "Let me get this straight. You just had to help carry the children earlier, too, when you were at...?"

"The zoo," Max confessed defensively.

"Ah, the zoo." Rand nodded gravely as if Max's explanation didn't border on the bizarre. "*With* two children and Kaitland," he added, nodding again.

"Kaitland is their nanny." Rand was enjoying every minute of this, Max thought, disgusted.

Rand lowered his head, rubbing his chin in amusement.

"Don't say anything," Max warned.

Rand only shook his head, then ignored his brother's warning and went on. "This is the same sweet, beautiful Kaitland who was caught in a compromising position with a senator, isn't it, Max?"

"You know it is. And I know you had trouble believing it when it happened. So, don't goad me. I don't want to discuss that, by the way." he added.

Rand, as usual, ignored him and continued. "But you're letting Kaitland work here, with these children you're worried about. Don't you think she wants to discuss the past?"

Max frowned. "We've come to an understanding. There will be nothing from the past brought up. We're just going to try to be friends. As a matter of fact, Katie is only temporarily a nanny. I told her as soon as Elizabeth got back, she'd be able to help me out until I can find someone regular. It would only be a few days at most. I'm sure by then we will have found the mother."

Rand was already shaking his head. "I'm afraid that's not possible, Max. Elizabeth's pregnant."

Max stared, stunned. "But she can't have babies. You told me the doctor said the damage caused by her ex-fiancé when he pushed her down the stairs had scarred her permanently."

"The doctor was wrong."

Max's shock turned to joy and a huge smile spread across his face. "Congratulations." He jumped up to shake Rand's hand. Rand stared at it distastefully. "We'll forgo another handshake until you can wash up. But thank you for the well-wishes. As for Elizabeth's barrenness... It's true there was a lot of damage when her ex-fiancé shoved her down the stairs. But evidently not as much as the doctor thought. She's definitely pregnant, morning sickness and all. But I'm not allowing her to work until she's further along. I'm afraid for both her and the baby."

"I understand completely," Max said.

"What I would suggest is to keep Kaitland on."

Max stared in disbelief. "But I can't do that."

Rand raised an eyebrow and Max almost groaned. Rand was always getting Max in trouble with that look. "Don't even say it. I'm not keeping Katie here. I have things that need doing. I don't want the distractions."

"So, she's still a distraction?" Rand asked, looking amused.

"I didn't mean distraction," Max amended, though thinking about her soft hand and gentle smile, he realized she was indeed a distraction—and more. *Obsession* was the word that came to mind.

"It would be easier on the kids if you kept her," Rand said. "And don't forget, she's an emergency foster parent—or used to be."

Max scowled.

Rand chuckled. "Face it, brother. You're gonna have to put your feelings aside—good or bad—and let Kaitland stay. You need her."

Rand stood. "I'm going to go wash my hands. I suggest

you shower and then I'd like a report on who's running the business while you've been running your life.''

He left.

Max walked over to a mirror and stared at his reflection. Rand was right. He looked as though he'd been mowed over by a crazy Weed Eater. His hair was sticking up every which way. His shirt had stains on it. And his face. His eyes had a haunted look that he didn't like one bit.

Going to the door, he headed up the stairs toward his room. He would not allow himself to care for Katie again.

No way. No how. Out of the question.

Trust must be part of the relationship. And he didn't trust her. Well, maybe he did, with the kids, *temporarily*. But not with his heart.

"May I come in?"

Kaitland glanced over to where a short perky redhead stood at the door. A soft tentative smile creased the woman's face and her eyes glowed with kindness.

"I'm just changing diapers," Kaitland said. "When Bobby and Maddie go down, it's for the count."

Elizabeth laughed, the soft, sweet sound quiet in the large room. "I didn't think kids this age ever took a nap. I'm Elizabeth."

"Rand's wife," she acknowledged. At Elizabeth's surprised look, she added, "I read the paper. And even if I didn't, Max has told me all about what a miracle worker you are."

"Max doesn't have much faith in his brother."

"Oh, no," Kaitland corrected. "He does. He thinks Rand is very intelligent, and when Max met you, he knew Rand couldn't let you get away."

Elizabeth chuckled again. Kaitland placed a blanket over the kids, took the diapers to the pail then went to the rest room to wash her hands. When she was done, she motioned to the sitting room off the main nursery room. "How can I help you?"

Elizabeth shrugged and seated herself next to Kaitland. "I

saw the children when you passed earlier and was just curious.''

"They're not Max's," Kaitland said, not wanting Elizabeth to think ill of her brother-in-law.

Elizabeth smiled. "I know that. Max isn't the type to hide kids in the wings."

"Someone left them on his doorstep. He hired me to be their nanny until he can locate the mother."

Elizabeth made a shocked sound in her throat.

"I think he's planning on asking you to watch the kids now that you're back," Kaitland said.

"I'm afraid he'll have to find someone else," Elizabeth told her. "I'll be glad to help, but I can tell you right now, Rand will say no. You see, I'm pregnant. We never thought I could conceive after some other problems." A dark cloud crossed her features momentarily then they brightened again. "Now Rand won't let me do anything. He wanted to extend our honeymoon two more months so I would take it easy. I promised if we returned home, I wouldn't lift a finger until we were certain I wasn't going to miscarry."

"I can tell you're very happy about the child."

"I am. Now, correct me if I'm wrong, but don't you usually run the day care at my church?"

Kaitland smiled. "I do. I didn't think you remembered me."

Elizabeth rolled her eyes. "I once tried to find you to introduce Rand to you. I was desperate to help Rand, and thought if he met a nice woman it would bring him out of his depression."

"I think he met the only one he wanted to," Kaitland replied, staring at Elizabeth's glow. "And vice versa."

Elizabeth nodded. "True. But at the time I didn't want to be involved with a patient. You see, I was his occupational therapist."

"I see," Kaitland said.

"And you," Elizabeth asked, grinning. "How do you feel about being involved with your boss?"

Kaitland paled. "It's not what you think."

Elizabeth's smile collapsed as she obviously realized she'd said something a bit too outrageous and had struck some unseen nerve. "I'm sorry. I shouldn't have said that. To me, it's just so obvious in your eyes when you say Max's name..."

Kaitland smoothed the creases in her cotton pants, refusing to meet Elizabeth's eyes. "Max and I were once engaged. It didn't work out."

There was a pause. "But you're working for him now."

"I took the job hoping God could heal the breach between us. I've been in limbo for years over things that happened between us five years ago. I had hoped to see Max, heal the breach and part as friends."

"But that hasn't happened."

Kaitland shook her head, unable to believe she was telling Elizabeth this. They'd spoken in church before, but had never been involved socially. "Please don't repeat this to Max."

Elizabeth reached out and took her hand. "Of course not. It's painful to still love someone who doesn't realize it."

"Oh, I don't love him," Kaitland protested.

"Don't you?" Elizabeth asked. "Well, it doesn't matter. These Stevens men can be real thickheaded. But I'd say if you're still here, that must be a good sign that you can handle them."

"But I was only supposed to be here until you showed up. I imagine when Rand shoots down Max's idea, he'll find someone else. So, either way, I'm sure to be gone."

"Ahem." Both women turned to see Max strolling through the door. "I hope I'm not barging in on a tête-à-tête, but I need to talk to Kaitland."

Elizabeth stood. "No welcome for me?"

Max smiled, momentarily distracted. Opening his arms, he allowed Elizabeth to step into them. She squealed when he hefted her up and spun her around.

Kaitland's heart squeezed painfully as she watched the interaction.

Planting a big smack on Elizabeth's cheek, Max said, "Welcome home, sis. If Rand gets too cautious with you over your delicate condition, you just let me know."

"I just might take you up on that," Elizabeth whispered, then hugged him back.

"Don't be swinging my wife around like that," Rand drawled, leaning against the doorjamb with a smile that said he wasn't totally serious.

Both Elizabeth and Max groaned.

Rand ignored them. "Come along, Elizabeth. The plane ride was long. You need a nap."

"Tyrant," she muttered, bringing a smile to Max's face.

"You're just learning that?" he asked innocently.

Elizabeth smiled and stepped over to Rand.

Rand nodded to Kaitland, slipped his arm around Elizabeth's waist and started out the door. Kaitland could tell by the way Rand's features softened that everyone else in the room was forgotten as he fussed over his wife.

When it was quiet again, Max turned back to Kaitland. Her stomach knotted painfully. She was about to be offered her last check and shown the door.

It was time to go and nothing really had been solved. Max had agreed to try to be friends and they'd spent time together, but she still had all of these feelings, feelings she hadn't recognized until they'd been riding the elephant together at the zoo, holding the children in their laps. She wanted more, wanted something special with Max.

But that was impossible, she admonished.

Still, it was there, the wanting, needing, yearning. Oh, why did that senator have to attack her? And who had taken those photos? Why hadn't she come to Max to tell him about the incident? If she had, she'd likely have her own children by now. Little ones just like the two in the other room, probably twins, since twins ran in her family, just as in Max's.

"So, what did you need to talk to me about?" she asked him.

Max paced to the balcony doors and stared out. "Elizabeth is pregnant."

Just as she'd feared. "She told me. We'd met once or twice before, though I wasn't sure she would remember me. I do go to a fairly large church."

Max laughed. "A hundred and fifty isn't large."

"For Zachary it is."

"Granted. At any rate, Elizabeth is pregnant and Rand has promised to have my hide if I dare propose to Elizabeth the idea of working with the children."

Kaitland smiled, though it was tinged with sadness. Rand just might say something like that. But she had a feeling Max was exaggerating. "I understand. Have you contacted the employment agency yet?"

Max turned around in surprise. "Are you that eager to leave? I thought since the kids knew you, it might be best if you stayed until we locate the mother."

Kaitland's heart soared, but she did her best to keep her facial expression neutral. "I'd like that very much. Maddie and Bobby are a wonder. I've enjoyed being with them."

"And you need the money," Max stated.

Kaitland nodded stiffly. "Yes, Max. I need the money."

Concern etched his forehead. "Why won't you tell me how much you owe? I'd be glad to help you out."

"Don't do it, Max."

"Do what?"

"Don't go snooping. We're no longer involved. This is strictly business. You have no right to ask questions about my life now."

"Who said I would do that?" he asked innocently.

"I know you. Once you get on the trail of something that interests you, you don't let up."

She saw something like a flash of pain in his eyes, then a melancholy look that lingered. "I don't, do I?"

She shrugged, uncomfortable, looking away.

"I thought we'd agreed to be friends," he said.

"Friends don't confide everything," she replied.

Max sighed. Finally, he crossed the room. The sofa gave as he seated himself by her. Kaitland felt his nearness, wanted to turn into his arms where she had once found comfort, but knew she'd run into a brick wall if she did. So, she sat, waiting to hear what Max said.

"With Elizabeth pregnant, it's doubly important we get

along. Rand is afraid she'll lose the baby, and any undue tension might affect her adversely.''

Kaitland smiled. "You're as bad as Rand. Elizabeth is stronger than she looks.''

"She was almost killed a few months ago.''

It was Kaitland's turn to stare, shocked. "What?''

"We kept it out of the newspapers. But an ex-fiancé caught up with her and attacked her. She was shot. She lived, but barely.''

"I had no idea.''

"We want it that way. You know how people pursue anything to do with our name. I'm only taking you into my confidence because you won't spread the information to the news.''

"Thank you.''

"I still trust you, Katie.''

"A little.''

"As much as I can,'' he replied, and there was genuine pain in his voice. "But this isn't about us. This is about Elizabeth.''

"I understand. I won't do anything to worry Elizabeth,'' Kaitland agreed.

"Thank you,'' Max said, standing. "I'll have your paycheck on the desk this evening.''

"And I still get Sunday off?''

"No problem. Sarah has agreed to help in your absence.'' He walked to the door. "With Rand back, things should settle down some and one free day is only reasonable.''

"Thank you.''

With sadness, Kaitland watched him leave. She knew he still didn't trust her. He was back to treating her coolly, as if she was an employee again, too. *Why, God? What must I do to make him trust me?* Even as she asked, Kaitland realized there was nothing she could *do* to make Max trust her. She'd just have to hope the longer she was around Max the more he would come to see she wasn't what he thought.

And then what?

Could there ever be more?

Kaitland wondered about that a long time. With a slow smile, she decided Max's keeping her on as nanny was a good beginning.

Chapter Nine

"Marjorie! Come on in." Kaitland wiped her hands on her shorts, and opened the door wider. "I was just finishing some scrubbing in the kitchen, then I have to work on my car. Unfortunately, it gave out just as I got back from the store."

She glanced at her watch, then at the pretty redhead in front of her. "So, what's up?"

Marjorie smiled, shook her head ruefully and strolled into the house. "You should get rid of that piece of junk in the driveway and get you a new car, if you want my opinion. And I just stopped by to visit. Can't I visit an old friend?"

Kaitland laughed, walked back into the kitchen to finish her work and replied over her shoulder, "There's always more with you, isn't there, though?"

"Shame on you, Kaitland. Not *always*."

Kaitland finished wiping down the stove she had decided to scrub to take out her frustrations on before she went out to try to fix the car. It was better, she had learned, to be relaxed when you tackled something with the car, and she certainly hadn't been relaxed when the radiator had sprung a leak in her driveway just as she'd pulled in from shopping. "So, you want to know what I'm up to?" Kaitland asked. "Just like any good reporter who loves the Stevens, you've come to find out why I'm out there."

Marjorie laughed again. "I'd give anything for the scoop, Kaitland. But I would never come to you." Kaitland turned from the stove in time to see her friend's expression turn serious. "Yes, I'd heard a woman was at the Stevens' house, and people are wondering. I called to ask you to lunch and found out you weren't at the day care for the next three weeks, and put two and two together. You're out at Max's, aren't you?"

Kaitland smiled. Marjorie might be a reporter for a local newspaper, but she'd never before printed anything without Kaitland's permission. And she was sure the woman wouldn't start now. "I'm working for him temporarily, that's all I can say."

Marjorie nodded. "Are you okay with this? I mean, I know bills have been tight, but if they're so tight you have to go back working for him after everything that happened..."

"It's an opportunity to get over the past hurts so I can get on with my life."

Marjorie didn't look as if she believed her. "As long as you're sure. My offer still stands. If you're having trouble meeting your bills..."

"You're a good friend, Marjorie. But I couldn't accept the help."

"Look, just because I'm an avid follower of the Stevens doesn't mean I'd expect information from you," she said, sounding hurt.

Kaitland sighed. "I know that. I guess I just have too much pride. Besides, all of the articles you've written about Max and Rand have been tongue-in-cheek. No one does humor better than you."

"Because I don't take them as seriously as other reporters do," Marjorie said, smiling. "Hey, they're celebrities, but they're human, too. They deserve some breaks sometimes."

"I never will forget the article you wrote when Rand's wife died. Highlighting the good, not wondering how he would survive another day blind or without his wife."

Marjorie blushed and then shrugged. "Enough about them. I did come by hoping you might be willing to drop a tidbit about what's going on. But my main reason was to find out if you're okay. I know you were hurt years ago by Max. You were devastated, actually. I was shocked when I realized you might be working for him again. I just wanted to make sure it wasn't a necessity.''

What could Kaitland say? Yes, it was. She had to have the money. But she liked being around Max, too. Oddly, at the same time that it was a painful reminder of the one disastrous event in her life, it was also a comfort. ''Don't worry, Marjorie.''

''So, what about that lunch?'' Marjorie asked, changing the subject. ''Do you feel like getting away and just shooting the breeze like we used to do?''

Kaitland smiled. At one time, she and Marjorie had been very close. Over the years, they'd drifted apart and only got together occasionally. ''Can I take a rain check on that? My car kaputed on me. I have to plug a leaking radiator and be back at the Stevens' house before dark to relieve—'' She caught herself just in time.

''Sure. No problem,'' Marjorie said. ''I've been swamped and, to tell you the truth, I was on my way to an appointment but thought to put it off if you were available. I guess I was lucky to catch you home since you're living out there.''

''Yeah, Marjorie. I'm living there. Now turn off that curiosity. If things weren't so touchy with Max I'd be glad to tell you more. I'm just afraid to risk it right now. Later, I promise to tell you all.''

''How many times have I heard that in the past,'' Marjorie said, grinning. ''Nope. I'll get my sources elsewhere, thank you very much. I'd never get the whole story out of you. You can't blame me for my curiosity, either. It comes with the job.'' Her expression turned sober. ''You just be careful. I don't want to hear you've been hurt again. You're too good a friend.''

Kaitland hugged her. ''Thanks, Marjorie. Call me with a date when you're available. I'll try to get some time off.''

She walked her friend to the door.

''Will do,'' Marjorie said.

She watched Marjorie leave, a soft smile on her face. Growing up together through all three schools had forged a bond between her and Marjorie. However, as much as she liked

Marjorie, when she'd met Max, her relationship had cooled simply because Marjorie wrote the local stories that had to do with Max. Kaitland hoped one day Marjorie would get transferred to a different part of the paper and they could be close again.

Marjorie had once told her she loved the job but hated the strain it put on their relationship. And they usually did good, as long as nothing unusual was going on with the Stevens. Her editor insisted that stories about them sold papers, and tried to get them in as much as possible. So, Marjorie did the stories, or approved the stories, or bought the stories that had to do with Max or Rand.

Since her breakup with Max, it had been easier to go out to lunch with Marjorie. Still, now that she was working for Max, she worried about going out with her friend and Max hearing about it. It would be better if she and Max resolved what was between them first before she told him about Marjorie. He'd never met her. Marjorie had been on a leave of absence having a baby when she and Max had been dating. Since then Marjorie had lost her child and husband. She'd come back to work for the paper shortly after Max had broken their engagement.

And now she wasn't sure how to tell Max that one of her dear friends was a reporter. He'd just love that.

Oh, well. It was none of his business. She wouldn't say anything to hurt him, and Marjorie wouldn't use her friendship to approach Max. Things should be okay.

She went to the hall closest and grabbed her box of tools. The car had to be fixed or she'd be late to Max's. She'd learned a lot about fixing a car in the last year and a half. She could change the oil or tires. She knew how to check belts, work on the timing, change a fuel filter. One of the men at church was a mechanic and he sometimes came over and helped her. He'd even invited her over a few times when he was doing something new so she would have an idea how to do the job if she ever had to later on.

Joe was a swell guy. She thanked God for his help.

She pushed open the door and was surprised to see Max's

sleek Mercedes pulling into the driveway. Why in the world would he be here? The look on his face as he climbed out of the car told her he was angry about something.

"Why didn't you tell me?" he demanded, coming toward her.

Uh-oh, she thought. She'd done something to upset him. She started toward her car with the tools. "Tell you what?" she asked, not sure she wanted to know.

"About your finances. You're going to lose the house if—"

"You had no right!" she accused, dropping the tools and swinging around on him. "I told you not to go snooping around."

Max didn't even have the decency to look abashed. "I was worried."

"Well, worry about someone else. I'm fine. As soon as my job is done with you, I'll be able to pay the taxes and the last of my grandmother's outstanding bills and be in the black again."

"But you shouldn't have to struggle—"

"Pu-leeeze!" she groaned. "Max. People struggle every day. I'm making it."

"Just look at what you're driving," he said.

"I knew you'd overreact if I told you," she grumbled. "And my car is just fine." She lifted the hood and started examining the radiator.

"If it's just fine, then what are you doing?"

She scowled. "My radiator is leaking. I'm going to plug it until I can get a new one installed. The plug will work for a while."

"You're going to… Since when do you know anything about cars, Katie?"

"Since I've had to learn," she replied sharply.

"Oh, Katie, che'rie," Max said, his voice filled with sadness.

"Don't you dare pity me!"

Max immediately wiped the sad look from his face. "That would be like a mouse taking pity on a lion and going into the cage so he could eat him. You have a bite in you when you're mad, Kaitland. One I don't remember being there before.''

She shrugged. "As long as you remember it's here now.''

Max slipped out of his casual jacket and rolled up his sleeves.

Kaitland stared as his muscular arms appeared inch by inch. He was so gorgeous, she thought dispiritedly. "What are you doing?''

"I'm gonna fix the car.''

"Oh?'' she asked, arching an eyebrow, her mind temporarily off those strong arms that he was revealing to her. "And you know how to fix a car?''

"Of course. I'm a man, aren't I?''

She glared. "That was sexist!''

He smiled smugly. "I know.'' Inching her aside, he began to poke around under the hood. "Actually, Rand and I went through a stage where we rebuilt cars. It was fun. We learned a lot.''

"Well, I've learned a lot, too,'' she said defensively.

He lifted his head and stared at her in surprise. "Che'rie, I was only joking with you. Obviously you have learned a lot if you know your radiator is leaking and know how to plug it. Not many people ever learn more than how to tell the mechanic to change the oil.''

A small smile lifted the corners of her mouth. "Well, I did that at one time. But a friend at church has been giving me lessons on how to fix things on my car.''

"Good going, Katie. You've always been resourceful.''

A pall fell over the conversation as Katie realized how that could be applied to the past. Max went to work on the car, Kaitland helping him as he asked for tools or handed her something to hold.

"I'll change the oil while we're doing this,'' he said finally as he finished working on the radiator.

"Did it two weeks ago,'' she said.

"Very good.'' He wiped his hands on a cloth Kaitland handed him. "Why didn't your brother help you out?'' he asked at last.

Kaitland sighed. "Why should he?" Kaitland explained how her grandmother had inexplicably cut her stepbrother out of her will and how he'd blamed Kaitland for it.

"That's no excuse," Max said. "I'd like to get my hands on him and have him try to hand me that rubbish," he said. "But right now, I want to take you out to dinner."

Kaitland stared, shocked. "Me?"

He rolled his eyes. "No one else is around. And I missed lunch."

"Oh, Max! Why didn't you tell me. I can fix you something—"

"I want to take you out to dinner, Katie. That was one of the reasons I came by."

Suspiciously, she asked, "This doesn't have anything to do with my finances, does it?"

Max scowled. "Don't mention that to me. I'm still mad over that. But no. I just thought it would be nice to go out for dinner, as…friends."

He sounded as if the word was hard to pronounce. But at least he was trying. "Just let me change," she said, deciding to go along.

"I'll finish this up and wait for you on the porch."

He watched Katie go and wondered how he was going to tell her this car was going to need a major overhaul if it was to keep running. It looked like a wreck waiting to happen. The idea that she was driving around in this, with the kids. It gave him cold chills. It might have been a decent car when she'd bought it, but it was just too old now. She was going to keep putting in more money repairing it than it was worth. He had taken a moment to examine the wiring and saw many frayed places in it. And that was only the beginning.

He sighed.

"So, it *is* you!"

Max hadn't heard the person approach. But he knew the voice. His eyes narrowing, he stepped back from the car. "Hello, Robert."

Robert, looking suspicious, glanced toward the house. "Just what are you doing over here, and to Kaitland's car?"

"Fixing it," Max said, his anger at the brother seeping out. "It's a shame Katie has to drive something like that when you drive a brand-new sports car. But then, I suppose you don't care that she is about to lose everything she owns."

Robert scowled. "What are you talking about? She's not about to lose everything. If she was, she would have told me."

"Robert!" Katie had just come out on the porch. Her eyes glanced back and forth between the two and she hurried down the steps. "I didn't know you were coming by."

"Yeah, well. If I'd known Don Juan was here, I wouldn't have."

Max knew it for the lie. Robert could have driven past if he hadn't wanted to see Kaitland while Max was around. "Did you tell your brother that you're in the red?" Max asked.

Kaitland gasped.

Robert looked at her. "He's lying, isn't he, Kaitland?"

Kaitland shot Max a furious look, then addressed her step-brother. "You've been upset lately. I never got a chance to mention it. Besides, I knew you were estranged from Mimi and so I saw no reason to ask you to help pay her medical bills."

"Medicare should have covered them."

"It did most, plus her other insurance. And some of her money covered the rest."

"But cancer is a very expensive illness," Max added. "So, Kaitland had to sell her car, sell off stocks and bonds and now is working for me so she can earn enough money to pay the taxes on this house."

"I'll be fine once those are paid," Kaitland said. "You make me sound like a pauper. In a month or two my struggling will be over."

"Why didn't you come to me, Kaitland?" Robert demanded. "I might not have liked your grandmother, but I would have helped you out."

Max was surprised at the earnestness in his expression. But Robert ruined it when he added, "Anything would have been better than going back and working for him."

"Robert!" Kaitland admonished.

"Spoken like a true—"

"Max!" Kaitland warned him.

He sighed. "I am sorry, che'rie. But the fact is, your brother did not care enough to look out for you and it is upsetting."

Robert scowled at Max. "I will see to any other outstanding bills, Kaitland. You have my word on that. However, as for coming back and visiting you, you'll have to get rid of him first."

He stormed off.

Kaitland's shoulders slumped.

"I'm sorry, Kaitland. But why do you let him come by when he only hurts you?"

"You show a true Christian attitude, don't you, Max?" she said. "He's my brother. I would never turn him away, just like you'd never turn Rand away."

"But Rand and I get along."

"What if you didn't? Would you still turn him away."

Max opened his mouth to retort, then paused. "I have really wronged him, haven't I?" Max said ruefully. "I was so angry that he let you live like this, barely scraping by…this whole thing was my fault. Next time I see Robert, I'll be sure to apologize."

He reached out and caught her under the chin. When her eyes reluctantly met his, he said, "And I apologize to you now. You're right. It was very unchristian of me to react that way. I lowered myself. Please forgive me for hurting you, che'rie."

She shrugged. "Fine."

He grinned. "You're cute when you pout. But I guess it's better than you being truly angry and taking a swing."

The corner of her mouth quirked up.

"I would be laid out on the sidewalk, groaning in pain," he said, "and all of the people passing by would recognize me and call the papers and then I would end up on the front page with the headline that you had laid me low."

Both sides of her mouth quirked up, then she giggled. "You're ridiculous, do you know that?"

"I try, che'rie. It's worth it to see you smile. Now, let's go get some dinner."

She hesitated.

"I owe you at least that after the total jerk I made of myself."

She smiled. "Okay. But nothing expensive."

Chapter Ten

"I thought I said nothing expensive," she said, looking around at the steak house uneasily. She'd only been inside Ruth Chris's with Max before. She would never be able to afford it on what she made.

He shrugged. "I feel like a steak."

Kaitland looked at Max. His casual suit still made him look more elegant than any other man she knew. She wondered if Max knew what grunge was. Didn't he ever just pull on any old thing? She was exceedingly glad she'd put on her white sleeveless dress and pinned up her hair. She'd known this wouldn't be a fast-food date.

Looking around, she was grateful to see she didn't look out of place. She smiled at Max. "Well, I feel like seafood, if that's all right with you."

Max looked up and his eyes darkened, just like the old days, she thought, her heart suddenly tripping. "Whatever you want tonight is all right, che'rie."

The low drawl of his voice, combined with the dim lights and soft music, sent shivers up her spine.

The waitress chose that moment to arrive and take their orders. When she left, Max turned back to her. Reaching out, he touched her hand, casually stroking it. "I again want to apologize for my behavior tonight. It was inexcusable."

"Why do you dislike my brother so much?" she asked, trying to ignore the warmth of his hand on hers.

He smiled, though it was a tight smile that conveyed displeasure not uneasiness. "I've never mentioned this before, che'rie, but there are rumors that Robert plays dirty. No one has ever said anything specific, but still, it's hard to discount so many rumors. And an acquaintance of mine once mentioned, before he realized what he was saying, that your brother had ruined a man's career. He never went into details. But watching the way he treats you seems confirmation enough for me. It hurts me to see him use you."

"He's my brother. I can only hope one day he'll change."

"I know, che'rie. One day, with God's help, perhaps Robert will change."

The food arrived and the conversation lapsed as both tasted their entrées.

"Have you heard any more on the missing mother?" Kaitland asked, before taking another bite of her scampi.

Max shook his head. "I expect Dugan will find something any day. He likes to say he can find a mosquito in the middle of a desert."

Kaitland chuckled. "In a desert, huh?"

Max shrugged. "What can I say? He is from Texas. Their sayings are strange there."

"You have several stores in Texas," she said, surprised.

He grimaced. "And they all do wonderful business. The people are nice, but, as I said, they are very different from the people here."

She nodded. "If you say so. As I've never left Louisiana for more than a short vacation, I wouldn't know."

"You'll have to go with me sometime..."

Kaitland looked up.

Max cleared his throat.

"I meant to mention that everything went fine at the church," Kaitland said.

"What are you talking about?"

Kaitland blushed. "I thought Sarah told you. I'm...it's not important."

Max laid down his fork. "If you felt the need to bring up the subject, then it's important, Kaitland. What is it?"

She shrugged. "Jake called me. He was worried about the

publicity. I told him everything was okay, but I was going to use the rest of my vacation, even if you find the mother first, simply because I didn't want the publicity to adversely affect the church.''

"Jake asked you to take the time?" he demanded quietly.

"No!" Kaitland replied, horrified. "I didn't say that. I said, I insisted on taking the maximum vacation whether you found the kids' mother or not. Jake is a wonderful man. He has worked hard at building the church and he has just started on a major inner-city project. The way the media is, I was afraid they'd trace me to the day care and start hounding the church, trying to dig up anything they could. And not everyone on the committee is as understanding as Jake. Jake does his best to avoid controversy where his teachers and assistants are concerned. A few have even stepped down temporarily if anything questionable came up until all was cleared up. He's a good man and I don't want to see him hurt.''

He shook his head. "I understand and I'm sorry my thoughtlessness caused this problem.''

"No, Max," Kaitland said, reaching out and taking his hand. "It wasn't you. *It* was the paper.''

"But it caused you grief. No one likes that.''

She shrugged. "I suppose it happens and there's nothing we can do about it no matter how distasteful it is.''

His eyes darkened with what she thought was pain and then the expression was gone.

"Has Jake ever stepped down, I wonder?''

Kaitland shrugged again, her eyes not leaving his, very aware of how he held her hand and refused to release it. "I have no idea. Like I said, he's a good man.''

Suddenly she stiffened.

Max saw her face pale, before she pasted on a serene smile and stared him in the eyes. But the Kaitland he knew was gone. Her eyes were blank, lifeless. "What is—" He stopped as he was interrupted from behind.

"Max Stevens. I thought that was you. It's been simply ages since I've seen you. Where have you been keeping yourself?''

Max looked up to see Winna Richardson and her husband, the senator, standing by his side. He felt Kaitland's hand become clammy and her gentle tug.

He released her fingers and stood. Kissing Winna's hand, he smiled. "I've been so busy with the store, dear lady, that I've had no time for other pursuits."

She laughed. "Well, we're having a party in two weeks. I'll be sure to send you an invitation. And who is this?"

She turned to Kaitland. That serene smile was still there, but Kaitland looked as though one wrong word would crack her emotions wide open.

He introduced her and both Winna and the senator shook her hand.

"Ah, yes," Winna said. "I've met you before. Your brother attends a lot of the charity functions, does he not?"

"Yes. Yes, he does," Kaitland replied.

The senator's wife turned back to Max. "Bring her along if you'd like. We'd love to have her." She winked.

The senator nodded, and then both strolled away.

Max resumed his seat. Kaitland looked green around the gills. She placed her napkin by her plate but didn't look up.

Max tossed his napkin onto the table. Guilt was written all over her. How could she have done *that* with the senator? A senator who was married? He couldn't believe his Katie was that type of person. Why? Why? Why?

He motioned for the check. "I'll drop you off to pick up your car." He had no intention of bringing up the painful subject. But he couldn't miss the relief in her posture when he avoided it.

He paid the bill, escorted her to the car and drove her home. Not a word passed between them.

"I'll see you in a little bit," he said just before driving off.

"Father, I can't stand this," Max said as he drove home. "At one time, I thought not knowing was the best route. It hurt too much. But now...I just don't know. It hurts too much to think about it. Katie looked so defeated, so guilty and I just can't understand why. If she had planned her liaison with the senator on purpose, she wouldn't look that way. But what other reason was there? She is not the type to casually fall into someone's arms. She's always been quiet, serene, careful. Of course, once you get to know her, she's not the same person. But she wouldn't do something like that...except for those pictures.

"Please help me. Help her. No, help *us*. I can't do it. I need Your help, Your guidance. Because without You, I've already made a mess. I think I'm beginning to agree with Kaitland. I only want the pain gone so we can go on with our lives."

Then, because no one else could see him, he allowed the tortured expression to show on his face. "Your will be done in this."

Peace flooded him and he realized that by letting go and allowing God to take care of the problem, a tremendous weight lifted from his shoulders. True, the problems weren't solved, but he knew, with a certainty, that the solution would be forthcoming.

Chapter Eleven

"I was sorry to hear about your grandmother."

They were at dinner. Kaitland had one child on each side of her, while Max sat next to Maddie. Elizabeth was across from her and Rand next to Elizabeth. She smiled at Rand's words. "I got the flowers. Thank you. She was a Christian so it makes it easier, even though I do miss her."

"It gets easier as time goes by."

Kaitland knew he was speaking from experience.

Elizabeth reached over and placed her hand gently on Rand's arm.

He smiled and dished up some asparagus then passed the platter to Max.

"Tell us about the trip," Max said, taking the asparagus and avoiding the grip of the little girl, who protested loudly. Max passed the vegetables on, then speared one of the green stalks from his plate and handed it to Maddie, who promptly quieted and began chewing on it.

Rand gaped. Kaitland smiled at his expression, but covered it by wiping her mouth with her napkin. Bobby, clearly feeling left out, pounded on his tray. Kaitland stabbed a piece of baked chicken and held it up to Bobby. He wanted none of this fork business—as usual—and peeled the chicken from the fork then popped it in his mouth. Kaitland was careful to keep a watchful eye on the children as she fed them tidbits while Rand talked about his trip.

She also noted that Max did his share of feeding Maddie.

She wondered if he realized how attached he was becoming to the children.

"Want!" Maddie interrupted, reaching for Max's plate.

Max smiled, patted Maddie's hand, waiting to see to her as Rand continued talking about the island he and Elizabeth had visited.

"Want!" Maddie demanded again.

Kaitland saw the stubborn look on her face. Maddie was getting ready for a tantrum. In the weeks she'd been here, Kaitland had come to recognize that look.

"Max," she interrupted.

He looked around just as Maddie tossed her plate.

It hit him in the chest. "Oh, no!"

Kaitland started to stand.

Max waved her down. "I'm getting used to this." Turning to Maddie, he gave her a stern look. "No, no. Maddie, bad. You don't throw your food." Then his face softened. "But Max was bad, too. I shouldn't have ignored you." With amazement, all three watched Max fix another plate, make sure it was suctioned down to the tray this time and then give the child another stalk of asparagus.

"You're going to ruin your reputation if you let anyone see you this way," Rand finally drawled.

"What?" Max asked.

"The fun-loving bachelor. People are going to worry if they see you like this."

Max looked to where he had gotten distracted with Maddie, then to his spoiled shirt, and an embarrassed smile crossed his face. "Well, you know how rumors are."

"Yeah, I do," Rand said, though he was grinning as if he was reveling in the scene.

Kaitland enjoyed their banter, but with a bittersweet ache. The more Max played with the kids, the more she realized what she'd missed out on with this man.

"Well, it sounds like you had a wonderful time, but I think these little ones need a bath," Max said.

Rand laughed.

Max sighed. "Two kids takes more than one set of hands.

Darlene has the night off tonight. Katie will need help. So, just get used to seeing me helping around here the next few weeks, Rand, unless you want to help her,'' Max added defensively.

Rand lifted his hands, but didn't stop laughing.

Elizabeth socked him in the arm. "You've been laughing at the situation ever since we returned. Cut your brother some slack.''

"I am. I am. I think it's very good training for when he's an uncle.'' He patted Elizabeth's still-flat tummy. "Go on. Go give them a bath.''

Kaitland stood. "Let me take Maddie. She's the messiest.''

Max lifted Bobby into his arms and Kaitland turned toward the stairs. "Are you ready for a bath, buddy?'' she heard Max ask.

Rand suddenly broke into more gales of laughter.

Even Elizabeth chuckled.

Kaitland turned to see what was the matter. "Again?'' she asked, dismayed, seeing the stain spread down Max's shirt.

"Again?'' Rand asked, his eyebrows shooting up.

"We'll have no trouble potty training this one,'' Max said to his brother. "Just put one of my shirts over the potty-chair and he'll do it every time.''

Mortified, Kaitland hurried over to Max. "I'm so sorry, Max. Why don't I just give them a bath tonight? I appreciate your offer, but you don't have to...''

"I want to,'' Max said, his gaze reassuring her. Then with a rueful smile, he added, "Besides, I'm already a mess.''

They walked up the stairs together. Kaitland could easily imagine them as a family taking their children to bed. Realizing how dangerous those thoughts were, she instead asked Max, "Are you sure you want to do this?''

Max smiled. "Believe it or not, I'm having fun.'' His smile faded. "I've been restless lately, bored with life. Like I was missing something. These children have filled a void I didn't know existed. I need to get out more, do more charity work, get in touch with people, I suppose. But because of the publicity the family attracts, I tend to isolate myself.''

Kaitland didn't comment. Max was looking at these kids as more than charity, she was afraid. He truly enjoyed them. She knew, from being a foster mother in the past, that you could easily grow to love the kids in your care only to have your heart ripped out when it was time for them to leave. But she also knew she wouldn't trade that experience for anything in the world. She wasn't married, would probably never marry, so the only kids she would ever have would be those who passed through her doors from Social Services.

"If you'll watch them while I prepare the bathroom?" Kaitland asked.

"No problem," Max said, and sat down in a chair. The two children, released, began to squeal and run around the room. Maddie, of course, danced back and forth in her exuberance. Bobby quickly made his way to the toy box where he collapsed and began to play.

Kaitland laid out the towels on the floor and along the rim of the tub. She ran just enough water to fill the bottom of the tub, then went to get the children.

Max was on the floor making childish faces at Maddie, who was suspended over his head. When he saw Kaitland, he immediately stopped. "She was bored. I had to find something to do." Scooping up one child under each arm, he started toward the bathroom.

Horrified, Kaitland took Bobby.

Max chuckled. "Don't worry. These two, I have decided, are indestructible."

He looked around in approval at the bathroom. "I take it they must make quite a mess."

"It's an experience," Kaitland replied as she stripped down Bobby.

Max removed Maddie's clothes and put her in the tub. "Wheee!" she cried out and splashed.

Max blinked as water splashed him in the face. "A definite experience."

Before Kaitland knew what he was up to, he had snagged the bottom of his shirt and lifted it off. "I'm going to need a whole new wardrobe of things that aren't *dry-clean only*. That, or buy up a line of dry-cleaning stores.''

Kaitland didn't comment. She couldn't.

She'd forgotten how beautiful Max was. That was one of the reasons she'd always enjoyed swimming with him. His body was a work of art. She could sit back and appreciate how well in shape he kept himself. Hair was sprinkled across his tanned chest and narrowed down to his pants. She had thought one day to be able to claim that body as hers, too. She'd always been dowdy-looking, as far as she was concerned, and it had flattered her outrageously that such a beautiful man found her beautiful, too, wanted her as his wife, loved her and was willing to promise to be hers for the rest of his life. Tears pricked her eyes.

She swallowed and turned her attention to Bobby.

Max's strong, tanned hands joined hers in the tub as they bathed both children in silence. Finally, Max said, ''I can't understand why the mother deserted her children.''

''Who knows,'' Kaitland replied, soaping Bobby's arms as he splashed and gurgled. ''As you pointed out to me earlier, there are any number of reasons. You're rich. You could give them a better home. Or maybe she just couldn't take care of them.''

''I'd find a way for these two little cherubs.''

''Maybe this was her way,'' Kaitland said. Turning her gaze to his, she continued earnestly, ''She's got to know you and know what type of person you are or she wouldn't have named one of her babies after you. Maybe she knew you were kind and gentle.'' Her gaze slid away, focusing on the children once again. ''I know that's why my mother left my stepbrother and me in my grandmother's care.''

''You never talked about her with me—before,'' Max said quietly.

''Maybe I was caught up in the romance of dating *the* Max Stevens,'' she replied. ''I don't know. I do know that my grandmother was a sweet but stern lady who loved Robert and me very much.''

''Did you ever...did you miss your parents much?'' Max

continued questioning as Maddie slowly relaxed in the tub
and let Max bathe her.

"I suppose I did. But whereas Robert ran hard, using alcohol and women to fill that void, I ran to God. God gave me
a peace and acceptance I needed. I found out He could be a
comforter when my grandmother didn't understand what I was
going through."

She lifted Bobby into her arms and wrapped him in a huge,
fluffy, peach terry-cloth towel.

"And despite that, you still talk with Robert." He sounded
amazed and just a little humbled, but couldn't help it. Kaitland
had such a forgiving heart. More so than anyone he knew.

Holding Maddie, Max followed her into the next room. He
chucked Maddie under the chin before grabbing a diaper and
watching Kaitland skillfully wrap it around the child.

"He's my brother. I'd never stop talking to him. I do pray
for him though. I keep hoping he'll come back to God, turn
away from the life he's leading."

"All you can do is trust God and pray," he agreed. Taking
the sleeper that Kaitland had laid out, he tried to get Maddie's
feet into it. Just as he'd get one in and start on the other, the
little termagant would pull out the first foot then wiggle her
toes.

"Here, let me dress Maddie," Kaitland said. "You finish
up Bobby."

Max realized Bobby was almost asleep. Without arguing,
he brushed past her and worked Bobby's feet into the sleeper.
He noted Kaitland had put the sleeves on first. A much more
effective way, he was sure. Snapping up the garment, he carefully lifted the sleeping child into his arms.

Bobby only stirred a bit. Tenderly, he brushed a lock of
hair off Bobby's forehead. "They're so small, so innocent. I
hate to see a strike against them already."

"What do you mean?" Kaitland asked, taking Maddie to
the rocking chair where she sat and began to rock her.

Max sat on the edge of the bed and watched Kaitland,
thinking how beautiful she looked sitting there, how maternal.
Even as he had the thought he realized that he had a child on

his shoulder and that he was patting the boy's back. He wondered how he looked to Kaitland. "I wonder if the mother realizes these children will have to go into foster care.if she doesn't come back."

"Who knows what was on her mind. Maybe she thought you'd just keep them."

He laughed, though it sounded unsteady. "Keep them? I'm not a father. I could never be a father. I mean, there's more to being a father than this."

Isn't there? he asked himself. You had to be married and wait nine months while you read scores of books on the subject and then you had to go through the labor and delivery and they would have a mother and you missed many nights of sleep...or at least, that's what he'd always thought being a parent meant.

"I wonder if, when I find the kids' mother, she'll agree to let the children be adopted out to someone. I'd be more than willing to contact a lawyer and arrange everything."

Kaitland glanced up at him. "I'm sure she'd want that. Max, she wouldn't have left them if she could've kept them. I know people do that all the time, but look at the diaper bags, and the clothes. Whoever was their mother cared for these children deeply. She only wants what's best. When you find her, I'm sure she'll thank you for your help."

Kaitland stood and quietly glided across the floor to the cribs. She lay down Maddie. Leaning over, she placed a kiss on the little girl's cheek. "Good night, sweet one." Then she said a soft prayer over the child.

Turning, she held out her arms for Bobby. Max stood and handed her the child then stepped back and watched while she did the same with Bobby.

Max stepped forward, and for the first time, placed a kiss on Maddie's cheek. It was soft and warm. A shuddering little sigh escaped her mouth and she popped her thumb in it. The he turned to Bobby, placed a kiss on his cheek—he was already sucking his thumb. Turning to Kaitland, he intended to tell her good-night. But when he saw her quickly glance at his chest, then avert her gaze, he forgot his intentions. When he'd stripped off his shirt, he hadn't thought about Kaitland being in the room. How many times had they gone swimming together? He didn't realize Kaitland would even notice.

The longing he'd seen so briefly in her eyes—he realized it mirrored what was in his own heart. Before he could think better of it, he stepped forward and took Kaitland in his arms. "Good night, Katie," he whispered huskily, and then, lowering his head, he touched his lips to hers, a gentle kiss, nondemanding, but exquisitely tender, and filled with longing.

The kiss brought back good memories. Too many. And with one last gentle kiss, he lifted his head.

Staring down at her soft features his heart twisted with remorse. *Why? Oh, Katie, why?* his anguish cried out.

Dropping his arms, he turned and left the room.

Katie opened her eyes, saw Max scoop up his discarded shirt and leave without another word. Gently, she touched her lips, shaking with old desires she'd forgotten existed.

How could she have forgotten how much she'd enjoyed kissing Max, how sweet and tender his embraces were? Trembling from head to toe, she sank onto the edge of the rocker.

She wondered if Max had forgotten, too.

Or was that why he'd left in such a hurry?

With a sigh she remembered other times she and Max had shared a tender kiss or look of longing and wondered if Max recalled them. But more important, she wondered what he would do tomorrow after what had just happened tonight.

Would he acknowledge the feelings still between them or pretend that nothing at all had happened?

Kaitland wasn't sure she wanted to know.

Chapter Twelve

He did neither. He completely avoided her. It had been five days since the kiss they'd shared and she hadn't seen Max. She knew he'd been in to visit the children. Darlene had told her that. Evidently, he was scoping out her schedule and working around it.

She'd explained to him once before that the children needed him in their life. Well, she needed him too…at least occasionally. True, she was an employee, but that kiss changed things.

You didn't kiss your employees. At least, that was the excuse she was using concerning Max.

Both Rand and Elizabeth were giving her strange looks. She figured they blamed her for Max's absences from meals and the odd hours he now stayed at work. She knew Max blamed her for that accidental kiss or he wouldn't be avoiding her. And she didn't want him avoiding her because she wouldn't get the problems between them solved if he kept hiding out.

Therefore, now that the kids were taking their morning nap, she was going to hunt down Max and try talking to him. She'd come up with the perfect excuse—the children needed to get out and she wanted to make sure it was okay to take them on an all-day excursion.

Of course, she shouldn't take that kind of trip with them without making sure it was okay with Max. She never took them off the property without letting him know since there were always reporters hounding his steps.

She checked her hair in the mirror, to see if her French braid was neat. Her jeans and soft baby blue top brought out the green of her eyes and the blush... Realizing she was checking her appearance for his sake, she rolled her eyes. If she went down there looking as if she'd dressed ready to kill, he'd run even farther away. She only wanted to set things straight, get back on an even keel, not chase him off.

She went downstairs, checking room by room as she passed them. In one room she stumbled onto Rand and Elizabeth hugging.

"Oh!" Her cheeks pinkened. "I'm sorry." She started to back out, embarrassed to catch them in an intimate embrace.

Rand grinned, but didn't release his wife. "Honeymoon, you know. What do you need?"

He looked so much like Max it made her remember Max's embrace. "I was just looking for Max."

"The study."

She nodded and backed out.

"Close the door, please, Kaitland."

She heard a muttered exclamation from Elizabeth, but didn't stop to hear what Elizabeth was berating Rand for. Rand's husky laugh followed her out the door.

She didn't remember Rand ever being this carefree five years ago. He'd always been at the office when she'd visited before. Rarely had she seen him around the house. Come to think of it, he was *very* carefree, laughing, joking, his eyes twinkling with a merriment she'd never seen in him, but often seen in Max.

Except that she never saw it in Max now, only occasionally, when one of the children did something to amuse him.

Going to the study, she found him there. He was sitting with his back to the door, holding something in his hand and staring out the balcony doors. "Excuse me, Max, but I had heard you were home and..."

Max whirled, his eyes widening in surprise. Quickly, he

slid a paper under a manila envelope on his desk. "What can I do for you, Katie?"

Curious, she eyed his desk. She watched him nonchalantly fold his hands over the envelope.

"Look, Max, I know you've been avoiding me and we need to talk."

She hadn't been going to say that at all. She wanted to call the words back, start out softer instead. But it was too late and Max reacted the way she thought he would.

He sighed, a look of pained frustration on his face. "It was a mistake. I was feeling close to the kids, enjoying the intimacy they offered, and I stepped over the line. I shouldn't have. I hope we can just forget it."

She shouldn't be hurt by his attitude, knowing it was purely defensive on his part, but she was. "Forget it? Well, now, Max, that's going to be pretty hard to do unless you tell me you go around kissing all your female employees like that."

She waited. When he didn't answer, her anger at his continued rejection made her fist her hands on her hips. She was bursting over everything that was between them. All she wanted was peace again. Was that so much to ask?

Max blew out a breath. Shoving himself up from the desk, he went to the balcony doors and resumed staring out. "It doesn't matter what I do with *all my female employees,*" Max replied sarcastically. "You and I are no longer dating."

Kaitland reeled as if she'd been slapped. But instead of retreating, she went forward. "I was out of line," she said quietly. "You're right. But, Max, I'm working in this house. You can't wash hot and cold like this. If we're going to work together, then we need to establish some ground rules, forget the past and go on from here."

She was by his desk now. She absently glanced down to what he had hidden, wondering what it was. Kaitland would like to think, under normal circumstances, she wouldn't have looked. But when she saw a corner of the picture that showed a bed, a man and a woman's leg...a sick feeling rose inside her. Surely it couldn't be, not after all this time.

She reached down and pulled the picture out from under the envelope. Cold sweat broke out on her.

"No, Katie. Don't look."

She and the senator. The senator pinning her to the bed as he kissed her. Her dress hiked up to her thighs with his leg wedged between hers.

She was going to be sick.

Across the bottom was scrawled the word *Remember.*

"Oh, Max," she whispered, tears coming to her eyes. After all these years, she would have hoped he'd at least forgiven her her part in the whole mess.

"Listen to me, Katie," Max said, coming toward her, but her eyes were so full of tears she couldn't see what he was feeling, could only hear desperation in his voice. The desperation of someone guilty, caught in his crime.

The picture slid from her fingers, and without another word, she turned and fled.

"Katie! Katie, come back here now!" Max ran after her, but stopped at the door, watching as she raced up the stairs. "Katie!" he called out, anger in his voice.

The door down the hall flew open and Rand came out. Seeing Katie's flight, he turned on his brother. He strode angrily toward Max. But as he watched Max, anger slowly left his face until concern was left. "I was about to blast you for upsetting her again, until I saw your face, little brother. Want to talk?"

Miserable, Max nodded. "I thought maybe she had something to do with it. But I don't think so now. I should have made sure it was put up..."

"What are you talking about, Max?"

"Close the door, will you?"

Rand pushed the door closed. "Now, will you explain why you scared ten years off Elizabeth's life and left Katie in tears...again?"

"You've always blamed me for our breakup, haven't you, Rand?"

Rand sighed. "I don't blame you. I think you should have talked with her, tried to work things out. It was obvious the way you grieved that you loved her, Max. I don't understand why she would do something like that, but maybe she was being blackmailed, or she had to have money. I don't know. But you never gave her a chance to explain."

"That's just it. She had a month to tell me, but never did."

Rand sat down by Max on the couch, staring off in the distance. "I know that. And I've always really liked Kaitland. That's why I can't understand what happened. She just wasn't that type of girl." He sighed. "I wish it could have worked out. But, it didn't. And no one's to blame if you choose to go separate ways. But if that's the case and she's now tormenting you so, why do you keep her here?"

"This has nothing to do with my feelings for Katie." Max stood and went to his desk. He brought back the picture and handed it to Rand.

Rand took one look at it and started to discard it, then paused. "Where'd you get this?"

"At least *you* believe I haven't been tormenting myself with old pictures of Katie. This was in today's mail."

Rand frowned, sitting forward. "Why?"

"My question exactly. When it happened five years ago I could understand why. Someone was warning me about what was going on behind my back. But why now? Katie and I aren't involved. These pictures are old. I know all about her."

"Unless someone is worried you'll become involved with her again."

"But why would it matter? The only thing I can come up with is that Katie is somehow involved and it's the precursor to getting blackmail money."

"You think whoever was trying to blackmail you five years ago has come back?"

Max shrugged.

"And you think Katie is involved."

"It seems strange that when she shows up, the pictures suddenly show up again." He handed Rand an envelope with two more pictures inside.

"Katie saw these and thinks you kept them around to remind you of her betrayal."

Max nodded. "And I started to go after her. But now I'm not so sure if I should. I'm tempted to try and mend the fences, Rand. I'd like to date her again. But these pictures, it brings it all back. I don't see how we'll ever be able to let go of the past."

Rand was quiet a long time. "You're going to have to forgive her, Max."

"I have forgiven her," Max argued, appalled.

"Have you forgiven yourself, too, then?"

"What do you mean?"

"I know you. You blame yourself for her going to someone else. I saw it in your eyes right after it happened." Rand's voice dropped, more emotion than he usually showed sounding in every word he spoke as he stared Max in the eye. "And no matter how much you say you've forgiven her, you haven't. You may convince everyone else, but you won't even listen to an explanation from her. Why?"

Max turned from Rand's stare but wouldn't answer.

"Because you're afraid of what you might hear?" Rand asked.

Max scowled. "I don't want to hear that I wasn't what she needed. Call me vain, but I loved her. I can't face that."

"You're not vain, just hurting. Go to God, Max. Let Him heal your heart so you and Kaitland can both be healed. Even if you don't end up together, you need to go on, let go of this pain."

"But someone isn't going to let us, are they?" he said, motioning to the picture.

Rand slipped the picture into the folder and turned back to Max. "I'll get these to one of our lawyers. It's time someone else knew about this, so don't argue. We'll take it one day at a time. Don't tell Katie, if that's what you feel like. I won't interfere, but we have to consider that someone out there hasn't forgotten. This isn't some whim like we thought five years ago. Whoever wanted to blackmail us before is making it clear they're going to try again."

Max dropped his head back on the sofa. "I'm really sorry,

Rand. This isn't much of a thing to come back to after your honeymoon.''

Rand grinned. "I hate to tell you, brother, but the honeymoon ain't gonna end just because we have a few fiery trials to face. God will see us through, and Elizabeth isn't as worried about her reputation as Carolyn was. She's a real trouper and will thumb her nose at the media if this leaks out.''

Max smiled, though he knew the expression looked weary. "I only hope Katie will be able to do the same, since these pictures are of her.''

"Kaitland? It's me, Elizabeth. Can I come in?''

Kaitland quickly wiped the tears from her face before opening the bathroom door. "Are the children awake?''

Elizabeth rolled her eyes. "Do you really think I'm going to be distracted that easily? You know why I've come here. Rand and I almost had a cow when Max shouted downstairs. He never shouts. His voice just gets low and his eyes narrow when he's angry.''

"Not this time.''

"I know a woman in distress when I see one. That's why I came up to check on you when I saw you tear up the stairs.''

Kaitland felt tears coming again. "Thank you, but there's nothing you can do.''

Elizabeth grabbed her arm and dragged her over to the sofa. "Usually with my patients I tell jokes. Wanna hear one?''

"I don't think I'm exactly in a mood for a joke,'' she replied, the tears still sounding obvious in her voice.

"Then that's just the time you need it,'' Elizabeth said, then, "So, how many Stevens brothers does it take to screw in a lightbulb?''

Kaitland shook her head. "I don't know. Two?''

Elizabeth smiled. "Are you kidding? They're too thick-headed to realize they can do it themselves. They get a servant to do it.''

Kaitland did smile. "That's awful.''

"Well, those men can be pretty awful sometimes, too. I

swear, there are times I'd like to hit Rand with a two-by-four...several times.''

Kaitland laughed. ''I know. Max is so stubborn. I thought he'd forgotten...'' Her voice trailed off.

''What?''

Kaitland sighed. ''You know Max and I were engaged to be married. It was a great time. We were so in love. I admit I was naive, a little awed by all of this.'' She swept her hand around the room. ''Even my brother tried to convince me I wasn't in love with Max. But I was, very in love, despite how shy I was over the media attention and Max's money. And I thought he was in love with me.''

She sighed again, her shoulders sagging as she remembered.

''My brother is a user,'' Kaitland continued. ''Actually, he isn't really my brother. He's my stepbrother, as he will point out, but to me he's flesh and blood. When we were small, my mom married his dad. They died in an auto accident not too long afterward. We had nowhere to go, so my grandmother raised us both. Robert always felt like the outsider, claiming he didn't belong.''

''And you felt guilty for that,'' Elizabeth concluded.

''Just a little. I love him. He had no family left after our parents died...except me. And he and my grandmother didn't get along. Anyway, he's gotten involved in lobbying and attends huge balls and fancy dinners. I'm very uncomfortable at these functions...you aren't going to discuss this with anyone, are you?'' she suddenly asked, wringing her hands.

''Of course not!'' Elizabeth said. ''What you say won't leave this room. Gossip is a very distasteful thing.''

Kaitland felt the trembling start deep down in her soul as she began to explain.

''I went to a party one night that my brother begged me to attend. During the party I got a note. I thought it was from Robert, asking me to meet him in his room. So, I went up there. Instead, a drunk senator was waiting. He—'' Kaitland's eyes dropped. ''He tried to rape me.''

''Oh, dear.'' Elizabeth moved closer.

Kaitland felt her slip her arm around her and she gratefully leaned into the silent support Elizabeth offered.

"Rand's going to kill me for upsetting you."

"I'll handle Rand. If he kicks up a fuss, I'll just faint in his arms."

Despite the seriousness of the situation, Kaitland giggled. "You really are awful."

"I know. But don't you just love me."

Kaitland giggled again.

"So, what did Max say when you told him?"

"I didn't."

"You didn't tell Max?" She sounded incredulous.

"I was so embarrassed and ashamed. How could I look my fiancé in the eyes and tell him that at the party I'd gone to with my brother, a party, I might add, that Max had asked me not to go to with my brother because he believed Robert was only using me." She shuddered. "Anyway, how could I tell him that while there I met a man in my room and he was drunk and almost raped me."

"He needed to know."

Kaitland pulled away. "You're telling me. I kept wanting to tell him. Things became strained. I was awful. I pulled away from him whenever he hugged or kissed me. I couldn't deal with being touched. It wasn't Max. I needed him, but felt suffocated. It's hard to explain." She shuddered at the memories. "I also couldn't handle the hurt and confusion in Max's eyes, either. It killed me that whenever he would try to kiss me, I would stiffen up, only for him to pull back, and with such a look of hurt and confusion in his eyes. How could I explain what I felt?

"Just before the wedding, I decided to tell him. You see, it wasn't fair to Max. And I wanted to go to counseling and I didn't want to hide that from Max. Besides, I had decided I could trust him, that he wouldn't turn away in betrayal or disgust. After all, look what he'd been through the month after the incident, and he was still there despite how shabbily I had treated him."

"What happened?" Elizabeth asked softly, taking Kaitland's hand. Kaitland noted her knuckles were white where she gripped them together.

What had she done? she mused. "He walked into the room where I was sitting and dropped some photographs in my lap. They were photos of me and the senator, lying on the bed in what looked like a very intimate embrace.

"Max knew which party they'd been taken at since I hadn't attended any others," she continued. "He made an unimportant comment inferring my betrayal. Then he turned around and walked out."

"Oh, Kaitland." Elizabeth's voice ached with remorse.

"That was five years ago. I thought it would be good to see him again, work through the past so we could get on with our lives. I even thought God was leading me here. But now I'm not so sure. Just now, when I went down to his study, he had one of the pictures, he was looking at it, and across the bottom was the word *Remember*."

"Oh, Kaitland," Elizabeth murmured again.

"I don't know what to do." Kaitland allowed the tears to flow again, crying out all her hurt and pain. Elizabeth murmured soft words of comfort as she held Kaitland.

"You know," Elizabeth said when Kaitland finished crying and pulled away. "Sometimes healing can be very painful. And a lot of times it doesn't happen overnight. We have to take it one day at a time. The blind patients I work with have to relearn the layout of their houses, the way to dress, to eat, to converse, everything. Our spiritual healings are like that, too. We have to take one day at a time and let God pull out each fear and pain and deal with it. That's one of the most painful processes you can go through, especially if the wound has set for very long. Like a broken bone that has to be rebroken and set, we sometimes have to have everything dredged up and the air cleared before the trust can be reestablished."

Elizabeth handed her several tissues. "I guess what I'm saying is, if you think God sent you here, then play like a bulldog and clamp those teeth into this and don't let go, no matter how rough the ride. Keep smiling no matter how painful and let God do His work. I'll be praying for you and I know Rand will. He really likes you a lot. And, believe it or not, I bet Max is praying about this, too. Trust God to do His work, Kaitland. And trust Him to work it out for what's best for both you and Max.''

Kaitland leaned over and hugged Elizabeth. ''Thanks, Elizabeth. You're right. I will.'' She stood. ''Now, you'd better find Rand before he comes to make sure you're resting.''

Elizabeth groaned.

Kaitland chuckled. ''And I'm going to go check on the kiddos. It's about time for them to get up. And every time I've been late getting them from Darlene, I've caught at least one of them eating something that's not edible!''

''I wish I could help,'' Elizabeth said, grinning.

''No you don't. You want to be with your husband. Now go.''

She watched Elizabeth leave. Her smile left her face as soon as Elizabeth was out of sight. Elizabeth was right. She had to trust God to handle the mess she'd made five years ago. And no matter what, she just had to grin and bear it and know God would work it out for the best.

Father, I'm leaving this in Your hands. My heart. Max's heart. Our future. Please handle this as You see fit and give me the courage to face Your answers.

As if on cue, one of the children could be heard from down the hall. *Thank You,* she added to the end of her prayer, then headed out of the room. Time to get back to doing what she was hired to do and just let God handle the rest.

Chapter Thirteen

Crash!

Max jumped up from the chair in his study. Tossing down the papers he'd been working on he hurried around the desk and to the door. He skidded to a stop just outside, staring in dismay at the scene before him.

He should have known not to come out here. Something had warned him. Kaitland was in a red bathing suit, holding both kids, who were wearing blue suits, with a broken vase scattered around her. And of course she wasn't wearing any shoes.

"I didn't mean to disturb you. Could you, um, possibly call for Sarah and we'll wait here?"

Max thought about doing exactly that. He hadn't wanted to be involved with Kaitland. He had decided to treat her as an employer would an employee and be courteous. He had figured that would set everything to right and they could go on. But seeing her here, like this... She was so vulnerable. Enough was enough. Rand was right. He should put forth the effort to be a friend. He walked forward. "Let me take the kids."

"No. Really. That's okay."

"Katie. Don't argue." Bobby came willingly and Maddie lunged. He took them across the floor, handing them to the butler who had just rounded the corner, and who immediately gaped like a fish out of water. Max grinned when he saw

Bobby pull his wet fingers out of his mouth and rub them on Timms's shirt.

When he turned back to Kaitland, she was still standing in the same place staring in dismay at the mess around her. Smiling, he decided to enjoy her discomfort, only for a moment. After all, it had been he who had been miserable this last week. And maybe his sense of humor would restore her good mood. He hated seeing the cautious look in her eyes whenever he was around.

"Well, are you going to send for Sarah?" she asked.

"I don't know. What will you give me if I do?"

Kaitland glanced up, unsure.

He was happy when he saw her features relax. "I'll break some more stuff trying to climb up this table to get around these pieces of pottery if you don't," she retorted, placing her hands on her hips.

"You'd ruin my house?" he asked, feigning astonishment

"I don't see that I'd have any choice, Mr. Stevens."

"You could ask me for help," he replied smugly.

"I thought I did that."

"No, you wanted Sarah's help. How about asking me specifically?"

She crossed her arms.

He sighed. "Well, I suppose I'll have to help you anyway. So, where were you headed, the pool?"

"How'd you guess?" she replied sarcastically.

He came forward, pottery crunching under his feet. "I had a feeling."

Wary again, she watched his approach. "What are you doing?"

"Helping you out." He scooped her up. "You've lost weight," he commented.

She hit him on the shoulder. "That's none of your business. Now put me down!"

"I dunno." He lifted her, bouncing her slightly in his arms. "I might want to find out why you've gotten so skinny first."

"Max," she warned.

He grinned, carried her over to where the kids were and

allowed her to slide down out of his arms. He saw that her cheeks were pink. The old heat warmed his body as he realized how much this woman still meant to him. Why *not* try to be friends? If that was all she wanted, surely he could work his way toward that.

"You're not going in alone with both of the kids, are you?" he suddenly asked, not seeing Darlene around.

"Of course I am. I'm a good swimmer."

"But I know these two," Max said, and making a sudden decision, added, "Go on, I'll be out in a minute."

"No! I mean, that's okay."

"Nonsense," Max replied, already heading up the stairs. "I was only doing the boring fiscal reports. Rand is back so my workload is much lighter, but I still need a break."

In minutes Max joined them at the pool, dressed in a pair of green and black bathing trunks. Kaitland watched him dive in and swim toward them. Maddie and Bobby were both in life preservers, having a blast. "Catch, Maddie," Kaitland called. She tossed a small floating ball to Maddie.

Maddie squealed and reached out for it. Grabbing the ball, she threw it, and caught Max in the middle of the chest just as he surfaced. "Whoa, che'rie," Max drawled, fumbling and finally grabbing the hand-size ball.

"Mine!" Maddie demanded, holding out her hands.

Max chuckled and threw her the ball. Maddie threw the ball aside and held out her arms again. "Mine!"

"I think she means you," Kaitland said.

Max smiled. "Indeed she does." He moved forward and bussed Maddie on the cheek. Waving her arms wildly, she threw up water, squealing again.

Bobby blinked, shook his head from the drenching and then held out his arms, too. Kaitland intercepted Bobby, holding out her fingers and letting him pull himself along through the water. He was enraptured with the game, kicking his feet, laughing, shaking his head whenever he accidentally splashed water in his face.

All in all, it was a wonderful time of fun. "I told Sarah

we'll have lunch out here," Max told her when he saw Darlene bringing food out to the table.

Kaitland was surprised. Not only at his thoughtfulness but at how easygoing he'd been all day. "Okay," she agreed, wanting to prolong their camaraderie. "It's probably time for the kids to get out anyway."

She climbed from the water, feeling as if she'd put on at least twenty pounds when her feet hit solid ground. Picking up Maddie, she headed for the table. Max followed, carrying Bobby.

They strapped both kids into the high chairs that had been brought outside. Then soup and sandwiches were served.

"No!" Maddie replied when Kaitland tried to feed her the soup.

"No!" Bobby echoed.

"I thought they'd be hungry," Max said and again offered the soup. Bobby rubbed his eyes and pushed the spoon away.

"They're tired. They've had a full morning. Maybe they'll eat if they can feed themselves," she added. Cutting up one of the sandwiches into small pieces, she set it before the children.

Bobby immediately ate several bites. Maddie had to peel back the bread and examine what was in it, making disgusting faces when the mayonnaise caused the bread to stick to her fingers. She ate the meat inside, though.

With an eye on them, Kaitland sat back and enjoyed the soup.

"I enjoyed this morning, Katie," Max said, tasting his soup.

"The kids are fun," she replied.

"I enjoyed you, too," he added.

Kaitland's spoon paused.

"I've been thinking over what happened the other day," Max said. "I want to apologize for my actions. Rand pointed out to me that I've been pigheaded and I should do my best to let go of the past and get on with my life. I'll be honest. I don't know how well I'll do, but if we could start out working toward one goal, I think we might do it. I'd like to work toward being friends. Maybe if we can just take one day at a time, be civil and promise not to look back, each day it will get easier to forget. I think five years ago, we both ran from the pain instead of confronting it.''

''You ran, Max. Not me.''

''But you never bothered to tell me, just pulled away from me at every opportunity.''

Tell him, a voice whispered, but she couldn't. She couldn't sound as if she was giving him an excuse for her behavior when it had been so wrong. ''You're right. We both made mistakes. All I'm asking is when you find the kids' mother, we part as friends. Nothing more. I'd like that.''

Max nodded. ''I'd like that, too.''

''There's a children's show at the library next week. They're having a clown. It's a lot of fun. I usually volunteer each summer...but you know that.''

''I think Maddie and Bobby would like that.''

Kaitland smiled. ''I'd like that, too.'' Looking to where Maddie was beginning to nod off, she stood. ''I have to get the children up and changed for their nap. You want to help?''

''Sure,'' Max replied, standing. Something had finally been accomplished. He pushed the fear that she might be involved in the latest blackmail scheme to the back of his mind. He was going to take this one day at a time. Only one day. Everything was fine today, he'd deal with that.

He juggled until he could pick Maddie up.

''Max, you have a phone call from a private investigator. Dugan Lawrence.''

Max looked up to where Sarah had appeared. He glanced back to where Kaitland held Bobby and saw the disappointment in her eyes. ''Can you do this alone? That's the people who are working on finding the kids' mother.''

''Do you think they've found her?''

''I don't know. But Dugan rarely calls in the middle of the day like this. I'd say it's promising.''

He started to hand the baby over to Kaitland, but Sarah intercepted her. ''I'll take her, Maxwell. You go answer that call.''

He smiled. "Thank you, Sarah. I'll be up as soon as I'm off the phone and let you know what they said," he told Kaitland as he turned toward the doors that led to the den.

As he left, he wondered at his feelings. He was excited to be talking with Dugan, but worried, too. His gut was clenched as he wondered if he was about to lose the kids after searching so long for the mother, and he worried about Kaitland, too. They'd just resolved to try to work out their problems. Surely their time wasn't about to end now, was it?

Going into the den, he picked up the phone.

Chapter Fourteen

"She's dead."

"What?" Kaitland stared at Max's strained features.

"That's why Dugan has had so much trouble finding her. The mother is dead. But we do know who she is. Her name was Samantha Jenkins. Dugan traced her back to a shelter for unwed mothers. She evidently was dropped off there by a man late one night, aeons ago. According to the woman at the shelter, Samantha wouldn't say who the father was, just that she wanted to keep the babies, was running from an ex-boyfriend and that a man had picked her up alongside the road and given her a ride."

"You were that man?"

Max nodded. "I was driving home one night and saw her walking along the road. She was huge. I thought she was going to have the babies any minute. She assured me she had a month to go. I bought her a meal, prayed with her, gave her some money."

Max sat down in the outer room of the nursery. "According to Dugan, she had the babies two weeks later, was up on her feet and went to work at a restaurant in town. From what he can find out from her co-workers, Samantha was being harassed by her old boyfriend to go back to whatever she had once done. She didn't want to, so she decided she had to run. Her co-workers said she was afraid he'd use the kids against her—probably why she left them with me."

"So, who is the father?"

"No one's listed on the birth certificates and she never mentioned his name to anyone."

"So, what are we going to do now?"

"Kaitland, do you suppose we could get your pastor to help us pull some strings and get them temporarily assigned to you, here at my house, just until I can get my lawyers to find someone to adopt them? Or until I get temporarily certified as an emergency foster parent?"

Kaitland's eyes widened. "I might be able to. We'd need to make an appointment with Jake, go in and talk to him. Then we can see what he says."

"Good. Make the appointment for tomorrow. We'll get Darlene to watch the kids.

Kaitland nodded. "I hope you know what you're doing," she replied, but in her heart, she knew he was doing the right thing. He would make sure the children went to a good home. She trusted Max on this.

He stood. "I need to get back to work. Give the kids my love when they wake up."

"I will," she replied, her heart flopping over at his words. Those babies didn't know how much Max loved them yet. Nor, Kaitland was afraid, had Max himself figured it out yet, either.

"So, what is it that you needed to talk to me about?" Jake asked, leaning back in his chair and studying Max and Kaitland.

Max sat with his legs crossed, the picture of elegance in his casual gray suit, while Kaitland wore one of the drop-waist dresses she referred to as her day-care attire. Loose, simple and able to take any stains. Her hair was pulled back in a braid and she squirmed as Jake studied her.

"Kaitland and I have come to you for help," Max said. "I'm not sure if you know that Katie has been an emergency foster parent for years."

Jake smiled. "As a matter of fact, I do. I'm just surprised she told you. Kaitland isn't a very talkative person."

He had been joking, but Max took him seriously, Kaitland

could tell by the strange look he shot her. *Oh no,* she thought. *Don't tell him. He doesn't know* you *are the one.* "Katie and I go way back," Max said, not catching the mild panic in her eyes.

She saw the moment Jake made the connection. His smile dropped away and his eyes shot to Katie in shock. Max was still looking at Kaitland so he didn't see her pastor's reaction.

"I've known for a long time she wanted to be a foster parent," he continued. "I even knew her when she filled out the paperwork." A shadow crossed his face before his expression was once again impassive. She knew he was remembering that was just before the ball that had ruined their lives, though she hadn't sent off the paperwork until after their breakup. She'd told Max she wanted to hold on to the documents and pray first.

"You know of the children that were left on my doorstep anonymously," Max said. "We finally found the mother. Unfortunately, she's dead. She was killed in an auto accident in Texas. There's no father listed."

Jake nodded, then addressed Kaitland, "What's the problem?"

"We want help talking with the agencies about me keeping the children at Max's house until he can get his lawyers to find someone to adopt them," Kaitland said.

Jake looked from one to the other, his hands steepled in front of his lips. Finally, his gaze rested on Max. "Why?"

Kaitland would have worried over Jake's statement had it been delivered to her in such a blunt tone. But Max, used to big business deals, was unflappable. He uncrossed his legs, folded his hands over his flat stomach and met Jake's stare with one that was deadly serious. "I feel responsible for these children. The mother left them in my care for a reason. True, I only fed her and gave her a lift to the unwed mothers' home. But in her mind, she felt that was enough to judge me as a responsible person to leave her babies with. I've watched Maddie and Bobby over the last few weeks. They're very attached to each other. If they go into foster care with someone else, it's not guaranteed they'll be kept together...especially if someone adopts them. I'd like to keep them at my house with temporary guardianship until I can get my lawyers working on finding someone to adopt them. I'm rich. In this world, money does talk. I'm willing to use the money to help these children. And though prayer doesn't matter to the world, I do pray and think it's God's will that these children stay here. God tells us we should feed the hungry. I can provide for these children while my lawyers find adoptive parents.''

''And you know it'll take a while to certify Max since he's never been a foster parent, but I'm already certified,'' Kaitland added.

''Many will assume you wish to adopt because you're the children's natural father, Max. What about your reputation, should this get out?'' Jake said. ''Or how about Kaitland's reputation?''

Max flinched a tad and Kaitland was sure he was thinking of her reputation with him, or lack thereof. She'd had a sterling reputation once. How those pictures had stayed out of the papers, she didn't know. But the only one who knew she had a soured reputation was Max, and her pastor. And probably Rand. And Elizabeth. The list seemed to be getting longer as the years went by.

''I can't speak for Katie.'' He gave her an unfathomable look that sent a trickle of worry down her spine. It was as if he was seeing someone else, some other time, and that made him sad. Then his eyes refocused and he was his normal self again. ''But you've seen what the magazines print about me. I have a black heart and am a love-'em-and-leave-'em type of guy. Of course, it's not true, but I've learned that any storm can be weathered if you just ignore it. I have to depend on God to fight my battles in that area, though I'm not above calling the TV stations and telling them I'd be most displeased if they ran something particularly obnoxious.'' He smiled.

Kaitland wondered if he actually realized how powerful he was in the business world. Not everyone could do that. She knew he'd made his displeasure known on several occasions. Of course, the media knew he had the money to sue if they did print lies that hurt his family or business. That's the only time she'd ever seen Max carry through on a threat. He and Rand would allow no one to touch their family with cruel lies. Many retractions had appeared. But the everyday hounding and petty lies, he tended to ignore.

Knowing if this news hit the papers, who'd have a field day examining his life and those of the children, Kaitland realized Max must be much more wary of the situation than he let on. To keep a scandal at bay, he would need as much secrecy as possible until the arrangements were a fait accompli. And he would see to it, or heads would roll.

"Kaitland?" Jake asked.

"I don't think it'll get out. If it does, no one will be interested in me," she replied. "At least, not that much. I won't be under the pressure Max will be under."

Max and Jake both studied her incredulously. "I can handle it," she replied stubbornly.

"Even if the board hits the ceiling over this?" Jake asked.

"Yes. Even if the board hits the ceiling." She knew two people on the board who would have fits if it came out in the newspapers that she was working for Max. Even though nothing was going on, it would still look bad for the church. She could hear the arguments now: "She's living with a man who has two illegitimate children," they'd say. Kaitland felt sure that Max wasn't the children's father. But, she thought wearily, that would be the popular assumption. How will that look to the parents of the children she is in charge of? What about the moral clause in her contract? How will it effect newcomers to the church if a scandal is cast over this church?

And they were right, to a point. Heaven knew there had been enough church scandals in the past five years that hit the paper. But, despite how she felt over the possible repercussions, Kaitland knew she had to work out her differences with Max before she could go on with her life. She believed God was in this even if no one else did.

Jake sighed. "Very well. Max, can you give all the information to Shirley and then I'll make some calls."

Max wasn't stupid. He eyed Kaitland before standing. "I'll be out here when you're ready, Katie."

Kaitland nodded.

When the door was closed, Jake's hands fell to his desk. He leaned forward, crossed his arms and stared at her for several moments. "He's the one, isn't he?" Jake finally asked.

Katie had known that was coming. "Yes, he is."

"Why didn't you say something before I sent you to his house?"

Katie shrugged. "I felt it was time to clear the air. It was nothing against you. But you *are* a friend of the Stevens brothers. I thought maybe one of them had mentioned my relationship with Max, until you suggested I go out there."

"Correct me if I'm wrong, dear one. But don't you love him?"

Katie looked around the office, not meeting his eyes. When Jake didn't comment, she finally said, "Okay, yes, you know I do. But I specifically went out there so I could put the past behind me and go on with my life."

"You're setting yourself up in a dangerous situation, you know that, don't you, Kaitland?"

"I don't think you have anything to worry about. Max is no longer interested in me that way."

"I wouldn't be so sure. The air crackled every time he looked at you when you weren't paying attention. He might be hurting, still feel betrayed, but you're a lovely woman, one he planned to marry. I don't want you in a situation where you might end up getting hurt again."

Kaitland sighed. "I know, Jake. I promise. If things get too intense, I'll move out. But we've spent lots of time together since I started caring for the children and nothing has happened."

"Not yet," Jake said. "Just be careful."

There was a pause, then Jake asked softly. "Since you've had time with him, have you told Max everything yet?"

She flushed. "No. I'm not sure he'd forgive me even if I did tell him."

He studied Kaitland before finally saying, "Then maybe you just need to forgive him for his mistakes and leave it at that. We can't make anyone forgive us. And yes, you should have told him when it happened, but no one's perfect. If Max can't understand that and is still angry with you, then he's not the man for you. God will have someone else for you."

Jake came around the desk and took her hands. "I'm here, Kaitland, if you need me. Day or night, just give me a call."

Kaitland smiled. "Thank you."

"Let me make some calls."

She went to the door. Outside, Max was waiting for her. They walked out into the main sanctuary while they waited for Jake to make his calls. "What did Jake want?"

Kaitland sighed, dropped her head back and stared up at the vaulted ceiling. She'd love to lean just a little to her right and rest her head on Max's shoulder, but knew he wouldn't accept her need for security right now. Instead, she answered him honestly, blunting any emotions from her voice. "He didn't know you were the one I was engaged to until you mentioned it to him. He wanted to make sure I had made the right decision in staying out there with you."

"Wise man."

Kaitland turned to look at him in surprise.

"We were engaged once, Katie. Of course your pastor would be worried about the situation. And you can't deny that the attraction between us is still there. Otherwise, I wouldn't be tempted to kiss you at the most inopportune moments."

Seeing the look in his eyes, she realized this was one of those moments. He reached up and touched a loose strand of her hair. "We're both adults," she argued. "And besides, what good is attraction if there's no trust."

Max sighed, a resigned look coming to his eyes. "You're right. Without trust there's no reason to carry anything further, is there?"

Ask me why. Just ask me why, she wanted to say. Instead, he only stared at her. "No," she whispered, her gut churning as she fought and tried to tell him, then finally lost the battle. "No, no reason at all."

They sat in silence in the darkened church, the only noise from the day-care children in the background and the occasional sound of beeping from the computer in Shirley's office.

"By the way," Max said casually, looking at the nails on his right hand instead of at her, which immediately warned Kaitland she wasn't going to like what he had to say.

"Yes?" she asked when he paused.

"There is a car being delivered to the house tomorrow."

She knew immediately where this was going. She saw red. "I told you, Maxwell Edward Stevens, that I wouldn't—"

"Now, che'rie," he said, smiling congenially and holding up his hands. "I worked on your car, remember? What type of person would I be if I let you drive around in that—especially with the children in it."

"But—"

"Just think," he interrupted. "Your car is, unfortunately, a breakdown waiting to happen. What would happen if you were on the road with the kids, followed by a reporter…or at night and followed by something worse. Please accept the gift. It's not a too expensive car that would embarrass you as a gift."

Kaitland softened at those words. Even when they still had those problems between them, he was thinking of her, and what people might say if he were to give her a very expensive car. "Oh, Max," she said, dropping her head.

"Please, che'rie. Please accept the car."

She struggled. Pride wanted her to say no. But he had a good argument. "You chose your words carefully, using the kids against me, didn't you?"

He smiled a boyishly handsome smile. "It worked, didn't it?"

Reluctantly she smiled. "Yes, it worked." But it worked even better on her heart. She realized how much she truly loved this man. Not as in past tense, but now, and that she would somehow, sometime, find the courage to tell him about what happened because maybe, just maybe, he might actually be ready to understand what had happened five years ago. She hadn't thought so until now. But whether he'd meant it to or not, his concern had shown her a glimpse into his heart. The man she thought she'd known was still there, just buried under a lot of excess baggage that he had to get rid of. Exactly what it all entailed, she didn't know. But maybe they could work this all out.

"Please, Father," she whispered.

Twenty minutes passed before Jake came walking out of his office.

He propped a foot on the pew in front of him and rested his arms across his knee. "Well, it's done. Believe it or not, all I had to do was mention your name, Max, and people bent over backward. You'll have to tell Rand I might be using his name in the future when I'm dealing with some hardheaded businessman." He grinned and Max chuckled.

"I'll do that."

"The papers will be drawn up. Your lawyers should contact the social worker on the case and then you'll have documents to sign and, to make a long story short, it looks like you'll get to keep the kids without losing them any time soon. They'll process the paperwork to certify you as a foster parent just in case Kaitland wants to leave."

Kaitland flushed, knowing it was an out Jake had suggested. "Meanwhile, you need to take the children to the doctor. According to the people I spoke with, there are probably some shots and stuff the kids need, plus social services will need a medical record on file of the kids' health."

Max stood. He stuck out his hand. "Thanks, Jake. Rand was certain you'd help us, but I had my doubts, especially with our past." He glanced to Kaitland.

"Yeah, well, about that. I'll reserve judgment and trust that since both of you are Christians, you'll put God first in your relationship—or lack of one," he added when Kaitland started to object. "Just as long as you put God first."

"We'll do that," Max said. Grabbing Kaitland by the hand, he pulled her up to stand beside him. Jake, of course, didn't miss that. Kaitland's heart didn't, either, though she tried to act nonchalant. She was disappointed when he released her and placed a hand to her back. "We'll go make a doctor's appointment for the kids right now and have them examined by my store's physician. A family doctor should be all right, I suppose. I mean, they don't have to go to a pediatrician today, do they?''

Jake chuckled. ''Any doctor will be fine. Family doctors handle kids, too.''

''Good. Well, you take care and hopefully we'll bring the children to this church to visit sometime soon. We've been looking around for a new church, Rand and I. He suggested Elizabeth's church.''

''We'd be glad to have you,'' Jake said.

''Thanks again, Jake.''

Kaitland breathed a sigh of relief as they exited the sanctuary.

''Now what?'' she asked as he held the passenger-side door of the Mercedes open for her.

''Now, my dear Kaitland,'' he said, resting his hand on the door and dropping to where he could meet her eyes, ''We get to play doctor.''

Chapter Fifteen

"No, no, bad!" Maddie slapped the stethoscope away from her chest, frowning severely at the elderly doctor who was trying to do the examination.

Max had gotten quite an education about children and doctors while he was here. "Come on, che'rie," Max cooed. "Be nice."

Her lower lip jutted out. Bobby, who was confined to Kaitland's lap while he waited for his turn on the examining table, jutted out his lip, too. "Baaaaad!" he bellowed then clapped.

Dr. Weston laughed, and put his listening device back into his pocket. "They both seem to be in fine health and very well developed for their age. This little one has quite a stubborn streak, doesn't she?"

Dr. Weston lowered Maddie to the ground to watch her walk as he began filling out the paperwork. Max wasn't surprised when she toddled over to the plant on the floor and tried to eat it. "No, no, Maddie, dear," the doctor began.

"Mine!"

Max lifted Maddie into his arms, dug the plant out of her mouth, ignoring the teeth that clamped down on his finger. "Don't worry. She usually doesn't swallow it, unless you leave it in there very long. She just likes plants."

Weston chuckled again. "Well, she can like them, but teach her not to eat them. Some are poisonous."

"Believe me, I know. I've had my gardener go through the house and get rid of any that are. I'm having my gardens redone where the children might come in contact with any of them, too.''

"I'm glad to hear that. Each year poisoning is a danger for young children.'' He turned back to the children and smiled kindly. "She's walking fine. So is Bobby. The only thing left are the shots.''

Max tensed. He felt harried after an hour at the doctor's office. They'd pulled two bugs from Bobby's mouth, and taken away a bottle that Maddie had snatched from a baby. Then, of course, he had made the mistake of taking a turn holding Bobby while Maddie was examined and Bobby had christened him again. He was getting good at holding the child at arm's length. Max was afraid Bobby thought it was some game and peed on him just to be thrust out in midair. He always chortled afterward.

Max decided he was going to invent a diaper that didn't leak, except he figured Bobby would find some way around it.

And now he had to wait for the children to get shots. He knew they would throw a fit—especially Maddie. "Are the shots necessary?'' he asked.

"I'm afraid so. These are their first shots, their MMR. It's more important to get the shots than risk the diseases.''

"I understand,'' Max said, resigned. The doctor nodded and left.

"Don't worry,'' Kaitland reassured Max as they waited in the small room. "They'll do fine.''

Just then a nurse walked in with two injections in her hand. The doctor stuck his head in behind her. "I'll fax this paperwork to the office that needs it and you can go when Colleen is done.''

Max thanked the doctor, who immediately went back out the door. The coward. Pronounce his sentence then leave the kids for the parents and nurse to handle. "How do you want them? On the table?''

The nurse smiled. "No. You hold the little girl, I'll inject her in the thigh.''

Max nodded. He gathered Maddie close. He loved the way

Maddie smelled like powder and was so soft. He rubbed his nose against her silky hair, before wrapping his arms around her.

He wasn't sure if he could do this. Until now, the children had been something special, exciting, sweet. But this was different. He didn't want to cause them pain. He knew, logically, that it was necessary, but the thought of them going through any more than they had already...

"Max, do you want me to hold her?" Kaitland stared, concerned, noting the way he was stroking Maddie's head and how she was gurgling.

"No. I just hate that she'll feel more pain." He looked at the nurse and nodded. "There's going to be a little stick, che'rie, then Max will make it all better," he whispered.

He saw the needle descend.

Suddenly Maddie's eyes widened and her face crumpled. A loud wail broke from her throat. She sounded as if her world was ending. "It's okay, che'rie," he whispered, patting her back. "Max loves you and will take care of you."

His heart rose to his throat when he realized what he'd said, *Max loves you.* It was true. In the few weeks they'd been with him, the kids had become more than just a responsibility but two people he loved and cared deeply about. "Max loves you, che'rie," he whispered again, patting her back.

Her cries turned to whimpers and suddenly, against his cheek, he felt a tiny hand patting him. "Me love," she blubbered through tears. "Me love."

"I love you, too," he whispered again and again and she continued to pat his cheek and he her back.

Another wail filled the room and he looked over to see Bobby's face crumpled into a scowl as he wailed out his displeasure. It was funny how he could tell the differences. Where Maddie had been truly distressed, Bobby was just plain mad.

"Come here, Bobby," Max said, surprising Kaitland. Of course Kaitland was surprised. He avoided holding Bobby because of Bobby's leaky bladder every time he picked him up. He held open his arm and Bobby willingly flung himself into his embrace. Maddie patted Bobby, ''Bobu, Bobu,'' she repeated over and over and Max hugged him close until the little boy's wails ceased. In seconds Bobby was gurgling and talking his baby gibberish to his sister.

He heard Kaitland thanking the nurse and then she gathered up the diaper bags. He stood there holding the kids, feeling like an idiot, but soaking in their presence.

After weeks, it was disconcerting to think he wanted these children to be his own, that he was actually disappointed that they weren't. His heart felt protective over the idea of them getting shots, over what they wore, what they ate. Looking back, he realized he'd slowly been falling in love all along.

Seeing Kaitland walk up, he thought that if they'd gotten married years ago as they'd planned, his kids would be around four years old by now. Kaitland had wanted kids immediately. Was that why she liked being a foster mother? Why hadn't she had kids?

Those new questions rose in his mind, questions he'd never asked himself before, as well as old ones of why had she been sleeping with someone else when she was engaged to him? She was a Christian. He just couldn't mesh the two images. She believed in chastity and they both had agreed to wait, yet the pictures showed, to the contrary, that she hadn't waited.

Maddie patted his cheek again, drawing him back to the kids. He couldn't desert them. How did he know they would be adopted by someone who loved them? How could he trust someone to take care of them right? How could he live without them?

''You're gonna have a hard time letting them go,'' Kaitland said, as if reading his mind.

''No, I'm not,'' he replied.

Going to the door, he arranged payment and left.

''Of course you are, Max. I can tell just by looking at you how attached you're becoming to these kids.''

They strapped the kids into the car seats then climbed into the front seat.

''You're right, but I'm not letting them go. I'm going to adopt them.''

Kaitland stared, aghast. "But how? Why? I mean, I know you care for them, Max. But you're not married."

There was a heartbeat of silence, then Max replied, "You don't have to tell me that."

She didn't recoil even though his words hurt. "I meant they should have a father *and* a mother."

"They have no one right now."

"But maybe, with time, someone can be found..."

"*With time* being the operative words. I've been thinking. They're getting used to me, and how can you guarantee that we can find someone who will take them both? That's going to be hard. Plus, once we do find adoptive parents, can you guarantee they'll love the twins and make sure they have what they need?"

He backed out of the parking lot and pointed the car toward home.

Kaitland knew he wasn't talking material possessions. Max wasn't that shallow. Still, it rankled that he could adopt these children if he wanted, and probably be accepted as a parent.

With shock, she realized the reason the idea bothered her was that she wasn't in the picture, too. Ashamed, she looked off into the distance. He had made his choice a long time ago. The past was over.

"You care for them now, Max. But isn't it possible that when you marry, your wife wouldn't?"

"I wouldn't marry someone who couldn't love my children."

She knew that. She wasn't thinking clearly. "What if you get tired of them? I mean, it'll be just you. Will you grow bored with all of the childhood diseases and sibling rivalry that goes on. And two get into more mischief than one."

"I think I, of all people, would know that. Remember the trouble Rand was always getting me into. And boy, was it something else. Yes, I think I'm qualified to understand the workings of twins."

He was right there.

"But how is your brother going to take it?"

Max smiled. "He'll be enthused, I'm sure."

* * *

"You're going to what?" Rand's voice rose and Kaitland watched as, with effort, Rand forced himself to calm down. "I knew you'd been going through something the last week or so, but I didn't think it was that." He glanced toward Kaitland then back, indicating just what he'd thought it was.

"It's what I think is best all around. Samantha Jenkins left her children with me. They have no one now. I want children." He shrugged. "I'll love them."

Kaitland could tell Rand struggled before finally nodding. "I'll have the lawyers get on it immediately."

Kaitland was surprised Rand took this so easily. But then she remembered the special link the brothers shared. Rand evidently knew more about what Max was feeling than she did.

However, Elizabeth wasn't so quiet. "I think you're avoiding the real issue here, Max," she said, glaring at him as if she was an older sister about to chastise a child.

Max scowled at her. "And that is?"

"Your heart. You want a family, and are opting for the easy way instead of letting God heal you first."

Max's scowl turned darker. He shot a look at Kaitland then back to Elizabeth. "That, my dear, is none of your business."

Elizabeth opened her mouth to argue. Kaitland saw Rand unobtrusively reach over and lay a hand on Elizabeth's thigh. She closed her mouth a moment, then said, "I'm family. But you're right. There are other ways to handle this." She grinned cheekily. "I'll just pray for you and God will work it all out."

Max groaned. "One day, Elizabeth... Rand, you must talk to your wife about her mouth."

Rand grinned, turning his eyes down on Elizabeth. "Oh, I will, brother, as soon as I get her upstairs."

Elizabeth blushed.

Max cleared his throat.

Kaitland looked away from the loving stare Rand gave Elizabeth.

"Excuse me, please," Kaitland said. "I need to go check on the kids and then run by my house. I'll see you later."

She turned and left, unable to bear the banter anymore.

"She still loves you."

Max glanced to Elizabeth, who, he saw, had been watching him watch Kaitland leave.

"I care for her, too," he told his sister-in-law. "And before you start nagging again, Kaitland and I are trying to work past the hurt so we can be friends again."

"Just friends?" Rand asked, studying Max with concern.

"If she would only talk to me, maybe, just maybe I could begin to understand her betrayal. I could never trust her again, but I could at least let go of the pain."

"Have you asked her what happened, Max?"

"No, Elizabeth. I don't think I can."

"Why?"

"Because..." Because why? Because Max was afraid of her answers. It might destroy the wall around his heart? He'd have to face that he might have been wrong in his judgment? Why? Exasperated, refusing to face the questions, he said, "Nothing. I need to go see to some things Jennifer was going to fax over to me."

He got up and headed to the library, thinking about not only what his sister-in-law had said just now, but earlier, too. He was afraid Kaitland would say something like she didn't love him, or had decided she really didn't want to marry him. He was almost certain she was here to search out forgiveness for something she'd done. Guilt was a powerful motivator. If that were true, then they might be able to get over everything and be friends, but it would soon be obvious that love wasn't motivating her at all, only the guilt. How did you bare your heart to someone like that? She very well might say she loved him and they'd be in the same mess again. He found he really didn't want to face whatever she might have to say. And what if she said something else? Was he ready to deal with part of what had really driven him to let her go in the first place? Could he bare that part of him to anyone?

As for the kids... Yes, he wanted kids of his own. Elizabeth was right about that. And he yearned to have them, something a bachelor wasn't suppose to admit to. But that wasn't the only reason he wanted to adopt Maddie and Bobby. There Elizabeth was wrong. He loved them. He would one day have children if he married.

Bobby and Maddie would be as much his as any other children. He didn't believe in separating out the kids as some did, calling them stepkids, or adopted kids. They would be *his* kids. As far as he was concerned, he would accept them as if they were flesh of his flesh. And as much as he could he would protect those kids from the media and any other negative effects. Unlike his father, who had been unable to protect Rand and himself from the many harsh realities of what the media could do to destroy a family. Or the realities of a mother who got so caught up in the negative effect of a media exposure that all she could think about was getting out.

He forced his mind away from that past sorrow. Instead, he thought about the kids.

Elizabeth would see in time that he could provide for the children. Max thought Rand might actually have glimpsed that determination in Max's spirit or he would have objected more. As for Kaitland...the future was a blank where she was concerned. She would see his determination...if she was here long enough.

Kaitland.

What was he going to do about the dark murky situation with her?

Chapter Sixteen

"**H**ello there, little one!" Max scooped Bobby up off the floor and held him above his head. "What's say we go celebrate?"

Kaitland grinned with indulgence. The last few days she'd seen a change in Max. He was no longer the moody, careful man around her, he was more the carefree person she'd once known. They had come to an uneasy truce and were doing their best to forget the past and become friends again.

The only problem was, she couldn't sleep at night for the memories that haunted her. Over and over the near rape played in her mind. She and Max could play at being friends, but there was always going to be a small barrier between them because of the one small piece of the puzzle she held. Yet, if she revealed it to him, she wouldn't be able to stand the disgust on his face. Or worse, she might have to face that he wouldn't believe her. So, she held the missing link in her heart and prayed God would provide the opportune moment for her to reveal it.

In the meantime, they both did their best to talk and act as if nothing were wrong. If they practiced long enough, she hoped that Max would open up and she would find a way to explain the past to him.

Now, she simply pushed the unpleasantness behind her and smiled. "What has you in such a good mood?"

Max grinned at her as he put Bobby down and lifted Maddie who was demanding his attention. "My lawyers called.

They've started adoption proceedings. I feel like celebrating and thought I'd take the kids to a fast-food restaurant.''

''When was the last time you went to a place like that?'' Kaitland questioned, amused.

''There's a first time for everything, isn't there? I remember seeing playgrounds there. We could take the kids, feed them, let them play, then bring them back and put them down for a nap.''

She laughed at Max's hopeful expression. ''And then?''

''And then some peace and quiet. You and I could play Scrabble on the patio or just sit and enjoy the spring day. Sound good to you?''

Kaitland smiled. It sounded heavenly. Max was putting forth the effort and she would go along with him. ''I'd love to. Just let me fill the diaper bags.''

''I'll drive. I don't want to look too obvious with a chauffeur.'' He put Maddie down. She objected loudly and hung on to his leg.

''If you don't want to look obvious, I'd suggest you change out of your casual suit.''

He grinned. ''I've bought new clothes. Meet me in the library and you'll see. After all, I can't afford to buy new shirts and slacks every time this one wets on me,'' he said, glancing down at Bobby who had toddled over to the toy box. Maddie let go of Max's leg and followed Bobby.

Kaitland shook her head. ''Cotton?''

''Right from the JCPenney catalog.''

''I'll believe it when I see it, Max.''

She changed and dressed the children then packed the diaper bags.

Taking the children by the hands, she escorted them down the stairs to Max's library. Maddie, who had taken a fancy to the plant in this particular room, toddled right over to where it should have been. But it wasn't there. In consternation, the little girl began to explore the room—looking for the plant, no doubt. Bobby went to the coffee table and began to remove the magazines one by one.

Kaitland sighed, gathered up the magazines to move them, but was interrupted. "Well, how do I look?"

Kaitland turned, and gaped. *Gorgeous,* she thought. Tan cotton pants and a berry shirt tucked into them with a slim dark belt circling his middle. It was a shame that any man could be so gorgeous.

"Well, well, well..."

Kaitland heard Rand's voice and looked beyond Max to find Rand gaping in astonishment, too. Rand came in and made a show of circling Max. "Little brother has decided to finally discard the swinging-bachelor image, I see. Where did you get these clothes?"

Max glared at his brother. "Penney's. And they're fine. They're washable. I made sure of that."

"Oh, I'm not saying that at all, little bro. What I am saying is that it's about time. I just never thought to see my brother give up his wardrobe of Armani suits for cotton knit and permanent press."

"Well, now you have, so stop harassing me and go find your wife. I'm sure she'd appreciate your humor. She did enough while you were ill to get you laughing again."

The brothers stared at each other a moment and Kaitland could tell they were doing that twin thing again that she'd often witnessed—communicating without saying a word. Then Rand smiled and said, "You look good," and walked out.

"Maddie and Bobby do that, too."

"Do what?" Max asked, coming over and scooping up Maddie, blowing strawberries on her stomach before settling her on his hip.

"That silent-communication thing."

Max glanced at Kaitland in surprise, then he smiled and there was a mystery to his eyes as he said, "It's just always been that way between us. I tend to forget that's not common with other people. Rand just...well, he was letting me know he approved of the changes in me."

"It's important what he thinks, isn't it?" Kaitland asked.

"Yeah. Very. I don't know what I'd do if I ever lost Rand.

That's one reason I want to adopt Maddie and Bobby. They shouldn't be separated.''

"Does it bother you or Elizabeth—your relationship with Rand?''

"Nah. Elizabeth understands. She's not the jealous type. As a matter of fact, she really likes being part of a close, loving family. I'm afraid if I marry, Elizabeth will put the woman through the third degree before she'll allow it.''

He strode out the front door and to the car Phil had brought around. He now had car seats that were transferred to whichever car the twins were going to be in.

Both children were placed in the back seat and strapped in. Then Max slid behind the wheel and they were off. In minutes they were at a fast-food restaurant. "So, what do you want to eat?'' he asked, going inside.

Kaitland watched him study the menu. "This is all fried stuff,'' he muttered.

Kaitland laughed. "It's fast-food. What do you expect?''

"And there's really no choice. Hamburgers or hamburgers,'' he added.

"They have chicken sandwiches, too. Stop being so critical.''

"The food isn't good for kids.''

Kaitland rolled her eyes. "One meal isn't going to kill them.''

She stepped to the cash register. "Let me order.'' Without waiting for a reply, she ordered for all four of them. Max paid and then smiled his thanks when a young lady took the tray to the table for them.

He strapped Bobby, who was closest to him, into the high chair and then dug out the hamburgers from their wrappings. In consternation, he stared at Bobby then at the burger. "He can't eat this.''

"Like this, Max,'' Kaitland replied. She tore the hamburger into tiny finger pieces and laid two or three in front of Maddie. The burger was joined by two fries.

Max followed her instructions. "They're making a mess,''

he added when a piece of bread went over the tray and onto the floor.

"Don't worry. Grab a bite of your hamburger before one of them starts complaining and wanting down. We don't have help here to take them while we finish our meal."

Max bit into his hamburger. His forehead wrinkled. "This is very poor-quality food, but good."

Kaitland rolled her eyes again. "Yes, it's good. And it's not *poor*-quality, Max. It's just different from what you've always eaten."

"I've eaten out," he complained.

"How many times have you eaten in a fast-food restaurant."

Max opened his mouth, then paused. "Once or twice, I'm sure, as a teenager. Rand used to love this stuff and would drag me with him. But I can't remember what restaurant it was."

Max took another bite.

"Dink!"

Bobby pounded his tray then pointed. "Dink! Dink! Dink!"

"Stop that," Kaitland admonished. "Yes, you may have a drink."

Bobby chortled then latched on to the straw Kaitland stuck between his lips.

"Dink! Dink!" Maddie called.

Kaitland turned to Maddie and gave her a drink, too. Max set down his food, helped Bobby, then went back to eating.

It was soon apparent this was how the entire meal was going to go. "I see now why parents sometimes look so frazzled when they come into Stevens Inc. They're full and we haven't even finished half of our meal. But the stress of trying to answer to these two demanding fiends has robbed me of my appetite."

"Save your food in the bag. We'll take it with us outside. Once they start sliding, you might find you're still hungry."

They wrapped their food, cleaned up the messy kids, then went out to the playground.

Kaitland took off their shoes and helped both children into the plastic-ball tent. Max smiled as the children squealed and threw balls into the air. "Why didn't they have stuff like this when we were kids?" he asked, grinning over their exuberance.

"They had skateboards."

Max groaned. "I remember. I have an ankle that aches to remind me of how much we enjoyed skateboards as kids."

"Why do I hear a story in this?"

"Did I ever break a bone that Rand wasn't somehow behind it?"

"According to you. But one day I'd like to hear Rand's side to all of these stories you tell me."

"He thought it would be fun to tie ropes to Dad's car bumper, and when he left for work we could catch a ride. At the end of the driveway, we'd let go and see who went the farthest. However, we hadn't thought about the way the driveway curved. Or the trees that lined it."

"What happened?"

"I was scraped and bruised from the low-hanging branch of one of those historic oaks outside my house, and my ankle was broken in three places. But Rand took the blame and he stayed with me the entire time I was in a cast. It ruined both of our summers."

Max watched Kaitland laugh. She was beautiful when she relaxed and enjoyed the situation. He couldn't remember her being this beautiful or carefree so many years ago. She'd loved him, but had been so awed by his money. He worried again that it had been his fault she had turned away from him. And wondered as he had at least a thousand times, if it had been for the best. Had he married her back then, no matter how much he had loved her, he had to wonder if she would be this self-assured now, this carefree. Or would she have come to resent living in a glass house?

She was dressed in a loose top and floral full skirt. Her hair was again in a French braid, from which tendrils escaped, softening her features. He wanted to reach out and touch her cheek.

Lifting his hands, he almost did exactly that...until Maddie squealed, "Slide!"

"Are they old enough?" Max immediately asked, eyeing the slide with a little trepidation. "I don't want them to fall."

"We'll stand at the end and catch them. Don't worry."

Kaitland reached in and helped Maddie and Bobby out of the balls. Holding their hands, she walked them over to the slide.

With great patience she guided them up the slide. "Go!" she called out, smiling when Maddie edged her rump to the edge of the slide.

She walked to the end, waiting. Max came up beside her. She stepped forward, to catch the kids and misstepped. Automatically reacting, Max caught her in his arms. "You okay?" he asked, holding her gently in his embrace.

Her pupils dilated just slightly and her breathing was shallow. Max recognized the signals she was sending out. He wanted to kiss her, too. But not here, not in a public place where she might regret it.

"I'm fine," she finally said.

Hearing a squeal, they both turned toward the slide where Maddie came sliding down, feet in the air. Max dropped his arms and scooped up Maddie, just in time, too, for Bobby was right behind her.

Kaitland started to step forward and winced. Immediately, without thinking, Max slipped his arm around Kaitland again. "You okay, Katie?"

"When I misstepped earlier I must have sprained my ankle a bit. I'll be fine."

He watched the yearning in her eyes, saw her bring it under control and then break away. He allowed it. He knew she still cared, that it wasn't just guilt leading her down this road. And it gave him hope.

He would wait for the right time and then find out what Kaitland hid in her heart, what had driven her to betray him as she had, and he would pray that God could heal the breach between them and they could have more.

She scooped up Bobby, kissed him on the cheek and walked them both back to the slide again.

Yes, he was going to pray more for Kaitland. Because Kaitland had too much love in her not to open up and share it with those kids—and him. Despite the resolve, there was a small niggling doubt that reminded him that his mom and dad had once had that, too. He pushed the thought aside. That no longer mattered. Kaitland had gone through the fire just as he had when he'd received those pictures. They could survive anything the media threw at them. She wouldn't eventually get tired of him and the kids and want to leave.

But as much as he believed that, he watched Kaitland as she laughed when the kids both came barreling down the slide again. Would she be able to love him and be willing to stay with him no matter what?

Chapter Seventeen

"So, sister, have you quit working for Max already?"

Kaitland whirled from her car to find her brother sitting on the porch swing.

"Where's your car?"

"In the garage. I didn't want tree sap on it."

She pulled out her keys and opened the door to her house. "So, what brings you here?" she asked, going into the dark interior of the house, already knowing what brought him here, realizing she was going to have to face him after she had been purposely ducking his calls since going to work for Max.

"Why haven't you returned any of my calls? I needed to talk to you last week. It was urgent."

Kaitland went to the rolltop desk in her living room, her low heels clicking across the wooden floor before she crossed onto the rug. She sorted through the bills, placing each in its place, thinking she was finally seeing a light at the end of the tunnel. Just one more week and she'd have enough to pay off the last of the creditors and then she could work on building up savings. She knew she only had two weeks left with Max. She thanked God things had worked out the way they had.

"Kaitland! You're not listening."

She sighed. "Yes, Robert, I am. You said it was urgent. Your urgency wouldn't have anything to do with that dinner party I read about last Saturday?"

Robert flushed and looked petulant when he said, "I'm in between girlfriends. I really needed an escort."

"What happened this time?" Kaitland felt sorry for Robert. He didn't seem to be able to hold down a relationship and she blamed herself in a way. If only she could have helped him understand that she and Grandma had loved him.

"She just didn't work out. I haven't found anyone I like as much as my last girlfriend who left me a year and a half ago. They're all so self-centered. I've had to hire other women to help me and that gets expensive."

Kaitland's eyes widened in dismay. "You've hired professional escorts to go with you to these dinners?"

"What did you expect? I can't do this alone."

"Do what alone?"

Robert stopped whining and his face closed up. "Dating," he said. "What do you think? It wouldn't hurt you to answer my calls once in a while and just go with me. You're a good distraction. They all love you."

Memories of that night long ago returned. "Well, I don't like the shallowness of most of the people who attend those functions. We've been through this before. I don't drink. I don't like flirting. I just don't fit in with the rich crowd."

"You seem to be doing okay with your boyfriend," he muttered, his countenance turning red as his temper rose.

"What do you mean? I don't have any boyfriend right now."

Robert shot her a dirty look. "Just a minute." He stormed through the house to the side door that led to the garage. Kaitland followed to the kitchen where he was already coming back in. "I'm tired of you lying to me and treating me like pond scum, Kaitland. I'm your own brother and you won't do me one little favor. But I just wonder what type of favors you've been doing him."

He slammed three different papers down on the counter.

"Oh dear heavens," Kaitland whispered, her face draining of color. The top paper was a national rag magazine that showed her in Max's embrace. And they certainly did look cozy. Her eyes were half-closed, her lips parted, and Max was leaning close as if he had just kissed her or was about to. It looked very, very intimate. Wedding Bells Ringing, the headline read. The day at the fast-food restaurant, she realized bleakly.

Quickly, she moved the magazine aside to find another one. On it, was another picture of her and Max. He was holding Maddie in his arms and had an arm around her. Stevens' Secret Family, it was captioned.

The third picture showed Max holding Bobby above his head, her in the background with Maddie. Bachelor Father, the headline read.

As she scanned each article, she found three different stories. She was his mistress and these were his children; she was his wife and was kept hidden because she wasn't rich enough to be accepted by Max's crowd; she was the live-in nanny and she was helping with the kids but Max and her had a thing going and were planning marriage.

"Well?" Robert demanded.

She looked up, her head whirling at the thought of what this was going to do to her reputation and Max's, as well. "I've got to call Max."

"You don't deny this?" Robert pointed toward the papers.

"Of course I do, not that it's any business of yours."

"I'm your brother," Robert argued. "Of course I have a right to know. You won't help me out, but you're willing to ruin my position as a lobbyist by having your name splashed all over the front page of these national magazines."

"Trash-zines," she corrected, going toward the phone. "And don't try your guilt on me. You'll revel in this at your work. The more notoriety, good or bad, the better known you are and the more likely people will know your name."

Robert advanced, furious. "Don't push me, Kaitland. You and that grandmother of yours got everything. Everything. I was left with practically nothing. I'm trying to make a living at a very difficult job. And you, who professes to be so loving and kind, won't even help me when I ask it."

"You're rich, Robert."

Robert's eyes narrowed. "Not in my circles I'm not. According to those I hang around with, I'm an upstart with barely enough money to qualify for their clubs. Certain things are expected of me. And to see me escorting my sister around would certainly help my reputation, even if she is a tease.'' He swung his arms at the photos. ''You're right about that. But that doesn't mean I have to accept your actions when you've all but ignored me.''

Kaitland's temper sparked. ''I don't have time for this, Robert. I'm due back at work by two so Darlene can have the rest of the week off. If you don't mind, I have some phone calls to make.''

''You're throwing me out?'' he asked incredulously.

''Unless you have something nice to say, I'm asking you to leave. You know I've never thrown you out.''

He turned and stormed out the door. She heard his car start and then the engine roar as he shot out of the driveway.

She was immediately contrite. He was her only brother, whether he was blood or not. She shouldn't have talked to him that way. He always sought her out to blow off steam.

She sighed. Had she not been so upset over the pictures, she wouldn't have lost her temper. Now she was going to have to apologize. She also understood why the scriptures said not to be unequally yoked, believers with unbelievers. She couldn't imagine being married to someone who was like her brother.

At least Robert looked better, as if he was off the alcohol now. And she hadn't smelled any on his breath. Yet he was on a course of self-destruction and she didn't know how she could turn him around. Need. He always needed more money, more power, more favor with the senators... It was going to ruin him if he didn't get control of himself.

The phone rang, sounding loud in the quiet house. ''Hello?''

''Katie. I've been trying to catch you all morning.''

''Max.'' Tired and now worried how she would handle this new problem, she sighed.

''You've seen,'' he said curtly.

Kaitland leaned back against the couch. ''Yes, I've seen. So, what do we do about it?''

''Are you okay?'' His fury subsided and concern echoed

across the phone lines, warming Kaitland's heart. "I didn't mean for this to happen. You know how those reporters hound my family."

"I'll be fine. I guess I'm still in shock. And Robert was here when I arrived..."

"What did Robert want?"

"Don't sound so sour, Max. He's my brother."

"Stepbrother who enjoys using you. He hurts you every time he's around, Katie. I can't help worrying whenever you bring up his name."

"He was upset over the headlines. That's all. But at least he told me before I found out from some reporter who might have managed to track me down or something."

"You need to come back over here. We have security. You'll be better protected. I'll get to the bottom of this, and make sure there are retractions printed."

"Max, please. It'll only flame the fires."

"I won't let them get away with this. I can't help it, Katie, but I draw the line at my personal life being splashed across the papers...especially when it might jeopardize the adoption proceedings."

Kaitland shivered at the renewed coldness in his voice. She knew from experience Max was not a person to cross when he used that tone.

"Come back and let me handle this," he said, his voice almost abrupt. "They won't bother you here."

"I'm fine, Max. I have bills I must pay. Then I have a few more things I need to do. I'll be back over after that. Don't worry about me."

There was a pause on the other end. "But I do. And soon, Katie, very soon, I think you're gonna figure that out and either open up to me or run away again."

"I didn't run away the first time, Max," Kaitland replied, her heart rate accelerating.

Her breathing turned shallow and her stomach clenched. She could tell by the silence on the other end that Max regretted confronting her so directly. "I want to tell you, Max.

I want to tell you everything. But you'll hate me when I do and I just can't face that.''

Finally, he sighed. ''When you feel the time is right, then. I think I might just want more than friendship. My feelings are becoming more involved and I need to know if we have anything else before it's too late and I open my heart completely to you again.''

Tears filled Kaitland's eyes and streamed down her face. ''I don't know, Max. I really don't know.'' She heard a beep and latched on to that as an excuse to get off the phone. ''My other line is beeping. I'll see you later this afternoon.''

''As you wish.''

She clicked to the other line. ''Kaitland? This is Jake. I think we need to talk.''

Kaitland sighed. She'd known this was coming, had in fact been going to call her pastor before the phone had rung. ''When would be a good time to stop by?''

''I'm here all day.''

''I'll be right by.'' She hung up the phone.

What had started out as a nice day was rapidly deteriorating. She wondered if it could get any worse.

''What in the world is going on?''

Bewildered, Kaitland stared at Rand, who was laughing his head off, to Elizabeth who was punching him in the arm, crying, ''Stop laughing and help him,'' just before she herself giggled again, only to repeat the process.

Several of the staff stood behind them, all gawking into the children's nursery.

Kaitland set down her purse and papers and edged her way around the gaping servants. ''Max, what are you doing on the floor? Where are the children?''

Max lay on his back near the low-set twin bed that was kept in the room in case she wanted to lie down with the children. His left arm was extended, and on his face he wore a look of extreme frustration. ''The…children…are right—'' *huff* ''—here.''

"What's in your hair?" she asked when she noticed his hair was sticking up on end.

"Vaseline."

A high-pitched giggle escaped from under the bed and Kaitland realized the children were ducking Max's grasp. "What happened?"

"What does it look like?" he questioned, making another foray with his hand under the bed, which brought another round of giggles from the two culprits.

"It looks like they're playing hide-and-seek."

Max paused to stare incredulously at her.

She sighed. "Grab a shirt and reel one in, the other will follow."

"I would, if they were wearing any clothes," he said tightly.

"He's been at this at least five minutes now," Rand said, doing his best to remove the grin from his face and failing miserably.

"You see," Max continued, moving his hand back and forth as he ignored his brother's words, "evidently, Bobby finally learned to undress himself. As you know, Maddie is already proficient. And I was only gone from the room a minute..."

"And they slipped under the bed." Rand chuckled again.

"Can't you snag an ankle?" she asked, a little alarmed at the shade of Max's face.

"Oh, he has, several times. That's what's the matter with his hair. What Max isn't telling you," Rand said, "is that the little angels found the Vaseline while he was gone and now they're both slick as ice on an asphalt road in the middle of winter."

He started laughing again.

"I swear, Rand, I'm not going to protect you if Max comes after you." Elizabeth smacked him on the arm for good measure then turned to Kaitland. "The children think it's a game, as you can tell, and no one can get them out."

"Oh, dear," Kaitland said. She clasped her hands together,

trying to decide what to do. "Move away from the bed, Max," she finally said.

"But..." He looked to where the children were, then back to Kaitland. Without another word, he slid his arm from under the bed and moved away.

Kaitland grabbed a blanket and lay down on the floor. She turned her head to where the children were. Max, Rand and Elizabeth, plus all the staff, were staring at her as if she'd lost her mind, but she ignored them. "Well, there you are, my two little termagants," she said sweetly. "Hi there."

Two little stark-naked babies, their eyes round, stared back at her. "Peekaboo," Kaitland said, and shot a grin to both kids.

Maddie clapped.

Bobby chortled.

Kaitland took the blanket and eased it up over her eyes, then jerked it down again. "Peekaboo," she called out again.

Maddie squealed and wiggled around in the small space.

Kaitland lifted the blanket twice more then dropped it, eliciting responses from both children.

"I don't see what—"

Kaitland cut Max off with a wave of her hand. She finally pulled the blanket up and left it over her face. There was the expected chortle, clapping, then another squeal. Then the sounds changed, to demanding.

Finally, Max said, "Well, I'll be..."

Kaitland felt two hands jerk on the blanket. "Pee-boo!"

She wrapped the blanket around Maddie. "Pee-boo yourself," she said, grinning and hugging her close.

Max quickly wrapped another blanket around Bobby.

"Let's get them washed up and then we'll have that bed blocked so they can't get back underneath."

"Amen to that," Max said. He touched his hair with disgust. "At least it'll wash out of the clothes I have on."

Kaitland looked at the cotton pants and light blue top he wore. As usual, he was gorgeous. Not even a little Vaseline could detract from that. She reached up and slicked his hair back. "There. You look fine now."

"He looks like James Dean," Rand commented.

"Well, maybe I just like the James Dean look," Elizabeth said and walked over to Max. Bussing him on the cheek, she said, "You have much patience. I don't know how you put up with him."

"Long-suffering, that's what I am," Max said, grinning superiorly at Rand.

Rand snagged his wife. "Come on. I think we need to have a talk about just who you're suppose to be loyal to."

Elizabeth giggled, winked at Kaitland and Max and left with her husband. Seconds later they heard a squeal, a giggle then absolute quiet.

Kaitland glanced at Max and cleared her throat.

Max smiled. "I like Rand's way of getting her loyalty. Lead the way," he added. "Let's get these two monsters cleaned up."

They put the children in the bathtub and began to scrub them. "You're amazing with children, Kaitland," Max said as they soaped up each child.

Kaitland shrugged. "You will be, too. I've had years of practice, don't forget. This is all new to you. With time, everything will come to you."

"I don't know. I was so angry and frustrated. I only walked out for a couple of minutes to go retrieve an outfit from the other room. I couldn't get to these two. I kept thinking, if they can get undressed and into trouble that fast, what if something serious happens? What would I do then? Would it mean their lives because I was inattentive?"

"Oh, Max," Kaitland murmured. She washed Maddie's hair, ignoring the splashing. "Don't say that. Children are children. I sometimes think it's in their nature to explore and get into mischief. You'll learn that things like this are just going to happen. It's not something to get upset over. Save getting upset for the other dangers they'll drag you through, not the minor things."

"I don't consider this minor," he said.

"By tomorrow you will. Or when you realize you could have moved the bed to get them."

Max's shock was priceless.

"Careful what you say," she warned.

He decided against saying anything.

"Of course, they would have still played catch-me-if-you-can if you'd moved the bed. It would have probably taken two of you, one on each side, to catch them. And it wouldn't have been as entertaining to Rand."

Max sighed, then a reluctant chuckle slipped out. "I imagine I looked pretty silly."

"You reminded me of one of those kids on the black-and-white TV shows that wore his hair straight up. It was pretty comical-looking."

"Gee, thanks."

He wrapped a towel around Bobby and stood. Going into the other room, he dried the boy off and automatically dressed him. "I've already lost an hour's worth of work up here with these two."

"Which you can do later," Kaitland said.

"Yeah. I never realized how nice it is to be able to work out of your home. I go to the office three days a week and the other two days my secretary works on what I give her. Then, of course, on the weekend I go through our company's local stores. I imagine I'll have to make three or four trips a year to the other apparel stores as things come up," he told her. "However, I'm thinking on expanding Dugan's job from head of security at our store to problem solver. The man is brilliant. He's a former cop who enjoys a challenge. If I brought him on full-time, he could be the one going from store to store, trouble-shooting for me and then I'd make the decisions. That way I could be with the children more until they're older. I'd only have to make a couple of trips a year, with Rand only making a couple, too."

Dressed, Bobby jumped down from the bed and toddled over to the toys. He pulled out colored plastic blocks and began to bang them together.

Kaitland, done with Maddie, patted the little girl's bottom and sent her off toward Bobby. "Have you heard anything about the adoption proceedings?"

"The lawyers are filing the papers. It'll be a little longer before everything is settled. They warned me, though, that negative publicity could really hurt the case, especially since I'm single and already have such a bad reputation thanks to the newspapers. What's so disgusting is that the reputation is false, but it just doesn't matter. Maybe my mother was right to want..." He glanced at her, then away.

He sat down next to Kaitland on the bed, then reached out and took her hand. Tracing the back of her fingers, he asked, "So, how'd it go today? Any press catch up with you?"

Kaitland shivered at his touch. Forcing her voice out, she replied as calmly as possible. "No. They haven't figured out who I am, yet, I don't think."

"I'm sorry about this. I'm usually so careful. I won't tolerate the children's chance at adoption being hurt by this. I've set wheels in motion for retractions."

His hand continued to stroke hers. Kaitland watched, mesmerized at the sight of his darker skin against her lighter tone. His hands were neat, clean, his fingers long and slim.

She raised her gaze to find him staring at her.

Her heart fluttered at his concerned, almost wary look. Suddenly she wanted to tell him everything. She could tell he was thinking about the incident five years ago. But she was afraid he would hate her when she told him the truth. She was so ashamed. Logically, she knew it wasn't her fault. But there was that small part that told her if she hadn't gone to that room, answered that note...it wouldn't have happened.

"Actually," she said, fear rising in her. "I think I'd like a kiss. That might help me forget about today." *And the other, too,* she added silently.

She leaned forward and placed her lips against his. His kiss was gentle, yet reserved. She could feel it as if he had said it out loud: I can't release myself to you until I know what you did.

She tried to deepen the kiss, desperate for only a moment to forget the past. Max's hands rose. He gently disengaged himself from her. Definite concern was etched on his features. "What is it, Kaitland? Tell me."

A scream pierced the room.

Kaitland and Max both jumped and whirled. Maddie was covered with blood, holding her head. Bobby held a metal jack-in-the box in his hands. "Oh my goodness!" Kaitland cried, jumping up.

She ran over to Maddie and scooped her up. A cut about a half an inch long slashed across her head. It was deep enough that it would need stitches. "Max?" she called.

Max, who had Bobby and looked almost as white as the paint on the wall, came over to her, shushing Bobby as he bounced him. "Is it bad? Look at all the blood."

"She'll live. But this is one of those times I told you about earlier. She's gonna have to go to the hospital and have stitches."

"I'll get Darlene to stay with Bobby and then we'll go."

He headed toward the door with Bobby. While he explained the situation to Darlene, Kaitland found a cloth to press against Maddie's head, then grabbed the diaper bag.

Downstairs, as they were getting in the car, Max totally surprised Kaitland with his attention to priorities. Instead of worrying about the leather upholstery of his car getting stained, he strapped Kaitland in, because she was holding Maddie in her arms, and said, "Just take care of my little angel there, and we'll worry about everything else later."

He went around the car and climbed in and Phil shot off toward the hospital emergency room.

Kaitland held Maddie close, rocking the child who was now only sniffling. She was relieved that she'd been given a reprieve from telling Max about the incident. But she wondered now if it wouldn't have been better just to get it out and deal with his shock rather than wait until another opportunity arose. *Dear Father, help me make a decision. Give me the courage to do what is right.*

Chapter Eighteen

"So, what's the trouble?" Rand asked, walking into the study where Max was sitting.

Max glanced up at his brother. "Home early today, aren't you?"

Rand shrugged. "I had a feeling."

Those feelings they shared. Max wasn't surprised Rand had picked up on this. He sighed, tossed down the reports he was working on, opened a drawer and pulled out a plain manila envelope. Tossing it onto the desk, he waited for Rand to pick it up.

He watched Rand slide out the pictures. His mouth tightened. "These are new. Same incident, just different poses."

Max's gut clenched. "Yeah, I noticed."

Something in his tone must have alerted Rand to how he was feeling. His gaze shot up to lock with Max's. "How serious is it between you two now?"

Max sighed. "I never stopped loving her. I realize that now. I don't know when the realization came, maybe seeing her with the children, or hearing her laugh, or just having her around where I couldn't hide behind other things. But it's still there."

"Along with the hurt."

"Yeah. Along with the hurt. She almost told me the other day. I mean, call me perverse, but I just have to hear why she decided to cheat on me. Maybe if I hear the reason, I can get on with my life."

"What about your feelings?"

Max shrugged. "We don't choose who we love. But we do choose who we forgive. I can't completely let this go until she tells me where I failed."

"Where you failed?" Rand looked at him oddly and Max knew he was wondering what he meant.

Rand hadn't heard the final fight between their parents. He'd never shared that one thing with Rand. How his mother had accused their father of failing to protect her and the children from the press. How she wanted a divorce. Max's father had insisted they take a vacation to get away from it all…and then they had died. His mother hadn't been able to handle the pressure of the family's notoriety, the fast rise her husband had made in the business world. And his father had failed their mother. It reminded him too much of his situation with Kaitland and how afraid he was that he was going to fail her or that she would get tired and leave. That was his real fear. Maybe she had gotten tired of seeing reports about his alleged romances and decided to prove something to him. But that was something he would not discuss with anyone. He never had and never would.

"Maybe she failed?"

Max shook his head. "I only know I love her."

Rand shifted the pictures, then frowned when he came to the note.

"They want a pretty penny for these," Rand murmured, scanning the note. "Or they'll release them to the press."

Slipping everything back into the folder, he passed it to Max. "What are you going to do?"

Max liked that about Rand. In important matters, he didn't try to force his will on him, he treated Max as an equal. Rand was the best friend he had. And he needed to discuss things with him, knowing it would go no further, knowing he wouldn't be condemned for any decision he made. "I don't want Kaitland hurt."

"If these pictures hit the stand, you know they'll ruin her career at the day care."

"Jake knows about this incident," Max told him. "But

you're right. Being splashed across the front page, being exposed to the public eye in such an intimate position, even if Kaitland and the senator are completely clothed, would be a guilty sentence. But I won't pay hush money. There's never a good ending if you do that.''

"There's something else bothering you, isn't there?'' Rand asked.

"I'm worried about how this turn of events is going to affect the adoption of Maddie and Bobby.''

Rand leaned back in his chair and crossed his legs. He wore a business suit and conservative silk tie. His hair was slightly rumpled after a full day at work. He rubbed his eyes, which meant his contacts were bothering him. He usually came home and changed to glasses. But instead, he'd come straight to his brother.

"I don't know what to tell you, bro. The evidence is incriminating.''

He sighed, saw Max's stricken look and shook his head, disgusted with the situation.

"Kaitland will probably lose her job at the day care,'' Max said. "She's also primary foster parent for the kids right now, though I should receive approval in the next day or so. Still, the church's board of directors would probably take a dim view of the publicity the media would generate when that was also found out.''

"And we know the media will do anything for a story, they would, of course, exploit this state of affairs no matter how loving and caring Kaitland is,'' Rand added. "If the outcry is loud enough, it could very well affect the outcome of the adoption. And here's something we haven't thought of before. What will the senator do when these come out?''

"Do you think he's being blackmailed too?''

Rand shrugged. "If he is, I doubt he'd tell us. Maybe the best thing to do is to contact the police at this point. I admit, when things happened years ago, you were too upset to deal with it. But for it to come back now...to torment you twice. This guy is a treacherous blackmailer. He's not going to go away. Unless he's caught, this is going to hang over you and Kaitland for the rest of your lives.''

"Isn't that just the truth," Max muttered.

"You know, if it's any help, there's a verse in Psalms that tells us not to worry about the world, that our enemies will soon wither. God takes care of His own. Maybe you just need to pray and leave it in His hands. Let Him guide your next actions.''

"Yeah. I've been praying. All day, on and off. But I fear that something is going to happen to the kids—''

"They're resilient," Rand interrupted. "Sometimes we have to go through a few trials so that we're strengthened.''

"Like Katie and me?" Max asked, knowing his brother.

"Yeah. Kaitland wasn't ready to marry you five years ago. You weren't really ready to marry, either. You've both grown, been through some hard times. Your love is deeper now.''

"Are you saying I was shallow?" Max asked, surprised.

"No. But weren't we both just a little naive, living in our own world, thinking we controlled everything that went on around us?''

Max was astonished at how open Rand was being with him. He realized something else, too. "You're right. We were pretty arrogant back then. The great Stevens empire. No troubles, the world loved us, everything was going smoothly.''

"Pride goes before the fall," Rand added.

"And fall we both have." Max relaxed, peace flooding him. "And now God is restoring.''

Rand's eyes widened at Max's meaning. Then he smiled. "Let me know when you convince Katie of that.''

That was the first time Rand had ever called Kaitland by her nickname. He knew now she would always be a part of their family. "Well, learn patience, brother," he said as he shoved the paper back into the desk. "She'll have to come to some decisions herself and we still have to work out what happened five years ago.''

"You'll do it," Rand told him. "We'll all be here for both of you. But you're gonna have to trust her, Max.''

"I do, basically." Max said.

Rand shook his head. "Let go of the pain before it ruins your newfound love. Then pop the question." He stood. "Let me know what you decide about that." He nodded toward the closed drawer. "Now I've got to go find my wife. I've been home too long without telling Elizabeth hello."

"Did I hear my name?" Elizabeth said, breezing into the room, her purse on her shoulder.

"Uh-oh," Max said, leaning back in the chair and watching Rand's smile drop.

"You're not going out, are you?" Rand said.

Elizabeth chuckled, leaned forward and slid her arms around Rand's waist. "And hello to you, too. You're not due home for at least three more hours." She nuzzled his neck, placing a trail of kisses there until she reached his mouth.

Max felt sorry for Rand. He looked disconcerted, trying to concentrate on what he'd asked her, and deal with the havoc his wife was playing on his senses. "Stop that," Rand finally muttered. "You'd drive a sane man crazy."

She laughed again, her smile lighting her eyes. Rand's features immediately softened. "I'm worried, honey. Tell me you're going right back upstairs to rest."

"Oh, Rand," Elizabeth said, attempting a pout, then giving up when it didn't work. "Why did the..."

"And no jokes," he warned.

Max knew how she used jokes to distract as well as make them all look foolish. It was the latter she'd probably been about to try on Rand. And Rand was unable to withstand her jokes. He was learning to cut her off early before she could reduce him to a pile of mush.

She shrugged. "My friend Laurel is meeting me for a late lunch."

"But your pregnancy..."

"Is perfectly normal," she said, taking his hand and placing it on her abdomen.

Max felt suddenly out of place. He shifted in his chair, thinking of how he'd have felt had it been Kaitland who had almost been killed.

"Maybe Rand is right," he offered.

Both of them looked at him incredulously. "Hey, I can side with my brother once in a while," he added defensively.

"Traitor," Elizabeth muttered. Turning back to Rand, she said, "You know Laurel was off freelancing for some newspaper when I was working for you. She arrived back just in time for our marriage and then we went on our honeymoon—it seems almost six months since I've seen my dear friend."

"We've only been married..."

"I know how long we've been married. I said it only seemed like six months because I didn't have much time when we planned the wedding. I'll be back in an hour or so. She and I have a lot to catch up on. Besides, she's the one who called me! She asked if I'd be available today at this time to talk."

Rand rolled his eyes. "You should be resting."

"Trust God to keep that which has been firmly planted right where it should be," she said softly, earnestly.

Max saw his brother sinking to that pile of mush again and knew Rand was lost.

"Be careful," Rand muttered, looking as if he couldn't figure out how he'd ended up giving her his blessing. "Call me if you need me. And take your pager with you."

Elizabeth squealed happily. "You're such a teddy bear," she said and hugged him.

She gave him a kiss and was out the door in a flash before Rand could change his mind.

"Teddy bear?" Max asked, his voice reeking with laughter.

Rand actually flushed. "She has these crazy names. And I don't want to hear them from your mouth again, little brother, or we'll have to take it outside."

Max's eyes widened as if to say, *who me?* "Teddy bear..." The phone rang.

"Answer that," Rand said and strode out of the office.

"Hello?"

"This is Marjorie Wiscott calling for Kaitland Summerville."

"I'm sorry, she's not in right now. May I take a message?" *Marjorie. Marjorie? Where did he know that name from?*

"Just have her call me, please, when she gets in. It's about a story for the local paper."

Max's blood turned cold. "Thank you." But the woman had already disconnected.

Marjorie Wiscott. Yeah, he knew the name. He'd seen her byline several times, she'd written about his family in the newspapers here. What in the world was she doing calling Kaitland and what story was she talking about?

"Hi, Max. I just wanted to let you know we're back."

As if thinking about her had summoned her there, Kaitland came striding in the door, wearing a tailored pink shirt tucked into loose gray trousers. A slim belt around her waist and loafers, both dark, completed her ensemble. She looked like a poster for middle-class motherhood.

He looked in her eyes, trying to see any reflection of pain or bitterness that might send her to a newspaper. It wasn't there.

"What's the matter?" she asked, hesitating near the chair.

He waved her to be seated. "Tell me, Katie, are you still angry at me? Would you be willing to betray me again to get revenge?"

He could have slapped her and caused less pain, if the look on her face was any indication. But after that call…

"I'm not running this time, Max. I'm trying to stay here, prove to you that we can put the past behind us." Kaitland dropped her head. "I never explained, just turned my back on everything years ago. I realize how wrong that was now."

"Katie, che'rie," Max said softly, standing and coming around the desk, his anger over Marjorie falling away. "I didn't ask you for an explanation, either. We were both hurting and yet I was arrogant enough to expect you to say you were sorry. You might say we were both at fault."

"I didn't see it that way," Kaitland whispered.

"Nor did I," Max admitted. "I don't know why you betrayed our trust, or why you suddenly found my touch so repulsive, but I know now I should have tried harder to work things out." But he knew part of the reason he hadn't tried.

Part of that fear...that dark monster that ate at him, the one he'd never let go of years ago, after his parents' deaths.

"Oh, Max," Kaitland replied, her pain in her eyes. "Please don't blame yourself."

"How can I not when those children up there could be ours now if I'd only tried harder with you."

Tears filled Kaitland's eyes. "It wasn't that easy. We both had to grow."

"You sound like Rand." Max finally accepted that Kaitland wouldn't betray him again. He was almost certain of it. Rand had told him to let go of his bitterness. Until that call, he hadn't realized how much pain was still stored up inside him. *Father, forgive me,* he prayed. He just had to let go or he was going to be eaten alive.

But that call. Why would the woman call here as if she knew Kaitland?

"I always thought he was a smart person." Kaitland smiled, her eyes meeting his.

"Don't tell him that, he'll get an ego."

"He already has an ego," she said.

He just couldn't let go completely, he realized. That one small part of him remembered the photos and the betrayal, as well as the call. He had to ask. Maybe soon he would be able to trust her. He'd even thought maybe he had started to, but that call... "Do you know a Marjorie Wiscott?"

Kaitland stiffened.

The hopeful part in Max withered at the suddenly shuttered expression on her face. *No, God. Please, not again.*

"I've met her a few times."

He felt it starting all over again. He'd been ready to confess his love, and now this. There had to be an explanation, he told himself. Maybe she likes the woman and isn't ever offended by anything the press says. If he pushed it, maybe this time things could be explained. And if she decided to marry into the family, maybe she wouldn't eventually get tired of what the press tried to do to her to leave. "She called here for you a few minutes ago, about a story."

He watched her closely. Her eyes widened, then she sighed.

"I'd hoped to tell you before anyone else got a hold of you..."

"What?" he asked, anger seeping into him. "Katie, you know how I hate the press. What does Marjorie want? She's one of the people who has written stories about my family in the past. Why was she calling here for you?"

"You know, Max, you're going to have to get over your aversion to the press. Not all journalists are total jerks that would sell their souls for a good byline."

"But Marjorie is," he replied, remembering some of her stories.

"No. She wouldn't sell her soul. But she would buy a story. And she would pursue one too. She found out I asked for an additional week of leave from the day care. I thought it would give you a little more time to get your license as an emergency foster parent and a little more time for the furor of the rag magazine's story to cool down before I went back to work."

Max felt bad. "I'm sorry, Kaitland. I didn't realize. I didn't think about that. I bet you're in hot water over this at the day care. I want to apologize for not thinking about the press following us to the fast-food place."

"It's no big deal." But he could tell by her eyes that it was a big deal, as was his doubting her. She sighed, then smiled. "And no. I'm not in hot water. Jake was concerned. He wasn't angry, he was dismayed that I was taking an additional week. But you have bigger problems to worry about. You see, I found the perfect way to appease Jake's dismay about my additional week of leave. As of today, you're going to have to look for a new secretary."

Confused, Max asked, "What does Jennifer have to do with this situation in the press and Jake and u...and everything?" He wasn't going to say *and us*.

"She's the new assistant day-care director at the church. I needed some help. She loves kids. I approached her. Did you know she once owned a day care?"

"Jennifer?" He was still lost. Kaitland had the ability to do that to him.

"Yes. She had to close the day care because of her

mother's death. Actually, it was her mother's business. But I think Jennifer will be wonderful working for Jake.''

"You stole my secretary.'' It was beginning to sink in. She really wasn't worried about the story in the press. He'd hurt her, but instead of dwelling on his blundering mistake, she was going on to something else.

"I'm also paying her better than you are.''

"When is she leaving?'' he asked, astounded, and just a little touched by Kaitland's ability to go on despite the circumstances. She was strong. She wasn't a weak person. It made him wonder if he had been wrong about five years ago. Could there have been an explanation other than the obvious one? Could his Kaitland have actually been innocent in it all? Could the pictures have lied? She was too strong to let herself get messed up in such a situation unless she had been behind a deliberate attempt to hurt him and to extort money from him.

"Two weeks. She's going to give you her notice tomorrow. And be nice to her.''

"I wouldn't be anything but nice,'' Max replied, indignant. "I guess if Jennifer's leaving means things will be easier for you at the day care, as well as here, with the kids, it's okay.''

She smiled. "Good,'' she said as she stood.

Max felt bereft. "Katie?'' He stepped forward and took her hand.

Startled, she looked up at him. He didn't know what to say. So many questions whirled in his mind. He rubbed his hand over her fingers, gently, back and forth. "Your hand is so soft.''

She smiled, her features softening. "I want you, too, Max.''

He leaned forward, touching her lips to his. When she didn't resist, he dropped her hand and wrapped his arms around her. He felt her own arms wrap hesitantly around him, then she was returning the kiss. Her lips were soft, yielding, seeking warmth and comfort. He gave what he could and accepted what she freely gave.

Finally, he lifted his head. He leaned against his desk, pulling her more securely against him and dropping his head on top of her soft honey blond hair. "I just don't know what to do, what to believe."

"I want to tell you, Max..." He waited. Her voice was so weak, vulnerable, that it actually sent chills up his spine. "I can't stand the ultimate rejection again. I just couldn't go through that. It hurt too much the first time."

He realized it was his fault that Kaitland sounded so defenseless. He was at fault because in a way, he had betrayed her own feelings all those years ago by not staying and confronting the problem. And because he still didn't trust her, was afraid of what he'd hear, he still might hurt her again. "I want to know, Katie. When you feel up to telling me."

The spell was broken. With his words, she pulled back. A sad smile touched her lips and her eyes reflected years of pain that he'd never realized she felt. His gut twisted at the sight. "I just can't," she told him. "Not until I know you won't turn your back on me."

He stared helplessly. "I want to say I'd never do that, Katie."

"But you did, five years ago."

He nodded wearily. "I did, to my great regret."

She turned and headed toward the door. "You know, Max," she said as she paused at the entrance. "I never stopped loving you."

He watched her walk out and knew he couldn't concentrate on work now. All he could see was that sad resignation in Kaitland's eyes. And he knew, somehow, that he had put that look there. And it scared him to death.

Chapter Nineteen

"I think you'd better sit down."

Max turned from where he'd been staring out the window to see his brother striding into the room. His face wore a thunderous expression and he clutched a newspaper in his hand.

"What? What is it?" Max asked, coming forward.

Max's surprise evidently registered with Rand, for he slowed, and actually held the paper back. "I'm sorry, Max. I didn't mean to startle you. I just wanted to get here before anyone else."

It was six-thirty in the morning. Max knew the paper had only been delivered, just after six. "What is it you're trying to tell me without telling me?" he asked, seating himself on the sofa and waiting for Rand to do the same.

He didn't. He stood in front of Max with a look of regret on his face.

For the first time, real alarm grabbed Max in the gut. He'd seen that look on his brother's face before…always when bearing bad news. Slowly, feeling as if his arm was made of lead, he lifted it toward the paper.

Rand hesitated again, then finally handed over the paper. "Front page of the State section."

Max opened the paper to that section…and sucked in his breath at what he saw. Instant Daddy, the headline read. A picture of him lifting Maddie into his arms at the fast-food restaurant was underneath the headline.

"'Max Stevens as he lifts his soon-to-be daughter into his arms,'" he read under the photo.

His glance jerked up to Rand's, whom he realized recognized the implications. Who knew he was adopting these children? A few pictures in a rag magazine was one thing. But someone close to him had given this story to the state paper. They wouldn't have printed it otherwise. And with such accurate details.

He felt sick at the implications. "'Bachelor or Daddy or both,'" Max read the article out loud. "'Our local celebrity, the most eligible bachelor in the tristate area, who has done an admirable job of matching wits and avoiding the matrimonial knot, has finally met his match in a set of twins that were left on his doorstep just a month earlier. According to sources, the twins, Maxwell Robert and Madeline Renée were deserted on multimillionaire Max Stevens's doorstep with a note asking him to take care of them. And that he has done, falling head over heels in love with the two small cherubs, insofar as he has decided to adopt them as his own...'"

Max let the paper drop. He was going to be sick.

"Maybe it was someone else, Max. There's no proof it was Kaitland."

Max looked up bleakly. "The byline is Marjorie Wiscott's." He paused, then added, "The same woman who called five days ago to talk to Kaitland about a *story*."

Rand ran a hand through his hair, pushing at his glasses because he hadn't had time to put in his contacts, then finally sighed. "I can't understand why she'd do this. She knew how you felt about keeping this information out of the newspaper, didn't she?"

"Oh, yeah, she knew," Max said, even though his heart felt as though it were shattering into pieces at his feet. "I told her exactly how I felt. But she just seems to do things over and over like this, doesn't she?"

"Who does things over and over?" Kaitland asked, strolling into the room with Maddie in one arm. The cut on the little girl's head had completely healed. Kaitland gave Max a smile. "Darlene has Bobby and we're heading for breakfast.

I thought you might..." She trailed off and frowned at Max's expression.

Rand was frowning, too. "I'll leave you two alone," he said, refused to meet Kaitland's eyes and walked out.

"What's the matter, Max? What's up?"

Kaitland was concerned. She'd never seen Max look quite so stricken, except...

The blood left her face. "You're scaring me, Max. What is it?" She sank into a chair, releasing Maddie who was wiggling. In the background she could hear Bobby and noted Maddie took off at a toddle for her brother's voice. She thought to stop her, but the slap of the paper in front of Kaitland froze her to the spot.

The picture stood out like snow in a jungle. But what was even worse was the headline and what the article said.

Total silence greeted her when she was done reading. She didn't want to look up. Feelings of that time so long ago mixed with feelings now. Dread, fear, nausea. It was happening all over again. The silent accusation in his eyes had said it all.

She started to stand. She would leave, go up to her room and give Max time to think this through. As she'd told Max a few days earlier, she couldn't go through the pain again.

"Why, Katie?" he asked, his voice full of anger and confusion. "You knew how I felt about those children being exploited. You aren't cruel enough to have done it for revenge. And I know you don't tend toward gossip. So, that only leaves the money. But I offered you money to help pay your grandmother's bills. So, why would you go to a stranger and sell her a story only you know? It's just like five years ago. Questions but no answers. Your actions are that of a malicious, conniving money-grubber. I didn't want to believe it five years ago...nor when I started receiving these." He opened his desk drawer and pulled out a manila envelope. Pouring out the contents, he let the pictures fall in front of her.

Pictures of her and the senator spilled out. Dizziness engulfed her. "But what am I to think when I get blackmail notes both last time and this time when you are in my house?

Not a single one the entire time you were gone. But as soon as you return..."

Blackmail notes?

He'd been getting blackmail notes and pictures? Strangely, she thought, she was relieved. Maybe then, the picture she'd inadvertently seen on his desk that day had been one of these. Yes, there it was. She saw it now, partially covered by another one. At least he hadn't been holding on to it and using it to remind himself of what she'd supposedly done years ago. Yes, that was a relief, wasn't it?

Max didn't wait for her to comment. He only swiped a hand through his hair and continued, "I just don't understand your game, but I'm tired of playing, Kaitland. I won't risk my feelings anymore and then end up with the heartache you dish out."

"How do you know it's me who leaked the story?" she said feebly, thinking to argue the article.

"Marjorie's byline. Are you going to tell me it wasn't you?"

Looking at the condemnation in his eyes, Kaitland finally gave up. What was the use? He'd never really forgiven her for five years ago. She'd known, on some deep level, that he hadn't and that's why she'd always been afraid to tell him what had happened.

And if she argued now—his mind was set against her. "No, Max. I'm not telling you it wasn't me."

She had to get out of here, out of this house, now! "Darlene is quite competent at handling the children," she told him. "Please send someone with my things."

"What do you mean?" Max demanded, standing, too.

"I'm quitting. Effective immediately. I'm sure you don't want a conniving—what was it? Manipulating...no, malicious, wasn't it? Yes, malicious, conniving money-grubber. I'm sure you don't want that kind of person in your house any longer. Heaven forbid, she might steal the china, or the strongbox you keep unlocked in your drawer."

At his surprised look, she nodded. "Oh, yes, remember, you once showed it to me—before." She started toward the door. "You know, Max, I was a fool. I had prayed and thought God had opened this door so we could work things out and go on with our lives. But I see you don't want to go on. You want to harbor that hurt and nurse it and baby it so it never goes away. You'll never learn, will you? I would say you're going to be hurt over this when the truth comes out...but just like five years ago, it probably won't come out—the truth, that is. So, Max, have a nice life. Stay hurt, and buried in your fears and insecurities."

She turned at the door and faced him. "I'm tired of trying. I'm closing the chapter on this part of my life and going onward. Goodbye, Max."

She walked out, past Rand who was holding one of the children with Darlene, past Timms, the butler, out the door to her car. The only thing in her car were the keys, since they always left the keys in their cars. Her clothes, her purse, everything, was still up in her room. But she didn't care. She would take no more of Max's pain. She had to get out, go away where she could lick her wounds. For, as she'd told Max, she gave up. She would not try anymore.

"Father, help me," she whispered, starting her car and driving down the driveway. "Just help me get the car home in one piece before I fall apart."

Chapter Twenty

The sound of the front door brought Kaitland's head up. She'd been lying on her bed for almost an hour, crying until her nose was stopped up and her throat raw. For some reason, she hadn't thought she could hurt again the way she had hurt the last time.

She'd found out she was wrong. Uncurling from the pillow she clutched, she moved her Bible to the side and stood. Only one person entered her house without her permission.

Her brother.

Just what she needed to top off a disastrous morning.

"I see by your face you saw the paper this morning. Or rather, your ex-fiancé has," Robert said, stomping into the living room. "Who ran the article—you or him? Well, that was a great way to thwart any blackmail," he continued, confusing Kaitland.

She rubbed the tissue across her nose. "What are you talking about? No. I don't want to know. Look, Robert. I really don't want company right now. Can't this wait until later?"

"If you want Max to lose those two little brats he's trying to adopt, then by all means throw me out," he sneered.

"That's ridiculous. You have no control over that. Why are you so angry?" Her head was beginning to throb. She just didn't have the patience for Robert today.

Robert raised a haughty eyebrow. "Are you willing to risk that?"

Kaitland sighed. It did no good to argue with her brother.

He was totally self-centered. If he thought he needed something, he would go to whatever lengths possible to get it. If she threw him out, he'd only rant and rave for the next month until she finally listened to what he had to say. "Fifteen minutes. That's all you get."

She only wanted to go back into her room and crawl under the covers and cry. She had three more days before anyone would expect to see her at church. She could hide and pray and cry until some of the pain left and the numbness set in and then she could start to function again.

"I need some help at a function in two days and I want you to do it."

She stared at him, dumbfounded. "Do I look like I'm in any condition to go to one of those parties?" she asked, unable to believe how callous her brother was. "Besides, I've told you before, I don't like those events. What makes you think I'm going to change my mind now?"

"Those children."

"You're not going to get some senator or someone to help you against Max. Come off it, Robert. And your power doesn't extend past there."

"It will eventually. And you're going to help me. Why not take a look inside this envelope here."

Kaitland picked it up and dropped into a chair near her dining-room table. Nothing could be worse than what she'd been through this morning. It was simply easier to go along, then when Robert was done asking, tell him no. Opening the envelope, she shook the contents into her lap, and gasped when pictures of herself and the senator were revealed.

Her stomach churned but she managed to keep her voice steady. "Max already knows about these."

So, someone had told Robert about this, too. Her whole life was going to end up on the front page pretty soon and she didn't have any idea who had taken these pictures.

Max's words came back—his accusatory tone. No, it wasn't someone Max had hired, though she had wondered at one time. Could he have been so jealous as to take the pictures? She knew better now. Then the senator maybe? No. She'd been over this hundreds of times in the last few years and had come up with a hundred different people, but had discarded each one. Who could it have been?

"I know that," Robert said scathingly. "You lost your fiancé because of these. You wouldn't have been happy with him. He'd keep you up there in their house like some princess and never let you out again. You wouldn't be able to work or enjoy life. You wouldn't be able to help me anymore or even be my sister. He'd see to that."

"You've talked to Max about these pictures?" she asked, not understanding what he meant by his statement about losing Max. How could he have known that so fast...unless he'd gone by the house? Oh, no, she thought miserably. No wonder he was so angry.

"Not exactly, Kaitland. I'm the one who gave Max those pictures."

"But how did you get them?" she asked, then realization dawned. Kaitland thought she was going to be sick. She was wrong. The day could get worse.

Pain tore through her heart and her eyes filled with fresh tears that she refused to let fall. She gulped in a breath, forcing the bile back down her throat.

"You set me up." Her voice was barely audible over the roaring in her ears. Black spots danced before her eyes and her head spun crazily. A hard jerk on her arm, the biting pain from Robert's fingers, brought her back from the brink of darkness.

"You're my brother. How could you?" Her heart was bleeding pain as she stared at the man whom she had always loved like a blood brother.

"Come on, Kaitland. I was never really your brother. Your grandmother made sure of that."

"That's not true. You were always my brother to me. Grandmother just wanted you to be a little reasonable."

"No. Your grandmother wanted me to be more like her family than my family, whom she told me several times was below your family's lineage. She always thought your mother married beneath her family. And whether you realize it or not, she didn't want me near you. She said I was a bad influence.''

Kaitland wondered if that was true. She couldn't remember her grandmother being that way. But that wasn't the issue. "So, that's what my grandmother might have done. But why take out your anger on me?'' she asked, her voice sounding weak to her own ears.

Robert shook his head. Finally he said, "You don't get it, do you? This isn't about you. This is about power. I want power so no one will ever have control over me again. I was desperate with the senator. I had to get something on him because he wouldn't listen to reason on a bill that was coming up. I knew you wouldn't let him under your skirt. But maybe just a few pictures of him with you might do the trick—and they did. Both of you fell for the notes so easily.''

"You've been playing some sick game with my life?'' She remembered the pain of the past five years and couldn't believe her own brother—no, her *step*brother—had done this to her.

"You're going to help me again,'' he said, not answering her. "I need some more pictures of a couple of different men. I'm losing some of my power over various committees in the state senate and I've got to get these guys in compromising situations. You don't look the part of vixen and would be perfect for my scheme.''

"You can't seriously believe I would help you. You're crazy.'' Rage was boiling in her. She could feel herself beginning to tremble over how this person had destroyed her life.

"Oh, am I? Well, let me share a little fact with you. Those two kids Max loves so much just happen to be mine.''

Kaitland laughed, albeit a little hysterically. "Well, you've certainly kept them a secret if that's so.''

Robert shot her an ugly look. "Those pictures of you worked wonders with the senator. But you refused to go to any more dinners with me. I had finally found a way to get to some of these men. They all have families, and whether it's their actions or that they're lured there, none of them could explain pictures away. I found someone else who would help me. But Samantha got pregnant.''

Kaitland felt sick again and her hysteria was instantly cured. She knew that was the name of the children's mother. She remembered Max telling her that. With clarity she realized that Robert was telling the truth. ''Bobby,'' she whispered, remembering that Maxwell Robert was Bobby's real name.

''That's right, sister. They're mine. However, Samantha ran off in the middle of the night. As I couldn't use her when she was pregnant, I decided to find someone else. But I haven't been able to find anyone I really trust. I'm desperate. Some of the men don't believe I'm a formidable foe because the ones I bribed are gone from office. I need more pictures. And if you don't help me, I think I might just have to claim those brats.''

''I won't do it, Robert!'' she said fiercely. ''You know I won't.''

''It's your choice. You keep going back to this Stevens jerk. Fine. You want to marry him, go ahead, but you're gonna have to do this for me first,'' Robert said. ''It's critical I get at least this one senator in a situation. Senator Bradley is against gambling. If I don't find something on him, he's going to sway some of the others to ban gambling in this state. I have too much invested in a gambling venture to let that happen. Once I control him, some of these other conservative bills he's been pushing will be under my control, too.''

''What's to stop you from claiming the children anyway?''

''What's to stop me from sending these pictures to the newspaper and ruining Max's chance in a custody suit when it comes out what type of person he has allowed to take care of his wards? Just think what that would do to his very family-oriented business. Or what it would do to you, too, not to mention those kids, who I will then immediately claim and of course get custody over. I can just see the court when I explain that Samantha ran off without telling me and that when I saw today's story, I realized I'd finally found my children.''

''You don't even care about Samantha, do you?''

He shrugged. "I saw the kids that day at the house. They looked like Samantha. I hired a detective and found out she was dead. She was too clingy anyway."

Kaitland stood, despite how shaky her legs were and went to the door. She pushed it open, using its solid strength to hold her up.

"You make me leave without an answer and I'll ruin your boyfriend."

"Do your best," she replied coldly. "He and I are not involved."

"What about the kids?" he asked, his shock evident, though he tried to hide it behind bravado.

"Go for it," she replied only after a slight hesitation. "Just leave now, Robert, and don't come back. It's going to take me a lot of prayer before I can ever face you again."

He sneered as he walked past her. "Fine. Don't help me. I'll find someone to do the job before Saturday. But let me tell you, Kaitland. You're gonna be sorry you didn't help. Those kids sure did mean a lot to Max."

He sauntered out. Kaitland knew it was because he thought he'd struck a nerve. And he had.

As soon as he was out of sight, Kaitland rushed into the bathroom and threw up, until there was nothing left in her. Then she lay against the tile floor and cried.

"Father, what do I do now? This is all such a mess. I don't want him touching those kids. I'm so angry I think I honestly hate him at this moment. How could he have turned out this way?"

But she knew. Just as Saul, who had been called by God and anointed king, had turned his back on God and sought out a soothsayer for his guidance and assurance, so had her stepbrother turned his back on God and had been given over to a reprobate mind.

"I can't think about him, Father. It hurts too much. You work on him and change him," she begged. "I don't want to see him. I can't help him anymore or even be a friend to him. And I can't let him take those children. Or hurt another senator. What am I going to do?"

An idea came to her. She realized there was really only one thing she could do. But to do it was going to require more courage than she had shown in the last five years. She was going to have to walk right back into the lion's den and deal with one of the Stevens brothers.

"Just don't let him eat me up and spit me out when I face him, Father," she said.

She rose and washed her face and prepared to face Rand Stevens at the headquarters of Stevens Inc.

Chapter Twenty-One

"Who let you in here? Get out. Now!"

Rand looked like an avenging angel when he was mad. And boy was he mad. He had been sitting bent over his desk looking at some papers when she'd managed to sneak past the secretary. She'd told the woman she was waiting for Max and they would go in together when he arrived. As soon as the secretary had left her station, she'd slunk in.

Now Rand stood, pushing up his sleeves as if he was getting ready for a fight. She'd never known Rand to be physical, but he scared her just the same. She backed up against the door. "I'm not leaving until I tell you what I came to say."

"You'll leave right now." He came forward, striding across the carpet like an angry lion about to pounce.

She turned her head, closed her eyes and gritted her teeth, pushing her hands against the door and digging in her heels. This had been a stupid idea. She knew Rand and Max were close, had remembered Max saying Rand had taken her side years ago, but of course, she hadn't seen him right after the incident. He was going to throw her out of the office—physically.

When nothing happened, she opened one eye and peeked at him. He stood a foot away, staring at her strangely. "You know I'd never hurt you, Kaitland. God knows I'd like to throttle you right now for what you've put Max through, but I wouldn't physically assault you. So stop cringing like that."

"Well, the way you came after me gave me my doubts," she replied hesitantly, not moving from her position.

He sighed. "It's Elizabeth. She never gives an inch. I forget how intimidating I can be." As if realizing he had relaxed, he stiffened. "You have exactly five minutes to tell me whatever you think is important."

She sagged against the door. Where to start? She was so relieved, her mind went blank. Overload of all that had happened today, she was sure.

"Well?" Rand asked, but his voice had softened. He hesitated only a moment before coming forward and taking her by the elbow. "You look like you're about to fall down. Come over here."

That one act of kindness was her undoing. She burst into tears—again. Embarrassed, she tried to keep her face down where he couldn't see, though she was wailing loud enough that Max's secretary could probably hear her in the other wing of the building.

She felt a hesitant pat on her head, then her shoulder, heard a grumbled statement and then she was hauled into Rand's arms. "Okay, che'rie, take it easy. Cry it out and then tell me what's the matter."

"I love Max!" she blubbered through loud wails of distress.

"You have quite a way of showing it."

She slapped his chest, which caused a grunt from him. "Ah, all women, they are the same," he murmured, his accent thickening, so much like Max's. "You have the same spirit as my Elizabeth when she's ready to pull my hair out. I do not envy Max," he said. "Now tell me. Why did you go to the press?"

She cried another five minutes before she was able to talk. "I'm s-sorry," she stuttered, sniffling loud and blowing her nose. "I had to tell you. The senator. Jonathan Bradley, your friend, only an acquaintance of mine," she said in disjointed sentences. "It's my brother. He's behind it. You need to tell him. I love him."

"I know you love your brother, but let's go back..."

"Not my brother," she cried. "*Your* brother. I love him. I hate my brother." She paused. "Well, I don't hate him, but I really want to at the moment. He's ruined my life."

"And the senator?"

"He's gonna ruin his life," she said.

Rand sighed. He released Kaitland and stood. Going over to a small bar area, he poured her a glass of ice water and wet a cool cloth. "Wipe your face," he said when he returned to where she sat. "Drink this, and we'll try again."

She did as she was told. "Now, che'rie, tell me what is the matter," he said as he resumed his seat next to her.

"I told you."

He looked as if he was getting upset. "Do you mind if I ask a few questions?"

Realizing she was still making a muddle of her explanation, she nodded.

"What is this about Senator Bradley being your brother?"

Kaitland's eyes widened. "I didn't say that."

"Then what did you say?"

"Senator Bradley is on a committee about gambling. You know Robert does some heavy lobbying. He's known as a man who can get the job done. Or he was. Evidently, he's losing some power in his reputation. He wanted me to help him with Senator Bradley. I had to do what happened before—lure Jonathan to a room and then let Robert snap pictures of me and the senator in a compromising position. I couldn't do it. I refused, but he's going to find someone who will do it and I knew you were friends with Jonathan and he wouldn't believe me since we are only passing acquaintances and it *is* my brother..."

Rand had stiffened and his face turned thunderous. "Your brother was the one who took the pictures? Then you and he *have* been trying to blackmail Max."

"No!" Kaitland cried. "You see, I was almost raped—" She gasped.

Rand's eyes sharpened and focused on her.

"Oh, please," she whispered, almost moaning in shame. "Please don't tell Max."

She dropped her head and began to weep softly. *"Juste ciel,"* Rand said softly in French.

Good heavens. She'd heard Max say the expression enough times.

"I think I am beginning to see, che'rie. Tell me then, if I am mistaken. You were in that room with Senator Richardson without knowing what was about to happen? Your brother took pictures. He used them to break up you and Max. You held your tongue because you love your brother."

"No." She shook her head, negating his words. Taking a deep shuddering breath, she whispered, "I'm so sorry. I'm not usually so emotional. I just feel as if I've lost everyone in the short span of three hours. I didn't know until today that it was my brother who had taken those pictures. He told me, at the same time he threatened to take the children from Max."

Rand sat up. "Maddie and Bobby? How?"

"Oh, Rand. That's one of the reasons I'm here. I'm no longer speaking to my brother. As I tried to explain a moment ago, Robert wanted me to lure Jonathan Bradley up to a room and help him get incriminating photos on the senator. I refused. He told me that Maddie and Bobby are his children. He was using the threat of taking them back, as well as exposing those pictures, as leverage. I told him I didn't care about my reputation. I plan to resign from the day care, of course, so he can't hurt the church. But I won't let him use the children, or hurt Senator Bradley." She paused for a moment, then, "There has got to be something you can do to protect the children and help the senator. Robert plans to tell the authorities that he has been searching for the children's mother and the story this morning led him to them."

"This would have been a lot easier if you hadn't gone to the press with the story."

"I didn't."

Rand looked at her in shock. "Then who did?"

She shrugged. "I have no idea. It's true Marjorie Wiscott and I are on-again off-again friends. But she never interviewed me for this story. I know it's under her byline. I plan to call her later and find out where she got her information. I'm not sure she'll tell me, if the person who gave it to her asked to be anonymous. All you have to know is it wasn't me. I'm not the source.''

Rand studied her, then he looked grim. "Max is never going to forgive himself for this. Nor am I likely to forgive myself. Forgive me, che'rie, for not coming to you and finding out the truth. You have been through more than you should have had to go through.''

Kaitland's shoulders slumped. "It doesn't matter, Rand. I had hoped Max loved me enough to forget the past. I just couldn't confess to him...'' She trailed off.

"He wouldn't have blamed you,'' Rand said softly.

"Five years ago, he tried me and judged me without an explanation, Rand. And did it again. He would have blamed me. Please don't tell him about the incident I mentioned. Let him believe what he wants. It's better than him knowing my secrets and then rejecting me...or worse, apologizing out of guilt.''

"You misjudge my brother. You're right—he should have forgiven you instead of holding on to the pain and keeping it close to his heart. But we aren't perfect. Sometimes it's easier to hold on to it than risk our hearts again. It's wrong. God tells us to forgive *and* forget. We cannot forgive and then make the person pay a penance for their mistake. However, that's what we often do...and if not them, then ourselves.''

Kaitland was jolted by his words and looked up into Rand's understanding eyes.

"Forgive yourself, Kaitland,'' he said. "Let God heal your heart. You did nothing wrong five years ago except not come to my brother and explain. This is the same thing you have done today. I will tell you, Max will find this out and will come to you to hear the truth. You must stop hiding behind your walls and confess all.''

"He'll pity me,'' she whispered. "And probably feel guilty.''

"Good. A nice dose of guilt should help clear his mind, make him stop pitying himself.'' He smiled at Kaitland. "If nothing comes of it between you two, then that's fine. But at least you will again be able to live and go on and you will be stronger, as will my stubborn-headed brother."

She chuckled. "That's what he thinks of you."

Rand chucked her under the chin. "He's wrong. I'm happily married and very biddable now." He stood. "Go home. Rest and pray. I'll make sure Jonathan knows what's going on. And I'll make sure Robert can't get the children."

At the pain in her eyes, Rand added softly, "I know your heart must be breaking over what you must do to your brother. But you're doing the right thing. Let God wrap you in peace, che'rie."

She nodded. "Please don't tell Max about..." She looked him in the eye. "About what happened five years ago."

"It's not my story to tell. When he comes to you, you will tell him."

She thanked him and left, keeping her head down so no one could see she'd been crying. As she walked to the elevators, she thought it unlikely Rand would be right this time. She was certain Max wouldn't ever darken her door again. But Rand had been right about one thing...she was doing the right thing. No matter how much her heart felt as if it was being ripped out, she couldn't let Robert hurt someone else.

Chapter Twenty-Two

"We need to talk—again," Rand said, going into Max's study.

Max looked up and met his gaze. "You said that once. I don't care to hear it again."

"You may look like a wreck at the moment, but I can guarantee you, Kaitland looks worse."

"Kaitland? When did you see her?" Max's eyes widened in shock and in them was a hint of wariness mixed with hope.

Rand shook his head in disgust. "What is it with you, Max? I love you, but you're so mule-headed stubborn. Why have you ostracized Kaitland so thoroughly without finding out what was going on?"

"She's the one who went to the paper. I should have known…" He trailed off and shook his head.

Rand strode forward. "What, Max? What should you have known? I never bought that you just broke it off with her. You're the type to be easygoing with most things, but I could tell you cared for Kaitland. When this fiasco happened five years ago you ran from it, I would say it was in relief, if I didn't know better. And now, again, a newspaper article and you just let her go once more. There's something more behind this and I'm not letting you get away without telling me this time."

Max glared at his brother. "It's none of your business."

Rand walked over to the desk, slammed his hands down on it and leaned forward, scowling. "It is when my own flesh and blood is tearing himself up over it. What is it? What should you have known? Tell me!''

Max erupted. "I should have known she was just like our mother.''

Rand's eyes widened, then he nodded with understanding. "I never realized you knew, too,'' he said and sank down wearily into a chair. Max sank down too as if his outburst had exhausted him. "Why didn't you ever mention to me, in all of these years, that you knew of our mother's betrayal? Especially when Carolyn died in a car accident?''

Max shook his head. "I know it sounds crazy, but there were so many times I'd wondered if we drove her to leave Dad. We were such a handful. Had she not been leaving him, he wouldn't have insisted on one last vacation alone so they could try and work things out, and they both wouldn't have died together.''

"Oh, Max,'' Rand said. "It's been so long.''

Max shrugged. "Dad loved Mom. Too much. He should have let her go and he would be alive. They both would. He wanted her too much.''

"And you think that's the problem here? That Kaitland is going to find she doesn't like the life of the rich and famous like Mom and ask for a divorce? Or is it that you're afraid of loving her too much and chasing after her like Dad chased after Mom,'' Rand said with dawning realization.

Rand shot out of the chair and began to pace. "I have heard some stupid things in my life...but fearing you love Kaitland too much takes the cake. You would rather let her go than risk loving her? You would rather make her absolutely miserable than go after her.''

"But with Kaitland it's different. She did betray me before we were married and again with the reporter. Are you suggesting I actually go after someone like that? No matter how much I love her, I'd be a fool if I did.''

"You're a fool if you don't,'' Rand told him. "You're so busy trying to find some way she might leave you like Mom tried to leave Dad so you can prove to yourself that you shouldn't love her that you've missed out on the one person who loves you more than life itself."

"Just what do you now about it?" Max demanded.

"I know she didn't betray you with those pictures."

"How do you know?"

Rand scowled. "You'll have to ask her. I promised not to say anything. But I can tell you she didn't betray you with that article, either."

"She told you that, too."

"Yeah. And if you weren't so bullheaded, you'd figure that out just by knowing Katie. And I know she didn't break off all contact with her brother and come to me to tell me he was going to try to get the kids—his kids—away from you because she just happens to be planning to try some other way to hurt you."

Max fell back into his chair, shock on his face. "She did what? Maddie and Bobby are...*pooyah-ee!*" His *good grief* came out in French he was so agitated.

"I'm afraid so," Rand said. "I have our lawyers on it. I just came by to tell you that you've made a major mistake with Kaitland and if you let it go this time without fixing things, I'm afraid I'll have to take you outside and beat the stuffing out of you."

Max blinked. "You and what army?" he asked, his own temper finally sparking at the way Rand was treating him.

"It'll only take me. Because when you figure out everything that has transpired, you'll feel too guilty to fight back."

Max sought for a hole in Rand's argument. "If you're so sure Kaitland wasn't the source for the article in the newspaper, who was? It had to be someone who knew our family inside out. That information could only have come from someone in here, and if you tell me Timms, Sarah or Phil did it, I'll laugh."

"It's my fault."

Rand and Max turned to stare at the door where Elizabeth stood looking absolutely awful over the situation. A newspaper was clutched in her hands.

"What are you talking about?" Rand asked, going over and gently taking Elizabeth's elbow and guiding her to a chair.

"Stop treating me like an invalid, Rand." Then, turning to her brother-in-law, "Oh, Max, I'm so sorry. I had no idea until I got the paper about fifteen minutes ago. I slept in this morning because I wasn't feeling well. When my friend Laurel called me the other day, it was because she wanted to interview me. I didn't realize she wanted an official interview. She has this instant-recall memory so she doesn't use tape recorders like most people. However, she asked me what was going on...we go so far back I didn't think anything of it. We laughed and joked. When I saw the article this morning, I knew what had happened. She sold the article to Marjorie Wiscott who had approached her about it. She thought it would be fun done as a tongue-in-cheek, which she said she's no good at writing. And I have to admit the article is like that. But she thought I had given my permission for the article. I've never been so shocked or embarrassed in my life. I'm so sorry," she repeated. "I'm planning to go over and tell Kaitland immediately it was my fault... Max? Are you all right?"

Max moaned and dropped his head to the desk. "Please leave. Both of you," he whispered, his mistake so glaringly obvious that he couldn't stand to face anyone.

"Max?"

"Come on, Elizabeth," Rand said. "Give him time."

He heard both of them leave, heard them pull the door closed behind him. When no one was around, he allowed his grief to pour out.

"Rand was right. Why have I held on to the hurt and pain all of these years? Why couldn't I accept Kaitland for what she was, a gentle soul who loved me? *Loved me.*" He pounded his fist on the desk again, his misery obvious. "Loved, as in past tense. There is no way she could have cared for me. At least, Father, that's what I thought. How could she love me? My mother was so unhappy that last year of her life. She didn't like being in the spotlight. She hated it. I just knew Kaitland would hate it and would pull some crazy stunt like my mother did to try to break off the marriage.

Of course, my mother's crazy stunts had been just disappearing for a week or two at a time, telling my dad she needed time away, until that last time when she told Dad she wanted a divorce. I just knew Kaitland wasn't the type for the limelight. She's so quiet, gentle, kind and loving. She reminds me of a flower, so fragile.''

He stood and walked over to the chair where he knelt and dropped his head to his arms. ''But she's not the one who's in the wrong. She's never been in the wrong. I've run her off both times. I've wronged her more than anyone deserves. What a fool I've been. What am I going to do?''

He continued to pour out his heart until the pain lessened and God finally restored a peace that had been missing from his life for many years, a peace that passes all understanding.

And he knew what he had to do.

Chapter Twenty-Three

"We got him."

"Jonathan?" Kaitland asked. She hadn't talked to Jonathan in over six months. "Senator Bradley?"

"Yes, Kaitland. It's me. The police told me the part you played in helping me. I appreciate that, though I wish it would have proven unnecessary. However, I called to thank you and tell you personally that Robert had a woman approach me Saturday. He came with the *evidence* today that the under-cover policewoman he solicited helped him acquire. The circle is completed and he was arrested. If it helps, he actually looked resigned to what had happened. I think there might be hope for eventually reforming him."

Kaitland sighed. "Only with God's help. He has so much anger in him. But I appreciate your call."

"I wish it hadn't been over such circumstances," the senator said. "However, now that I have you on the phone, I remember about six months ago you promised one day you might take me up on my offer of a date. I have something special planned, a nice quiet dinner at my house tonight. Only two or three friends. Do you think you could fill in as my date?"

She had thought Jonathan wouldn't remember that or their few meetings at different functions. She was wrong. And she was wrong about how forgiving this man was, too, if he could ask out Robert's sister. "Oh, Jonathan, I don't think so. I really don't feel up to it."

"It's important, Kaitland. I know we're not very close as acquaintances. I won't pressure you that way. I know you've been through a difficult time."

"News travels fast."

"Indeed it does. But please, consider coming over to my place at seven. Like I said, I wouldn't ask if I really didn't need this. Consider it me collecting on an old debt."

"I would think, Senator, that my information could serve as that," she said warningly.

He sighed. "You're right. Then I might as well give you a hint. It's about Max. If you won't do it for me, then would you come for Max and the kids?"

Kaitland dropped her head in defeat. She'd only met Senator Bradley a dozen times. They weren't intimate friends the way she and Jake or Shirley were or even Jennifer, with whom she had become close in the past few weeks. But all he had to do was mention Max's name… "I shouldn't, Senator. But I'll come. I'll stay for exactly one hour and then make an excuse. If you haven't told me what you need by then, I'm gone. And you understand I'm only doing this for Max?"

That husky voice of his rumbled across the lines. "Oh, yeah, sweetheart. I definitely hear that. See you then."

He hung up.

Kaitland immediately called herself ten kinds of fool. She should have refused. Max was a closed subject on her life. Today had been her first day at the day care and everyone was treating her as if she were made of spun glass. It was driving her crazy—maybe because that was exactly how she was feeling. She'd actually agreed to go to Jonathan's house so she could tell everyone tomorrow she'd gone out on a date with one of the most handsome and eligible men in Baton Rouge—next to Max, of course. That would shut them up and hopefully stop their looks of fear and pity whenever she walked past.

Going upstairs she decided to take a quick shower and then determine what to wear. Something cute and flashy—the exact opposite of what she was feeling. She would wow them to-night, even if she didn't feel as though she could wow poison ivy at the moment.

"Senator Bradley," she greeted, walking in, glancing around curiously. She'd never been to Jonathan's house before. She was impressed. It was very nice, low-key, conservative just like the man, though it hinted at money in its simplicity.

"Let me take your wrap."

She looked up at Jonathan. He was taller than Max, probably six-two. His light hair and tanned skin glowed from the lighting in the other room. His green eyes were twinkling and his lips twitched with a smile. She turned and allowed him her wrap.

"Are your other guests here yet?" she queried, clutching her purse.

He gave her another one of those quirky smiles and nodded. "They're on the terrace. I have a few things I need to do. Won't you please go on out and...introduce...yourself." He motioned her ahead of him toward the living room. Across the way she could see a dimly lit patio that led to gardens beyond.

She hated this. She absolutely hated this. "About Max?" she said, wanting to find out why he had insisted on her presence.

"Later," he replied and headed down the side hall, leaving her standing in the living room.

Her emerald green dress was long, slit up the side to her knee and sat just off the shoulders. Small flashes of silver glitter sparkled on the material.

She'd coiled her hair up in a French twist and carried a small purse that she could hold in one hand, hoping to feel sophisticated.

All she felt was foolish.

She didn't want to socialize with people she didn't know. But if this was about the children and Max...

Taking a deep breath, she walked outside, thinking the

party must be farther in the gardens. She hesitated just through the door.

The night was crisp, cool, and the smell of flowers wafted to her on the air. Stars shone, just coming out as it was twilight. Patio furniture, very nice wood with cushioned seats, was scattered around in an artful display of disarray. It was dark enough that at first she didn't notice the shadow off to her left near one of the paths through the jungle of gardens.

Something, though, must have alerted her to his nearness because she stiffened and searched the area until she located the shadow. As if sensing another person's presence, the shadow straightened and turned.

Her heart began to hammer against her chest. "Max?" she whispered, uncertain if her eyes were playing tricks on her. Unconsciously, she took a step back, her purse falling from numb fingers.

The figure froze.

"Max?" she asked louder.

A squeal to her right forced her head around and she saw Maddie and Bobby toddling up the path with Darlene. When the children spotted her, they let go of their nanny and lunged toward her.

"Maddie up!" the little girl demanded, thrusting her hands up toward Kaitland.

In shock, unsure what to do, she responded automatically. She lifted Maddie into her arms and bussed her on the cheek, wiping off the extra lipstick, tears filling her eyes when Maddie gave her a very sloppy kiss back.

"Me. Me! Me!" Bobby demanded and she awkwardly bent and scooped up Bobby, too.

"They missed you," Max said.

Pain lanced her heart and she trembled at his voice. She kissed Bobby, who immediately pushed her face away and began playing with the earring in her left ear. She chuckled, though it was a very unsteady sound. "I missed them, too," she said. What did he want? Why was he here? She would have sworn he wouldn't have anything to do with her again. Yet here he was, staring at her with those deep dark eyes, revealing nothing of what he felt. How odd. With Max, she pretty much always knew what he felt. He was very open and vocal. Or at least he had been with her.

Maddie immediately wiggled, wanting down. Bobby, of course, followed his sister. "Darlene, Jonathan said milk and cookies were waiting for them inside."

Darlene immediately herded the children toward the prize. A small smile touched Kaitland's mouth as Maddie and Bobby jabbered on about cookies while eagerly toddling through the doors.

"So, where are the other guests?" Kaitland asked, looking around in expectation once the children were gone.

"There are no other guests, che'rie." His voice was soft, husky, deep with feeling.

No. She couldn't handle this now. Not today. She was still too raw from everything that had happened this last week. "You asked Jonathan to call and set this up, didn't you?" she accused, eyeing the door with longing.

"I thought we should meet on neutral ground. Please don't go," he added when she turned to do just that.

She froze. Max never begged. But it sounded as though he was pleading right now. Without turning around, she asked, "What do you want?"

"I want to know what happened five years ago."

Bitter pain twisted inside her. "You know. I betrayed you. Remember the pictures." She was trembling so badly she knew if she took a step on these heels she would fall off. But which would be better? Making a fool of herself running away or breaking down in front of him? He didn't give her a choice as he stepped into her line of sight, inadvertently blocking the exit.

"I know there were pictures of you taken. But you're not that way, Kaitland. You're too gentle to ever do something so underhand."

"Oh? And what finally convinced you of that?" she sneered, furious suddenly that this topic was about to be dredged up again.

"I think I always knew the truth. But as my brother pointed

out today...*juste ciel,* it wasn't you, Kaitland. It was never you. It was me. I just couldn't accept that you might not get tired of my way of life. I was looking for an excuse. And I found it in spades with those pictures."

Kaitland felt unexpected tears overflow at the pain in his voice.

He continued, "I found a lot more than I was expecting in those pictures. And *oui, che'rie,* I was hurt. But I held on to my pain instead of letting it go like I should. I held it in my heart. Instead of forgiving you and forgetting like the Bible commands, I harbored the pain and allowed it to grow, using it as proof that you would one day leave me like my mother..."

He stopped.

His mother? Max had never been insecure. At least, she'd never known him to be insecure. Seeing a dawning light in what had only been a dark void before, she asked a question that would continue what she had thought a hopeless subject. "What about your mother?"

Pain darkened his gaze, his eyes making her heart break. She watched as, instead of facing her, he turned and stared off into the sky as if contemplating the origin of the stars. "My mother was very unhappy the last two or three years of my parents' marriage. She didn't like the media and what they were doing to our family. My dad kept telling us that publicity would help the store and just to ignore all the erroneous things that were published. But she couldn't handle the way they exploited us. I can remember many times finding her crying. I never told Rand, never shared that with him. It's the only thing I've ever kept from him. But I swore if I ever married, I'd find a woman who didn't mind publicity and I would make sure my children were protected from the barbs and things the media threw out. And then I met you, and fell in love with you. But you were so soft, tender, innocent, I knew the press would eat you alive if they ever sank their claws in you. I knew you'd be unhappy and would eventually leave."

"You sure didn't have much confidence in my love, did you?"

He shrugged, still avoiding her gaze. "It wasn't that. I guess I never got over the way my father fell apart that last year as he tried to convince my mother to stay and the nightmare of my brother and I being left to our own devices when we had been such a strong family up until then. I was afraid to risk it with children. So, it wasn't so much that I didn't trust you as I didn't trust marriage. I love you, che'rie. More than life itself. I only realized during prayer, after I'd run you off a second time, what an absolute fool I've been, not allowing God to heal my pain and trust Him to see us through to the end."

He held out his hand. "I won't do again what I did five years ago. I wanted to come to you and find out just what happened. No more hiding behind walls. No more running. If our love is to last, we must be honest—no matter what."

Kaitland's knees knocked together. She couldn't reach out, afraid she was going to faint at his words. *Be honest—no matter what.* Well, what did it matter? How much worse could it get? Unable to stand still, she went over to a path and started down it. She could hear Max by her side, but refused to look at him. If he touched her now, she would finish the crying jag she had started at his confession. Instead, she inhaled the fragrance of azaleas and honeysuckle as she walked.

And she remembered.

"The party I went to five years ago was really something," she said finally. "I've been to plenty of parties, but this one was different. It was just before Mardi Gras and the women's gowns seemed more glittery than normal, the men more jovial. The people there had had a good year and were in the mood for celebrating. Of course, I enjoyed how outgoing and friendly the guests were since I tend to shy away from situations where I have to talk. However, I'm still the old Kaitland and prefer to have someone I know by my side even if someone else is doing all the talking. That's why I never minded going to parties with you, Max. The people at those functions are low-key, they're polite and you never leave my side."

She sighed, a lonely broken sound that echoed loudly in the garden. "That's why, when my brother, Robert, disappeared and then I got a note asking me to come to his room, I assumed it was from Robert.''

''It wasn't Robert?'' Max asked.

''Oh, yes, it was. But the note to the senator was from him, too.''

''I don't understand. Why would your brother do that? Why did he want you there?'' Max asked. ''Your own brother?''

Kaitland shuddered. ''Yes. My own stepbrother. He's the one who set up the senator to get some pictures of him in a compromising situation so that Senator Richardson would have to vote Robert's way. He's also the one who, because of his note and stupid plan, almost got me raped.''

Tears started.

Max didn't force her to explain more, just reached out and pulled her into his arms and held her as she cried for what had happened, for their own disaster and for all of her disillusionments in the past few hours. And as he held her, he murmured words of love and soft soothing sounds, stroking her back, her hair, her arms.

All the while rage ate at him. Rage at what her stepbrother had let occur, rage that she had held this in and rage that he had been such a thrice-cursed fool and not insisted on finding out the entire story when it happened. Because of him, his Katie had suffered untold sorrow and had had no one to turn to for help. *Ah, Father, help me. Forgive me for my excessive foolishness,* he prayed.

Kaitland clung to him and cried until there was nothing left in her, then she collapsed against him.

He pulled out a white silk handkerchief and fluttered it in front of her face. ''Well, che'rie, it looks as if the children aren't the only ones to ruin my suits. However, you, I don't mind.''

She sniffled again, a pitiful sound on the cool night air. Wiping her face, she tried to move back.

''No, che'rie. I'm not letting you out of my grasp this time. I was more than an idiot last time not to ask you. However, *ma petite,* I'll hear it all.''

Never had his accent been so strong. She knew how much

he was hurting for him to lapse into his own language. Her
heart cried out for the pain of it and the new pain she would
cause him with the explanation. "Don't blame yourself, Max.
I didn't try to stop you when you turned your back on me.
I'll tell you though, I never stopped loving you. I couldn't,
though I was tempted to try after the newspaper article appeared."

Running her hand down his shirt, she stroked his chest in
comfort. He tightened his arms around her. "That was Elizabeth's fault, che'rie, for which she has profusely apologized.
Just one more sin to add to my list," he muttered.

"No, Max. Never. God forgives. He forgets. I forgive you.
And I will forget. I want you to forget, too, never again to
condemn yourself for your mistakes. Because what I'm asking
of you now is forgiveness in what I am going to share with
you."

She shuddered. "My stepbrother has never felt as if he was
accepted by me or my grandmother, so he feels no blood tie.
Even though we aren't blood-related, I've always considered
him my real brother."

Until now could have been added easily, the way Kaitland
paused after that statement.

"He has this unhealthy need for control," she continued.
"Evidently, as long as he has control, he has power over other
people, and he feels superior. His greed knows no end. More
power, more control. By getting into lobbying like he is—
was," she corrected, "he was able to feed that need for
power. But it wasn't enough. He couldn't make people do
what he wanted..."

"Until now."

"Right. That's why he lured me up to the bedroom where
Senator Richardson thought I was waiting for him. He
snapped a few shots, threatened the senator and then he had
that man's votes."

"He's not a Christian, sweetheart." Max said simply.
"And he has a lot of bitterness in him. I'll talk to him and
make sure he understands he's not to bother you again or I'll
bring additional charges against him."

"For bothering his sister?"

"No, che'rie. For trying to blackmail money out of me. Those pictures you saw me with that day and the ones I've received since were sent with a note threatening me if I didn't do what he wants."

"But that would hurt your reputation."

"Who cares? Maybe once I worried about the paper. But I let the fear of what the press would do to my eventual family consume me so much that I ruined our chances before we could start. They can print what they want as long as you promise never to leave me over the erroneous things that will crop up."

"I haven't left you yet and look at all the lies they've printed about you so far? Including," she added, a small smile in your voice, "that you just got back from Colorado where you were secretly meeting with a certain European princess who was there on vacation."

He chuckled. "I had forgotten about that story that happened when Rand was in therapy with Elizabeth. Of course, it was quite a shock, coming back to find my brother had regained his sight. So, it's understandable that I forgot about that one."

"My point," Kaitland said, "is that the stories have never bothered me. That's how these magazines are. They thrive on sensationalism. And it's good for business," she teased before sobering when she pulled back and met his gaze. "I'll confess now that I didn't come to you years ago because I was ashamed of what had happened. I was afraid you'd look at me differently. Please forgive me for that."

He shook his head. "Never would I look at you differently, che'rie. And of course you're forgiven. As you said, God forgives. He forgets. And starting today, after the harsh lesson we have both learned, I promise you I'll do my best never to look back on a wrong but to forget it and go forward. Nothing else matters but that I love you, Katie. I want you in my life the rest of my days. I love you, and I need you. The children love you and need you. And I wouldn't be averse to adding a few little ones to the brood, either. We can forgive the past, accept the lesson we have learned from it and look forward if you're willing.'' Max reached into his pocket and pulled out a small box.

Kaitland accepted it from his hands, opening it reverently. Inside was nestled an emerald and diamond ring. "Oh, Max," she whispered.

"It's the same as the necklace and earrings I bought you years ago."

Looking up, she asked, "You kept this all these years, even though you believed I'd betrayed you?"

Max shrugged. "Despite what an idiot I was, I never could let you go."

Kaitland smiled, her luminous eyes shining from the tears there. "I guess I was right when I felt it was God prompting me to take the job."

She held up the box and held up her hand. Max readily slipped the ring onto her third finger. She stared at it, murmuring, "God has certainly worked out many problems between us and cleared up so many questions I had about the past."

She lifted her hands and placed them on his shoulders. Looking into his eyes, she allowed her regret to show. "I'm sorry, my love, I didn't come to you sooner and ask forgiveness for my stubbornness. I have no excuse. I used my hurt to hide behind, thinking you were the one who should have come forward."

Max stroked her cheek, gently tracing the curve of her delicate bones. "God works on His own timetable. As Rand said, neither one of us were probably ready five years ago. And remember. *Forget.* It is over, to be remembered no more. I'm ready to go forward with the certainty that God is leading us and guiding us and will protect our steps every day of our lives. How about you?"

Kaitland stared up into the dark brown eyes brimming with love and promise. Her heart swelled to overflowing with her love for this man. "Oh, yes, my love. I'm more than ready. Ready to take you on, the kids, and your obnoxious brother."

Max laughed huskily. His eyes, though, burned with his

love. "That's the spirit. And you're gonna need it if, as my wife, you're going to help me keep Rand from corrupting those two little termagants."

Kaitland's heart lifted, soaring to the heavens.

"But first, let me do something that has been long overdue." Max leaned forward and placed a loving kiss on her lips, pulling her into his arms. She reveled in the sweetness as he molded her lips to his, consuming her with his tenderness and yes, love, with no inhibitions between them. Her fingers slipped into his silky hair and she stroked his neck, her heart almost beating itself right out of her chest.

Finally, he lifted his head. Kaitland rested in his strong arms, allowing him to hold her weight against him. Slowly, she lifted heavy eyelids. "That is what you wanted to show me?" she asked, confused though pleased.

"That," he replied, grinning very smugly at her reaction, "and my promise to cover you with those each night for the rest of our lives."

He lowered his head and their lips met again, this time with a promise of bright things and the future ahead.

* * * * *

Acknowledgments

Wow. A second book. And so many people to thank. My GEnie pals, Kathi Nance, Judy DiCiano, Shannon Lewis and Nancy aka Igor; and Yvonne Grapes, my mail critique partner. And Gayle Anderson who willingly read over the manuscript for mistakes. They are wonderful to bounce ideas off of.

And of course, Jean Price, my agent, and Anne, my editor, who have been unfailingly patient with me as I learn the process of what goes into publishing a book. And Anita Slusher and Debbie Weaver.

But most of all, my daughter, Christina, my son, Jeremiah, and my husband, Steve, who are so wonderful about eating spaghetti or leftovers when I'm at the computer.

Dear Reader,

Ideas come from many places. I love baby stories and I love twin stories. And I like happy endings. When I started Max's story, I thought about how we sometimes are urged to forgive, but it's so often only lip service. "I'll forgive you. But you're gonna have to really earn back my trust. And it's gonna take time!" And yet that goes against what the Bible teaches us. God tells us to be like Him. Forgive and forget. *Forget* being the word we usually leave out! I thought, wouldn't it be nice to see a story about a man who fears that pain from his past and is betrayed on top of this. We see him gun-shy, yet not so sure just how badly he wants to love. So he professes forgiveness, but hangs on to the memory of the pain—until God points out the error of his ways. And of course, I always like the humorous things children get into, considering I have two of my own and always have a brood over. I hope you enjoy Max's story of tenderness and triumph. Not just with Katie, but with those two little lively angels that are left on his doorstep. Write me and let me know. P.O. Box 207, Slaughter, LA 70777.

Yours truly,

Cheryl Wolverton

Books by Deb Kastner

Love Inspired

DEB KASTNER

is the wife of a Reformed Episcopal minister, so it was natural for her to find her niche in the Christian/inspirational romance market. She enjoys tackling the issues of faith and trust within the context of a romance. Her characters range from upbeat and humorous to (her favorite) dark and brooding heroes. Her plots fall anywhere between, from a playful romp to the deeply emotional.

When she's not writing, she enjoys spending time with her husband and three girls and, whenever she can manage, attending regional dinner theater and touring Broadway musicals.

DADDY'S HOME
Deb Kastner

To my daddy, Jim Larkin,
for never letting me give anything but my best.
And for my girls' daddy, Joseph C. Kastner, Jr.,
who never stopped believing.

Chapter One

"Christopher's back in town."

Jasmine Enderlin stiffened at the statement. Keeping a carefully neutral expression on her face, she met her grandmother's shrewd gaze. "And you're telling me this because…?"

"Don't be obtuse," Gram snapped, shaking a wrinkled finger under Jasmine's nose. "Don't you pretend I need to spell it out for you. I'm not buying. You know exactly what I'm saying, and you know why. Now, do you want to know the details, or don't you?"

"Yes," she whispered, not even sure Gram would hear her. She released an audible sigh and turned back to the thick olive-colored sweater she'd been folding moments before.

Jenny's sweater.

Brushing the soft material across her cheek, she caught a whiff of Jenny's light, breezy scent on it.

She wouldn't have thought something as simple as the smell of her sister's perfume would set her off, but for some reason, today it did. Her eyes pricked with tears, and she brushed them away with a hurried swipe of her fist, hoping Gram wouldn't notice the furtive action.

Why would Christopher come back to Westcliffe at all, and especially now of all times?

As if to answer Jasmine's unspoken question, Gram shrugged her age-bent shoulders. "He wants his son."

"What?" She sprang from the bed, tipping a pile of freshly

folded blue jeans into a heap at her feet. "What do you mean he *wants* Sammy? He can't have him," she added vehemently, hugging her arms to her chest as if protecting an infant there. *Her* infant.

A moment more and she would have dashed from the room to snatch up the baby boy sleeping soundly in his bassinet in the next bedroom, but Gram held up a finger in protest. "You haven't heard the story."

I know the story, she thought, her heart clenching. *Love. Betrayal. Desertion.*

That chapter of her life was over, she reminded herself, fiercely determined to remain in control of her emotions. She shook her head to detour the advancing thought, but it came anyway.

Jenny's dead.

Ugliness folded over her like quicksand. God didn't help Jenny. He could have, but He didn't. Guilt stabbed at her conscience, and she briefly wondered if her thoughts constituted blasphemy.

Maybe they did.

But how could she change the way she felt, the way she viewed things? What else was she to think? Three months ago when *she* hadn't been able to save Jenny. Not with all her years of medical training, not with so much love that she would have willingly taken her sister's place.

And God had done nothing.

"It isn't your fault, my dear," Gram said as she hobbled over to a high-backed Victorian chair and seated herself with the sluggishness of age. "You shouldn't blame yourself."

Gram, she reflected with an inward wince, had the annoying ability to read her mind. Even as a child when Jasmine lost both parents to a tragic car accident, Gram had known what she was thinking and feeling. Gram had raised her, knew better than anyone what she suffered now.

"Because Christopher came back all of a sudden, after a year away?" she asked, knowing full well it was not the question Gram was answering.

Her keen silver eyes fixed upon Jasmine. If she was disturbed by her granddaughter's persistent avoidance of the obvious, it didn't show in her gaze.

"I had my hair set in the salon today," she said, relating the story as if it were of no consequence. As if Jasmine's world hadn't come crashing to a halt the moment she'd heard Christopher's name. "Lucille Walters came in for a perm. She told me everything she knew. Said since it's January and all, he's looking for a new beginning. Clean slate, you might say. Seems he's bunking with her boys at the Lazy H."

"He's rooming with ranch hands?" she asked, surprise sounding in her voice. His parents, like hers, were with the Lord. And as an only child, he had no family to return to. But ranch hands?

"Seems a bit peculiar to me." Gram raised a gray eyebrow and cocked her head to one side.

Her laughter was dry and bitter. "Yeah, for someone who's scared to death of horses, I'd say it is." How quickly the old anger returned to course through her. Righteous indignation swelled in her chest. She embraced it, welcoming the heat that surged through her bloodstream like electricity.

It was her way of dealing with what she couldn't stand to face. Anger filled the empty spaces, leaving no room for more painful, tender emotions to surface.

It was a welcome relief. "Did you talk to him?" she queried, her voice unusually low and scratchy.

"No." Gram leaned forward and cupped a hand to her mouth as if to whisper a secret. "But he told Lucille he wants his son."

"Sammy is *not* his son!"

Sammy! Would Christopher take him away from her? That sweet baby had given new meaning to her life, given her a reason to live when all she wanted to do after Jenny's death was crawl into the nearest hole and die.

And Christopher could take it all away. The thought pierced her heart like a stake. Sure, she had the papers that said she was Sammy's legal guardian, but Christopher was related by blood. She pumped her fists open and closed to release the tension swirling through her.

Oh Jenny. Why did God take you away from us?

"Sammy's *my* son," she said again, more to reassure herself than to answer Gram.

"Not sure the law will see it your way." Gram's age-roughened voice broke into her thoughts. Her eyes were full of compassion as she reached forward to squeeze her granddaughter's hand. "Seems to me Christopher had some part in making that baby."

Jasmine didn't want to think about that. "Jenny's will makes *me* his guardian. Besides, a romp in the sack doesn't make a man a father." She snorted her derision. "He doesn't deserve to be a father to baby Sammy, as I'm sure the courts will agree. He abandoned Jenny long before his *son* was born. What kind of a *father* does that make him?"

Gram held up her hands as if to ward off a blow. "I'm not disagreeing with you, honey. No-sirree! I'm just concerned that he's going to fight you every step of the way. Mark my words! You know as well as I do that Christopher Jordan is a strong, stubborn man. He won't stop until he gets what he wants."

She knew. Better even than Gram did. Once, she'd known his heart and soul. Or at least she thought she had. "He won't get Sammy," she vowed, her voice tight.

Gram raised an eyebrow. "Well, girl, I've gotta say you can be just as determined as any ol' man when you put your mind to it." She chuckled. "My money's on you."

"Thank you for your confidence," she replied with a wry smile. "I'll fight him if I have to." No one would take Sammy away from her. *No one.* He was her baby now. And he was all she had left of Jenny.

Sammy's cry pierced the gray haze of rage and frustration that flooded Jasmine's mind. She dashed into the other bedroom and tucked the crying baby to her chest, speaking to him in an incoherent, soothing whisper.

At three months old, Sammy was already well able to make his desires known, she reflected with a smile. Not all the anger in the world could dim the gentle glow of love that filled her heart every time she held this sweet, precious child.

With the palm of her hand, she smoothed the tuft of light brown hair covering his head. He had a cowlick on the left side of his forehead. Just like his father.

Christopher.

She shook the thought away. "Gram, if I change Sammy's diaper, will you take him for a while? I want to go through the rest of Jenny's clothes before I quit for the night."

Gram came around the corner, smiling and cooing as she approached Sammy. "Let's get you changed, little fellow, so I can take you. Your Mommy needs to get some work done."

Mommy. Jasmine felt less awkward after three months, but still the term hovered in the corner of her consciousness, taunting her to prove herself. She wrapped a fresh diaper around Sammy's waist and pinned it securely, barely giving a thought to her actions.

Some things, at least, were beginning to come easier for her.

It was she who rose each night for the two o'clock feeding, she who burped and cuddled and changed the boy.

She hadn't planned to be anyone's mother. Not for years yet, in any case. If only...

"Don't you think you've done enough for one day?" Gram asked, reaching for the infant and bouncing him against her shoulder, patting his back in an age-old, soothing rhythmic gesture. "You have to go to work early tomorrow. Besides, you've been called out three evenings in a row. Can't the people around here stay out of trouble for a single night?"

She chuckled. "I don't mind, Gram. Really. That's why I went to medical school. I survived my residency with far less sleep than I get here. This town rolls up the carpet at six o'clock in the evening! In Denver, our worst hours were late at night."

"Be that as it may," Gram argued, "things have changed. You've got a little one dependent on you. You need to keep yourself healthy. For Sammy's sake, Jasmine, if not your own."

She laughed. "Gram, I've never been sick a day in my life, and you know it. I rarely even catch a cold!"

"For Sammy's sake," the old woman repeated, kissing the infant's forehead.

Jasmine sighed. "For Sammy's sake. Everything I'm doing is for Sammy's sake. Not that I regret a minute of it." She stroked one finger down his feathery cheek, enjoying the loud giggle that erupted from him. Staring down at him now, her heart welled with love.

"Take care of my baby."

Her sister's voice echoed through her head as if it were yesterday, and not three months past. Would that fluttery, empty feeling in the center of her chest ever really go away, or would she eventually learn to live with it? It caught her unawares at the oddest moments.

She closed her eyes and took a deep breath to steady her quivering nerves. "I've got to get back to these sweaters, or I'll never get this done."

Gram settled herself on the rocking chair in the corner of the baby's room and adjusted Sammy on her lap. "We'll be fine, dear. Just don't be too long. I think he's hungry."

"I'm not surprised. That baby eats more than most kids twice his size," she commented as she moved into the opposite bedroom. "There's a bottle ready in the fridge if he gets too restless."

She eyed the open closet defensively. Jenny's clothes—blouses crammed haphazardly onto hangers, blue jeans rolled and stuffed on the shelf top above, the one dress she owned to wear for special occasions—beckoned to her.

She'd already put off this unpleasant task too long. The time had come for her to finish packing Jenny's things away and to sell the bungalow.

She reached up to the shelf above her head and tugged on a pile of jeans, which came fluttering down on top of her. Something solid hit her head, making a loud, clapping noise and stinging her skin where it slapped. She instinctively threw her arms over her to protect herself from being beaned with further projectiles, but none were forthcoming. It was just one book.

A book had been rolled up in a pair of jeans? That was

something she didn't see every day. Curious, she reached to retrieve the errant missile.

A Bible. Jenny had a Bible, hidden away like a treasured possession. Somehow she'd assumed Jenny had left the faith, if her actions were anything to go by.

Curious, Jasmine thumbed the pages, recognizing the flowing loops and curves in the margins as Jenny's handwriting. Even though Jenny said she hadn't made peace with God until the end of her life, this Bible obviously had held some significance for her. Bits of paper were carefully folded into the book, as well as a single white rose, carefully pressed and dried, softly folded onto the page with the family tree.

Jasmine brushed her fingers over the crisp, dry calligraphy. "February twenty-fifth. Jennifer Lynn Enderlin married Christopher Scott Jordan."

Tears burned in her throat, and she bit her lip to keep them from flowing. Would the pain never lessen?

She ran a finger over the black ink, the carefully formed letters. Jenny's handwriting had always been so much neater than her own. It had been a source of endless amusement for Jenny to be able to harass her older sister about the chicken-scratching she passed off as handwriting. It was, she had often teased, God's sure sign to her that Jasmine was meant to be a doctor.

She curled up on the floor against the edge of the bed, staring at the Bible. It was a tangible piece of Jenny. She could run her fingers down the cracked leather binding, read the notes Jenny made in the margins about the Scriptures she read.

Slowly, almost reverently, she opened the Bible, silently flipping page after page, pausing to read a comment here and a highlighted Scripture there. Jenny had obviously spent a lot of time in the Word before her death. Jasmine's throat constricted around her breath.

The doorbell sounded. She snapped the book shut and stuffed it under Jenny's pillow. Her thoughts whirlwinded as she considered who might be at the door. Perhaps someone was here to look at the bungalow, even though it wasn't listed yet.

"I'll get it!" she whispered, peeking into the extra bedroom. Sammy was sound asleep in Gram's arms, and it appeared Gram, too, had taken the liberty of a small nap. Her chin nestled against the baby boy, and her mouth had dropped open with the light buzz of snoring.

Jasmine chuckled quietly and moved to the front door. It was only when her hand was already on the knob and she'd half opened the door that it occurred to her who might be waiting.

"Christopher!" Jasmine confirmed, staring up at the tall, ruggedly handsome man before her. "What are you doing here?"

Her heart skipped a beat, then thumped an erratic tempo in her throat, blocking her breath. Anger, shock and a dozen other emotions buzzed through her like a swarm of angry bees.

A smile tugged at the corner of his mouth, but it didn't reach his eyes, which gleamed like cold, gray stones. Despite herself, Jasmine remembered how those eyes used to twinkle, changing in shade from a deep gray to a cobalt blue whenever he was happy.

He clearly wasn't happy now. The quirk of a smile changed into a frown, matching the twin creases between his light brown eyebrows.

"That's a fine welcome for an old…friend," he commented slowly, his scowl darkening.

"What do you want?" she snapped, her voice cold. She felt a stab of guilt for her rudeness, but she brushed it away.

The man didn't deserve better. In her book, anyone who deserted his family didn't deserve much of anything. Except maybe a swift kick in the backside.

"Cut to the chase, Christopher." The determined gleam in his eyes left no doubt he wasn't here for a social call. And the sooner he was gone, the better.

Every muscle in her body had tensed to the point of physical pain, but that was nothing in comparison to the wrenching agony of her heart at seeing him again. She had no idea it would be this difficult to face the man she'd once loved with all her heart. She clenched her fists, her fingernails biting into her palms.

I'm not ready.

She knew she'd eventually have to confront him, but she'd hoped to be doing it on her terms, in her time, on her own turf. Three strikes and she was out before she even got a chance to bat.

He was taller than she remembered, with a lithe frame and broad shoulders. He curled a steel gray cowboy hat in his fists, leaving exposed the cowlick that made his light brown hair cock up just over his left eyebrow. She remembered once telling him it gave him a roguish appearance. He'd just laughed and shaken his head. Maybe if he'd known just how much she'd wanted to spend her life with him—to marry him and raise a family with him—things might have been different. If only...

"Medical school has done wonders for your manners," he commented gruffly. "What do they teach you there? How to offend your neighbors in one easy lesson?"

The barbs found their mark. "You're not my neighbor." She scratched out the words, since her throat had suddenly gone dry.

He raised one eyebrow. "No? Whatever happened to the Good Samaritan? Or didn't you learn that one in church?"

Jasmine cringed inwardly. It wasn't like him to throw Scripture at her that way. He possessed a strong, quiet faith, which he neither took lightly nor tossed in someone's face like pearls before swine.

She wondered where that faith had gone. The past few months were proof of his decline. Choosing to marry Jenny over her without even the courtesy of a phone call, then up and abandoning the poor girl once she was carrying his child—the change was too great to fathom. The icy-eyed man standing before her was a virtual stranger.

"Maybe you haven't heard," he continued. "I'm living at

Lucille's place now.'' He rolled the brim of his hat once more, then jammed it on his head.

''With the ranch hands,'' she added dryly.

''Mmm. So you did know, then. I was wondering how long it would take for the news to get back to you. Small town and all.'' He peered over her shoulder into the room. ''Aren't you going to invite me in?''

She heard Sammy cry out, and wondered if Christopher heard it, as well. With lightening swiftness, she stepped out onto the front porch and quietly but firmly closed the door behind her.

''No. I'd rather not.'' She wondered if he heard the quavering in her voice, and determined to control it with all the force of her will.

Christopher appeared unaffected by her intentional rudeness. He placed a hand on the door frame above her right shoulder and leaned into her, his face only inches from her own.

Her head spinning, she tried to inhale, tried to steady herself mentally. Instead, she breathed a heady whiff of his western-scented cologne.

Her favorite. The brand he used to wear especially for her.

Panicking, she stepped backward until her shoulders hit the solid strength of the door. This furtive movement was no deterrent for Christopher, who simply crooked his elbow to narrow the distance between them.

The brim of his hat touched her forehead, and he tilted his head to move in closer. His breath mingled with hers, his steel gaze never leaving hers for a moment.

She felt the way a mouse must feel when hypnotized by a snake's haunting eyes—knowing she would be consumed, yet powerless to look away.

He was going to kiss her. The snake wasn't even going to ask. Just take. And she wouldn't be able to stop him, so mesmerized was she by his gleaming eyes that looked so serious beneath the brim of his hat.

She closed her eyes. Despite her head screaming to the contrary, her heart beckoned him closer. It wasn't rational; in fact, it was quite out of the question. But knowing that didn't stop her from wanting his lips on hers just one last time. Perhaps it was a move toward resolution. She leaned closer, anticipating the moment their lips would meet.

"Where is he?" His low voice resonated in her ears.

Her eyes snapped open to meet his amused gaze. The twinkle had returned, and the dimple in his left cheek was showing. He was completely relaxed, and he was smirking at her!

Hurt and anger warring within her, she pushed both hands into his chest and shoved as hard as she could.

Christopher stepped back, but only because he wanted to. He didn't want to admit that his feelings hadn't changed, not in all these years, and not with all that had happened between them.

But now was not the time to pursue his feelings, though surely that time would arrive. He would *make* that time come, one way or another.

There were bridges to be built to gap the distance between them, and that would take some time. He'd known from the moment he decided to return to Westcliffe that it wouldn't be easy. Not for him, and most definitely not for Jasmine.

She could be one stubborn woman, he thought, pressing his lips together. But then again, he was a stubborn man. He clamped his teeth down hard and stared her down.

"Get out of here, you snake." Her voice was a low rasp.

Snake? He cringed inwardly at her animosity. He'd hoped her anger at the situation would have dulled enough with time for her to listen to reason, but it was obvious she was no closer to being ready to accept the truth than she'd been a year ago. He set his jaw and narrowed his eyes on her. "Not until I've seen my son."

"*Your* son? *Your* son is doing very well without you, thank you very much. When did you decide to be a daddy, Christopher? Yesterday? It's not like a hat that you can put on whenever you please. What right do you have to waltz in and demand to see him? He's a twenty-four-hour-a-day responsibility, which I have been facing alone, I might add. He's a flesh-and-blood human being, not some toy you can play with whenever the urge strikes you!''

"Yeah," he agreed, tipping his hat backward and raking his fingers through his hair. Some things hadn't changed.

Jasmine Enderlin was as pigheaded as she'd always been. If she hadn't jumped to conclusions a year ago, he wouldn't be standing here like a stranger on her front porch. God willing, they would've been married.

But God wasn't willing. And Jasmine wasn't budging.

"Give me a break, Jazz. I've been busting my tail to get back here."

"Is that so?" she snapped. bracing her arms on her hips. "And I'm supposed to feel sorry for you because you worked so hard to get back here?"

He leveled his gaze on her and stepped forward. "That's *so*," he said, his tone hard. "And at the moment, I don't give a wooden nickel how you feel about me. I want to see my son. Now."

Chapter Two

Jasmine's breath came in short, uneasy gasps. Her head swirled with emotion. To have to see Christopher again, to face not only what he'd done to her heart, but to her family, was enough to daunt the strongest of women. But to have him waltz into town and demand to see his child with all the arrogance of the perfect father was positively the last straw.

Anger welled in her chest.

"What right do you have to demand *anything?*" she growled through clenched teeth, willing her throbbing heart to slow before it beat a hole through her chest.

Christopher pulled the hat down low over his brows and leaned toward her, his posture firm and menacing. For a minute he just stared at her, the ice in his gaze freezing her insides. When he finally spoke, it was in a whisper. "I'm his father, Jazz."

His voice cracked on her name, and for the briefest moment, she saw a flicker of pain cross his gaze, so deep and intense she almost felt sorry for him.

Without even realizing what she was doing, she reached out a hand to stroke his strong jaw, then withdrew it just as quickly, curling her fingers into her chest as if she'd been burned.

She didn't feel *anything* for Christopher Jordan, she reminded herself harshly. Not anymore. He didn't deserve her pity, or her compassion. Scriptural verses flooded her mind, words about mercy and forgiveness, but she refused to concede. Not for him.

It didn't take a genius to read the change in her demeanor, and his eyes quickly shaded, resuming the tint of frosty steel.

"I have rights," he reminded her, his voice as cold as his gaze.

Jasmine steeled her heart, preparing to do mental battle with the man who'd once been the love of her life. She'd fight him tooth and nail for Sammy, and in the end, that was all that mattered. Not the past. The good or the bad. She wouldn't let her heart betray her a second time.

"You lost any rights you had the night you left Jenny alone and pregnant," she snarled.

His lips thinned. He opened his mouth to speak, then abruptly shut it again.

"You *aren't* Sammy's father," she added abruptly, sensing her advantage.

The barb met its mark, if his sharp intake of breath was any indication. She rushed on before she lost her nerve.

"You can threaten me with a lawsuit if you want, but I'm not backing down. Jenny made *me* Sammy's guardian. I've got papers to prove it—papers that will stand up in *any* court of law."

Jasmine wasn't as certain of her claim as she sounded, but she wasn't about to let on. She made a mental note to speak with the family attorney, feeling pleased that she'd struck Christopher dumb, at least for a moment.

He swept off his hat, his gaze genuinely hurt and confused. "Who said anything about a lawsuit?" he demanded, blowing out a breath. "Shoot, Jazz, don't you know me well enough by now to know I wouldn't do that to you? Or to Sammy," he added, under his breath.

Hat in hand, he reached out his arms to her, beseeching her with his gaze as well as his posture. "Just let me see him. I won't stay long. I just want to see that he's safe and—" His voice choked, cutting his sentence short. "Please, Jasmine. Just for a minute."

She felt herself relenting even as her answer left her lips.

''Forget it. Not now, and not ever. Go back from whatever rock you crawled out from under, Christopher. There's nothing here for you now.''

Her heart felt like it had been through a paper shredder, and she whirled away from him before she gave in to the earnest pleading in his tone. She had to get away from him until she could think things through, knowing she couldn't put two straight thoughts together when he looked at her that way.

How could she not remember the man Christopher once was, the strong, gentle man she loved? But that man was gone, her dreams shattered by the same disheartening reality that was responsible for creating the sweet little boy in the bedroom.

Which only served to prove that good really could come from something bad.

No matter what, she had to protect Sammy. She opened the screen door and slipped inside, glancing behind her shoulder in time to see Christopher punch his hat on his head and move to follow her.

Her heart pounded as she reached for the door and slammed it behind her, barely locking Christopher out before he began pounding.

''And good riddance,'' she whispered, leaning her forehead on the door.

Jasmine was terrified Sammy would wake up and start wailing. If that happened, and Christopher heard his baby, he'd never leave. She slid down against the wall, cupping her hands over her ears. Why wouldn't he just go away and leave them alone?

After ten minutes, when she'd finally concluded he'd never quit pounding, she heard him stomp back to his truck and slam the door. She felt both relieved and yet strangely desolate now that she was once again alone.

Her heart was still in her throat as she peeked from behind the front curtain and watched him drive away in his old Chevy truck, relaxing only when she knew for sure he was gone.

He would be back. Christopher Jordan was a stubborn, vigorous man who actively pursued what he wanted. He wouldn't let this episode stop him from seeing Sammy. But at least it would give her time to think, to sort out her feelings so she could face him again without the emotions that earlier clouded her judgement.

Running a palm over her hair to smooth it, she took a deep breath and forced a smile to her lips. She knew Gram would see right through it, but she had to try.

Head held high, she walked as quietly and serenely as possible into the bedroom. Gram sang softly to the baby, rocking slowly back and forth with Sammy tucked in the crook of her arm.

It was such a peaceful scene, and so much at variance with the frantic pace of Jasmine's heart, that she nearly turned tail and walked out again. But Gram caught her eye and smiled.

"He's sleeping soundly, dear," she said softly, continuing to rock. "I fed him the whole bottle. He's probably down for the count. Can you help me lay him in the bassinet?"

Jasmine nodded and moved forward, holding Sammy a moment longer than necessary, inhaling his sweet, baby scent and enjoying the feel of his soft skin against her cheek. It was only the threat of losing him that made her realize that she couldn't live without him.

It was more than just the schedule changes, the responsibility that came with having a newborn. More even than knowing there was someone completely dependent on her for his every need.

It was the space in her heart that grew larger every day, ebbing and flowing with love for this little one.

There was no way she was going to let Christopher take him away. She'd once thought the gaping hole he rent in her heart would never be mended. But loving Sammy forced her to open up her heart once again, to feel and live and hope.

She kissed the infant on his soft forehead and pushed the thatch of downy hair from his eyes. She wouldn't let the little guy down. No matter what.

"Is he gone?" Gram asked gently.

With an audible sigh, she took her grandmother's elbow and led her to the kitchen, where she seated the elderly woman on a foldout chair. Jenny's financial straits were obvious by the card table she used in place of a regular kitchen table.

Sammy had the best of everything, most of which had been bought by Jenny before her death. She had sacrificed everything for her unborn son, showing the kind of sweet, giving person she was all the way up to her last breath. She would have done anything for her Sammy.

Jasmine felt a tug of grief, and made a pretense of looking through the cupboard in order to have a moment to fold those feelings back into her memory. She already knew what was in the cupboards, which amounted to a box of peppermint tea and a box of saltine crackers.

"Do you want some tea?" she asked, hoping her voice didn't sound as high and squeaky to Gram as it did to her own ears. It annoyed her to betray her feelings in her voice, especially to Gram, who was already much too perceptive. With a determined effort, she steadied her voice and continued. "I think I'll have a cup, myself."

"Are you okay?"

She took her time pulling two mugs from a shelf and filling them with water, before turning to face her grandmother. "Yes, of course. Why wouldn't I be?"

"I can't imagine," Gram replied dryly.

She set the cups in the microwave and turned it on, then sat down across from her grandmother. "You're too wise for your own good."

Gram met Jasmine's gaze over the top of her spectacles and chuckled. "I haven't been alive for eighty years without learning something."

Jasmine reached for Gram's hand and squeezed it. "You've been so much help to me these past months," she admitted, her voice quavering with emotion. "I couldn't have made it without you."

"What's family for?" Gram said, waving off her comment with a slight grunt of protest.

The microwave buzzed, and Jasmine jumped up. As she dipped the tea bags into the mugs, she took a deep breath and plunged ahead. "It *was* Christopher at the door."

"Who else would it be? Didn't sound like he was in a hurry to leave, either."

"That's the understatement of the year," she agreed quietly. "I should have realized he'd be back, that he'd want to see Sammy at some point. I just wasn't prepared for him to show up today."

"And you sent him packing." It was a statement rather than a question, punctuated with a dry chuckle.

Jasmine laughed, but it didn't reach her heart. "You could say that. I slammed the door in his face."

"He'll be back." Gram nodded her head as if confirming her own words.

The flatness Jasmine felt when Christopher left wound itself more tightly around her chest. "I know," she whispered.

"What are you going to do about him?"

Gram was nothing if not direct, she reflected. No games. No beating around the bush. She just said what she thought and was done with it. One of the perks that came with age, Gram always said just before blurting out something outrageous.

Jasmine shook her head. "I don't know yet. Seeing him again confused me. I thought it would be easier. I thought..."

"That you hated him?" Gram queried gently, finishing the sentence for her. "Love doesn't give up so easily, my dear."

She shook her head fiercely. "No. I'm not in love with Christopher anymore." If her heart believed that, she wouldn't be quaking in her shoes, she thought acerbically. But she'd never admit it, not even to herself. "I've been over him for a long time."

"Have you?" Gram's questioning gaze met hers, and she looked away, afraid her grandmother would read the truth she knew must shine through her tears.

She couldn't love Christopher! Not after all these years, and especially not after everything he'd done to her and her family.

Then why did her heart leap when she saw him again?

She'd loved him since they were both in high school, she rationalized. For years they'd been inseparable. He'd been the man to whom she pledged her life, with whom she was ready to tie the knot.

Was it any wonder she would have such a polar reaction at seeing him again?

How could she not? It was only natural, after all, for her to have lingering feelings for a man who was such a large part of her past. Some of her happiest memories were with Christopher Jordan, and that was something his recent actions couldn't take away.

"My feelings don't matter," she said at last, shaking her head. "This isn't about me." She paused and took a deep breath, giving the bassinet a pointed look. "He wants to see Sammy. For all I know, he wants to take him away. And somehow, I've got to figure out a way to stop him."

Gram slowly stood and stretched, then shuffled to Jasmine's side, placing a consoling arm around her shoulders.

That the arm around her didn't have the power of former years mattered not a bit. Strength flowed from the elder to the younger with an intensity that only came from inner peace.

"I know this is hard for you, dear," she said, patting Jasmine's shoulder as she would to comfort a child. "But don't ignore your feelings. They are God given. Pray about it. Search your heart. And, Jasmine?"

"Mmm?"

"Talk to Christopher."

"*Talk* to him?" she screeched, her anger returning in spades. "Gram, I never thought *you'd* be on his side, after what happened to Jenny! Why should I *talk* to him?"

Gram's eyebrows creased as she frowned. "Don't you speak to me that way, young lady," she said, her tone brooking no argument. "I may be eighty, but I can still take you over my knee!"

Jasmine stepped back, surprised, then broke into a tired laugh, serving as a valve for the release of her anger. Gram was right, of course.

She hugged her grandmother as hard as the older woman's frail bones would allow. "I'm sorry," she said, her heart contrite. "I'm just confused. I'm sure I'll be all right after I pray about it.'' The words slipped out of her mouth from years of training, and she just wanted to bite her tongue. Pray about it, indeed.

Gram nodded, not appearing to notice the grimace Jasmine made. "I'll pray, too. It's the best we can do. The first thing, and the best. It'll all work out. In God's way, and in God's timing. We just have to look to Him and trust that He knows what's best."

Well, on that point, anyway, Jasmine couldn't agree more. God, if there was one, must certainly have something spectacular planned, or else He had a very peculiar sense of humor. If only she knew what He had in mind—and what role she was to play.

Christopher pulled a hard right off the gravel mountain road and drove into the brush, not caring that the pine trees were probably scratching the truck's exterior. When he was in far enough that he couldn't see the road, he slammed the gear into Park and shut down the engine.

This wasn't the way he'd meant it to be. He thumped a closed fist against the steering wheel. He hadn't meant to alienate Jasmine with the first words out of his mouth. What a big lug he was. Talk first, stick his big, dirty boots in his mouth afterward. He could certainly add his first encounter with her in a year to his ever-growing list of failures.

This one, however, he had to take full credit for. Much of what happened to him wasn't in his control, a part of God's will he couldn't understand. But this was completely his own doing, and he'd blown it big time. Not exactly a surprise, with his track record.

He'd been so certain he was meant to come back to Westcliffe. What else could he do? He loved Jasmine. He always had. To think of living without her—and Sammy—was unbearable.

But if his first encounter with her was anything to go by, he had a long way to travel to get back in her good graces. Her closed attitude left him shaken and unsure of himself. She didn't even try to hide how much she loathed seeing him again.

He lifted his hat and raked his fingers through the short ends of his hair. Frustration seethed through every nerve ending until his whole body tingled.

All he wanted to do was see Sammy, not run off with the boy like some criminal, though that's how he'd been treated. And Sammy had been in that bungalow. He'd heard the baby's cry and the soothing sounds of Jasmine's grandmother coming from the other room. What kind of a fool did she think he was?

The point of it—and that's what hurt—was that Jazz didn't want him to see the baby.

He understood her hesitance. He'd done a lot of things that needed explaining. But in the meantime, he'd hoped their years together would count for something.

He wasn't foolish enough to expect that he would be able to knock on her door and resume their relationship, where it had broken off before she'd gone off to med school, but couldn't she at least listen to him?

"Ha!" he said aloud, the sound echoing in the small cab of his truck. She hadn't listened to him then, and she wouldn't listen now.

Especially now. She wouldn't trust him any more than any other of Westcliffe's residents did. Far less, even, for she had more reasons to doubt him than the small town that virtually shunned his existence now that he was back.

The neighbors he could live without. Jasmine, he couldn't.

He'd hurt the woman he loved most in the world, and the knowledge sat like lead in his stomach. It was a burden he'd been carrying since the day she'd turned away from him and walked right out of his life. The day the world discovered he would soon be a father.

Jasmine thought he'd betrayed her, and mincing words didn't change anything. Pain seared through his chest.

He wasn't denying his actions, no matter how questionable the whole thing was in his mind. What else could he have done, under the circumstances? He thought he was doing the right thing. He thought Jasmine would understand, that she'd want him to take the actions he'd decided on for Jenny's sake.

But she wouldn't even listen. What she'd learned, she hadn't learned from him, and he would regret that for the rest of his life. He should have made the trip to Denver as soon as he found out about Jenny. But there was so much to do, and not much time in which to do it.

He'd been so wrapped up in the tailspin his life had taken that he'd put it off, thinking he'd approach Jasmine when the ruckus had died down. After he'd taken care of the necessities, and before she'd heard the truth from someone else.

She still didn't know the truth. He'd hoped to tell her today.

He'd even hoped she'd forgive him. It was part of what drove him back to town—to ask her forgiveness for his part in the tragedy that had become their lives, and to ask for a second chance.

It was obviously not going to happen that way. He clamped his teeth together until he could feel his pulse pounding in his temples. What he wanted didn't matter. Not yet, and maybe not ever.

He had another responsibility—Sammy, the baby he'd never seen. He wasn't going to let that boy down. And if that meant postponing the inevitable confrontation with Jasmine on personal issues, so be it.

His resolution did, however, present a unique set of circumstances, since he had to go through Jasmine to get to Sammy. Emotional issues aside, Jasmine was a formidable woman. If she decided to make things rough for him, there was no doubt in his mind she would succeed.

Which meant he had to convince her otherwise. Make her see reason. They needed to put the past aside, sit down together and discuss the issues like the adults they were.

This wasn't some high school spat they could just ignore and expect to go away. They were dealing with the welfare of a child. For all intents and purposes, *his* child.

His throat tightened. He had actually been relieved to hear Jasmine had been appointed Sammy's legal guardian, though he would never tell her so. He couldn't think of a better

Chapter Three

Three days later, Jasmine stared over the rim of her coffee up at the soft-spoken cowboy across from her. The term *cowboy* used loosely, she thought wryly. Christopher had been born and raised in this mountain town, but he couldn't ride a horse to save his life. Ranching wasn't in his blood.

He looked the part, though, with his form-fitting western jeans, snap-down western shirt and a steel gray cowboy hat. Of course, he'd taken off the hat when he'd entered the café, exposing his thatch of windblown brown hair.

Another cowboy trait.

Her mind was being perversely obtuse this afternoon, she thought. How she could find anything humorous to laugh about in her present state of mind was beyond her comprehension. It was as if her subconscious were seeking to avoid the inevitable confrontation.

The determined gleam in Christopher's eyes and the hard set of his jaw gave him away. Why else would he have asked her to meet him in a small café in Wetmore, a half hour's drive from their home town and well out of the public eye?

She'd been surprised when he'd called yesterday and asked to meet her, but now she was as prepared as she'd ever be for whatever he would throw at her, though she still couldn't come up with a single acceptable reason for a man to abandon his wife and unborn child. And then return to claim his son after Jenny was dead. If he didn't want the boy before...

The familiar swell of anger rushed through her, but she

mother for the boy. He could depend on her to take Sammy as if he were her own.

And he could leave.

He recognized that the moment he'd seen the deter on Jasmine's face. He could turn around, walk righ Westcliffe, and never look back, knowing Sammy w pable hands. Loving hands.

And he would be doing no less than what every pected.

Maybe that would be best. How was he to know? H ready to be a father. What did he know about bab hadn't planned to be a father for a few years yet, afte Jasmine had settled down. Blast it anyway, he didr know how to change a diaper.

What kind of hole had he dug for himself? And all he was trying to do the right thing.

He blew out a breath and started the engine, gunnin Reverse and making the wheels spin as he pulled ba the dirt road. He shifted into gear and put the peda metal.

Heading back toward town.

He couldn't leave. He couldn't go without Samm knowing he was in Jasmine's capable hands. And tho knew he would cause a lot more pain before he coul mending hurts, it had to be done.

He had to go back. He needed Sammy in his life.

Sammy—and Jasmine.

tamped it down. She would listen. She owed him that much, whatever sort of torn and twisted man he'd become. He claimed he wanted Sammy, and today he would attempt to explain why.

Not that his words would make any difference. She already knew what her answer would be, despite anything he told her.

He couldn't have the baby. Not in a billion, trillion years.

Sammy was her son now. The papers declaring it so were firmly in her possession and valid in a court of law.

She'd fight him tooth and nail in court if she had to, but she prayed it wouldn't come to that. That was her true objective—to reason with him, to try to touch the man she once knew, the man buried deep inside the monster sitting across from her.

To make him leave quietly. And alone.

"What'll ya'll have?" said a waitress, tapping her pencil against her pad of paper. Her cheek near her bottom gum was plump with tobacco. Jasmine had heard of gum-chewing waitresses, but the thought of a tobacco-chewing waitress was more than her stomach could handle.

"A cup of hot tea for me," she said weakly, shifting her attention from the woman to focus on her queasy insides. "Peppermint, if you've got it."

She wasn't sure she could swallow even tea, but it occurred to her the peppermint might settle her stomach a little. She'd used it on Sammy's colic to good effect, so she could only hope it would ease some of her own distress.

"Double cheeseburger with everything, onion rings and a chocolate shake," Christopher ordered, smiling up at the waitress as if his entire life weren't hanging in the balance of this conversation.

Maybe it wasn't. Maybe he didn't care. Jasmine didn't know whether to feel relieved or annoyed.

It was obvious *his* appetite, at least, wasn't affected by their meeting. And *he* wasn't keeping his hands clenched in his lap to keep them from quivering, either. She pried her fingers apart and put her hands on the table.

Christopher cleared his throat and ran the tip of his index

finger around the rim of his mug. "Remember when we used to sneak up here on Friday nights?" he asked, chuckling lightly. His gaze met hers, the familiar twinkle in his light gray eyes making her heart skip a beat.

Jasmine felt her face warm under his scrutiny. She knew what he was thinking, the memories this café evoked. Two carefree youths, so much in love, their lives filled with laughter and happiness. And hope.

"We thought we were being so underhanded, slipping out of town." His light, tenor voice spread like silk over her. "Remember? We were so sure nobody noticed we were gone. We really thought we were pulling one over on everyone. And all the time, they were probably laughing and shaking their heads at us."

Jasmine laughed quietly despite herself. "I'm sure Gram knew all along. She had such—" She was going to say high hopes for the two of them, but the thought hit her like a slap in the face, so she left the end of her sentence dangling sharply in the air.

How ironic that he'd picked this location to meet today. She'd been so wrapped up in dealing with her crisis that she hadn't realized the poetic justice in his choosing this café. She swallowed hard, trying in vain to keep heat from suffusing her face.

It was the place where they'd first said *I love you.* The night they'd pledged themselves to each other forever. The night he'd asked her to be his wife. Before med school. And before Sammy.

She could see in his eyes that he was sharing her thoughts, reliving the memories right along with her. Her chest flooded with a tangle of emotions. Anger that he had brought her here. Hope because he remembered, too.

Had he brought her here on purpose, she wondered, as a way to have the upper hand? Or was this simply a convenient spot to meet, away from the prying eyes of the world? Did he mean to remind her of their joyful past, to taunt her with what could never be? She pinned him with her gaze, asking the question without speaking.

In answer, he swiped a hand down his face. "I'm sorry," he said, shaking his head regretfully. "It was thoughtless of me to bring us here. I should have realized—"

"It's okay," she interrupted, holding up a hand. "Better here than in Westcliffe, where we might be seen." She closed her eyes and eased the air from her lungs. At least he wasn't trying to rub her nose in the past, and for that, she was grateful.

He let out a breath that could have been a chuckle, but clearly wasn't, from the tortured look on his face. "I prayed about this meeting before I called you," he admitted in a low voice.

He clenched his napkin in his fist and looked out the window, allowing Jasmine to study his chiseled profile. There were small lines around his eyes, and dark furrows on his forehead. They weren't laugh lines, she noticed sadly. He looked ten years older than his twenty-eight years.

"Truth be told," he continued, still avoiding her eyes, "praying is about the only thing I've been doing for weeks."

His admission wasn't what she expected, and it took her aback. She remained silent for a moment, trying to digest what he was telling her.

She'd assumed from his actions that he'd played his faith false, that he'd given up on God and was taking his own way with things.

Abandoning his family was hardly the act of a man walking with his Maker. But now he was telling her, in so many words, that his faith was still intact. That he believed God was in control. That he believed prayer would help this wretched situation. That God was *here*.

She barely restrained the bitter laugh that desperately wanted to escape her lips. Irony seethed through her. How had he kept his faith in God when hers so easily disappeared?

He smiled, almost shyly, as if his revelation had taken great effort. It probably had, though there was a time when there had been nothing they couldn't share between them.

In so many ways, she wanted to close her eyes, embrace his belief, wipe the slate clean and start all over again. To return to the time in her life when she believed, and when her belief had given her hope.

But that was naiveté. She wasn't a child, to believe in miracles. To believe in a close, personal God who would help her through life's problems. Her faith was ebbing and flowing like waves on rocks.

She wasn't even sure she believed in God, at least in a personal God who watched over His flock like a shepherd watching over His sheep.

She couldn't—and didn't—pay Him more than lip service, and at this point she was hardly doing that. Although she hadn't denied her faith outright, she hadn't set foot in a church in months.

The subject humiliated and frustrated her. All those years she considered her faith strong, yet it wilted with the first attack of trial.

Some Christian she was. Or maybe she never had been. She was too confused to know.

How could she believe in a God who would allow Christopher to get away with what he'd done?

And Jenny—what about Jenny? If God was there, why hadn't He helped her? Why hadn't He healed her? He'd forced Jasmine to stand helpless and watch her sister die, her head crammed full of medical knowledge and unable to do a thing to save her.

"Would you pray with me?" he asked when she didn't answer.

Prayer. Gram suggested it before, and now Christopher was bringing up the issue. Her heart clenched. It wasn't as if she never tried.

She had. Last night on her knees beside her bed. But the words wouldn't come, and the space between her and the heavenly realm seemed unbridgeable. God wasn't listening. Or He had cut her off. As she had once cut off Christopher.

She shook her head. "We're in a public restaurant, Christopher. Let's just get down to business."

She cringed inside as she said the words. It wasn't *business.* It was a baby's life they were talking about.

He looked vaguely astonished, but he didn't argue. Instead, his gentle smile tipped the corner of his lips as he reached for her hand, which she quickly snatched from his grasp.

Shrugging, he plunged into the reason they were meeting. "You know what I want. I want to see Sammy. I want to—"

"Take him away from me?" she snapped, heedless of the fact that she hadn't given him a chance to finish his sentence. Suddenly she felt completely unsure of herself as Sammy's guardian, of her ability to provide what he needed. Without thinking, she took her insecurity out on the man sitting across from her. "I don't think so, Christopher."

He opened his mouth to protest, but she gestured for him to stop.

"You need to understand something," she continued, her voice crackling with intensity. "You weren't around when Sammy was born. You didn't walk him up and down the hall at all hours of the night because he had colic and didn't want to sleep. You haven't changed him, fed him or bathed him."

"I haven't even—"

She pinned him with a glare. "I have. *I* was the one there for Sammy. And *I* am going to be the one to raise him."

"But I want—" His voice closed around the words and he coughed. "I want to do all those things. I want to be there for the boy. My..." He hesitated. "My son."

He looked petulant, and his eyes pleaded for her mercy.

Why, oh why did his mere physical presence affect her so? He once used those very same big blue-gray eyes to get his own way with her when they argued over which movie to see or where to go for dinner.

This wasn't one of those times. Nor was it a debatable issue.

"Let me explain something to you," she said, her voice splintering with restrained anger. "I very frankly don't give a snip what your story is. I don't even want to hear it, though I'm sure you've spent many hours rehearsing for my benefit."

His scowl darkened and he grunted in protest.

"No, really. It doesn't matter. Nothing you say matters. What *matters* is that I've bonded with this baby, and nothing is going to convince me to give him away. Most especially to you."

With a sharp intake of breath, he sat back in his seat and pounded a fist on the tabletop, making the silverware rattle.

Water from her cup splashed onto the surface of the table, and she quickly wiped it with the edge of her napkin, her face flaming with anger and embarrassment. She hazarded a glance at the neighboring booths, wondering if anyone had noticed his outburst.

"Even before you've heard what really happened?" he asked through clenched teeth, his chest rising and falling with the exertion of each angry breath.

She lifted one sardonic brow. "Astonish me. You were abducted by aliens. You've been in a coma. You had amnesia. What, Christopher? What's your story?" As much as she tried to keep her voice low, it lifted with each word to a higher crescendo until she'd reached well beyond shrill and piercing.

Now *she* was the one causing the scene, and it was *his* fault. She didn't care how irrational and childish the thought was. She clamped her jaw shut and glared defiantly at Christopher, and then at the patrons staring at her. Life had freeze-framed, with everyone's attention on her.

She blew out a frustrated breath, furious that he had provoked her to make a display of herself.

"Jazz," he began, reaching out with both hands in a conciliatory gesture.

She threw her napkin down on the table and stood. "I thought this meeting was a good idea when you first suggested it," she said slowly, articulating each syllable in a low, precise tone. "I was mistaken."

She looked blindly out the window, then back to Christopher. "I love Sammy, and he's staying with me. End of subject." She met his gaze briefly, willing her strength to hold out until she could flee from his presence. "Goodbye, Christopher."

She turned and walked away from him, holding her chin high and staying steadfastly determined not to look at the patrons she felt were staring at her.

Christopher could pick up the tab on the check. It served him right. Her blood boiling, she wished momentarily that she'd ordered a full-course steak dinner instead of just hot tea.

When she exited the café, she pulled in a deep breath of mountain air, closing her eyes as fresh, cool oxygen flooded her lungs. If only she could dissipate the heat in her brain as easily.

Walking away from Christopher was the hardest thing she'd ever done. He was suffering in his own way, she realized, and her presence affected him as much as his did her.

All the more reason for them to stay away from each other, she decided, fortifying her decision with every justification available to her.

Her heart said a father should be with his son. Her mind said Christopher forfeited that right when he walked away from Jenny and his unborn baby.

She had to cling to reason, no matter what her emotions were doing. Sammy's well-being depended on it. Probably her own happiness, too. She loved that baby. And for now, maybe for always, that love would have to be enough.

Christopher ate his food in silence, ignoring the curious stares and speculative talk around him. His mind was so pre-occupied with his troubles that he barely tasted his food, and had to order a second milk shake to wash the hamburger down his dry throat.

He loved Jasmine more than ever. He thought the feelings had faded some with time, but sitting across from her today, he knew he was fooling himself. The ache in his chest only shaded his deeper feelings. He would do anything to wipe the pain from her eyes, and it was the ultimate irony to know he'd been the one to put it there in the first place. Sure, Jasmine was being harsh and stubborn, but who could blame her? He knew it was her fear of losing Sammy that was speaking for her. She'd always been an all-or-nothing kind of woman, a fact Christopher admired. Her obvious devotion and loyalty to her nephew only made him love her more.

Pain lanced his temple, and he reached a hand up to rub it firmly across his brow. Nothing was going as he had hoped.

He knew without a doubt that when she walked away today, she wouldn't meet with him again, at least not intentionally. She'd run the other direction whenever she saw him, screaming inwardly if not in reality.

Which meant his next move must be furtive. He'd have to follow her around until an opportunity presented itself to speak with her again—in a time and in a location where she had no place to go except into his arms.

God would give him that opportunity. Or maybe he'd have to make his own.

Jasmine didn't immediately return to Gram's apartment, where she was staying with Sammy. She knew Gram would take care of the baby as long as necessary. And right now, Jasmine needed to be alone, to have time to think.

Not entirely conscious of where she was going or why, she found herself parking in front of Jenny's cottage. There was still a lot of work to be done, she supposed. And it was quiet here, a far cry from the hustle and bustle of the medical clinic.

Once in the small cabin, she started to absently box up Jenny's things, beginning with the books in her room. She picked up an empty apple box from the pile and began stacking various romance novels spine up, mixed with some hard-backed classic literature.

Jasmine laughed to herself, trying to picture her flighty sister reading the classics. Fashion magazines were more her style.

Had been her style. Jasmine quickly sobered. How well had she really known Jenny? She suspected not as well as she should have, especially in the last few years.

They'd been close as children, though there was four years difference between them. But they had drifted apart when Jasmine reached high school and got interested in friends, makeup and boys.

In Christopher.

And when Jenny caught up, she'd taken a different road

than Jasmine, who'd been class president and received straight A's. Jenny hung out with the flashy crowd, the ones with too much money and too much time. Jasmine had always wondered what Jenny could have in common with her friends.

She didn't have money, and she wasn't college-bound. She just didn't seem the type. But she appeared to be happy, and Jasmine had left it alone. How she'd ended up with a simple cowboy like Christopher was beyond Jasmine.

And then she'd gone off to college herself, thanks to the grant from the city, increasing the emotional distance between the two sisters. As far as she knew, Jenny had grown into a beautiful, self-assured adult, a relative stranger she greeted with a kiss on the cheek when she came home from the holidays. Had Jenny been seeing Christopher even then?

There was always laughter in the house during vacations and holidays. Jasmine puckered her brow, straining to remember if her sister had been part of the joyous festivities. Or had she been off with friends? Jasmine couldn't remember. Probably, she'd been too busy with Christopher to notice, a thought which gave her a guilty start.

Shaking her head to clear her introspection, Jasmine carried the box of books into the living room, where the rest of Jenny's boxed goods were stored, and went to Jenny's room to begin stripping the bedclothes. Her sister's sweet, airy scent still lingered on the sheets, and she brought a pillow to her face, inhaling deeply.

"We never said goodbye," she whispered aloud, hugging the pillow to her chest. She wished she had one more minute, just one, to give Jenny a hug and tell her how much she was loved.

Jasmine shook herself from her melancholy with some effort. Funny how grief hit her at the oddest moments. She'd think her emotions were under control, and then in a second's time, grief would wash over her and overwhelm her, sometimes for no apparent reason.

Those were the toughest times, the moments before she found the strength to tuck her grief back away and go on living, because that's what she had to do. Because she was here and Jenny was not, and baby Sammy depended on her.

She reached for the other pillow, but when she yanked at the corner to pull off the pillowcase, Jenny's Bible fell to the floor.

Jasmine had forgotten all about it. She'd slipped it under the pillow when Christopher had shown up. She was relieved to find it now. It was a part of Jenny she wanted to keep.

Heart in her throat, she reached down and scooped it up, tenderly smoothing the bent pages before closing the cracked leather. Sitting on the stripped bed with one leg tucked under her, she ran a hand across the front of the Bible, considering whether it would be right to read more of the notes Jenny had written in the margins.

She was so confused, so hurt. And she missed her sister terribly. Would it be a breach of trust to read a little, to bring Jenny near through her words, her thoughts and dreams and faith? Who knew but that maybe, in some small way, it would help her know what to do about Christopher and Sammy.

She could only hope for such a miracle, even if she didn't believe in miracles anymore.

Chapter Four

The next morning, Christopher eyed the two-room log cabin, turning over the possibilities in his mind. After leaving the diner, he'd phoned an old high school football buddy, who'd lent him this place for the weekend. If God was willing and he planned right, it would be his and Jasmine's for at least one completely uninterrupted, if not happy, day.

Loose gravel and pine needles crunched under his feet as he approached the cabin, his friend's fishing hideaway. Nothing spectacular—it didn't even have electric heat. But for what Christopher had in mind, it was perfect.

He'd purposely picked a cabin tucked up just far enough into the Sangre de Cristo mountain range to keep the clinic from sending in emergency equipment right away, yet far enough from town to warrant Jasmine's personal attention.

Not to mention high enough in altitude to get a good snow, if the weather cooperated.

He eyed the sky critically, wondering when the snow would start. The weather forecast indicated a major storm heading their way. It could snow five feet in a day here, given the right conditions.

He only hoped these *were* the right conditions, external and internal. And that Jasmine would come when he called, even if she knew about the impending snowstorm. If they sent a couple of paramedics from Wetmore after him, he was in a world of hurt.

He laughed despite his sour mood.

She would come. Jasmine Enderlin was the singularly most compassionate woman he'd ever known. She wouldn't give a second's thought to risking her own life and health in order to help someone who needed her, a quality that made her a terrific doctor and an even better person.

His respect for her was only superseded by his love.

If he could just blurt out the truth of the past and wipe the slate clean, things would be much simpler. *If* she would listen. *If* she would believe him.

And *if* he had only himself to consider. He wouldn't waste a second before telling her everything. And he sure wouldn't be at 9500 feet constructing ridiculous undercover adventures better suited to spy novels than to an old-fashioned man who couldn't give up his dreams.

But right now he'd do just about anything—including spy novel antics, in order to see her again.

Again he glanced at the sky, wondering how long he had left to prepare. He had wood to chop, dinner to make and a leg to break.

He chuckled softly at his own joke, then quickly sobered, drawing in a breath, clenching his jaw and pressing his lips together as he determinedly went to find an ax.

I married Christopher tonight. Mrs. Christopher Jordan. Jenny Jordan. How awkward that sounds!

I still can't believe things worked out the way they did. Everything seemed so hopeless, and then there was Christopher and...

He gave me a rose at the altar. A single, beautiful white rose. I've pressed it into this Bible as a keepsake— the only one I really have of my wedding day.

It all happened so fast. No photographer. No wedding cake. No guests. Except for Gram, who stood up for me, and Christopher's brother from Texas, his only living relative, for him. Jasmine was there in the back, but she didn't say anything.

Jasmine cringed inwardly. She'd only gone because she thought it would be spineless not to. And she wanted to show them she was bigger than that.

Oh, she was bigger, all right. Pouting in the back and glaring at everyone. She'd never even wished the couple happiness.

She shook herself from her thoughts and continued reading, picking up where she'd left off.

But at least I can keep this rose. I know what he was trying to communicate with a white rose rather than a red one. He doesn't love me. He loves Jasmine, and he always has.

But he's committed himself to me, now. Me and my baby. And Christopher is an honorable man. He won't go back on his word.

I hope, in time, he'll learn to love me, though I know it will never be the kind of love he has for Jasmine. But no matter how he feels about me, he'll love the baby. And he'll be a good daddy. If there was ever a man who was meant to be a father, it's Christopher.

Jasmine barely restrained herself from crumpling the piece of paper in her hands. She'd found it tucked into the page with the family tree, where Jenny had carefully written hers and Christopher's names on the appropriate lines. She'd drawn a heart where their baby's name would go.

She tucked the paper deep into the binding and closed the Bible with a pop. Her throat constricted until no air could pass through, but it didn't matter. She wasn't breathing anyway. Constrained air lodged squarely in her chest, throbbing mercilessly against her rib cage.

Christopher still loved her, even when he married Jenny? Oh, sure, but Jenny was carrying his child.

She was more confused now than ever. Nothing Jenny had written made sense! She stared at the Bible for a moment, then tossed it away with a frustrated groan.

Jasmine nearly launched herself off the bed at the sound of her pager. Placing a palm to her chest to slow her rapidly beating heart, she reached her other hand for her pager and turned it off.

The sweet strength of adrenaline pumped through her, clearing her head. While she wasn't like some of the residents she'd linked up with when she was in Denver, to whom the excitement of the moment was their reason to serve, she couldn't deny the pulse-pounding anticipation of being needed. It thrilled her to have something to give back to the little town that had given her so much.

She reached the phone and dialed the clinic number. Jill, the county nurse, gave Jasmine a quick rundown. A man had called from a mountain cabin just above Horn Lake. He'd been fishing, apparently, when he slipped off a wet log and fell.

"He's all alone, and he's afraid to drive. And Jasmine— he says he doesn't have insurance and can't afford a hospital. Or a doctor."

Jasmine made a noise from the back of her throat that signaled her compassionate understanding of his situation.

She pictured a gray-haired widower finding solace fishing in a mountain lake, afraid even to call the clinic because of the expense. An old man, all alone, with a broken leg and no one to help him.

The picture in her mind was too much for her heart to take. She'd work for free if she must, knowing that her actions would open a whole other can of worms should she be discovered dispensing her charity.

"What are the coordinates?" she asked, balancing a pad of paper on her hip so she could write them down.

Jill gave her the exact location of the cabin, someone renting the old Wallaby place. Then she paused expectantly.

"I'm going up there," Jasmine said, answering Jill's unspoken question. She reached into her jeans pocket for the keys to her four-by-four. "I have my bag with me. As long as it's not too major, I can handle a broken leg on my own. If it's too bad, I'll drive him back to the clinic myself. An ambulance crew wouldn't want to hike up into the lake area anyway."

"It's starting to snow, Jazz. The weather forecast says we might be in for a blizzard," Jill warned. "You never know how bad it's going to be. Maybe you ought to let Wetmore's EMT take care of it."

There was more than one EMT, and they were all men. Jill didn't have to say it for it to be true. And she was probably right.

But this was Jasmine's call, and an inner prompting was telling her to go.

"No, it's okay. I can get there faster. The poor old guy is probably in a lot of pain." And it would give her something to do to keep her mind off Christopher and her problems, she added silently. "I have my cell phone. If I have any problems, I'll give the guys in Wetmore a ring. I promise."

"Jazz, I didn't say—" Jill began, but Jasmine didn't let her finish as she put down the phone and raced to her car. Checking her sports utility vehicle for gas and equipment, she quickly got on the road. It took her half an hour to drive the dirt road as far as it ran toward Horn Lake.

When she reached the end of the line, she pulled her parka snug around her chin, gathered her gear onto her backpack, and began the hike up to the lake. A breeze had picked up, stinging her cheeks with bitter cold. Gritting her teeth, she ignored the icy pain and concentrated on putting one foot in front of another.

Just when she was getting to where she was no longer able to ignore the cold, she spied the cabin she was seeking. It was a run-down old place, more of a summer home than a winter hideaway. Jasmine wondered at the old man living in such conditions year-round.

Could a broken heart cause such misery? Her own heart clenched, answering the question on its own. Jasmine knew too well the feeling of abandonment, and she prayed she'd be able to help this neighbor, whoever he was, in more ways that one.

It occurred to her then that she hadn't asked for her patient's name, a major oversight not like her to make. Maybe those short nights *were* getting to her.

Her mind had been preoccupied, trying *not* to think about Christopher, she reminded herself, knocking firmly on the door. When no one answered, she tried again. And again.

Finally, she pounded on the door with her fist, wondering if her patient had been hurt worse than she'd first imagined. "Hello? Is anyone in there? Can you hear me?"

She'd break the door down if she had to, but it occurred to her to try the handle first. It turned easily in her palm and the catch switched, making the door swing inward. Jasmine shivered and swallowed hard. It was odd for the door to be unlocked.

She ignored the uncomfortable feeling of a stranger making herself welcome and stepped inside the cabin. "Hello? I knocked, but no one answered! Sir? Are you here?"

The scene inside the cabin was anything but frightening. In fact, if she didn't know better, she would think it was the setting of a lovers' secret rendezvous.

The only light came from a fire crackling in the old stone hearth. It basked the room in a soft, flickering glow similar to candlelight, but with the sharp, pungent scent of pine. The wooden floor had been recently swept, and firewood was stacked neatly in one corner.

A meal was set on a checkered cloth on an old, rickety table whose spindly legs looked like they might collapse at any moment. A tingle went up her spine as she realized the meal was set for *two*.

Clearly, she was not the one expected in this cabin. Her first thought was that she'd made a mistake, gotten the coordinates wrong and entered someone else's cabin.

But that couldn't be. This was the old Wallaby place, though others owned it now. It was too hard to keep track of all the summer residents who came and went. She struggled to remember who might have rented the cabin after Grace and Chuck Wallaby moved to Arizona.

Suddenly she noticed that the rocking chair facing the fire was slowly tipping back and forth without so much as a squeak to give it away.

Someone was in the cabin. But why didn't he answer when she called?

She tensed, then forced herself to relax. Fear and mortification warred within her for prominence. There was no reason for her to feel embarrassed, necessarily, but heat flamed her cheeks nonetheless.

She was a doctor responding to a call, she reminded herself sternly, taking a deep breath and squaring her shoulders. His broken leg might not be much, if he was rocking in a chair with that pain, but his hearing left a lot to be desired.

"Excuse me," she said loudly enough to cause an echo. She moved into the firelight, wanting to see and be seen. She didn't want the poor guy to think she was sneaking up on him. "I guess you didn't hear me knock. I'm Dr. Enderlin, and I've come to see about your—"

She paused, the breath cut off from her throat, as her eyes met a warm blue-gray gaze and her heart slammed into her rib cage.

"Christopher!"

"I see you made it," Christopher said, tipping his head toward her in greeting. "I was going to go looking for you if you didn't show up soon."

He neglected to mention that it had taken all the force of his will not to bolt into the winter chill to search for her when she didn't arrive as quickly as he'd expected. Only knowing he'd ruin any chance of convincing her to stay and listen if she discovered his scheme too soon kept him glued to his chair and praying for her safety.

Night came swiftly onto the mountains. Horn Peak quickly blocked out the feeble rays of the winter sun as it set for the night. It would be dark in a matter of minutes.

Her cheeks, already flushed a pleasant pink, rose in color, contrasting starkly with the silky weave of her sable hair. Her mouth opened briefly before she clamped it shut again and stood arms akimbo, a glare marring the sheer beauty of her face.

"You're angry," he said aloud, realizing as he spoke that he was stating the obvious.

She made a pointed glance down one of his legs, which were crossed loosely at the ankles, and up the other one before coming to rest back on his face. Her gaze made his skin tingle all over, and he shifted in his seat like a man with poison ivy.

Guilt tugged at his chest, and he shrugged at her unspoken question. When she looked back at his wool sock-encased feet, he chuckled and wiggled his toes.

"Please tell me you didn't call me up here on a ruse," she said, her voice hoarse, whether from restrained emotion or from her walk in the chill night air, he couldn't say.

He cleared his throat, struggling between feeling mildly guilty and very self-satisfied. She was up here, wasn't she? Even if she *had* come under false pretenses, his intentions were good.

"Well...if you mean do I have a broken leg, then I guess the answer would have to be no," he drawled, tipping up the corner of his lip in a half smile he hoped would endear himself to her and not further raise her ire. He wasn't nearly as cocky as he used to be about the easy cowboy charm that had always worked with Jasmine.

"I see," she said, swinging her backpack off her back and holding it in front of her like a shield. Her fists clenched the material, her knuckles white. Christopher flinched inwardly, offering a silent prayer for the right words to say. Why did it have to be like this between them, when it used to be so good?

"I didn't call you up here on a ruse," he denied flatly.

"Really? Then what *do* you call it?"

"Embellishment. I stretched the truth a little because we need to talk."

"A little?" One eyebrow rose as she glared at both of his perfectly sturdy legs. "I drop everything to make a risky call in the middle of a major snowstorm, and you say you exaggerated a *little?*"

"If it makes you feel any better, I think I sprained my ankle chopping wood for the fire."

Her eyes were glowing, and he knew her well enough to know she was holding back a smile. But he could tell she was still harboring her irritation and resentment, and with good reason, he had to admit.

"I'd never do anything to hurt you, Jazz. Five more minutes and I would have come after you. I'd never put you in danger or let you get hurt, not when it's in my power to protect you."

"How comforting," she said dryly, turning away from him and surveying the room. "A knight in shining armor who tosses his damsel in distress to the dragon before attempting to save her." She turned back and smoothed a hand down her hair, which was attractively disheveled by the hood of her parka. "Does this place have a phone I can use?"

"Of course. On the far wall, next to the table."

Shedding her coat, she walked over to the antique phone and dialed a number, talking in hushed tones to the person on the other end of the line.

Christopher watched, a smile playing on his lips, as she picked at the cheese, crackers and fruit on the table as she talked. Things were working out far better than he'd anticipated. He half figured he'd have to hog-tie her to get her to stay with him, and here she was taking off her coat and eating the food he prepared for her all of her own volition.

Perhaps she knew how critical it was that the two of them worked things out. He was the first to admit it would take far more than a good talk to untangle this mess. But it was a start.

And afterward, he was prepared to follow up those words with action, to slay her dragons and bring her home to safety. Jasmine—and Sammy, too.

He wondered if she noticed the bouquet of red roses lying next to the bottle of sparkling cider. And if she did notice, would she realize the flowers were for her? Hope swelled in his chest and he swallowed hard.

He sat back in the rocking chair, giving her privacy to finish her conversation. She was probably calling Gram about Sammy, and he didn't want to pressure her.

She hung up the phone and went to stand by the fire, holding her hands palms out toward the flames. It was all Christopher could do not to join her at the hearth, wrap his arms around her tiny waist and bury his face in her long, soft hair.

It was something he would have done, in the past. They would have stared at the fire and talked in hushed tones about their future, reaffirming with every look and caress the strength of the love that passed between them.

It was like being run through with a bull's horn not to be able to hold her now. He stopped rocking, holding his breath through the endless moment of silence.

Finally, she turned and met his gaze, her dark eyes warm with emotion and the glow of the fire. "I want you to know that I'm just warming up here by the fire for a few minutes before I head back to my truck. I'm not staying, if that's what you're thinking."

"Jazz, you can't just turn around and walk out of here!" he began, but she cut him off when he tried to continue.

"I made it up here just fine, and the hike is downhill from here." She blew out a breath. "I can't stay, Christopher. Please. Don't try to make me."

The spur in his gut raked his insides like a cowboy's heels on a bucking bronc.

She wet her bottom lip with the tip of her tongue and continued. "Since it appears there's no medical emergency, I'm needed in town."

"I didn't call you up here to be a doctor, Jasmine, no matter what I said to the nurse on the phone."

She paused and breathed heavily, as if testing her words in her head before speaking them aloud. "I know," she said, her voice a low purr. "And I think I understand."

"Then stay."

She shook her head. "I appreciate what you're trying to do here, but—"

He would have interrupted her again, but her pager beat him to it.

Jasmine turned the blaring instrument off and glanced at the number. "I need to use your phone again," she said, her voice dull.

"Go ahead."

He rose and stood behind her as she made contact with the clinic in town. This conversation he wanted to hear, and he didn't think she'd mind his eavesdropping.

"Doctor Enderlin here," she began, then stiffened. "What?" Her voice went unnaturally shrill, sending a shudder of premonition through Christopher.

He reached out with a tentative hand and withdrew it again twice before finally laying a gentle palm on her shoulder. She tensed for a moment, then eased back into the stronghold of his arms. It only seemed natural to wrap his arm around the front of her shoulders in a move that was equally firm and gentle.

A silent offering to lend her strength. Her whole body quivered beneath his touch, and he knew it was the voice on the other end of the line that was making her shake.

And it wasn't good news.

"Forward her call to me," she said in a pinched voice. As she waited, she pulled a notepad and pen from her breast pocket, scribbling madly when the voice on the other end of the line resumed. She paused every so often to ask a question or clarify a response, but through it all, her trembling increased.

Moments later, she hung up and redialed the clinic. She put her notepad down and plastered her grip on his forearm, her gaze seeking his for reassurance. He gave her everything he had, tightening his hold just enough to let her know he read the terror in her eyes. And to let her know he was there for her, no matter what.

He watched in amazement as the doctor in Jasmine surfaced, masking the fear. Her features composed and relaxed and a determined gleam lit her eyes. So complete was the transformation that Christopher wondered if he hadn't imagined her alarm.

She squared her shoulders, which he took as a cue to drop his arm from around her and step back. "No, his leg wasn't broken. Minor *sprain,*" she said, tossing him a glance that made him cringe. "I've already taken care of it."

No you haven't, he disagreed mentally. *We haven't even started.*

But if someone needed her medical attention, she'd leave. And he'd let her go, of course. Shoot, he'd go with her.

"I'm only a ten-minute hike at most from that cabin. I can reach her."

A ten-minute hike. In this weather? Ten minutes would seem like an hour. He picked up her parka. It was soaking wet. He moved it close to the fire, knowing it wouldn't have time to dry before she left. And a damp coat would make that hike every bit more excruciating.

"Who's injured?" he asked when she hung up the phone. She drew a breath and pinned him with her gaze.

"Not injured. Amanda Carmichael is stranded alone in her cabin, and she's having her baby. *Now.*"

He didn't miss the fear that briefly flashed in her eyes. Was she remembering Jenny's death?

He muttered a prayer for her comfort under his breath, and steeled himself to do what he could to answer that prayer on his own. If all he could do was stand by her and support her, then that's what he would do. And he might even surprise her.

His mind clicked into gear, reviewing the things he had learned. During the last year away from Westcliffe, God had given him the opportunity to prove himself as well as to help people in need.

The Carmichaels lived a short distance away, thank God. "We'll use the snowmobile," he said, thinking aloud.

"What?" she said, looking confused.

"I'm going with you."

Chapter Five

"There's no need," Jasmine said. The words were so firm and frosty they would have rivaled the air outside, but he wouldn't be moved from his purpose.

"I know there's no need. I *want* to help."

"You'll just be in the way."

"Maybe," he agreed, reaching for her parka and wrapping it around her, wincing at how cold and damp it still felt. "But I'm going anyway."

Jasmine met his gaze square on. Probing. Testing. He held perfectly still, barely breathing as he let her see inside his heart.

After a moment, she shrugged and turned away from him. "Whatever. But I'm leaving now."

Christopher snatched his own coat from a rack near the door and quickly zipped it up. "It'll only take me a minute to warm up my snowmobile." He planted his cowboy hat on his head by the crown and straightened the brim with his fingers.

"Good idea. We'll get there in half the time. I'll wait," she said, looking as if she weren't very happy about it but was determined to follow through.

Christopher warmed up the engine, then went back inside the cabin to get Jasmine, who was by this time pacing the floor. He hid a smile. She never had been the patient type. Probably why she was a doctor.

Ugh. He shook his head. His puns were getting worse by

the moment. Could stress do that to a person? The thought nearly made him chuckle, if he wasn't so cold and the situation so serious. "Bundle up, darlin'. It's a raging blizzard out there, and we're heading right smack into it."

He wasn't kidding, Jasmine thought as she mounted the snowmobile behind Christopher. It was freezing and then some. The wind was blowing so fiercely the falling snow was almost horizontal to the ground.

"Hang on tight!" he yelled over the wind, and Jasmine tentatively wrapped her arms around his waist. It was funny how an action could be at once so awkward and yet so disturbingly familiar.

She clung tightly to him as the vehicle bounded over the snow toward the Carmichaels' cabin. In the brief conversation she'd had with Amanda, she was reassured that the labor was progressing along normally, if quickly.

Amanda was certain she would have the baby any moment. Unusual to have such a short labor with a first baby, but Jasmine had seen odder wonders in her time at the hospital in Denver. The best and the worst.

She swallowed hard and squeezed her eyes shut, trying not to think about Jenny. Trying not to think about death, when she should be concentrating on welcoming a new life into the world.

There was nothing to worry about, she reassured herself, praying all the while God would make it so. She'd spent her requisite time on the maternity ward during her residency. She knew how to deliver a baby. She had all the necessary equipment, unless there was a problem, in which case she'd call for a back up.

She'd known coming back to Westcliffe that, while most expectant mothers made it to the hospital in Pueblo for their labor and delivery, she would be called on from time to time to deliver a baby.

And she'd had confidence in her baby-delivering skills until Jenny died. Watching her sister hemorrhage and knowing she was powerless to stop it was nearly the end of her medical career, never mind the permanent scars it left on her heart.

She knew how irrational it sounded. Jenny's death didn't have anything to do with delivering Sammy. But that didn't stop Jasmine from remembering, and the memory made her shaky.

It had taken all her effort to continue serving as the doctor to the town, and it was only her sense of obligation to its people that kept her there now.

What she really wanted to do was run away, hide her head in the sand like an ostrich. Now more than ever. How could she help Amanda and act as if nothing troubled her?

She could, and she would. She clenched her teeth together and concentrated on reigning in the strong wash of emotion coursing through her.

She was a doctor. Doctors sometimes lost patients, and it wasn't their fault. If she internalized guilt every time something went wrong that was beyond her control, she would go crazy.

But Jenny wasn't just any patient, and Jasmine couldn't just lightly brush it away. The knowledge that she might not be able to help Amanda Carmichael shook her to the core. Women died in childbirth, even in the twentieth century. The shiver that coursed through her had nothing to do with the cold.

Christopher took one hand away from the handlebar and placed it over her clutched fingers. She leaned her cheek into the strength of his back and sighed. It felt good to be in his company again. Good, natural and right, as if she'd never left.

And despite the offhand manner in which she'd answered him back at the cabin, she needed him now. Desperately. She needed his strength and assurance, and most especially his faith.

He pulled the snowmobile up to the front of the house, a small, A-frame log cabin similar to the one from which they'd come. Modest, but made for the weather, the building was a solid fixture against the raging of the storm.

Christopher removed the key and dismounted in record time. He held his gloved hand out to her, his lips pressed together grimly.

By the look on his face, Jasmine couldn't tell if he was angry or worried. Maybe a little of both. But she knew him well enough to know he'd put his own feelings aside long enough to help another human being out of a jam. Even if she was that person. And Amanda, of course. He would ignore the tension between them for Amanda's sake, as well as the baby's.

He saw her face and flashed her an encouraging smile. Reassured, she reached for his hand.

She expected him to release her fingers when she was free of the machine, but instead he tucked her hand under his arm and gave it a reassuring squeeze. "I'm here for you, Jasmine," he whispered gruffly, then gave the thick oak door a solid knock.

It wasn't likely Amanda would hear them knocking over the wind, so she wasn't surprised when no one answered. Christopher knocked again, then looked to her for guidance.

She stepped forward and tried the doorknob, which moved easily in her hand. "Amanda?" she called, stepping into the cabin out of the snow and wind, noting that Christopher followed her in. She heard a muffled cry from the back of the cabin and gestured for him to sit while she found Amanda, who was in the back bedroom, looking tired and peaked. Her pale green eyes gleamed with a mixture of anxiety and excitement. Her short, curly auburn hair was stuck to her forehead where streaks of sweat had dried, and the freckles that marked her face became more pronounced with her pallor. Her small frame looked thin and skeletal, except for the pronounced bulge of her abdomen.

She was a small woman, like Jenny. Small women sometimes had more trouble delivering. Jasmine cut off the thought before it could reach its completion.

"Dr. Enderlin!" she exclaimed, attempting weakly to sit up on the bed. "I'm so glad you're here! My water broke, and these contractions hit me real hard! I thought I was going to be popping this kid out all by my lonesome!"

"Well, that isn't going to happen," Jasmine replied, laying a comforting hand on her arm. "We're here now. Lie back on the bed and rest while you can. You're going to need all your energy for pushing.''

Amanda nodded.

''Do you know Christopher Jordan?'' she asked, her voice clipped with the calm, emotionless demeanor she used with her patients.

''Sure.''

''He's here to lend me a hand. Is that okay with you?''

''I don't care who helps,'' she said sharply, curling into herself as another contraction hit. ''Just get this baby out of me!''

Jasmine ignored Amanda's terse words, knowing it was pain speaking and not the voice of her neighbor. ''I'll be right back with Christopher, and we'll see what we can do about getting you out of pain and introducing you to your new little one.''

As she went back to get Christopher, she took a moment to breathe deeply and regroup. She hadn't been prepared for the stab of panic that attacked her when she saw the writhing woman on the bed.

Contractions were a natural part of childbirth. Pain, too. But it still rattled Jasmine to see a woman in so much agony and not knowing the outcome her pain would produce.

A healthy baby, she reminded herself. A big, beautiful, healthy baby to lie in his mother's arms. She couldn't bear even to consider anything else.

''Can you give me a hand?'' She gestured to Christopher, who was sitting in a wicker chair that appeared two sizes too small for his long legs.

''She's okay with my being here?'' he asked, his voice and his face lined with compassion.

''Sure. And I can use all the help I can get. She's on the verge of having this baby. I've got to check both mom and baby out, then prepare her for delivery.''

''You can count on me,'' he said, tossing his hat onto the chair and moving quickly toward the bedroom. Jasmine followed on his heels, her medical mind clicking into gear, going over the procedures she'd need to accomplish in the next few minutes.

Christopher stepped into the room and combed his fingers through his hair. "You're in good hands, Mrs. Carmichael."

Amanda smiled weakly. But to Jasmine, his words had the same effect as turning on her hairdryer and dumping it in the tub while taking a bath. She darted him a surprised glance. He'd been told how Jenny died, and she'd bet her last dollar he knew she'd been there when it happened. He nodded solemnly, his gaze full of compassion.

She swallowed hard as he flashed her a reassuring grin. It will be okay, his eyes said. He knew, and he cared.

Amanda grasped her abdomen and groaned.

Jasmine and Christopher broke eye contact and rushed to her side, each taking one of her arms as she breathed through the contraction.

In-two-three-four, out-two-three-four. Jasmine counted the age-old rhythm in her head, verbally cheering Amanda on as the contraction peaked and receded.

"How often are they coming?" Christopher asked quietly, adjusting the pillows for Amanda's comfort.

Jasmine shot him another startled look. *She* was the doctor here. She should be the one asking the medical questions, and he was playacting someone out of a medical drama.

What did he know about a woman in labor? A tide of animosity washed over her, though she quickly stemmed the flow as she'd been trained to do in medical school.

She knew more than anyone that this was no television show where everything always worked out. The last thing she needed was some couch potato playing EMT.

Christopher's body didn't suggest he spent a lot of time watching television, but his attitude reeked of it. Maybe he just watched medical thrillers.

Amanda smiled weakly. "About every two minutes."

Jasmine settled her attention back on the woman. "Are you more comfortable on your side or on your back? Have you tried walking around?"

"On my side," she said, her voice dull. "I'm too tired to walk." Suddenly she doubled over as another contraction hit.

Christopher looked across the struggling woman and met Jasmine's gaze. "That wasn't two minutes."

"No," Jasmine agreed, "It wasn't. Amanda, I think this baby's ready to meet you face-to-face." Her heart leaped into her throat to do a little dance, then moved up to pound furiously in her skull. This was where the rubber met the road. And she hadn't even assessed Amanda's health yet, or the tiny infant whose life depended on her care.

Jasmine quickly searched through her case for her fetascope and a number of vacuum-packed sterile instruments. She didn't know how much time they had left before the baby would come, and there was a lot to do in the meantime.

"A stack of clean sheets?" Christopher asked, reading her mind.

"Yes, please. And some blankets to wrap the baby in. Warm them in the dryer first. And kick up the thermostat. We need to keep the baby as warm as possible." She wondered again if his baby-birthing information came from the television, maybe an old western. She didn't have time to ponder.

Amanda curled in bed, screaming in exasperation, as another contraction racked her small frame. The hair on the back of Jasmine's neck stood on end. "I hope it's soon," Amanda mumbled through clenched teeth. "I can't stand this much longer."

"You're doing fine," Jasmine soothed, brushing Amanda's sweat-soaked hair away from her forehead. "I'm going to have a listen to this little guy's heartbeat when this contraction is over."

Despite the fact that she hadn't used a fetascope in awhile, she found the baby's heartbeat with ease. It was strong and steady, without a hint of fetal distress. She let out a sigh of relief and offered a silent prayer of thanks.

Christopher returned, his arms laden with sheets and towels. Without a word to Jasmine, he unloaded his burden and began systematically laying out fresh, folded sheets on the bottom edge of the bed, gently moving Amanda's legs when necessary, offering quiet words of encouragement as he worked.

Jasmine took a quick breath and watched him with the woman, amazed by his careful thoughtfulness and the capable assurance of his movements.

He left the room momentarily and returned with several pillows. "I picked up every pillow I could find," he told Jasmine before focusing his attention on Amanda. "These will help support your back while you're delivering," he explained, laying the pillows next to her on the bed.

"Sit up?" Amanda queried with a weak smile. "I don't think I have the strength to move my little finger."

He chuckled. "You don't have to sit up until Jasmine says it's time," he reassured the groaning woman. "Hang in there, Amanda. Breathe through it. You're on the down side of this contraction. You're doing great, and you're going to be a terrific mother."

He looked to Jasmine, a question in his eyes. She answered with an infinitesimal shake of her head.

"Not quite yet," she said, speaking to both of them. "Probably within the hour. But Amanda, this is your first baby. We may be pushing for a long time."

Amanda winced. Christopher wet a washcloth and draped it across her forehead, his soothing tenor reassuring the tired woman.

If Jasmine was honest, it reassured her, as well. His *presence* reassured her. His instinctive knowledge of childbirth was a sight to behold, but that didn't shock her nearly as much as his bedside manner. Unlike the proverbial fainting man in the delivery room, Christopher was a pillar of strength, holding Amanda's hand in place of her husband.

"Where *is* Bill, anyway?" she asked aloud in a conversational tone, preparing the iodine solution she would use to disinfect everything and keep the area as sterile as possible. Keeping germs to a minimum was crucial. She couldn't have another woman die like Jenny had done, and infection was always an issue.

Please, God.

"He..." Amanda paused and gritted her teeth, breathing only when Christopher reminded her "...went out of town for a sales seminar," she finished, gasping as the contraction passed.

She realized too late the kind of question she had asked, how it might affect Christopher. She hadn't even considered the fact that he hadn't been present for the birth of his own son, and wondered how he felt about it now, watching another woman labor. Did he realize what Jenny had gone through to bring his son into the world?

She darted a glance at him. His jaw was clenched, and she could see the anger in his eyes. Anger at Bill for not being there for his wife, or at himself for the same offense?

Jasmine was definitely angry with Bill. What kind of a man would leave his wife in the middle of nowhere when she was due to deliver a baby?

Despite her misgivings, she picked up her thread of dialogue. Even if Amanda was angry at her husband, it would keep her mind off her pain. There was little or no break between contractions now.

Sweat was pouring from Amanda's brow. She appeared as frightened as she was tired. Jasmine knew, from her schooling though not firsthand, that the contractions at this stage were fierce and unyielding.

"His timing could have been better," she said lightly, glancing at Christopher.

At least he had the grace to look ashamed, she thought, noticing how the tendons in his neck tightened as if he were wincing. As well he should be. His own actions were reprehensible.

"It wasn't Bill's fault," Amanda exclaimed, panting for breath. "Not that I care *what* his excuse is at this point!" She stopped and panted. "His boss forced him to go. He'll be so disappointed that he isn't here for the birth."

Amanda cried out. "I've got to push, now, Doctor." Sweat broke out anew on her forehead.

Jasmine checked her again. "You're right, Amanda. You're fully dilated and effaced," she informed her patient, who looked as if she were beyond caring, now that the contraction was over. Amanda's eyelids drooped for the few moments between contractions, and her face was pale and haggard.

It was no wonder they called it labor. Jasmine wondered how a woman could fall asleep between contractions that were obviously wrenchingly painful. Some "experts" said it was a bad idea to let a patient fall asleep, but the poor woman looked so exhausted, Jasmine had to believe that any relief she found must help, be it ever so little.

"Your baby's coming!" Christopher said enthusiastically, gently wiping Amanda's face with a cool rag, and never letting go of her hand. "You'll get to see him any time now!"

Tired as she was, Amanda smiled.

"Christopher's going to prop you up with some pillows," Jasmine explained. "When your next contraction comes, take a deep breath and push for all you're worth."

Christopher gripped Amanda's hands and coached her through several contractions, each one tiring Amanda more. Jasmine wondered how much longer the laboring woman would be able to hold out.

"He's crowning!" she announced excitedly on the next contraction. "Amanda, I see your sweet baby's head!"

Amanda laughed weakly. "Can you...does he...?"

Jasmine smiled. "He's got a full head of thick, dark hair like his daddy," she confirmed.

"Oh!" This time it wasn't so much an expression of pain as it was of wonder.

Jasmine's heart jumped into her throat and lodged there. A baby was a miracle, and it was a joy to be a participant in the wonder of birth.

But they weren't out of the woods yet, and her mind wouldn't let her forget it, not even for a second. "Let's give another really good push, and I think his head will be out."

Christopher tucked the woman into the crook of his arm and wiped the sweat from her eyes. "This is it, Amanda. Give it your best."

Amanda nodded and gritted her teeth determinedly.

"C'mon, kid, let's get this over with," she breathed. "I don't know about you, but I'm getting tired out here."

Jasmine and Christopher shared in her laughter, until another contraction hit and it was time for everyone to go to work. As Jasmine predicted, the head appeared, and she quickly turned the baby a quarter and suctioned the nose and mouth, clearing the air passageway.

"All right," Christopher said calmly, though excitement lined his voice. "The head was the hard part. The rest is easy. Just one more good push, Amanda, and you're finished."

How did he know that? Jasmine wondered again. Christopher continued to amaze her with his medical knowledge.

One more push was all it took. "It's a beautiful baby girl!" Jasmine announced, accompanied by the happy sound of the baby's first wail.

"She's beautiful," Christopher agreed, his voice hoarse.

Their eyes met, and Jasmine was surprised to find he had tears on his face, running unashamedly down his cheeks. Excitement and wonder and joy skirmished for prominence in his gaze. But above all, there was love.

The other emotions confused her. Love made her swallow hard and turn away, focusing her attention on completing the afterbirth and getting Amanda resting comfortably in her bed beside her new daughter.

Again, Christopher was a great help, washing and caring for the baby as if he handled brand-newborns every day. He talked and gurgled to the baby in the helium-high-pitched voice men automatically use with babies. Jasmine tried and failed not to let the scene affect her.

How could she help it? Seeing Christopher holding an infant brought up too many memories. Too many questions. And far too much pain. She gathered her equipment and tried not to think at all.

After spending several more hours monitoring Amanda and her daughter, Jasmine promised to visit her first thing in the morning. Jasmine gave Amanda instructions on what to do if she had any concerns as she prepared to leave.

Christopher interpreted her actions and pulled her aside.

"I'm taking you back to the cabin," he said in a tone that brooked no argument.

As if she had enough strength left to argue. She didn't much care *where* he took her, as long as it was warm, and quiet, and she could find someplace to lie down and curl up under a blanket. It was after midnight, and she was physically and emotionally exhausted.

She wondered if Christopher could sense she was near her breaking point. He was solicitous on their way out, taking her bags for her and insisting he keep an arm around her to prevent her from falling on the ice.

She yawned and tucked her head into his shoulder. Tomorrow was soon enough to ask him the questions that had paraded through her mind in constant succession throughout the entire ordeal. For now, all she could think about was sleep.

Chapter Six

Christopher woke to the sound and scent of bacon being cooked in a skillet over an open fire. His neck crimped painfully and his shoulders were unbearably tight from sleeping in the old wooden rocking chair in front of the fire, leaving Jasmine to the privacy of the only bedroom.

He'd carried her in to bed the night before. By the time they'd reached the cabin, she was barely holding on. He'd gripped her hands tightly around his waist for the last mile, hoping she wouldn't slide off the snowmobile. The cold had been her breaking point, and she hadn't made a whimper when he pulled her off the back of the snowmobile and into his arms.

Admiration rose in his chest. She was so strong for others, giving every bit of herself until she was completely drained. She was the type of person who naturally put others' needs before her own. He wished he could voice his respect for her, but she wouldn't believe him anyway.

What saint wanted praise from a sinner? And that's what he was, at least in Jasmine's eyes.

He figured she'd sleep, at least, but it appeared *he* was the slugabed this morning. He yawned and stretched, ruffling his hair with the tips of his fingers.

He couldn't help but enjoy the sight of Jasmine, dressed in the rumpled clothes she'd slept in and looking all the more attractive for it, humming quietly as she turned bacon.

His breath caught in his throat at the domestic scene, the

warm, cozy atmosphere she'd unintentionally created. The world had ceased to exist except for the two of them in this cabin. Maybe today, finally, they could work out their problems and move on with their lives. He didn't dare to hope they could move on together. Yet.

"Smells wonderful," he said, moving to crouch beside her under the pretense of warming his hands at the fire. "Breakfast for two?"

He heard her breath catch as she swung her gaze up to meet his. The flash of startled surprise in her eyes stabbed him like a dagger to the chest. The guilty knowledge that he'd placed himself in this position was his penance, his punishment.

He'd have to live with the pain he'd caused her for the rest of his life.

"I was kidding, Jasmine. Relax. I'm not trying to put you under any pressure." He restrained himself from brushing back the lock of hair that had fallen in her eyes. Her beautiful, shimmering green eyes.

"I know," she said, her voice low. She gave him a wavering smile. "I'm not afraid of you, Christopher."

He swallowed hard, certain his heart had stopped beating altogether. "I'm glad to hear it," he said, his voice gruff.

"I couldn't find any muffins, but I mixed up a batch of pancakes. I thought we could fry some in the bacon grease, if you think your cholesterol can handle it," she teased, a sparkle in her eye.

It was good to see her smile. "You don't have to worry about me," he said, puffing out his chest and flexing his biceps. "I'm the very picture of health."

The smile dropped from her face as she hastily turned back to her cooking.

"What did I say?" he asked gently, laying his hand on her arm.

She shook her head. "Nothing. Can you get the pancake batter from the table?"

"Sure." The message was clear. She wanted him to back

off. He was invading her space. He thrust his hands through the spiked tips of his hair and moved to do her bidding.

Grabbing the batter, he handed it to her, then stepped back, folding his arms with his open palms tucked close to his chest. If she wanted room, he had no choice but to give it to her. Even if what he really wanted to do was take her in his arms and erase the distance between them entirely.

"Why didn't you wait for me?"

Her question was spoken in such a soft tone, Christopher wondered if he'd imagined it. But when she turned to him, there was no denying the challenge in her gaze. Challenge, and pain.

He had no doubt of her meaning. She'd bridged the gap between them, said the torturous words that would open dialogue.

And now the ball was squarely in his court. They'd promised to marry as soon as Jasmine's internship was complete. He'd been so young, and so in love, the wait had seemed short. Now, it loomed before him.

"I couldn't wait," he said, surprised at how difficult the words were to say, though he'd rehearsed them a thousand times. His voice was rough and gravelly. "I had no choice."

Her shoulders tensed, and she turned back to her pan, breaking eggs one by one into the skillet. The hiss as each egg dropped into the pan reminded him of the torment of hell he was in.

"Oh, I see," she said finally, sarcasm lacing her voice. It was obvious she didn't see at all.

"Oh, Jasmine," he groaned, slumping back into the rocking chair and holding his head in his hand. The pulse at his temple threatened to burst through, and he pressed against it with the palm of his hand. "If you only knew what really happened!"

She picked up the skillet with a towel wrapped around the handle and slid the eggs onto a platter, then stood and wiped her fingers on her jeans. Christopher dropped his head, unwilling to see her perform such a normal, everyday task when real life was so off-kilter.

He didn't see her approach, but suddenly she was there in front of him, kneeling down before him and reaching for his hands. "I want to know, Christopher. Tell me."

He expected her to yell, to argue with him the way she had the other times they'd met. She had every right to be angry, and she was a spirited woman. But her gentleness, the glimmer of tears in her eyes, was his undoing.

He wrapped his arms around her and pulled her into his chest, burying his face in the glorious silky softness of her thick, black hair.

He inwardly groaned, expressing the agony that was his. For no matter how much he wanted to be with Jasmine, she could never know the whole truth. How could he confess it and risk losing Sammy? It would hurt so many people if the truth came out, including Jasmine. He couldn't be so cruel. He pulled her tighter, closer to his heart.

Jasmine didn't think. She just wrapped her arms around his neck and tangled her fingers in the short ends of his hair. For just one moment, she would give herself the pleasure of being in Christopher's arms again, feeling the strength of his arms like steel bands around her waist, taking joy in the sheer, masculine power of his broad shoulders.

She'd missed him, more than she'd thought possible—until this second.

She'd been only half-conscious when he'd brought her inside his cabin the night before. There was a moment of panic when he tucked her into bed. They'd never been intimate, saving that most precious of relationships for the time when they joined as man and wife; but Christopher was a different man now, and she wasn't sure what he was capable of.

In the end, he'd placed a gentle kiss on her forehead and she'd drifted off into peaceful dreams. If she were honest, it was the best sleep she'd had in months. Sammy was safe with Gram, and though the dear old woman wouldn't get a good night's sleep, Jasmine realized it was probably in everyone's best interests for her to have this night away from all her responsibilities.

She clung to Christopher a moment more, wondering how

she could ever have left his side in the first place. If she hadn't gone away to medical school, they'd be happily married right now, probably with two-point-five kids and a dog and a cat.

But she had a dream to follow, responsibilities that went beyond her own limited vision and encompassed the world. At least she thought so at the time. She'd been so sure of herself when she'd expressed these thoughts to Christopher, urging him to go on with his life. It wasn't fair of her to ask him to wait for her.

He'd argued, but she'd been firm, certain she was doing the right thing. Sometimes now she wondered if that vision she'd so readily embraced was nothing more than a specter created by an overzealous teenage girl who desperately wanted to be part of something bigger than herself.

A husband, two-point-five kids and a dog and a cat would never be enough for her. She'd wanted to be a doctor for as long as she could remember, and had never veered from that objective. Again, she questioned her convictions, and came up with nothing but a blank.

Not that it mattered now. She shivered when Christopher moved his head down, his lips grazing the tender skin of her earlobe before planting tiny kisses against the nape of her neck.

With a surprised gasp, she pushed him away. "Christopher, no."

The tortured look on his face was almost enough to send her back into his arms. *Almost* enough. The memory of Jenny's casket being lowered into the ground stopped her cold.

Her stomach lurched, and she wondered if she was going to be ill. Jenny was dead, and she was consorting with the enemy! It was enough to make even the strongest constitution weak and queasy.

Christopher stood suddenly and walked away from her, raking his fingers through his hair. "I'm *sorry,* Jasmine," he growled before stomping to the side of the room and slamming his fist into the thick log wall. He winced with the impact. "What else can I say?"

She remained silent as he shook his grazed knuckles, pressing her lips together to keep herself from murmuring something sarcastic or unkind. She'd never seen him angry enough to punch something. Christopher wasn't prone to emotional outbursts, which made him all the more unpredictable now.

"You can tell me the truth."

He turned on her, his eyes dark as granite. "The truth?" He laughed cynically. "I don't know what the truth is anymore."

"No? Let's start at the beginning." She paced the room, ticking off a list on her fingers, beginning with her thumb. "I distinctly remember you saying you loved me, that you'd wait for me as long as it took."

He grunted in defense.

She shook her head. "I know. I was the one who insisted we break up while I went to medical school." Her throat closed around the words. "But I didn't exactly mean for you to take up with my sister!"

When he stayed stubbornly silent, she continued. "I guess any old Enderlin woman is good enough to date, doesn't matter which one," she jibed sarcastically.

"I never *dated* your sister!" he snapped back. "Not ever, Jasmine. I was faithful to *you*."

"Except for when you tied the knot with Jenny, you mean," she corrected acerbically. The knowledge that he'd been intimate with her before their marriage slashed just as deeply as the wedding itself. Maybe more so. It gave a new dimension to her pain, making her feel unattractive and unwanted.

It was irrational, she knew. Christopher had never denied his physical attraction to her, and it was a mutual decision to honor God and wait for the wedding. And she had been the one to break off their relationship before med school. But she still felt he'd turned his back not only on her, but on *God*, when he welcomed Jenny into his arms.

Poor, sweet, innocent Jenny. At least he'd married her when she discovered she was pregnant with his child.

Married her and then abandoned her.

All the old anger came rushing back, and she turned on him, her face flushed with fury and her gaze condemning him before he opened his mouth.

"You said you would listen," he said quietly, shaking his head. "But you've already accused, tried and found me guilty."

"Aren't you?"

He swiped a hand down his face. "I don't know, Jasmine. And that's the honest truth."

"Please tell me you're kidding."

A dry laugh burst from his throat. "I wish I was. Every-thing was in such an uproar. But I didn't—" His words dropped abruptly and he turned away.

Christopher had been about to say *sleep with Jenny at all.* Not even after the marriage. He was there to give the unborn child a name and a roof over his head, and that was as far as it went. Jenny's health was declining rapidly, to his dismay. But if everyone knew the marriage hadn't been consummated, others had leverage to use against his claiming Sammy as his son.

"I did things in the wrong order," he said gruffly. "I'll admit my responsibility to that."

Jasmine winced, then straightened her shoulders and pierced him with a cold glare. "How gallant of you."

"I'll tell you what happened," he said, his voice low and scratchy. "You can figure out the rest."

She nodded miserably and slumped into the rocking chair, wrapping her arms around herself protectively. He wanted *his* arms wrapped around her. But she needed to hear this story, and she needed to hear it from him.

"Jenny called me up and asked me to come over and spend the evening with her and Gram." This wouldn't be news to Jasmine. She knew how close he was to her grandmother. "But when I got there, Jenny was in tears and Gram was nowhere to be found. Jenny told me later she was out of town visiting relatives."

He was silent a moment, allowing Jasmine to sort through

the issues. It didn't take her long to reach her own conclusions.

"Are you telling me she called you over on a ruse?" she asked, disbelief gleaming from her jade green eyes.

He paced over to the rocking chair and squatted to her eye level, wanting to be sure she could see the truth in his eyes when he spoke. "That's exactly what I'm telling you."

"Hogwash," she snapped. "Why would Jenny need to trick you? She could have just called you."

"Yes. And I would have come. I'd do anything for your family." He'd certainly proved that, even going to the length of ruining his own life in the process. He *had* to win Jasmine back, or his life was *worth* nothing.

He took a deep breath, wondering how to tell her what happened next. "Jazz, your sister was…emotionally unstable. She was a basket case by the time I got to the house. That's the only reason I stayed."

"Jenny was sensitive. She cried easily. But she was *not* a basket case!"

Christopher held up his hands. "I'm sorry. I don't mean to upset you more. I know Jenny was a sweet girl. But she was really upset that night. Smashing glass vases against the wall, turning over furniture—"

He stopped when he heard her sharp intake of breath.

"What…" Jasmine swallowed hard. "What happened? What was wrong?"

"She didn't tell me. At least not then."

She pinned him with a glare.

"I'm serious. She wouldn't tell me. She kept mumbling something about a low-life scumbag, but I never got her to elaborate any further than that. She just burst into tears again."

Jasmine's jaw clenched. He stood and put his hands in his front pockets to keep from touching her. She needed someone to ease the lines of strain from her face, to knead the knots from her shoulders.

Someone. But not him.

"This had something to do with a man?" she asked, her voice choked.

"I believe so. I stayed with her. Cleaned up the mess. Cooked her dinner. She'd calmed down by that time, and... she begged me not to leave her alone."

Compassion and sympathy flashed across her face, replacing the fierce lines of anger. Christopher swallowed hard. Jasmine had the gift of looking beyond the obvious to find the heart of the matter. Hope flared in his chest and his pulse raced.

"So you reached out to her, trying to comfort her, and..." She left the end of her sentence dangling.

"No!" Christopher closed his eyes and willed his emotions to the back of his mind. Her words weren't full of condemnation anymore, but reluctant understanding. "It wasn't like that! You don't understand!"

"I think I do."

"No. I didn't *comfort* her...that way. I went out and rented a couple of those old movies Jenny liked so much and popped some popcorn."

"And?"

He pulled in a breath. "And fell asleep on the couch, somewhere in the middle of the movie. That's all I can tell you."

"A woman doesn't get pregnant by a man sleeping on her couch, Christopher." Her sarcasm was back, a sure sign she was getting defensive again.

Anger tore at him as his face warmed with the necessity of talking about something so personal, so intimate, in such a clinical way. There was no love lost here.

He couldn't tell her why he left, or one of the two main reasons he returned would be null and void. He couldn't let that happen. "That's all I can tell you."

"That's all I want to hear." Jasmine stood suddenly and whisked around the room, gathering her personal items and her doctor's bag. "I'm going back to Amanda's to check on her and the baby."

"I'll take you."

"No," she countered far too quickly. "I want to walk."

"Walk?" he protested. "In case you didn't look out the window, there's over a foot of new snow on the ground!"

She tilted her chin up and glared at him. "So?"

"So...you can't just go *walking* to Amanda's."

"Watch me."

"Of all the stubborn, mule-headed women..."

She wrapped her parka around her and pulled up the hood. "I'm sure you've known plenty."

The barb met its mark. He clamped his jaw shut and scowled. Stubborn. Mule-headed. And he loved her with every beat of his heart.

"You don't believe me, do you?"

"What's to believe? That Jenny's baby was an immaculate conception? I don't think so, Christopher."

"I'm telling you the truth." He faced her off, his head only inches from her own. Her green eyes were flashing fire. Anger rose in his chest. All their history together, and she couldn't see the truth when it was staring her in the face. Maybe he couldn't say the words aloud, but she should *know*.

The injustice of it branded him through the heart. "You don't believe me?" he asked again. He willed every bit of his heart into his gaze. Surely she would be able to see that of all the people in the world, he could not lie to her. Not now. And not ever.

"As a matter of fact, no," she said, tipping her chin up to pierce him with another glare. "I don't believe a word you say."

"Then believe this." He took her firmly by the shoulders, tightening his grip when she tried to squirm away. If she didn't know his intentions to begin with, he was aware of the very moment when she read it in his gaze.

He waited until that moment, until she knew what he meant when his lips descended on hers, tormenting him with their sweetness. In his kiss, nothing would be hidden. She would know the truth.

He shifted his weight so he could draw her closer and slid his hands up her shoulders so he could cup her face in his palms, sliding the smooth material of her parka hood away from her head. She was so soft, so sweet, and the unusual, tropical scent that was Jasmine enveloped him.

"And the truth shall set you free." The Scripture flooded his mind even as she melted into his embrace.

Would the truth set them free? In the eternal sense, he knew the answer to that question, but what about the rest of their lives?

She clutched at the front of his shirt like a drowning woman. Instead of pushing him away as he expected, she pulled him closer, hoarsely whispering his name between kisses.

Warmth rushed over him at the sound of his name on her lips. He loved this woman.

He'd always loved her, since the first time he'd looked up into a giant elm and seen her dangling from a branch when he was seven and she was six. Nothing had changed. And everything had changed, leaving him with nothing but the tattered cover of his life. And leaving him without Jasmine.

He broke the kiss off before his passion overrode his good sense, knowing she was too emotionally drained to be the strong one now. He tucked her into his chest and inhaled sharply, trying to slow the runaway rhythm of his heart and steady his ragged breathing. He wanted the moment to go on forever, but knew that his wish went beyond the bounds of reality.

After a moment more, as he expected, Jasmine stiffened and tried to pull away. He caught a glimpse of regret in her eyes and reached for her elbow, but she yanked herself out of his grasp. With a huff of breath, she pulled up her hood and marched determinedly for the front door.

She opened the door and a snowy gust blew in, chilling Christopher instantly. She appeared not to notice, stepping out onto the porch as if it were a bright summer day and not the aftermath of a Colorado blizzard.

At the last moment, she paused, then turned back to him. A single tear slid down her cheek.

His breath caught in his chest as his gaze met hers. He clenched his fists at his sides, hating that he'd hurt her, wondering if kissing her had been the wrong thing to do. He wanted so much for them to be together, but...

"I believe you," she said quietly. "I'm very confused right now. I don't know how to reconcile the facts. But I believe what you told me today is the truth."

"And the truth shall set you free."

Chapter Seven

"*One more push, Jenny, and you're finished! Your baby is almost here!*" *Sweat poured from Jasmine's forehead, rivaling that of her laboring sister. Breathing heavily, she wiped the sting of salt from her eyes with the edge of her sleeve, careful not to contaminate her iodine-splashed hands with germs.*

"*I can't do this anymore,*" *Jenny whispered, her voice cracking in agony.* "*I can't! I'm too tired to push.*" *Panic in her voice rose to a fevered pitch, then dropped suddenly as her head sagged back onto the sweat-soaked pillow and her eyes drooped closed.*

"*You can do this,*" *Jasmine said, giving Jenny's leg a reassuring pat.* "*With the next contraction. Then you can rest all you want.*" *She noticed her voice quavered slightly. She couldn't quite maintain the clinical detachment necessary for a doctor. Not with her own little sister.*

Well, not so little anymore, she reflected, automatically clearing the baby's airway as she worked. Jenny was having a baby!

Christopher Jordan's baby.

Jasmine felt a slight rush of envy, but didn't allow the feeling to persist. Christopher might be the biological father. But where was he now?

Gone. And it was just as well.

Jenny groaned. Another contraction was coming. One more

*good push and Jasmine's first niece or nephew would put in
an appearance. Excitement mounted.*

*Jenny rolled up and clenched her jaw as she pushed, but it
was not enough to keep her from screaming when the baby
slid out into Jasmine's waiting hands.*

*A perfectly formed little boy. Jasmine counted quickly—ten
fingers and ten toes, then cut the cord as the child let out a
lusty yell.*

Worse than a nightmare, the memory of Jenny's death
haunted her waking moments. Jasmine pulled her four-by-four
into the driveway of Jenny's house and wiped a hand across
her eyes to dispel her thoughts. She sighed and gripped the
steering wheel, steadying her labored breath. In the semihyp-
notic state that driving sometimes induced, she'd let her
thoughts run away with her.

Jenny's bungalow was becoming more and more of a haven
to Jasmine, and she was beginning to wonder at the wisdom
of selling the quaint old place. She unlocked the door and
stepped inside, inhaling the light, lingering scent of cinnamon
potpourri—her sister's favorite aroma. Jenny was an almost
physical presence here, where her thoughts, hopes and dreams
had once meandered through the hallways.

Where Sammy had been born. And where Jenny had died.

Jasmine didn't want to remember the sad things anymore.
She was tired of trying to think through the issues, wrestle
with the nuances of truth she was learning. She couldn't stop
the thoughts from coming, but she continued to shove them
into the back of her mind.

That, and trying to forget what Christopher had said. How
would she ever sort through the mess that had become her
life? His revelation, and her response not only to the words
but to the man, had her running from that cabin at top speed,
afraid to look back lest her heart become more entangled than
it already was.

After visiting Amanda and reassuring herself that the
mother and baby were fine, she'd hiked back to her vehicle
and made the treacherous trip back into town. She'd spent a
couple of hours with Sammy, then she put him down for a

nap and headed straight for Jenny's, determined to finish the bittersweet job of preparing the bungalow for sale and get it over with.

Grabbing a box, she opened the drawer to Jenny's night-stand. She'd left this job until last, because she suspected many of her sister's personal items would be in this drawer.

Low-life scumbag. That's what Christopher said Jenny had been mumbling that night. It almost sounded as if she were talking about a man, the sort of statement a woman used in regard to a relationship gone wrong.

But Jenny hadn't been involved in a relationship. Surely not? That she hadn't said a word about a special guy was proof positive that Christopher was lying—wasn't it? She'd certainly never brought a man home to meet the family that Jasmine knew of.

A beat with the echo of a canyon pounded in her temple. She and Jenny were too close for Jenny to keep secrets, es-pecially about romance. Her sister had been the first person Jasmine shared her secrets with, and thought Jenny had done the same.

You kept your engagement to Christopher a secret, her mind taunted. If she'd just told Jenny the truth, maybe none of this would have happened. Jenny wouldn't have run to Christopher, and he wouldn't have—

She cut the thought off. Her whole thread of thought was assuming Christopher was telling the truth. She'd told him she believed him, and she did, though it was completely ir-rational to do so. Something in his look when he told her the story was so honest, so sincere, that she could do no less than give him the benefit of the doubt.

Of course, his explanation did nothing to the fact that he'd neglected to tell her of his upcoming wedding to Jenny, nor his subsequent abandonment of his wife and unborn son.

With a grunt of protest, she pulled on the drawer, wonder-ing if it would reveal answers to her questions, or if it would merely reveal more secrets to unfold.

It was locked.

"Great," she said aloud, fuming inside. "Calm down and

think this through rationally," she demanded of herself, willing her blood pressure to settle. "Where would Jenny put the key?"

She ran her mind over the possibilities. She'd already been through the dresser and the closet. She'd packed Jenny's kitchen items into boxes. She hadn't run across any keys, much less a small drawer key.

She sighed, frustration seething from her lungs. One obstacle after another, with no end in sight. Weariness spread through her bones, dragging her down with its weight. Maybe Gram was right, and she did need a break. But that would leave Westcliffe without a doctor.

Unless...

Jasmine made a dash for her purse and dumped the contents onto the bed. She snatched her date book from the hodgepodge of items and flipped through the pages, then reached for the telephone, which she'd not yet had disconnected.

"Marcus? It's Jasmine," she said without preamble when a man answered. She could tell from the deep sound of his booming bass voice that it was her dear friend from med school, so she didn't see a need to make small talk.

She'd met Marcus White at a campus Bible study during her first year as a resident. When her world had fallen apart, Marcus had been a rock, believing for her what she couldn't believe for herself.

He showed her in the best way, in word and deed, that everything she'd grown up believing wasn't in vain, and that God still worked in people's lives. She wasn't sure she believed it still, but not for his lack of trying.

He knew her present circumstances, at least about Christopher's dumping her for her sister. He didn't yet know about Jenny, never mind Sammy, but that could wait until later. She would explain the particulars when she saw him face-to-face.

She refused to give a thought as to what Christopher might think of Marcus's sudden arrival in her life. She knew he wouldn't be happy about it. Just one more obstacle he had to surmount. At least that's how he'd look at it.

Her eyes clouded as she remembered telling Christopher

about Marcus. She and Christopher were secretly engaged at the time, and though he hadn't said anything, the left corner of his lip had turned down. He'd looked for all the world like a little boy who'd just been told to share his favorite toy. She'd kissed him and promised him the world that day, and he'd quickly lost his surly mood.

She shook her head and swallowed hard, dislodging yet another memory. They seemed to plague her today. It was none of Christopher's business who she brought to Westcliffe, she quickly reminded herself. *She* would be happy to see her old friend, and that's what really mattered, wasn't it?

As soon as they'd discussed how Marcus's own plans to return as a doctor to the inner-city neighborhood he'd grown up in had backfired, Jasmine enlisted his professional help.

"I'd be there even if you didn't need me as a doctor," he replied immediately. "I told you that you can always count on me. I'm here for you, girl. You just give me directions from the airport."

Jasmine breathed a sigh of relief. "I'm glad to hear that. I didn't dare to hope when I called you. And of course I prayed that your situation would work out in your home neighborhood."

"I appreciate your prayers," he said, sounding as if he were choking out the words. "Rest assured, God answered them."

Jasmine felt the familiar flare of animosity rise in her chest, the anger that jumped out when she was least prepared for it.

That he was holding back his emotions was blatantly obvious to her, yet his words were filled with strength and calm. For some unexplainable reason, that riled her.

"It was just a figure of speech, Marcus. How can you say God answered your prayers?" she demanded. "You aren't accepted as a doctor in your very own neighborhood. It was your dream."

"That was God's answer," Marcus explained patiently. "He wants me to serve elsewhere. When He's ready, He'll change my dreams."

His voice was firm. He really believed what he said, and that shook Jasmine to the core. She'd once believed herself to have the kind of faith that could move mountains. She made a grunt of disgust.

Deep down, she couldn't deny God existed. The beauty and artistry of His creation was enough to prove otherwise. But she'd come to believe He stood aloof, didn't dirty his hands with the affairs of men and women—at least not common, everyday country girls like she was. Where her life was concerned, she was on her own.

"I wish I had your faith," she said, her tone petulant.

"You don't need my faith," Marcus replied, laughter echoing from the deep recesses of his chest. "You have your own. It just hasn't resurfaced yet." He paused as if giving her time to consider his words.

When she didn't respond, he continued. "Now, getting down to business. What is it you need me to do for you? Tell you to take two aspirin and call me in the morning?"

Jasmine laughed weakly before filling him in. When she hung up, she returned to the locked drawer, deciding it wouldn't hurt to attempt to pick the lock. She tried a hairpin, a credit card slid into the top of the drawer, and the keys from her own chain, but nothing worked. She racked her brain for another idea.

Determined pounding on the front door interrupted her work, and she sighed in frustration. Yet another difficulty was just exactly what she didn't need right now. And she had no doubt it *was* a major trial on the other side of the door. A six-foot, broad-shouldered, sweet-talking problem.

No one but Christopher Jordan and Gram knew she was here. The rigorous beat on the door left no doubt which of the two wanted to see her. And it was not Gram.

"Pizza man," he coaxed from behind the door. "Open up, Jazz, I know you're in there."

"What do you want?" she demanded as she stomped to the door and swung it open. "I'm really not in the mood for company right now."

Christopher tipped his cowboy hat from his head and smiled as he tucked it under his arm, extending the pizza box he held in the other. "Why is it every time you answer the door you bite my head off? Something about knocking make you churlish? Maybe I should install a doorbell to make things easier for you.''

His tone was so light and flippant she had to chuckle, and the aroma of sizzling pepperoni was making her mouth water. ''Oh, that would help,'' she quipped back. ''Then you could interrupt me with a bell when I'm loaded under with a ton of boxes, instead of pounding my door off its hinges.''

''Man with food doesn't work for you?'' His smile was adorably contagious, and she found herself smiling too.

Just food would be best. The *man* in question was already making her heart skip erratically, something she could do without.

''I knew you wouldn't be able to resist pizza,'' he said, stepping around her and into the bungalow. ''I stopped by your place first and talked to Gram.''

Sammy! Panic stabbed through her, but quickly ebbed. If he'd seen his son, he sure wouldn't be here now, offering her a pizza.

''She said you hadn't eaten—did you catch lunch in town?''

She sighed. ''I haven't been to town. And no, I didn't have lunch. We had a big breakfast, remember?''

He shook his head. ''You've got to eat regular meals, Jazz, or you're going to hurt yourself.'' Placing the pizza box on the table, he tossed his hat onto the counter and pulled out a slice of pizza, waving it invitingly beneath her nose.

''You sound just like Gram,'' she said, scowling.

Even as she wished everyone would stop trying to run her life, her fickle mouth was watering at the tantalizing aroma. She licked her lips.

''Hungry?'' he asked, cocking a grin.

''Starved, actually.'' She didn't realize just how hungry she was until he'd arrived. She snatched the slice of pizza from him and bit into it, savoring the rich flavor of the mozzarella cheese and the tangy spice of the pepperoni. ''Mmm. My favorite.''

''I remember.'' His voice was husky.

She tried to catch a glimpse of his face, but he'd turned back to the table to get himself a slice. "You still haven't said why you're here," she reminded him, a little annoyed and a lot confused.

"Isn't it enough that I want to be with you?"

Her breath caught. "Under the circumstances, I'd have to say *no*."

The smile disappeared from his lips and his eyes turned a smoky gray. "Gram said you might need some help finishing up here."

"Gram talks too much."

"Now, is that any way to talk about your grandmother?" He squinted one eye at her, and she could see laughter lurking just below the surface.

"It is when she butts her nose into someone else's business. Especially mine."

"She's worried about you."

Reaching for a napkin, Jasmine wiped tomato sauce from the corner of her mouth. "I know she is."

Their eyes met and locked. Christopher's eyes were the smoky blue color that radiated love and passion and made her heartbeat triple. He was a vibrant, passionate man, applying everything he had to whatever he did, just as the Bible said. Whether it be in work, or play—or love. How often had he teasingly reminded her of that verse as his eyes turned smoky?

"In case you're curious, Gram wouldn't let me see my son," he said gruffly, answering the question she hadn't asked.

"I figured."

"I didn't ask." His voice sounded strained, almost tortured, when just a moment ago he'd been laughing.

Her eyes widened. She wouldn't blame him if he'd sweet-talked Gram into seeing Sammy.

When he'd first shown up on her doorstep, her only thought was protecting Sammy from his clutches. But now, despite the myriad of unanswered questions, she wondered at the wisdom of keeping Christopher from his son.

It was clear he cared about the boy, though he'd never seen

him. Christopher was acting very much like the man she once knew and loved, the man who put others' needs ahead of his own, who always tried to do the right thing. Who would love and cherish his children.

"I'm not ready," she said aloud. "I know you want to see Sammy, but—"

"He's my son, Jazz."

"I know." *But you ran away.*

The barrier was still there between them, as potent and ominous as the Berlin Wall had once been. She blew out a breath. They'd been down this road before.

She needed more time to think, to sort things out, before she made any decisions. If she allowed herself to be led by her emotions, she wasn't the only one who stood to get hurt. "Did you come here to talk about Sammy?"

He wolfed down another large bite of pizza and shook his head. "No. I came to help. But—" he continued between bites, gesturing toward a pile of boxes "—it looks like you're finished."

"Almost finished," she corrected. "Everything except Jenny's nightstand. I'm going to give it to charity, but I wanted to clean it out first. The stupid drawer is locked, and I can't find the key."

"Have you tried to pick the lock?" he asked, wiping his hands on a napkin.

"Yes, but you're welcome to try again. It's not like I'm a master thief or anything."

"What did you use?"

"Hairpin, credit card, screwdriver. Any other ideas?"

"Do you have any idea where Jenny might have kept the key?"

"I don't have a clue. This is my last project. I've scrubbed this house from floorboards to ceiling, and haven't found a single key."

"Would she have put it somewhere special?"

It was as if a lightbulb had flipped on in her mind, so quickly the answer came to her.

The Bible.

It had lots of pages marked with lumps made by various items—maybe the key was one of them. It was worth a try.

She rushed to the living room, where Jenny's Bible was sitting on top of a small stack of boxes of items Jasmine was keeping.

Jenny's favorite sweater. A photo album to give Sammy when he was older. And she was keeping the Bible, whether or not she ever read it.

She could throw it away, she supposed, but someday, maybe, she would give it to Sammy so he could know a little more about his mother, have something personal of hers, something to remember her by.

His *real* mother.

That he would only remember *her* as his mother both thrilled and terrified Jasmine. And now, if Christopher had his way, the boy would know his father, too. The situation suddenly didn't seem so awfully bad, for the boy, at least.

If Christopher wanted to play a part in Sammy's life, which appeared to be the case, Sammy would be able to benefit from a male role model. But it also meant she would be forced into close proximity with Christopher on a regular basis for the rest of her life.

Any hope she had of getting over him and moving on with her life, perhaps even finding someone else to love, died an instant death in her mind. There could be no other man. It was as if Christopher had been made for her, complementing her strengths and augmenting her weaknesses. She glanced to where he stood, his arms crossed over his broad chest, one shoulder leaning casually against the far wall.

She used to think that he *was* made for her, God's choice for her perfect mate. She squeezed her eyes shut against the tears that burned there, then opened the Bible and shuffled through the pages.

In the middle of it, tied with a small piece of golden embroidery thread, was the key. Jasmine pulled it out and snapped the book closed. "I've found it."

She felt rather than saw Christopher follow her into the bedroom. His gaze on her was almost tangible, and though he remained silent, she knew he felt her tension at the questions yet remaining. She sat on the edge of the bed, her spine stiffly straight, the key poised and waiting in her hand.

It slid easily into the lock, clicking softly as she turned it. "It fits," she said, knowing the verbal confirmation was unnecessary. He dropped his large hand on her shoulder, lightly rubbing the tension from the back of her neck.

The drawer wasn't nearly as full as she expected it to be. A box of tissues, a couple of paperbacks, a pair of reading glasses. And a picture, an old newspaper clipping that looked like it had been handled frequently.

Curious, Jasmine picked up the photograph. A clean-cut young man dressed in tennis whites with a sweater draped over his shoulder stared dully at the camera, as if annoyed that he was once again being photographed. He was leaning against the railing of his yacht. A smiling bleach blonde had her arms around the man's neck. She, at least, didn't mind being photographed.

There was something disturbingly familiar about that woman, she realized with a start. She looked closer.

"That's *Jenny!*" she said aloud, astonished. Without thinking, she looked to Christopher for help. He merely clenched his jaw and looked away.

How could the woman in this picture be her sister? The Enderlins were a far cry from the country-club type, of which there were none in Westcliffe. A few in Pueblo, maybe, and definitely Denver. But not from around here.

What disturbed her most of all was the foreign look the woman who was her sister had on her face. There wasn't a trace of the sweet girl she'd grown up with. The woman in the picture looked comfortable on a yacht on Pueblo Reservoir where the rich hang out, and in the newspapers. Excited, but not giddy.

Jasmine swallowed hard. "How?" She choked out the word, then gasped for a breath.

"I didn't want to have to tell you." Christopher's voice was low and strangled. Turning toward her, he clenched and unclenched his fists. He opened his mouth to speak, then closed it again, scowling.

She waited, barely remembering to breathe. Her fingers were shaking where she held the worn photograph, the last picture taken of her sister. Nothing was as it seemed. Everything she believed in played her false.

Christopher. God. Now even Jenny. She wondered if she had the strength to hear what he had to say. Christopher reached for her, enfolding her in his arms without a word. Her quivering turned to trembling, and her trembling to quaking as the events of the past few months caught up with her.

She didn't cry. Her tears were spent. But the tension in her body welled up in her like lava in a volcano, finally exploding into tremor after tremor.

He buried his face in her hair and stroked her temple, murmuring until the shock had passed. When she no longer shook, he kissed her forehead and released her.

"Things changed around here after you left for med school," he said, carefully enunciating each word as if the syllables themselves caused him pain. "There are some things about Jenny you need to know."

Chapter Eight

Christopher didn't know how much to tell her. He wasn't sure he should be telling her anything at all. She'd been through so much already. But there was still so much she didn't know.

How could he make her understand how her leaving affected those closest to her? With both their parents dead, Jenny had been dependent on Jasmine, looking up to her as a role model, almost as a mother figure, though they were only four years apart.

All through junior high, Jenny had walked in Jasmine's shadow, doing the things she knew would please her sister rather than developing her own interests. But when Jasmine left for med school, Jenny changed.

Jasmine sat on the bed staring up at him, her wide, green angel eyes shimmering with emotion. Words he never planned to say hurdled over one another to leave his mouth. Without conscious thought, he related the story.

"After you left for med school, Jenny got into trouble. She made new friends—friends apart from the church and the community. She made a lot of trips to Pueblo, staying away for days at a time, even."

"I didn't even know she was hanging out with the jet-setters," she whispered.

"You had all you could do to keep up with your studies," he reminded her gently.

"But I could have *helped* her!"

"Maybe. Maybe not. Jenny had the strong will of an Enderlin, Jazz. She could be nearly as stubborn as you." He tipped up the corner of his lip, trying to smile, but feeling like he was grimacing instead. "I'm sure Gram thought it was just a stage, that she'd grow out of it."

"And she did, didn't she?"

"In a way. When she found out she…was carrying Sammy, she walked the straight and narrow."

What had her sister been seeking? The urge to pull her back into his arms was strong, but he resisted. Since he'd been back, he'd been reaching for her.

This time, he wanted her to reach for him first.

"She went back to church. Got straight with the Lord. Grew up in a hurry so she could raise a baby. She would have been a good mother to Sammy," he concluded softly.

"Do you know the man in the picture?" she queried, handing him the worn newspaper. Steeling himself for what he might see, he glanced at the picture. He had ample reason for his hesitance.

This was the man.

He handed the picture back to Jasmine with such alacrity her eyes widened in surprise.

He'd seen the young man in the photograph, though he couldn't place him right away. He knew it hadn't been with Jenny—he would remember that. The face was familiar, but beyond that he couldn't say.

Bart Pembarton. The biological father of Jenny's baby. That was the man pictured, Christopher realized a minute later.

"I don't think I know him," she said slowly, taking the picture back. She stared down at it another moment, as if trying to read something into the picture that wasn't there. "You know what's odd?"

"Hmm?" he murmured distractedly, his gaze tracing the line of her jaw to her full, wide mouth, which was even now curled down in a girlish frown.

"This doesn't look like Jenny at all, but even so…she looks happy."

"I don't see how."

"Maybe *happy* is the wrong word. Content? No, not that, either. I would have thought she'd be uncomfortable with rich people. But something in her eyes, I guess, makes me think…oh, I don't know. Like she really cared for the man in the picture. Maybe my overactive imagination is running away with me."

"If you want to believe she was happy, then believe it."

"But you don't."

He clenched his jaw. "I can't say. All I know is that she ran with a bad crowd. She made sure she was quite visible— almost as if she *wanted* you to hear about her behavior."

"I'm surprised I didn't."

"Like I said, Jazz, we all thought it was just a stage she was going through. If I would have guessed—"

"No, you're right," she interrupted. "You had no way of knowing."

Christopher picked up the nightstand and balanced it in his arms. If he stood still a moment longer, he would spontaneously combust. "Where do you want this thing?"

Jasmine pressed her fingers to her temples and squeezed her eyes shut as if staving off a headache. "Out in the living room with the rest of the boxes."

Just before he left the room, he saw her tuck the picture into the front pocket of the flannel shirt she had on over her T-shirt. Anger flooded through him.

He wished Bart were here now. He had two fists to introduce him to. He didn't even want to talk to the man, just show him in a way he could understand what happens when you mess with one of the Enderlin women.

But that was impossible. Bart was dead.

He wanted—no, needed—to help Jasmine. But all he succeeded in doing was to dig himself in deeper. He wasn't able to ease her pain. All he could do was stand by and watch, powerless, as the plot thickened.

More than anything, he hated this feeling of helplessness. He needed to do something, to take some positive action instead of just sitting here twiddling his thumbs.

There must be something he could do. But what?

He ground his teeth in frustration, barely resisting the urge to slam the nightstand to the floor and stomp it to pieces. It wouldn't do him any good to break Jenny's furniture.

Jasmine shuffled from the bedroom, refusing to meet his gaze as he stooped to settle the nightstand next to the boxes.

"Sammy..." she began, then hesitated, looking every direction except at him.

He dropped one knee to the floor, afraid his legs might buckle from the powerful, potent force of the single word. His breath jammed into his lungs and refused to be released.

She cleared her throat and tried again. "Sammy and I will...be walking in the park tomorrow afternoon."

She stopped again, and this time pinned him with a gaze so direct and open it knocked the stubborn breath from his chest in a whoosh of air. "At one o'clock."

Swallowing hard, he forced a trickle of oxygen back into his burning lungs.

Her meaning was unmistakable.

She would let him see the baby!

The memories haunted Jasmine even in her dreams.

Jenny was fading fast.

Instead of the regular joyful recovery of bringing new life into the world, Jenny was growing more peaked by the moment.

Jasmine felt for a pulse. It was weak and erratic. Something was terribly wrong.

"It hurts," Jenny rasped weakly, rolling her head from side to side on the sweat-soaked pillow.

It shouldn't hurt. The baby boy, wrapped in a blanket next to Jenny's side, was wiggling and gurgling contentedly. The afterbirth should have been easy.

Jasmine wiped her hands on a clean towel and stood slowly so as not to alarm Jenny. Her mind was screaming in panic, but her training as a doctor pulled her through. She would remain calm. If Jenny sensed her anxiety, it would only make things worse.

She needed to use the phone, she'd said.

To tell everyone the good news?

Sure. That was it. Her voice quavered with the lie. She'd only be a minute.

But the helicopter couldn't come soon enough. There wasn't anything anyone could do.

Not even a doctor. Jasmine knew it, and so did Jenny.

Her sister had looked up at her with the pained, wise gaze of someone who knew her time was near. She reached for Jasmine's hand, and it was all she could do to keep from shaking, from bursting into tears. From screaming to God for mercy.

"Grieve later," Jenny had said. "There are more important things to do right now." The hospital helicopter was on its way, and there wasn't much time. At least that's what Jenny said. The truth was much harder to hear.

Jasmine merely nodded, unable to speak. She wanted to run, to cry, to scream in rage. Instead, she took her sister's hands and waited.

"I've already made arrangements for my funeral," Jenny whispered, her voice hoarse.

Jasmine felt as if a thousand pins were pricking her body. This couldn't be happening.

Jenny nodded. "Yes. I knew I was dying. I've got cancer, Jasmine."

Jasmine gasped in pain and shock.

"I'm okay with it," Jenny was quick to assure her. "I've made my peace with God."

"How...when?"

"I found out about the cancer the same day I found out I was having Sammy. He's the sole reason I've been hanging on. It's my time, Jasmine. I'm not going to fight it anymore."

"What about your baby?" What Jasmine really wanted to say was "What about me?" but she knew how self-centered that sounded.

How could she ever live without Jenny?

Jenny laughed weakly. "He's going to be fine. I know you'll make the best mother in the world. He's a lucky little boy."

"Me?" She swallowed around the lump in her throat.

"The papers are already drawn up. I want you to be Sammy's legal guardian." She reached weakly for Jasmine's hand. "Please."

"Of course," she assured, her voice scratchy. "Of course I will."

There was a moment of silence as Jenny's spirit seemed to fade away. Her breath became shallow and her eyelids drooped. Then, with what appeared to be a monumental effort, she opened her eyes and focused on Jasmine.

"Take care my baby." A single tear formed at the corner of Jenny's eye, then meandered slowly down her face.

Jasmine watched the progress of the salty drop of water as if in a trance. "You can care for him yourself when you get better."

"You and I both know that won't happen."

Jenny's fingers were cold as they squeezed her hand. "Promise me."

"I already did." The sting of tears met with Jasmine's stubborn opposition.

Jenny pulled the infant close to her chest, her tears coming in earnest now. She stroked his cheek, his nose, his ear, then planted a gentle kiss on his forehead. With a sob, she handed him to Jasmine.

"I'm so sorry." Her words were growing slurred and faint. "Forgive me."

Jasmine wasn't sure if Jenny was speaking to her or not. Her eyes had closed, her face contorted in pain.

"And Jasmine, find...Christopher..."

Jasmine sat bolt upright in her bed, sweat pouring from her brow. Sammy's shrill infant cry had wakened her from the nightmare that was so much more than just a dream. Her breath came in deep, angry waves, her lungs burning with exertion. Jenny's final words echoed in her head, and she wrapped her arms around her legs, hugging her knees to her chest.

And tomorrow—or rather, today, she amended, glancing at

the clock on the nightstand—she would introduce Sammy to his father.

She scooped the boy from his bassinet, murmuring gently and rocking him against her breast. She used her index finger to peep through the venetian blinds, which affirmed that the world still lay heavily under the shroud of darkness.

She yawned and rubbed her eyes. Sammy was pretty much sleeping through the night lately. She wondered what woke him, and hoped she hadn't inadvertently yelled in her sleep. She put a bottle of formula in the microwave and settled with Sammy on a rocker, humming softly.

She didn't even recognize the song she was singing, at first, but as the melody progressed, the lyrics soon followed.

"Great is Thy faithfulness...morning by morning new mercies I see."

There was no mercy for one such as she, though seeing the innocent, wide-eyed pleasure of the chubby baby boy in her arms made her wonder.

Where did God's plan end and hers begin? The road was narrow—had she missed it altogether?

She certainly felt she'd wandered off onto some mighty big highway, covered with cars and semis, without a shade of grace or mercy.

She closed her eyes, hesitantly pointing a prayer toward the ceiling, nudging gently to see if the wall between heaven and earth was as firm as she'd once felt it to be.

It budged. No, it did more than budge. The floodgates of heaven opened and God's grace shone upon her like the sun, lighting even the darkest recesses of her heart. The experience was at once so jarring and so gentle that she barely heard the beep of the microwave signaling the baby's bottle was ready.

Sammy heard it, though, and began doing baby jumping jacks in her arms, flailing his round little limbs wildly to get her attention. She opened her eyes and laughed, breathing in the peace that passes understanding. Not really knowing, but *knowing* anyway.

Nothing had changed, yet He had changed everything. She was still meeting Christopher to introduce him to Sammy.

They still had a wide gap to bridge between them, and a million details to work out where Sammy was concerned.

What was different was *her*. She'd just made a tiny step toward the right road. A step toward discovering what God wanted her to do. She prayed for the strength and courage to do His will when she knew what it was.

She wasn't the wide-eyed innocent she'd been before she went off to school, she thought, appeasing the squalling baby with his bottle, then settling back down on the rocker.

She was a world-worn woman with a chip the size of Texas on her shoulder. She knew life wasn't full of easy answers. She no longer expected black to be black and white to be white. There were lots of other colors in between black and white.

But then, she reflected, tired but content as she rocked her baby boy, maybe that was why God made rainbows.

Chapter Nine

Christopher was as nervous as a teenager on prom night. After all this time, he was finally going to be able to see Sammy, maybe even hold him. Checking his image in a mirror, he smoothed back his hair with his palm and planted his hat on his head.

He didn't know why he was making such an all-fired effort to look good today. It just seemed right for him to present himself in the best light for his...*son*. The word stuck in his mind and refused to dislodge. He swallowed hard.

It wasn't every day a man met his son for the first time.

He was nervous about holding Sammy, even though his EMT training in Pueblo had taught him how to hold a newborn. He'd been fine with Amanda's baby, but his own son was another question entirely.

Thank goodness Jasmine would be there. She would show him how.

Funny how he fell into his easy dependency on Jasmine after all this time. She was his beacon in the night. Suddenly, he recognized the care he was giving his grooming was as much for her as it was for Sammy.

A family.

No. He wouldn't think about that now. He would meet the baby, and let Jasmine see his dedication to the child with her own eyes. Then she would understand he meant what he said.

The park was a mere five-minute drive from the ranch. He arrived early, thinking he'd find a seat on the bench next to the playground to wait. But when he got there, he changed his mind.

He didn't want to inadvertently put Jasmine on the defensive. Better to wait in his truck until he saw them, so he could approach from a distance, and make sure he didn't catch her off guard.

Not that she'd really be off guard. He knew the herculean effort it had taken her to comply with his wishes. She was offering her trust when no one else would give him the time of day. He wasn't only asking for *her* trust, either, but for her to risk what was dearest to her in the world—Sammy.

His breath caught in his throat when he saw her crossing the lawn toward him. She'd clearly seen his truck, waving in his direction when he looked up. He swallowed hard and waved back.

Her long black hair waved like silk in the breeze, gently caressing the smooth skin of her cheeks. She glanced down at the carriage and made a face, laughing at whatever response she created.

He bolted from the truck, then stopped short at the lilting sound of her croon. "That's a good boy, Sammy. That's my big boy."

He *was* her boy. The knowledge jolted through his system. All of his senses snapped to life, appearing to magnify of their own accord. The scent of fresh-clipped grass assaulted his nostrils, an unusual aroma for the middle of winter in Westcliffe. The wind was crisp and sharp against the edge of his jaw. And Jasmine's sweet voice melted into him like liquid gold.

One thing was sure—she would never give up Sammy. To him or anyone. Without the boy, she would wilt up just as sure as any mother deprived of her infant. He'd already caused enough of a ruckus in the Enderlin family to last a lifetime and beyond.

But he couldn't just turn around and walk away. He wouldn't. He clamped his jaw against a bitter chill that swept through the air. For better or for worse, Sammy was his responsibility. And for better or for worse, Jasmine would have to get used to his presence in her—in *their* lives.

She startled visibly when he tentatively reached for the carriage, her movement as instinctive as a deer caught in headlights. She might be here, but there was obviously still a part of her that was afraid he would grab the baby and make a run for it. That knowledge didn't hurt him as much as the uncertainty in her eyes.

Would he ever be able to prove himself? He resisted the impulse to turn and stalk off the way he came. Frustration and anger seethed through him, vying for prominence, but he held it in check and tipped his hat off his head.

"How is the little nipper?" he asked, awkwardly opening the conversation.

"Good."

Terrific. She wasn't going to help him any. He met her gaze and stepped forward slowly, his movements painfully obvious.

Releasing her breath, she nodded toward the carriage. "I suppose you want to see him."

A low rumble of laughter left his chest as she stated the obvious.

She laughed with him. "That was dumb. Sorry. I'm as jumpy as a rabbit today."

"Me, too," he agreed. Somehow it was easier knowing she experienced some of the same awkwardness he was feeling. Even if it was awkwardness *he* had created.

"You can pick him up."

"I..." He hesitated, unsure of himself. What happened to showing Jasmine what a perfect father he was? He was afraid to pick up the baby.

He scooped Sammy up and cradled his head, making soothing noises. He tried to remember everything he'd learned. Support the neck. Tuck him in your arms.

Suddenly Sammy pumped his arms and legs wildly, nearly rolling off Christopher's arm. He made an exclamation and grabbed for the boy, who let out a delighted squeal which sounded very much like, "That was fun, let's do it again."

Christopher and Jasmine both laughed with him.

"You don't have to support his neck," Jasmine said. "He's old enough to do that on his own."

"He's a sturdy little guy," he commented, reaching tentatively to touch the baby's hand. His throat tightened as Sammy wrapped his little fist around his index finger and brought it to his mouth, smacking noisily.

"Sure he is. Sammy's my happy baby, aren't you, big boy?" she asked in a sweet croon. "Mommy's big boy."

Mommy.

She called herself Sammy's mother. He supposed he shouldn't be surprised. It was best for Sammy and a natural thing for Jasmine to do, but for some reason it made his throat constrict until he couldn't draw a breath.

"How old is he?" he asked gruffly.

The question made Jasmine scowl. "Three months."

Had it been that long? He would have been back sooner, had he not been in the middle of his EMT training in Pueblo. It had been his way of dealing with Jenny's death, losing himself in his studies, following God's call. But it kept him from Sammy. And Jasmine. Guilt stabbed at his chest.

"Can you show me how to hold him?"

"You said yourself he's sturdy," she replied, the lines creasing her eyebrows together easing as she stroked the boy's downy hair. "Just grab him under his shoulders."

He released the breath he'd been holding and adjusted Sammy, holding him under his arms. Christopher was surprised to discover how heavy the boy was already, and how slippery, when Sammy began wailing and squirming.

He tightened his grip on the boy, still holding him at arm's length. This baby-holding business sure was awkward. "Easy, little fellow," he coaxed.

Jasmine laughed. "He likes to be cuddled close to your body, Christopher. Give your son some loves."

He flashed her a surprised look, but was quickly diverted by his wiggling son. He pulled the boy up to his chest until the baby's soft cheek rested against his rough chin. He gave the boy a hesitant kiss on the top of his head.

To everyone's surprise, Christopher's most of all, Sammy immediately settled down. The baby lounged back into the crook of Christopher's arms and gurgled contentedly, one fist planted firmly in his mouth.

"He likes me," said Christopher, astonished.

"Well, of course he does. Babies know these things, you know. I'm sure he can sense you're his father."

That was stretching it, Christopher knew. He would hate to find out what would happen if Sammy had been exposed to his *real* biological father. Not that Bart wanted anything to do with him.

If only he could tell Jasmine. But everyone was better off if he kept his mouth shut. Sammy was safe, and Jenny's name wouldn't be dragged through the mud.

In all the ways that counted, he was Sammy's father. The baby sensed his sincerity, if not his genetic connection. It would be much harder to convince Jasmine, but he'd manage. He was Sammy's dad, and he'd prove it.

"Does he like to swing?" he asked, gesturing to a swing set.

"He loves to swing," she answered, nodding for him to lead the way.

The three of them spent over an hour playing in the park. He carefully pushed Sammy in the baby swing, laughing out loud when he squealed. Jasmine held the baby on one end of the teeter-totter while he worked the other end. She even convinced him to climb up the ladder and squeeze through a narrow opening to take Sammy down a slide.

He couldn't remember being happier. He was with his son and the woman they both loved. And they were happy.

He hadn't laughed so much in years, and it was nice to see Jasmine with a grin on her face and a rosy glow on her cheeks. She'd been so unhappy lately.

Somehow the time they shared was unexpectedly intimate, something special only a family unit could experience. He wondered if Jasmine sensed it as well. It was almost as if it were floating in the air, permanently binding them together with every moment they spent together. They were a family.

A *family*. That was the answer.

"I've got to get Sammy back to the apartment. His little hands are like ice cubes."

Jasmine's statement dashed his thoughts and brought him abruptly back to the present. "I wouldn't want him to catch a cold," he said, concern lacing his voice.

She chuckled and adjusted the baby's hood over his head. "He'll be fine, Christopher. I just think we need to be heading home."

"I—" He floundered, having so much to say and not knowing how to begin. "You can't go yet."

She lifted an eyebrow. "Oh? And why is that?" He could still hear laughter in her voice, and he crooked a smile in return.

"I have a question to ask you."

"Ask away, then. I've got to put Sammy back into his stroller anyway."

"Okay." He took a deep breath of the fresh mountain air and hoped desperately the words forming in the back of his throat came out in English and not in some alien language.

Stalling, he crouched down to stroller level and kissed Sammy on the cheek. He was feather soft and smelled so sweet and clean. Christopher had a feeling it was going to be difficult to walk away from the little nipper, even for a day.

"We're off," she said brightly, turning the stroller around.

"Wait!" His heart hammered double time.

She turned toward him, looking mildly annoyed.

"Marry me."

Jasmine's jaw dropped, and she struggled for a good minute to wipe the stunned look from her face. "Excuse me?"

"That didn't come out right," he said, color rising on his face. "I'm sorry, Jasmine. You deserve a marriage proposal with all the trimmings, but under the circumstances, I thought it best to bring up the subject now. Best for Sammy, I mean. And…er…us."

She sat down on the cold grass, not trusting her weak knees to hold her weight. Her insides felt like gelatin. Marry Christopher?

She pulled her knees up to her chest and wrapped her arms tightly around them, as if she might fall apart were she to loosen. She wanted to marry him—it was what she'd always wanted. That was what made the moment so difficult. What she wanted didn't matter.

"Give me one good reason I should marry you," she snapped, deciding to take the offensive.

He crouched down to her level, hat in hand. "I can give you two," he said, his voice low and strong. "Number one, Sammy."

"Sammy?" she repeated dumbly. She didn't know what she expected Christopher to say, but it certainly wasn't to start off discussing his—*their* son.

She shook herself mentally. What else would he be talking about? Surely not love. "What about Sammy?" she asked suspiciously.

"He needs a family."

"He *has* a family. *Me.*"

"I won't dispute that, Jasmine. I've seen today what a good mother you are to Sammy. Great, actually. But doesn't Sammy deserve a home with both a mother and a father present?"

She remained silent, feeling his argument weighing her down like a cement block on her feet. She wanted to bolt from the scene and from Christopher's logic, but instead simply set her jaw and tightened the hold on her legs.

"Don't you see?" he continued, softly pleading. "I can give Sammy a name. I can give him security. I can be a good male role model for him. And most of all, I can point him to his Heavenly Father by being a good father on Earth."

Jasmine shut her eyes, unable and unwilling to meet his persuasive stare.

"I'll do right by him. By both of you. And Jasmine—"

She opened her eyes then, to find Christopher's face only inches from her own. He was looking at her with such love and passion that she couldn't mistake his meaning.

He crooked his adorable grin and Jasmine felt her heart do a loop-de-loop. Why couldn't she resist him? She should, but when he was this close to her, all she could think about was holding him near to her and never letting him go again.

"The second reason our marriage is a good idea is because I love you. I always have, and if you search your heart, I think you'll discover that truth for yourself."

He was speaking the words she wanted to hear. But he was also presumptuously speaking of their marriage as if it were a fact. She embraced the anger that welled in her chest, finding it much easier to deal with that emotion than the frightened tremor of a cornered animal.

There were too many questions, facts Christopher was elusive on or flatly refused to discuss. It was time to throw the ball back at him in spades. "Okay."

"Okay?" He tipped off balance and landed hard on one knee on the frozen ground. "Yee-haw!"

Jasmine cleared her throat. "But before you throw your hat in the air and start celebrating, you might want to hear the conditions to this agreement."

He smacked a big kiss on her lips and stood, anxiously shifting from foot to foot. She stood as well, dusting off her backside and cringing at the feel of ice on her jeans. She'd been so steamed up she hadn't realized until this moment how cold the ground was.

She glanced at Sammy, afraid it was getting too cold for the baby, but he was sleeping soundly, his head tilted awkwardly to one side, his breath coming in little white puffs. It calmed her heart just to look at him.

"Honey, I'll do anything for you and Sammy. Just ask."

"Then tell me the truth. I know why you married Jenny, but why did you abandon her? How do I know you won't do the same thing to me?"

His scowl darkened. He looked like a man frozen in ice.

She nodded. "I thought not," she drawled acerbically. "What else could I have expected?"

"You could admit your love for me," he countered. "You could follow your heart for a change, instead of rationalizing everything."

"Oh, like how a man runs out on his wife? That's a tough

one to rationalize, Christopher.'' Inside, her heart was breaking, but she was cool and crisp on the outside.

It was happening again, the betrayal, the utter abandonment she felt when she'd first learned about Christopher and Jenny. The pain felt every bit as fresh and new as it had way back then. Only now she stood to lose Christopher a second time, and with him, Sammy.

Christopher was Sammy's blood relative. His father. She wasn't sure, but was afraid the courts would find in his favor. It was a blessing, really, that he hadn't already filed a law suit. Instead, he'd come up with the ridiculous notion that marrying her would solve everyone's problems.

Well, it would only add to hers. ''Then I guess the answer is no,'' she said, surprised at how even and stable her voice sounded.

Christopher clenched his fists, fighting desperately to control the anger and hurt warring inside him. He couldn't tell her why he left. ''Why can't you just love me enough to trust me regardless of the way things look?''

He saw her wince, and reached out to hold her, only to withdraw again when she pierced him with a glare.

''How dare you lay this on my shoulders?'' she snarled through gritted teeth.

Because I love you, and I think you love me. He was about to answer when he was interrupted by a man's low bass calling Jasmine by name.

Jasmine whirled around, relief evident in her expression. Christopher broke his gaze away from her, seeking the man that could bring such happiness to her features. He felt his insides crunch as she launched herself into the big African-American man's arms.

''Marcus!'' she shouted merrily. ''I'm so glad you've come.''

Christopher didn't see why she had to be quite so jubilant, unless she was just putting on a show for his benefit. He'd startled her with his sudden proposal, and he knew it. But she didn't have to hang on the man just to make a point.

Marcus kissed her firmly on the mouth, and she joined in

his low laughter. He swung her around as if she weighed nothing, then gently placed her back on her feet.

Christopher scowled. Marcus. He'd heard this name before. He searched the recesses of his mind for the occasion.

Of course. Marcus White. Her friend from college. But what was he doing here?

And what was he doing kissing Jasmine?

Chapter Ten

"You arrived just in the nick of time, you knight in shining armor, you," she teased, giving Marcus one more affectionate squeeze before releasing him.

He chuckled, a sound that echoed from the depths of his barrel chest. "You need saving, fair damsel?"

"Call me distressed," she promptly replied.

"And I suppose the man with the stroller glaring daggers at me would be your Christopher?"

"He's not—" she began, but Marcus cut her off with a look.

"Save it for someone who'll believe you."

Jasmine made a face. "I forget how well you know me."

He wrapped an arm around her waist. "Are you going to introduce me, or do I wait until he knocks my block off first?"

They walked arm and arm to where Christopher was standing, scowling at Marcus and rocking Sammy in his arms.

"Marcus, I'd like you to meet Christopher Jordan," Jasmine said shakily.

"And who's this little fellow?" Marcus reached for Sammy as if he held babies every day, causing Christopher's scowl to darken even more.

Jasmine knew there was going to be an eruption the size of Mount Saint Helens if she didn't avert a disaster here and now. She laid a hand on Christopher's arm and said, "That's our baby, Sammy."

Marcus started so abruptly he almost dropped the baby. "But that's impossible," he muttered under his breath.

Christopher relaxed his posture and reached for the baby. "Nope. This is my son. Say hello to the man, Sammy," he said in a high, tight voice. He waved the baby's pudgy little arm at Marcus.

Jasmine laughed at the astonished look Marcus flashed her. *I'll explain later,* she said with her gaze. He nodded imperceptibly.

"Christopher, I really do need to get Sammy indoors."

He eyed Marcus again, then held the baby to his chest. "I can take him for a couple of hours if you want to—" he stopped and ran his tongue slowly over his bottom lip, eyeing Marcus with distaste "—renew old friendships," he concluded, his voice low and coarse. "I'll drop him at Gram's apartment in a couple of hours."

Jasmine didn't know what to feel, never mind what to say. Christopher obviously loved Sammy, but could he be trusted to care for the boy? What if he ran off and she never found him again? She couldn't bear the thought of losing both of them.

But she couldn't very well confine him, big ox that he was. And even if she could, freedom was a rare commodity. She felt God nudging her to trust Him, and to trust Christopher.

"The stroller converts to a car seat," she said, standing on tiptoe to give Sammy a kiss. When she moved away, Christopher took her elbow and drew her back, brushing a gentle kiss across her lips.

His eyes met hers, and they were gleaming with joy and relief. "Thank you," he whispered for her ears only. "I won't let you—or Sammy—down."

She believed him. Despite his past and the web of mystery still entangling them, she believed him, and her heart was at peace.

"Be sure and buckle him in real tight. Oh—and there's a diaper bag stuffed underneath the seat of the stroller. You should have everything you need—formula, bottles, diapers.

You do know how to change a diaper, don't you?'' she asked half in teasing and half in distress.

He smiled down at her, his eyes twinkling affectionately. ''Think I can handle it.''

His mouth straightened to a firm, thin line as he nodded grimly at the other man. ''Marcus.'' He turned away and put Sammy in the stroller, then straightened. ''Take good care of my lady.''

Jasmine's heart nearly bolted right out of her chest. *His* lady? It gave her shivers just to think about it, but she didn't let herself smile. Instead, she attempted to look every bit as grim as Christopher. ''I can take care of myself.''

Marcus burst into low laughter. ''You got that right, girl.''

Christopher just shrugged, indicating his frustration, and stalked off in the other direction, pushing the stroller ahead of him.

Jasmine turned to Marcus. ''You, dear friend, are a lifesaver.''

''Sweet as candy, you mean?''

She chuckled. ''Oh, you!''

''Well, whatever else I am, color me confused. I haven't the slightest idea what just happened over here, but I can tell you one thing—one and one aren't adding up to three, if you know what I mean.''

''I told you it's a long story. Things have gotten rather confusing.''

After filling him in on the past three months, Jasmine sighed. ''I've missed you, Marcus.''

He settled an arm on her shoulder. ''Missed you, too, girl. I have this peaceful feeling inside me like this is really where God wants me to be.''

''I hope so. I need you.''

''I'm here in the flesh, girl. Now you just tell ol' Marcus what he can do for you.''

''Well...'' she begin, then hesitated. ''You can't wave a magic wand and wipe the past away, nor can you wipe *my* slate clean, so let's try helping me keep the town clinic run-

ning. It's turned out to be more than I can handle with a
baby.''

"I'm not surprised.''

"Yes, well, Gram helps out as much as she can, of course,
but she has her own physical limitations to worry about.''

"You're living with your Gram?''

"Yes. She was gracious enough to take me in. Nags me
incessantly about taking care of myself. She'll be glad to hear
you're here to lend me a hand.''

"Hand, foot, eyeball. Whatever you need.''

"Gross!''

"Sorry. Male humor.''

She rolled her eyes. "That's something I don't think I'll
ever get used to. Christopher always comes up with the most
outrageous—'' She cut her words off abruptly, mortified by
what she'd said.

Marcus hadn't missed her hesitance, for he squeezed her
shoulder lightly. "What are you going to do about him?''

For some reason, Jasmine wanted to break out into bitter
laughter. She remained silent as her emotions warred within
her, guilt, bitterness, anxiety, anger, pain, grief. She closed
her eyes and felt herself weave against Marcus.

He tightened his hold on her. "Question of the day?'' he
asked seriously.

"I guess.'' She took a deep breath of the crisp mountain
air and let it cleanse her insides. "Christopher—asked me to
marry him just before you got here today.''

"Really?'' Marcus ran his free hand across his jaw. "No
wonder he was glaring at me, poor man. What did I do, interrupt the romantic moment?''

"Oh, no, quite the opposite, in fact.''

He cocked an eyebrow.

"I was trying to figure out how to gracefully disappear off
the planet after I declined his offer.''

Marcus dropped his arm from her shoulder and whirled her
around to face him. "Girl, you continue to astound me! The
guy you moped around med school for asks you to be his
wife, and what do you do? Say no.''

"It's a little more complicated than that."

"Don't you let a little jealousy get in your way. If Christopher was a big enough deal to mourn about for a year, he's a big enough deal to marry."

"I'm *not* jealous," she denied, even as butterflies of envy fluttered through her stomach.

"Seems like a perfect solution to me. Christopher is Sammy's biological father, and you are his adoptive mother. Christopher loves you, you love him and everyone loves the little tyke. Talk about your fairy-tale endings."

"Don't I wish." Jasmine paused, trying to figure out how to phrase her next statement. "Christopher abandoned Jenny, Marcus. Before the baby was born."

"*Abandoned* her?" He brought up a fist and shook it as if threatening an intruder. "Why, I'd like to—"

"We all did. And he was such a good Christian, too."

"Good Christians don't knock a girl up and then abandon her."

"This one did."

"Then why did he come back?"

Jasmine sighed. "I've been asking myself that for days now. Naturally I'd assumed he'd walked away from his faith, but he hasn't, Marcus. I can feel it in my heart."

"Then what?" His voice, a deep bass to begin with, dropped another octave, and he scrubbed a hand across the short, tight curls of his hair.

"I don't know. And every time I ask, he clams up like a soldier at Buckingham Palace. All he says is that I need to trust him. Oooh!" she exclaimed, releasing her pent-up frustration. "I think I'm getting a headache."

"That's what you get for trying to think," he teased, attempting to lighten the mood.

"How would you know?" she rejoined, glad to back off from the subject of her life. She'd rather not think about it at all, much less talk about it.

"Do you trust him?" Marcus asked, breaking into her thoughts.

She met his gaze. "I don't know. Right now, my heart is saying one thing and my head is saying another."

"Then wait," he said, grinning to show a full, straight line of shiny white teeth that were enhanced by the dark features of his face. "You'll know when the time is right to act. God will put your heart and your mind in one accord, probably in some incredibly amazing way. All you have to do is wait."

Chapter Eleven

"*What now, Lord?*" Christopher whispered, tucking Sammy's head under his chin. "Where do I go from here?"

He'd spent his two hours with Sammy just rocking him in his arms. His little cabin on the Walters's ranch wasn't exactly secluded, what with all the other ranch hands living in similar quarters all around him. But cozy was just right for the afternoon with his son. He fed him a bottle and even changed a diaper. He'd done well for his first try at diaper duty, even if he did say so himself.

Sure, he put it on backwards the first time, but he quickly realized his mistake and had everything in the right place in no time flat. And no one could accuse him of making the same mistake twice.

He wished Jasmine could have been there to see. Then, perhaps, she would see what a great father he wanted to be. He'd be a great husband, too, but that would be harder to prove. Especially since she'd turned him down flat.

How could he walk away? This baby was as much a part of him as if he *were* the biological father. Sammy was his responsibility. But he was also his son.

Marrying Jasmine had seemed the obvious answer to everything. They could be together, and he could be with Sammy. And it *was* best for Sammy.

Darn the stubborn, mule-headed female race, one woman in particular. Why couldn't she trust him, look past his actions and into his heart?

And to think that this whole blinking mess got started because he was trying to help her sister, thinking that's what Jasmine would want him to do. Remind him never to attempt to read a woman's mind.

So, what was the next step? Somehow, he had to make Jasmine see reason. He had to make her see what a good husband and father he'd be.

Or else he needed to show Jasmine what her life would be like if he and Sammy weren't in it.

He stroked his chin and pondered the thought. It could work. Jolt her so she spoke with her heart and not her head. Whether she was ready to admit it or not, she was meant for him. He, Jasmine and Sammy were meant to be a family. He felt it in the very core of his being.

He tried to focus and pray, but he was too jittery, unable to sit still. He laid Sammy in the middle of his king-size waterbed, placing pillows on either side of him to keep him from rolling off.

"Sleep well, son," he whispered, kissing Sammy's forehead. "Daddy's home."

He paced the halls for another hour, trying out one scheme in his head and replacing it with the next. By the time the clock struck five, he had a mental wastepaper basket full of shredded ideas.

Glancing at the clock, he felt his shoulders tighten. Jasmine would be expecting him to return Sammy any time now. Well, she'd just have to wait. The boy was sleeping, and Christopher wasn't about to wake him up. He'd wait until the boy woke on his own.

Or at least that was the excuse he gave mentally. Deep down, he was glad he'd be a few minutes late. Maybe missing Sammy would give her time to think. Think about what life without him and the baby would be like. Maybe she'd meet him at the door with open arms and welcome him into her heart and home. And maybe his tennis shoes would sprout wings and fly.

She'd no doubt think he'd up and run off with the kid. His jaw tensed. He'd actually considered it. For at least a millisecond. How could he not, with the possibility of being torn from his son forever lingering on the horizon?

But he wasn't a fool. Running away would be the absolute worst thing he could do. Jasmine already didn't trust him because of the last time he'd left Westcliffe. And the fact that then, as it would be if he left now, there had not been a single moment where his soul didn't long for Westcliffe and to return to Jasmine's side, wouldn't hold much weight with her.

If he ran, it would be with the thought of eventually reconciling with Jasmine. But if he ran, reconciliation could never happen. So he had to find another way.

There *was* another way. It came to him clearly and quietly, a way to startle Jasmine into searching her heart for the truth. She'd mentioned it herself the first night he was back.

It was difficult to consider the option, but what other choice did he have? He had to do something to shock her. And this was going to make Jasmine fighting mad.

"Where is he?" Jasmine demanded for the tenth time in as many minutes. She peered through the front window shade, watching the parking lot below for lights or movement.

Marcus was stretched out on Gram's sofa, snoring quietly. Gram was sitting in a rocking chair, sipping at a cup of hot tea.

"You're sure you knew what you were doing when you let him take Sammy?" Gram asked, her voice scratchy. She often coughed at night.

"Of course I knew what I was doing!" she snapped, then grimaced. "Or at least I thought I did. What's taking him so long? Do you suppose they got in an accident?"

"He's probably just enjoying time with his son, Jasmine," Gram said gently. "It's their first time alone with each other. Don't rush them. Besides, you should be enjoying this time off baby duty. It's going to be nice to have another parent around."

"He sure swung you over to his side in a hurry," she commented acerbically.

"I wasn't aware there were sides," Gram snapped back, every bit as brittle.

Jasmine sighed. Even she had to admit the sides were getting a little gray around the edges.

"Why don't you grab a cup of tea and sit down? We haven't had a good chat in ages."

Jasmine did as she said, feeling more relaxed just holding her steaming cup of tea.

"That Marcus fellow is certainly nice," Gram said in a transparent attempt to change the subject.

"Yes. He's a good friend. It was really great of him to agree to help me out at the clinic. I hope you don't mind his crashing here overnight until he can find a place to live."

"I'm always open to entertaining strangers," Gram agreed quickly. "You never know when you're going to offer your hospitality to an angel."

Jasmine laughed. "Marcus is a real sweetheart, but he's hardly an angel. He'd be the first one to tell you that. But I'll concede he's prayed me out of more than one pinch. His faith in God is strong."

"Is that the only reason you invited him?"

Jasmine stiffened. "If you mean do I have feelings for Marcus, no. At least, not in that way. We are dear friends, and that's all we will ever be. He knows how I feel about—" She wasn't about to finish *that* loaded statement.

"Christopher," Gram concluded for her.

She winced, folding her hands in her lap to keep them from shaking. Gram would notice her anxiety in a moment if she wasn't careful to hide it from her.

"But that wasn't what I was asking. It appears to me you might use Marcus to hide behind so you don't have to deal with said *problem*."

Jasmine didn't fail to notice how Gram avoided speaking Christopher's name a second time. "I'd never do that to Marcus!"

"Maybe not intentionally, honey, but it would be easy to do without even meaning to."

"I don't think so."

"Think about it. You and Marcus are close. It would be easy to give Christopher the opinion you were more than friends, without ever letting on to Marcus what you were doing."

"What are you getting at, Gram? Are you trying to plot me a way to get rid of Christopher for good?"

"No, of course not. I'm just trying to point out what might happen. You're bound to get hurt. You could lose Christopher *and* Marcus."

"I don't *have* Christopher," she denied, her mind freezing on the first part of Gram's statement.

Gram cocked a silver eyebrow. "No? I've got news for you, sweetheart. That man loves you within an inch of his life."

"I don't see what difference that makes." Gram of all people knew how impossible the situation was.

"It's your call, Jasmine. I just want you to remember the Lord's admonition to forgive. Christopher has done a lot of bad things. But he's back now, and it looks to me like he's trying to atone for his sins."

"I don't know what that means to me."

"Give yourself time. God will help you work it out."

She had God to help her work it out. That was a comfort, anyway. She'd been praying and reading the Scriptures every day since she'd made a commitment to walk in His steps. He'd been opening her heart to considering new paths.

It was part of the reason her feelings about Christopher were so contrary. And another of the many reasons she could not even consider marrying Christopher at this point.

"I've been feeling restless lately," she admitted quietly.

Gram nodded.

"I always thought the only thing I wanted in the world was to become a doctor and move back to Westcliffe. I wanted to be a country doctor, taking care of the people I've known all their lives. I wanted to bring all my high school friends' babies into the world. I've never even considered any other path. But lately..."

"You've discovered there's more to life than just your career."

"Yes, for starters. I'm sure you remember how much a newborn baby changes your world. I view everything as a mother now, not just a woman. Family means more to me than I expected."

"Enough to give up your career?"

"No. I don't think I could ever give up being a doctor, at least in some capacity."

"Dr. Mom," Gram teased.

"I don't think that's quite enough," she said, laughing. Tears followed close behind the laughter, for no reason she could fathom. "I'm a small-town girl who is strongly tied to her roots. I love the Wet Mountain Valley, the beautiful mountain range. History runs through the town like Main Street itself. Two years ago, I was pining for home, thinking that once I was back I would never want to leave Westcliffe again."

"Come here, love," Gram whispered, opening her arms.

Feeling like a young, frightened girl again, Jasmine knelt before her grandmother and laid her head against the old woman's breast. She closed her eyes, inhaling the powdery scent that was distinctly Gram, and losing herself in the gentle caress of Gram's hand on her hair.

"I think God's calling me somewhere else," she admitted, reaching for a tissue.

"Any place in particular?"

She wiped her tears away, her mind wandering to the missionary information packets she'd been studying in every bit of her spare time. "I think I'm going to take Sammy and go to Ecuador."

She expected Gram to be surprised, but she just nodded like a sage old owl.

"Why do I get the feeling you already knew this?"

"I didn't know where. I just knew. Why Ecuador? Are you going down as a doctor?"

"There's a hospital in Quito. And I already know Spanish.

I learned it in college and used it a lot in Denver at the hospital.''

"I'm glad you're seeking God again, Jasmine.''

She smiled through her tears. "Me, too. But I'm scared to death to be stepping out in faith.''

"He's ahead of you, on the left and right of you, and behind you as well. He's your fortress, and a twenty-four-hour-a-day watch guard. Rest in Him.''

"I will, Gram.'' She blew out a breath. "Whew. It sure is nice to have that off my chest. I do worry about you being here all alone.''

"I'm not alone. God is here. And I have lots of friends in this town. I was born here, you know.''

And I'll die here. The words were left unsaid, but hovered in the air anyway, putting a damper on Jasmine's rising mood. She made a mental note to explain Gram's situation to Marcus when she talked to him, so he would look in on her regularly.

That is, when she had that big, long, unavoidable heart-to-heart talk with Marcus. The mere thought of it made her stomach cramp. What would he say when he learned she was prepping him to replace her rather than just help her out?

Her thoughts were interrupted by the doorbell. She jumped to her feet and lit to the door like someone had set her tail on fire. Behind her, she was aware that Gram had stopped rocking, and that Marcus was wearily rousing himself on the couch.

No one said a word, but she knew they'd all thought the same thing. Deep down under layers of reassurance was the lingering doubt that Christopher might have been planning to steal Sammy away all along, and she had conveniently handed the baby right into his hands.

"Christopher,'' she announced loudly as she swung open the door, her hands shaking with relief. Her heart wanted to burst with happiness when she saw him and the baby, but instead, she scowled. "You're late.''

"Sorry, Mom,'' he replied, tipping his hat back and giving her that toe-curling grin of his. Her heart was hopeless to resist his physical presence, but her mind was pressing for answers.

"This is where you come into the house, remove Sammy from his seat and give me a really good excuse why you thought it was okay to worry me half to death."

"I had you worried?"

"A figure of speech, I assure you."

Gram burst into laughter, but when they both turned to her, she was looking away out the window and humming softly to herself.

"The little nipper was sleeping," he offered, unbuckling the straps on the baby carrier and lifting Sammy out of the seat. He kissed the baby's cheek and handed him to Jasmine.

Her heart immediately settled now that Sammy was back in her arms. He was a perfect fit. His sweet, baby scent was pleasant to her nose, and his happy squeal music to her ears. She really was becoming a mother.

She didn't feel quite whole without him any more. And maybe just a little of it had to do with Christopher being here with her as well.

"Were you giving your daddy a hard time?" she asked Sammy, who bounced and kicked in her arms.

"Da!" he said, then, pleased with himself, said it again. "Da!"

Christopher whooped in delight. "Did you hear that? My baby boy just called me Dad!" He thrust his chest out like a rooster and strutted around the room. "How 'bout that? Sammy's first word is *Daddy*."

He couldn't have been grinning any wider, Jasmine thought, somehow irritated, feeling as if she'd been betrayed. Of course the baby didn't know what he was saying, and she'd be hearing *Mommy, Mommy* soon enough. Still…

He pulled his hat off his head and rolled the brim in his fists. "Will you walk me out to the porch?" He glanced covertly at Gram and Marcus.

She stared at him wide-eyed for a moment, then nodded slowly. "As long as you promise this won't be a repeat of this afternoon. I can't handle that yet."

"Oh, it's definitely not a repeat of this afternoon," he muttered under his breath.

"In that case, let me give Sammy to Gram and I'll be right there."

He nodded and planted his hat on his head, sauntering out to the porch. He took deep breaths to try to slow his heartbeat. It was downright cold once the sun went down. He could see his own breath coming in white puffs of mist, and the breeze nipped the skin on his face despite his five o'clock shadow.

She appeared suddenly, and immediately wrapped her arms around herself against the cold. Christopher wished he'd thought to remind her to bring a coat out with her.

"I won't be long," he promised.

"Um, okay," she said, looking perplexed. Her bottom jaw was starting to shiver. She looked small, defenseless and entirely adorable.

He put his hands on her shoulders and rubbed down her arms to help restore the circulation. Then he lightly swept his fingers back up her shoulders and cupped her face in his hands. He brushed a light kiss on her forehead, her nose, her lips, her jaw.

Then he took a deep breath and plunged ahead. "I can't live without my son, Jazz," he began.

"I don't expect you to."

"But you won't marry me."

She stiffened in his embrace. "You promised you wouldn't ask me that. I can't think about it right now."

"I wasn't asking, just stating facts. I know you feel it's more than you can handle right now, but it really is the best thing for everyone concerned."

"I asked you not to talk about it anymore," she snapped, turning away and staring off toward the shadowy, jagged outline of the Sangres.

He moved up behind her, putting an arm around the front of her shoulders and drawing her firmly against his chest.

She stiffened in his arms, but didn't try to move away.

"Can you really not trust me?" he asked, his voice husky. "Isn't it enough that I've returned?"

"No. And no. You've given me no reason to trust you, and how am I supposed to know whether or not you are staying for good?"

He *wouldn't* be staying in Westcliffe for good. It was part of what held him up from returning for Jasmine and Sammy. But now wasn't the time.

"What if I told you leaving was something I had to do, that it wasn't meant to hurt anyone? And that the reasons are, at this point, beyond explanation?"

"In other words, you plain just don't want to tell me. You don't trust me, but you want me to trust you. To be your wife." She turned in his arms until they were face-to-face. She looked up at him, confusion rampant in her deep green eyes.

He wanted to forget his intentions and kiss Jasmine like he did in the old days, when they dated in high school.

But he was a man now, and the kiss he would give her would be a man's kiss. It was far too dangerous to risk. His self-control was thread thin as it was. And he had an agenda tonight.

Cupping her hips, he pushed her back a step. She stroked a hand down his face and sighed. "Don't you see, Christopher? I can't marry you with secrets between us. A husband and wife are one. They should share their lives in every way, and that includes trusting the other enough to tell the truth."

Her voice cracked and she stopped, nibbling on her full bottom lip as she considered what to say next. "If you believe I love you, then you've got to know that whatever dark things are in your past, I can hear them. I can forgive you. And I'll go on loving you."

It was incredibly tempting just to blurt out the truth and have it done with. He more than anyone was sick to death of keeping secrets. If it would be like Jasmine said, he'd willingly divulge the whole agonizing truth.

If she loved him and forgiveness was real, she'd understand why he'd kept silent, and would join in his silence to keep Jenny's memory untarnished and Sammy's reputation pure.

There would be no more bitterness between them. They'd marry and raise a big family, with Sammy as their eldest son.

But it wouldn't happen that way. Anger would overwhelm the lesser sentiments, and then Jasmine wouldn't allow him to see Sammy at all. If he told the whole truth, she'd have ample authority for making it so Christopher never saw Sammy again.

And that, he could not risk. It wouldn't be right. He owed it to Sammy to keep the truth to himself. More important, he loved the boy.

"I can't tell you, Jazz. I'm sorry, but I can't."

"Then it appears this conversation is over. I'm freezing out here, anyway. Good night, Christopher." She ducked under his arm and started toward the door.

"Wait!" he called, reaching for her elbow to stop her. "If you won't accept my marriage proposal, what are we going to do about Sammy?"

"Sammy?" she asked, looking perplexed. "Oh, I see. You mean can you see him again?"

Christopher nodded.

"You've proven yourself, as far as I'm concerned. We'll make plans for you to see him on a regular basis. Every other weekend or something."

His jaw dropped, then he clamped it shut. He was good enough to see Sammy every other weekend? What was this, some kind of contest or something, and Sammy was the door prize?

"Why don't you go out and buy yourself some baby furniture? You can use my car seat-stroller, but you'll need a crib, some baby blankets, diapers and a few toys."

She sounded so detached, too clinical. He yanked his hat off and slapped it angrily against his thigh. "I'm afraid every other weekend isn't good enough for me."

"What's that supposed to mean?" she snapped, sounding alarmed.

"It means if you won't marry me, I'm taking you to court for full custody of Sammy."

Chapter Twelve

The cabin was cold and empty when Christopher returned. He poked at the ashes inside the wood stove in the corner and got some kindling ignited, then slumped into his large easy chair and spent ten minutes staring blankly at the television and channel surfing with no real heart.

He was bluffing, and he was more afraid than he'd ever been in his life.

The whole thing was nothing but a ruse to catch Jasmine off guard. It had as much chance of failure as success—the act of a desperate man.

He looked around at the cabin and snorted in disgust. This place wasn't fit for anyone, much less a tiny baby. Besides, it wasn't his. He couldn't even imagine what the Walters would have to say about it if he brought a baby on their land.

He supposed he could look for something else, except he really wasn't looking for something more permanent. Because he wasn't going to be staying in Westcliffe.

Now, however, it looked as if he *would* be staying, at least until he could prove to Jasmine his heart hadn't changed, that he wasn't the scoundrel of a man who walked out on her sister. He was still the man she had once loved and to whom she'd pledged herself.

He wasn't leaving without Jasmine. And if that meant another six months or another six years, then so be it. God's timing was better than his, he knew, but he was impatient.

He'd played his ace. Now all he could do was sit back and

see if he won the hand. This was Dead Man's Draw, winner take all.

The irony of it was the secret he was carrying was the reason he *couldn't* take Jasmine to court for custody of Sammy. There, under oath, he would have to tell the world that he was not Sammy's father. And even if he lied, which he wouldn't do under oath, the paternity test they'd no doubt make him take would be just as revealing, probably more so.

And in Westcliffe, real news was scarce. They were sure to make the front page of the newspaper, maybe even as far as Pueblo. And Sammy would become a public entity.

He couldn't let that happen. He *wouldn't* let that happen. Bart Pembarton hadn't been man enough to own up to what he'd done, to do the right thing, marry Jenny and claim his son—not when Mommy and Daddy might object. And object they did, when Christopher confronted them with the facts after Bart's death. Bart's parents had warned Christopher not to let Sammy become a public entity. He sensed their threats were real. No matter what, Christopher had to protect Sammy.

Without realizing where his thoughts were heading, the night of Bart's death replayed in his mind, as clearly as if it had happened yesterday. It was a hot, damp night in Pueblo, and he'd been working on duty as part of his EMT training.

They'd been called to the scene of a fatal traffic accident. The wreckage was a once shiny BMW lodged between a light pole and a building, as if the driver had been attempting to drive on the sidewalk.

There were no drugs or alcohol involved, and the fatal accident remained shrouded in mystery. But the driver had been the man in Jenny's photo. Why had Bart crashed his car?

Christopher's stomach knotted. He'd made a decision to forgive the man for getting Jenny pregnant. It was a conscious struggle to make that decision truth. He still got angry just thinking about it. But forgiveness, he reminded himself, was an act of the will. His feelings would eventually fade, and God would help him through.

Responsibility definitely hadn't been Bart's middle name.

Of course he hadn't wanted a child to slow down his jet-set life-style, especially with his parents holding the purse strings.

The Pembartons might have money, but money wasn't what a child needed most in life. Only he and Jasmine could give Sammy the home he deserved. He knew he couldn't do it alone. The picture wasn't complete until Jasmine was in it, binding their hearts together as one.

Which is why he'd taken so great a risk in announcing he was taking her to court. The last thing he wanted to do was hurt her, and he knew his words had hurt her. But it couldn't be helped. He'd tried affection, now he hoped intimidation would work.

If it didn't, he was in a world of trouble. He clenched and unclenched his fists, wanting to punch something just because it was there.

He was a man of action, and he'd just relegated himself to sitting back and waiting for Jasmine to come to him. All he could do was pray she'd want to talk about a compromise, which would give him another chance to convince her marrying him was the best solution.

If only he didn't hate waiting so much.

"Oooh! That lousy, no-good, rotten—" Jasmine vented, stomping across the floor and back again. "If he thinks he can intimidate me, he has another think coming."

Marcus grinned up at her from the kitchen table, where he was eating a big bowl of oatmeal. "You were so quiet last night, I knew there was something wrong."

"I didn't want Gram to worry. But Marcus, what he did to me last night was like a slap in the face."

He chuckled, a low, deep sound from his chest. "You haven't exactly let the cat out of the bag yet, girl. What exactly did he do?"

"He said he's suing for full custody of Sammy."

"He wants *full* custody? He wants to take Sammy away from you?" he said quietly, in wonder. Then he took her firmly by the shoulders and reassured her with the strength of his gaze. "You've got rights, Jasmine. And friends who will fight tooth and nail to keep Sammy with you. Myself being first and foremost, of course.''

"I know." She sighed wearily. It had been a long, sleepless night, fighting emotions that ranged from passionate, self-righteous ire to fear and apprehension such as she'd seldom known before.

She'd spent at least an hour raging in her own fury before it occurred to her the best thing to do was to seek a Higher Authority in the matter.

She'd sought God on her knees, begging for His interference in her cause. She knew that God, more than anyone on this earth, understood what it meant to be separated from His Son.

She'd pondered through the middle of the night on the incredible mercy and love of a God who would give His own Son to die in her place. What sacrifice Jesus made for her, to come down from heaven and be made a Man. And His Father willed Him to go.

She knew she was not that strong. She couldn't give Sammy up, not even to Christopher, who she knew would love and care for the baby.

She prayed for peace, and she prayed for answers. But by morning she'd still not been able to come up with any long-term solutions to the problem, short of running away and changing her name as she'd seen ladies on television crime shows do.

Would she be a hunted woman? Would Christopher put the FBI on her case? Her mind had raced with the possibilities, and the questions answered themselves.

She couldn't force Sammy to live that way, living hand to mouth and always looking behind her for shadows. It wouldn't be fair to him. She had to find another way to fight Christopher and keep Sammy.

"Are you taking me to the clinic today?" Marcus asked, cutting off her thoughts.

"Actually, today would be perfect. I'll show you around and get you settled. This afternoon I've really got to try to hook up with one of those charity organizations in Pueblo so they can come by Jenny's bungalow and pick up all her things.''

Marcus nodded, but didn't comment.

''I hate to be leaving you on your own on your first day, but the county nurse will be there, and being such a small town, the receptionist is very knowledgeable.''

''No problem. Relax.''

''Of course, I'll be wearing my pager, and I always have my cell phone with me, if you have a problem.''

He barreled out a deep, hearty laugh. ''Will you *relax?* I've been alone in a clinic before. I think I can handle it. Besides, I'm getting kinda fond of this country living.''

''You've only been here a day.''

''Fondness grows quickly. I feel like I'm home here in Westcliffe, with its horses and hayfields. Funny for a man born and raised in the ghetto, I guess. But I can't help it. This place just feels right to me. Like I could put down roots here. It'd be a great place to raise children,'' he concluded, with a pointed look at Jasmine and a sly grin.

She was relieved to hear it, more than he could possibly know. That Marcus might want to stay on as the doctor for this town was looking like more and more of a possibility.

And if that happened, she'd have the freedom she desired to pursue the new dreams God had given her. If she could work things out with Christopher and Sammy. At the moment she was bound hand and foot.

She had three choices. She could run, but she'd already ruled that one out. She could go to court, but with Christopher's paternity proven, she had the sinking feeling he'd get Sammy in a heartbeat, no matter what she said on the witness stand.

The other option, and the one that galled her to the core of her being, was that she could go back to Christopher and beg. Beg for time with Sammy, even if it were just every other weekend, as she had suggested Christopher do.

For a moment, she found herself in his shoes, only able to see their son once every two weeks, and then for only a couple of days at a time. It was no wonder he'd said it wasn't good enough. If he felt even half the agony that she did at the thought, his heart was being ripped out of his chest in little pieces.

It startled her to have put herself so much in Christopher's position, and she immediately shut down her thoughts and emotions on the subject. Her only desire and responsibility was to see she kept Sammy, whatever the cost.

"You look like that famous thinker statue guy. The de-e-e-ep thinker," he said in an exaggerated tone. "Keep that up and you're going to make your headache worse."

"Are you ready to go down to the clinic?" she asked, her voice sounding annoyed despite her best efforts.

"Not thinking about Christopher won't make him go away," Marcus said gently. "Eventually you are going to have to face him again and try to work this out."

"That may be," she snapped, seething in frustration. "But I don't have to think about him, talk about him or most especially talk *to* him, today. I would appreciate it if you didn't bring his name up again."

"Hey, girl, whatever you say," he replied easily, ignoring her tone. "I think we ought to get to the clinic right away. Do you think I might be able to search out a place to live after work?"

"Well, sure. The clinic closes at three today."

"I'm looking to buy, Jasmine. I hope that doesn't alarm you."

"On the contrary, I'm very pleased."

He opened the front door and gestured her through. "After you, Dr. Enderlin." She'd been called a doctor since the beginning of her internship, but suddenly the title felt too tight, as if it were strangling her.

Funny how something she had worked so hard for and been so single-minded about could feel so awkward and uncomfortable to her now.

Well, no matter. She loved being a doctor. At least *that* hadn't changed. She'd just discovered there was a big, scary world out there and shades of gray all over the place.

"Jasmine? Are you coming?" Marcus asked in his soft, low voice.

Jasmine. At this point it was all she could do just to be Jasmine, never mind mother, doctor, friend. And now Christopher was asking her to be his wife. She wanted to scream in frustration.

That is, if he still wanted her as his wife. Taking her to court was a pretty drastic move in the opposite direction. But she wouldn't think about that now, she reminded herself again.

Today, she would just be Jasmine. Okay, and Dr. Enderlin, at least for the afternoon.

As it turned out, Jasmine wasn't able to contact a charity group in Pueblo as she'd planned. An avalanche at the nearby ski resort kept Marcus and her busy well into the night, tending to major wounds, X-raying broken appendages and arranging for helicopter flights and ambulances for those who needed to be hospitalized.

Days flew by as Jasmine made rounds, introducing Marcus and caring for the less serious injuries. It seemed to Jasmine that at least a third of the town had been skiing that day, though she was certain she was overestimating.

Her real surprise was in Marcus. She already knew he was a fine doctor with a heart for the people, but she was truly amazed at how well everyone had taken to him. She'd heard compliment after compliment from those healed by his medical expertise.

He was so patient with the children, kind to the elderly and straightforward when a patient needed to hear something about their recovery. More than once she'd just hovered in the background and watched him work his magic on others.

Marcus found a house, and because it was vacant, the closing went quickly. At the end of the first week, he'd moved into his new home.

By the end of the second week, Jasmine was physically and mentally exhausted. The only good thing was that she hadn't had time to think about Christopher. She checked on baby

Sammy during her lunch hour and tried to spend time with him in the evening, but more often than not she fell asleep on the rocking chair with a wiggling, bouncing Sammy in her arms.

Marcus insisted that she take a week off. The clinic had slowed down to a dull roar, and she needed time to recuperate so she could be at her best for Sammy.

She didn't even argue, which was very unlike her. Instead, she went to bed and slept for two days, rising only to eat and care for Sammy. Gram assured her everything was under control and that Jasmine should rest before she became ill.

It wasn't until after her extended session of sleep that she felt ready to face the world again, and the first order of business was finding a charity to take care of Jenny's things. After arranging for one to come that afternoon, she put a sandwich together and took off for Jenny's bungalow.

As always, the smell was the first thing that caught her when she entered the house. Jenny's smell. She wondered why a house would have the owner's smell about it once the owner was gone. She didn't notice any smell in her own house. She wondered if others did, and if so, what kind of smell hers was.

Jenny's was light and breezy, just as Jasmine remembered her personality as being. But then she remembered the newspaper photograph.

The newspaper photograph! What had she done with it? Her hand flew instinctively to her left breast pocket, where she vaguely remembered placing it. But of course it wasn't there now, since she wasn't wearing the same clothes.

What *had* she been wearing? She strained to remember. She'd worn her grubbies that day, which meant...

The jeans with the holes in the knees. A black T-shirt. And...

Her red plaid flannel shirt. That was it. The photograph was in the pocket of her red plaid flannel shirt. Except, where *was* her flannel shirt?

She leaned against a wall and slid slowly to the floor, cupping her face in her hands. How could she have been so stupid as to lose the picture?

She was overreacting, she knew. It was just a lousy newspaper photograph, and not even one that showed Jenny in her best light. But for some reason, it was important to Jasmine, a part of Jenny that she wanted to keep.

Odd as it seemed, she felt it must have meant something special to her sister, being locked up in her nightstand as it was. She could just picture Jenny carefully unlocking the drawer and pulling out the picture, staring at it with the glassy-eyed look of someone in love, and then hugging it close to her heart with a sigh.

She threw her head back until it was touching the wall, and it was there that she spotted her red plaid flannel shirt. Jasmine broke into strained laughter. Here she was getting all stressed about a shirt that had been right in front of her nose all along. Now that she'd noticed it, she remembered getting warm— more by Christopher's gaze than the heat in the house—and shedding her flannel to work in her T-shirt.

The doorbell rang, and Jasmine jumped, putting a hand to her chest to still her racing heart. Why was it every time the doorbell rang in this place she jumped out of her skin? She'd be glad when this was over and she could sell the bungalow. The strain of Jenny's death was getting to her again.

She welcomed the charity people in, gesturing at the boxes to be taken. When one of the men picked up the apple box with her personal items in it, Jasmine reacted immediately.

"Wait," she exclaimed. "I'm sorry. That one's mine. I apologize. I meant to get it out to my car before you gentlemen got here."

The trucker, a boy in his late teens, grinned and handed the box to her. "Sure thing, ma'am. No problem."

She took the box and turned away from him before she scowled. She hated when people called her *ma'am*. It made her feel like her grandmother. And this young man was no exception.

Where did that come from, she wondered as she packed the box in the back of her four-by-four. She shook her head.

It wasn't as if she were an old maid or anything. Lots of people established themselves in their careers before they married and settled down, didn't they?

Besides, she'd already had two bona fide offers of marriage, right? Okay, so both were from Christopher. But still... She tipped her chin in the air and marched back into the house, determined not to let it bother her.

"This is yours, miss?" the other trucker, a middle-aged man with jocular features asked, waving her flannel shirt. *Miss.* Now that was *much* better. She smiled widely. "Oh yes, that's mine."

She heard the crumple of newspaper as she took the shirt. The men would be there for a while loading the truck, she decided, and it would be best to stay out of their way.

She found an out-of-the-way corner where she could watch them without fearing they would trip over her, and sat down cross-legged on the floor. Gingerly, she felt for the pocket and pulled the newspaper clipping from it.

It was crumpled. She laid it against her thigh and smoothed out the wrinkles with the palm of her hand. The same proud man stared at her, and there was Jenny with her arms thrown around him and a silly grin lighting her face.

But there was love in her eyes as she looked at that man. Jasmine had no doubt of it now. Jenny had found true love, the way she had with Christopher.

Probably no one but a sister would notice. And it did make her wonder about Jenny's relationships before Christopher. The man in the picture obviously had money. It was odd that Jenny would settle for a penniless, small-town cowboy, even a guy as wonderful as Christopher.

Her skin tingled at the thought, and she shook her head. Back to the man in the picture. He was blond, buff, and, if the look on his face was anything to go on, conceited as all get-out.

She read the caption, searching for his name. "Barton Pembarton III," she read aloud, as snooty and regal as a butler announcing a guest.

She glanced back at the picture. "Barton Pembarton III

enjoying a Valentine's Day cruise with his yacht *Celebration* on the Pueblo reservoir.''

Of course, no mention of Jenny. She wasn't media material, even in a skimpy bathing suit. Jasmine wondered how Jenny had taken that slight, or if she'd even noticed. Perhaps she was used to playing second fiddle to the rich playboys she hung out with.

Jasmine, that's not fair! she chastised herself. She didn't know for a fact Jenny led that sort of life-style. She was the last one who should be judging another on circumstantial evidence, especially her sister.

She tucked her thoughts away with difficulty and returned her attention to the truckers. The men were finished with the boxes and bid her farewell on their way out.

There was a strange mixture of sadness and relief swirling through her chest at finally putting an end to all that was Jenny. It was almost as if she were being forced to say good-bye once again. She clutched the newspaper clipping to her heart.

The house was so empty and barren, devoid of life. Even the boxes had given it some sense of humanity. But now there was nothing. Nothing except herself and the photograph she held in her hand.

Chapter Thirteen

Jasmine glanced at it one last time, intending to tuck it into her wallet when she was through. She stared at Jenny for a long time, then ran her fingers over the caption.

Suddenly she noticed the date in the upper right corner of the clipping. *It was dated last year!*

Last year. Last Valentine's Day. But how could that be? She was with Christopher by then, carrying his child. Jasmine was a doctor—the math involved in pregnancy came naturally to her.

Sammy was born in early October, and he was two weeks overdue. That put his conception somewhere square in the middle of January. Which meant what?

She stared at the newspaper clipping in disbelief. Had Jenny been two-timing Christopher with this Barton What's-his-name? Christopher appeared to stiffen a little when he'd seen the photograph, but not nearly enough for her to believe he'd just discovered he'd been cuckolded.

He was a proud man. Whatever else he would do, he wouldn't accept his future wife out *playing* with another man. Besides, why would any woman want to cheat on Christopher? He was the most gallant, loving man a woman could want.

She swallowed hard, trying not to think of Jenny in Christopher's arms. She'd conquered her anger, but the stab of pain that accompanied any thought of those two together would never go away. Some wounds even time couldn't heal.

Jasmine turned her mind back to the puzzle at hand. Okay, so Jenny was pregnant with Christopher's baby and was hanging around with Bart. Where was Christopher?

She struggled to recall exactly when she'd learned about Christopher and Jenny's impending nuptials. She closed her eyes, trying to remember what she'd been doing when she heard the news.

Maternity. She'd been serving on the ward, learning first-hand how to bring new life into the world. And dreaming every time the miracle of birth happened of her own children, the ones she would have with Christopher.

Okay, technically, they weren't speaking to one another. And she was dating Richard, a radiology intern. But deep in her soul, there was only Christopher, and she knew she was kidding herself to believe otherwise. Richard was a nice, sweet guy, and that was it. It was only pique and pride that kept her from apologizing to Christopher and making things right.

She'd just finished a twelve-hour shift and was getting ready to drop into bed when her phone rang. Groggily, she answered, only to find Mrs. Rulitter jabbering something about Christopher getting married and was Jasmine going to be able to make it back to town for the wedding day, short notice as it was, and all?

A dazed Jasmine had pulled the handset away from her ear and stared at it, bemused. Of course Christopher was getting married. To her. But it wouldn't be until after she was finished with her internship here in Denver. And anyway, it was highly unlikely she'd miss her own wedding.

Mrs. Rulitter was spouting nonsense. She was on the verge of telling meddlesome gossip so when she heard something else on the line. The constant chatter hadn't ceased. Apparently Mrs. Rulitter wasn't even aware she didn't have an audience.

Somewhere in the prattle, she'd heard her sister's name. Jasmine pulled the phone back to her ear and cleared her throat loudly. When Mrs. Rulitter didn't take the hint, she resorted to rudeness.

"I don't mean to interrupt you, Mrs. R., but I'm afraid I missed what you said about Jenny. Is she in some kind of trouble?"

She couldn't imagine what her sweet sister could have done to have become the object of town gossip. Whatever it was, though, it was good and juicy enough to warrant Mrs. Rulitter's long-distance call.

"Has she asked you to be her maid of honor?" Mrs. Rulitter answered a question with a question.

"Maid of honor!" she exclaimed. *"Jenny is getting married?"*

"Of course. That's what I've been telling you. Jenny and Christopher are going to tie the knot in a month's time. Shotgun wedding, if the gossip—er, news—I've gotten has the least inkling of truth. Can't say I blame the girl. It's tough when you've got a good-looking cowboy like Christopher."

Jasmine's head was spinning, and she sat down hard on the bed.

"Shotgun wedding," Jasmine repeated dully, her extremities going numb. Now she was not so much afraid of passing out as simply turning into sludge and melting into the sheets.

That meant a baby. Jenny was having a baby?

Christopher's *baby.*

She tried to breathe, but couldn't. *"Are you sure about this?"* she squeaked through a dry throat when she could speak again.

"Sure as shootin'," Mrs. Rulitter promptly replied. *"Jenny probably hasn't asked you to be maid of honor yet because of—well, you know, your past with Christopher. Bless me, I thought you and he were gonna tie the knot. You sure were little lovers in high school. Oh well, I'm sure you both grew up and grew out of each other. Happens all the time."*

Grow away from Christopher? Her every thought, at least in her free time and often at work, was about Christopher. But of course, that was how it must look to an outsider.

It was almost laughable, if her stomach didn't hurt so much. Jenny was bubbly and flighty. She'd drive calm, cool Christopher mad in a day. And as far as Jenny was concerned, *surely she considered Christopher as more of an older brother than a love interest.*

Lines were crossed somewhere. That was all there was to it. She'd make a simple phone call to Gram's apartment, and it would all be straightened out in a heartbeat.

Or else she'd pinch herself and wake up. This was more like a nightmare than reality. Christopher and Jenny. What a laugh!

Or was it? Her mind flashed back to the night before. She'd just come in from a date with Richard when the phone rang. A glance at the call display screen on her telephone warned her the call was from Christopher.

Annoyed, she'd handed the phone to Richard and requested he answer, knowing that would bother Christopher more than any futile argument. Looking back, she recognized how juvenile it was, and felt a moment of regret.

It appeared his call had been much more serious than she could have imagined. Had he called her to tell her he was getting married?

With shaky fingers, she punched the numbers on the keypad. She hoped Gram would answer. At least she would be straightforward. Gram always told the truth, no matter if it hurt.

The phone rang, then rang again. Finally, a light, tenor voice answered on the other end of the line. She might have thought she had the wrong number, but she recognized that voice instantly, and intimately.

Christopher.

She cleared her throat, suddenly flustered. Why was Christopher at Gram's house? Talking to him was even worse than trying to sort it out with Jenny.

She blew out a breath, hoping he couldn't hear how shaky it sounded. "Hi, Christopher. It's me."

"Jasmine!"

Under usual circumstances, she would have thought he was excited to hear from her. But what she heard in his voice was shock and alarm.

So it was true. Suddenly Jasmine knew, without his having

to say the words. Their souls had been connected for so long she could even tell long distance what he was feeling.

"I understand I'm to wish you happiness," she said, trying but not succeeding in masking the bitterness lacing her tone.

She heard his deep intake of breath. "Jazz, I—"

She cut him off. "Save your breath, pal. Let me talk to Jenny."

"I tried to call you. I was going to drive up but—"

"Frankly, I don't really want to hear. Will you get Jenny for me, please?" she asked, annoyed that she couldn't keep her voice from shaking.

She'd heard Christopher curse as he put the phone down. He never cursed, and Jasmine felt a perverse pleasure in driving him to it. It was the least he deserved.

Jenny picked up the receiver, exuberant. "Oh, Jasmine, I'm going to have a baby!"

Nothing about Christopher, only the baby.

"So I heard," she said dryly. "When?"

"Well, Chris just took me to the doctor in Pueblo this morning. He says the baby is doing great, and I should expect her in early October. They did an ultrasound, and I got to see her little heart beating."

Jasmine had cringed at the use of Christopher's name. In elementary school, he'd given anyone who called him Chris a black eye. She'd always thought of him as her Christopher. But Jenny had broken all the rules.

"You know it's a girl already?"

"Well, no. Not really. I'm only ten weeks along. The ultrasound technician said she wouldn't be able to tell me the sex of the baby for sure until she was much bigger. And if it is a girl, they might not be able to tell me at all. Little boys are easier to spot," she concluded, giggling.

After that came the quick calculation. How long had they been seeing each other behind her back? It was Saint Patrick's Day, so Jenny had been seeing him for at least two months, probably much longer, since they were intimate.

Christopher simply wouldn't pressure a woman on the first date. He'd never pressured her at all. Maybe Jenny had pres-

sured him. But in any case, they'd been seeing each other awhile.

Yet he'd been with her, Jasmine, during the Christmas holiday, which meant he'd been lying to her. The time they'd spent together was a hoax. He'd probably been with Jenny all along, right behind her back.

She'd felt as if gravity had tripled, pulling her whole body down into the earth.

Jenny had filled the silence with her babbling. "Can't you just see Chris bouncing all those curls and pearls on his knee? Or teaching his little girl to dance? He's going to be the greatest daddy in the world."

She'd paused and waited for Jasmine to answer her questions. As if Jasmine hadn't pictured Christopher as a father a million times.

"This is okay with you, isn't it? I mean about Chris and me?"

Jasmine gasped for air, but her throat was closed.

"He said it would be. That you'd understand. I really hope you'll wish me happiness, Jasmine. It means a lot to me. And of course I want you to be my maid of honor at the wedding."

A maid of honor. When she should have been the bride! she felt her head spin, and nausea was coming in waves. "Yes, of course. Congratulations. Unfortunately, I'm calling long distance, so I won't be able to stay on the line. And I have a class in just a few minutes, anyway. Goodbye, Jenny."

Jasmine had clanked down the phone in the receiver, grimacing at her lie. She had no class to go to. She was done for the day. She just couldn't stand to listen to the sound of Jenny's happy voice while she was in such agony. She lifted a prayer to God, asking Him to forgive her. She hadn't known what else to say.

She sank down beside the bed, seeking heavenly comfort. Only God could help her now. She'd been so exhausted when she first came into her room, but now she wasn't sure she'd ever sleep again.

After what had seemed like hours of praying and crying out to God, she'd dozed off, still on her knees.

* * *

Jasmine awoke with a start. The little bungalow was shrouded in darkness. Feeling displaced, she wrapped her arms around herself and took deep breaths.

She rolled to her knees, exclaiming as the cramped muscles in her neck, arms and thighs made themselves known in spiked bursts of pain.

Her voice echoed in the small room, making her feel even more alone. Something crunched under her left knee. Her newspaper clipping! She carefully set the clipping aside, then continued her slow, laborious crawl to the other side of the room. She reached the door and barely missed smacking her head against the solid oak before she reached the light panel. She flicked the switch, flooding the room with bright, cheery light.

Jasmine breathed a sigh of relief. She wasn't afraid of the dark, or of being alone, but the light was certainly welcoming to frighten away her dark thoughts. The day her own dreams died. A day she'd never forget.

March 17! Of course. That's what she'd been trying to remember. She dashed back across the room and snatched up the newspaper clipping.

She pieced it together in her mind, bit by bit, trying to create a timeline that made sense.

Sometime in early January, Jenny gets pregnant.

February 14, Jenny is seen on Barton the Snob's boat. At least he looked like a snob. She's clearly in love with him, or at least is making cow eyes at him.

March 17, she's engaged to Christopher.

She hadn't learned about the engagement all that long after it happened. Jenny had assured her they'd only made the decision to marry the night before. She went over the facts again. There was something she was missing. Jenny had cancer. Did she know of her illness at that point? Was she trying to live it up as much as possible before her death, even if she made Christopher suffer?

And Christopher—did he know about Jenny's illness? Is that why he allowed her to play around with another man?

He wasn't the type of man to sit around blindly ignoring the obvious while he was being cuckolded.

Or...

Jasmine's thought was so astounding she felt as if her entire body had been pricked with thousands of pins and needles. Her blood pressure skyrocketed.

Or Sammy was not Christopher's son at all.

It made sense. Jenny and Bart. The thought was enough to make her cringe. Could Sammy's biological father be Barton Pembarton III?

She cringed, and her stomach swirled. That possibility was far worse than Christopher sleeping with Jenny, though that, too, must have been, or else why would he have married her?

The questions collided in her head like bumper cars. None of it made any sense, and yet it did. Too much so. And if Bart *was* Sammy's biological father, that created the possibility, however slight, of *his* claiming the boy, a thought that chilled Jasmine right to the core.

She shook her head, astonished. Things weren't anything like they appeared, and for every answer she concocted there arose five or six new questions. Like why wasn't Bart in the picture now, if Sammy was his son?

Bart's son. That meant Christopher *couldn't* pursue custody of Sammy in court. He had no right if he couldn't prove his paternity. That he was married to Jenny would mean nothing, especially in light of his past behavior in running out on his wife and unborn baby. They'd surely ask him to take blood tests or whatever it was they did to check for DNA. And if the court didn't order it, she would, knowing what she now knew.

And if she could disprove Christopher, she would be free and clear to claim Sammy as her own. She'd work off the assumption that Bart didn't want anything to do with his son, or that he didn't know about him in the first place. She wasn't sure what was ethical in this situation, but she'd work that out later.

For now, she needed to find out the truth. And the one person who could tell her what really happened was Christopher. It was time to pay the man a visit and lay it all on the line.

The more she thought about it, the more she believed she was right, despite the nagging doubt that Christopher wouldn't take her to court in a custody battle if he wasn't absolutely certain he was the father of the child.

Well, there was only one way to find out. Confronting him would only save her the time and effort of having to go to court to make Sammy her son, if her hunch was correct. Sammy's adoption could proceed as scheduled, and her life could go on as well.

She refused to consider that life wouldn't truly go on without Christopher. She loved him, and she always would. It was more than likely she'd never marry. How could she, with Christopher always on her mind?

But she didn't have to be married to have a full life, did she? She had Sammy, and she had an exciting missionary vision she believed God had placed in her heart. Surely she could be happy with that. The question was, what to do now? She had to take *some* kind of action.

There was no way Christopher would continue this mad ploy to take her to court for custody if he discovered she knew the truth about him. About Sammy. No wonder he was so closemouthed about the whole thing.

She wondered again why he would take her to court when he wasn't the biological father. He had to know they'd demand a paternity test, and he'd be disproved in front of everyone.

Which meant, if everything she suspected was true, all his huffing and puffing about taking her to court was nothing more than a worthless threat.

The realization hit her like a bullet in the chest. Why that foul, no-good beast of a man! He wasn't really trying to take her to court to take Sammy away from her. That had *never* been his intention. He was bullying her into accepting his marriage proposal! It made perfect sense and explained nearly all his actions over the past month, save why he left Jenny after marrying her. *That* he still needed to explain.

And if he thought his little ploy to get her to tie the knot was going to work, he had another think coming. He was probably sitting around right this minute waiting for her to come begging for mercy.

Oh, she'd fulfill his wishes all right. She wasn't even going to wait until morning to pay that man a visit. But boy would he be surprised when she showed up at his door and cut the line to his threat like a snip with a pair of scissors.

She was out the door, her car key in her hand, when a thought occurred to her, one that put the brakes on her anger and sent her head spinning again.

If Christopher wasn't Sammy's father, why did he call him his son? And why did he want the baby boy as his own?

Chapter Fourteen

Christopher was tired of waiting.

He clamped his freshly shaved jaw closed as he pulled his left boot on, then his right. It was time for action. He'd considered and discarded a number of scenarios before settling on one. The right one. And the toughest.

He was going to tell Jasmine the truth. He stared at himself in the mirror, scowling at the man he'd become. A man of secrets. And what were secrets but lies left unspoken?

He should have told her the truth in its entirety the moment he'd crossed the town line into Westcliffe. No, that wasn't right. He should have driven up to Denver the second he and Jenny made their plans.

He *should* have talked to Jasmine before he made any plans at all.

He swiped a hand down his face and turned away from the mirror. A million *should-haves* wouldn't mend his broken world. He had to deal with the way things were now. And right now he had an irate, stubborn, wonderful woman on his hands that he couldn't decide whether to shake silly for being so headstrong or kiss thoroughly just for being herself.

He hoped for the opportunity to kiss her again. Over and over for the rest of their lives. But come what may, he couldn't keep up this ridiculous ruse and sit around waiting for her to come meekly and mildly offering to compromise.

He knew it wasn't Jasmine's style. He should have known it wasn't *his*. He'd spent the better part of the afternoon praying, asking forgiveness for his deception and for strength to reveal the truth to Jasmine when the time came.

He stuffed his cowboy hat on his head by the crown and adjusted the brim with his fingers. Now was that time. And it wasn't getting any easier by putting it off.

His mouth set in a grim, determined line, he opened his front door, then stepped back with a muffled exclamation of surprise.

"Jasmine!"

"Christopher." She was dressed in black jeans and a fringed western shirt. A small gold cross, set with a tiny diamond in the center, was the only jewelry she wore. Her long, shiny black hair was pulled back from her face with a clip, exposing her firm jaw and determined eyes.

If he didn't know better, he'd think he was looking at his reflection in a mirror. Jaw set, eyes sparking with stubborn pride and resolve, shoulders squared with purpose.

"Going somewhere?" she asked, gesturing to his hat.

"Er, yes. I mean, no. Actually, I was going to see you."

"You were?"

She looked every bit as flustered as he felt.

"Would you like to come in? The place isn't much to look at, but it's a roof over my head and walls to keep out the cold," he rambled, suddenly overaware of his humble surroundings.

"Not a problem," she said, shedding her coat and draping it across his armchair. She seated herself on the floor near the woodstove.

"Okay," he said, recovering slowly. He shut the door and tipped his hat off his head, returning it to the rack behind the door where he usually hung it.

He wondered where he should sit. If he sat in his armchair, he'd be sitting above her. Same with his desk chair. It might give him a slight mental advantage, but he wasn't sure that kind of advantage was what he wanted tonight. Then again, he was a gawky jumble of long arms and legs sitting on the floor.

But at least then he'd be face-to-face with Jasmine. He sat on the floor.

Actually, he stretched out right in front of her and propped his head on his hand, like he would have in the old days. With only a single lamp for lighting, it was dark, comfortable. Intimate.

"So..." Jasmine began, then stopped.

"So..." he repeated, feeling suddenly nervous.

"Did you want to go first?"

He swallowed hard. Did he? He probably should. She might have come to ask for compromise, which would be unnecessary once he'd spoken. But how did a man start such a conversation?

It was going to be a long night. Maybe he should offer her some coffee or something.

He took a deep breath and opened his mouth to do just that when she jumped in and beat him to the punch line.

"I could use some coffee." She gestured to a worn aluminum coffee percolator sitting cockeyed on the woodstove. "Is this the pot you use for coffee? You don't happen to have a microwave, do you? I don't much have experience with cooking on a woodstove. I'm a modern woman, if you know what I mean."

She was babbling, a sure sign that she was nervous. Christopher grinned inwardly and reached for the pot. "Now, don't you go fussin' over this here coffee," he said in his best imitation of John Wayne. "Why, this is the way the old cowboys used to make it. Threw the grounds right in to brew, they did."

She made a face, indicating she didn't believe him for one moment. She still knew him that well, at least.

"It'll put hair on your chest," he drawled, laughing when her mouth dropped open.

"Oh. Now *there's* something I need," she said, laughing. "A furry chest."

Christopher felt himself blush to the roots of his chest hair. He coughed and made a bee-line for the door, unable even to come up with another line of conversation that would put the old one to rest.

Excusing himself, Christopher stepped outside to the pump and filled the pot with fresh spring water, then filled the aluminum cup with coffee from the barrel on the porch. Settling the lid on top, he took a deep breath.

Thankfully, she didn't follow him out, and he had a few moments to collect his thoughts and clear his head. He was going to be the first to reveal what was in his heart. It was imperative he be thinking about what to say, but Jasmine's presence made it excessively difficult for him to think of anything besides how much he loved her, how he wanted to take her into his arms and never let her go again.

It had startled him immensely when she'd shown up at his door at the very moment he was leaving to see her. But he had to admit in some ways it made what he had to do easier, in the privacy of his little cabin where they wouldn't be disturbed.

And she couldn't kick him out if she got mad at him, he thought dryly. He chuckled, creating a puff of mist in the night air.

When he could stall no longer, he picked up the pot and returned to the cabin. She was seated where he'd left her, her arms wrapped around her knees as she stared vacantly at the warm glow of the woodstove.

Seeing her there, her gorgeous black hair gleaming like silk in the dim light, he once again wondered how things could have gotten so far out of control.

He loved this woman with every beat of his heart. And he sensed that her feelings for him hadn't died, no matter how well she attempted to mask them with other emotions. He'd always been able to read her gaze, and he'd caught glimmers of what used to be in her eyes, especially recently.

But her eyes were shaded as they turned to look at him. Shaded, and angry. He wondered how her mood could have switched in the time he'd been outside, but he was afraid to ask.

Instead, he put the coffeepot to boil on the stove and seated himself on his desk chair. "Are you sure you wouldn't be more comfortable sitting on the armchair?" he inquired gently.

"No, thank you."

They sounded like strangers. It was enough to make Christopher want to pound something, but instead he leaned forward with his elbows braced on his knees, clenching his fists behind his forearms so Jasmine couldn't see.

She wanted him to go first, and go first he would. "I needed to see you today, Jasmine, because—"

"Wait!" She stood abruptly and began to pace the small room. "I don't want to hear it. All you've ever told me about what happened between you and Jenny are lies."

He shook his head in vehement denial, but she held up her hands in protest when he tried to speak.

"Half-truths then. You're hiding something, Christopher Jordan, and I've come here tonight to find out what."

"Jasmine, if you'd let me explain," he interrupted, biting off his frustration before he lost his temper. What was with her tonight, anyway? She wanted answers to her questions, answers he was finally ready to give, but she wouldn't let him get a word in edgewise.

It was almost as if she were subconsciously trying to avoid hearing what he had to say.

"Are you going to tell me the truth, or aren't you?" she demanded, looking down at him with her arms braced on her hips.

"I'm *trying* to tell you," he snapped back, standing to tower over her. "*If* you'd let me speak."

Her sparking green eyes widened slightly, then narrowed upon him. She was not the least bit intimidated by his greater height.

"Good," she said firmly, reaching up and caressing his jaw with the palm of her hand, gently bringing his head down until his face was mere inches from hers. He closed his eyes, savoring the feel of her gentle fingers.

"Since you're in the mood to talk," she whispered, still

stroking the line of his jaw, "Why don't you start with the fact that you're not Sammy's biological father."

Jasmine wouldn't have gotten such a strong reaction if she'd slapped him hard in the face. And in that moment, she knew that her theory was, indeed, fact. Christopher *wasn't* Sammy's biological father.

She'd come here with the intention of confronting him and being done with it. But she certainly hadn't meant for things to happen as they did. He'd stepped out to get water for the coffee, and she'd sat inside and stewed. It was a nervous reaction to coming face-to-face with him when he'd returned. He was standing over her, near enough to touch, his broad shoulders like a shelter. It had taken all her strength not to step into the haven of his arms. As it was, she couldn't help herself from touching his face, running her fingers across his clean-shaven jaw.

His cologne, a western scent, was strong, wreaking havoc on her senses. She'd almost succumbed to the love she still felt beating strong in her heart.

And then she remembered the impassable wall between them, the wall created by Jenny. And Sammy.

She'd just blurted out what she knew with no warning, no warming up to the subject.

Christopher had exhaled as if someone had sucker punched him and whirled away from her, raking his hands through the tips of his short brown hair. He stood facing away from her, and she could see his hands trembling.

"I see you're not denying that you really aren't Sammy's biological father."

"How long have you known?" he asked, his strained voice a good octave lower than his usual smooth tenor.

"I only began suspecting it this afternoon. I didn't know for sure until this moment." In an instinctive move borne of love, she stepped forward and reached out for him, stopping just short of touching him.

"I guess you're really laughing now, aren't you? I played my trump card and lost everything."

He sounded so genuinely miserable that Jasmine flinched.

What he said was true, but she knew she had put some of that agony in his voice. Oh, *why* hadn't she gone home and spent the night praying before blustering up here like a misguided whirlwind?

She muttered a quiet prayer for God's help to untangle the entire mess once and for all. Then she reached up and gently placed her hands on his shoulders. "I'm sorry, Christopher," she whispered, her voice cracking. "I shouldn't have blurted it out that way. I've hurt you."

He stepped away from her touch and turned to face her. Instead of the tortured expression she expected to see on his face, she found him scowling so darkly she took an instinctive step backward.

"Don't apologize, Jazz. I've had it coming for a long time. I'm not surprised that you loathe me."

"I don't—" she began, but he cut her off.

"It's time for you to hear the whole story. It isn't pretty. But it's time you knew the truth."

Jasmine sighed. "Well, at least we agree on one thing."

He led her to the easy chair and bade her sit. Reluctantly, she did, and he knelt before her. It felt too much like a knight paying homage to his queen for Jasmine's tastes. She would have preferred to be on an equal level. She tried to move onto the floor, but he wouldn't let her.

He took her hand and turned it over, palm up, staring at it so fiercely it was almost as if he were trying to find the answer to their dilemma in the lines of her palm.

"I'm asking for forgiveness, Jasmine, though I don't expect you'll be able to give it right away. I want you to—" his voice cracked and he paused, swallowing hard "—to be able to put this episode behind you. To go on with your life and…find happiness."

This sounded like a eulogy. Jasmine's heart sank. She'd been so angry. She still was. But even so, she wasn't sure she was ready to say goodbye to Christopher forever.

God was calling her to missionary work in Ecuador. She'd have to say goodbye to Christopher one way or another. But it just didn't feel right.

"Go on," she said at last, when he didn't continue.

"I also want you to know I never meant to hurt you."

She lifted an eyebrow. That was pushing things a little bit. He had, after all, dumped her for her sister and then—but no, Sammy wasn't his baby.

"It might not seem that way now."

She nodded, barely restraining a bitter laugh. Lately she'd discovered nothing was as it appeared.

"I told you how Jenny called me one night, asking me to come to dinner with her and Gram. Gram wasn't there, and Jenny was a wreck."

Jasmine pictured the scene in her mind. "I remember. You said she was throwing things."

"Yes. She was hysterical. Completely beside herself. But Jasmine," he said, his voice low and earnest, "that night—it was the night I tried to call you and that guy answered."

"What?" she shrieked, then clapped a hand over her mouth. "I thought—"

"That the night in question had been much earlier. Otherwise, how could I have been Sammy's father?"

"But you're not..."

"Exactly. Anyway, to continue the story, I calmed her down and we watched a movie. After the movie, Jenny was herself again. She told me the real reason she invited me over. She needed help. She—" Again he cut off his sentence.

"She was pregnant with Barton Pembarton the Third's baby," Jasmine concluded, the scene coming clear in her mind. "She'd tried to call me, but I wasn't home. I remember the message on my machine, now. It said to call her right away, but I was pulling an all-nighter."

She had closed her eyes as she pieced the facts together, but snapped them open when Christopher's hands closed firmly on her arms.

"How did you know?" he asked in amazement.

"How did I know what?" She was having trouble following him, steeped as she was in chronologizing the facts.

"Know Pembarton's name?"

"The newspaper clipping we found in the drawer. Remember?"

"Yeah. That's the first time I'd ever seen what he looked like." He clenched his hands. "Man I'd have loved to give him a piece of my mind."

Jasmine chuckled. "You'll have to stand in line. I expect there's a number of people in that category."

"When Jenny told him about the baby he refused to acknowledge it."

"What?" Jasmine stood. "Why, that—"

"That's not the worst of it." Still on his knees, Christopher reached for her hands and drew her down beside him on the floor. "He told her he was engaged to marry a Denver socialite. His parents' choice for his bride."

"Poor Jenny," Jasmine whispered.

"Well, you can understand why she was so upset." He looked away. "And she'd learned she had cancer and didn't have long to live. I didn't even know what to say."

"I can imagine."

"I was her sister's boyfriend. I felt so awkward even discussing such private issues. But she was hurt, and needed to talk."

"Is that what she wanted you to do?"

"Yes. She already loved her baby, and despite everything, loved the baby's father. It was her family she was worried about—the stigma of her having a child out of wedlock."

"She should have known we'd all stand by her and support her."

"Yes, but Westcliffe is a small town. Things like illegitimate children are remembered forever. It isn't like Denver where single moms are the norm and a person can just fade into the background."

"That still doesn't explain how you and she ended together," she reminded him, bracing herself for the answer she'd been waiting so long to hear but in truth was afraid to know. "Or why."

"I thought it was the right thing to do, that God had placed

me where He did for that reason," he said with a bitter laugh.
"I thought it's what *you* would have wanted me to do."

"Marry my sister and not tell me about it?" she snapped,
the old hurt rising to the surface. He'd known about Jenny's
cancer. "Where did you get a cockeyed idea like that one?"

He blew out a breath and looked away. "I meant to tell
you everything." Suddenly he stood and pulled on his jeans
to straighten them. "Coffee's ready. You still want some?"

"I guess." She looked away from him. Coffee didn't even
sound good anymore.

He returned with two steaming mugs and handed her one
before sitting back down. He propped one arm on the seat of
the easy chair and sighed. "Jenny was more concerned for
you and Gram than she was about her own reputation. And
of course, she worried about the baby."

Jasmine drew in a loud breath. Of course Jenny would think
of Sammy first. Hadn't she been that way the whole time she
was pregnant?

Christopher continued. "She didn't know what to do. She
was just talking it all out, really, trying to come up with a
feasible solution that wouldn't hurt anyone."

Her breath froze in her chest. Did they really think their
actions wouldn't hurt anyone? Did they not consider the ache
ripping through her heart when they planned all this?

But of course, Jenny had sacrificed so much more. She'd
given her life for her baby. Who knew but that chemotherapy
would have prolonged her life, perhaps even saved it?

Jenny hadn't so much as mentioned her cancer to Jasmine.
Did she fear Jasmine might try to change her mind? But how,
how could she have believed it would be okay to marry Christopher?

"I was the one who convinced her," he said, answering
her unspoken question. "She wanted nothing to do with it,
not knowing what you'd say, how you'd feel. But I knew
you'd understand, so I talked her into it."

"You knew I'd understand," she repeated dumbly, wondering why everyone else in the world presumed to know what she would think and feel when she couldn't even figure that out herself.

"She was young, alone and scared. And pregnant. If we announced our engagement, everyone would just assume the baby was mine. He'd have a name, and he'd have my protection."

He paused and made a fist. "Bart Pembarton was a weak, irresponsible boy, still tied to his mother's apron strings. I wouldn't let him near someone I care for, much less a baby. Jenny knew it as well."

"Then why was she with him?" Jasmine blurted angrily. "Where was her head, Christopher, for her to go and get pregnant by someone like Bart?"

He pinned her with a glare. "That's exactly what the town would have said. Don't you see that?" She was shocked into silence.

"He's dead now, so the point is moot."

He didn't say how Bart had died, and Jasmine didn't think to ask. The news only added to the depth of her wounds. Poor Jenny. She'd been so fortunate that a man like Christopher would come into her life when he did, would offer her the solace of his name and take on the burden of her illegitimate child.

"That explains who, what, where and why," she said, ticking the list off on her fingers. "But there's one thing you haven't answered."

He lifted an eyebrow.

"How were you planning to handle *me? Oh, Jasmine, by the way, I decided to marry your sister instead of you?* Only you never got a chance, did you? Because dear old Mrs. Rulitter thought she should be the one to break the news to me."

"Oh, come on, Jazz," he snapped, his face flushing. "Give me a break, here. I'm sorry you had to hear it that way. But that's not how I meant it to be. You know I tried to reach you."

Jasmine stood and crossed her arms to stave off the chill settling in her heart. She was trying to understand, she really was. But the sense of betrayal that she'd been struggling to tamp down just wouldn't stay put. It bubbled up in jealous swirls all around her insides.

"Tell me then, Christopher, how it was supposed to be."

"Yeah, well, think about this, Jasmine. What if you had been there that night? What if you had picked up the phone and heard Jenny wailing on the other end? What if she had told *you* her story. What would you have suggested she do?"

The air seemed to get thicker in the room. Her mind raced for a pithy answer, or even a serious one, but nothing came.

"Yeah, that's what I thought," he drawled. "It was the only thing I could think of. And it would have worked. If things hadn't gotten out of hand so fast."

"Meaning if I hadn't found out the way I did."

"Well, yeah, sure, that's what I mean. I tried to tell you. But obviously, I didn't succeed," he finished miserably.

"Just for curiosity's sake, what were you planning to say? Were you just going to break things off with me and leave me dangling?"

"Of course not!" he nearly shouted, then looked away. "I was going to explain everything. You were supposed to see how heroic I was being, and how perfectly everything would turn out. I mean—" he cleared his throat "—as perfect as things could be, under the circumstances."

"In spite of the fact Jenny was dying."

"You're still not seeing the whole picture, are you?" he demanded, thrusting his fingers through his hair.

"Evidently not," she said wryly. "I haven't quite figured out how I was supposed to play into all this. Or whether I was just supposed to fade out of the picture completely," she added on a pique.

"You were supposed to marry me, you mule-headed woman!" he stormed. He stalked across the room and leaned one arm against the wall.

She laughed out loud, but it was a dry, bitter sound. "Oh, I see. You were going to be a bigamist. That surprises me. Somehow I always pictured you as a one-woman kind of guy."

"I am," he declared, the passion of his statement making

his neck redden. He was by her side so quickly she didn't even see him move before he swept her into his arms and kissed her firmly and thoroughly.

She was breathless by the time he raised his head. His eyes were glowing with conquest. Her heartbeat roared in her ears, and she thought if he let her go, she might well fall to the floor.

Never in all their years together had Christopher kissed her with such strength and passion. To her surprise, she wanted more. If he leaned down and kissed her again, she wouldn't so much as mew a protest.

But he didn't kiss her. He gently pushed her away and into the easy chair, where he knelt before her.

"I'm a one-woman man," he said, his voice husky. "And I always have been. Jasmine, that woman is, was and always will be you."

"But you married Jenny, anyway." She could have slapped herself once the words were out of her mouth, but she couldn't help it. Her wounds were recently reopened and raw to the touch.

He tipped her chin so their eyes met. "Yes. I did. And I'd do it again. Jenny was dying. She wanted you to raise the baby. She knew I was going to marry you, so it was the perfect solution. I would marry Jenny and proclaim myself the legal father of the baby. When she died, you, Sammy and I would be the family Jenny wanted us to be. She really loved you, you know. You were supposed to be in on the plan."

Tears rolled down her cheeks at the thought of her sister sacrificing everything for her baby. And all Jasmine had been able to think about was the way she'd been jilted. Her sister hadn't told her about the cancer, and now, perhaps, she knew why. Jasmine had backed away from her relationship with Jenny, letting her sense of betrayal get the best of her when she should have been trying to forgive.

She should at least have been trying to find out the truth. She hadn't even done that. How many actions had she based on misconceptions? How much hurt could she have spared everyone? She knew Jenny suffered from the breach in their relationship at least as much as she had.

Maybe more.

And how much more she would have made of the short time with her sister. If only she had known.

"You okay, Jazz?" Christopher asked uncertainly, reaching for her hand.

She snatched it back and cradled it against her. She was so ashamed of her words and actions, she could barely think. "Why didn't you just tell me the truth?"

He groaned. "If you remember, we weren't exactly on speaking terms when we first saw each other again. I lived in constant fear of flying projectiles."

She couldn't even find it in her heart to chuckle. Her sorrow was nearly overwhelming, and she knew if she didn't escape Christopher's cabin soon, she'd break down completely and wouldn't be able to go anywhere.

"And then it became too difficult. Insult piled on insult until no one could break their way through." He paused and wet his lips with his tongue.

"I'm as much at fault as you."

"I was going to tell you everything the day I came back to Westcliffe. But then when some of the facts came together, I stood to lose Sammy. I knew you'd be a great mother for him, but I just couldn't rest until I was part of the picture. I wanted Sammy to have my name. And my protection, what little I could offer."

"But he's not your son. You could have just walked away." *Like you did before.* But she didn't need to say the words.

"That boy is my son, Jasmine, in every way that matters. I love him, and I want to take care of him. I didn't want him— or you and Gram—to face any more scandal than you'd already dealt with. And I guess I didn't really want to be the one to have to tell you about Jenny. Or that Bart's parents rejected Sammy as their grandchild. It seemed easier to remain quiet."

Revealing Jenny's shame would only add another scandal

to the family record. Dear Christopher had done all he could to shield the Enderlins from harm. It just appeared that they—*she*—got into trouble faster than he could play the rescuer.

"I've got to go," she said suddenly, snatching up her coat and dashing out the door without looking behind her.

Christopher called to her, but she refused to listen, to stop her headlong flight into the darkness of the night. It was where she belonged, in the dark.

She knew the way back to her four-by-four, and her feet put themselves one in front of the other without conscious thought.

He'd given everything, and she'd done nothing. She hadn't proved her love with faith and trust. Instead she'd made every one of his gallant actions twice as hard for him to make.

He must hate her. And if he didn't, it was only because he was the best, kindest, most honorable man in the whole wide world.

And she didn't deserve him.

There was a new wound in her heart, one that made the others small by comparison. She wanted to cry but her eyes were dry, for what use was crying when the wound in question was self-inflicted?

She was every kind of fool. And she'd discovered the truth too late.

Chapter Fifteen

So much for confessing the truth, Christopher thought, lifting himself gingerly from his easy chair. It was very early in the morning, judging from the thin stream of light beaming through the window. He'd spent the night half-sleeping, half-praying on the chair, and every muscle in his body was screaming for release.

And he was no closer to resolution than he'd been when Jasmine had left the night before. He didn't know what he expected God to do.

He knew better than that. God wasn't going to solve his problems for him, or undo the mess he'd made. A man had to live with the consequences of his actions, even when it meant watching the woman he loved walk out on him.

He deserved it, of course, but that didn't make it any easier to swallow. To have fought so long and hard for their happy ending, and then to have it dashed from his hand by his own foolishness was its own penalty.

She wasn't coming back. He'd seen the disillusionment and disappointment in her eyes, heard the anger sounding from her voice. She no longer trusted him.

And not all the words in the world could unscramble the disaster that his life had become.

Heading out the door the night before, his heart had been light. He'd found hope that she might hear what he had to say and forgive him. That they might have that happily-ever-after ending they used to dream about. Sammy would only add to their bright future.

His chest clenched, thinking about Jasmine and the baby. Despite the circumstances, God had given him such a love for baby Sammy he could barely contain it. It was like a fountain overflowing. And now he'd lost Sammy, too.

He found himself at the stable, where he looked around uncertainly. It occurred to him that here was a good getaway, to ride off into the Sangres until he figured out what to do next.

He had plans, at least. He'd felt God's call into ministry. He finally knew what he wanted to do with his life. But he'd hoped with all his heart his future would also include Jasmine and Sammy.

A dark bay nudged Christopher with his muzzle and he jumped back, laughing shakily. "Guess you just want some hay, now, don't you, fellow?" he asked, not knowing if he spoke aloud to reassure the beast or himself.

"Hey, Chris. Whatcha doin' in the barn?" Old Ben, one of the ranch hands sidled up to him and slapped him on the back. "Goin' riding?"

"Thinking about it," he admitted, sliding a glance toward Ben.

"Kinda green with horses, ain't ya?"

He chuckled. "You could say that. I've been on a horse all of twice in my life."

"I still don't see how you could have been raised on a ranch in Westcliffe and don't know how to ride."

He sighed quietly. This wasn't his week. He was going to have to divulge another secret just to get a horse. "Twice being when I fell off backward," he clarified. "I was six."

"Shoot, boy, you should've climbed back on. Who was teaching you? They should've known that."

"Unfortunately," he commented dryly, "I was teaching myself. And as far as I was concerned, taking one topple was enough to prove I wasn't cut out for the rodeo."

"But you want to ride now." It was a statement, made with an undertone of humor.

"I expect so. If you'll help me saddle a horse, that is."

"Well, I'd hate to keep a cowboy from his cows, if ya know what I mean. But I gotta tell you, I don't have a broken nag in the bunch."

"You don't have a single horse I can handle?" Maybe this was a bad idea and he should take his truck up to Horn Lake or something. At least his truck wouldn't throw him off. But for some reason, maybe it was guilt, he wanted to ride a horse.

"Commander might be a safe bet," he said, stroking the white stubble on his jaw. "Recently gelded. Ought to be a safe ride."

"Which one's Commander?"

"This dapple gray over here." He reached into his pocket and produced a carrot, which he fed to the nickering gelding.

Christopher tugged his hat lower over his brow and set his jaw. Commander. Sounded intimidating to a man who didn't like horses. He reached out a hand to stroke the horse's muzzle, but quickly withdrew it when he bucked his head and whinnied.

Old Ben laughed. Christopher scowled.

"Are you *sure* you don't have another one for me to ride?" he asked, ready to give the plan up completely. "I only want to go up by Horn Lake for a while."

Old Ben scratched his head, then his eyes lit up. "As a matter of fact, I think I *do* have something you can handle."

"What's his name?"

"He's a she. And her name's Fury."

Fury. And he'd thought Commander was bad.

A good night's sleep could make a world of difference to a woman, Jasmine reflected as she rose and glanced at the clock. Nine o'clock. She never expected to sleep as well as she did. It was amazing how clean a freshly scrubbed soul could feel. She'd come straight home from Christopher's cabin and slipped into the apartment so as not to wake Gram or Sammy.

She'd dropped into bed, exhausted from thinking and sobbing. So depleted, in fact, that she wasn't sure she had enough left in her to pray. Which is why it surprised her at how easy confession came from a quiet mind.

She didn't have to speak aloud and list every sin, or kneel in the proper posture of prayer and make her pleas to heaven from there. She merely had to lie still and *be*. God did the rest, sweeping in and taking the burden away from her, replacing it with the peace that passes understanding.

Be still and know that I am God.

The Scripture had soothed her wracked nerves, unhinged the stress from her shoulders. She'd made a thousand mistakes, but God was greater. Thank God, He was greater.

This morning, all that was left was to go back to Christopher, this time for good. She'd unjustly condemned herself, she realized now. Yes, she'd made more than her share of mistakes, but then again, so had Christopher. Surely they could forgive each other and finally be at peace.

She laughed out loud. He was every bit as stubborn as she was, the big lug. They'd butt heads more than once during their marriage, but she couldn't think of a rosier future or a brighter dream. She'd have the two men she always wanted, Christopher and Sammy, to love and spoil for the rest of her life.

"Where are you going looking so chipper, young lady?" Gram asked suspiciously as Jasmine entered the living room where Gram was rocking Sammy, who sucked noisily from his bottle.

"Hey there, little guy," she said, kissing Sammy on the forehead and Gram on her weathered cheek. "And hello to you, too, lovely Gram."

"Now I know something's up," she complained good-naturedly.

"I'm going to see your daddy! Yes I am!" she said in baby talk, as Sammy wrapped a pudgy hand around her finger. "Daddy's going to take good care of his little boy."

"Now, this *does* sound interesting," Gram said with a crackly laugh. "Do tell."

Jasmine couldn't help but smile. "I love him, Gram."

"Oh, now *there's* news."

"And I think he loves me, too," she concluded with a sigh.

Gram rolled her eyes. "And it took you *how* long to figure that out?"

"He's not the bad guy in all this."

"I never said he was," Gram reminded her.

"No, I guess you didn't. But you never offered me an easy way out."

"The easy way out isn't always the best way out. The road is narrow, and that sort of thing. Besides, I didn't know anything for certain. I just suspected that young man of yours wasn't the type to change his character so radically. He's always been a good fellow, that one."

"Oh, he's that," Jasmine agreed with a laugh. "That, and *so* much more."

"You've ironed out all the issues?" she asked gently. "Come clean with each other?"

"Well, pretty much. I guess." She experienced a sudden flash of apprehension running through her, but it abated as quickly as it came.

"Good. Then you can tell me why he left Jenny before Sammy was born, especially since you knew she was dying. That's the one thing I've never been able to figure out."

She blanched. "I...er...that's one of the things we haven't discussed yet."

"Jasmine," Gram exclaimed in exasperation. "Don't you think that's one of the biggies you want to have cleared up before you make any long-term plans with the man?"

"Well, yes, sure," she agreed, stammering slightly. "But Gram, the point is, I trust him. I don't know why he did what he did, but I trust that he had a good, honorable reason for doing it."

Gram raised a bushy white eyebrow, and Jasmine held up her hands in her own defense.

"Even—maybe especially—about his leaving Jenny."

"I cannot even fathom."

"Well, neither can I. But I'm not going to speculate, either."

"There you go, girl," Gram said, her voice filled with encouragement. "You're off to see him, then?"

"Yes, after I check on Marcus at the clinic. I need to have a long chat with him, anyway."

"Just don't get distracted," Gram teased.

"Oh, Gram! You know I won't. There's nothing to keep me away from Christopher now."

She made a beeline for her four-by-four, hoping to corner Marcus as fast as possible and be off to see Christopher. She still hadn't mentioned to Marcus that she wanted him to be her permanent replacement, but then it occurred to her that she hadn't yet mentioned Ecuador to Christopher, either.

Well, of course she hadn't. They weren't exactly on speaking terms. She couldn't just blurt out that God was sending her to a foreign country to work as a missionary. And it could be that Ecuador would have to wait.

She felt it so strongly, so certainly in her heart, this need to serve as a doctor in that little hospital in Quito. But if God allowed her to be with Christopher, she would choose that first. If God really meant her for Ecuador, the rest would fall into place in His time.

For once she would trust God and see what happened. It could only be good. She was certain of that.

She was more nervous about speaking to Marcus than she was to go see Christopher. Somehow she felt she'd deceived Marcus, and perhaps she had at that.

She found him in a back office, cheerfully working on a pile of paperwork higher than his head. He was singing a hymn under his breath and tapping his pencil in time to the beat.

"You can take the man out of the music, but never the music out of the man," she said with a laugh.

He looked up quickly, a startled look quickly replaced with a welcoming grin. "You said it, girl. Don't be thinking you'll be takin' the music out of *this* man any time soon."

"It's good to see you so happy," she said gently, her heart welling up with joy.

"I've never been so content, Jasmine," he agreed, placing a hand on her shoulder. "I'm glad you brought me out here. New York wasn't the place for me. I just didn't know it."

She smiled up at him and gave him an impromptu hug, which he returned.

"I told you God changes your dreams. Now all I want is a small country clinic like this one and a roof over my head. Beautiful mountains on one side and a gorgeous valley on the other."

"I've been meaning to talk to you about that dream," she inserted, taking the opening.

"Oh, so the time has come already. You feel rested enough to get back to work?"

"No, no," she exclaimed, shaking her head fervently. "I didn't mean that at all. I was wondering if you'd like to stay on here as *this* clinic's doctor!"

His face brightened immediately, but then his brows fell in confusion. "You know I'd take this job in an instant," he said, his voice low even for him. "But if *I'm* the doctor, where does that leave you?"

"Happily unhindered and pursuing the Lord's work," she replied promptly.

"Huh?" he asked, justifiably confused. "But I thought *this* was the Lord's work for you."

"Maybe it was. But not anymore." Her excitement bubbled over, and she smiled widely. "I'm getting married, Marcus!"

"To Christopher, I assume," he commented, sounding mildly cynical.

"Well, he hasn't asked yet—again—but I'm hoping he will today. And I plan to accept. There's more," she said, and she proceeded to fill him in on her plans to go to Ecuador to be a missionary.

Marcus laughed aloud. "Girl, you better be goin' to tell your honey that information right away. That isn't the kind of news you surprise him with on your wedding night."

"I know. I'm on my way to see him now. I wanted to see you first."

"Tell him I wish you both the best."

"I will, Marcus. Thanks." She blew him a kiss and dashed out of the clinic, eager to find Christopher and throw herself into his arms.

Nerves finally hit her as she walked up to Christopher's cabin. She hadn't actually planned what she'd say when she got here, and now she could think of a million reasons why she shouldn't be there at all.

She knocked on the door and waited, tapping her toes in time with the hymn running through her head. The same hymn Marcus had been singing, she realized with a smile.

When he didn't answer, she searched his empty cabin, then headed to the mess hall. Frustrated and feeling her anxiety rising, she decided to find a moment's peace and shade inside the stable. She inhaled deeply despite the crisp air. She loved the smell of horses.

Quite a contrast, really. Next to the hustle and bustle of a hospital emergency room, there was nothing she liked quite so much as the respite of a stable, with its pungent combination of fresh hay and fresh manure, and the horses stamping and whickering lightly in the background.

She walked up to a friendly gray and rubbed her hand along his neck, making soft, horsey sounds with her tongue. She'd been riding since she was three. Though they didn't own any horses now, she occasionally borrowed a mount from here at the Walters to take a picnic into the mountains.

"That's Commander," said a voice from behind her.

She jumped and put a hand to her pounding heart. "You startled me, Ben," she said, turning back to the horse. "Well, there, Commander, aren't you a pretty boy?"

"That he is," Old Ben said fondly. "The poor fellow was recently gelded, so he's still got some stallion to wean out of him. But he'll be an excellent mount after a month or two."

"Yes," she said, speaking to the horse. "I'll bet you'll be a beauty, won't you, my boy? I'll have to take you on a ride sometime so you can show off what you can do, won't I, big boy?"

Old Ben laughed behind her shoulder.

"What's so funny? I've been riding since I was three," she said, offended.

"It's not that, Jasmine. I know you can handle this mount. But this morning—" He snickered and wiped the corner of his eye with the sleeve of his flannel shirt. "This morning, Christopher Jordan wanted to ride Commander." He promptly burst into another round of laughter.

Jasmine knew it was polite to laugh along, but she couldn't. She didn't know what jolted her more—the fact that Old Ben had seen Christopher this morning, or that the crazy love of her life wanted to ride a horse!

"You didn't let him, of course," she prompted.

He chuckled again. "Not on your life. The guy was heading into the hills. Said he wanted to go up by Horn Lake. On a *horse*. Oh, man."

Jasmine smiled along with him as her mind processed the information. Christopher was clearly trying to find somewhere quiet to think things through. Up to that point, he was being rational. But why on earth did he want to ride a horse, when he could just as well have driven himself up to Horn Lake?

"Thanks for not giving him a mount," she said, smiling at Old Ben.

His pale blue eyes widened and he scratched his day's growth of beard. "Oh, I gave him a mount."

"What?" Jasmine screeched, clasping her hands together.

"Sure." He smiled. "I put him on Fury."

"I don't believe this." She turned and stomped out of the barn, heading straight to the mess hall. Christopher was somewhere in the Sangre de Cristo mountain range on a horse called Fury. And he was alone.

Ben might think it a joke, but to Jasmine, Christopher on a horse was deadly serious. He knew nothing about trail riding, and there were a million hazards to best even a good rider.

After getting Cookie to pack a lunch for two, Jasmine rushed out the door and made her way steadfastly back to the stable. Ben stood where she'd left him, looking bemused.

"Don't just stand there," she barked. "Help me saddle up Commander."

He raised his eyebrows at the order, but did as she requested. Jasmine ran back to her car for a few emergency items she always kept with her and stuffed them in the saddlebag. Ben had already tied her lunch to the other side.

"You going to be warm enough?" he asked, concern in his eyes.

Jasmine picked up the reins and led Commander to the front gate. The horse had a nice, easy pace, and Jasmine didn't anticipate any trouble. "I expect so, Ben. Don't worry about me."

"Okay, I won't," he responded, walking out beside the horse. "But, Jasmine—"

She cut him off with a "Hee-yah." She set off at a canter, leaving the stable, and Old Ben, in the dust.

The last thing she heard as she turned around the corner of the drive, was Old Ben muttering, "—about Fury…"

Chapter Sixteen

Christopher lay flat on his back with his hands clasped behind his head, staring at the clear blue Colorado sky. A cushion of snow and pine needles made his bed a comfortable one, and it wasn't too terribly cold with the sunshine streaking through the trees.

God's country. He didn't get up here enough to ponder God's creation and wonder at His magnificence. It sort of put things in perspective for him.

His life was in God's hands, and he wouldn't have it any other way. He'd apologized to Jasmine, and tried to set things right. That was all he was able to do. He regretted the fact that he'd let his temper get the best of him, but he supposed he'd apologize for that too, when the time came.

He was trying to imagine a life without Jasmine and Sammy, but it just wasn't fathomable. They *were* his life. But he'd done everything he could to make them a family, and everything he'd done had failed. He could only hope for a miracle, now.

In the meantime, he supposed he should go on pursuing the call God had given him for the ministry. He'd put his application in to the local seminary, right here in the Sangres, only about a mile from where he currently lay. The president of the seminary had already assured him of a spot in the next class, which would start at the beginning of summer.

At least he would remain close to Jasmine and Sammy this way. He couldn't even consider not being able to see his son, and his dear, sweet Jasmine on a regular basis. He thanked God again for the blessing of Sammy, who would bind him to Jasmine forever, in a way, even if it wasn't the way he would have chosen.

He heard the sound of hoofbeats approaching only seconds before Jasmine launched herself from the saddle and landed in an ungraceful heap of arms and legs right on his chest, knocking the breath from his lungs.

If the shock of her landing didn't stun him, the fact that she was feathering kisses across his face and neck certainly did. And there were streams of tears rolling down her cheeks. He stared up at her stupidly, unable to move.

"Oh, my darling Christopher. Oh, my dear, crazy love. I came as soon as I heard. I brought supplies in the saddlebag. Oh, just tell me where you're hurt, my love, and I'll make it better." She was half laughing and half sobbing as she continued to rain kisses down upon him.

It occurred to him that he didn't really *want* to move, or to be taken from the heaven in which he'd suddenly found himself. He had no idea what Jasmine was about, but as her silky hair fell down around him, he thought he might have found the most pleasant way to smother to death that the world had ever known.

She stood up as quickly as she'd descended on him. For a moment she just glared down at him, then turned and stomped to her horse, yanking a paper grocery sack off one of the saddle strings.

She stomped back and threw it at him, again pelting him in the chest. He grinned despite his best efforts, and swung to his feet, casually leaning his back against a convenient pine tree.

"I thought you were injured," she said, enunciating each word unnecessarily, "because Old Ben told me he let you ride out on Fury. And—"

He tried to interrupt her, but she held up her hands and continued on.

"*And* there you were, lying on the ground like some corpse

or something and I thought... Oh! Who cares what I thought? The point is, you're fine."

"You sound as if you'd rather I wasn't," he remarked dryly.

"At this point, don't push it," she said, and then broke into laughter.

He laughed with her, relieved. Apparently she was here with some purpose other than to cause him bodily harm. They met each other's gaze and laughed even harder. He reached out and hugged her to him, wanting her back in his arms. She didn't resist.

"Uh, Jazz?" he asked when they'd both somewhat recovered. "About Fury..."

"You must be a better rider than I thought. Or else a quick learner."

He shook his head and tried not to grin. "Not exactly."

She lifted an eyebrow, and he shrugged and pointed to the glen, where Fury was tethered.

Jasmine had been honestly terrified when she tracked him up here, but she turned her gaze to where he pointed and felt her mouth drop open in surprise. "That's *Fury?*"

An ancient gray donkey with one droopy ear looked back at her, his expression one of mild annoyance. He had a clump of grass in his jaw and was chewing slowly. He couldn't move beyond turtle speed, she was certain of that just by looking at him.

At least now she knew why Old Ben had been laughing. "He's a little short for a man with your long legs, don't you think?"

Christopher turned a deep shade of red, and reached to retrieve his cowboy hat from the ground. "Fury is a she, thank you very much, and it just so happens that we got along fine."

"In other words, no one saw you trying to ride the beast," she teased.

He tugged on his cowboy hat and grinned from underneath it. "That, too. But really, she's perfect for me. One speed, slow. And since my legs can almost touch the ground when

I ride her, I don't have that *liable to take a digger* sensation I get from riding a horse."

"Oh, Christopher." Before she could consider her actions, she slid forward, framed his face in her hands, and kissed him soundly on the lips. She loved him, every crazy inch of him, and she wanted him to know that.

"I didn't think you'd be back," he admitted, settling her into his arms. "I was trying to figure out what to do next."

"And what did you decide?" she murmured, locking her arms around his waist and snuggling under his chin. "There's food in that bag, by the way."

"Then we should eat. I missed breakfast this morning."

"Yes, I know." Kneeling, she ripped the sack open to bare the contents—fried chicken, cheese, biscuits and a couple of apples.

Christopher shined up an apple on his flannel shirt and took a big bite. "You make it your business to know whether or not I eat breakfast?"

"I make it my business to know a lot of things," she teased. "Like how you planned to get along without me."

"I couldn't do that, and you know it. You and Sammy are all the world to me. But—" he paused and stared down at his apple.

Jasmine felt her chest tighten, as if she were once again going to lose control. But control wasn't hers to begin with, she reminded herself. It belonged to God.

"What I was thinking about up here," he said, crouching down to face her, "is that I'd like to go to seminary. In fact, I've applied to the one here in Westcliffe. I believe God is calling me to the ministry."

She took in a deep breath, then laid a hand on his arm. "Oh, Christopher, that's wonderful." She stroked his forearm up, then down again, loving the texture of flannel under her fingertips. "Are you going to pastor a church?"

"I'll do whatever I have to in order to stay near you and Sammy, but—" He removed his hat and swept a hand through his hair before planting the hat firmly back in place, brow low over his eyes. "But recently I've had other ideas with what I might do for the Lord."

"Such as?" She sensed his hesitance, and wondered if she ought to tell him she'd follow him to the ends of the earth if necessary. That was, after all, what true love was about.

Still, though Christopher was being affectionate enough, he'd spoken of being *near* her and Sammy instead of *with* them. She kept her thoughts to herself and her mouth firmly closed.

"I want to go to Ecuador, Jazz. There's a hospital there where you could do some work if you wanted. After I left Jenny, I got an EMT certificate in Pueblo."

"So *that's* where you learned to deliver a baby," she said, the lightbulb in her head going off.

She was still reeling about his wanting to go to Ecuador. It cleared up any lingering doubts she had about whether or not the two of them should be together, but she wasn't quite prepared to express her thoughts in words. For now, she simply wanted to experience the sheer joy of a match made in heaven.

After a moment, she sighed aloud. "Will you be angry if I ask you a question?"

He sat down beside her and laced their fingers together, squeezing gently. "I love you, Jazz. I want to marry you. If there's anything else we need to clear up between us, let's get it over with now. Let's start fresh from today, okay?"

"Okay." Her heart thumped loudly in her chest as she wondered how to phrase the delicate question. "I want you to know up front that it doesn't matter what you say. I love you and I'll marry you, and the answer to this question isn't going to make a bit of difference."

His Adam's apple bobbed as he swallowed. "It means a lot to me that you trust me."

"I do. But there's no sense in leaving a nagging question behind. Why did you leave Jenny, Christopher? Everything else makes sense, seen from your viewpoint. You acted in a gallant and honorable manner. But then how could you leave?"

She held her breath, wondering if she'd been too harsh.

He smiled gently, and sadness lurked in his eyes. "Another thing I didn't want you to know about Jenny." He blew out a breath. "She knew when I married her that my heart did and always would belong to you. She knew I planned to tell you, though the thought humiliated her. But you had to know, for the baby would one day be your own."

"Yes, but you didn't tell me."

"No, I didn't," he replied gravely. "And because I didn't, Jenny got it into her head that I might come to love her, and that the three of us might be a real family."

"I can see how that would happen." It hurt to think about it, but Christopher was a magnetically attractive man. What woman could sleep with him and not fall prey to his natural charm and stunning good looks?

"She was young," Christopher explained. "And idealistic. I tried to ignore the tension building between us, but she wouldn't let us be. One day she demanded that I—well, uh…"

Understanding dawned on her, and she swiped a hand down her face as if clearing the cobwebs. "What are you trying to say, Christopher? That you didn't consummate the marriage?"

"That's exactly what I'm trying to say. Jasmine, you didn't think that I'd—"

"I'd think that if you gave me no reason to believe otherwise."

"I love you, and I've always loved you. We made a pledge long ago to save ourselves for each other, and I've never broken that promise. Not even when I made my pledge to Jenny."

Tears pricked at the corners of her eyes. After all this time, all she'd been through, they would still have the joy of a previously unexplored wedding night together.

"The long and short of it is, Jenny threw me out. She was in love with me and couldn't bear the thought that I was in love with you."

"But why did you leave? Everyone blamed you." *She* had blamed him, when all the time he'd been suffering for her.

"One takes the bow, one takes the blame, Jasmine. That's just the way things are. Jenny threatened to expose herself if I didn't leave town. She told me not to contact her at all, and not to ever try to see the baby."

"Do you think that was jealousy talking?"

"Oh, I'm sure it was. And immaturity. I'm not holding a grudge."

"Another man would," she said, feeling as if she were missing some fact, something important that was lurking just outside her reach.

"I'm not another man."

"That's the understatement of the year." She hugged him close and closed her eyes. Jenny's face sprang to mind, just after she'd had Sammy. Her last words—she was trying to say something about Christopher.

"I love you, Jazz kitten."

"I love you, Christopher cat," she replied, using the pet names they called each other in high school. "And honey?"

"Mmm?" he asked, his face buried in her hair.

"I think Jenny wanted us to get back together. At the end…she kept saying your name."

"There you go, then. Happily ever after."

She smiled, knowing he couldn't see. It was time to share some of the joy in her heart with him. "Not completely, my dear."

"No?" He leaned down on one elbow and looked up at her, his normally gray eyes a smoky blue, shining with love for her. "What have we missed?"

"Oh, something about Ecuador."

He smiled up at her. "God will work it out in His own time, if it's meant to be," he said, reaching a finger up to stroke the line of her jaw.

She leaned into his caress. "He already has. I've had my application to Quito in for months now. I'll just tell them to put me on hold for a couple years so you can finish seminary and I'll continue to work part-time at the clinic with Marcus."

"Yeah?" She put a hand to his chest and could feel his heartbeat pumping wildly. "Well, praise God!"

"Yes, let's," she said, smiling.

"Marcus is going to stay and work at the clinic?" he asked belatedly.

"Marcus found he has a liking for country living. We've already made arrangements for him to stay on here."

"*Now* can we have our happily ever after?" he whined like a petulant little boy.

"*Now,* my love. And let's not rush it. We have the rest of our lives together."

Epilogue

Considering the fact that the Enderlins were still in questionable social status, nearly everyone in town showed up for Jasmine's wedding three weeks later—the soonest Christopher and Jasmine had been able to convince Gram she could arrange a proper wedding.

The church was so full they were bringing folding chairs in, and it occurred to Jasmine, as she stood in the back of the room to watch the proceedings, that perhaps they should have used the grange hall.

But of course she wanted a church wedding, with her pastor decked out in his finest vestments up in front, and she gliding up the aisle in her white gown like a fairy-tale princess.

She felt like a princess, on this happiest of days. The only sadness to mar the event was that her parents and sister were not here to see her wed to Christopher. She wondered if they could see their loved ones from heaven, if they knew that today was her wedding day.

People quieted as the organist began the wedding march. She had no bridesmaids, as a sign of respect to her sister. She tightened her grip on Marcus's arm and bowed her head, saying a little prayer of remembrance.

"Hey, girl, you aren't nervous, are you?" he whispered, sounding surprised. "This here's your big finale."

"No it's not," she whispered back, scowling. "It's only my grand entrance."

"Touché," he said, and bowed. He was handsome in a

white tux with tails, especially when he smiled in that big, toothy way of his. "We're on."

Jasmine gathered her dress and her thoughts, but in the end, all she could think about was putting one foot in front of the other. She didn't even look up until she reached the front row, and then she was so stunned she couldn't think at all.

Christopher stood waiting, his eyes alight with love. In his arms, in a matching silver tux with ruffles and gray cowboy hat, was his son. He'd insisted Sammy be part of the ceremony, and Jasmine was glad he was. Now she was walking up the aisle to her two handsome men, and her future couldn't look any brighter than this moment.

Marcus patted her hand as they reached the front, and the minister held his hands up for silence. He intoned the requisite opening and asked who would be giving the bride away.

"I am," Marcus boomed in his resonant bass. "In place of her mother and father, and in memory of her sister."

He placed Jasmine's hand in Christopher's, and she was relieved to feel his own hand shaking beneath hers. Or maybe it was her hand shaking them both.

"Thanks, buddy," Christopher whispered as Marcus moved away.

He turned back and winked at them both. "You take care of my girl, Mister."

Usually Christopher would have bristled, but today he merely grinned. "You can count on it."

The minister directed them to face one another and hold hands in order to exchange vows and rings. Jasmine had seen a dozen real weddings and who knew how many more on television, but she had no idea how completely her life would flash down to this one moment. She was certain she wouldn't be able to say a word.

"Are you ready?" Christopher whispered, squeezing her hands.

"I've been ready for years," she whispered back.

It seemed only moments later that the ceremony was complete and they were turning around to be introduced for the first time as Mr. and Mrs. Christopher Jordan. And their son

Samuel. The many times she'd dreamed it as a teenager didn't hold a candle to the real thing.

Tears ran unbidden down her cheeks, but she didn't even bother to wipe them off. They were here, the three of them, a family at last.

"Happy, my love?" he whispered in her ear.

"Oh, yes."

"Then promise me you'll never look behind, but only to what's ahead." He gestured down the aisle and out the door, to where a limousine waited to take them to the airport.

It was an easy promise to make. And one she intended to keep.

* * * * *

Dear Reader,

The apostle James tells us the tongue is a fire, and likely to burn out of control if we aren't careful what we say. Sometimes, however, it's what we don't say that gets us into trouble.

That's what happened with Christopher and Jasmine. Assumption built on assumption and was never confirmed. Pretty soon it became impossible to tell what was truth and what was a lie.

I hope you enjoyed journeying with Christopher and Jasmine. As is always the case when an author puts her fingers to the typewriter to create characters, I ended up learning more than they did. It's my very great privilege to be able to live with my characters and share in their conflicts—and, of course, their resolution.

I love hearing form my readers. Please feel free to write me at P.O. Box 9806, Denver, CO 80209.

Blessings,

Deb Kastner

Hideaway

E.R. doctor Cheyenne Allison seeks a break from her stressful life, but instead finds a dangerous vandal and terror.

Will trust in her charismatic neighbor and faith in Providence get her through a harrowing ordeal?

HANNAH ALEXANDER

Available October 2003 wherever hardcovers are sold.